One

CW01499052

Earth; March 26th, 2008 (Federation Year 5615)
Although the sun was bright and warm that early spring day, Danielle was in no hurry to get out of the car parked in front of M-Town's Court of Disciplinary Action.

"Come on," her lawyer Jed Harris said with a light touch to her shoulder. Danielle had spent half an hour that morning ironing the wrinkles from her uniform, both as a meditative detachment from the stress compounding in her skull and to prove to the judgmental dipshits about to decide her fate that she was, in fact, a decent soldier. *Maybe I don't have that record in this life,* she thought, staring out the window overlooking M-Town's central plaza, *but I used to be. Or so I hear.* She doubted some old Federation documents were enough in this life.

"Can I have a moment?" She inhaled a deep breath, closed her eyes, and folded her hands in her lap. Jed was silent as he perused a document he pulled out of his briefcase.

"I've gotta get going," their driver said. "The mob is coming for us."

Indeed, here they came, having recognized the markings of a khaki-clad officer about to walk the Green Mile. The rabble grew louder as protestors and national media crews followed the rope barriers separating them from the goings-on at the courthouse. They had been a common sight for the past few weeks, but it wasn't until that month that the signs went up and the marching affected a typical day in M-Town. What was once a place of mundane military office work, training, and fooling around, had now become the political epicenter for the country's moral stance on homosexuality.

"Hell no, they won't go! Hell no, they won't go!"

The chants hit Danielle the moment Jed opened her door and extended his hand to help her out. She brushed him off, insistent on rising from her seat with nothing but a dour demeanor and her hat shielding her eyes from the fervor exploding around her.

"Queer love is real love! Queer love is real love!"

Rainbow flags flew. Signs depicting gay soldiers embracing waved above protestors' heads. Signs begging the American government to overturn Don't Ask, Don't Tell rose the highest. The loudest and proudest were invited in front of the TV cameras and interviewed by local and international news stations.

"This is a mockery of American freedoms!"

One large man was the loudest of them all. Although he was dressed in civilian clothing, his Marine tattoos suggested he knew what it was like to serve. Danielle didn't recognize him. She barely recognized anyone after the mental dissociation began.

It was bad enough she was paraded in front of these people. Armed courthouse guards hustled Danielle and her lawyer past the crowds shouting her name and asking her to stay strong. *Get them all away from me!* she begged the universe, which had already proven to be against her more times than not. Because when it wasn't bad enough that she was doomed to be reborn again and again for all eternity, she had to deal with this shit.

"Don't look at them, and don't talk to them," her lawyer muttered as he shoved her up the stairs. "They are *not* here."

Yet how could she avoid most of the uproar when it was right in her ear?

"Danielle! *Danielle!*" A familiar voice finally caught her attention in the end. "Keep your head up so you can kick them in the balls!"

She did exactly what her lawyer told her not to do—she turned to Ben Kallman, straining against the rope barrier that separated officers like her from black-marked civilians like him. Ben was part of the first wave of court-martials that tore apart whole departments of M-Town. Danielle had avoided that first wave. Then the second. But when the third went out? She was caught by the tide.

Friday, March 26th at nine in the morning. That was her court date, and that was all she would get, because there were more people who must be tried before the end of the month. She was lucky she got a whole morning for herself.

"Lucky." Her lawyer had seen the witness list. The government had brought out enough evidence to all but ensure her rank and benefits stripped by the end of the day. *I'd cry,* she thought as she looked Ben in the defiant eye, *but I'm not crying for any establishment that doesn't want me.*

Sure. She said that now.

Silence overwhelmed her as she stepped into the courthouse and the guards closed the doors behind her. The halls were filled with both civilian and uniformed clerks, lawyers, and the witnesses about to air out Danielle's dirty history. Jed hustled her toward their assigned courtroom on the second floor. The only priority she was allotted was a hassle-free trip through security. Probably the last time she would ever enjoy something like that in her life.

The second floor hallway was even quieter than the first. Danielle was already exhausted by the time she finished climbing the steps and saw how many wrinkles were in her damned uniform. Good thing the first person she saw was her grandmother, who stood from a bench with a lint roller in her hand.

"Good morning, sweetie." Regina held herself together as she brushed the lint off her granddaughter's body. "Lovely day, isn't it?"

Danielle's eyes slightly widened. "If you want to call it that."

"No matter what happens, I'll be there, all right?"

Regina wasn't usually the Pollyanna type, but Danielle also knew that this wasn't some unfettered sense of justice possessing her grandmother. This was a woman who had seen her fair share of court-martials in her career as a captain. How many times had she been called to the stand to testify against the very officers she oversaw—and even took care of, sometimes? Danielle would never make it to captain like her grandmother had. Then again, many argued that Regina was robbed of further titles since her gender was a hindrance during the time she served. *"I was one of the only female captains in America back then, hon,"* she had told Danielle more than once. *"One day you'll be a colonel. Just you wait."*

Yeah, right. Danielle never hoped for more than captain, and that would only come with a few retirements. Ones she would never get to see now.

"We've gotta go." Jed motioned for Danielle to pull away from her grandmother, the only person in this hallway she dared to touch.

Because it sure as hell wasn't the woman standing outside the courtroom doors.

It was the strangest thing. Although Miranda Hotchner had been a rare sight around the office ever since she started attending court-martial after court-martial, Danielle still didn't expect to see her there. Nor did she anticipate the salute she received. Indoors. While her hat was still on.

Regina rushed up behind Danielle and yanked off her hat.

Danielle gave what would probably be the last salute of her military career. She remembered the day she first saluted Miranda. How long ago had it been? Four years? *Jesus. Time has gone by so slowly,* Danielle thought. The past year alone felt like ten. It didn't help that Miranda had been there for all of the crazy shit that befell their little corner of Earth.

"At ease." Miranda remained in front of the doors. It was still fifteen minutes before the start of the trial. Until then, they could both pretend that things were business as usual.

But they weren't, were they?

This was it. Jed had all but said that Danielle was toast. Not that the odds were ever good for someone as soon as she got to the court-martial stage, but Danielle was guilty of everything charged against her. Not only did she have lust for her sex, but she had indulged in it. A few times.

Just like she had indulged in a few things she should not have with her own commanding officer.

Miranda would surely be called to the stand that morning. The only reason Danielle was allowed to speak to her right now was because Miranda was her commanding officer for a few more hours. That and there had been so many hearings so far that year that some things were overlooked, for better or worse.

Right now? Danielle wasn't sure if this was for better, or definitely worse. She certainly did not appreciate the strange feelings welling up within her when she locked eyes with the one woman who busted her up the most.

"Good luck, Lieutenant." Miranda tucked her coat over her arm and stepped to the side. "Do your best to be in the office later this week, would you?"

Danielle allowed herself one small smile. "I will do my best, ma'am." They both knew her best wouldn't be enough.

Jed opened the courtroom door and escorted Danielle to her fate. She knew more than one person stared into the back of her head. It was a feeling that haunted her for the rest of the day.

"Where the hell are the discs, man?" The joke Clyde uttered was lost on himself as he rummaged through the band members' bags in search of the elusive CDs they spent the whole week burning. "The whole point of the show is to sell some tunes!"

Devon looked away from the setlist he was about to confirm with concert management. He didn't have time to deal with his best friend's nerves, nor did he have the countenance to bear yet another thing going wrong on the day of their biggest show yet. Because he didn't have enough to worry about already... Devon was supposed to be *gone* and at some courthouse in M-Town within half an hour.

"Check the red bag!" he called over his shoulder. "I saw Serge put them in there last night!"

"Hey, May!" The loud game of telephone made its way across the room until it finally reached May, who was wrapped up in the world of her phone. She dropped it to her chest and rolled her eyes. "Check that out for me, would you?"

Sure enough, the burned CDs in their jewel cases were ready for the merch stand later that night. Devon confirmed that another crisis had been averted before turning back to the manager, whose slick ponytail and denim jacket proudly said that he had seen more than a few fledgling bands get their big break under his watch.

"Seven songs. Under a half hour." He squinted to see the handwritten time stamps on the sheet. The band had spent two whole weeks fine-tuning the setlist to best show off their catalog while also maximizing their allotted half hour. A good mix of original and cover songs—the ones they could get the rights to cover at a large outdoor festival, anyway. It was the first one of the concert season, and while *Opening Night in Late March* wasn't the biggest event in the world, it was a huge step up for Karma, a band that had spent the past few months hustling local shows when they weren't recording their first official EP. This was in between work and the hell that emerged when Devon received a very stern and *very* demanding subpoena to show up as a character witness for one Lt. Danielle Cromwell.

The fact it was her lawyer who requested his assistance meant he was keen on doing whatever he could do to save Danielle's career. It was the least he could do for a woman who had saved his hide more than a few times over the past millennium.

"I can't hang around long," he said after giving a genial slap to the manager's arm. "I'll be back in time for sound check this evening, but I have to go to the M-Town courthouse like... right now." Nine in the morning. What a time to be grilled about one's sexuality. "Any of the other guys can fill in for me while I'm gone." What a *time* for the band's de facto leader to have to bail.

The manager took the setlist with him out the door. Devon likewise grabbed his things and hoped to the Void that he was dressed well enough for a courtroom. He had worn his best work pants and a plain turtleneck, which was quite the sight backstage at a rock music show.

If only his ex-girlfriend could see him now. *She might soon...* Odds were good that Alicia was also at the hearing, and she would be the best dressed person there.

He said goodbye to his bandmates before booking it to the parking lot, where he had scored a decent spot near the main building. He needed that good luck to get him to the courthouse in time. It was a fine thing for a civilian to think he had every right to show up fashionably late to something the government wanted him at, and he wasn't about to be the ninth person that month to find out what happened when a bastard like him was held in contempt of military law.

Unfortunately, he didn't make it all the way to his car. Not before another car cut him off in the marked walkway leading from the ticket booths to the parking lot.

"Devon Anderson?" An elderly man dressed in a three-piece suit and sporting a large ebony earring in his lobe lowered his window in the backseat. "That's you, correct?"

It took Devon a few seconds to reorient himself, and in that time the driver hopped out and opened the other back door. Both he and the elderly gentleman looked at Devon with expectant faces, as if he were supposed to hop in without asking any questions.

"Excuse me?"

"My name's Pauloso d'Whain. But most people on Earth call me Paul." The gentleman extended his hand through the back window. "I'm from the Federation. Not affiliated with its government, however."

Devon took a step back. "I'm sorry, but I don't have time for this. I must –"

"Yes, you're heading toward M-Town. Come. Hop in and let me give you a ride. We need to talk." When Devon still wasn't moving, Pauloso continued, "It will be worth your while to chat with me, Mr. Anderson. Or do you prefer to be called Mr. Gardiah?"

Devon narrowed his eyes. Lest this man continued to call attention to who they were, he became obliged to sit in the back of a luxury vehicle he couldn't name. Rich, coming from a man who was once accustomed to some of the finer modes of transportation the Federation had to offer.

"It is such a pleasure to meet you, Mr. Anderson." The hand that had hung out the window now reached across Pauloso's chest for Devon to shake. It was met with a firm yet hesitant touch before Devon crossed both arms and kept a respectful distance from this stranger who already knew so much about him. "I don't expect you to recognize me as well as I do you. I'm not a famous man who has transcended time and generations to keep showing up when the going gets tough."

His Federation accent betrayed him then, a linguistic tic that Devon had noticed after months of talking with Federation-born citizens who spoke both fluent Basic and English. Many, *many* Federation-types vied to enlist him for endorsements and events sure to bring in trillions of Federation dollars which, he was assured, were worth much less than American dollars, so a trillion was not that impressive. Until it was. Because he was there, and that's why they needed him!

Devon was completely within reason to suspect another such pitch from Pauloso. Yet he would be remissed to not hear the man out, even as he was dragged into the back of an unknown car and possibly dumped in M-Town a few minutes late and held in contempt anyway.

"I'm the CEO, if you will, of a multimedia company that deals primarily with Earth-based entertainments," Pauloso began as Devon gave into panic that he was about to testify on the military stand. "My enterprise is responsible for broadcasting many of your fine films and shows to homes within the Federation. Perhaps you've heard of 'Channel 1000,' as it's called in English? No? It's like the Federation channel we receive here, except it features shows such as *Survivor* and *Neighbours*. Both are incredibly popular on Terra III and other astral bodies."

Devon was listening, but said nothing. All he knew about *Neighbours* was that it was Australian and had something to do with Kylie Minogue.

"We also publish and distribute Earth-based music throughout the universe. Quite the market for that as well."

Pauloso didn't mention it, but he had every right to be proud of how his family's company had cornered the Earth-based media market in the past fifty years and turned it into a profitable niche. A few music and acting stars were Federation-born, but beyond that, it didn't involve in-person promotions, let alone concerts or stage productions. The d'Whains made a bulk of their fortune through sales and subscription-based services they curated. One day, Earth history books would refer to them as, *"Netflix, but for the Federation."* The one-stop shop for the latest Prince compilation and every episode of *The Simpsons* available for instant download. (Now with dubs in Basic, Huling, Rothyyl and, if one could possibly believe it, Julah.) "We've recently opened a new department, locating raw talent here on Earth and turning them into Federation superstars out of the box."

He let that sink into Devon's tired skull. Unfortunately, Devon was so worked up over the events going on that day that he barely heard a thing Pauloso said.

"You are one of the most famous Earthlings in the Federation, Mr. Anderson," Pauloso said to get Devon's attention again. "You and Ms. Cromwell, but I don't believe she's big into the arts, now is she?"

He said that name. The one Devon was already obsessing over. *Her lawyer prepped me on what I was going to be asked...* he thought, trying not to gulp down more bile escaping his stomach. *Fuck me. Fuck me sideways, and don't be gentle.* No wonder he was sweating. That was exactly what he would talk about on that stand as soon as they got there.

"I understand that you have a band. I also understand that one of your bandmates is named May d'Eran, the daughter of famed reincarnation psychologist Rea d'Eran. I bet you don't know this, but Rea's parents were accomplished musicians. Runs in the family."

Devon was still not talking.

"I saw your band—Karma, is it?—perform at The City's Bar two weeks ago. I was very impressed, and plan on catching tonight's show as well. I know the head organizer and plan to be in the front row to fully appreciate your talents on the stage."

That finally got Devon's attention. He wasn't about to give Pauloso all of it until he was sure they were actually heading toward M-Town. "Huh?"

"I'm interested in your built-in fame and your natural talents, Mr. Anderson. I'm also interested in your connection to a few well-known families, such as the d'Erans and, dare I mention them, the Marlows."

There was another name that sent chills down Devon's back. Bad enough he had last seen Ramaron Marlow only a week ago, when he went over the final arrangements for an upcoming trip to Terra III. *Because I don't have enough on my plate right now.* This trip had been planned far in advance, long before this festival gig came up or Danielle was court-martialed.

"Wow me tonight, Mr. Anderson…" The car pulled up to the outskirts of M-Town. It was left idling while the driver hopped out and opened Devon's door. They were instantly bombarded by the ecstatic chants of protestors and security attempting to keep them away from the courthouse doors. "And we may have a very fruitful relationship ahead of us."

Devon left his gaze lingering on the old man's lined face before climbing out of the car. "We'll see. Thanks for the ride."

The door was shut behind him. Pauloso remained in his seat, heaving a sigh of satisfaction as he withdrew his intergalactic communicator and hailed his personal assistant on Terra III. (Not to be confused with the one he worked with on Earth.)

"Yeta, dear," he said in formal Basic, "make sure my schedule is cleared the day Devon Anderson is scheduled to be in the capital. I plan on dropping by the office. Oh, and call my contract lawyer. I have a *lot* of work for him to do."

Pauloso had been in the business long enough to spot the exact type of personality he could mold into a moneymaker. It didn't matter if the rest of the band were competent or even aware of the Federation and its machinations. The details with that could come later, when a few heads were blown and souls shattered with the knowledge of a vast, technologically and culturally rich world beyond Earth.

That wasn't Pauloso's problem, however. *His* deal was finding the raw talent and innate fame that could rock the whole universe. He was already set on having Devon's signature on a few contracts. Yet that cool if not distracted demeanor that left Pauloso's car? He knew how to market that. Not only to the Federation citizens searching for the next "mysterious" musician to fawn over, but to the Earthlings who claimed to care about natural talent more than anything else.

Here was hoping the band was as good as he had heard so far. Because Pauloso was set on making billions of American dollars while the rest of the universe burned around him.

Two

The prosecution's first witness shifted in her seat, the sweat on her brow glistening as if she had walked through Bay Area fog instead of sitting in a courtroom.

It didn't help that Alicia Greene was living in one of her own personal hells. Specifically, the one where she had to face her past relationships and the details she had planned on taking with her to the grave.

"You and Lt. Cromwell were in a sexual relationship for a year, correct?" The prosecution, primarily comprised of a gruff, middle-aged man who took no pleasure in reading the sordid details of every person's sex life, stood before Alicia with his shoulders squared and his back straight. The man was already six feet tall. Now he looked seven. "That is what you told the court in your original statement."

Alicia shrank beneath the man's imposing figure. He reminded her of her father, a military man who dealt with no shit, least of all his daughter's frivolous follies. That was the man who ultimately led to the end of Alicia's first gay relationship. With the woman sitting at the defense table, no less.

"Y... yes." Alicia cleared her throat. She also sent a sympathetic look in Danielle's direction. It earned her a slight nod, and Jed's unwavering gaze. Alicia couldn't help it if she had been subpoenaed to testify *against* Danielle, a woman she never wanted to see harmed by an institution that couldn't give two shits if she was a decent officer if it meant she went home to sleep with women. From the sound of it, Jed and Danielle knew she was screwed. The most important thing was that Alicia tell the truth so she wouldn't get herself into trouble.

Didn't make this easy. Far from it.

"You're saying that you engaged in sexual intercourse with Lt. Cromwell?"

Alicia's face was so red that anyone who could see he held at least a little pity for such an embarrassed young lady. Even the prosecution politely looked away while she momentarily lost her voice. "Yes," Alicia eventually squeaked. "I was her girlfriend."

"Which included regular sexual intercourse."

"Oh my God!"

The stenographer looked up from his typing, shrugged, and continued with business as usual.

"Objection," Jed said. "The witness has already answered this question. More than once."

"Sustained. Move along, please."

The focus soon shifted from her own personal sex habits to, well, Danielle's. "Did Lt. Cromwell ever tell you about past homosexual relationships? Such as with girlfriends before you, Ms. Greene?"

"Yes. She had a girlfriend in high school, I guess."

"So her pattern of behavior went all the way back to adolescence?"

"I suppose so." Alicia was quick to amend that. "She had boyfriends too."

The prosecutor ignored that statement. "Was Lt. Cromwell comfortable in her sexuality? Did she attend functions for LGBT people?"

"Yes. Much more than I was."

"Did she give herself a specific label?"

"Yes."

"What was that label?"

Alicia exchanged another glance with Danielle, who sat up straight in her chair and looked less affected than ever. "She called herself bisexual. I never knew her to call herself anything different."

"Implying that she was firm in her attraction to women?"

"And men," Alicia pointed out, though it was a fruitless cause.

She was soon let go. The hesitant steps she took off the platform almost brought her to lay flat on her face if it weren't for a clerk jumping in to save her at the last second. It wasn't out of the goodness of the clerk's own heart, however. There were more witnesses to shove through, and Alicia needed to get the hell out.

"Mr. Anderson," Jed said to the young man attempting to keep his cool in his tight turtleneck. Way too tight. Devon had been pulling against that collar since he put it on that morning. "You claim to be close to Lt. Cromwell."

"Yes. I know her well."

"Would you say you're one of her closest... confidants?"

"Yes."

"How do you two know each other so well?"

Devon pulled his bottom lip into his mouth, mulling over the words he and Jed had practiced earlier that week when they went over the questions he'd be asked on the stand. "We met through a third party a year ago. We casually dated for a while."

It was the strangest thing to say, since what they had was *far* from "casually dating." The Process mandated that two souls shoved into it together were forever bound, spiritually, emotionally, and physically. While Devon and Danielle would never get married or approach their attraction to one another as anything more than cosmic crusading, they couldn't deny that it still existed. Yet he couldn't exactly tell the court that. Not even Jed knew about Danielle's connection to the Federation. Nor did he know about the Federation. Everyone who did considered it a boon that she had such an ignorant lawyer. It kept him focused on the Earth-based facts.

"Casually dated. With romantic intentions?"

"Yes."

Jed nodded. "Did this include sex?"

Devon inhaled another deep breath. The whole room was focused on him. That included Danielle, whose elbows dug into the table, hands plastered over her face. One hazel eye peered at him between her spreading fingers.

"Yes."

"Had Lt. Cromwell mentioned any other male lovers around you?"

"Yes. I know of at least one boyfriend she had in college."

"I see. Do you know if she had any other male lovers after you and she first... casually dated?"

He winced. Having those words thrown back in his face was like taking an ax to the skull. "Yes." It was only the smallest of lies. Devon knew that Danielle had fooled around with some other guy, but not much else.

"When did you first begin seeing Lt. Cromwell?"

"Last May."

"And when is the last time you and she..." Jed glanced at his client, who looked like she was on the verge of death, "made love?"

The reason Devon was so nervous didn't have anything to do with lying—he wasn't about to lie. Nor did he fear the look coming from Regina in the front row of the public gallery, where she sat right behind her granddaughter. Nor did he fear Danielle having a conniption because now it was on public record that she slept with this random guy a few times. No, what scared him almost shitless was the *other* look coming from the *other* side of the room.

Yes, Miranda was quite interested in knowing the answer, now wasn't she? She was also the only person Devon had to fear in the whole room.

Which made him the only person who knew *why* he should fear her.

Oh well. This was for Danielle. In a way.

"This past Christmas," Devon said.

The daggers instantly stabbed him in the chest. Devon spared only one glance for Miranda, who had furrowed her brows so hard that she looked like she was about to explode. Devon might as well say goodbye to his manhood now.

"No more questions." Jed returned to the table. Unfortunately for Devon, that did not mean he was finished on the stand.

"I have only one question," the prosecutor announced, as he stood up on his side of the room. "Mr. Anderson, are you or are you not also the ex-boyfriend of the Ms. Greene who was on the stand before you?"

Not so far away in the audience was Alicia, who had all but covered her head in further embarrassment. Danielle may have been the one on trial, but due to the nature of these proceedings, everyone was finding out who had slept with whom at some point in their lives.

At least it's only in this life, Devon thought, grateful for once that his love life had not been as active as it was a thousand years ago. Then again, he wasn't using women, gambling, and drink to cope with the scars and traumas this time.

"Yes," he said.

A low murmur went throughout the courtroom. There went everyone's credibility. Devon might as well have said he and Alicia were part of some great conspiracy to make Danielle look like some giant sex freak. Or at the very least, everyone sounded like a big ol' liar.

"I can't believe this," Danielle muttered to Jed. "Could this get any worse?" Who was next? Brandon, her ex-boyfriend from college? Although Jed had considered him after Danielle reluctantly submitted a rather detailed history of her sexual activities, that affair had been too long ago. And while the military was not above dragging witnesses across the country for court-martial hearings, Brandon now lived in Baltimore, with his wife and two young children. Jed had decided to stick with Danielle's recent sexual history. Too bad Devon was as good as it got for their defense, and there was no explaining the tricky ways of the Process when it came to how he ended up with her ex-girlfriend.

Danielle glanced over her shoulder. Regina still sat resolutely behind her granddaughter, but the confusion on her face was palpable.

The consternation on Miranda's face, however, all but said she would rather rip out her toenails than sit through this.

That went for almost everyone else too, although even Miranda had to concede defeat to Danielle when the last of the prosecution's witnesses was brought into the room. Danielle's jaw dropped. Devon slowly shook his head. Alicia squeaked into the back of her hand, instantly recognizing that head of dark hair and the smirk the size of the sun that announced the whole world existed in the palm of his hand.

Well, Danielle's world. That was the only one Seth Elliot was interested in destroying.

"Mr. Elliot," the prosecutor said, "could you please tell the court the nature of your relationship to Lt. Cromwell?"

The smirk never left his face, not that he had anything to proudly admit. The prosecution called him up, after all. This wasn't about his skill as a ladies' man. If anything, he was also about to embarrass himself. Danielle already wondered what the hell angle he could possibly take on the behalf of the prosecution. She was the only one, for Devon and Alicia sat in the audience, correctly calculating what this man was about to say.

"We dated. Once."

"Only once, Mr. Elliot?"

Seth shrugged. "It didn't go anywhere. We went back to her place at the end of the date, but... ah, let's say I ended up going back home shortly after."

"Why is that, Mr. Elliot?"

Danielle furrowed her brows. *Because you didn't have a condom and were too lazy to go get one!* She was halfway to shouting that at the top of her lungs. What was the point of keeping it to herself anymore? Like so many of her old coworkers, she was about to go down in military history as a slut. *Three whole people!*

She couldn't help but think of her coworkers who had to endure one gay lover after another taking the stand, until the judge announced he had seen more than enough. That had basically been Ben's trial. Funny. Was anyone going to bring up the fact that Seth's brother, the man caught fooling around with Ben, had testified at *that* trial? Danielle burned a hole into the back of her lawyer's head, willing him to tear Seth apart. Man was a jackass. It was the least he deserved.

"It became very apparent that Danielle wasn't experienced with male lovers," Seth said. "I'm a busy man. I don't have the patience to teach women how to make love."

Danielle gasped. Regina blew out a noise that said she'd like to teach this boy some manners. Devon couldn't decide if he was more upset by the implication that Danielle was a lazy lover, or that there were men out there who were *that* lazy themselves.

This guy needs a fist to the face. Again, he thought. He had no doubt that part of Seth's testimony was rooted in Danielle punching his lights out a few months ago. For *Alicia's* honor, no less!

The prosecutor continued. "So you forwent sexual relations with Lt. Cromwell because you would have rather spent your time elsewhere?"

"It didn't seem worth it to me, no. Besides, she had spent the whole night telling me that it was her first time dating a man in years. I thought that she, like so many other women these days, was too busy to bother. Then I realized she was talking about her history with women for most of the night."

"Did she tell you about her former lovers?"

"She mentioned she had mostly dated women before, yes." The little smirk grew. "The L word had dropped more than a few times."

"What L word is that, Mr. Elliot?"

"Why, lesbian, of course."

Danielle had half a mind to pound her fists against the table. She had never once called herself a lesbian around Seth. She hadn't even mentioned her bisexuality, fearing that he would fetishize it. Her goal that night may have been to achieve something casual, but she didn't want to go through with it if she believed she was nothing more than nighttime fodder for a man who didn't carry his own damned condoms.

It was almost amazing how many little lies Seth told on the stand. Little enough that it would be difficult for Jed to poke significant holes into them, but big enough that they would leave an impact on the prosecution's behalf.

Danielle remembered so many details from that not-so-long ago night. How flirtatious she had been. Boldly inviting the man up to her place for some *Irish coffee,* of all things. Making out with him, bearing *no* reservations because it wasn't like she was shy around men when she put her mind to it. Sure, it hadn't been the healthiest thing when she went for it, but since when did Danielle Cromwell consider the health of the matter when her sex life was on the line? This whole trial was a good example of that!

Jed did his best to lure the truth out of Seth, but the problem remained that he was their star witness after Alicia. He spun a tale that told of a nervous and inexperienced Danielle, who was "experimenting" with men more than indulging in her tastes in them. Alicia and Devon may have outright said that they had sex with her, but Seth was the one who made her sound like a sad, *sad* woman who was desperate to please but so off the mark. Why would a woman keep talking about "all her girlfriends" when she was trying to sleep with a guy? Made no sense to Seth, who hadn't actually heard a single thing about Danielle's same-sex relationships on their one lousy date. He simply liked to pretend that he had.

"What was that?" Danielle hissed to her lawyer as he sat back down with a sigh. "That guy lied for half a damned hour."

"He didn't necessarily *lie,* Cromwell," Jed spat back. "That's the problem. You said yourself that he left your apartment before anything actually happened. What do you want me to do? This isn't TV. I can't pull shit out of my ass and deflect."

The final witness of the morning was a mark of propriety. Yet the court had no idea what they were doing when they called Capt. Miranda Hotchner to the stand.

The woman was a professional by now, having testified at seven other court-martials over the past several weeks. Because *seven* was the number representing how many good officers she had lost to the witch hunt, spearheaded by penny-pinchers who wanted to move bodies out of M-Town and replace them with "good, wholesome soldiers" coming back from the Middle East. It had always been an open secret, one that DADT barely kept together, that many of the data entry and clerical offices around M-Town were home to LGBT officers who had been granted a final pardon by their former commanding officers. As long as people kept their heads down, stayed out of the public eye, and did a decent enough job, their careers in the military were probably safe. Until people started violating the *Don't Ask* part of the glib, anyway.

"Are you Lt. Cromwell's commanding officer, Captain?" the court asked.

"Yes," she responded, posture perfect and voice firm yet non-threatening, a stance she had perfected over the past several weeks. Some may even say she had perfected them for this moment. If there was anyone she wanted to keep in the military, surely it was *Danielle,* the woman whose secrets she kept... and some other things too. The kind of things that got a woman discharged from the military in those days.

"How long has Lt. Cromwell served at her post?"

"Almost five years now."

"And in that time have you ever known Lt. Cromwell to date women or otherwise engage in homosexual activities?"

Miranda told this court the same thing she told all the others. "No. I don't make a habit of knowing much about my officers' personal lives. It has no bearing on what we do in our office. I don't ask about it, and I don't expect them to tell me about it."

Everyone who knew the truth had to hand it to her: she lied with professional grace. Almost as if she had been doing it for so long that it came naturally to her now. Because if there was anyone in Danielle's life who knew how *gay* she could be, it was her commanding officer, the woman who had made it more than obvious that they were welcomed into a sexual relationship at any time. All Danielle had to do was say yes.

Danielle had never been more aware of how much she had wanted to always say *yes* until this moment, when Miranda sat in that seat as if she owned it, and nobody could tell her what to do or what to say. She always had that kind of confidence about her. The kind that both attracted Danielle like a hot magnet *and* made her insanely jealous. For God's sake, they had been kissing more often than not the past few months. Well, not since Danielle showed up at Miranda's doorstep on a cold November night and announced nothing would happen between them until she started getting a hold of her memories.

This woman knows everything about me, Danielle thought, and that included details about the Process, the Federation, and a renowned mercenary named Sulim di'Graelic. The problem was that Danielle knew nothing about *her*. With everything else going on in their lives, it seemed pertinent to hold back on their mutual attraction until things stabilized in Danielle's life. Ha! How was *this* for stable? *That was back before she told me I was being court-martialed!*

Most awkward day of their half-hearted relationship thus far.

"There is word around M-Town, you know," the prosecutor said, elbow leaning against the edge of the stand and haughty voice implying it had something on Miranda, as well, "that says you have a closer relationship to Lt. Cromwell than you do with your other officers."

Miranda furrowed her brows. Luckily, she had a good idea where he was going with this. "If you mean my relationship to her through Capt. Biggs, then yes, I do. Her grandmother, Ret. Capt. Regina Biggs, is my former commanding officer in the same department. I received a promotion and took up her post after she retired. It's a coincidence that Cromwell came by afterward."

"I see. Is that the *only* relationship you have to her?"

Miranda was about to tell him that *she* wasn't the one on trial, although there were already enough bets around M-Town insinuating it was only a matter of time before she joined the ranks of the court-martialed. Yet one of the reasons she had lasted this long, outside of certain familial connections keeping her out of trouble, was because she knew how to play the game. "Cromwell and I maintain a very professional relationship, if that's what you're asking. She has been nothing but an officer in good standing for as long as she's served in my department. She causes no trouble and keeps to herself. Honestly, I wish half my officers were so gracious."

"But you still personally know her through her grandmother, whom you've already admitted is your former commanding officer."

"Yes. If the military had a problem with that connection, I should think Lt. Cromwell would have been reassigned long before it came to this point."

Danielle was simply happy that the prosecutor didn't start grilling Miranda about her own sex life, let alone how a certain someone may have been a part of it. The truth that they *had* kept most of their hands to themselves would only carry them so far if it came out those kisses they shared could have easily turned into something more.

Honestly, it wasn't until Miranda took the stand that Danielle felt like she really was a guilty sinner. *Gay, gay, gay.* That's all she could think when she looked into those brown eyes, and it wasn't *just* an admonishment toward her commanding officer's very obvious, *very open* sexual proclivities. Danielle could rattle off a few of Miranda's girlfriends, and those were only the ones paraded about in private company over the past few years. God only knew about the others.

"So you're confident in saying that you know not of Lt. Cromwell's sexual history while under your command?" the prosecutor asked.

Miranda scoffed. "Of course I don't. She never told me, and I never wanted to know. I was under the impression that's how it worked."

A few whispers overtook the courtroom. That was perhaps the most critical thing Miranda had yet to say about any of this.

"Thank you for your time, Capt. Hotchner." The court dismissed her without prying any further. No one should have doubted the desire, however. There were more than a few discerning eyes around M-Town who would have *loved* a chance to dig into Miranda's own private life, but a lack of time and a need to stay on track with current candidates for court-martials made them too nervous to ask. Even if this was perhaps the only time they *had* to ask.

The court went into recess for a "short deliberation." Danielle, who had already taken the stand on behalf of herself earlier that morning, let out a shaky breath while people stood around her and the rabble began.

"Honestly wasn't as bad as I thought it would be," Jed muttered. "Helps that you haven't had the most robust love life, it seems."

Danielle scoffed. "Yet here I am, getting court-martialed."

"Don't lose all hope yet."

Hope? What hope? Danielle's military career was over the moment Miranda informed her she was being court-martialed. Even if she was somehow, miraculously found innocent of this asinine charge, it would still be a mark against her for the rest of her life. She could kiss any future promotions goodbye. Hell, she'd definitely be reassigned, and it would *not* be a pleasant post. The old friends she once had no longer talked to her out of fear they would be singled out next. Even her own grandmother looked askance at her half the time.

I'm never coming back from this, she thought. Good luck to her finding a new job, let alone career, after this was over. Most of her friends fled the city, never to be heard from again, or got minimum wage jobs to tie their bills over. Minimum wage employers were some of the only ones willing to take a chance on a freshly court-martialed man, regardless of the reason for the trial.

She was better off packing a bag for the Federation and cashing in her chips on her new-found fame out there. Sounded like that's what Devon was doing. *Hmph.* Danielle distracted herself from her fate by staring at Devon, still sitting on his bench with a glum look about him. *Might not be a bad idea.* The man was about to embark on some cosmic tour while Danielle wallowed in self-pity.

Shit wasn't fair. Then again, there were a hundred discrepancies between them, none of which were the least bit *fair.*

Three

"Hey."

Alicia looked up from where she sat in the hallway. While she wasn't the only one on the bench, she was the only one to give Devon a response. "Hey."

"Mind if I sit?"

She glanced at the empty space next to her and shook her head. "Help yourself."

Devon hugged the arm of the bench and drew his feet in before they tripped anyone, a flurry of pantsuits and military uniforms fatiguing his eyes. It wasn't his first time in a court-like setting. It was, however, the first time he had gone to watch one of his loved ones lose everything they thought they had. "You were great on the stand today," he said. "Couldn't tell how nervous you were."

"Then how did you know I was nervous?"

"Because I know you." Alicia wasn't the first person Devon thought of when it came to someone baring their life on trial. Hell, if he had to choose between her and Danielle... he'd pick Danielle to deal with it every time. Besides, Devon still had plenty of sympathy for the woman he once loved and still talked to on a semi-regularly basis.

Granted, most of that talking was done over text. This was the first time he had seen her face since November.

"Yeah," Alicia finally said. "That sucked. A lot."

"To say the least."

"At least nobody is going to jail for this stuff." Alicia held her bag closer to her chest. "Right? You haven't heard of anyone going to jail for being court-martialed over this, right?'

Devon shook his head. "I guess it's rare they're being court-martialed at all," he said. "But they're pushing through so many people that it's like they have no other choice."

"I really don't get it. Why now? When there's always been..." Alicia pressed her fingers against her lips before she said too much. "People have always known."

"I don't know. Maybe somebody has an agenda. Elections are this year. I... well, I don't pretend to know much about what goes on behind the curtain, so to speak." Until that past year, Devon was blissfully unaware of many things, including what really went on in places like M-Town. He was also ignorant of the worlds beyond his own. Of course, now that he had regressed to his previous life, he couldn't imagine an existence where he didn't fluently speak a dead language or knew about alien worlds. "Shit's crazy, though. Danielle's never done anything wrong. They should honestly be commending her for the role she played in protecting this godforsaken planet."

Alicia's shoulders bunched up, allowing her to inhale a deeper breath. "They don't care about that. They only care about making her feel like the wrong kind of slut."

"Yeah, well..." Devon shrugged. "They're a bunch of bastards. What are you going to do?"

She placed a hand on his and gave it a tight squeeze. "Seems like I should be sorry that we're meeting again in times like these. One of these days we'll have to meet up because somebody's world *isn't* ending."

"And to think, I'm leaving the planet in a couple of days—" Devon stopped before a passing officer had the chance to hear him. There were definitely members of the Federation among them, some of whom might even be internally screaming to be so close to so much action, but they would never betray their origins.

Still, there were ways to tell if someone knew of his fame or not. Otherwise, how would Federation citizens find one another on a planet that wasn't supposed to know about them? Golden F pins on lapels were the first signs of a possible friend. Then there were coded words that sounded a lot like phrases in Basic. As for the man passing them? He may have been a member of the Federation—even keeping his cool around Devon, a man he instantly recognized as soon as he entered the hallway—but there was no way for anyone who didn't know him to tell. He liked to keep it that way.

"You're going out there again, huh?" Alicia glanced up at the ceiling, as if she could see beyond the atmosphere and catch a glimpse of a world beyond her own. "How about you bring me back a souvenir this time? Not that I know what kind of souvenirs they have out there. Maybe a keychain. Shot glass. Spoons..."

Devon chuckled. "I'll see what I can do. Clyde is already pissed enough he can't come with me. Was probably a huge mistake letting that guy know anything about alien humans. And the other aliens."

"If anyone needs to stay here on Earth, it's that boy."

"Agreed. Luckily, one of my band members... you remember May? I think I've told you about her... is going with me for part of the trip. It's old hat for her, even though she was born here on Earth."

"Is that so?" Alicia steeled herself for the possible answers to her upcoming question. "Is May your girlfriend?"

That got a sound of disbelief out of Devon. "No. She's a bandmate." He almost said it too quickly. Too defensively. Because nothing said a woman wasn't his girlfriend like vehemently saying she wasn't. "I mean... it's not like that."

It didn't matter how much Alicia nodded or told herself that Devon must be espousing the truth. The fact was that he was about to leave the planet, and she would be crawling back to the apartment she shared with her friend Jenna. The amount of moving Alicia had done in the past few years had streamlined her life and invited her to try a minimalist approach to her belongings. It had not, however, made dealing with her conflicting feelings for Devon any easier. "Is Danielle going with you?" Alicia asked.

"No. I think she has enough going on here to keep her preoccupied for a while." Danielle had been invited, of course. They both had been, since they were often billed as a pair over the past millennium. Yet Devon was the only one in a situation to accept an invitation to a tour around the Federation, giving interviews about his existence and meeting with a few important people to go over the continuous hunt for Nerilis Dunsman. As if Devon had anything to do with it anymore. "That's why May is coming with me. It'll be nice to have a fellow Earthling who is familiar with a few things along for the ride."

"I can understand that," Alicia said. She didn't mention that it might also be nice if it could be her one day. Whether because she longed to spend time with Devon again, or she was a slave to the curiosities that summoned her to parts unknown... well, all of it was better than being here, where she had to look upon her ex-girlfriend's misery.

"Are you going to hang around for the verdict?" Devon asked.

Alicia slowly turned toward him. "Of course I am. Are you?"

"It feels like the right thing to do."

Alicia looked around the hallway, littered with people in uniform and the kind of manners she had always seen in her own family and when dating Danielle. "Feels so weird to be back in a place like this again," she said. "I hate it."

Devon didn't have to ask why. "Come on. I think they're about to give the verdict." While he didn't take Alicia's hand on their way into the courtroom, he stayed instinctively close. He wasn't sure what he thought he was protecting her from, other than a few of the demons that lurked around them every time they hashed out old history.

The verdict was swift. Although Danielle had prepared herself for the inevitable, she still held back a few tears when her rank and benefits were unceremoniously stripped away from her.

At least you didn't make it to the final stretch of your service, only to have it yanked away from you. That's what she thought while putting on a brave face and thanking the people who had come out to support her that day. The courtroom was already fixed up for the next poor son of a bitch about to have his life demolished. *At least I'm not Ben, who only had five more years to serve before he got full retirement.* Danielle had only served ten. While she intended to stick with the military until retirement, she couldn't say she felt bad now. They clearly didn't want her.

It was strange to hug her supporters, thank her lawyer, and turn down offers to go out and make a mess out of their lives. Danielle still had paperwork to fill out and things to hand in. While she didn't have to figure out her future right *now,* she still wanted some space to breathe and think. That meant accepting a ride home from her grandmother, where they sat around the counter talking about nothing in particular.

"I'm so sorry, honey," Regina finally said. "I don't know what's come over people, but I don't want you worrying about money or any of that. If you need to come home..." She stopped. She knew Danielle didn't need to hear reassurances that grandma's house would be around.

"Thanks. I'll figure something out." Danielle already had a backup plan. She may officially no longer be in Earth's military, but she had heard there were others out there. All it took was the right connection. Like Regina had secured her granddaughter a spot in M-Town, there were people Danielle knew who could get her a position somewhere else. Preferably there on Earth, but there reached a point in a woman's life where she didn't care what planet she was on anymore.

"I know, dear. You always do."

Danielle encouraged her grandmother to drive home to the countryside before the day grew too late. Her phone blew up with calls from her best friend Troy, from Ben, and from more people in the media who wanted to interview her about her trial. She didn't recall people like Ben garnering this much interest from the media. Was it because she was a woman? Because she once lived as a woman named Sulim di'Graelic, although she no longer remembered it?

Did she care?

She stood in front of her mirror for a long time, beholding the uniform she had worn for years. *Never thought anything about it until last month.* Taking off her uniform now would mark the final time. The badges no longer meant anything. Her nametag might as well have said *Loser.* Although she had pressed her uniform and shined her shoes like she was taught in Basic Training ten years ago, back when she was young, dumb, and searching for meaning in her life, they bore the evidence of a woman who had lost everything.

Her job, anyway. But her job had been her life for the longest time. Office workers may have sold their souls to the corporations they worked for, but the military existed on another plane of reality. It was *everything.* Job. Training. Benefits... family. Danielle would feel that hole in her life for years to come. Although she never got along swimmingly well with military life, she knew how to do it. She had come from the influence. Her grandmother had set the stage for Danielle's decisions, whether she meant to or not.

Finally, Danielle unbuttoned her shirt, pretending that this was another day after work. She was changing into civilian clothing because it was the thing to do. Not because she *was* a civilian now.

Even though she was.

Funny how quickly that happened. She had gone from First Lieutenant Danielle Cromwell to... Ms. Danielle Cromwell. She wondered if this was how she felt in her first life. She heard she was once the niece of a well-to-do lady on some planet far, far away. Back before she was kidnapped to a more desolate wasteland of a planet, where mercenaries sold themselves to the highest bidder. Had Sulim gone from privileged princess to heartless warrior? Was that why this didn't feel so foreign now?

Unfortunately, there was no one to really ask, not that she desired the answers. She had been dragged to Cerilyn a while before Devon witnessed the slaughter of his parents. According to him, however, Sulim had been one of the only mercenaries to show him kindness on Cerilyn, forging the bond between them that lasted the rest of their lives.

Hell, the rest of their *existences,* apparently.

Nobody can really tell me what I used to be like, she thought, sitting on the edge of her bed. *Not the real me.* She had a feeling that, whoever she was on Cerilyn, it was nothing like the old her that had grown up somewhere else entirely. The American military had taught her enough in *this* life that most people didn't come out of it the same person they were before, for better or worse.

That crushing loneliness she often felt throughout her life returned at that moment. She had always assumed that it was a feeling most people suffered from time to time. Not until she learned the truth of her soul and talked to a therapist who specialized in reincarnation had Danielle realized this sensation was another wonderful side-effect of the Process. That Void-forsaken wringer that had squeezed Danielle's soul of everything that made it whole, over and over.

Her phone rang, pulling her away from madness for another evening.

"Hey." She had immediately recognized Troy's number. There were few people she could stand to hear right now, and maybe he was one of them. She would find out within a few seconds.

"Heeeeey."

How was a man supposed to sound when he had lost his best friend from the office? Granted, Danielle definitely suffered the worst between them that day, but the universe would allow Troy to be upset on behalf of himself as well. As long as he didn't let Danielle hear the sniffing he had courted from the moment he heard the news on the military grapevine. There were more than a few people who reported the verdicts the moment they were handed. Troy had actually heard of Danielle's military demise before word reached her mentor in the Federation ten minutes later.

"Heard about what happened. I'm so sorry."

The heavy sigh leaving Danielle's lungs had the power to knock her unconscious. Instead, she flopped back onto her bed, the headboard smacking against the wall and her eyes slamming shut. "Me too. You put in ten freakin' years, and this is what you get." Danielle only had to put in ten more and retire at forty. Still plenty of life left to do other things, like travel the world and universe. That was coming for her now, whether she liked it or not.

"Where are you now?"

"Home."

"Really?" Troy's surprise was only matched by Danielle's disbelief. "I just finished my shift. Let me buy you a drink. A bunch of us will..."

"No, thanks."

Danielle knew what he had in mind. The same thing the department did every time one of their own was court-martialed that year. Drinks. Lots of them. Both for the dearly departed and everyone else, who was either covering their own gay asses or mourning the loss of another decent coworker. While only half of the officers assigned to their data entry division stuck around for longer than a year, it was like a family. A highly dysfunctional family with a woman—who had relations to international terrorists—for a mother. The thought of receiving the pity she had dished out for the past few months made Danielle want to throw up. She could get drunk on her own. Assuming she dared to part with the money she should be saving.

"You have other plans?" Troy asked.

"Yeah. There's a place nearby I might go and hang out. I want some peace and quiet. There's a lot of shit going on beyond my own woes at the moment." Devon had invited her to his big moment on stage that evening... hell, wasn't he going on stage *right now?* Danielle glanced at her alarm clock and realized she didn't give a shit. The man had known she wouldn't be in the mood, anyway. Had she *not* been court-martialed, she might have gone, if only to say she had been there at Karma's first big festival performance. But that was still a big maybe. Danielle preferred to avoid crowds. Perhaps there were some people who preferred them in the wake of terrible shit befalling them, to blend in with the masses and forget about the pain for a while, but that was not Danielle's style. She was better off moping and stewing. Preferably, with a hard drink. "I might be up for something tomorrow. Dunno. Ask me twenty-four hours from now."

"Still time for you to go on that big intergalactic tour, I guess."

"Can't think of anything worse right now!"

Danielle had been invited, of course, but Devon was better suited for that kind of bullshit, anyway. He got along better with people. Hell, he had regressed, so picking up Modern Basic and dealing with the strange ways of the Federation came more naturally to him. This was a man who now spoke fluent Old Basic. Supposedly, Danielle could do it too, although the ability remained locked away in her stupid, dormant brain.

"Well," Troy continued, while Danielle pushed herself up to her feet and finished dressing down in her civilian clothes, "if you need anything at all, Danny-Lynn, you be sure to let me know, okay? I'm going out with some of the others to drink our problems away so I might be too sloshed to help later tonight, but... yeah, I'll give you a ring tomorrow. Take care."

Danielle was ready to go when she hung up on him. She had the perfect, quiet little bar from a few blocks over in mind. Drinks were a bit pricier than she liked, but that also meant the place wasn't likely to explode in chaos while she drank and stared at her phone, as if it held any of the answers she sought.

Whatever answers those were. Danielle was so hungry for answers about her own existence that she had all but given up learning a damn thing.

She was better off letting the universe decide for her. Whatever came her way? She could take it. She had taken on much worse before, apparently.

Four

Minor improvements had been made to Commander Yara d'Alacron's hospitality in the months since she ascended to her lofty position. Before, whenever Master Ramaron Marlow was summoned to her office in the heart of Terra III's capital, he was appalled to be served iced water and the occasional cup of caffeinated *wao-su,* the closest thing to coffee the Federation came to consume on a regular basis - before coffee was discovered on Earth, anyway.

Now, however, he was served a type of *cageh* that had all the aromas of home. He took special notice, however, that the stamp on the bottom of the infuser did not contain the Vallahar family crest. They may have been renowned for their *cageh* plantations, but the Federation was in the midst of quietly blacklisting the family's goods in the light of Master Janush Vallahar's involvement with recent events.

Because stepping down as the ambassador to Terra III hadn't been a big enough shame, apparently. Now his family, for which he was responsible for, faced dire financial straits if the Federation placed a silent embargo upon their crops and drinks.

Too bad, wasn't it!

"Woo, fancy." Lanelle Lanerak, Marlow's first and foremost assistant, whistled at the delicate *cageh* serving set placed before them. Fragrant steam rose from the opened lid as the servant stirred the leaves and placed a small drop of *hedpah* oil into its midst. Much too small to be considered an illegal substance, but enough to make Lara's guests feel cozy. Either way, Marlow took a hard look to ensure that really was *hedpah* going into the communal drink, and not something else.

Like a truth serum. He wouldn't put it past his hostess. "When's the last time the Federation government went this far out for us, hmm?"

Marlow sat back in his plush seat, his old and weary hip muscles enjoying the light murmur of a massage from the motor resting deep inside the chair. "We're actual guests this time, I suppose. Far cry from when we were all dragged into interrogation one by one." It had only been a few months ago. Surely, Lanelle wasn't that easily swayed? Then again, her humanity usually chose moments like these to leap out and show her employer that, at the end of the day, she had a human's mind. Easy to be swayed when a woman only lived a hundred and fifty years...

Unlike Marlow, who didn't want to talk about the birthday that had recently passed. He was well over three thousand by now. Past the point of desiring to recite his age to anyone. Why, he was practically *sixty* in human age.

Ahem. Definitely sixty. Not seventy. Or seventy-five, like some calculators liked to speculate. Just because he needed a cane these days to get around...

Ask me how I hurt my hip, Lara, he thought, as the doors opened and a small contingent of armed guards brought their commander into the receiving room of her own office. *Unless you already know.*

His people's healing skills couldn't help him by the time he finally saw someone about the limp he had acquired. Then again, to properly heal any injury, the healer needed to know the direct cause. Something Marlow was often too embarrassed to admit.

"Master Marlow." A large folder hit the table before Yara had a seat on the other side of the table. "Ms. Lanerak. So grateful that you could both meet with me on such short notice."

They waited for the servant to pour the commander a cup of *cageh* before returning the greetings. Eyes burned holes into the servant until he bowed out of the room. The only other people sitting in on this private meeting were the two armed guards by the front door. Marlow was well within reason to wonder if they were there for general security, or to ensure that a certain sorcerer didn't throw a conniption because he didn't get his way. Honestly, they *should* be concerned.

Marlow followed the law as much as he could reasonably consider, but there reached a point when a man had to pull rank with his race, age, and magical abilities.

Never his gender, however. That wasn't the gentlemanly thing to do.

"Regarding tomorrow's arrival of Mr. Gardiah..." Yara stopped herself, the false humility in her nonplussed demeanor almost more comical than it was honest. "I'm sorry. Mr. Anderson. I'm still getting used to it."

"Imagine how we feel," Lanelle muttered.

"My extended apologies. Regarding tomorrow's imminent arrival of Mr. Anderson, I'd like to ensure that his lodgings have been properly swept for devices and his ensuing entourage have had all their backgrounds checked..."

This was a perfunctory meeting, and while Marlow was not above making sure things were in order before big events—he was a noble *julah,* after all—he sensed that there was something particularly condescending about these proceedings. Lanelle and her partner, Evan, had taken great pains to ensure Devon's tour of Federation bodies went off without a hitch. Accommodations were arranged. Security procured. Translators, therapists, and even a chef who could recreate simple Earth-based dishes were hired to follow them for the next two weeks. (Evan was especially excited about that chef, but would be most disappointed to learn that he did not, in fact, know how to make sponge cake.) The only way things could go drastically wrong was if Yara herself interfered. Considering this was a project assigned to her by the President of the Federation, since Devon was a celebrity of great cultural importance, Marlow was right to assume that Yara was invested in everything going to plan. There must be something else lurking in that diabolical head of hers to drag this out for Void knew how long.

"I've made sure to reserve the entire suite, ma'am." Lanelle pointed to the western portion of a certain hotel's map. "Devon will be secured in the innermost room, with Master Marlow taking up the adjacent suite and..."

"Yes, very nice. Good work." Lanelle closed the cover on her tablet and sat back in her seat. "Ms. Lanerak, would you be a dear and give your employer and me a little space? We have something confidential to discuss."

Lanelle and Marlow exchanged a furtive glance. Marlow nodded, sending Lanelle off, although neither knew what for.

He'd find out as soon as the door was closed behind Lanelle.

The pleasant yet fake demeanor immediately dropped from Commander d'Alacron's face. Quite the feat to make an intimidating woman look even more unapproachable, yet there Marlow was, sharing a table with one of the most powerful people in the Federation. More powerful than the president, if enough people would argue it. *Maybe* more powerful than the Master Chancellor of Yahzen, but that was Marlow's bias speaking. She held more legal clout than Marlow, that was for sure, and she also wasn't afraid to use brutish intimidation to get the answers she sought. Like now, when she said, "Master Marlow, I'd like you to assure me that at no point in this venture will I find cause to take Mr. Anderson into custody for conspiring to help a known criminal."

All right. He was *not* expecting that! "Excuse me, Commander?"

She sniffed while reorganizing her folders and tablets, as if Marlow were a foolish nuisance who didn't understand his true standing in this situation. "My ongoing investigation into the whereabouts of Nerilis Dunsman keep bringing me back to the theory that not only do *you* know where he is, but that some of your closest confidants—of which I include Mr. Anderson—may also know. Why, I even have reason to believe that you and he may keep constant contact with him. Isn't that something? All of my research, all of my investigations… keep bringing me back to you and yours."

Marlow fought to keep his demeanor in check. Fine thing if he showed off the shock that this woman was *still* on his ass over things he could not control. Like that *fossup* egg of a criminal who kept contacting Marlow whenever the hell he felt like it. Last time Marlow heard from his old friend, the universe-renowned Nerilis Dunsman, the deposed High Priest of the Void was gallivanting between outposts and crossing into parallel universes. He had a long-term goal of learning how to fuse them together although, as he put it, *"The calculations behind the soul merges alone… let alone on a cosmic scale… it makes my head hurt, Ramaron. You wouldn't believe the thumping going on in there right now."*

Yet Marlow couldn't let on that he knew any of this. Yara was always five minutes away from arresting him and throwing him into the Federation's highest security prison, which wasn't that far away. Terra III may have only had one moon, but half of it was dedicated to housing some of the worst criminals, many of whom were condemned to death.

Not quite the company I wish to keep, Marlow thought, as he maintained gracious eye contact with his hostess.

"Probably because we've had the most dealings with him over the millennia, Commander. You're talking to the man who can remember when Nerilis Dunsman threw up all over himself in the middle of a lecture. He had drunk a little too much *yaya* the night before." A little. Too much. More like half a cask of Void-begone Brew. The humans weren't the only ones who partied hard at their colleges. If Marlow had a coin for every drink he had, he'd have all of his family's money amassed before him. *And I'd still have a bum hip.*

"I already know that about you, Master Marlow. Which is why we keep having these frustrating conversations about where he is. You keep insisting you don't know where he is."

"I've told you, he does as he pleases, and he has his ways of staying under your radar."

"Yet you will not tell me what those ways are."

"Because it goes even above *my* head. How many times do I have to tell you that he's more powerful than myself? He's the most talented *julah* our kind has ever seen. Even back in our days at the Academy, it was like that. Really went to his head, if you ask me."

Nerilis wasn't the kind of lad who took his power humbly. Nor did he succumb to the plights of creative genius. He partied, partook in coming-of-age ceremonies, and for Void's sake he fell in love and eventually got engaged. Aside from rising in the ranks to become one of the youngest High Priests of the Void ever recorded and conducting the kind of experiments that resulted in young sorcerers being expelled from the Academy, he was completely normal.

Until he wasn't anymore, of course.

"Yes, well…" Yara opened one of the folders. Although there were half a million *CLASSIFIED* indicators on it, nothing about it looked like it had anything to do with Devon's impending arrival. "I'm about as tired of talking about him as you are, Master Marlow."

Doubtful. This woman was hell-bent on formulating a legacy that would make her one of the most famous—or infamous, depending on who was asked—commanders in the history of the Federation. She wanted whole classes dedicated to her. Footnotes in textbooks weren't good enough.

Yara was far from the first woman to make it to commander. She was born and raised on Terra III, so she didn't have some interesting background to propel her to automatic stardom. Her conventional beauty would only play a part if she were the modeling type. However, even if she were, she still had that giant gash over her left eye. She needed something big. Some grand action to cement her place in finicky, forgetful human history. Bringing in Nerilis Dunsman and ensuring his death would be one mighty fine way to prevail.

Rumors churned that she was working with the president to ensure both of their legacies. Two women bringing down the greatest terrorist history had ever known? Oh, even Marlow could taste the accomplishment.

Too bad she was always barking up the wrong tree.

"I've had some intelligence come my way recently, Master Marlow." Yara stared at a piece of paper before turning it around and placing it before Marlow. Most of the text was written in Basic, the official language of Federation documents, but there were a few handwritten lines in Julah. It may have been Lara's own hand, since most of the grammar made little sense and there were egregious spelling errors, as if a novice had tried their hand at translating. "Very fascinating intelligence. The source is decent too, so it's been worth my time to personally investigate it. Take a look. Tell me what you think."

That was all she would offer before Marlow perused the typeface. Yet the first thing to draw his eye was the grainy photograph at the bottom of the paper.

"Does she look familiar to you, Master Marlow? She certainly looked familiar to me. I've seen that face a few hundred times in my life, yet never with that name attached to it."

Marlow politely put the paper back down. "I have no idea who she is."

"Really, Master Marlow? You're telling me you don't recognize one of the most famous faces of your people? I've personally seen her portrait hanging in the Temple. She's venerated as a demigod by strict adherents. My own mother prays to her before she goes to bed every night."

Marlow picked up the paper again, pretending to give it a second look. Of course he recognized her. Any *julah,* let alone one who personally knew her for so long, would recognize Joiya Lerenan's face. Even if she was styled *nothing* like the Joiya he once knew and loved.

Because that wasn't Joiya. That was a completely different woman who happened to look a lot like the High Priestess of the Void.

"She does look mighty familiar, but I'm afraid you've lost your mind, Commander, if you think this is Joiya Lerenan. She is dead. Hmph, as dead as you can be when your soul has Ascended to the Void." Her body was long dead too, but Marlow would rather not implicate himself in her so-called murder. *Worst fucking night of my life,* he thought. By far the worst night of Nerilis Dunsman's life as well.

"I know she's dead, thank you." Yara reclaimed the paper. Her eyes lingered on the photograph, a smug smile slowly spreading across her face. "I also know that my intelligence tells me this is Dunsman's daughter."

Genuine surprise gripped Marlow. Not because the news was unheard, but because *nobody* was supposed to know about it. Hell, the mere fact that such a woman was officially a part of Lara's investigation did not bode well.

"Do you know this woman's name?" Yara continued to hold the paper as she showed it to Marlow. "Miranda Ann Hotchner. Known alias is Michiko Kawazama. Her mother is listed as some woman from one of Earth's countries. Her father is supposedly named Gregory Hotchner. However, there are absolutely no records of such a man existing on Earth. Not one of his description or fitting the correct time period, anyway."

"I'm not sure I follow. Why are you looking at this woman? Facial recognition? Commander, there are trillions of people in this universe. We're bound to see doppelgangers across the generations."

"I told you, Master Marlow, this is coming from my source, who tells me that Nerilis Dunsman has a daughter. This is the woman who comes up when I do some deep digging. What do you think about that? Do you know anything about him ever procreating? It's not in any records *I* know of, besides some unfortunate..."

"I know what you're talking about in regard to that." It had been nearly fifteen-hundred years since Joiya's ascension, but her life leading up to those days had been far from joyous. She and Nerilis had been plagued with miscarriages, enough that their elders asked them to reconsider marriage in case they were a poor match. Now, it was believed that Joiya's fate as the High Priestess of the Void prevented her from carrying any child to term. Her soul may have been constructed of endless life, but her body was never meant to be long for the world. "I've never heard of him having children with other women."

That was a lie. He had heard. Recently.

Then again, if there was one thing Marlow was good at, it was lying to Commander d'Alacron.

"Very fascinating. So you're saying that, although nobody in this universe knows him better than you, he may still have a child that even you don't know about? But my sources do? Very, very fascinating."

"Your sources are probably wrong, Commander. There are a lot of unscrupulous people out there who will say anything to sound important and make a dollar." He might have been looking at one such person now. Fancy that.

Yara crossed her arms and leveled her gaze on the man she knew was lying. Not that she could prove it. Marlow was too good at covering his lies—and being Void-knew how many years older than her helped. He also had his race to back him up. There wasn't a *julah* alive who wouldn't take his side against hers if push came to shove. They were all like that. *Julah* only worked against Nerilis Dunsman, and that wasn't all of them—and only because he had given them a bad name.

Still, she had rattled him a little. He was surprised by something. Either the knowledge that his old colleague may have had a child as recently as thirty-five years ago, or that Yara knew about it. Of course, the grandest conspiracy in all of this wasn't necessarily the fact that Nerilis Dunsman was a father. It was the appearance of his supposed daughter.

Yara was bound to keep digging, of course. And the deeper she dug, the deeper she would realize the conspiracy went.

She couldn't wait to ask Mr. Anderson a few questions when he arrived on the morrow.

Rather than stew in *woe-is-me* misery or freak out about her impending financial situation, Danielle took to the quiet bar with two goals in mind: to drink a glass of the best whisky in the house, and to draw up a list of her prospects now that she was officially unemployed and not likely to get a nice salaried job with a court-martial on her record.

No big deal! she thought as she sat near the corner of the bar's large and inviting square shape. *I'll get a job flipping burgers, am I right?* Those kinds of thoughts made her want to smack her forehead against the bar.

The bartender looked askance at her as he brought her the drink and took her money. She had been slowly saving up to buy a small house in the next... decade. So much for that now. Danielle would probably burn through what savings she had trying to pay her rent and job hunt at the same time. Ben had gotten a job at one of the gay bars in the Castro, both because he had great connections there, and because it was the best he could do with his record. It harkened back to the blue slip days, when gay discharged soldiers wandered around their old, assigned ports, searching for work so they could afford a ticket back home. A lot of them ended up staying, which gave rise to the neighborhoods so many of them now took for granted. Danielle didn't have those kinds of connections, though, and the few lesbian bars that were left probably couldn't afford to hire new staff. Not that Danielle knew the first thing about bartending. She knew how to make Irish coffee, but that was about it.

"Let's see..." She tapped a pen against the small notebook she had pulled out of her coat pocket. A humble list of monetary pursuits lay before her, although she hadn't made it past selling her plasma. Her grandmother had offered help in the form of letting Danielle move back home. At least she wouldn't have to worry about bills. But she also wasn't about to give up her life she had built here in the city. Where her friends were. Where the people who knew about her *brain* and *soul* were. "Yup. I only have one choice."

She wrote down, *Make Marlow give me money.* Solid plan. The bastard owed her for the millennium's worth of spiritual torment she had undergone because of him. Plus, he was from an old, wealthy family. He could totally afford to make her his lazy employee who didn't do jack shit on Earth. *Just pay my bills, asshole.*

The bar wasn't that large. All it took was one person stumbling in to catch Danielle's attention. And most of the bars' patrons, since there were only a few of them in there that early on a Friday evening. Besides, it was the kind of "classier" place in the neighborhood that attracted the upper middle-class on dates, meeting friends, and holding business meetings that spilled out of the office. There were no TVs showcasing the local sports games. No jukeboxes. No fried foods. Just the square bar and a few outlying tables with two or three chairs. Danielle hadn't merely walked all this way for the top-shelf whiskey. She wanted the calm while she sorted her thoughts and prepared for a life without half the things she had known.

"Oh..." came a familiar voice. "I didn't... Sorry."

Danielle was hardly surprised when she looked up and beheld Miranda standing around the corner of the bar. She was halfway to taking off her coat and the bag hanging from her shoulder. The khaki uniform was gone. So were the barrettes she used to keep back her bangs for work.

She looks like another woman who belongs in a place like this, Danielle thought, and not only because Miranda always looked like a million dollars in her civilian clothes. She had that effortless ability to move around spaces as if she absolutely belonged there. If it weren't the hundred people saying hello and attempting to get her attention, it was how readily staff waited on her. Like the bartender, who asked her what she wanted to drink before she sat down.

Because Miranda had no idea Danielle would be there, huh? To be fair, Danielle had wandered closer to Miranda's residential neighborhood than she usually did for a long drink. That's why this place catered to those wealthy enough to afford single-family homes in the middle of the city. Something Danielle had always questioned about Miranda's finances, since a woman on a meager captain's salary wasn't about to stretch her dollar far in the Bay Area.

"I didn't know you were here." Miranda pulled her bag back up her shoulder and grabbed her coat.

"No, no." Danielle leaned against her elbow as she motioned for Miranda to sit back down. "Have a seat. Not like this is weird anymore." It had stopped being weird months ago, when Danielle realized there was a cosmic reason for Miranda's constant presence in a certain somebody's life. Sometimes, a woman had to pick her battles when it came to the machinations of the Void. Miranda's arrival may have been a coincidence in a mortal's terms, but they both knew better now. Better to watch things play out than attempt to push them away.

Yet Miranda wasn't in a hurry to either grab her things or sit down. When the bartender asked her again if she'd like anything, she muttered that a scotch suited her well. A far cry from the martini she was about to order to get her started. *"Go straight for the scotch,"* the universe said. *"You're going to need it."*

"All right." She pulled out the stool and helped herself. Without her coat, she represented the kind of dressed-down woman Danielle rarely associated her ex-commander with, if only because Miranda rarely went anywhere without a skirt and blouse. Tonight, however, she was in a pair of jeans and a long-sleeved scoop neck that allowed her two prominent collarbones to stick out in ways they never did at work. Good damn thing. Danielle would've had bigger problems than merely crushing on her captain.

Except she wasn't Danielle's captain anymore. Not someone she worked with, either directly or on contract. She was just another woman now. Danielle was a civilian, and as long as they didn't get caught and cause trouble for Miranda in the court-martial-happy culture...

Danielle kept her eyes on her notepad. She hoped her handwriting wasn't big enough for Miranda to read from a few feet away. Bad enough Danielle could smell musky perfume that must have been placed directly on the skin. Right on the throat. Maybe a little on the shoulders. Shoulders in a thin, off-white shirt...

This was a different kind of nightmare. Why did they have to know each other? Had Miranda been any other beautiful woman—let alone *exactly Danielle's type*—Danielle would have taken it as a sign that she should flirt and try to get lucky. A little bone thrown her way to make up for the shit she endured earlier. As it was? It still felt taboo. She simply didn't know if it was the rules drilled into her skull, or something else that gave her such a strange feeling around Miranda. The one that told her to be wary. *Danger, danger, danger.*

Danger from what, though? For the longest time, she attributed the "danger" to their work dynamic. Then Danielle discovered that the commander she had silently lusted after for a few years was somehow a part of the Federation, let alone privy to intimate details about Danielle's past life that even *she* didn't know. The answer was always on the tip of her tongue too. There were nights when Danielle closed her eyes and saw the flickering face of someone she desperately wanted to meet again. To touch. To hold. To cry against, for as long as she was allowed.

Damn it. Things were getting weird again.

"So... how you holding up?" Miranda asked, shortly before thanking the bartender for her drink. "That was one of the rougher trials I've seen."

"How so?" Danielle doodled something in the corner of her notepad. She probably should have turned the page so Miranda didn't see the name "Marlow" in there. Not that it mattered anymore. Miranda knew everything. Danielle knew nothing. This was how their worlds spun.

"The case they built around you was based entirely on your exes. I mean, I've seen a lot of exes on the stands recently, but because you were so on the downlow when it came to queer events... ah, they couldn't get you on that."

Yes, that definitely had backfired on Danielle. She was never big on the events Troy and others tried to drag her to, but part of the reason was the wariness that came with being so "out" in a career that didn't appreciate it. Without explicit proof that she was at "lesbian night" once a month or cavorting with women she fancied in public, the courts had to dig into her homosexual history. That was how women like Alicia got trotted onto the stand, forced to drink in the horrific embarrassment for the rest of her life.

Danielle and Miranda were silent for a moment. Miranda shot some of her scotch down her throat, eyes remaining locked on the ceiling even after lowering her glass to the countertop. Danielle looked away before she was captivated by the movements of Miranda's throat. The perfume continued to invade her space, however, and it made her think of something she couldn't quite remember.

That warning bell clanged in her head. But she didn't know if it was because Miranda posed a physical—or spiritual—threat, or because the truths she carried in that head of hers were too much for Danielle to bear.

Sometimes, she swore she knew Miranda from another life.

"Christmas, huh?"

Danielle shot a defensive look in Miranda's direction. She sat with her arms crossed beneath her breasts, head turned toward the bartender as he served a group of friends at the opposite corner of the square. Yet Danielle would win the bet that said Miranda didn't care that much about the woman with buck teeth or the young woman who snorted every time she was greatly amused. She was thinking about something that had been bothering her from the trial.

"Don't judge me," Danielle snapped, although her tone carried a good-natured ribbing she hadn't intended. "I don't have to explain myself."

Scoffing, Miranda shook her head and pushed her elbows onto the counter. Fingers combed through shoulder-length brown hair. Her black roots were prominent on her scalp, with streaks of shadows dancing between the brown hair dye that illuminated the bright amber of her eyes. People from the Federation whispered that she looked suspiciously like a prominent figure for a reason.

Although Miranda styled her body to suit her tastes, she would never escape the hue of her eyes, the type of hair growing from her scalp, or how her lean body chose to distribute fat, if at all. She had been born with a *julah's* form reincarnated as a human. Things changed from life to life as the genetics of her mother of the moment held minor sway, but in the end, Miranda was cursed—or blessed, depending on how one looked at it—to inhabit a body originally belonging to someone else. The first soul in the history of time to ever achieve such a damning feat.

Not that Danielle knew those details. All she knew was that the otherworldly quality to Miranda's appearance wasn't only from how she dyed her hair or wore her makeup. There was a spiritual component that attracted them together. One they had both been fighting since they encountered one another on Earth.

"I'm just saying," Miranda continued, her eyelashes fluttering in Danielle's direction, "you can do so much better than him."

"It's not like that."

"I know he's not your boyfriend." Miranda didn't utter the other words attempting to follow that. *"He wouldn't dare."* Danielle wouldn't understand. Hell, Miranda felt guilty for thinking it to herself. Her qualms with Devon were personal. Sure, Danielle's relationship with him played its part, but even if she never, ever kissed the man, animosity would rear its ugly head every time Devon and Miranda were in the same room. Which happened *way* more than either of them cared to admit.

Danielle had no memory of a few months ago, right? When Miranda and Devon stormed the Temple of the Void, intent on saving her from ritualistic sacrifice. Miranda had barely escaped the aftermath. Devon could afford the interrogations on her behalf. She had to stay low.

Nobody was supposed to know she existed.

"So why give me crap about him, then?" Danielle asked.

"Why? Makes me feel better about myself, I suppose."

"At least you're honest."

"I try to be when I can get away with it." Miranda sensed the need to change the subject. She consulted her glass of scotch before saying, "So, any plans now that you're a free agent?"

"If you mean to ask if I have any job leads, then no. Not outside of attempting to get a job through the..." she lowered her voice. "The you-know-whos. The F people."

Miranda held back a laugh. Too bad it instead came out as a guffaw. "The F people. That's precious." She was encouraged to apologize when she saw the mild annoyance on Danielle's face. "You can say Federation, you know. Hell, the bartender's from the Federation. He absolutely knows who you are."

Danielle dropped her pen, wide eyes absorbing the sight of a slight man who cleaned glasses and faced labels on the shelf. "How in the world do you know?"

"You pick up the signs after a while. Overhear the code words most of us Earthlings don't recognize, until we do. Lots of transplants come here to talk about 'back home' and all that. It's one of the reasons I like coming here. Great amusement. Most of them don't know you understand Basic. It's up there with eavesdropping on Japanese tourists."

"I don't know Basic." Danielle supposedly knew Old Basic, but not only was it still dormant in her brain, Devon's difficulties with translating Old Basic into Modern Basic seemed tricky enough for Danielle to eschew getting in on that in a hurry. "I won't ask how you do."

"Probably for the best. I like keeping a low profile."

"Because people aren't supposed to know about you, right?"

Miranda leveled her gaze on Danielle for the first time since sitting down. Eyes as bright as the lights above them threatened to slice Danielle in two if she didn't stop asking questions. Yet why would she do that, when she had nothing to lose now? Nothing aside from her sanity, perhaps.

"It's a precarious situation I've been born into," Miranda said. "I work with the choices I'm presented with. Keeping a low profile is a part of that."

Something about that only made Danielle more curious. "Yet you were cavorting with a known intergalactic crim –"

Miranda "accidentally" knocked the napkin stand over. The loud clang giving half the bar a heart attack brought with it a sweet *"Sorry!"* while she cleaned it up and continued to fire warning shots in Danielle's direction. Right. Probably shouldn't bring up someone like Syrfila Tograten in a bar full of Federation citizens.

"Sorry," Danielle apologized. "I'm sorry for a lot of things."

Miranda's countenance softened. "For what?"

"I don't know. Just feel like I should apologize. It's been a long day. I'm... tired." To put it lightly. Her hell wasn't quite over, either. There were still more meetings with her lawyer. Some publicist wanted her to give an anonymous interview. God only knew what else she'd have to endure before she was officially "free" from the military's grasp.

The saddest part? She'd probably go back to how everything used to be if they waved the magic wand that made it so. Danielle was in a part of her life that craved stability. The universe was in enough flux around her. Losing her steady job that provided its own culture and tracks to success? Not great.

"You don't have anything to apologize for. What happened was out of your control. Wasn't fair, either." Miranda sighed. "You were a model officer. Most days." She said that with a small grin. "Could've done without you dragging your ass in late so many times. A meaner commander would have made you do ten times as many pushups as I did."

"I think you only did that much because you wanted to see my biceps flex."

Danielle had chosen to say that when Miranda was stealing another sip from her glass. Out came the scotch again, burning new holes into her nose and making her choke on her own spit. "Excuse you," she said between outbursts. "More like I let you get away from harsher punishment because you're so gosh-darn cute."

"Uh-huh. So it's true. I was one of your favorites, which meant I got away with more antics."

Miranda shook her head. "I have no way of answering that without incriminating myself in some way. You should look into law school now. You'd make a brilliant lawyer, apparently."

"That's more my ex-girlfriend's thing." Assuming Alicia was still going to law school. When she wasn't taking a break because she was dealing with PTSD from what happened last spring, she was having quickies with nefarious fellows who brought their brothers to their fights. "Probably my ex-boyfriend's too, although the thought of Seth being a *boyfriend* is pretty hilarious. I literally had one so-so date with him last November." Danielle didn't regret the urges she had that night. She did, however, regret directing them at Seth. When Miranda said that Danielle could do "better," she certainly didn't mean Seth, even if he was technically more attractive and more successful than Devon. At least Devon cared about her. *Enough to get a condom...* Danielle couldn't believe this was the comparison she was forced to make in some Federation-approved bar on the night of her court-martial.

"Are you seeing anybody right now?"

Well! That was a brazen thing to ask. Somehow, Danielle wasn't surprised, and she shouldn't have been. Miranda may have been good at sounding like she asked that in good faith, but the ulterior motive was *definitely* there. She might as well have grabbed the neon OPEN sign hanging on the door and propped it up on the counter in front of her. *"Miranda Hotchner, Open for Business."* All sorts of business. This was a woman who was always unattached, even if she had a date for almost every function. Even Danielle could see from a mile away that they were Band-Aid dates to hide whatever emotional scars she bore alongside the fading lines on her back. Syrfila Tograten had been the only woman who came close to claiming the title of Miranda's significant other, and she would smack the person who verbally suggested it.

"I haven't 'seen' anyone since my ex-girlfriend. I don't really have the time or mental energy to date," Danielle said. "Life has had a way of monumentally sucking this past year." She left it at that.

"I understand."

"I bet you do."

"What's that supposed to mean?" Miranda asked.

"You know what it means." Danielle sipped more of the top-shelf whiskey still lingering in her glass. "The reason the bartender knows who I am. Like it or not, I'm a celebrity in parts of this universe." That's why Devon was going on some tour, right? Sure, the talking heads told him and Danielle that it would be about building goodwill between Earth and the Federation. They were basically the most famous Earthlings *ever* now. Their faces, both old and new, were in books and TV programs across the Federation. *The Mercenaries.* They might as well form a band and call themselves that. Danielle might have a writing bone in her. With her and Devon's powers combined, they could write a bunch of punky screamo about the Process and why it should rot in hell.

Miranda looked away. "Yes, well," she began. "You're definitely ahead of me on that curve."

"Didn't ask for fame. You're terrified of it." Danielle snorted. "What a pair we make."

The subtext of that statement was not lost on either of them. Miranda held her arms close to her chest while staring at the polished wood of the countertop. Danielle gazed off into the distance, yet no matter how much she turned her head away from Miranda, she still smelled that damnable perfume.

She still felt the other woman's presence. A woman who could be stripped of her name and identity, but still be *that woman.* The one haunting Danielle through multiple lives she never asked to have.

There it was. That muddled face before her eyes. The panic-stricken light overwhelming her made her teeter on her stool, but she caught her balance and returned to the present before Miranda even noticed.

"Damn it all," Danielle muttered. She pounded back the last of her whiskey and pocketed the pen and notepad before it could slip to the floor. Like she was about to slip when the alcohol hit her the moment she got off the stool. "I'm gonna go. I need some fresh air."

She met Miranda's eyes for a final time. What was that lurking behind them? Concern that they would no longer have excuses to see each other again? Ha! With the way the Void and the cosmos played their cards, Danielle would see Miranda every time she went to the supermarket. Every corner of a bar would be filled with her presence. Her own damn car probably had an excuse for Miranda to be tied up in the trunk. Nothing shocked Danielle anymore.

Nothing except the hand appearing before her for one last shake.

"Good luck, Cromwell," Miranda said with the tone she usually reserved for work. "I have every confidence that you'll figure things out and be back on your feet in no time."

Danielle hesitated before lifting her hand to shake Miranda's. "Thanks." Their fingers instantly intertwined, thumbs curled together and palms squeezing. While they were both used to giving firm handshakes, they were not accustomed to receiving them. Let alone firm handshakes that could be construed for other things.

The other words Danielle wanted to say were lodged in her throat. It didn't help that she couldn't pry her eyes off the woman touching her. Because perfume and scoop-neck tops weren't enough. Danielle had to also endure torture from a hand she didn't expect to be so damned *soft*. There were terms for officers like them who had never seen "real action" and instead served their country in domestic office spaces. *Soft Hands* was one of them. One of the politer ones, really. Yet Danielle couldn't be offended when this was the reality she now encountered. A woman's soft hands were like Kryptonite.

She had to get away. Now.

"Thanks for everything," she said. "I appreciate it. See you around."

The last thing she wanted to do was turn around and behold the face watching after her. There was more than enough evidence that postulated Danielle was likely to run into those arms and beg to know what was going on. What was between them? How were they related? Why were they always pushed together, even when the timing was all wrong?

The answers, of course, were always swimming around her brain, unafraid to exist but too shy to show themselves. Except for now, when one answer hesitantly presented itself the moment Danielle stepped into the cool night.

"Who says the timing's all wrong now?"

Five

Drinks flowed at the post-festival party Devon and the rest of his band were invited to that night. He needed it too. While the thrill of performing on stage was always a welcome addition to his life, that morning had been such a clusterfuck that he was likely to get smashed on cheap beer and wake up with a hangover—in time to do some light intergalactic travel.

"Did you *see* all those people?" Serge, the primary guitarist of the band, represented the crowd with the breadth of his arms. "One thousand people! Can you believe it!"

"Definitely not bad for being one of the opening acts," May said, her bottle of beer already half empty. She was about to do some light traveling as well. So if she was okay with drinking a little more than usual to celebrate? Devon was right behind her, knocking back beers and high-fiving the other bands and their roadies who swept through the bar. "Our MySpace page is gonna skyrocket. Y'all watch it!" She had put a lot of time and effort into that MySpace page, although Clyde bugged her about Facebook. *"Lots of college kids on there, May! Get on it!"* She was more concerned with putting up a proper website for the band, however. Whenever she was supposed to have the time for that.

"We completely sold out of CDs and shirts, guys!" Here came Andy, Serge's girlfriend and the band's #1 hustler. When she wasn't helping them set up their gear, she was at merch booths ensuring the marked-down CDs got into the hands of people who even slightly liked the music. The demo had been cut for this event, after all. Six songs—four originals, two covers—and a promo single featuring the song they opened with that day. "Easy" was the song that came together when

May and her keyboard were officially added to the group. It had been a big hit with the crowd too. There had been crowd surfing. And a little headbanging. Enough that Devon had to step back from the front of the stage.

"Jesus, can you believe it?" Clyde was nearly a mess of tears as he drank his beer and slapped his hand against Serge's shoulder. "It hasn't even been a year since our first real gig at that little dive bar. Just like this one!" Here came the tears. At least he could embrace them now. "And in time for Devon to get the hell out of here and tour the galaxy or whatever."

That sobered Devon up fast. Luckily, Serge, Andy, and their new drummer Hank assumed Clyde was drunk and indulging in hyperbole. "It's just a little international trip. Been a long time coming, right?" He held his bottle up for a toast. "Gonna have a lot of new music material when I get back!"

The cheers flowed. Serge and Andy abandoned the table to go dance. Hank spotted a gal he knew from his neighborhood. At least Clyde could mutter about whatever he wanted in present company.

"I'm going too, you know," May said in his direction. "I swear, both of you keep forgetting where I'm really from."

"*You're* the one hiding it from everyone!" Clyde shoved a handful of peanuts into his mouth. "Devon almost shat his pants when he figured it out."

"Don't know if I would put it that way." Devon turned to May, who was three chairs away. "But I am pretty grateful for it. Kinda hard to get shit done when I'm tiptoeing around the truth around everyone." For the longest time, Clyde was the only one who knew about Devon's spiritual misery. They called it that "reincarnation stuff," since if anyone ever overheard them, they simply assumed they were two stoner Buddhists going through a phase. Maybe that was the case for Clyde... "Having you on the trip will be a big help. Still can't believe you said you would do that, though."

"Why? You're going to parts of the Federation my parents have only told me about." May snorted. "They're way too settled here on Earth to go on big trips like that anymore. I'm going, because it may be my only chance. Besides, I need a vacation as much as you do. Let's write some damn music."

"Speaking of music..." Something was on the tip of Devon's tongue. Something about a guy in an old car. *What was his name again?* Devon thought, retracing his steps between sound check that morning and testifying in a military courtroom at lunchtime. *Kinda hard to remember what strangers said to you in their car when you told a whole bunch of people in uniforms who you had sex with on Christmas.* Was that dread rising through him like a bulging tide? About the upcoming trip and the inappropriate questions people would ask about his personal life? Oh, absolutely. Couldn't get through another few minutes without that in his chest.

"Just promise me," Clyde said, interrupting Devon's thoughts. "When you two come back ready to get married, I'm invited to the wedding."

Devon almost dropped his drink. "Excuse me?" That was followed by a more colorful phrase from May's mouth. She was excellent at getting her point across without speaking English—or her parents' mother language, for that matter. "Care to explain yourself?"

"Maaaan." Clyde's chuckle was almost more erratic than his movements. Nobody had counted on him being the designated driver that night, but that only meant he drank *more.* And when Clyde drank, he was likely to overshare and extrapolate all the wrong ideas. About his love life. About *others'* love lives. Like Devon's! "You guys make such a cute couple. I'm totally jealous, man. You always get the cutest chicks, Dev. Even before Alicia the uptight babe, there was that theater kid who you said gave the greatest..."

"*O-*kay!" With his cheeks on fire and May's face shyly turning away, Devon reached across the table to grab Clyde by the arm and give him a firm, distracting shake.

"Danielle totally ain't my type but even she has a killer bod, man. She's gotta be what, less than fifteen percent body fat? Whoa. How much is that? I don't feel great."

"You're itching for a smack, huh?" Devon said through gritted teeth. May joined him by Clyde's side, and right on time, for he was slipping down his chair and toward the floor. "I've got him," Devon said to May, who attempted to help prop Clyde back up in his chair. "Shit, he's such a lightweight." He meant that both in the literal sense and referring to Clyde's ability to hold his liquor. Or none at all, in this case.

They passed Clyde to the large group by the wall. Other bands had gathered to talk shop with Serge and Andy. They were also keen on talking to Devon and May, especially when they realized Karma's bassist was drunk off his ass and now complaining about his left butt cheek going to sleep.

"I think I'm going to go," May said, grabbing her jacket from the corner pile of coats, hats, and jackets. Devon had refrained from adding his to the pile after he heard someone call it the "lice hump." The Void only knew what he would pick up during his travels through the Federation. Last thing he needed to bring was *lice.* "Are we still meeting at your place tomorrow for takeoff?"

Devon looked around to make sure nobody eavesdropped on their personal—yet coded—conversation. "Yeah. Eleven. Bring only what you can carry on your person. Or that's what they told me, anyway." They would not be taking the convoluted, particle-rearranging and blasting mode of transportation most humans endured when traveling between planets without a ship. Instead, they would enjoy the much more comfortable mode that was "magical teleportation." That was the official description, according to Devon's hazy understanding of Modern Basic. He wasn't far from the truth, either. The Federation clearly defined their science-based (all right, with a little of a *julah's* magical influence) teleportation devices and how a skilled *julah* sorcerer could simply "bend" the world around him and stroll from one planet to another in about half a second. Unfortunately, there were limitations, such as extraneous luggage left behind. "Anyway, about what that dumbass was saying..."

"Don't think anything of it. If I worried every time a guy assumed I was dating a male friend, I'd be a bigger mess than even my own mother could handle."

A helpless chuckle shook Devon in his core. *That's one way to put it,* he thought. Besides, May's mother wasn't the kind of therapist who dealt with anxieties and paranoia. One could only imagine how Rea d'Eran dealt with her ignorant Earthling patients who knew nothing of their reincarnation drama that probably single-handedly led to them having past-life nightmares. Eventually, Devon would ask how a woman from the Federation helped people completely oblivious to it.

"I'll see you tomorrow. Be safe getting home." May finished putting on her jacket and left the bar without another glance in Devon's direction. Yet he would be correct to assume her reason for that. He would've made the same exact exit had their situations been reversed.

Miranda sat in her living room, basking in the dim lights she set to their lowest settings and the warmth of the central heat she cranked up higher than most guests liked. She had no guests tonight. Having come in from a cold, late winter's night, she was inclined to sit in nothing but her jeans and top—*and* not be cold.

Besides, looking at the letter left on her coffee table made her sweat more than enough.

She knew who it was from without a return address or a signature. The first giveaway was the language: Julah, the *lingua franca* of the people of the same name. While Miranda was far from fluent, she knew enough to parse the layered meanings of this seemingly simple correspondence. Her penpal asked how she was doing before launching into poetic praise of the flowers that grew around the Marlow Estate that time of year. *Clever,* Miranda thought. Her father, the notorious Nerilis Dunsman, protected them both against a Federation officer's interception of this letter by making it look like it came from his old friend Ramaron Marlow. Miranda knew jack shit about the old family estates of Yahzen, the home planet of the *julah,* but she wouldn't be wrong to assume that the Marlows enjoyed a fragrant and colorful explosion every spring. Still, that wasn't the true meaning of the letter. When Miranda looked between the lines and digested the words she read, she saw the cryptic message her father sent her.

Another one to add to the pile.

Miranda's system consisted of reading her father's letters, transcribing them to Japanese (or Old Basic, but Japanese would be harder for a Federation officer to translate in a timely manner), destroying his original letter, and picking the details out of her own handwriting. Eventually, she would receive a good enough description or coordinates to where they were to meet next. Then? Brace for an obnoxious chat with Daddy.

Sighing, she tossed her letter onto the coffee table and got up from her couch. A bottle of wine and a cigarette were the best ways to calm her nerves after a long day of watching the woman she loved have her sexual history scrutinized and used to ruin her life. Not the first time Miranda sat in on a court-martial hearing and witnessed the downfall of another decent officer. Yet it was the first time she had to swallow the bile rising in her throat every time the court implied Danielle was a godless heathen because she once kissed a girl.

If only they knew she's kissed me. Miranda stared at the wine labels in her cabinet, not comprehending a single one. Not the Napa reds she picked up whenever she went for a short drive north, and not the Tuscan or French imports she sometimes indulged in when she wanted to further distance herself from the brutal savage she once was. *And that's in this life.*

She chose one of the Napas. They were easier to replace, and she may as well embrace her domestic roots tonight. The memories forever burned into her psyche were at the forefront of her mind . There was no escaping the screams of torment she caused, or the angry, mutilated faces of the people who got in her way or went against her orders a thousand years ago. A good bottle of wine couldn't wash away the sins a woman named Cairn committed, but it could loosen her thoughts.

So could use a damned cigarette, not that she knew where her half-empty pack had run off to between leaving M-Town and coming home. The short-lived cigarette she had on the courthouse steps hadn't been enough to get her through the rest of the evening. So much for her constant fight to cut back to one or two a day. *I need to go cold turkey,* she thought while pouring herself a glass of wine. *It's the only way I'll commit to anything.*

Sure, she'd go cold turkey. As soon as she finished this bottle and pack of cigarettes. She could start her sober, nicotine-free life on the morrow.

A glance out the window would have told her that she was about to have an unexpected visitor. And, usually, Miranda would have looked toward her window to decide if that's where she wanted to have her cigarette like she sometimes did. She was a woman who preferred to keep the smoke out of her house, after all. One never knew when they might entertain a guest who would rather drown than set foot in a smoker's house.

Like that moment Miranda had been anticipating for the past ten years, not that she ever thought it would actually happen. Which was why she didn't bother looking at her window as she brought her glass of wine over to her couch, fixated on locating her cigarettes.

She nearly jumped out of her skin when her doorbell rang.

Paranoia wasn't a stranger to her existence. This was a woman who carried the trauma of a mercenary's bloody life on her soul, and this life alone had seen one nosy parent with boundary issues and a plethora of criminally-inclined associates who courted bounty hunters and Federation police alike. Miranda couldn't shake the immediate fear that she was about to die. Nor could she set aside the hope that this would be nothing more than Girl Scouts selling cookies or the neighbor asking if she had seen his missing packages.

Even so, she had a drink of wine before going to her door. If she were to die tonight, the last thing she wanted on her lips was alcohol.

You're not going to die, you hysterical bitch. Miranda rolled up her sleeves before peering out her peephole. *Or maybe we are.* She had to step back and swallow one of her heavier breaths. Clearly, her eyes were playing tricks on her.

"What are you doing here?"

This wasn't the first time Danielle showed up on her doorstep. The last time she beheld the only woman with the power to make her stand down from a fatal fight, Danielle had declared she knew Miranda to be a key player to retrieving her dormant memories. *That wasn't all she said...* She had asked Miranda for patience while she pieced together the mysteries of her past lives and why it may prove too dangerous to ever remember who she once was or what she had done. *I know. I know everything.* Miranda saw a flicker of that uncertainty in Sulim di'Graelic's hazel eyes as she briefly recognized the other woman for who she was.

A friend. A comrade. A coworker. The love of her life.

The worst part was not being able to say a word about it.

"Is this a bad time?" Unlike the November night when she graced Miranda's doorstep, the Danielle of March hesitated. Granted, she had been through a bit of a rough day. Yet the last anyone had seen her, Danielle was sitting with her hand in her head at a neighborhood bar. After a long walk around town, Danielle's feet brought her here. Back to where she knew the answers lurked. Back to where she constantly fought a temptation she would eventually succumb to, like a moth drawn to a flame that promised eternity.

An eternity of suffering, perhaps, anyone would think in her position. Or Miranda's, for that matter.

"N-No." Miranda cleared her throat. "I actually just got home." She looked over her shoulder. The wineglass wasn't out of place. The letter written in Julah, however? Danielle might not immediately recognize the language, but Miranda shouldn't take her chances. All it would take was one hard look, and Danielle would recognize the flowing letters of a cursive-based script. She had seen it in her travels of this life. What if she thought Miranda wasn't to be trusted? *Don't be conspicuous about it. Come on,* Miranda thought. She should have put her father's letter away when she was finished with it. "Is there something you need?"

Danielle shrugged, her jacket flapping against her black T-shirt. "You mean besides a new brain? Or a new soul, for that matter?"

Miranda was speechless. How in the world was she supposed to respond to that?

"Can I come in? We need to talk."

The first thing Miranda did was head to the coffee table, leaving the door open behind her. Although she hadn't given verbal confirmation, Danielle helped herself in, staring at the décor details of Miranda's house. Beige walls, white trim, hardwood floors and stainless steel appliances didn't only represent the design aesthetics of most move-in ready homes of the neighborhood. They were Miranda's preferred accents, since she was a woman who appreciated earthy tones and the subtle, soothing colors that kept her paranoia in check. The only non-Western expressions of her background she indulged were some Chinese calligraphy prints along the staircase. She didn't even display her own artwork she painstakingly created in her spare bedroom. There wasn't a brass butterfly on the mantle or her favorite book that had been considered classic literature a thousand years ago. Nothing that pegged her as anything more than a red-blooded American woman who knew not of worlds beyond her own. Not even the other Earth-based cultures she was technically a part of in this life. Such references were dangerous both with the xenophobic types and her own psyche at times. This was a woman who wouldn't be surprised if Commander d'Alacron sent a Federation SWAT team through the doors and windows one day. If Miranda went down, she was going down with all the evidence she could amass on her side.

All of it was rather silly with Danielle standing in its midst, though. She was so modern in comparison. *A fantastic representation of the current state of her soul,* Miranda thought before looking away. *Stuck in the present. Always looking forward and never looking back at her roots.* Miranda had never been in Danielle's apartment before, but she would be right in assuming the colors were black and white with only a hint of accidental color. Even Danielle's wardrobe was simple and understated. When she hadn't been wearing her khaki uniforms, she was dressed in nothing more than jeans, black or white T-shirts and pullovers, and the same jacket she had for the past three years. How that jacket had survived at least two attempts on Danielle's life would always remain a mystery to them both, but Danielle never complained. She hated shopping.

"You want a drink?" Miranda asked after stashing away her father's letter beneath a pile of Japanese and Western fashion magazines. "I was about to get drunk on wine. Start this weekend off right."

"Californian or Italian?"

Miranda's eyebrows lifted in mild appreciation. "What if I told you it was Oregonian?"

"I'd call you a liar, because everyone knows the only American wine you drink is Napa Valley reds."

"Everyone, huh?"

Danielle snorted. "Ben talks."

"Yes, well, that's why Ben was one of the first to get kicked. Doesn't take a good military lawyer to figure that one out." Miranda took one last drink of her wine. "Although his fascination with me will always be weird."

She met Danielle's eyes from a few feet away. Miranda's desire to know what Danielle so fervently wanted to discuss in private almost overrode her ability to play a decent hostess. Good thing she hadn't found those cigarettes. No faster way to make Danielle run in the other direction than to overwhelm her with tobacco stench. One of the few things Ben fed to Miranda over the past decade.

"You're really pretty, you know that?"

Miranda almost dropped her glass. Slowly, she turned around, eyes as wide as the first time Danielle showed up at her door wanting to *talk*. That time had definitely not gone in this direction, however.

"Sorry." Danielle looked away, pink tickling her cheeks. "I've always sucked at this."

"Sucked at what, exactly?" Miranda had a million other questions she could have asked, but decided to go with the kind of thing Danielle expected. "Complimenting a woman?" She offered a smile of reassurance. "What do you want to talk about so badly that you came straight over here as soon as you thought about it? I can't imagine it was to finally blurt the one thing you've been thinking since we met, but were too chickenshit to ever say."

Danielle lost the ideas she had been considering since leaving the bar earlier that evening. What had been so resolute in her mind the moment she decided it was now lost to the Void and its inability to keep her soul from decomposing wherever she was reborn.

Yet it had chosen Earth this time. Out of all the places to send the chess game that was fighting over a planet's soul, the Void decided that three relative strangers were cursed to this out of the way planet. It wasn't the tiny mining planet that had occupied one life again, with a population small enough to ensure Cairn and Sulim crossed paths multiple times before even realizing who the other was. Nor was it the now obliterated hub of Paxoah, one of the largest planets to have ever existed outside of the Federation's knowledge, let alone contain billions of people. Earth was a humbling yet comfortable location for three souls to know so well by the time they officially crossed paths.

And crossed paths we have, like a hundred times without realizing it, Danielle thought, as she finally allowed herself to openly admire the woman she had not-so-secretly crushed on for the past however many years. How could Miranda be so casual *and* fashionable? Was she naturally built to accommodate such an infuriatingly captivating style? Or did she spend untold hours in front of her mirror ensuring she looked as "natural" and "effortless" as possible? Even in a military office, where she had to keep her bangs out of her face and hold back on the makeup, she was the prettiest one in the room. *Doesn't help that every time I see her, I suddenly remember... something.* A something always on the tip of Danielle's tongue and always imploring her to act on her instincts.

Perhaps their mutual attraction was more forbidden than being commanding officer and a lowly recruit reporting for duty. For all Danielle had known, the song and dance they did over the past several years was due to Miranda's manipulative nature playing the long con and waiting for the perfect moment to kill Danielle in her sleep.

She didn't see Miranda as a potential threat now. Nope. She was back to being that strange, attractive woman who held the keys to Danielle's identity. An identity she had to remember on her own, if she wanted to live to enjoy what few positive memories she had. The threat of a forced regression always hung between them. Miranda would lose everything if she accidentally caused Danielle's forced regression. And Danielle would die, doomed to the Process's machinations beyond the end of time.

"I had a lot of things rehearsed in my head before I came in here." Danielle sweated beneath her jacket. Nerves, mostly, although Miranda's love for cranking up the heater wasn't helping. "I went through a whole improvised script based on how you greeted me. This is the positive outcome. Except... I don't remember what I was going to say now." She further blushed when she realized her words were dashed the moment she saw Miranda again, dressed for a comfortable night at home while still looking like the kind of goddess who stole Danielle's heart again and again.

"Maybe you don't have to say anything," Miranda suggested. "Maybe it's better to act."

Did she know what she invited into her home? If Danielle acted... if she dared to be so bold and give herself completely over to the instincts that threatened to consume her...

She'd either be the most suave bitch in the universe, or she'd be the biggest fool.

Which would she rather gamble?

This was a diverging path neither Sulim nor Cairn had encountered since they died a thousand years ago. Never, in the past one hundred lives, had they the chance to pursue the feelings that had survived the annihilation of their planet. There was either no time or they were pulled apart by their warring factions. Maybe Sulim was so traumatized by her bruised soul that she took one look at Cairn's face and died on the spot. Sometimes, neither of them reached adulthood, doomed to a plague on their planet or not reaching maturity before Nerilis made his move.

But three things had always been certain: Cairn would be reborn first, the worlds would conspire against her finding Sulim again, and Sulim never, ever had the chance to embrace the one good thing she felt whenever she was around the soul that had followed her across time and space.

No wonder Danielle's chest heaved, her eyes glazing over as she fought to remember what she had wanted to say. All she could remember was what she wanted to *do*. The welling emotions that had no name. The whispers of words nobody but her could remember. A full and loving life that not even Devon knew about. The greatest secret burdened by the Process had nothing to do with Relics, planets, or the Void, and everything to do with how powerful one forbidden love could be.

Danielle walked past Miranda, stopping long enough to consider the staircase before her. When she took the first step, it was with her eyes locked on the calligraphy hanging on the wall. She didn't read Chinese, but she felt their meaning deep in the marrow of her mortal bones.

"Together... One Day... In this Home..."

"H-Hey..." Miranda's voice followed her as Danielle rushed upstairs, taking a sharp turn down a short hallway. Two doors were opened. Bedroom one. Bedroom two. The second bedroom was dark, but the outlines of an easel and the carefully organized canvasses brought Danielle inside. Paints weren't as well organized. They cluttered this corner and were strewn about that ledge by the window. Enough light filtered through from the streetlamp to illuminate Miranda's current work in progress. An abstract representation of the feelings they conjured whenever they were in the same room. Violets. Rosy pinks. Glittering gold dripping down burnt orange and sienna. A splotch of aquamarine to bring out the violet. A yellow butterfly streaking toward the corner, both escaping the emotional chaos and chasing after its unknown destiny.

"Is that you?" Danielle asked the moment she sensed Miranda's presence behind her. "Or is it me?"

"Do you remember?" That tone was cautious, both for Miranda's sake and the woman who stared at a shadowy canvas in a room that was not her own. "Do you remember anything at all?" If Miranda allowed a drop of desperation to enter her voice, she might as well strike them both down where they stood. Try again in the next life.

"I remember this feeling."

"What feeling?"

Danielle swallowed, the painting fading away. The blur overtaking her vision didn't present anything new. No memories. No indications that either of them shared anything more than the space they inhabited.

"*This* feeling." How else could she describe it? The presence. The fears. The jubilations and desires. The jump in her step when she raced to the person she wanted to see the most.

"She's there," said the damnable voice that occasionally haunted her head. It was Sulim's voice. One that sounded suspiciously like Danielle's, yet came from a place Danielle could never hope to access. It was the reason she argued against the concept of reincarnated souls being exactly the same person. How could she really be Sulim when that woman existed separately in her subconscious?

How?

"For the love of God, go to her. Please. Do it for me. I want to feel like that one more time."

Danielle wiped a single tear from her cheek. It would be the only one she allowed for the rest of the night.

"Who are you?" Danielle whispered.

Miranda sucked in her lips before she said something trite, like, *"I can't tell you."* Or, *"I am nobody."*

She wasn't nobody.

"I am the chief of your tribe," she said in Old Basic, hoping against hope that Danielle might understand even a sliver of it in her thick head. "I'm the one who saved you from a life of misery, but you're the one who saved me from a life of torture. I will always be in your debt. You will always be in mine."

Danielle stood, unmoving.

"My body is older than yours, but my soul is as young as yours. I couldn't control who I was born as. Not today, and not a thousand years ago. But the Void decided that nothing was more important than us crossing paths one day. I've regretted every time I've let you out of my sight since."

That head of blond bowed, a hand covering her face.

"You don't remember me because of something we did. Something we can't take back." Miranda switched to English. "We can't take it back. But it's not our fault. We did what we had to do." Miranda wasn't as strong as Danielle. She had to shed more than a few tears as she fought for the words to say that would get her point across without potentially damaging Danielle's soul. "I wish to the Void you could remember. Anything. Even the worst day of our lives."

Danielle turned back around, her eyes as hollow as the heart Miranda had been carving since she first realized she had to protect herself from the pain following her wherever she was born. *I am cursed to always remember you, Sulim,* she thought. *While you never remember me. I am repenting for my grievous sins. This is my purgatory.* A thousand years of torture.

"I could never tell you in words," Miranda said. "But I could show you in other ways." The opportunity was closer than ever before. Dare she believe the day had finally come? When the fiery angels guarding the gates to purgatory finally let her step outside for some fresh air?

Danielle dashed out of the spare bedroom and down the hall. Before Miranda could assume that her beloved was leaving the premises once again, she realized that Danielle was in the master bedroom, removing her jacket and tossing it onto the stool before the vanity.

"What in the..." This wasn't really what Miranda had in mind. It had to be a trick. A new level of eternal damnation, after God decided she hadn't suffered enough. "Have you lost your mind?"

The woman sitting on the edge of Miranda's bed was no longer hollow. Full color had returned to Danielle's eyes, including the glint Miranda always beheld whenever they locked gazes from across a room. Yet instead of her telepathic plea for Danielle to remember leaving her head, she accepted one. One she hadn't heard in a thousand years.

"Come here."

"This is crazy." Why was Miranda so flustered? Did she refuse to believe that this was really happening? That Danielle could be the instigator when dreams finally came true? Miranda had never foreseen this. Not the coy, flirtatious look in Danielle's eyes or the confident way she took up space in another woman's bedroom, as if she belonged there. "What are you doing?"

"We no longer work together." Danielle shrugged. "Why fight it any longer?"

The timbre of her voice punched Miranda right in the heart—or, perhaps, the loins was more accurate. It had been a damnable long time since the two were connected in Miranda's body. *A body I stole from someone else.* It may have been hers now, but she would never forget the all-consuming love another soul once experienced in this cursed body.

No wonder Miranda was destined to this existence. Her soul had been marked for an exceptional time from the moment it emerged from the cauldron of the Void. Danielle was sucked into the gravity of one soul's destiny. Now here she was, making the best of it.

"I'm honestly shocked," Miranda said.

"Hey, if you don't wanna…" Danielle hopped back up and brushed her shoulder against Miranda's. She might as well have shoved her. "Just say so. Don't jerk me around. Tell me that you want me as much as I know you do." She squared her shoulders as she faced Miranda, a look of obstinate consternation flooding the crevices of her visage. "Or do you not want me?"

Those words dared Miranda to lie. To say that it wasn't the right time. That it was too soon after so much drama. That she didn't want Danielle at all, not today, and not after the past thousand years of begging her to remember even the *slightest* thing. The gauntlet dropping on top of Miranda's head might as well have told her to go screw herself.

Scoffing, Danielle took another step toward the door.

Miranda's reflexes had never acted so quickly. When she snatched Danielle by the arm, it was with the understanding she wouldn't be letting go for a long, *long* while.

"Don't play that game with me," Miranda spat.

Danielle glanced at the hand wrapped around her wrist. The transference of desire from one body to another easily collided when both directions demanded dominance. Yet it was Miranda who overwhelmed the dispersing energy first. All it took was an aggressive glare and the squeezing of her hand.

"I'm not playing a game," Danielle said coolly.

She was soon against the wall, her chin tipping up so her lips could accept the kiss coming for them.

Six

The world cracked against the energy exploding from one corner of its shell. A ripple traveled to the ends of the earth, awakening those who were asleep and striking those who were awake right in the chest. A ripple that wasn't confined to just the earth. While few of the Federation's busy inhabitants felt a single thing, the Void rumbled around them, beneath them, above them, from that other plane of existence it occupied, both seen and invisible. Everyone acknowledged powerful spiritual energy. But not everyone bowed beneath it like the entirety of the Void.

The only people who were completely oblivious were the ones at the center of the ruckus.

Words seemed both imperative and absolutely unnecessary as Miranda pressed her body against Danielle's and reveled in a response she could have never anticipated. There wasn't a hint of hesitation or foreboding in Danielle's kiss. She was as much of a participant as the woman she touched, a woman she completely lost herself in as soon as it was safe to admit.

Besides, what words could they say that added a single thing to this experience? Wasn't it mindful enough living in this moment? An instance they had both been craving since they first acknowledged an attraction to one another... a thousand years ago?

I remember the first time I ever kissed you, Miranda thought, her mouth too busy to speak. Her hands were likewise occupied with the bottom of Danielle's shirt, ensuring it made it over her head and onto the floor. Skin as warm as the heat in their hearts pressed against the palm of Miranda's eager hand. *I had kissed a hundred girls before you, but you did it with such purpose that I almost forgot who I was. You made me believe in love from one kiss.*

A crazy conception. A woman like Miranda, in love? The barbarian who had killed more people than she cared to count by the time she met Sulim? The cunt who had broken hearts badly enough that they came back with violent vengeance? The sullied child of a pleasure moon, who had never known a hand that wasn't greedy and callous? *From one monster to another. That's how I existed. I was content.*

She hadn't been born with the name Cairn. It was a word she came across in one of the chief's illicit videos about a planet called Earth. *"A pile of stones. A grave marker. Death and decay."* She may not have known how to say the word, but she adopted it out of principle. She had left her old life behind when the chief purchased her for pleasure and pain. *I was ten years old. It was all I knew.* Whatever little girl she was meant to be had died long before puberty. She couldn't remember a time when she was a virgin, let alone innocent and naïve. Those weren't words anybody ascribed to Cairn. She was the woman they went to when they wanted to lose themselves for a night.

She wasn't meant to love. Or be loved, for that matter. She was meant to kill, to drink, to gamble, and bang the night away so she could forget about having to kill again the next day. Men didn't mess with her. It was women who got to her, though. The ones who manipulated her, promised her either riches or *love* until she learned to distrust both.

Then came little miss killjoy. The abductee from some boring planet who was given to Cairn to handle and train in the ways of being a terrible mercenary.

Sulim had been everything Cairn wasn't. She was the girl Cairn could have been before she shed that old life and gave herself a name with hollow meaning. Her naivete and refusal to see things with a barbarian's eyes had infuriated Cairn. But it was also what drew her to the teenager with impeccable aim and a stoic empathy who guarded her in a fortress of distrust while offering a touch of affection to those who needed it.

She loved me before I accepted my own love for her. The only person to see the soul within the monster. The only woman in the universe who could bring down one of the most effective chiefs Second Tribe would soon see.

The final chief of a tribe doomed to decimation.

It's not our fault.

There were still glimmers of that woman lurking beneath Danielle's aura. The one Miranda had instantly recognized some faraway summer day in another country. The one she was drawn to when she visited her commanding officer's house for Thanksgiving. The one who accompanied a piece of paper she saw in her office one day—a paper bearing Danielle's name as an upcoming transfer to Miranda's command.

The Void always found ways to bring them together again. Sulim was always so tightly locked away, however, that Cairn was likewise fated to stare into a pair of hazel eyes that no longer recognized her. It wasn't until this life, when a woman named Miranda encountered one named Danielle, that she finally, *finally* saw that flash of recognition whenever they were together.

Thank God, too. Because this was their last chance at bringing their lives together.

Miranda tried not to think about it as she caressed the soft skin of a woman she had yearned to hold again for over a thousand years. *It feels like longer,* she thought, daring to stop kissing Danielle long enough to gaze into her face, delicate blond hair on fingertips and breaths slowing as they gazed into one another's eyes. The film of dissociation had long disappeared from the bright eyes that now whirled in a sea of greens. Sometimes, they were a ruddy, earthy brown, one of Miranda's favorite colors. But she often didn't get to see that color in Danielle's eyes. That required staring at her for too long, and Miranda was careful to avoid that level of discomfort.

"What?" There Danielle stood, dressed down to her jeans and a bra that didn't do much to cover her chest. A twinge of embarrassment descended upon them, its weight great enough to buckle their knees and bring them both down to the floor. If Miranda had worried about scaring Danielle away? Danielle feared that she somehow didn't stack up as a decent lover. While it was a fear she courted every time she was with somebody new, there was an origin to that, whether she remembered it or not.

"You're always afraid you won't stack up to the other people they've been with," a faraway voice said deep in the annals of her memories. *"She could say she's been looking for you all her life, and you won't believe a word she says."*

It had always been the worst with women, whether they were experienced or not. Would she soon realize that such insecurities were a millennium old? That they stemmed from falling in love on a planet full of sinners who knew their ways around their favorite vices? Sulim hadn't been on her adopted planet for a week before she discovered how deep their depravities went. By the time she braved a taste of the forbidden for herself? She simultaneously cast away her insecurities while engaging in some of the toughest thoughts she ever entertained in her mind.

She had a feeling she should try that again. Hell, she had been well on her way to that conflicting freedom before Miranda stopped kissing her, both hands splayed against the wall while she cast her eyes downward.

Did she know that she was so beautiful that it only made Danielle's insecurities worse?

"I want to hear you say it." Miranda lifted her head, her long bangs sliding down her face and thinly veiling her eyes. The shadows cast across her face either invited further adoration or the keen feeling that Danielle deigned to sleep with the enemy, after all. That feeling wouldn't be reserved for Danielle, either. There had been other lovers, ones who knew not of Miranda's tumultuous past or the truth behind her sophisticated veneer, who occasionally gazed upon her visage and wondered what she plotted. Was she friend or foe? Was she a black widow preparing to strike as soon as the deed was done? Or was she simply in the business of playing mind games?

Danielle could be a fool for any of those angles. Like now, when she slid a little farther down the wall, the weight of Miranda's aura pressing upon her. "Say what?"

Although Miranda's eyes lingered on the generous cleavage Danielle boasted in her bra, they did not attempt to devour her. Not yet. That would be too convenient for someone like Danielle, who was prepared to throw herself into this moment, unsure if she would ever have the chance again.

"Say that you want this."

So it wasn't enough that Danielle had marched into her house, came up her stairs, and all but asked for it? Wasn't enough to make her blush yet again, considering she risked more than her pride should she be shot down, as if she had been misreading Miranda's flirtatious signals over the past few years. *Has it really been that long?* Danielle thought, one hand rubbing a small knot forming in her chest. She cleared her throat and looked up again, meeting the sultry gaze boring possibilities into her soul.

"Maybe I'd rather hear you say it."

A small snort of disbelief heated the space between them. Miranda's face was so close that her breath was warm against Danielle's clavicle. All it would take was a small dip of her head to leave a kiss on Danielle's throat. Didn't she want to? Didn't she realize that this moment had been simmering between them since they first crossed paths?

Of course she realized it. That's why she played these games.

"If I told you how much I wanted you," Miranda finally said, "I might instead scare you away. At least give me a little confidence first."

Danielle didn't realize it, but Miranda made a careful move that harked back to that first time they made love a thousand years ago, when Sulim was the one afraid of scaring her lover away. She hadn't said a thing, but Cairn saw the fear and insecurity in her face as she came in for the kiss that reignited the flames that still burned between them after a long absence.

"Besides," Miranda continued. "I asked first."

"I want this," Danielle said before she lost the nerve.

"How much?"

If this was foreplay, then Danielle was neither getting off on it nor completely turned off. She merely stared into the depths of Miranda's eyes, attempting to catch a glimpse of the old soul that lurked behind them. *If I could see it, I might figure out who she is.* That name always on the tip of her tongue. The memories slightly out of reach. The screams of delight and horror dancing at the edge of her memories. There were facts she accepted as the truth, although she knew nobody told her the whole story. *I was a mercenary. I was forced into the lifestyle. I made a name for myself, because I was so successful but never killed anyone. I was the chief's personal bodyguard before I died. The chief's name was...* She had heard the name, from both Marlow and Devon's mouths. Yet she couldn't remember now. The name Cairn was both a distant memory she no longer needed and a refrain she called upon whenever she needed reassurance. She always needed reassurance. Why couldn't she remember Cairn's name now?

Why did it seem so necessary to remember it while looking into Miranda's eyes?

Danielle gripped the bottom of Miranda's sweatshirt and attempted to pull it up. Arms slowly raised. Hair lifted and fell again as the heavy fabric landed on the floor. Danielle leaned forward, looping her arms around Miranda's midriff while wishing to God that she could discover a way to make everything else fall off this woman's body.

"So much that it's a miracle I haven't thrown you down on your own bed yet."

Miranda betrayed her girlish surprise for the minutest of moments. "What's stopping you? Honestly. We've proven before that we're of similar strength. You could do it."

"Maybe I'd rather you throw your weight around."

"I could. This *is* my house, after all. The one you helped yourself into, if I may remind you." Miranda didn't wait for a response. She slowly lowered her lips to Danielle's neck, leaving the lightest kiss there.

Then another.

And another.

Little by little, she unraveled the last of Danielle's conscience. The one holding her back and protecting her from her own instincts. Breaths to the ear and light kisses to bare skin were good and all, but none of them compared to the erratic beating of her heart every time Danielle recalled the real kisses they had shared until a few minutes ago. The ones that had allowed her to slip into that subconscious state of both semi-regressing and giving herself over to the kind of moments that ruined a woman, regardless of her spiritual state.

One last little kiss pulled the final string keeping Danielle's nerves together. Miranda got what she wanted. Danielle, who could no longer hold herself back from what she wanted more than anything, threw herself onto the woman teasing her so badly.

The more clothes they lost, the closer they came to reclaiming the feeling they shared long, long ago. Feelings that Miranda had chased for as long as she had been reborn, and feelings that Danielle yearned to know again, yet could never find. They were the sensations that claimed a woman's fantasies in the middle of the night, when she half-awoke from an erotic dream that never quite faded away. No matter how much she clung to the memories and touched herself to the desires bubbling within her, however, she floundered. *Must be unreal,* she'd think when she awakened hours later. *Nobody really feels like that when they have sex.* Feelings born from prose and sensations simulated in film. There was nothing, *nothing* that compared in real life. The military could parade every person Danielle slept with onto the witness stand, and she would gaze upon them with nothing but pity.

"You really tried, but never quite got there," she'd tell Alicia. *"You know the only thing driving our nights together was our spiritual conundrum,"* Devon would hear, followed by, *"there's a reason it never happened in our first lives, right? I wasn't into you like that. I'm only occasionally into you because you take away the loneliness for a little while."*

Seth? He probably would've been the worst lay of her life, had they actually gone through with it. That's what Danielle told herself, and she wouldn't be far from the truth. Even the first man she was ever with was better than Seth, and that encounter had been *sad.*

No, what she felt with Miranda in those seconds between grabbing her and slowly making their way to the bed wasn't supposed to be real. It was a lie. A dream. The inverse of every time Danielle was with someone else and fought back that little bit of nausea bubbling up from the pits of her stomach. She always wrote them off as nerves. What if they weren't?

Why didn't she feel it now?

The easiest way to forget everything was to sacrifice herself to the present. Emotions overwhelmed them in the form of deep kisses and the hesitant touches that turned powerful the moment they spiraled over the cliff of familiarity. Touching a woman's breast may have been exciting when it was new, but once that bra was on the floor and those lips against peaked nipples, it was nothing but *right*. Like a wild night in on what would otherwise have been a humdrum date night. Danielle could hardly believe that this was her first time making love to Miranda when she accurately anticipated the ripple of her stomach and the way she groomed her body hair. Was she merely lucky in guessing how her lover might look? Or was that so-called luck born from intimate knowledge she had long forgotten?

Yet nothing hit her like the scent of Miranda's body. She was barely undressed, her soft moans driving Danielle a little more insane, when that scent hit her like a hurricane wind.

I can't believe this is you, she lamented. *It's really you.*

The thing about coherent thoughts, however, was that they had a habit of currying favor from madness. For every time Danielle briefly met Miranda's eyes and recognized the woman she knew inside of her, there was the time that completely wiped her memory and made her succumb to another kiss of fervor or touch of desperation. The words they refused to exchange were replaced with mutually intelligible gasps of surprise and pleasure, or strokes of the hand that conjured images of love and pain alike.

It wasn't that they couldn't speak. *Yes. No. Please. Do it. There, there, there.* Those words existed in whatever language they thought in at the moment. Yet a mental block separated those words from their throats. Mouths were only good for moaning, and lips belonged to the heavenly realm of kisses, both gentle and fervent. When Miranda kissed a heady line from Danielle's lips to her thighs, she might as well have declared that the last thing she wanted to hear were measly *words.* Aural languages were for the mere mortals who lived one or two lives.

Effervescent beings like them were ruled by the basest of animal instincts. So base
that they transcended modern thought and encompassed the future of human
evolution. Because some things traveled from one age to the next, never changing,
always present.

It didn't matter how old Danielle's soul was or what her body of the moment
accomplished. When the woman she loved kissed her nether lips with the intention of bringing her to orgasm, it only meant one thing.

Bliss. Heavenly, soul-washing bliss.

To be sure, there was plenty of skill involved. But there was also that sweet
familiarity that Danielle was only able to take advantage of because one of them
had her memories. Cairn had never forgotten how to make Sulim respond with
the kind of furor that neither marked her as a virgin nor the kind of girl the others
in the tribe treated with derision.

Guess which one of us was which, Miranda thought, before giving in to her
own mindful ambitions claiming every inch of her being. She had been waiting
a thousand years for this moment. How long had it been since they made love
like this? *Like I could ever forget the last time.* The night before it all came burning
down in a ball of fiery fury, when they realized they may never get the happily ever
after they had spent the past five years building on a planet where happiness went
to die.

This time is different. She thought that while putting all of her focus into
making her lover happy. *It will be different. It has to be different. I didn't sacrifice
my own soul for it to not be different.*

She stopped thinking. How could she think when the whole world conspired
to bring her back to this moment and nowhere else?

It was where she wanted to be, after all.

Do you remember me now? That was the last thing she thought before driving
herself home.

Danielle pulled a pillow over her head to unfurl the scream that had been
simmering in her stomach for the past five minutes. Miranda rather wished she
hadn't. What better way to celebrate this night than hearing the peal of a voice

she had yearned to entertain for so, so long? *I'll give her all the pleasure she wants,* Miranda thought, foregoing air if it meant extending Danielle's happiness a little while longer. *She can take it all from me. I don't need a single kiss or word of adoration from her ever again. I'll give and give until my star fades.*

It was the least she could do for the girl who showed her kindness, even though Miranda was the one who ruined her life.

"Oh my God." Those were a few of the only words either of them uttered, and Miranda was privileged to hear them when she finally drew her nose up the length of Danielle's torso and rested her forehead against her lover's chest. Hands met Danielle's, their fingers intertwining and palms pressing together. Arms lifted above their heads. Miranda dared to push her hips between her lover's, ready to go and go until they lost the will the move. "That was amazing. You're... like... *amazing...*"

Miranda's stoic veneer faltered. The part of her that forgot what planet and year it was had not been expecting *that* from Danielle's sex-addled mouth. Miranda would have laughed, except she was still vain enough to cling to propriety. *I would laugh if she remembered me. I'd laugh until the day we die again.*

"Not as amazing as you." Miranda could be as cliched as the women who stumbled their way into her bed, especially if it made them smile the way Danielle did.

Or kiss like she did.

Miranda teetered the fine edge between sacrificing herself to the night they shared, or opening her big mouth in the hopes that Danielle had somehow remembered her in that moment. *There is no greater vanity than thinking I can single-handedly make her regress using nothing but my tongue.* Yet Miranda hoped it, anyway. A thousand years and hardly a few kisses. Finally getting Sulim back in bed should have been a breakthrough. Indeed, it was. But one that belonged solely to the night, instead of their furtive existences.

"You can have whatever you want," Miranda finally said. "I'll give it to you." *Take my body, take my mind, and for the Void's sake, take my soul.* Danielle long had her heart. She might as well take everything else, too.

"Just make love to me," Danielle said. "Kiss me and don't stop."

Miranda could certainly deliver that. The Void knew she had been dreaming of it since the day she first realized the girl she dragged from some nowhere planet looked at her in a curious way. Lots of girls and women had looked at her with lust and desire in their eyes, but it was the first time the lost soul named Cairn blushed to see it.

It meant nothing to be chosen by the world. It meant everything to be chosen by a specific person.

What was fate? Was it the machinations of the Void, weaving a concrete narrative into a colorful tapestry that told tales of war and peace? Or was it the natural spiritual energy born of those finite number of souls that came into existence billions of forgettable years ago? Miranda's soul had been born alongside Danielle's. She often liked to think that they were born either right next to each other or one after the other. Forever entwined, no matter what lives they lived. They didn't need the Process to ensure they always found each other. Even if Miranda's soul was born to those two *julah* making waves among their people, she still believed that she would have found Sulim, eventually. It was their destiny as two happy children of the Void.

"I love you..."

Those words were spoken in an ancient language that went farther back than Old Basic. It was the language of the stars and that old, reverberating hum that powered all life in the universe. In those mountains of books and musings her father insisted she read, Miranda discovered an old *julah* saying that went, *"And when you surrender your senses and transcend your mortal form, you hear the Song of All Life. Although the Void calls you home, you may wander for a million years, singing the Harmony that flows through the universe."* Miranda tried to depict that saying in one of her paintings. Traditional *julah* artistry used butterflies as the most common motif to represent the souls singing the Harmony. She would never contend with the masters of their craft, who had spent thousands of years opening their hearts and ears to the Song, but she knew a thing or two about flying from one life to the next. For a while, it was the only way she could communicate her frustrations to her fellow humans.

So to hear that ancient Harmony vibrate in Danielle's throat, and all from a single kiss? More than a part of Miranda had reached that troubled, delinquent soul. It had plucked its strings and, for an infinitesimal second, reminded it how to sing the Song of All Life.

Miranda didn't know how to speak that language on command. But she could play a minor role in the Harmony, using a language that she and Sulim once used to communicate their innermost thoughts in the nights they stole together.

"I love you too."

Old Basic didn't hold the same tenor as universal Harmony, but she hoped it got the point across. All she had was hope, most of the time.

Hope. The sweetest thing. The constant companion that got Miranda up in the morning and soothed her to sleep at night. Hope was that thing she had abandoned in her first life, when all she knew and understood was the terrible kind of life that sucks all the hope from one child's soul. *I don't want to say she taught me how to hope, but...* She had relearned what hope was, anyway, when she finally had someone to live for. Some*thing* to live for. Hope for the future. Hope for an eternal love. Hope that they could one day escape their dangerous lives and fulfill the rest of their days in sweet, wholesome peace. Unmolested. Unchained.

It's not our fault.

Cairn had never courted as much hope as she did when she was reborn as a woman named Miranda on the planet Earth. If they could survive this round of torture, there was endless hope. Because Earth was the holy grail. Earth was that place of endless temptation, regardless of its age or era. A thousand years ago, there had been promise of fertile valleys, quiet countries, and enough resources if a woman brought Federation money to the trade cities of Europe, the Middle East, or even East Asia. Earth wasn't a part of the Federation, but there were enough people there who knew how it worked and, dare anyone say it, moved there for the simpler life devoid of technological fervor. It had certainly appealed to a female couple searching for a place to make their escape. They may have been the two most protected people in the Second Tribe, but if their kind ever caught a whiff of them turning traitor, their heads would adorn the pikes and their bodies dumped into the ravines in the dead of night. Back then, the threat of death was enough to strike fear into Miranda's young soul.

Earth had been their possible salvation. When the time was right, when they had skimmed enough money from the tribe's coffers, and when they were brave enough to put their lives on the line... they would go to Earth and start all over again. It was their hope.

Hope...

Like the hope Miranda felt when she was reborn on that auspicious planet with the love of her lives right behind her. They had finally made it. They had arrived on Earth, like they always dreamed.

Their names didn't matter. Nor did their careers and aspirations. All that was left was to reclaim Sulim's heart and help her blossom in Danielle's mortal coil. Then they could truly start over again. They could finally live that life together far, far away from a hell that no longer existed.

Nobody would come after them. They would finally thrive.

So, yes, Miranda had hope. From the way Danielle kissed her and asked for more, more, more all night long, she could only imagine that hope bloomed in this beautiful form as well.

She did, of course, although she couldn't quite put a name to it. All Danielle knew was that giving herself completely over to the whim and movements of their lovemaking was more fantastic than anything else she remembered. But like the other memories dormant within her, soon, these would fade as well. Yet until she fell asleep, with the moon shining through Miranda's bedroom window, she courted that hope and wonder as if she had never lost it a thousand years ago.

Seven

It didn't take much to make Danielle dream, let alone about her old, forgotten life. Sometimes those snippets stayed with her long enough for her to remember days or weeks later. Most of the time, however, they lingered as long as the dawn before disappearing once again.

She did not dream that night.

Instead, she welcomed a lasting, blissful sleep that skirted the line between restful and coma-like. There were always reasons to fall asleep like this, weren't there? A hard day. Illness. The crushing weight upon her soul finally taking its toll on her. Danielle was no stranger to the kind of sleep that blessed the dead.

Yet this wasn't the result of her body shutting down, or of her heart begging for one night's decent sleep. It was her soul, however. For the first time in nearly a thousand years, she slammed her head into a pillow and simply *slept.*

No dreams. No disturbances. No trace of her soul stirring in the corner of her mind's eye, waiting for the perfect moment to leap from the shadows of her body and awaken her from an otherwise fitful sleep. That's what Danielle had asked for since she was old enough to remember her first nightmare. Back when she lived with her mother, a woman who had been dead for years.

On any other night, she would pause her sleep to wonder if her mother was even real. Danielle had plenty of mothers over the past ninety-something lives. She had a mother in her first life as well, although nobody ever mentioned her. Either she was critical enough to cause a forced regression, or she was so inconsequential that Danielle was better off never thinking about a *mother* again.

This was not a night like that, though. This was...

She awoke a little after dawn. She was disheveled, flummoxed, and bemused, but she knew it was dawn and that a warmth blanketed her more than the bedding of a stranger's chambers.

Where am I? she thought, temporary amnesia claiming her in those needy moments between sleep and wakeful realization. This disorientation was like waking up in one's childhood bed during a visit, and not remembering the initial arrival. *Where am I? Whose bed is this? Am I home? This must be a dream.* Danielle was familiar with that hell, yet she couldn't say she immediately recognized this room like she would her childhood bed. Nor did she recognize the warmth of the person lying behind her, one arm loose around Danielle's midsection.

She slowly turned over. Inch by inch, she remembered the moments leading up to her arrival at Miranda's house. *That's where I am,* she thought. *This is her room.* Danielle had been in it before. To steal from her, no less.

Oh, she had stolen something again. Danielle may not have been sure *what* she stole, but it was now in her possession, and she didn't have a chance in hell of ever giving it back.

Miranda retracted her arm, half-asleep as she curled it beneath her body and buried her face in her pillow. The steady rise and fall of her torso suggested that she, too, enjoyed the kind of restful sleep Danielle had risen from only a moment ago. Yet Miranda was not in a hurry to awaken. Her breaths grew in volume, each one blowing with greater strength against the crook of her arm. Danielle was so momentarily captivated that she forgot why she held onto a moment of panic that jostled her more awake.

You came here of your own volition, she reminded herself as the memories returned. *You came up those stairs. You came into her room. You practically threw yourself at her. Why are you freaking out like you didn't mean any of it?*

Danielle braced her naked body against the length of Miranda's queen-sized bed. A pillow crumpled beneath her hand. Sweat that had dried across her body now flowed again. Everything was sticky. Her brow. Her arms. Her stomach and thighs. She moved enough to remind herself of what she and Miranda had done the night before.

She made you say that you wanted it. Then she gave it to you. Are you so surprised, dumbass?

It had happened. Well...

Danielle sat up, wrapping her arms around her legs. Miranda muttered something in her sleep. It wasn't English. It wasn't any Earth-based language. It could have been Basic. Or Julah. Or a host of other tongues Danielle no longer recognized. *I don't remember. Who is she? Why did I come here?* She had to breathe deeply and collect her thoughts. The last thing she needed was a mini-regression in Miranda's bed.

What scared her more? That she had sex with a woman she had been attracted to for years? Or that *something* happened to make her black most of it out?

No, she hadn't blacked it out after all. That suggested her mind chose to dump it into the ether for her own good. The memories were still there. They drew her back in every time she entertained them for a single second. Tossed her around like she was a girl reliving her first real fling, or at least the first time someone touched her in a way that sent her spiraling into the atmosphere. *Let's play a game of count the orgasms,* she thought. *Oh, wait. I can't.* The problem was that each memory carried with it a layer of unfettered emotion she couldn't comprehend. She reveled in it while it consumed her. Whether she was wrapped in Miranda's arms or pulling her on top, there was that closeness, that *bond* that went beyond mere compatibility. Them having a good time was a given. What Danielle felt was jubilation. The kind that choked her in a fog of fear.

A name always on the tip of her tongue. Memories she couldn't quite grasp, no matter how far she reached.

Danielle had two options. She could try to go back to sleep, since God knew she needed it. She would wake up around the same time as Miranda, be treated to breakfast, and forced to face the sheer curtain of untouched familiarity between them. Miranda would attempt to give her the distance she clearly needed to make difficult decisions about what "they" had and, if pertinent, ask her out or attempt to end their affair for now. There was no way they could simply go their separate ways without a "talk." No matter how enticing it might be to eat breakfast and act like nothing happened.

Or... Danielle could leave. Now.

Lord knew she wasn't proud. It would be her first time bailing on a sleeping lover, simply so she could avoid the awkwardness sure to embrace them. She hated herself for considering it. What had Miranda done to her? Except turn her gut inside out and make Danielle eat her own promises.

Just because it had been forbidden until the day before... ah, shit. It still felt wrong. Danielle may not have been attracted to the *forbidden,* per se, but she wasn't a big enough fool to assume the veneer fell away because of a court-martial. Let alone the day *of* said court-martial.

Right. She had been court-martialed. Wasn't that a lovely thought to dwell on as she crept out of the bed and searched for her clothing around the room?

She followed the trail around the perimeter, grabbing her jeans, socks, bra, and underwear. Well! She had to grab Miranda's first, because they were in an unholy gob with Danielle's. Did they always wear the same kind of black cotton underwear? Because the cut may have been slightly different, and the brand a continent apart, but damn if they didn't look the same!

Danielle had to crawl toward the bedroom door to find her shirt. It was about ten inches away from Miranda's sweatshirt, which was a crumpled mess compared to the woman now sprawled across the bed. Danielle tore her eyes away from the naked form of the woman she slept with the night before, if only to keep a semblance of her sanity—and to get her moving.

She should leave a note. No. A note invited further interaction. Damn it, Danielle was between a rock and a hard place, both of which told her to get away now, before she faced an unfortunate circumstance. *What? Like potential happiness?* she thought with a snort as she finished buttoning up her jeans and ran her hand through her messy hair. *Can't have that, now, can we? Heaven forbid we allow any happiness for Danielle! Practically allergic to it!* Great. After one of the best nights of her life, she was going to do this to herself.

She took one last look at Miranda before showing herself out. The house was quiet. Even the staircase refused to squeak or creak as Danielle descended and entered the abandoned maw of half-drank wine and papers scattered across the coffee table. The lights were still on, and the faint scent of cigarette smoke permeated the place.

Strange. Danielle didn't recall the taste or stench of tobacco the night before.

The door clicked shut behind her. Foggy, crisp air welcomed her and awakened the final parts of her brain. Danielle had enough cash in her pocket to get a cup of coffee in a café near her apartment, but she thought better of it. *I look a mess,* she thought, hands in her jacket pockets instead of fixing her hair. What was the point? The early morning breeze would mess everything up, anyway.

This was her walk of shame. She deserved to look like a slob as she made the long trek home, where she could shower and make herself coffee. Until then? *Gaze upon me Void,* she thought, teeth slightly chattering from the fog, *because you clearly have nothing better to do.*

The Void was not the only one to gaze after her, although the High Priestess certainly took note of everything that happened over the past twelve hours on Earth. Yet she wasn't the only one roused from her slumber. Someone she had a deep and personal connection with also awoke the moment Danielle stepped out of the house she invaded the night before.

Miranda had been too late to intercept her, not that she knew what to say or do. She had merely gone to the window, dressed in nothing but the bathrobe she kept hung on the back of her closet door, and gazed after Danielle's form as it wandered down the sidewalk.

How was it possible to feel so defeated after she finally gained one of the few things she desperately desired?

"Man," Devon said, after popping two pills with a side of water, "I swear I didn't drink that much last night, but I feel like I've been hit by a truck."

His mid-morning guest was May, who had brought with her a duffel bag full of clothing and toiletries she claimed could not easily be found in the Federation. Devon offered her coffee, but was a bit slow hitting the shower and getting dressed for their big day. Oh, he had been clothed by the time May showed up, but coffee? Breakfast? They didn't exist yet. The man had been too busy nursing a headache and more pain in his muscles. Something told him this wasn't a mere hangover. Nor was it the natural side-effect of hitting the gym a little more than he realistically should. Devon was past those grueling first few weeks of trying to get back into some semblance of shape. He didn't intend to get back to *mercenary* size, but from the moment he regressed, he hated to see what a wimp he had become over a millennium.

This wasn't that. This was something deeper in his damned, regressed soul.

"You didn't drink much at all, no," May said, coffee cooling in its cup on the small Ikea table Devon called *dining*. "Not as much as I've seen you drink before. I hope you're not sick, honestly. Even using sorcery to travel isn't easy on you if you're sick."

Devon sat down across from her, happy to drink scalding hot coffee that burned a hole into his tongue. "Have you traveled via magical teleportation before?"

"No," May said with a large grin. "I can't wait. I despise regular teleportation. It's why I never visit my parents' home planet if I can help it. Give me air buses any day."

"Greyhound," Devon countered. "Nothing like a bus full of weirdos that smell like their amplified armpits trying to sell you whatever crank they cooked in their last hotel." He may have had some experience with that. *I'm never taking the bus to Phoenix again,* he thought with mild nostalgia.

"I'll raise you my mom driving between here and LA."

"Having driven between here and LA recently... and knowing your mother..." Devon laughed. "Sounds like a nightmare." Rea d'Eran in a sedan, attempting to navigate SoCal traffic on a typical day? She probably needed her own therapist after that.

Devon had hoped his final guests would be fashionably late, giving him a little more time to wake the hell up and shake whatever funk had settled over him between last night and that morning. *Almost feels like... I'm trying to regress again...* Both Marlow and Rea had warned him that he might have moments of severe disorientation and memory blackouts for the rest of his life, but this didn't feel like that, either. It was like it hadn't even happened to him. Almost as if he wrestled with the uncertainties of another person struggling to let go of their past.

He had the urge to text Danielle. *"Everything okay?"* That could pass for a million things. She had a pretty shitty day recently. He was her friend, if nothing else, and should make sure she was doing all right.

He wasn't shocked to go without a response before Marlow and his small entourage arrived.

"How about that, huh?" He lifted his hat in greeting as he helped himself into Devon's apartment shortly after rapping on the door. Devon didn't even have to get up and unlock it. Like a *julah* as magically advanced as the Great and Scholarly Ramaron Marlow couldn't pick a lock with the flick of his finger. He didn't even do it on purpose anymore. "Arrived right outside your door with five minutes to spare. Made Evan account for your daylight savings and everything. I'm telling you, that really is a crock. What daylight are you saving? Get up earlier like the rest of the universe."

The usual greetings commenced, followed by questions about the impending trip. Evan approached the couple sitting at the small table and didn't hesitate to ask, "You guys got the stuff?" in his laziest English. He would argue before the panel that reviewed his higher degree application that it was a sign of his mastery over "the most important Earth-based language." Even thirty-five years ago, when he received his honors in Earth Studies and applied to work for Ramaron Marlow, a professor had argued that Mandarin would one day be more important, and Evan should seriously reconsider taking another two years to study it as well.

(He had declined. A job awaited him.)

May opened her duffel bag and pulled out three boxes of Hostess goodies she bought on her way to Devon's that morning. Evan unceremoniously stacked them in his arms before taking a selfie and posting it to his Federation-wide social media account dedicated to American treats. Everyone had long learned to stop asking questions about what he did with his damned education. It was bad enough Earthlings never believed him when he said he was almost sixty years old when he barely looked a day over thirty. (And by the Federation's reckoning, he wasn't.) Much like May benefited from her parents' genetics that stipulated humans had longer lifespans and retained their youth for a few more decades. Yara d'Alacron was a few years shy of eighty. Not that anyone wanted to think about meeting her later that day.

"Are we ready to go?" Marlow asked after checking his pocket watch, a trifling gift from Evan years ago that had proven quite handy, especially when Marlow wished to blend in among the Earthlings. "We have a date with the dear commander in an hour. We need to get everyone to Terra III and properly processed before then." He turned to May. "Have you ever traveled by magical teleportation before, Ms. d'Eran?"

"No, sir."

"You're gonna love it!" Evan called over his shoulder while he juggled the Twinkie and Cupcake boxes. "You don't wanna vomit after it's done!"

"Always a bonus," Devon muttered. "I already feel like shit, and I swear I haven't been drinking that much lately."

Marlow waited for the three humans to gather their things, make final trips to the bathroom, and rinse out coffee mugs. "Hmm. I admit, there is a strange sensation in the air today. I thought it might be pollution, honestly. Every time I see that fog, I get queasy." Fog on Yahzen was a sign that the Void was feeling particularly out of balance that day. A grand time for all *julah* who were sensitive to the machinations of the Void. "Are we ready? We don't want to keep the good people on Terra III waiting. I have mastered instantaneous teleportation, but not time travel. Come along now."

The snap of his fingers and the tap of his cane against Devon's floor got them hustling with bags slung over shoulders and beneath arms. This form of travel did not account for anything not on someone's person. Devon and May would be absent from Earth for about two weeks. They were reassured there would be ample time for laundry, so it was folly to bring more than a few days' worth of clothing. Nevertheless, May recounted how many pairs of underwear she packed while Devon held his bag close to his body. Now, how had he...

Ah. Too late. He turned around to check if the bathroom window was shut and discovered that his apartment had faded away. Instead, they stood in a closed room with low lighting and a sign that said, *"All Aliens Must Register Beyond This Point."*

"Brilliant." Marlow removed his hat again, waiting for Evan to get the door for him. "Last time I teleported a group here, we ended up in the deportation chambers. That was a rough explanation that held us up a few hours..."

Neither May nor Devon were strangers to Federation bureaucracy at this point. May had often traveled to Federation territories with her parents, and Devon spent most of his November traveling from one place to the next. In so many ways, going through the post-teleportation process on Terra III was akin to traveling between countries on Earth. There was protocol to follow, whether it was standing in a certain line, having documents inspected, or answering questions in languages they might not understand. The only reason they put up with his pomp, however, was because of their special status on this tour. *Julah* were exempt from most of the rigmarole surrounding immigration—but only because the humans at the head of immigration gave up corralling the ancient race who were capable of *instantaneous teleportation*. Marlow was the first to quip about his own ancestor, Great-Great-Great-Uncle Finotol Marlow, who famously stood up to a line of immigration questioning on old Terra II by teleporting from the line and straight into his hotel room in the capital. Even after Federation forces came knocking on his door, he blew them off to enjoy his pot of evening *cageh*. It was one of the inciting incidences leading to their many exceptions.

Devon received his stamped passcard that was as good as a visa. It included a picture taken without his notice—and, of course, contained a *very* flattering rendition of him—and the name *Sonall Gardiah* under "known aliases." His understanding of Modern Basic only extended to what he vaguely concentrated upon when staring at words that were both familiar and mind-numbingly foreign. As soon as he started to think about it, the words were nonsensical.

"We've got plenty to do today!" Marlow waved for his human companions to follow him as he trudged forward into the immigration reception area. As soon as the guarded doors slid open, a flurry of activity announced that they had passed into official Federation territory. Speakers announced a security hazard in three different languages. An automated voice asked patrons to please not stand too close to the air and water purifiers, which used nuclear technology. The occasional hologram of a humanoid popped up to advertise "pain-free" inoculations for new and seasoned travelers. When Marlow stepped through the third advertisement to jump before them, May giggled at how the woman glitched out and all but malfunctioned when demonstrating a self-administered vaccine. Devon was too weirded out to notice.

Marlow was sure to keep his entourage from the more public areas, the ones littered with media who had heard rumors that Devon and May were due to arrive at any time. Instead, they took a more roundabout way that included heavily armed guards around every corner and signs asking "sensitive persons" to please report to the "Immediate Receiving Area." Devon hoisted his backpack higher up his shoulder as he took in the rambunctious sights and sounds of decorum in action. May girded herself to face the person standing at the end of a long walk with a number of armed guards, all fixated upon her.

One of the guards pointed to the people behind Yara d'Alacron, prompting her to turn around with a semi-shocked countenance. "Hello," she greeted from behind her veil of golden hair. "You are a bit early, aren't you?"

Marlow came to a complete stop before her, cane sliding off the ground as he tucked it beneath his arm. "I didn't want to keep you waiting, Commander. Nor did I want to leave your guests vulnerable to media attention."

"Yes, I have seen them for myself. We will have to make a controlled appearance later today, but for now, I have them sequestered. The fools think they're getting something soon." She cupped her fingers into Marlow's curling hands, the formal handshake known across the Federation. May was quick to mimic it, after having seen her parents do it a hundred times. Devon, however, went for the full Earthling shake that threatened to rip Yara's hand off her body. She adjusted to his strength with alacrity, although she could not hide the surprised yet pleased grin touching her face. She had not expected Devon Anderson to have such a grip. Sonall Gardiah? Yes. But the pictures of Devon she had on file didn't do his recent transformation into a more self-assured young man justice.

"Although we have arrived from their morning time," Marlow continued, "I think it pertinent to take them to their lodgings. Get them settled in before subjecting them to Terra III's unique... culture."

He didn't add that May had been here once before with her parents, or that Devon's regressed soul could hardly be scandalized by what he saw in the Federation, a place Sonall had called home a thousand years ago. Sure, technology and culture changed, particularly among the short-living humans. Yet the *julah* had a saying that went like, *"If one of our own can remember it, couldn't have been too long ago."*

Yara agreed that escorting the guests to their heavily guarded quarters in one of the capital's most luxurious hotels was, in fact, a grand idea. So much so that she was about to suggest it, and had already arranged for the rooms to be readied and her handpicked guards to be hard at work with nobody else there.

"I've heard a few things about this hotel," May said to Devon as they obediently followed their escorts down another long series of empty hallways. "Apparently, it's where they house foreign dignitaries and the most famous celebrities within the Federation. Even more guarded than anything you'll find on Earth."

Devon glanced at the back of Yara's golden head before turning his attentions back to May. "All the better for them to spy on their so-called guests."

"Huh?"

He snorted. "I guarantee our rooms will be under surveillance. Definitely bugged." When May's eyes widened, he explained, "I doubt that's changed in the past millennium. Was definitely kosher back when I was learning politics, both before and after my time on Cerilyn." As the second-in-command of his tribe, it was one of the few things meatheaded Sonall took seriously.

"Everyone is listening to you when we're on this planet," Cairn had told him when they dared to arrive on Terra III at the same time. *"Don't take it personally. They listen to everyone."*

He often wondered what juicy tidbits were stored on a server somewhere. Particularly any "private" conversations that occurred between Cairn and her personal bodyguard, a woman convinced that everyone was out to kill them.

I should try messaging Danielle again, he thought.

Yet before he could test the reception on his phone, which had been recently outfitted for Federation signals, Yara turned around and said, "I can assure that you and Ms. d'Eran will not be kept under any unnecessary surveillance."

Devon shot her a smile, but said nothing. Better to simply think, *"Yes, of course. Only the necessary surveillance will do."* Good thing he had no tyrannical plans.

Yara held his gaze until one of her men besought her attention. In that time, Devon sensed the same kind of foreboding nature that had haunted him the first time he saw women like Miranda or Syrfila. Women who clung to their aliases in a vain attempt at escaping their blood-soaked pasts. Did Yara have something to hide? Or was her status as the commander of the Federation Forces enough to put that wily look in her eye?

If it takes being a cold-blooded murderer to become the chief of a mercenary tribe, Devon thought as they boarded a private tube car in the depths of the capitol building, *I can only imagine what you must do to get her job.*

She was the kind of woman he didn't want for an enemy. That probably meant she would be, soon enough.

Eight

S weat soaked Danielle's T-shirt and brow as she collapsed onto her carpet, breaths racking her chest and fingers drumming against the back of her head. Wrists ached and biceps burned. Her cotton shorts rode high up her ass, but she didn't have the wherewithal to pull away the discomfort. Not after she had done two hundred pushups for the sake of doing them.

Perhaps there were a few reasons. Boredom, for one. Staying in shape another. When Danielle didn't hit the gym at work, she did pushups and sit-ups at home. On a good day she could go for the one-handers. Those weren't allowed when the CO doled out a little punishment for tardiness or insubordination. Miranda would laugh and tell Danielle to start all over again if she pulled that stunt in the office. *"Do it right this time, would you? This isn't an Olivia Cruise, and you're not impressing anyone on the dancefloor."*

Well. There was the third—and real—reason.

For God's sake, brain, Danielle thought, tapping her forehead against the carpet, *stop thinking about her for five damn minutes. Can you do that?* Physical exertion was a means to an end. A sleepy one, hopefully. Danielle had spent most of her day avoiding all thoughts and memories of the night before. A fool's errand, of course. Every time she closed her eyes or stopped running around the block for two seconds, she remembered that warm bed, those soft hands, and nipping teeth that threatened to tear her apart.

And I would've liked it too. God knows I liked everything else she did to me.

Danielle folded her arms beneath her head and looked up at the clock. It was barely ten. She usually went to bed around this time, although she didn't see the point now. What was she getting up early for? More running, pushups, and sit-ups? Nothing cleared her mind. Not of the hell she endured during her court-martial, and not of the conflicting feelings still waging war inside of her old, tired soul.

Admitting that she slept with Miranda wasn't enough. Neither was accepting how much she liked it. To really dwell upon it, Danielle must analyze every little thing she remembered for a swift second. Memories had always danced at the edge of her mind, but this? This was a level of foreboding she couldn't endure.

Nor could she stand the sound of her phone ringing a few feet away. The only reason she sat up to answer it was because she set that ringer to Devon's number, and he was off on another adventure, wasn't he?

Bastard. He was one of the only people who could possibly understand what she was going through right now. *Look at me,* she thought, *taking out my anger that I didn't go off with him.* A trip to the Federation would be a wonderful distraction right now.

"Hey," Danielle answered. Sweat stagnated on her brow, but at least she could control her breaths again. "How's it going out there?"

Devon took his time responding. "I'm never going to get over the toilets here. There, I said it. Bidets are less jarring than where they stick the water here."

Danielle couldn't remember what Federation toilets were like. Then again, she was more used to traveling to places that did things differently. "Thanks for basically telling me where you were right before you called me. Because that was clearly fresh on your mind."

Better than what she had been obsessing over all day. Even better when Devon entertained her with the stories he had amassed so far, from their dinner at a restaurant that served dishes from Sonall's home planet to the hefty reading materials about the next few days Devon was expected to peruse. "How do they expect me to read it?" he scoffed. "It's written in the Basic they have today. Not similar enough to what we used to speak a thousand years ago. It's like trying to read freakin' Beowulf. Only backward, I guess, because technically we speak Old English, and these people speak..."

"I get it." Danielle pulled herself up to her couch. "Get one of those translator things." The Federation had achieved real-time oral translations. Surely, they had them for the written word as well.

"Unfortunately, Evan's MIA. Said something about it being his wife's birthday."

Danielle wrinkled her nose. "I'm still not entirely convinced he's married. Sounds like something he made up to convince us all he's not a big ol' loser." Evan didn't *look* like a loser. He'd do quite well in his precious Earth's dating scene based on appearances alone, since the Void knew there was a dearth of Earth men who looked like a catalog model *and* had one of the highest degrees a person could obtain. Then he opened his mouth. A lot. *Usually to put Thin Mints in,* Danielle added. God. Evan and Girl Scout cookies. There was something she never wanted to behold.

"You there?" Devon asked. "I can't tell if my connection is dropping. I'm calling you from my phone. I dunno how many galaxies away..."

"Yeah, I'm here."

Devon was silent for a moment. "How are you doing? I haven't been able to check in since yesterday..." When his voice trailed off, it was to say, *"When your grandmother found out we banged last Christmas."* He left out who else found out. Like Danielle didn't want to think about Miranda right now, Devon could imagine a few better women to consort with.

"I have definitely been better," was all Danielle said at first. "I don't want to talk about me, though. Tell me more about what you're up to there. What time is it?"

She didn't pretend to know the intricacies of how many hours there were in a day on Terra III, let alone how that translated to the Standard Federation Clock. All Danielle cared about was distraction. An excuse to stop remembering the intimate sounds and kisses she experienced with someone so forbidden that it plagued her consciousness. *I can't tell Devon,* she thought while he regaled her with what was on Federation TV at that moment. *He would think I'm an idiot. Or get jealous. Or both.* She didn't want to deal with any of that. She could judge herself fine. Not to mention not giving a shit about his jealousy. They may spiritually be in an arranged marriage of sorts, but Devon would *never* achieve the kind of shit Danielle felt the night before.

A good thing too. Danielle could only handle so much.

"You sure you're okay?" Devon retracted that. "I mean, I know you're not *okay* right now, but..."

"I'm fine." Danielle did not mean to snap that. "It's been a really long two days. I don't know what I'm doing with my life. I barely know what I'm doing right now."

Their attempts to change subject fell flat. Devon eventually said goodbye and hung up. Danielle, however continued to stare at her phone. A few texts and missed calls from throughout the day advertised how much people cared about her in the aftermath of her court-martial. Troy, her grandmother, Ben and Alicia... Every Earthling she still had a bond with had either called or texted to tell her that they were there for her, whatever she needed.

Actually, there was one person who hadn't attempted to contact her all day.

She's not gonna call me, huh? Miranda must have known Danielle's number. She sure as hell knew where she lived. Yet short of them bumping into one another again, it looked like there was no hope of Miranda tracking Danielle down to get answers out of her. Or to even ask her out on a real date.

Not that Danielle wanted to be bothered. Honestly? She didn't know what she wanted. It was best for Miranda to keep her distance for a little while. Their night together was too fresh and real for Danielle to decipher her feelings. She was in no frame of mind to make dating decisions about anyone, least of all the woman who had moaned Danielle's name into a pillow.

She had the comfiest bed, though, Danielle thought. *And the way she held me while I slept...* Danielle may have awakened on the other side of the bed, but she had spent most of the night enveloped in Miranda's loving embrace. Danielle knew that much for sure. Yet would she ever realize long after she fell asleep, Miranda continued to gaze down at her face while caressing her hair and neck?

Something ached within Danielle's chest. Her heart hurt. So did her soul, but that thing had been hurting for a thousand years. Ever since she first gave herself to a woman who looked a lot like her forbidden love.

"Nobody can see us," the man wearing his graying blond hair back in a low ponytail said, "so why are you acting like you're on stage at the *orah?*"

Miranda couldn't help it. Even when she *wasn't* sneaking around the neighborhood in a hoodie and gloves, she was prone to surveying her surroundings, waiting for the moment someone attacked or otherwise compromised her safety. It went beyond her childhood with an abusive mother and a career in the military. Her whole existence was based on staving off death for another day. Usually from the man standing before her.

Her father. The most wanted criminal in the universe.

Fine thing for him to make references to the traditional *julah* art of stage, music, and song. The man hadn't enjoyed one of those stuffy performances in his life, and his family's affluence afforded him plenty of trips as a young man trying to live up to weighty expectations. One of the grandest benefits of becoming a wanted criminal? Never again having to sit in a booth and beholding the greatest diva of *julah* kind belting an operatic saga about generations of *julah* who feuded, wedded, and bedded. Not that Miranda would know a damn thing about that. She had seen only a few examples of *orah* in her many lives. *I remember the first time, though,* she thought as she stole farther into the shadows between two-story buildings. *I never visited Yahzen, but there was an* orah *theater in the Terra III capital when Sulim and I went...*

It always came back to that.

"Nobody can see us," Nerilis repeated. "I've made sure of that. Study hard enough and I could teach you to create simple temporal shifts like this one as well."

Miranda glanced up and down the dark alley. Didn't look like a temporal shift had been constructed around them, but she didn't know what they were *supposed* to look like. Glitches in the air? Rippling waves in the building behind her? A reverberation that entered her teeth? Her father may well have said he threw a blanket over them and called it good. Sometimes, she swore that's what he was saying.

It didn't help that Nerilis Dunsman was the most powerful manipulator of "magic" in the known universe, although the word magic was a misnomer that irritated *julah* scholars. As he often described to Miranda during these encounters, sorcery was nothing more than using the gift of the Void in one's blood to Sing the Song and call matters into being. Why couldn't she understand it? She had his DNA flowing inside of her. It should have been natural. Couldn't she do more than age slowly? That didn't count. That wasn't sorcery—it was biology. Any hybrid could maintain youthful appearances and vigor for decades of their long life. It shouldn't even matter that Miranda was *julah* on her father's side, often described as "inferior," genetically speaking. It may have been true for most hybrids, but her father was no ordinary man. He was Nerilis Dunsman, the youngest High Priest of the Void to ever serve the holy throne.

And her true mother was the effervescent spirit of the Void. How could Miranda *not* transcend her half-human biology and outpace the lazy students at the Academy? Nerilis didn't ask her to revive the dead, for the Void's sake. He only wanted her to add power to his. Was that really so hard to ask?

Naturally.

"Remember what we practiced last time?" Nerilis placed a red ball between them before moving ten paces away from his daughter. "You cannot move from one plane to the next without considerable concentration. You must void your mind of thought and consideration of mortal matters."

Yes, Miranda easily remembered the last time they played this foolish game. Her father had been dragging her to locations around town for the past three months, convinced that her genetic fortitude would amplify his own power as he pursued the impossible. Miranda didn't know if she was expected to join him in moving between dimensions, or merely act as a conduit for his experiment. In truth, he didn't know either. He had enough practice to storm into the Academy and declare himself the chair of a new Interdimensional Studies department, and nobody would have the grounds to object. Not based on his abilities, anyway. They would probably object to his background as a hellraiser and mass murderer, however.

That was what made this a frustrating endeavor for them both. Miranda didn't know the first thing about *sorcery*, nor had she ever fancied herself someone who pursued those ambitions. Not in her ninety-eight lives, anyway. This man could tell her she was originally destined to be born the daughter of the two most powerful people in the universe, but what the hell did that mean? It hadn't happened. There was no guarantee she would show exceptional talent. *I think I dodged a bullet,* she thought, while her father muttered in a language she barely understood. *Imagine being in that situation.* She'd take being the daughter of a madam on a pleasure moon any day.

No matter how she thought about it, though, one result was always the same. This man was her father. Her body and soul had followed his embarrassing sex life for the past thousand years. When Miranda really pulled herself down, she realized that this man celebrated her moments of murder with sex.

God, she really was his daughter. That basically described her life on Cerilyn.

"All right," Nerilis announced, this time in English. At least he remembered she didn't speak Modern Basic or Julah that well. Sometimes he slipped into Old Basic, although any *julah* would tell her that they focused on languages of the current age. It was the only way to make room in the brain for more and more. "You're going to move this ball with your mind. By the end of tonight, you will have moved it from that spot..." he took two more steps back, "to my feet."

Miranda had to refrain from sighing. The last time she showed a lack of enthusiasm, her father lectured her about the importance of sorcery for half an hour. *He disappears from my life for years at a time,* she thought, considering her childhood, *and now he's back to play Daddy when I'm thirty-five.* Typical.

"I'm not sure how this is supposed to work," she said. "I've never in my life shown any magical fortitude, and I think I would have remembered it if I did."

Nerilis scoffed. "Are you daft? Because I've seen you manipulate slivers of the Void more than once. Every time that woman..." He touched his chin and turned away, a new dawn of realization crowning his head. "Every time you exhibited a sliver of power, that woman was around."

Miranda didn't have to ask who he meant. "That woman" was not a phrase Nerilis reserved for his beloved Joiya, the woman who once owned Miranda's body and was not above possessing it when motivated. He could have only meant Danielle, who had been endangered more than once over the past year. *And those are only the times I know about,* Miranda thought, her own realizations prompting her to recall what happened every time she intervened with Danielle's untimely death. Perhaps her father wasn't out of his mind for assuming she had power beyond her own understanding. She merely needed to be inspired.

"Look." Nerilis lapsed into Julah, a language Miranda understood now that she had a reason to care. "I know what it's like to be in love. The Void knows it and makes my life hell for it now."

He was not impressed by the befuddlement dancing upon Miranda's countenance, but there was no going back on languages now. Nerilis didn't need words to convey his meaning, anyway. With his daughter's undivided attention now on him, he could look into her faraway eyes and see more than the bright shade of brown that once beguiled him when he was younger.

It's not the same, he thought, remembering another soul that once inhabited that body. *I can see her soul. It's not the same.* His gift of spiritual sight both protected him from heartache and threatened to destroy him from the inside. Just because he knew that wasn't the love of his life in that body didn't mean the memories ran away from him.

"I don't expect you to understand my kind of love," Miranda said.

"If you think I would have forbidden you from loving a woman," Nerilis continued with a snort, "well, I know firsthand that those things can't be helped."

Miranda didn't dare ask what he meant. She could guess well enough. She had even suspected it more than once, but she would never, ever say it out loud to a man who came off as sensitive about it.

"Had you been born to us a full-blooded *julah,*" her father said, "there would have been heavy expectations. They exist for all of us, including the imbecile you see standing before you."

Truly, expectations were what lifted and ruined him in his adolescence. Not even Marlow could understand the sheer amount of pressure resting upon Nerilis's shoulders when he enrolled in the Academy. The Dunsmans—now Ducah, a name he thought preposterous—were one of the most noble families within a race that knew nothing but prosperity. There had been countless rows with his mother and the matchmaker about who he would marry, since Joiya Lerenan came from a smaller, less noteworthy family.

I won out in the end, he recalled with triumph. *I am nothing if not stubborn.* Once Joiya accepted his proposal, there was no turning back. He was madly in love, the deep, all-consuming kind that would haunt him for the rest of his life. The foolish bastard merely assumed his beloved would be around for most of that torturously long existence, since it was unusual for a young *julah* to die without external cause.

"You would have suffered the pressure of being born to the High Priest and his talented, popular wife," Nerilis continued. "You would have been tutored by the greatest teachers to prepare you for the Academy, where you would have been expected if not required to specialize in spiritual matters. We would have asked you to become a priestess, regardless of your abilities, and your mother and I would have arranged a match for you when it was time. You would have had even less say in the matter than I did. The children of the High Priest marry whomever their parents say they will."

"I don't think I would have cared to be a *julah.*"

"Probably not. You may have rebelled. Perhaps to the point everyone but your mother shunned you."

"Is being who I am such a damnable offense?"

"It is when it prevents you from fulfilling your duties." Good Void, he sounded so much like a typical *julah* father, and that thought shook Nerilis Dunsman to his core. This was the man who railed against tradition, although he willingly embraced the aspects of it that suited him. *The Void spared her, I suppose,* he thought. The true reason Miranda was never born to her real mother was due to Joiya's calling to become High Priestess. But perhaps her soul also knew what torment awaited her should she be born to such cherished children of the Void. "Like I said, I understand where you're coming from. Homosexuality is not uncommon among our kind, but it's not something we flaunt when there are more pressing relationships to pursue." Same-sex dalliances were reserved for the young and curious. Maturation included giving up those desires in favor of the greater good. *Julah* did not easily reproduce, and their numbers had grown at a steady snail's pace over millions of years.

"Right," Miranda said. "Family connections and the propagation of the species above all else. Sounds familiar enough on this planet."

"That said..." Her father stared at the red ball, still planted between them. "One cannot prevent love from taking hold. You would have found ways to defy me back then as you do now. Except *now* I encourage you to tap into those inspirational reserves and do something productive with it." Nerilis chuckled. "The universe is on brink of collapse, and your lover is threatened with a fate worse than death. You may be one of the only people who can help me fix that. Surely, you can do it."

"That's different," Miranda said. "Nothing's happening right this moment."

"Everything you see here will collapse soon enough. When the Void loses its last dispensable soul, there will be nothing left. Not unless we do something about it."

Miranda hated to consider those implications. Both she and Danielle were spiritually compromised, trapped in the Process and facing nearly impossible odds of ever breaking free. *We're on opposite sides of this hellish spectrum,* Miranda thought. Danielle was trapped because she could not regress. Miranda had regressed years ago, but the conditions for breaking free beyond that? She might as well call herself Damned.

A fate worse than death was accepted long ago. Miranda's only hope was to spend her last life with the one she loved, latching onto a glimmer of that happiness they once shared a thousand years ago. Her father had to relate to that. The man knew love and loss for himself. He knew the consequences of being torn apart from one's fated match.

No wonder he always looked at Miranda as if she were cursed. Not only did she have the most compromised soul in the universe... but it was housed in a body that he once knew more intimately than his own. It didn't matter how much Miranda styled it to suit her personality. Nerilis saw his betrothed in the way Miranda walked and tilted her chin to the side. How much did it break his heart to know that this was their fate? Why did he always play his part in her creation every cycle?

He couldn't tell her that. All he could do was guide her, a thousand years too late.

"This ball will save your lives." Nerilis happened to glance at it, and a moment later, the ball rolled to the left as if it were kicked. The most powerful man in the universe didn't so much as blink or sigh. To him, moving a ball a few feet was like absentmindedly rubbing his fingers together. He thought it. It happened. There was no more to it than that. "But it must be placed back where it came from. Only you have the ability to make that happen. Well?" He *tsked*. "What do you do about it? Will you save our lives? Or will you allow the universe to collapse and seal our fates?"

All this to merge one dimension with another...

Miranda had already received instructions on how to perform simple acts of sorcery. They were the same lessons *julah* children learned when their parents and tutors tested their magical fortitude. *"See the ball? You want to play with the ball. Bring it to you so you can have some fun. How badly do you want it? What would you do to make that ball come to you?"* A boy like Nerilis had received murmurs and half-forgotten bouts of praise when he brought his ball over before the instructions were concluded. *"You're right,"* he had told his tutor, a man who would soon leave his post so someone with more foresight could take over Young Master Dunsman's education. *"I want to play with the ball. Sounds fun."*

I have to want it... Miranda stared at the red ball, brows furrowed and feet digging into the ground. *It's not enough to think it. I have to* want *it.* She also had to release her disadvantages into the ether. So what if she was only half-*julah?* So what if it was on her father's side? Did that mean she was less than? That she didn't stand a chance in this brutal hell she already courted? *This ball will save our lives. It must be moved.* Little children were taught magic by speaking to their base, unmatured desires. *"I want to play. That's mine. I want it."* A grown woman had to have something else on the line. Something that extended beyond her own soul.

Such as someone else's.

She remembered every time Sulim—whether that was her name or not—met her unfortunate end. Miranda, destined to always be born first, had sometimes seen the end before Sulim was cognizant. A hundred lives in a thousand years meant planets were destroyed long before Sulim learned how to walk. A blissful, forgettable death. Other times she was school-aged, and while she was tormented by fantastical nightmares, the woman Miranda was always destined to be only looked on while their worlds burned.

Nerilis had become so efficient over the millennium that he could destroy most planets before Miranda awakened as a new human being. Living to thirty-five on a place like Earth meant he either struggled... or he took a damned break.

That didn't matter. They were here now. This was what they were doing. Miranda must move the ball before not only Earth collapsed into oblivion, but the whole universe did as well.

The ball nudged two inches to the right.

"Good." Nerilis turned his attentions back to his daughter. "Move it more. Faster."

"I don't even know what I did..."

"You did the bare minimum. Now give it a little more effort."

The bare minimum? Miranda thought with a scoff. This man could not appreciate her position. Not if he tried.

"If you're going to stand there like a petulant child, then we're done here. I don't have time for this."

"Yet you need me so badly for your project, don't you?" Miranda could throw his shit back in his face. Didn't need to be his daughter to do that, either. "You wouldn't be wasting your time with me right now if you didn't."

"*Need* you? No. You misunderstand. I am merely after the convenience of having someone even slightly as powerful as myself onboard. I see the value when I consider what we're up against. Crossing isn't a simple matter, even for me. You're a convenience because you're not likely to turn me into the authorities, not that you could. And you're a convenience because my blood runs in your veins, and that must count for something. Every *julah* knows that sorcerous aptitude is highly determined by genetics. Why do you think my family poured so much into my education?"

Because Miranda wasn't enamored enough with her father already, she really needed to hear him sound off on his great, almighty, affluent family... which was a shell of its former self in the wake of his betrayal to his kind. His mother had died as a result of his treason. His family held a summit to change their name, any effort necessary to shake off their guilt by association heeded. The younger generations in his family struggled to find suitable matches, and the few that knew romance often found it in the arms of humans or soon discovered that they were a flight of forbidden fancy. What better way to rebel against Mother and Father than by sleeping with a Dunsman?

"They probably knew that if they didn't, you would whine about it like you whine about everything else." Miranda regretted it the moment she said it, but she might as well own her brand of rebellion. "Nobody gives a shit that your family is rich, powerful, whatever. Where are they now, huh? Where is this powerful blood family of yours to help you?"

Nerilis could have taken her bait for a fight. But three thousand years of life, much of it spent in solitude, meant he was not easily swayed by passion. Like most *julah* who approached the decline of life, he had tucked away his caches of enthusiasm.

But Miranda's was young and raw. Human too. For all of her latent *julah* qualities, such as her attraction to the finer things and entertaining pursuits of the mind, she was still more human in attitude. Centuries would past before she saw a glimmer of her full potential, but Nerilis didn't need that. She would die before then, anyway. Yet her humanly passion might be exactly what he needed to coax her power out of her. The more she fumed at him, the more that ball moved a little to the right.

"You want to know where my family is?" His smirk had to be checked before it gave away his game. "I suppose most of them are holed up in their estate, cursing my name while thinking of their glory days. I daresay the reason they've survived a thousand years of blacklisting and ridicule is because they once had so much wealth stashed away. Almost like they knew one of their own would go rogue and bring down the whole legacy. Oh, I have a few cousins who live out and about in the Federation." His cousin Calseeth was the steward for his oldest mentor at the Academy, a position he secured her some years ago. "Some of them even attend the Academy again, or so I hear. I doubt they'll let any in the Temple soon, though. A few thousand more years will have to pass. A shame. There are some bright enough minds in those lost generations."

"Am I supposed to feel sorry for you?" Miranda asked.

"On the contrary, I do not miss those people for the life of me." He supposed he missed his mother, but there was nothing to be done about that now. "I was never much attached to the elders still alive. Aunts, uncles, and such. My family has a reputation for sullen countenances and never-minced words. Just because you're used to it doesn't mean you fancy it."

Miranda looked like she would rather eat the dirt beneath their feet than hear any more.

"They blame me, and to be sure I did not help matters, but ultimately it is their demise they seek. No respectable family will marry any of my relatives, but those same relatives refuse to procreate at all, even with humans. Granted, such offspring are doomed to a tragically short life, but they fail to understand what a few hundred years of half-*julah* family members could do to refurbish the family's image. Nobody is as go-getting as mortals who only live for a few hundred years at most." That was being generous. Most hybrids lived for two hundred years if they were lucky. Longer than most humans, who had extended their lives to a ripe old age of a hundred and fifty, but mere footnotes in *julah* family history when compared to three to five thousand years. Did Miranda understand that even if she reclaimed her beloved's soul, that she would be doomed to watch that love snuff out before her very eyes? And possibly live a hundred more years?

"So your family is a bunch of bigots. Makes me glad I want nothing to do with them."

"Yes, it would be a hopeless endeavor. There would be no point in appealing to my family. Even if they believed you were my daughter, they would strike you down where you stand for speaking such heresy. I won't even mention what they would do to those you love."

Miranda furrowed her brows. "Good thing I have my big, strong father here."

"Oh, I would not interfere. What they do is none of my concern any longer."

He knew how to get to her, of course. Miranda had made it clear she was sensitive to how people genetically perceived her. Of course, a discerning father would have realized that it extended beyond half-human, half-*julah zazipah* politics and manifested in something as simple as Earth-based racism. Being half-Japanese (or half-Asian, for that matter) meant nothing to citizens of the Federation. Their acute ways of judging and excluding one another manifested on a more meta level, where a human's worth was based on whether they mixed with *julah, huling,* or even *isola-te* blood.

Nerilis didn't pay enough attention to his daughter's plights of identity, however. Not even when he regularly met her adolescent self in Japan. But he did understand *zazipah* perceptions. He also understood how his family would have treated his half-blooded child should he ever dare to bring her back to Dunsman Estate.

"It doesn't matter how much like your mother you look," he said with a sniff. "You would've been one of my mother's chambermaids at the very best. She would've told you that it was the greatest honor you could have hoped to achieve in her manor."

Miranda did her best to not show a sliver of disapproval. Yet her aura radiated that she would rather talk about the birds and the bees with her father than be reminded of every box she checked.

The ball hit the nearby wall.

"And the Void help you if you brought home a young lady to be your companion," Nerilis continued. "My mother had no patience for falling out of line. Some on this planet would call her a bit bigoted, I suppose. On my planet, however, she's merely a traditional woman overseeing the continuance of our line. If you proved to be an exceptional chambermaid despite your half-human blood, you can bet a suitable marriage would have been arranged between you and a nice young man. There would have been no room for your lady companion. And if you think I would have had any say in it as your father..." Nerilis threw his head back and laughed. "I would have been too busy ensuring my own happiness to care about yours."

The ball slammed against the wall.

"Now imagine what you could do if you really applied your passion to the application of spiritual manipulation."

Without a word, Miranda turned and exited the protective sphere her father had erected. Her sudden appearance garnered the attention of a man having a smoke on the sidewalk. He didn't ask any questions, though. Wisely, he had long learned to not ask questions when strange women magically appeared before him.

Nerilis learned one important thing that evening. His daughter still had untapped potential to match a fraction of his greatness. She also had but one attachment to the mortal realm, and that woman might prove to be the key to unlocking Miranda's true ability.

This was about to get messy again. At least he didn't have to worry about a motley crew of his own followers ruining everything this time.

Nine

Master Ramaron Marlow may have been busy with official Federation business on Terra III, but he had a small employ who continued his investigations on his behalf.

Sometimes in the most obnoxious places.

"The thought of drinking *cageh* makes me want to retch." Kalera Amyran, weighed down by the growth in her womb, spat that in Basic as she and husband Vikkel entered a *cageh* house in one of Yahzen's largest cities. "I'm pretty sure my doctor will ditch his degree if he finds me drinking caffeine at this stage of my..."

Her husband tightened his hand around the top of her arm. "You don't have to drink any," he said. "That's not why we're here, anyway."

Scoffing, Kalera plopped down into a chair at the first available table. A house maiden, bedecked in the conservative finery of an upscale *cageh* house, approached them with a specials' menu in her hand. Neither Kalera nor Vikkel failed to notice the look of recognition in her green eyes as she took in their appearances. Naturally, her sight lingered on the bump under Kalera's black blouse. *I would love to stick this ball up her ass and see how she likes it.* Fine thing for this young lady to give her such an eye too. What was she? A member of the Forsyth clan? Kalera was the daughter of Cornelius Ferran, the human ambassador to Yahzen! How dare this woman...

"I'll have a pot of the pungent *tesatah,* and my wife will have the new mother's herbal brew." Vikkel ignored Kalera's mutters that she hated being treated like a brood mare. If he waited long enough, she would have launched into a tirade about one of the young daughters of the Forsyth clan giving her a "dirty look" that would have only drawn more attention to themselves. Last he checked, anyway, hybrids were not forbidden from *cageh* houses—regardless of what some of the elders may have desired.

"Yes, sir." The house maiden plucked the menu from the table and slipped into the back. Vikkel folded his arms on the table and leveled a gaze upon his wife.

"We're here to work, not cause a scene," he reminded her.

"I can't help it. I'm so uncomfortable that..."

"I know, but you probably shouldn't swear either. Even in Basic. In fact..." Vikkel looked around the half-empty shop. He was one of the only men there, aside from two hybrid elders who swapped stories of their diplomacy work. Otherwise, it was mostly middle-aged and elderly *julah* women chatting over their pots and plates of snacks that heralded to contain ingredients from the student-tilled gardens of the Academy on Bah Zenlit. Granted, they were indeed scrumptious. But before Vikkel could think to order his wife a treat, he remembered why they were there.

"The tea will help," he assured Kalera. "Both your ailments and your concentration. I can't be the only one listening in."

"I thought you said we shouldn't be speaking in Basic?" Kalera chastised him in Julah. "Drawing attention to ourselves? Because I think it might be too late for that."

"What do you..."

Vikkel had his back turned to the woman quickly approaching them. Not quick because she had important things to tell them, but quick in that way most busybody women with nothing better to do make their presence known. Her periwinkle gown laced in *yeral* stones, so rare that they must have been passed down her matrilineal line, and the large *zatbah* ring that contained her most precious memories wasn't enough on a planet like Yahzen, where the female heads of families dressed themselves in ostentatious wares to show off status and personality.

Now, which family was this fine specimen of femininity and propriety from again? Neither Vikkel nor his wife could hear their thoughts over the loud clacking of heels.

"If it isn't the Amyran children!" That high-pitched squeal almost took an already irate Kalera and leveled her up to murderous. "Vikkel, right? Why, I knew your mother when we were girls at Lady Belan's School for Young Women! She had the most gracious curtsy out of all of us there! Absolutely gorgeous girl. You have her eyes, don't you? How is your darling little brother? I hear he is about to start lessons at the Academy! I almost fell out of my chair when I first heard of it! Is this your darling bride? Why, the ambassador's daughter, aren't you? I also knew Lady Ferran from the capital's *chazah* tournaments. She really was a wizard at the game. Does she still play? My gracious Void! Look at your stomach! It's about to explode! How far along are you, dear? My own daughter is about to have her child soon. Of course, she's a hybrid like you two, so it's like I'm becoming a half-grandmother instead of a real one, but I'm soooo excited to have a baby in the house! How excited is your mother, dear? You're Lady Ferran's only child, yes? Why, that makes your baby like a real grandchild, then! I can't wait for my Ellisia—she's my only full-blooded child since I married Lord Ithrah, surely you've heard about it—to grow up and have her own children. Oh, where are my manners? You *must* come sit with us at our table in the corner! We all know your mothers!"

Kalera picked up her stirring utensil, fighting back the urge to chuck it at Lady Ithrah (in case they missed that very important detail.) Her husband reached across their table and gently pushed her hand back down.

"We would be honored to join you, Lady Ithrah," Vikkel said. "My mother would greatly chastise me if I did not take this opportunity to catch up with you on her behalf."

"As indeed she should! Come tell us about the latest at Amyran Estate! We've bled each other dry about our own news."

The house maiden feared that the young couple had already left by the time she came out with their *cageh*. Yet she soon found them at the large table in the back, where Lady Ithrah and her entourage of lesser ladies, their daughters, and special handmaidens congregated to complain about their lives and the state of the universe. (Bonus if they could conduct some beneath-the-table deals that may or may not have included their children's personal lives.) Most of the ladies were delighted to welcome the fresh blood, and knowing that there was a young (albeit hybrid) man in their midst had them gussying up their hair and smoothing out their skirts.

"Isn't that Lady Amyran's child?" hissed a lesser lady of House Luram to one of House Hazurah. "The one that supposedly joined the League of Spiritual Awareness?"

"Shh!" Lady Hazurah mimicked the closing of her big mouth. "We don't speak of that in here." And for good reason. *Cageh* houses had been the hotbeds for clandestine meetings, particularly if certain families owned the shops. The Obello clan owned this particular house, and their own members had been interviewed by both Federation and Yahzen investigators before eventually being cleared. To say it was a touchy subject... "Besides," Lady Hazurah continued, "they work for Master Marlow."

That was the first topic everyone wanted to indulge after asking about the Ladies Ferran and Amyran. What *was* it like working for the great Master Ramaron Marlow? He paid fairly, yes? Oh, he had those very interesting humans he kept close by. Had they met the mercenaries? Did they know that one of them was currently touring Terra III, on what Lady Ithrah called a propaganda tour?

"He's a very agreeable employer," Vikkel said. He might as well. Marlow was the reason they weren't in prison. If Kalera thought she had complaints now? Wait until she enjoyed life in a Federation cell. While pregnant.

"Would you look at how high this child rides?" Lady Ithrah was bold enough to place both hands on Kalera's stomach. "It's obviously a boy."

"All three of my hybrid daughters rode that high," another woman countered. "Bless their departed souls."

A friend rolled her eyes. "You know what that means, yes?" When she met a few snickers, she continued, "It's an *inkep* baby."

The screeching laughter was reserved for the woman with three dead daughters, but Kalera was embarrassed enough to turn to her husband and say, "I can't take this anymore."

"Here." He poured her more new mother's herbal brew. "Drink your tea."

"You know they're gonna ask…"

"The hornier the mother is," the crassest woman in the bunch said, "the higher that baby rides." She turned to Kalera without another word.

"Get me out of here!" Kalera demanded with a hiss.

"If you do go," Lady Ithrah said, "Do say hello to Master Marlow for me. He and I have a smidgen of a connection, you see." For as much as the *julah* loved to flaunt their social connections with prestigious families, they never said something like that without a decent source to back it up. Even if that source occurred two thousand years before, and the man in question was not likely to remember it, as inconsequential as it was to his life. "He was briefly arranged to be married to my older sister, you see. Dearest Lalayra was mighty fond of him, too. Such a pity it didn't work out."

"Are you serious?" asked Lady Luram. "I had no idea that Master Marlow was ever engaged to anyone."

"I said it was *arranged,* dear. This was such a long time ago, you know. At least two thousand years. You may not believe it," she said to the young married couple who could not fathom such a forgotten age, "but your employer was quite the handsome young man back then. Everyone of betrothal age secretly hoped they would be paired with him. Even those from families too lowly to court any real hope." She tried to not look Lady Luram in the eye when she said that. Of course that woman hadn't heard of it. Two thousand years ago, the Luram clan were losing their coins to a Master of the House who liked gambling a little too much. It had gone on for over five hundred years. Quite the shame for a family that had built a sizable fortune trading with a fledgling Federation way back when. All of it gone in a *julah* generation!

"Oh, yes," said Lady Hazurah, who was the most senior of the high-born women at the table, "Young Master Marlow was quite the looker back when I first attended the Academy. Him and... the other one. They were quite inseparable. A very fine pair to behold, although nobody's wont to talk about Nerilis Dunsman's beauty these days like they were back then."

"Who the hell wants to admit they arranged an *inkep* with a terrorist?" Lady Ithrah scoffed. "Even though any keeper of the records will tell you he got around!"

Lady Hazurah ignored that inappropriate outburst. "Yes, he was a known philanderer at the Academy. So was Young Master Marlow, if you believed *those* rumors."

"So hard to believe he managed to con Her Holiness into an engagement," Lady Luram said.

"Not so hard to believe when you saw them together," Lazy Hazurah continued. "I came to the Academy before they left, and I saw them for myself. Incredibly handsome couple. He was utterly smitten with her. I don't doubt for two seconds that he would've been a faithful bastard to someone as beautiful and virtuous as Her Holiness. It's just too bad about the..." She was about to say the best kept, never-spoken secret of that young relationship that was never meant to be. Until she realized that there was a pregnant woman present, and it was bad luck to speak of miscarriage in front of a young pregnant *julah* woman, hybrid or not.

Kalera was hardly paying attention, however. Her husband urged her to drink her brew, but she was so damned bored of henpecking that she was liable to slam her forehead into the table and shake the *cageh* cups. Vikkel apologized for his wife's ill mood, citing the obvious afflictions that most of the women around them understood. Whether *julah* or human, pregnancy was no walk on Bah Zenlit.

The focus soon returned to the baby and the woman unfortunately attached to it. Although Kalera only thought herself so unfortunate because she hated nothing more than unwanted attention from full-blooded elders who thought themselves the experts on all matters. She didn't want their advice. Nor did she want to know which names they should name their firstborn, which everyone agreed was a boy. *No shit,* Kalera thought. She had known the obvious from the moment she first consulted the child she begrudgingly admitted grew inside her. When her mother-in-law bequeathed the gendered baby things that had helped raise Vikkel, one could have considered it a coincidence. But when Kalera returned to her natal home and discovered her own mother's purchases of the same gendered items, it was like the whole universe knew that a penis grew inside her womb.

The only thing none of these women could agree upon was what she should name her firstborn son, who would *obviously* go on to carry his father's line of Amyran hybrids. Lilla Amyran insisted that he be named after Vikkel's father, since "he wasn't a bad husband, for a human." But there was no way in hell Kalera was giving birth to someone named Barthametellow Amyran. (Everyone had called Vikkel's father "Bart," and that was almost worse.)

"Honestly," Lady Hazurah said in a hushed tone after Vikkel had to escort his paling wife to the ladies' powder room, "you have no idea what young men got up to at the Academy back in those days. When they weren't threatening to tear a hole into the sun with their kooky experiments, they were planting seeds from Sah Zenlit to Terra III. No woman my age or older should say a damn thing about Nerilis Dunsman's appearance when they were all racing to lift their plaid Academy skirts if it meant getting to tug his ponytail, if you know what I mean."

For every woman making a disgusted face at the table, there was another re-membering the photographs they had seen of a young Nerilis Dunsman. None of them knew what he looked like now, which was for the best. The reactions may have been the same. "We should be so lucky that the Void sent Her Holiness to put a clamp on that cock before it started breeding! Can you imagine what a child of his would really be like?"

The nods around the table were solely comprised of spite. "Absolutely insuf-ferable," said Lady Ithrah.

"But incredibly powerful, perhaps," Lady Luram added. "Unless we're talking a hybrid here."

They had changed the subject by the time Vikkel and Kalera returned.

By the end of their third full day on Terra III, Devon and May joked that the barrage of photos, videos, and interviews with every major news source in the Federation prepped them for life as famous rock stars. While May did not participate in the media frenzy, she had a front-row seat alongside Evan and Lanelle in seeing what buffoonery arose every time Devon grinned at a camera wrong or misunderstood a question asked in a language he did not understand. Marlow was his main translator for all languages *not* Basic (such an honor befell Evan), but not even a *julah* equipped with auto-translators could keep Devon from mishearing the word for "desires" as meaning something completely different.

"Desires for your future!" Marlow slammed his hand on the dinner table again, shaking his head as if he were offended once more. It had been two hours since that unfortunate interview with one of the Federation's leading investigative journalists, and he still wasn't over Devon blushing and saying he'd rather not talk about his philandering ways in his previous life. "Not *desires you had in the past!* And not those kinds of desires either! They are completely different words in Huling."

All Devon knew about the *huling* was that they were the race of humans who claimed Syrfila Tograten as one of their own. The woman interviewing Devon looked nothing like the dark haired, lanky featured woman who tried to kill him more than once over the past few months. Still, the reminder had not been appreciated. The fight erupting between him and Marlow after that unfortunate interview was part faulty misunderstandings, part Devon wishing to the Void that they would warn him about such a thing next time. *"You do know that not all Huling are terrorists, right?"* Marlow had said. *"Try not to paint a whole race of people with one stroke..."*

Nobody had pointed out to Devon that he was speaking near-fluent Modern Basic when he told Marlow to kindly go fuck himself. Well, he had peppered Old Basic obscenities in there, but the result was much the same. Lanelle had been alive when a word like *guldarpiloo* was still in use, and she had a grand laugh to hear it echo in the hallowed halls of Terra III's capitol building's media wing.

Yet Marlow was not the main source of Devon's irritation. Nor was the jet-lag or the overwhelming information coming at him from every angle. No, the thing that bothered him was something nobody else could understand. *He* barely understood it, probably because there was no way for him to understand the cause of his paranoia and the incessant feeling that something was about to *change* in his spiritual life. His Void-granted connection to both Danielle and Miranda meant he picked up on any momentous currents between them. Too bad Danielle had played coy on the phone and conveniently forgot to mention such a tidbit to him. That left Devon staring into the back of his hand while everyone around him ate dinner.

"You should *really* try the meatballs." Evan jerked his fork toward the food left cooling on Devon's plate. "They're not made of any animal you've heard of recently, but the seasoning includes paprika, and I know how much you Earthlings love paprika."

"Do I detect a bit of good old fashioned sea salt as well?" May asked in English.

"Obviously, but it's not from Earth. Far from the only planet with seawater, ahem. Should take you to the beaches near here..."

Lanelle rolled her eyes from across the table. "Only if you want him to get *mobbed*. Or us, for that matter. Nobody gives a shit who I am around here, but I can't go to the beach without at least ten people on top of me. Some of them even ask me out first. Usually the women."

"And you say yes, of course?" Evan asked.

"You'd love it if the answer were yes."

Marlow pushed aside his empty plate and popped open the tablet he carried in his bag. A holographic keyboard appeared in the space between the tablet and his hand. After a few cursory glances at his screen, he flew through typing a correspondence to the steward of his family's estate. Due to the many languages flying about him that day, he made no fewer than ten mistakes typing a simple sentence in Julah, the only language he hadn't heard in the past twelve hours.

"Would you two pipe down?" he spat in his native language, a cue that it was meant for his assistants' ears. Evan wasn't fluent in Julah, but he knew when he was being told to shut up. Sounded like the perfect opportunity for him to message his wife on his communicator.

"Have you heard from Danielle?" Lanelle asked Devon in a slightly hushed tone. Her boss continued to grumble to himself a few feet away. "I'd hate to think that you're having *so much* fun while she's back on Earth feeling sorry for herself."

"That's one way to put it." Devon finally tried a bite of the meatball. Someone had overcompensated with the paprika, but at least it was familiar after three days of trying foreign flavors. "I talked to her last night. Two nights ago? I don't remember what day it is. Either way, she sounded about as fine as one can be for being publicly tried and fired for sleeping with women occasionally." He maintained eye contact with Lanelle during that final statement. She may have known something about Danielle's proclivities. *Surprised she wasn't called to the stand because of Halloween,* Devon thought. Danielle was too drunk to remember, but at one fateful Halloween party the year before, she locked lips with Lanelle and claimed to like it.

Technically, Devon had locked lips with Lanelle too... in a previous life. Last November.

My head hurts. Devon pushed aside the rest of his meatballs and contemplated going to bed. Lanelle and Evan had devolved into speaking pure Basic with one another, and Devon didn't have the mental capacity to understand it.

"Gets tiring, huh?"

He turned toward May, who had finished her meal and now propped her chin upon her hand. "What?" Devon asked.

"Having everyone switch to a gajillion languages around you. My parents speak Basic, but I never picked it up that well. English is my first language, much to the consternation of my grandparents who don't speak a lick of it."

Devon fought back a yawn. "So you're the daughter of immigrants. Go figure."

May chuckled. "Certainly true. But most immigrants back home don't have to travel literal light years to see their extended families."

"They don't want to come visit you on Earth, huh?"

"It's difficult to get tourist visas to Earth. It's not part of the Federation, and our fellow Earthlings are what they call... ignorant. Except the word in Basic isn't as rude."

"You mean they're not supposed to know about the Federation."

"Nope."

"I'm still trying to figure that out," Devon said. "Earth seems like the exact kind of planet they would want in the Federation."

"You'd think, but from my rudimentary understanding of it, Earth was colonized by Federation dissenters thousands of years ago, and this kinda became the intergalactic equivalent of Australia for the longest time. By the time the Federation started thinking about Earth as a political entity, the Egyptian empire was in full swing and what we consider the ancient world was a great novelty to everyone living in the Federation."

"Yes, I vaguely remember." Sonall had loved watching reports from Earth a thousand years ago, back when William the Conqueror was deciding the fate of England. *I used to watch it with great interest, both as a youth and as a mercenary,* Devon thought. Only the higher-ups in Cerilyn's tribes were allowed news and entertainment from around the Federation, and one of the first things Sonall did when he was granted his first personal tablet was watch a documentary about the goings-on in what would soon be called the Crusades. "I wanted to travel to Earth as a visitor back then."

May's eyes widened. "I can only imagine how much harder it would have been a thousand years ago. How did people blend in like they do now? My parents barely assimilated, and they at least had cars to get around there."

"It was likewise difficult to get permission to travel to Earth back then. A lot of people did it illegally."

"But there were no teleporters back then... were there? Whoa. My mind is being blown." May tapped her finger against her lip. "Or they used space cruisers, which would've been so conspicuous."

"The only question I have," Devon said, changing the subject, "is how did humans begin to evolve on Earth if they already existed in our current form around the Federation?"

"There are some variances over the millennia, of course. According to my parents, anyway. The *julah* do most of the history record keeping in that regard, since they live so much longer. Perhaps we should ask your friend there when he's not cursing his email."

"Nah. I think my head would explode."

May chuckled. "Good call. Although if we were really worth our musical muscle, we'd create one helluva rock opera album about Earthlings from a thousand years ago."

"Or human evolution."

Evan stood up with a sigh grand enough to attract everyone else's attentions. "I'm heading home for the night, Boss. My mother-in-law is apparently visiting, and if I don't say hello at least once, it's my head on a pike."

"Speaking of a thousand years ago..." Devon muttered.

The only person to give Evan a proper sendoff was May, who asked if he might be willing to share some of his Earth history expertise from a Federation citizen's point of view in the coming days. Evan was more than happy to gush about everything he knew, but was too tired—and in too much of a hurry—to start that night. May walked with him to the door of their quarters and offered to lock the door behind him.

Evan turned around and helped himself back in five minutes later.

"Boss?" he called to Marlow, who was falling asleep at the table. "You really need to come see this."

Everyone understood that line of Basic. Even Devon, who glared at him with distrust. "What's going on?" he asked in English.

"Yes, what's going on?" Marlow said that in Julah. Evan jerked his thumb to the hallway behind him, prompting Marlow to get up and follow. Lanelle helped herself to the party as well.

"That can't be good," Devon muttered.

May nodded. "Let's assume it doesn't concern us."

It did, however, or at least Devon. Yet Marlow wasn't about to let him anywhere near their caller until he had a better idea of what was going on.

A woman who worked directly beneath Yara d'Alacron stood at the end of the guarded hallway. Her rigid posture and serious demeanor were nothing like the commander's dangerously casual approach to those she didn't consider a direct threat.

"Can we help you, Legate Ware?" Marlow asked the stoic woman who looked like she came to tell him his mother was dead. Again.

She bowed her head in acknowledgement before responding. "Master Marlow. My apologies for interrupting you on your evening off. However, there is a matter of pressing concern that I thought you should know about. Immediately."

"I'm guessing nobody's on the brink of death. Unless you share your commander's propensity for dry humor."

Legate Ware did not respond to that. "There is a man here who wishes to speak with you and your party at your convenience. He says his name is Fanar Gardiah and hails all the way from Arrah."

Lanelle was the first to recognize those names. She was already halfway to demanding more answers when Marlow said, "That sounds quite familiar. I'm guessing there is some veracity to his claims if you have not immediately turned him away."

"I took the liberty of checking his credentials," Legate Ware explained. "He is indeed named Fanar Gardiah and originates from the planet of Arrah. Whether it is vanity or not, however, I cannot say. I will leave it up to you whether you should like to speak with him."

Marlow glanced at the closed door behind him. "I will talk with him. Lanelle, come with me. Evan, go on home."

"Aww, come on." Evan stayed behind while Marlow and Lanelle went with Legate Ware. "This is finally starting to get interesting. You know what happens when I go home?"

"You sleep with your wife?" Lanelle cheerily asked over her shoulder. "Your life is so damn hard, Evan. I bet she even drew your bath for you and turned down the bed."

In truth, Evan was going home to chores, and Lanelle knew that, having spent many nights in his home when she didn't feel like being by herself. Evan rather wished she was coming home with him tonight. The banter between his wife and Lanelle would often leave him with a headache, but there were worse ways to end a workday.

Like going home knowing that everyone else was solving cool mysteries and watching Devon try more Federation food—sometimes with explosive results.

"Mr. Gardiah is sequestered in the interview room," Legate Ware explained, as she guided Lanelle and Marlow down a long hallway. She further assured them that an extra guard would be posted before their suite, to ensure that their Earthling guests would not be disturbed—or wander away too far. "He has been patted down for any hidden weapons and decontaminated for your safety."

"One never knows what bioterrorists are up to these days, indeed," Marlow drolly said. "Infecting themselves because they have some issue with us..."

Legate Ware remained unimpressed with his wit. "Right this way," she said.

Neither Lanelle nor Marlow knew what to expect. The name Gardiah was intimately familiar to both, of course, but not only did they not anticipate the arrival of someone with that name, but they also, like Legate Ware, had every reason to believe he was a zealot.

The young man sitting in the Federation Forces' local interview room, however, looked far from a zealot. He was of moderate height and thin, with moppy black hair and a prominent nose that almost detracted from the wide smile that appeared on his face the moment he realized he was joined by the great Master Ramaron Marlow.

"Hello, sir." His Basic was enunciated, but the accent one Marlow was not immediately familiar with. If this young man really was from the planet Arrah, then that might explain the strange, isolated tongue that pricked his corner of the universe. "I am very sorry for interrupting your evening. I forgot about what time it would be in the capital when I arrived two hours ago."

"All the way from Arrah, yes?" Marlow made note of Legate Ware standing in the corner of the room. "That is quite the trip, unless you teleported."

"Oh, no, sir. I drove here."

Lanelle almost choked on her breath. "That has to be a nine-day journey by cruiser. Even if Wormgate #3 is open right now, and I'm pretty sure it's *not*." The third Wormgate was notorious for always being down for repairs. Citizens like Lanelle often bemoaned her taxes going to such a deficient system when teleportation should simply be made more viable to the masses.

Fanar continued to grin. Whatever fatigue he might have been feeling at the end of his long journey was now washed away with a second wind. "We Arrahites are used to traveling such long distances to get anywhere, sir. Unfortunately, many of our closest inhabited neighbors have been... stolen, you might say."

"More like winked from existence," Lanelle muttered, referring to a host of planets that used to occupy that corner of the universe. Until Nerilis Dunsman made short work of them, anyway.

"Thank you so much for agreeing to see me, sir," Fanar continued. "I don't know what this lady told you, but I am a Gardiah of Arrah. I am, well... I am a direct descendent of Sonall Gardiah."

Lanelle could hardly contain her titters. Marlow, meanwhile, coolly said, "I was not aware that Sonall Gardiah had children."

"Yes, sir. My ancient ancestor was his son. You may have heard of the Gardiah Debate a few centuries ago? My ancestor challenged the government of Arrah for the rights to our ancestral lands, which had been ransacked by the mercenaries and picked up by the man who paid them. We had to prove our blood relations and..."

"If you don't remember it," Lanelle cut in, "I certainly do." It was her job to know as much about the mercenaries and Nerilis Dunsman as possible, after all. She often played the missing pieces of Marlow's memory after he had dedicated so much of his brain to utter nonsense. "It happened about seven hundred years ago, yes? Your ancestors claimed reparations on behalf of what happened with Cerilyn and the displacement of your family's wealth."

"We were blessed that the Federation courts sided with us, yes." Fanar's grin grew even wider. Such toothiness unnerved Marlow, who was still not used to some humans' love for oversharing their emotions. "We regained our family estate and portions of our old investments, but not our titles, unfortunately. We've kept a relatively low profile since then."

"Still breeding those horses?" Lanelle might have been having too much fun prodding the poor boy.

"We do breed horses, but a different stock from our ancestors. We're mostly farmers now. We provide over 40% of Arrah's *sarah* weed."

"Admirable," Marlow muttered, as if he could calculate how much that was. A planet like Arrah was lovely for a jaunt, the kind of place one went to "get away from it all" and to indulge in artistic endeavors for a few months. Its ties to the Federation were what kept it green and hospitable, thanks to intergalactic-wide mandates regarding overlogging, overfarming, and over-hunting. Three things Arrah was particularly known for. (And for the Gardiah horse stock that were once declared the finest in the Federation.) "I'm sorry to hear that horse breeding and rearing isn't what it used to be for your family."

"Yes, well... that was several centuries before my time." Fanar scratched his head. His willowy yet finely toned body suggested he spent more time farming and less time resting on his ancestors' laurels. It had indeed been several centuries since anyone by the last name of Gardiah was called Lord or Lady, a title Sonall was destined to inherit before the pillaging took him to a new life. The man sitting a few rooms away would never see such titles in his current lifetime.

Marlow considered that before responding. "Like I said, I had no idea Sonall Gardiah had children before his untimely end." He wouldn't mention the role he played in that. "Did you know this, Lanelle?"

"Only from what I knew of the Gardiah Debate. Thought I brought it up a few times, but I guess you were more concerned about other things, sir. My vague recollection says that the man who grew up to reclaim the Gardiahs' estate came from, how should I say... humble origins?"

Fanar cut in before Marlow could ask for greater details. "His mother was a refugee from Cerilyn. One of the lucky few to flee after heeding advanced warning. She fled to Eros, where my ancestor was born." Fanar cleared his throat and took on a young man's scarlet embarrassment. The moon called Eros was infamous for its one dominant industry, the kind that even the likes of Nerilis Dunsman once patronized when he hit the lowest of lows. "For what that's worth."

Marlow didn't have to ask any further questions, since *the woman was a sex worker* fit right in line with what he knew of Sonall's lifestyle. Certainly made more sense than assuming he had a long-term affair somewhere in the Federation. "What exactly can we help you with, Mr. Gardiah?" As if he didn't know where this was going...

"My family chose me to come to Terra III after we heard our ancestor would be here. As you can imagine, we are quite excited to meet him."

That was exactly what both Marlow and his assistant anticipated, since a young man like Fanar would not come all the way from Arrah without wanting something substantial. And requesting a personal audience with the busiest man any of them knew was definitely *substantial*. Marlow had a hunch that Devon knew nothing about any progeny he begat in his original life. Lanelle shuddered to think what this would do to their schedule—and what Evan would say when he found out he missed out on this brand of fun.

"Such a request may be difficult to indulge," Marlow said. "Please understand, Mr. Gardiah, it's rather out of our hands. Mr. Anderson's security is headed by the commander herself. She has the final say in who has access to his person." A convenient excuse for him to make. If Marlow really wanted Devon to meet somebody, he'd damn well arrange it with or without Yara's approval. "But I don't see the harm in running this by him first."

Fanar's face lit up. Lanelle slowly turned to her employer, her expression beseeching him to explain this to her later.

"I don't think you'll be meeting tonight, however. I trust that you have accommodations in the city?"

They exchanged contact information, although Marlow was sure to give the young man the number to an office line. This was the sort of situation Marlow wanted full control over, since exposing Devon to a strange truth about his first life might cause more harm than good.

After handing Fanar Gardiah back to the guards for escort, Marlow returned with Lanelle to the antechamber before their guest apartments, where Devon and May awaited them. Lanelle stopped halfway to the door, prompting Marlow to hang back and ask, "What is it?"

"This isn't going to cause some stupid paradox that threatens to bring down the whole universe, right?"

"What in the world are you talking about? What paradox?"

"Call me paranoid, but someone who has been through the Process probably should not be meeting their descendants from their first life. The Process nukes our fertility for a reason. Everything about this feels super unnatural."

"There has never been any indication of that being true. If you had descendants from your first life, I wouldn't see any harm in you keeping contact with them." Marlow put his hand on the door. "Then again, you are a much brighter woman than most of the people in the Process I've met."

"And how many would that be by now?"

Marlow chuckled. "There have been a few of you since my Academy days." He didn't mention that in the Academy, somebody was always in the Process so young spiritual sorcerers like him could become educated. Thus the cycle, like the Process, always continued.

Ten

The warm days kept coming, although the forecast assured residents of the Bay Area that spring wasn't *quite* there yet. Fog and rain were slated for the following week, but as far as anyone could see, it was sunshine and warm breezes across the remainder of the weekend.

Which meant Danielle was treated to a public grilling by her best friend.

"You've gotta be kidding me," she muttered while Troy folded his hands beneath his chin and bestowed a generous glare upon her. They had ordered their drinks at the hip brunch spot halfway between their apartments. Vehicles clogged the main thoroughfare, exhaust and raucous honking driving Danielle's nerves under the table. Yet Troy couldn't wait five whole minutes before demanding she share everything going on in her personal life. "It's only been two days since the hearing. You think I've got *anything* going on?"

"Hon," Troy said, lowering his voice, "you're a reincarnated badass who has saved the planet and seen things even *I* can't comprehend. You've always got something going on."

Between Troy and Devon, Danielle was likely to cut off every man she knew. They were nosier than her female friends, and that was saying something. *Everyone's convinced I'm hiding something,* she thought, before contending that she was, in fact, hiding something big. But what happened between her and Miranda was nobody's business, especially since the two men in her life had *serious* opinions about it.

It's best I don't think about it at all, Danielle told herself. As long as she kept her sunglasses down and focused on the snacks and beer heading in her direction, she could start thinking about her future instead of what occurred in the past. Including a past as recent as two days ago.

"I'm trying not to think too much about things," Danielle said. "Focus on one thing at a time, you know? Like how I'm going to keep affording my rent. I know Ben picked up a few jobs in the Castro and moved in with some friends to save money, but I don't know if I could do that. I have to worry about health insurance as it is." Ah, yes, that thing that kept her going to the doctor every time she was due another cancer screening. Ever since her breast cancer scare a few years ago, doctors had been vigilant. Too bad those visits and tests cost money. "Plus, you know, it was a rather traumatizing ordeal. Although I'm glad they're in such a rush to boot us queers out that they didn't drag it out for me."

Troy sighed, his dour countenance not perking up even when the server brought them tapas and beer. The *patatas bravas* Danielle ordered was no longer appealing. Troy likewise did not immediately dig into his Spanish omelet. They both, however, dunked their faces into their beers.

"You're still taking this a lot better than I thought you would." Troy put his drink on the table and leaned back in his seat. "I was worried about you these past couple of days. You were shutting people out. If you hadn't answered my phone call last night, I would've thought the worst."

"Jesus," Danielle whispered with a hoot. "I'm not suicidal. Just going through a bit of a rough patch, yeah? I'm allowed to pull back from the world for a couple of days and reorient myself. Because next week I start seriously considering my source of income."

"You have any leads yet? Because I think you should wring that old rich asshole for some funds."

Danielle tapped her chin in contemplation. "If you're talking about who I think you are, then you're not the first one to suggest it."

"Because it makes the most sense. How long will it take you to find some crappy job with half the income and benefits you got from the military? This city's getting more expensive every year. Unless you plan on moving somewhere, you've gotta score something, right? Make the old guy pay you for your pain and suffering. Maybe something decent will actually come out of all the crap he's put you through. That's what I would do!"

"I like where this is going," Danielle said, finally sampling her potatoes. The spice hit her almost instantly, but that's what the beer was for, right? "He can be my benefactor. Climb into those coffers and cleanse my soul with Federation coins."

Troy laughed. "I have no idea what those look like, but I already agree."

"Not even sure they *have* coins up there." Danielle pointed to the sky for emphasis. "Wouldn't be surprised if everyone's bank account data was chipped into their skin, and you scan your freakin' hand in front of whatever they use to check you out."

"Reminder to self: don't get bank data microchipped into my skin."

"There really is something to be said for being a little analog now and then."

They toasted their beers to that. Danielle wondered what it would be like to live off Marlow's money for the rest of her life. *I've done what he hired me to do,* she rationalized while eating her appetizer and drinking her beer. *It's only right I charge for every life he took from me, the danger my soul is in,* and *overall interest!* She would take a few grand a month in US dollars. Surely, he could swing that. Even better if there was a way to make that untaxable, although Danielle would soon regret that line of thinking when she encountered the potholes on her street.

"My grandma keeps bugging me to come stay with her for a while," Danielle said, changing the subject.

Troy spoke with his mouth full of eggs and potatoes. "Might be a good idea. Get out of the city and regroup."

"There's a lot going on here, though." Danielle referenced Devon's trip to the Federation... and what happened Friday night. *That doesn't count as something going on right now, though,* she thought with a snort. Troy looked askance at her, but she was not compelled to share what she was thinking. *Once I tell him about that,* she thought, *I can't take it back.* If sleeping with Miranda was a one-time thing, then Danielle was content to keep it to herself.

"Your grandma's worried about you. Can't blame her. I'm worried about you, too!"

"You should also be looking out for your own ass." Danielle could hardly believe that Troy had made it this far unscathed. He was as likely to get court-martialed now as Danielle had been.

"Helps that I haven't dated in months. They'd have to go back farther than last summer."

"Last summer? I thought you had gone out since then."

"I've gone to parties and clubs, hung out with friends..." Troy shrugged. "Something about the world almost ending last summer kinda killed my loving spirit. Guess my priorities have changed. For example, I don't regret taking extended leave around Christmas to go to Cabo with my family. Not sure I would've done that a year ago."

Danielle finished her beer, although the spice from her potatoes lingered on her tongue. *Why am I sweating?* she thought, as if she couldn't guess that the mixture of a warm day, hot food, and black clothing that covered most of her body wouldn't do the trick. "My priorities have changed too," she said. "I've gotta figure out how to break out of the Process before it's too late."

Whatever Troy was about to say was soon replaced with renewed thoughts. "I'm sorry. I wish I knew how to help." Because, as he astutely forgot to consider a few minutes ago, Danielle had bigger problems in her life than losing her military career ten years into the game. Like Troy—and Miranda—she had signed on for a full twenty-year career, complete with the benefits and pensions that came from formally retiring. Most of their friends from M-Town and beyond were like that. Most of them queer, too. That's how social circles worked when Don't Ask, Don't Tell hung over their heads. Either they all covered each other's asses, or they all went down together.

"I need to figure out what's holding me back." The anxiety Danielle had swallowed at the start of brunch now came back up her esophagus. She was liable to spit it onto the table at any moment, but with a little luck, she'd refrain. "Everyone's agreed without my input that I'm repressing some horrible memories that won't let me regress. Can't say I'm excited about unlocking those kinds of memories, but I guess I better think about the long-term health of my soul. I'm currently at a point where if I die... well, say goodbye to any chances of returning to the Void before the end of time. Or beyond. Something like that."

"I thought you were seeing that therapist who specializes in past life stuff?"

"God, she's so insufferable. They keep telling me she's the best in her field, but what the hell is she doing on this shithole planet if that's the case? She wasn't born on Earth." Rea d'Eran claimed to have moved to Earth because research told her that's where all the tortured reincarnated souls were born. Lovely. "Ugh. This is why I'm all worked up and making stupid decisions."

"Stupid decisions?"

Danielle bit her lip and looked away, grateful that Troy's gaze couldn't penetrate her sunglasses. "I keep trying to make them, I should say. You know, booking trips around the world I can't afford? Going skydiving?" *Ending up in a certain someone's bed for most of the night...* Danielle blushed so hard that she swore the air heated up ten more degrees. Great. Troy could definitely see that.

He could also sense that Danielle kept a pivotal piece of information from him. Under any other circumstance, he would have goaded her until she either left in a huff or finally confessed her sins. But this was different. She teetered on the edge of a breakdown, and he had the power to tip her over the edge if he weren't careful.

So he would pull back, discontent with their current situation, but happy to keep her somewhat sane for a few more days.

Besides, Danielle was momentarily checked out from their conversation. Her eyes had glazed over as she looked beyond the scope of her tinted sunglasses, past the edge of their quaint table and well outside the boundaries of their humble metro area. Where was she? In her room, trying to forget what she had done? In Miranda's room, embracing more than another woman's body?

Or was she on another planet, during another time?

"Danny," Troy said. "Come back to Earth, Danny-Lynn. Your boy Troy misses you."

"Huh? Sorry. You suddenly reminded me of something." What it was, though, she could no longer remember. Like so many minor flashbacks she had in her life, they were gone as soon as she realized she was having them.

Yet the residue of everything that had been on her mind remained with her long after they paid their tab—well, Troy's tab, since he insisted—and parted ways. Danielle assured him that she was going for a walk to take her mind off things and nothing more. Unfortunately, even she knew that was a lie. The moment Troy disappeared around the corner, Danielle immediately embraced the fog overcoming her on such a sunny day.

Although the sensation was familiar, something about it struck fear into her mortal heart. Her immortal one, the one that pulled her in whichever direction it sensed most pertinent, screamed into her ear that she must walk. This way. Now.

She knew this feeling like the back of her own hand. Any hand she ever had in any life she now forgot.

This was the feeling that drew her down the path of near-insanity.

She knew where she was going. She knew what drew her down into these unfathomable depths of memories swimming in her mind and sensations she once knew coming to claim her again. They didn't always happen when a certain person was involved. But they always happened around people who potentially held the keys to who she once was.

The keys that unlocked the part of her that was *Sulim.*

Was that the force propelling her down the sidewalk, one heavy step at a time? Did it take one little trigger to awaken that woman inside of her? The woman she wasn't yet ready to embrace as another facet of herself, instead of a completely separate identity? Her envy that Devon could contentedly live as two different people in the same body had driven her away from him. She couldn't bear the way he looked at her, as if he pitied her.

That was all in her head, of course. Devon often felt sorry for her, but he rarely pitied her. Fear wasn't pity. Concern wasn't, either. He loved her, that was all. Cared about the state of her soul and was invested in helping her break free from the Process like he had. He often described it as "the most liberating moment of my life, like a weight I never before noticed had been lifted from every muscle in my body." Danielle had always felt those weights in her limbs and in her gut. They tortured her soul as much as her heart cried out in pain. The few times she ever felt the slightest bit *liberated* was when she gave herself over to making love.

She wasn't stupid enough to believe that sex was the answer to her problems. But everyone with the slightest bit of knowledge about the Process asserted that people who went into it together were often sexually drawn to each other. It was supposed to be comfortable. A reassurance that the other person was alive, that their soul was intact and that one didn't have to suffer alone. Maybe there could be pleasure. Maybe there could be joy. The number of times Sulim and Sonall had been married over the past millennium attested to their quest to find that in each other. Yet what held them back? *Me.* Danielle had always known it. Devon knew it. The reason they could never try a real relationship in their current incarnations had nothing to do with desire and everything to do with someone's heart already belonging to someone else.

She used to say she would always choose a woman over Sonall. That had been true in every life they lived long enough to meet and realize what they meant to one another. But until Earth, until a woman named Danielle Cromwell, the soul that refused to regress had never figured out where she was meant to be.

Only the Void knew how much time had passed since Danielle first stepped away from brunch. Yet it couldn't have been that long. The neighborhood she now found herself in wasn't too far away from the trendy eateries and markets that signaled gentrification. She could have never hoped to afford a neighborhood like Miranda's. Now she really couldn't.

That's a lovely name, isn't it? Danielle stood on the sidewalk across the street from Miranda's house, which looked so much warmer and more inviting in the sunlight. Gone were the shadows Danielle used to cover herself whenever she went where she wasn't supposed to be. Every time she came here before, it had been at night. A night that played with her head and made her forget her plight for two whole seconds. *Wasn't that a name Shakespeare made up? I wonder how the Federation people feel about Shakespeare's work.* Sounded like something Evan used to bolster his ego. *"I can recite all of his tragedies by heart... and know what they mean!"* Danielle would rather not think about him. She'd rather suck in a deep breath and calm down her heart before it burst from her body.

While Miranda was a perfectly fine name and suited the woman well, there was another name always tickling Danielle's eyelashes. Shorter. Harder. Some might say *barbaric.*

The street was lively. Of course it was. Sunday afternoon on a bright, warm day after a dreary winter. Neighbors mowed lawns, washed cars, and played with their kids. Bikes whizzed by every time Danielle slightly came back to reality. More than one resident cast suspicious glances in her direction. Who was this woman who kept hanging around their neighborhood? What did she have to do with that military spinster who lived in the house in the middle of the block?

Miranda must have been home. Not only was her green SUV parked in the driveway, but the tiny garage door was open. *It's not a garage,* Danielle thought. *It's a storage shed built into the house.* A woman couldn't fit most modern cars in there. But she could store a motorcycle.

It was parked upright next to the SUV. Tools were strewn about the driveway. Most of the bike glistened from a recent washing, although there were no buckets or towels around. Danielle had half a mind to follow her gut instincts and cross the street. She could knock on the door again. She had done it before. She knew where it might lead.

She thought about it a little too much. Before the door opened and admitted Miranda, dressed in an old pair of jeans and with a handkerchief covering her hair, Danielle was already at the end of the block. Her heart raced. Her mouth was dry. Sweat poured from her brow and made life in a jacket insufferable.

Yet she couldn't turn around and go back. Deep down, she was still too scared to face the things that made her Sulim.

Devon expected to learn a few things about his first life while on this trip. Now that he had fully regressed and was free from the Process, it didn't matter what anyone told him or exposed him to—there was no threat of a forced regression that could kill him and send his soul on that tiring, endless journey into oblivion.

He did not, however, expect to learn something so cataclysmic that it made him question everything he thought he knew about Sonall Gardiah.

"What do you mean I had a son?" Good thing Marlow and Evan took him into a soundproof room to tell him the news, for his voice reverberated enough to make Evan flinch. "No way. I would remember that." Not all of his memories had returned yet, but he was correct to assume that something as big as a *kid* would be one of the first things to come back to him. That could only mean he hadn't known.

"You heard us," Marlow said. "It's recently come to our attention that your direct bloodline is still intact. On Arrah, no less."

Devon sat back in his seat. "On *Arrah?*" There was a name he hadn't said so loudly in so long. There were plans for him to visit his old home planet on the last day of his trip, but it hadn't seemed so real until now. Arrah was where Sonall was born and raised, until a rival rancher his father had wronged called a lovely hit on him. All Devon knew since then was that Arrah was never one of Nerilis Dunsman's ill-fated targets. He assumed it continued to rotate its merry way around its sun for the past thousand years.

The thought his own relations could still be maintaining his old lands...

"I'm still not following this," Devon said. "I have descendants. On Arrah."

"Afraid the horse breeding business went out with your parents," Marlow glibly said, "but they've been farming your old lands for the past several hundred years. Rebuilt most of the properties, so I doubt you'd recognize any of it except for the old growth left around."

"But I had a *kid?*"

"Honestly, it's rather interesting that this has never come up before, considering your... reputation."

Indeed, Sonall had quite the reputation back then, hadn't he? *I had been with more women by nineteen in that life than I will probably have by fifty in this one.* Even then, he wasn't so sure. Yet Sonall never dealt with former partners coming forward to call him the father of his children. He either fooled around with his fellow mercenaries, who were quick to embrace the free birth control in the fortress, or he paid for the company of a woman who was likewise savvy with keeping children out of her chambers. The only male mercenaries who had children were those who begat them before coming to Cerilyn, or those who were as unlucky as Nerilis Dunsman on his wedding day.

"Who was the mother?" Devon demanded.

Evan slid his finger across his holographic tablet. Blue Basic letters were too quick—and too backward—for Sonall to read. "According to the current Gardiah records, the line traces back to you and a woman named Renarda di'Yarabon." Evan looked up from the file. "Sound familiar?"

"Not at all."

"Read him the alias," Marlow suggested.

"Right. It says one of her planets of residence was Cerilyn, where she was known as 'Vaus.'" Evan snorted. "Doesn't that mean..."

"Pleasure. In Old Basic. Yes." Devon drummed his fingers on the table, the knowledge of who he had been with in the days leading up to his first death finally coming to him. "You've got to be kidding me."

Marlow practically fell out of his chair in amusement. "Tell us where she worked, Evan!" Devon didn't need to hear it. Even if he couldn't remember, the boyish blush on Evan's cheeks said everything. "She listed her address as 69 Red Street. Really, ah, mature." He cleared his throat. "It says she was the owner of a place called..."

"Honeydew," Devon once again filled in. "I think we all know what that was." A brothel. One with the highest reputation in the small city attached to Second Tribe's fortress, where ornery mercenaries took their few coins to gamble, drink, and make merry with the ladies and lads who made their livings there. Red Street was practically Main Street. Only Blue Street was larger, and it fronted the city for the crotchety foreigners who didn't want to be reminded of who they cavorted with on their way to strike a deal with the tribe's chief. The finest inns, shops, and restaurants were on Blue Street. The place with the most locals was *Red* Street. A place Sonall had known as well as his family's lands. "I had a child with Madam Vaus," Devon repeated.

He barely remembered sleeping with her. Madam Vaus was mostly a clever businessowner by the time young Sonall came to Cerilyn, having put her own long nights of working behind her. She occasionally entered the fortress to look for young women who were willing to trade being a mercenary for coming to work for her. She was usually turned down when young ladies heard that the cleaning, cooking, and attendant positions were filled. But she could use some fresh flesh at any time! She had the best rates! She didn't beat any of her girls! If they were to choose that path, they couldn't do any better than Honeydew! Even the chief patronized it! Wasn't that a roaring recommendation?

"Ms. di'Yarabon was part of the wave of refugees from Cerilyn," Evan further explained. "One of the few who heeded the warnings to evacuate. She had her son several months later while working on... Erolys... oh, come on, now. This is reading like an article from *Husband's Room*."

"Read it often, do you?" Marlow asked.

"Please, Boss. I *am* a husband, after all."

Devon rubbed his hand against his head, elbow digging into the table. "I can't believe this. All this time... how do we even prove that they're my kin?"

"We can't do it now, because you do not share their genetics in your current life," Marlow said. "But the Federation courts settled the matter centuries ago, when your great-great-grandson won his case to take back your family's lands. They did most of the work back then. The line has continued ever since, even taking back the name Gardiah. You have to understand, by the time this happened, you and Sulim were a known entity in the public consciousness. They capitalized quite well off your name."

Devon didn't know if that pleased or offended him. *By all means,* he rationalized, *something good should definitely come out of me being drawn into this shitty mess.* Yet no man wanted to have his name used to further the gains of another. Especially if he did not personally know those people.

A fact about to be rectified.

"Mr. Fanar Gardiah is actually here in the capital," Marlow said. "He came here on behalf of his family to establish contact with you. We told him it was up to you, and whether we could work it into your schedule. As it so happens, right now is the perfect opportunity."

Devon's throat was dry. "One of them is *here? Now?*"

"Why do you think we're telling you? We found out last night. There hasn't been much time." Marlow shook his head.

Evan continued in his employer's stead. "Obviously, it's a lot to take in right now, but the Forces don't know about this yet, and..."

"And we fear that they might send the young man along his beleaguered way," Marlow finished. "We've invited him back this morning under the pretense he *might* be able to meet you. Our armed entourage will be here in ninety minutes to escort you to your lunch with the president. The more time you sit here, the more time you miss speaking with one of your descendants, Sonall."

He wasn't playing when he invoked Sonall's name. Marlow knew that would trigger a direct response from the innermost parts of Devon's brain. His soul would not go unnoticed. Nor would his heart refuse to be acknowledged. Every part that made up the remnants of Devon's first life reacted. *A son,* both sides of him agreed. *I had a son. My family's lands are still tended to by my bloodline. I could meet one of them right now. I could meet my heir. I could maybe see those views again...*

Manmade buildings and plots were destroyed and rebuilt over the years. Nearly a millennium guaranteed that the actual estate was unrecognizable from what Sonall once knew. But the mountains, the oceans, and even the forests might still be there. Arrah was a small planet that prided itself on conservation. It was difficult enough for a person to purchase land to cultivate, let alone obtain permits to drastically change the local ecology. The only reason the Gardiahs had enough land to breed and train horses was because the family's founder was the confidant of the planet's chancellor. He could've asked to become a lumberman and raze a whole continent.

"All right," Devon said. "I'm interested. Do they still speak Basic on Arrah?"

Evan grinned before getting up to make the last-minute arrangements. "Of course," Marlow said as soon as the door closed. "But it's their own dialect of Modern Basic. Not as much like the standard version you've been hearing here on Terra III and on the broadcasts. You might need Evan to –"

"After the introductions are over," Devon got up from his seat, intent on freshening up and maybe changing into something else, "I should like to be alone with him. I'll be fine."

Marlow did not deny the request. He did, however, secure Fanar's route from his seat in the building's lobby to the suite on the top floor. When the few Federation guards on duty asked who he was, Marlow quipped that Fanar worked for him and was of no great importance.

The boy nearly passed out when he was brought into the room where Devon awaited him.

"Holy High Priestess of the Void," Fanar said with a reverent breath. "It's actually you!"

Devon had intended to keep his cool when he met Fanar, yet the boy's enthusiasm and simple invocation of the High Priestess threw him off guard.

"Hi." Should he stand? Should he continue to sit like this was his house and he had every right to accept guests? Fanar didn't look completely out of his element, although his finest clothing from Arrah was a bit... dated, by Terra III standards. An old woman would have called him quaint. Young men snickered behind Fanar's back. Yet nobody ever said anything to his face, for he carried the demeanor of an Arrahite as clearly as he brandished his Federation coins every time he attempted to buy something out of a snack machine.

"Mr. Gardiah," Marlow said, his cane smacking the ground as he stood between the two men whom, he might add, looked *nothing* alike aside from darker hair, "allow me to introduce you to Devon Anderson, the reincarnation of Sonall Gardiah."

"Pleasure." Devon intervened before his kin fell over himself in excitement. An extended hand was graciously accepted, although Fanar looked at it as if he didn't know if the space-time continuum would shatter should they touch. (Why in the world would it, though? There were no paradoxes to speak of in the room.) "You must be the young man I've been hearing about today."

Fanar nearly yanked Devon's arm off his body. The boy was deceptively strong, since he hid his farming muscles beneath the cape of his coat. Devon may have been working out for nearly a year, but he was nowhere back to his prime as Sonall—and, thanks to his current genetics, he might never make it there again.

"Thank you *so much* for agreeing to see me on such short notice." Fanar tripped back into his seat. He removed his cape from his shoulders, revealing the dress tunic he wore to weekly services revering the Void. One of his buttons was askew, but nobody bothered to tell him. "I had no idea if you might have word of us over the past millennium. We had tried contacting you intermittently, but according to our records, this is the first time one of us has ever met you."

Devon managed a polite smile. The one he had practiced shortly before his trip, and the one he had been using every time someone blew a little smoke up his ass on Terra III. "I've had my mentor and his assistant fill me in." He looked to Marlow. "Thank you for accommodating this." That was the old man's cue to give them some privacy.

Begrudgingly, Marlow showed himself out, but not without the words, "You have one hour before the Forces show up for your escort," falling from his lips.

The silence between the two Gardiah men as soon as the door closed was not... expected. Fanar patiently awaited Devon to say something, anything, while he memorized every second—his family would demand a thorough recount of this event, after all. Devon, meanwhile, had no idea what he should say to the young man dithering on the other side of the table. Everything felt too self-centered, or too insulting to a long line of people who had done their best to keep his family's lands occupied.

Finally, Fanar spoke, his thick accent coming through in his excitement.

"It's okay if you've never heard of us," he said. "According to the records, our foremother might not have even known she was with child when she evacuated Cerilyn. I understand you can't have kids now. Is that true?"

Devon glanced away. "I suppose so. People in the Process can't reproduce, I guess to keep things like this from happening." There was also the threat of an unborn fetus getting caught up with its mother in the endless cycle of death and rebirth, but nobody had ever bothered to disturb Devon's mind with that detail. "But I'm not in the Process anymore. Can't say I know either way right now." He wasn't in the business of finding out. "Guess your family got really lucky, because this will be my final life."

"But you're so young, so you've got *years* left to enjoy it!"

"How old are you, exactly?"

"Nineteen. My father's in charge of the farm, and I'm his heir presumptive, I guess you could say. I've got a little brother and sister, though. Most of us stick around to some extent. Got all sorts of cousins all over the place. But they sent me because they thought I might get something more out of it. And maybe because I'm way closer to you in age than my father is. He got started on a family pretty late. He's almost thirty-five."

Devon's had to check his dropping jaw. *What in the...* he thought, not recalling a time in his first life when Arrahites were known for popping out kids in high school. Unless Fanar was joking. (He wasn't.) That was the only explanation Devon would accept right now. (Except he wasn't joking, so Devon was better off not thinking about the state of the planet's society after a thousand years since he last knew it.)

"You must be a young soul." That was Devon's pragmatic way of saying he felt a million years older than this kid, and he was only the ripe-old age of twenty-three come that following month.

"I wouldn't know much about that. Our local Priest of the Void is a hybrid, so he doesn't have any skills for seeing that sort of thing."

"I don't... well, to be quite frank, this is rather overwhelming. Excuse me." Devon sat back, the gravity of this moment pulling him down into the annals of his weary soul. *This is my descendent. This is Sonall's descendent. I didn't even know I had impregnated someone before I died. I don't know how I would've reacted had Cerilyn never collapsed.*

Devon prided himself on being better than Sonall, in every way except for perhaps physicality. He had a grander moral compass. His empathy was untarnished. The freedom to live life as he wished meant he could be the man Sonall could have been, had Second Tribe not come to his estate and destroyed everything. "How much do you know about our family's history leading up to my parents' murders and my kidnapping?"

The smile fell off Fanar's face. "Whatever's in the history books, sir. I don't know if it's a good or a bad thing that none of the original house is left, but I assure you we've done well for ourselves in the centuries since then. We've been farming *sarah* weed for a long time."

"I vaguely recall it." Every planet had its indigenous plants, of course, but *sarah* was notorious for growing anywhere. *Anywhere,* even in the Cerilynian deserts. Of course, the varieties and quality of *sarah* depended on the soil, atmosphere, and water of any given planet (let alone continent,) but the thought of Arrah becoming a huge *sarah* hub made Devon rightly wonder what had happened in the past millennium. Times truly did change, whether he was around for them or not.

"So..." Fanar said after a long, extended silence. "My family has asked me to extend an invitation to you to come see your ancestral home whenever you have the chance. I understand you're a very busy man and have your own life on that other planet, but..."

Devon wanted to give him an answer. He was due to visit Arrah sometime soon, anyway, but he had never imagined actually going back to his place of original birth and feeling the energy of everything that happened there. The thought of it was... surreal. It took every memory he heard of those times and triplicated them until he already felt like she was surrounded by the fresh, open wounds of the worst days of his first life.

As a mercenary, he always dreamed of going home. To the well-ventilated house on the edge of an evergreen wood. To the quiet lands that occasionally burst with the energy of ranch hands doing their jobs, and the housekeepers joking about what their own families did when everyone was home.

To his family—the parents who cautiously raised him to take over the family business one day, and the sister who dreamed of traveling to Terra III and seeing the expansive metropolitans of humanity's intergalactic capitol for herself. *We used to watch feeds from and shows about Earth,* Devon remembered. *Everything was medieval back then. Graella was obsessed with the European and Asian fashions, while I wondered how those people would react if they ever found out about us.* The irony almost killed him.

"I'll have to think about it," Devon finally said. "I'm grateful that there are people there taking care of the land. I'm sure my parents would have been pleased with that outcome."

Fanar picked up on his plummeting tone. The robot that now sat before the young man wasn't anything like the guy Fanar saw on the broadcasts. The Devon Anderson who was replayed on endless loops on every twenty-four-hour news network and talk shows depicted a man who was affable, easygoing, and slowly relearning what it meant to be a Federation citizen. Everyone, from the historians who dedicated their lives to transcribing Nerilis's reign of terror, to the public consciousness that dictated what was what, agreed that Sonall was the people person, and Sulim the more incommunicable, stoic one. There was a reason she wasn't on this tour, after all. Fanar would never recall that it had something to do with her career troubles, but he wasn't far off in assuming that she wanted nothing to do with a cross-universe tour.

So to see the man Fanar had always admired from afar act like this at the mere mention of his maintained ancestral homes... for the first time, Fanar understood that the Process did things to a man's soul that could never be repaired. It was one thing for Devon to no longer recognize the property he called his home a thousand years ago. Quite another for him to face that amount of time passing, while he waited on the sidelines.

Waiting...

For what? To finally have the chance to breathe?

The experiences that made up the soul before Fanar had long been decided before two *julah* flew through Cerilyn and made short work of an entire population. Sonall had been spiritually handicapped by the sheer amount of trauma he endured after mercenaries swept through his land and made short work of the people *there*. Fanar only had tangential knowledge of what happened to his ancestors. They were part of the history books, both on Arrah and in the annals of Terra III's grand library that claimed to catalog every piece of published work in the known universe. He had the privilege of distance. He could read about the atrocious details and shudder, but he would never be teenaged Sonall, forced to kneel in the breezy foyer of his family's home and witness his father's death on the other end of a firearm.

He never had to watch his eyes roll back into her head, or his bloody body fall limply to the floor, his handcrafted clothing he took such precious care of now torn and stained.

He also never had to see the fallout of that day on a young woman named Graella, who lasted three months on Cerilyn before joining their parents in the Void.

No wonder Sonall became a mindless mutant once he gave himself over to the realities of his new situation. He didn't have the favors Sulim procured the moment she stepped off the shuttle that hauled her to Cerilyn. He had to claw his way up from the bottom of the ladder and take on the mantle of the Second in Command who was more brawn than brains. So much so that it wasn't until now that he realized Cairn had probably planned to have him dispatched before he became too much of a threat to her power.

It was a miracle he lived long enough to have a son.

Fanar couldn't have known any of that. He could, however, stare into Devon's graying eyes and see the remnants of that faraway hell.

Eleven

F ew peaceful, quiet places existed in the city. Even fewer allowed motorcycle access, but that never stopped Miranda from parking her bike around a hidden corner and throwing herself into the greenery of Bridge Park.

The place was always crawling with tourists, even on a Monday. Then again, so was the boardwalk, China Town (never mind the sorry excuse they called Japan Town around there), and even M-Town. Miranda had called in one of her personal days. Someone would want a doctor's note, eventually, but she had a private doctor who was always willing to write her up a note for whatever she wanted. One of the few things her old friend Syrfila hooked her up with, because women like them needed doctors who spoke Green Dollar Bills.

Her brain was fuzzy and her mind full of the crap that made her second guess everything she said and did. Case in point: she treated herself to exactly one cigarette as she lay on the seat of her bike and stared into the sunny blue sky. Yet she couldn't enjoy the damned treat, for she kept telling herself it was rude to smoke in a public park.

Oh, and certain people didn't like kissing smoky mouths. Every time she lit up, she risked a big fat "no" the next time opportunity presented itself. She was self-aware enough to know some of her clothing stank, but not enough to know how badly and *which pieces*. (All of them stank, of course, but that was the one answer she wouldn't believe.)

She needed that cigarette, though. It gave her room to focus on the task she assigned herself before her father had the chance.

"Come *on*." She stared at the bouncy ball she picked up at a convenience store across the street. It lay in the grass, the most non-exciting entity to exist since somebody threw a potato chip bag into the bushes a few yards away. Miranda was lucky if she could kick the ball with her own foot. Never mind moving it with sheer willpower alone. "Move, you piece of shit."

None of this lined up with her father's lessons on manipulating Void energy to contour the universe to her specifications. (That was how he put it, after all. In Julah, because Miranda didn't really need to understand his truncated Academy lesson, right?) But it felt good to curse at a ball. Maybe her anger would be enough to get it rolling across the park. With any luck, it would end up at the Japanese Teahouse, where she finally had an excuse to pick something up for her cousins in San Jose, not that they deserved it.

Miranda didn't know why she bothered. She would never be powerful enough to move things with her mind, blow people back with a wave of her hand, or whatever the hell else Nerilis did on a daily basis. *I've seen things,* she thought, recalling those first few days she met the man who claimed to be her father. In a forgotten, dirty Tokyo apartment, he and Syrfila proved their worth by dazzling her with magic, weapons, and drugs. *Syrfila was most of the drugs,* Miranda thought. *And sex, but my dear ol' dad wasn't supposed to know about that.* Not that he cared. He only seemed to care when Miranda was physically harmed, and it had nothing to do with her being his daughter.

Heaven forbid I have any power, though, she lamented. Or was it really a lament? Miranda didn't want power. She knew what power was like, and no magic was included the last time she ruled over a people. *A benevolent dictator,* she thought with a snort. *That's what they thought of me.* No freedoms whatsoever, but those were the conditions she inherited. Besides, the whole point was that she was better than the tyrant that preceded her.

But she had no magic. Not then, not now, and she was the daughter of the same powerful *julah* every time. What made Nerilis think that this time was any different?

"Move," she futilely commanded the ball. "Before I find a way to rip open the cosmos and kick you into another dimension."

She was one of the privileged few who knew of her father's plan now. Nerilis found it pertinent when his resistant daughter refused to go along with his games of magical manipulation. Had she been shocked? Hardly. While the plan was utterly ridiculous, she couldn't fault her father for having it. He was the kind of man who sold himself to lofty ambitions and grand ideals. If Nerilis Dunsman were a mere human, he would have been the local, brilliant upstart who bypassed to first become mayor and went straight for presidency. If it were a true analogy, he would've been elected too.

So to hear he wanted to cross dimensions? Miranda barely knew of the concept, but it didn't surprise her. If there were anyone in the universe who could do it, Nerilis Dunsman was the man.

Still no idea what that had to do with her...

Miranda hugged the ball to her chest and stared at the blades of green grass brushing against her boots. Only when she looked up did she realize that she wasn't alone.

Of course she wasn't. It was a big park, and even on a Monday there were families, couples, and joggers making the rounds. Yet it was one of the grandest coincidences of her month when she beheld the woman standing on the nearest pathway.

And for Danielle to be there *was* a coincidence, although when the Void decides something must come to pass, there isn't much stopping it. Not even Danielle's reluctance to get out of bed, dressed, and stepping out of her apartment could go against the Void's true desires. How quickly she accepted this encounter, however, was purely up to her. Not much the Void could do about stubborn women who didn't recognize a gift basket when it slapped them right in the face.

"Oh my God." Danielle thought she recognized Miranda from farther away, but now that she was a few feet closer, she realized her hell had come to life. "It's you."

Miranda, who had loaded a completely different greeting, responded, "Yes! It's me! Minding my own business on this lovely day." She tossed her ball into the air, where it briefly grazed the underbrush of the maple tree sprawled above her before plummeting back into her hand. She may not have possessed her father's abilities in sorcery, but she had the cool, quick reflexes of a *julah* woman who put them to good practice.

"Sorry." Danielle remained on the walkway. Propriety told her to march over and give her former commander a more proper greeting, but nerves and adrenaline begged her to get away. This was a woman who had awakened that morning somewhat thankful that she did not have to report to work so early. She slept in until ten, and after a brisk breakfast, workout, and quick trip to the café to drink in the day, went on a long walk that could only be supported by the lovely spring weather. When the fog burned off around noon? It was like discovering the exit of a cloudy maze.

Now Danielle wondered if her wanderings brought her here because magnetic attraction was too literal at times.

"I... it's, uh..." A couple holding hands came up behind Danielle. They barely had the attention to spare her, but it moved her off the walkway and onto the freshly cut green grass. Miranda was within closer earshot, but Danielle was not compelled to lower her voice. "You know... kinda awkward."

"Why, whatever makes this awkward?" Miranda drew her knees to her chest, arms wrapped around them while one hand gripped her ball. "The fact that until three days ago I was the woman who could make or break your career?" She tilted her chin up, inauthentic bemusement settling into her complexion. "Or because we've had sex?"

Danielle should have suspected such a reaction. The Void knew she could often anticipate Miranda's moods, be they sarcastic or sour. (On a good day, she could be both.) This was a woman who always knew the right seductive things to say, regardless of the appropriate situation. Yet Danielle reeled where she stood, having already fought off the lovely sensations flooding forth from her memories. The day after leaving Miranda's bed may have been a strange, candy-laden haze that intoxicated her with that sweet hangover, but now? Oh, she remembered details. Enough, anyway. Like how she had been as willing a participant as the woman sitting before her. *And by willing,* she reprimanded herself, *that means she didn't do anything I wouldn't... or didn't...*

There had always been jokes around the office that Miranda had the prettiest nails in M-Town. They were also the shortest. Some of those gossiping geese at the watering holes would've loved to hear Danielle's proof of their use now.

"That one," Danielle said.

"Ah." A breeze rustled the leaves above Miranda's head. Several of them fluttered to the ground, as innocuous as the breeze itself. Yet the one landing in Miranda's hair prompted her to brush it out with a flick of her hand. It began an obnoxious descent down the front of her black riding jacket, until she had to drop the pretty-girl act and smack her hands against her chest like a baboon. *Really graceful,* she thought. *Danielle definitely thinks you're a suave bitch. Congrats.* "Well! I won't act weird about it if you don't. In fact, we could completely forget about it, if that's what you want."

Danielle shoved her hands into her jacket pockets. "If you're trying to offend me, it might be working."

"Offend you? I'm not trying to offend you any more than you were me."

"Uh-huh." Danielle finally looked away from the woman who always drew her gaze. Even now, she struggled to keep her eyes on the flags waving in the distance and not on the lips she often fantasized about kissing. Or the hair she had fisted while screaming for the Void to come save her wretched, orgasmic soul. *This is going really great,* she thought. *Super awesome.* "I don't want to forget." Ah, crap. The pathetic mess standing in the grass had said that out loud, huh. How unfortunate.

Miranda chuckled. "Uh-*huh,*" she spat back, her grin struggling to remain contained behind her lips. "Would you come over here and sit down? People are starting to stare. They probably think I'm asking you for money."

"I don't mean to interrupt you," Danielle said. "I was on my way to... well, nowhere."

That immaculately plucked brown eyebrow cocked its way up Miranda's fore-head. "You have plenty of time for that. Come sit down with me."

"I don't want to get you in trouble for being seen with..."

"Stop making up stupid excuses and sit your ass down."

That familiar snap of Miranda's commanding tongue brought Danielle over like she was responding to a direct order. *Some things are never going to change, huh?* Miranda may no longer be her CO, but shaking those old habits was like retraining her brain to speak another language.

Or to accept another soul living inside of her. One of those things were more likely to happen first.

Danielle kept a respectable distance when she crossed her legs on the ground and lifted her sunglasses from her face. Miranda softened her stance, as if that were supposed to make Danielle feel more comfortable. Perhaps they weren't meant to be comfortable around one another without promises of *escape* hanging between them. They would never be casual friends. They probably couldn't even do a casual sexual relationship without it exploding in their faces. Danielle had too many issues. Miranda had too many secrets. Who cared about attraction when half the words they wanted to utter were damning?

"You're not working today?" That was Danielle's way of breaking the ice.

"I called out this morning." Without Danielle's sunglasses obscuring her face, Miranda appreciated the slant of those eyes, let alone the hazel within. "Suppose I didn't want to walk into the office with the threat of somebody else's court-mar-tial hanging above my head." In truth, she didn't want to walk through those halls knowing that Danielle would never be back. This arrangement was arguably better for a romance to finally grow between them, but that didn't parse to the emotional side of her brain.

The one getting me into trouble with women like her, Miranda thought.

"You don't think they're done, huh?"

"Not until the top brass is satisfied. It's going to take someone even higher to intervene, if they dare."

"Who's higher than the top brass? Besides the president?" Commander in chief. Yeah, right. Danielle couldn't say she missed taking orders from any man sitting behind a desk. Especially if that man was never a soldier himself! Danielle may have never served outside of an office in domestic territory, but she came closer to shipping out than most civilians.

"You might be surprised," Miranda said. "There may be no global force on this planet like there are on others, but even our commander in chief has to answer to Federation brass now and then."

"You're kidding."

"Nope. One of the reasons the Cold War happened was because one of us wouldn't put our toys away, and the Federation kept dropping ultimatums like we kept wanting to drop bombs."

"Here I was going to guess that Russia was the one not playing along."

"That's because you drank enough of the Kool-Aid. Gorbachev was working alongside the Commander of the Federation Forces to get Reagan to see reason. All that other stuff we're supposedly taught is only partially correct. Mostly a fabrication based on somewhat real events."

"How do you know that level of detail?"

Miranda scoffed. "Anyone in enough of the know with the Federation knows about this stuff. Who convinced King George to finally let us have our independence? The Federation. Who warned Eisenhower to not drop Fat Man and Little Boy, on pain of immigration sanctions between us and Terra III? Federation. Bet you didn't know that America was intergalactically isolationist during that time. Japan, though... it was booming with cross-cultural exchange with the *huling* sub-race. Kinda funny to think about, considering the state of Earth-based immigration these days..."

Danielle pointed her nose toward an ant scurrying across the ground. "How long have you known about the Federation?"

Her defeated tone beseeched Miranda to *not* tell her, *"Since I was born."* If there was one thing Danielle needed, it was to know that Miranda wasn't in bed with Federation anything from the time she was old enough to read and write Basic.

"Since high school," Miranda offered, leaving it at that. She wasn't only with-holding information about her father the *julah*. She didn't want to bring up Syrfila Tograten, the *huling* who introduced her to a world beyond Earth—and a world of incredibly domestic intoxication. "Let's say I got a crash course and have been up its ass ever since."

"Meanwhile, I supposedly have a whole history's worth of knowledge stored in my brain," Danielle said. "But I don't feel like unlocking it, apparently."

Miranda didn't mention she likewise had such knowledge unlocked in high school. *What knowledge you could call it, anyway.* She had not received the kind of education most normal citizens of the Federation were privileged to access. Growing up on a pleasure moon barely gave young Cairn the access to her ABCs, let alone math and history. And on Cerilyn? Nobody got an education there. The more ignorant the masses, the easier they were to keep from accessing materials they had no business handling.

A sour taste rose in Miranda's throat. She had once been responsible for keep-ing the people of her tribe ignorant and docile. Although, at the time, she thought of it as keeping them from being *suicidal.* But what Chief Cairn considered a big step in quality of life when she introduced (heavily monitored) media usage, Miranda realized was nothing more than a benevolent dictator trying to win the love and respect of people who would just as well throw her into The Pit.

She could think of one person in particular who would have *loved* to toss her battered carcass into the ravine where all dead bodies went.

"You want to go for a ride?"

Danielle looked up from her spot on the ground. "What?"

Miranda's thumb jerked to the bike parked a few feet away. "I know a quiet spot a few miles out of town. Got an extra helmet, and a whole afternoon to burn."

She risked running Danielle off by saying that, but she had risked doing that a hundred times over the past few years. What did she have to lose now? So many walls had come down between them in the past few days alone. Her odds were better now than ever before.

"I don't know..."

"You ever ridden on one of these things before?"

"Clearly, you have."

"I'm nooooot talking about myself. I'm talking about *you*."

Danielle conceded defeat. "Yeah. Once or twice. Last time was a while ago, though."

"So you're a pro?"

That got a laugh out of Danielle. "You just want to take me out into the wilderness and do God knows what to me."

She took a calculated risk when she said that. Would she be taken for flirting? For accusing Miranda of nefarious motives? Or would it barely be acknowledged, because two young co-eds picked that moment to scream at one another about what a beautiful day it was?

"Not God knows what," Miranda said with a grin. "I have a pretty solid plan."

"Does this plan include enjoying the way I wrap my arms around you?"

"Goodness, Cromwell." Miranda reveled in calling Danielle by that name, as if they were back in her office, hashing out appropriate punishments for an insubordinate officer. "Are you always this flirty? Or only when you're about to put something like that between your legs?"

"You're bold to be talking about my thighs like that."

Miranda recognized her invitation to up the ante and decided to accept. "I only talk about a woman's thighs if they've ever had my face in them."

Danielle was left delightfully speechless.

The helmet barely fit her head, which Miranda accepted as a sign of her acceptance. Otherwise, Danielle would have made a great show of ripping off the helmet and declaring it too dangerous for her to tag along on a ride. She could complain all she wanted, however, if it meant she still got on the bike and settled her arms around Miranda's midsection.

"You take girls on the back of this thing often?" Danielle asked as Miranda fixed her hair in preparation for her usual helmet. "Or do I get to be special?"

A few responses lurked at the ready. Should Miranda tell her the truth and admit that more than a few of her casual dates had been wooed with double-entendres about riding with their loins pressed against the small of Miranda's back? Or should she lie, and insinuate that Danielle was so special that she was the only one invited onto this precious motorcycle?

"You're the first one I'm excited to take out for a spin." That was Miranda's way of leveraging the two possibilities. She prayed it was the winner.

Danielle cinched her grip around Miranda's stomach. The heat flooding into the pit of her gut reminded Miranda that they were two mortal women with a lot to lose if they died in a horrific crash that day.

Yet if there was anything she learned a thousand years ago, it was that life was meaningless without the occasional adrenaline rush. Even better if she enjoyed it with the right girl.

Because back then, she reminisced, as the motor kicked to life and her riding gloves grabbed the handles, *we really were just girls.*

Women never forgot the thrills of their girlhoods. Some of them may pick their first loves or their first brushes with true independence as the times to cherish, but the intensity never wavered. It didn't matter if those memories were from one lifetime ago—or a hundred. When Miranda pulled onto the road and maneuvered to the nearest highway, she immediately recalled the first time she took Danielle out for a joyride on one of the many vehicles equipped for a jaunt into the dunes.

No, it wasn't Danielle. It was the other one. The name Miranda longed to say out loud, and to have acknowledged as it had been a thousand years ago.

The crisp, generous air was a different beast from the hot sands and hotter breezes smacking them in the face on Cerilyn. The adrenaline rush they felt back then had manifested from the fear of being caught, and from acknowledging that their relationship was a first for the both of them. Sulim had been blessed by the vigors of a first-timer's foray into the exciting unknown, and Cairn acknowledged that the teenager she plucked off some rural planet had an unrecognizable power over her. As their current incarnations weaved around highway bends and welcomed the coastal air into their helmeted hair, like their past selves had screamed in delight at hopping over desert dunes and getting sand all over their faces, the circle of first love descended like a halo on a recently anointed angel.

We're no angels, Miranda thought, as she changed gears and took on a long stretch of two-lane highway. *We're two corrupted devils who have strayed from their dark paths.*

Whatever she felt in her heart had the power to fell her, whether she rode a bike or stood on the edge of a seaside cliff. Sandstorms could have claimed her. Avalanches could have come for her. Tsunamis waged war upon the turbulent seas, but none of them compared to the cyclone of lust and the thundering of first love she had felt then—and continued to court now.

But they couldn't even have *normal* lust, could they? Miranda was acquainted with it. Danielle knew her fair share of simple lust. Yet what they both acknowledged now went beyond a few coy looks, a brush of the hand, or an innocent kiss that soon turned into torrential passion. They could have spent the rest of their lives as the most celibate pair to grace Earth's sordid soil, and they would never, ever fail to note the simmering desires flowing between them. It was the kind that was both unsated by indulgence and the kind that could kill them if they went for it. What came first, though? What they experienced a thousand years ago? Or what the Process had wrought upon these two lovers' souls?

The Process doesn't help, Miranda mused, although she was not wont to lose concentration on her driving. *If it made her bisexual, it can make* us *a pair who doesn't leave the bedroom for a whole month.* God willing.

Danielle barely acknowledged any of that, however. Unlike Miranda, she had yet to regress, if she ever would. She didn't understand the source of her unbridled desires or why her sweaty hands shook when wrapped around Miranda's midsection. She lacked the privilege of comparing this moment to that first time she and a troublemaker named Cairn snuck out of the impenetrable fortress and cavorted on the desert dunes, turning only to discover their favorite oasis that offered refuge for them to confront the truth between them. Sulim had been inexperienced, but unafraid to fall for the most broken girl in the bunch. Cairn had so much experience that at the hardened age of nineteen she was incapable of ever learning the difference between real love and the same old story her breakers had burned into her brain.

It had been a miracle the one had ever shown the other how to come out of her shell. Sulim's shell of inexperience had broken long before Cairn's shell of fears and insecurities, but by the time they died, they were bound so tightly together that not even a *julah* could send one into the Process without the other.

I don't care about that. Miranda picked the easiest place to park her bike, not so far from a large, sprawling oak tree, and considered it good when Danielle's hands tightened around her stomach. *I only want to know if she'll ever remember the first time we taunted one another with forbidden desires.* The way Sulim played that game back then definitely did *not* scream inexperienced, innocent farmgirl.

But that was counting her chickens before the first hen laid a single egg. Miranda had to survive the drive to the meadows and not botch her seduction if she wanted to get anywhere on this blessed day off.

"Wow." Danielle removed her helmet and beheld their picturesque perch atop a gently sloping hill. Thick green grass blew in the breezes that tunneled between higher hills. The first wave of yellow dandelions matched the hue of her blond hair as it rustled in the breeze. "Where are we? Can't be that far from where I grew up, but I don't recognize it at all."

Miranda likewise removed her helmet and hung both off the back. She turned her whole body around, one leg gracefully swinging with the other as she faced Danielle and appreciated the support of her handlebars. With a generous back-bend that pressed one handle into her spine, she said, "Just one of many lovely hideaways in this fair country."

Danielle latched onto that lingering sense of first-time innocence when she admired the rise of Miranda's shirt and the flat stomach beneath it. Like Danielle, Miranda kept her physique in prime condition, as expected of her military superiors. Granted, Miranda had some powerful genetics on her side, but even without them, the curvature of her stomach was a sight to behold when she bent backward. "Yeah. Lovely." She looked away before Miranda popped back up and pulled her shirt and jacket back down.

"Plenty private for you?" Miranda asked.

"There doesn't seem to be anyone else around, that's for sure." Danielle counted one gopher hole on the other side of the tree, but besides the birds flitting in the air, she saw no other signs of life. "Is this the part where you have your way with me, then kill me? I mean, preferably in that order."

Miranda, who had her carefully selected words once more foiled, slumped her shoulders and puffed out her cheeks. "Do you *always* use black humor in moments like these?"

"Black is my favorite color," Danielle pointed out. With luck, Miranda wouldn't be in the mood to debate whether black was really a *color* or not. "Feels appropriate to indulge in that kind of humor whenever I want."

"Black... and pink, yes?"

Danielle finally met her verbal match when that was slung in her face. "How do you know that? What are they putting in personnel files these days?"

"A lucky guess." *It was your favorite color way back then, that's all,* Miranda thought. "Black is the color you shield yourself in. Nobody can see through it, and it absorbs everything *nice* people try to give you. Black makes very convenient armor, that's all. So it's only natural that your *real* favorite color would be something so stereotypically girly."

"Meanwhile, your favorite color is brown. *Brown!* Who the hell loves brown?"

"Hey." Miranda held up her hand. "I like Earth tones. I appreciate all shades of brown. And green. And, yes, even blacks and grays. Did you know that there are shades of gray?"

"Don't give me crap about shielding myself in black if you're over here throwing dirt on yourself and calling it an aesthetic."

"You've seen my house," Miranda countered. "You know I use the colors brown and beige very well."

Danielle didn't take that bait. There were a hundred things they could talk about, and she decided to stick with whatever didn't bring them back to sex and romance. Miranda had mentioned being willing to "forget it ever happened" earlier. While Danielle was not in the business of forgetting over the long term, she didn't mind using it as an excuse to treat this as an opportunity to learn more about the woman always in her peripheral.

Even if Miranda's words were coated in the kind of smooth honey that went down the throat in a matter of a few agonizingly sweet seconds. Even if her tangling hair framed her face to look like she belonged on the cover of a high-fashion magazine. Even if she could wear a riding jacket and a pair of old jeans and make them look as crisp and authoritative as her military uniform. She had the gaze of an old soul, and while Danielle could acknowledge that Miranda *might* be reincarnated, it always surprised her to see the span of one millennium in those bold, brown eyes. Muscles may have been concealed, but Danielle never forgot how firm they felt in her hands or how strong this woman was.

She could fling me over her shoulder right now and carry me off to do unspeakable *things,* Danielle wistfully thought. Miranda spoke of some embarrassing moment in high school while Danielle's eyes glazed over, and she thought of all the times Miranda demonstrated physical prowess, whether it was a hundred pushups in three minutes or besting every challenger in wrestling. *I'm pretty sure she's beat me up more than once.* Danielle hated to admit it, but she was absolutely correct when she guessed how many times Miranda had knocked her on her ass.

The most damning thing was realizing how many times that happened because they fought for the same Relic...

...or that little blue ring Miranda occasionally wore on her left hand, as if she were betrothed to a fate bigger than them both.

"What is it?"

Miranda had stopped talking about whatever distraction she entertained at the moment. Danielle had spaced out for too long. Gone was her chance to look like she listened along, or dared to comprehend anything Miranda said about her Earth-based childhood.

There was no denying it. Danielle had been a million miles away, entertaining thoughts that might open inoperable rifts between them.

"How much do you really know about me?" Danielle couldn't lift her head when asked that, although her eyes strained to search Miranda's face for a reaction.

"You mean..."

"I know you know about the... yeah." Danielle rarely felt so embarrassed, yet there she was, mortified that Miranda might know about Devon, about Cerilyn, about the Process of all ungodly things. *And she knows I'm a trainwreck that can't remember who she is.* "But how much do you know about it? And why?"

Miranda inhaled a deep breath. Gone was the flirtatious serenity that had descended upon them when they reached the top of this hill. "You know I can't tell you how I know."

"Because it might force me to regress and kill me?"

"Yes." Miranda's hands dug into the leather seat beneath her. She cocked one boot into the grass and drew the other up onto the seat. When she pulled her hair out of her face, she said, "Believe it or not, I don't want that to happen to you. Although I can understand why you might think I want you to..." Her voice trailed off. Dare she say *"You think I want you to die a terrible death, never to return to the Void like we're all supposed to one day?"*

"I don't think you do. I'm only trying to understand."

Miranda took one of those pale hands that turned whiter the more Danielle dug her fingers into the bike. "I know that you're in a terrible situation, where if you want to survive, you have to remember that your name was once Sulim."

Danielle couldn't contain the gasp gnawing a chasm of anxiety into the depths of her heart.

"What?" Miranda released her hold on Danielle's hand.

"Nobody's ever said that name like that before." This was a woman who couldn't remember a time when she *was* Sulim. She had only been told. She only knew as much as the general public, and they might as well have forgotten how to say their own names, let alone hers. Both Marlow and Devon said *Sulim* with an accent that she hadn't realized was so heavy until now. *SOO-lim.* What was it? A way people from certain Basic backgrounds said those sounds?

Yet Miranda's smooth and lyrical pronunciation suggested she had said it not only a hundred million times before, but had done so with loving reverence. *Su-leem.* That wasn't the correct pronunciation either, but it didn't bother Danielle like SOO-lim might have. Was it because Miranda's way brought with it the affections of a pet name?

"I'm sorry." Miranda withdrew, leg lowering back to the ground. "I've said too much already. I shouldn't have said that name at all."

"Why do you know it?" Danielle wiped something from her eye. She hated how she was always compelled to cry whenever discussing her past as a woman she had long forgotten. Did her soul cry out for recognition? For retribution? Was there any chance in the void that she might remember? That her soul might finally get what it so desperately sought? "I don't care if you can't tell me. Please. Tell me. I hate this feeling killing me inside. You don't even understand it, do you?"

"You'll remember. I promise. You'll regress."

"I'm not talking about me." Danielle finally lifted her head, gaze meeting Miranda's only two feet away. "I want to know who you are."

That was a stab to Miranda's hardened heart. The knife of truth might not have penetrated her stony shell, but the attempt was there. It scratched her, poisoned her, taunted her with what might could have been.

"Why do you know that name so well?" Danielle repeated. "Nobody's ever said it like that before."

"Yes, they have. Many people have said your name like that."

It was a lie, but one Miranda had to tell before she lost Danielle from this pivotal moment. *I was the only one who said your name like that,* she thought. *I'm sorry. I wasn't thinking when I said it just now.* That's what she should have said, but her tongue remained tied. How could she lie about *that?* That kind of pronunciation was born from late nights tangled in bed, when teasing turned into affection. *She got me back as hard.* One day, Danielle might remember the way she said Cairn's old name when she thought nobody else was around.

"I always feel like I'm falling into a pit of distant familiarity," Danielle said. "Do you know what I mean?"

Miranda desperately wanted to say yes. She knew exactly what that felt like. To have pure knowledge within her reach, but a little too far to grasp by herself.

But if she admitted it, Danielle might know too much. Miranda didn't know if it was safe to say that she, too, was trapped in the Process with no hope of escaping. Not alone, anyway.

She took Danielle's hand again. This time, she touched the left ring finger that held significance in more than one culture.

"You once belonged to somebody," Miranda said. "And somebody once belonged to you."

Danielle looked away, but did not reclaim her hand.

"You lived in hell." Miranda cupped her other hand over Danielle's. "But you didn't suffer alone. There are some things worth remembering. Whatever you're afraid of knowing again... the good things must be worth it, right?"

Danielle sucked in her breath. "I don't know," she said. "That's the problem. I don't know what's worth remembering, and what is..."

Her words were soon stifled by the kiss coming for her, whether she knew she wanted it or not.

Deep down, she knew she did, although the anxious part of her holding back tears begged Miranda to rethink what she was doing. But what was Miranda supposed to do? Watch Danielle spiral into madness, because she no longer knew who she was or why she was here? When she could give her *some* comfort, *some* form of memory that might circle them back to who they used to be? Miranda took a chance because she had to, before Danielle descended into those fabled pits of despair.

You didn't suffer alone. Miranda infused everything she remembered from those times into one kiss. The good, the chaotic, and the serendipitous. Her hand braced against a red-hot cheek. Her lips beseeched a small moan of utter acquiescence.

Miranda brought Danielle out here so they could breathe the fresh air and maybe remember what it was like to have not a care in the world. Instead, she realized the true meaning behind Danielle's presence was repentance. These were women who had wronged each other as well as an entire planet of people. Maybe they weren't innocent people. But they didn't deserve to be obliterated.

We can't take that back, Miranda thought, as she dipped back Danielle's head for a final, heady kiss that lasted an age. *We can't even learn from our mistakes.*

Slowly, Danielle released her grip on the leather motorcycle seats and wrapped her arms around Miranda's neck. When their lips parted, Danielle pulled away and sighed.

They said nothing for a long while. The only words worth speaking were variants of *I'm sorry* and *I know.* Two phrases that hardly held any meaning.

Twelve

While Danielle suffered with spiritual division, Devon was expected to act like he had always been two people fused into one.

"But what does it *really* feel like?" his interviewer asked in slow, methodical Basic. He thought it made it easier for Devon to understand him. But he might as well have been speaking Julah, since the slower he spoke, the more Devon second guessed his grasp of a language that had evolved since the last time he used it. Evan was on hand to translate into English, and Marlow sat in the corner, ready to intervene should the interviewer go too far. Yet Devon would have rather they got lost. It was too much pressure, and there weren't any cameras involved – yet.

"What do you mean?" Devon asked.

The interviewer, a man who represented the biggest print magazine in the Federation, struggled to understand Devon's accent. Where could he place it, so he could mention it in his article? *"Mr. Anderson, formerly Lord Gardiah, speaks with a renewed grasp of Basic that has come to him after regressing. Yet he speaks as if it's a thousand years ago. His mix-use of the sophisticated Arrah dialect and the more brutal enunciation of long-lost Cerilyn captivate his audience."* Yes, that should do it.

"What does it feel like to go through what you've experienced? Few people can hardly comprehend what the Process is like for one life, let alone a hundred."

Devon waited for Evan to go ahead and translate. He was instantly hung up on the insinuation that a hundred lives vs. one meant anything. "You make it sound like I can remember anything in between. That's the one nice thing about it, I guess. I don't have to remember a 'hundred' lives. There's only what I've experienced in this life, and who I was a long time ago. If I had died and was reborn again, I wouldn't remember anything about Devon Anderson." For better or worse.

"So what does *that* feel like? Knowing that this life might be deemed inconsequential by your soul?"

Devon snorted. "Exactly how it felt when my name was Sonall Gardiah. You don't think about it. Once you regress, you don't differentiate between the two. All of the memories that have slowly been coming back to me are like they never left. Feels like a really long time ago, that's all. You know that phrase 'in another life?'" He waited for Evan to translate the gist of that meaning. "That's what it's like. Only literally. The only weird thing, I guess, is that even though I'm barely in my twenties now, I still have a ton of hindsight. Not only for who I was as a kid, really, but who I was as an adult back then too. I was only a little older than I am now when I died."

"Fascinating." The interviewer spent the next few minutes going over his notes and hemming and hawing over what he wanted to say.

Devon couldn't wait for this to be over.

Terra III still offered a plethora of things for him to discover. Not only had his time there as Sonall been limited, but everything had changed so much since he last remembered this place. The food was an adventure. The sights—and associated histories—blew his mind in ways that nothing on Earth ever had. The rare excursions to simply be a tourist had been few and far between. May had more opportunities to go out and do as she pleased, but also complained about the security restrictions she also suffered. The only good thing to come out of it were late-night music writing sessions. The songs they had been working on would need a harder look over by the rest of the band, but they had a good feeling that they would be well received. The sensation of being an alien in a strange land was a universal one, after all.

Sheesh, he'd much rather talk about music.

"You know what the biggest difference is between then and now?" Devon said, unprompted by the startled interviewer. "I have a lot more freedom in this life.

Even before I found out the truth about who I really am, I was living with such a freedom that only a man like Sonall could have coveted. I don't know what you know about being a Cerilynian mercenary..."

The interviewer opened his mouth. Evan almost laughed out loud to see how quickly Devon cut him off.

"But we were like slaves. You're kidnapped, you're forcibly enlisted, and the next thing you know, you're taking orders from people who don't care if you live or die. They can't care. They don't have the freedom to care. Everything you do as a mercenary is about your personal survival. You don't only have to survive your missions, some of which earn your tribe a hefty bonus because they're basically suicide missions." He had survived his earliest ones. Barely. By the skin of his talented teeth. *Nothing taught me detachment like those missions.* "You're traumatized on a daily basis until you don't know where you came from anymore. You don't have hobbies outside of gambling and drinking. Nobody's allowed media. There are no connections to the outside world until you raise high enough in the ranks that your loyalty is unquestioned. Forget reading books or watching TV. You drink the tribe's dogma until they're convinced you're capable of killing on their coffers' behalf."

The interviewer's mouth dropped open. "I only know what's in the history books," he meekly said.

"Now, I've got so much more freedom. Even if I were working a dead-end job as Devon Anderson, I could read books. Watch TV. Go where I wanted and eat what I pleased. I could have never learned about computers and music on Cerilyn. By the time I had those freedoms, my brain was rotten."

"Music, you say?"

Got him. "I spent most of my childhood in this life learning music as a hobby. Now I have a band. I'm actually here with one of my bandmates right now. She's the daughter of two Federation immigrants, but only one other person in our band knows about this place. Earthlings, you know." Always kept in the dark.

"That sounds difficult to manage. How do you handle living on Earth, where most people don't know who you are?"

"Handle it? I love it. I get to be a normal person there. That's what that whole spiel was about. Normalcy and freedom." Sounded like the title of Karma's next EP.

"Surely, there is something you miss about your time on Cerilyn."

I miss the people we lost. It hadn't been all bad, no. He had friends. People he trusted. Women he had loved and men who respected him enough to let a little cheating in dice slide. But he wasn't about to open that bottle of desert sand in front of this man. "No. I don't miss anything I can't have in this life. People there weren't happy. They were brainwashed and tortured. Maybe Nerilis Dunsman did us all a favor when he..."

"That's enough," Marlow softly interrupted. To the interviewer he explained, "That topic is off limits. For the both of you."

Devon supposed he didn't have all the freedoms, after all. He had no freedom to share his true feelings.

He would've regretted it, anyway. Passions flared while he thought of Fanar and the memories that surfaced. *My mother. My father. My sister.*

Devon could still see that woman. Young and traumatized Sonall had clung to his sister as they screamed for mercy, but that woman with the soulless brown eyes merely told them to "shut the fuck up." Her blade was covered in their mother's blood. Devon would never forget how unaffected she was by her cold-blooded murders. Just some nineteen-year-old child mercenary from Cerilyn who no longer cared about anything, as long as the contract was fulfilled and she didn't get the shit kicked out of her by the chief and her goons.

"You know what I miss?" Devon offered after any awkward silence. The interviewer leaned forward. So did Marlow, who waited for him to say something off-color again. "The quiet of my own quarters when I first got them. When you were dragged kicking and screaming to Cerilyn, you shared a dorm with up to five other kids. If the higher-ups liked you, a promotion might mean you only had one roommate. Then when you had been around a while and a few more people above you died or were retired, you'd get your own tiny room. You still had to share everything else with the jackasses, though."

The interviewer was not impressed.

"Somewhere around a few months after I arrived, I decided I didn't care anymore. They beat me down, like they beat all those who survive down. You start doing what you're told, pick up a few skills, and next thing you know... well, you're at some villa on some planet sticking a bullet in some poor sod's head. It's true what they say about it getting easier after your first kill. Once you accept that's who you are now, the numbing really takes effect." He didn't wait for anyone to interrupt him. "I got so good I was rapidly promoted. I followed orders, got really strong, and became proficient in every kind of weapon we used. Learned how to fly spacecrafts, let alone repair them." Devon sighed. "So before I knew it, I was Second in Command, and I had my own quarters. Do you know what that's like?"

The interviewer shook his head.

"I had a big bed and my own bathroom. I was living on the top floor with windows and shit. If you don't live on the top floor, you don't get windows in your room. You were up and down with the sun, anyway." Days were about twenty-eight hours long on Cerilyn, and with year-round hot weather, nobody missed the sun that much. "I got access to the outside world. Monitored and highly regulated access, but I could watch whatever I wanted on TV, let alone connect on what passed for 'online' on Cerilyn. It meant they trusted me enough to not go AWOL. It meant they had broken me down so much that I was no longer a flight risk. I sat there at night watching stupid shows. Ironically, I was really bad with computers back then. I couldn't have arranged an online coup if I wanted. But I really loved having my own place like that. With sunlight. I could hardly believe it."

Even harder to believe that he directly served the woman who had killed his mother. *That's how hard they beat me down,* he thought. Only the separation of a thousand years allowed him to see it for what it was. It took a hundred reincarnations to face the real hell he had been through as one of Cerilyn's topmost mercenaries.

"Well..." The man cleared his throat, rubbed his jaw, and finished punching something into his holographic notebook. "Thank you very much for the heartfelt answers, Mr. Anderson. I admit, it wasn't what I anticipated when I came to interview you today, but I think the readers will appreciate your honest views more than the softball questions I originally threw at you."

"Of course," Marlow interrupted, "you and your editor will run the whole article by myself and Commander d'Alacron before it goes into publication, yes?"

Nothing made the interviewer tug on his collar more than a veiled threat from a powerful *julah* who could turn him into a mouse with only mild effort. "Of course. I will also forward a copy to Mr. Anderson's digital address. It will be written in Basic, though. Is that all right?"

"I was under the assumption we were mostly speaking Basic this whole time. It may shock you, sir, but I am also literate in my original native language." Devon had meant that to come out with a bit more bite than it did. Instead, the interviewer was treated to more blush in his cheeks as he asserted it did *not*, in fact, surprise him that Devon knew how to read. Honestly, he would better understand written Modern Basic than he could from listening.

Handshakes dominated the room before the interviewer bowed his head in thanks and was escorted from the building. Devon let out an exasperated sigh. Evan patted him on the shoulder and asked his employer if they should start making plans for dinner.

"You did the best you could with those inane questions." Marlow pulled on his coat and readjusted his hat. Evan waited on his communicator for the host of Terra III's "best" Earth-Chinese cuisine restaurant to pick up and take their impending reservation. After a day like Devon's, everyone silently agreed to treat him to something that would remind him of Earth. So happened that Evan and Marlow agreed that Chinese was the single-best cuisine to come from the isolated planet trillions of light years away. "Keep in mind that your average citizen these days only knows of Cerilyn through 'ancient' tales and the stories we *julah* tell. And most of us *julah* never set foot on Cerilyn, let alone made dealings with mercenaries, so stories get conflated. People don't understand what a hard life it was or the terrors of those wars back then. Aside from Nerilis's reign of meddlesome malarkey, the universe has been a peaceful place. As a whole, anyway. Civil wars always happen."

Devon chewed on the inside of his cheek as he followed the other two men out of the room. Was what Marlow said supposed to make him feel better? Of course 99.99% of humans alive today didn't personally know anything of Cerilyn, a planet that had been destroyed a thousand years before. The culture died with it. Even if another planet of mercenary tribes popped up somewhere else, it wouldn't have the same feeling. The environment would naturally change. Everyday rituals, from how people bathed, had sex, and dumped their dead would change. Cerilyn was dead. Gone. Anyone who didn't evacuate when Second Tribe's chief sounded the alarm was winked from existence. Those who lived on could have shared their stories for a few more decades, at most. Eventually, it went the mythical way of Atlantis.

If only Devon knew the level of romanticizing that occurred throughout the Federation. All levels of media, from rock ballad albums to blockbuster films, had their hands in the Legend of Cerilyn, a planet full of barbaric heathens who were barely above the level of dogs. Only those who could string a sentence together bothered to lead, and those leaders were often depicted as ruthless dictators unafraid to lop off the heads of their own tribesmen. Filming always took place on the Federation planet Dokto II, known for its lush jungles. Desert scenes were sometimes filmed in the Sahara on Earth, if permits allowed. The locals were often hired to play extras, which meant the human tribesmen were either Moroccan, Egyptian... or if on Dokto II, an ethnic group of humanity known for their short stature and lean, muscular figures. The people of Dokto II lived off the ground and in the thick brush of the foliage, and coaxing them to come down onto the sets of what people *believed* Cerilyn to look like took a good amount of money. (The number of sets that had been sucked into the sinkholes often appearing was unprecedented for Federation cinema.) A far cry from the melting pot of peoples absconded from around the Federation. Even in the end, Second Tribe's upper ranks were represented by the fair-skinned nobles of Arrah and the dark-skinned scholars of Orfinice. The few times Cairn di'Cerilyn was portrayed on screen, she was always played by whatever hot Federation actress had the "milkiest" skin, as the press loved to label them. But they had dark hair, so casting agents thought it perfectly representable of the woman who, in actuality, had skin closer to an Orfinician than an Arrahite.

Had Devon known that, he'd likely hole himself up on Earth, never to venture out again... lest he decided to single-handedly edit every single bit of media about Cerilyn until his head exploded.

"We'll get you some seriously good food and head back to the suite before you know it." Evan said that while they rendezvoused with May in another room. She looked up from her phone, noted the obstinate expression on Devon's face, and decided to say nothing. "Then you can..."

"What a riveting interview." Evan leaped half a foot into the air when Yara d'Alacron's voice sounded behind him. While Marlow was not surprised, he expressed his mild disdain for the commander's presence by pulling the brim of his hat down his face and folding his arms across his chest. Yara bypassed both Evan and Marlow, heading straight for Devon, who did nothing more to shield himself than square his shoulders and offer her his best *You don't scare me* face. The man had spent an hour relieving the shittiest days of his first life. Yara was scarcely a threat. "I really like your honesty about being a ruthless killer for hire. I know a few men like that even today. They're very... cagey about it."

Devon settled into a wide-stance while the men behind him continued to pretend Yara was not there. Her presence didn't intimidate them, per se—well, aside from Evan, who was always intimidated by a strong-willed woman—but she wasn't the kind of woman someone looked in the eye unless they wanted a conversation. Whatever that entailed.

And she only had the one eye to look into, a fact nobody around there was likely to forget.

"I was far from the most ruthless," Devon said. "I heavily self-medicated."

"If it's all right with you gentlemen," Yara continued, her hands behind her back, "I should very much like to treat Mr. Anderson to dinner at the capital. We have a few things we must discuss." She caught the heavy breath about to inflate Devon's lungs. "You're in no trouble, I assure you. But I'm afraid it's a matter of intergalactic security, and I cannot afford for you to be... influenced? We shall say *influenced.*"

Marlow looked up. Evan turned away. May minded her own business in the corner, although she certainly saw the tigress lurking beneath beauty, brain, and brawn. Everything the room knew about the commander's ascension to her post painted her as more ruthless than any of the killers on Cerilyn. It may have been a woman's political climate on Terra III, but that didn't mean the post of Commander of the Federation Forces went to someone afraid to "get the job done."

No, nobody assumed that Devon was doomed should he go off alone with Yara. But whatever she wished to speak with him about was probably not good.

"Let me put it another way," Yara said with a whimsical sigh. "It's not as much a request as it is a strongly encouraged demand."

"Well then." Marlow pulled his communicator out of his pocket. "Suppose we'll hold off on the Chinese for another day. Evan, Ms. d'Eran and I shall make other plans while you dine with the commander. Far be it from us to insist you ignore her."

Devon couldn't help but notice his lack of agency in this situation. Not that he assumed he had much to begin with. Not since he regressed and realized the weight dragging down his conscience had nothing to do with forgetting to vote in the last local election and everything to do with letting trillions of people die. Sometimes it was better to simply follow orders and absolve himself of that agency destroying everyone else's life.

"Sounds lovely." He refused to look away from that one gray eye peering at him through a vacuous veneer. He had yet to discover what happened to the other eye, always carefully covered by a large swathe of golden hair. Devon assumed it was either a patch or a giant scar. He was right about one of those.

He would also get a good look later. A look he was only now beginning to anticipate, whereas May had been trying to warn him ever since they left Earth.

May accepted an invitation to dinner with Marlow and Evan, if only to get rid of the bitter taste in her mouth. She never once spared the commander a trusting countenance.

Thirteen

The air in the city was thicker than the breezes in the countryside. That was the first and only thing Danielle cared to think about as Miranda's motorcycle whipped through downtown after spending a lovely afternoon on the empty country highways and county roads.

Thicker with fumes. Thicker with heat. Thicker with the foggy memories of a time long past.

She never told Miranda where she lived, not that she had to. Miranda knew damn well where the woman holding on for dear life rested her head. If the address weren't always in her face at work, it was in the overheard conversations with coworkers and civilians alike. *"You know that Soviet-looking building across from the good bagel shop? I said the good bagel shop! Yeah, that's where I live. You coming over to watch the game or what?"*

Miranda followed the faded signs leading to guest parking. Five whole spots made up the parking lot closest to the street, but they were empty at that time of day. Most of the parking garage was a desolate land of asphalt and flickering lights. There were no guards. Miranda could have parked closer to the elevator, and nobody would have cared.

She removed her helmet and ensured her keys were properly pocketed. Danielle eased off the back of the bike, her sore thighs taking a few seconds to acclimate to standing again.

"Thanks for the ride." Danielle wiped her hand on the back of her jeans before placing the helmet she borrowed on the seat. Miranda remained in the driver's position, elbow leaning against one of the handlebars as she pretended to be unaffected by her unflattering helmet hair. "I mean... thanks for... yeah."

Miranda hid her grin behind her fingers. It was either that or boldly ask Danielle if she liked to act so adorably awkward on purpose. *I wouldn't put it past her,* Miranda thought, although she knew better than to assume it. When Danielle acted this way around her, it was because she desperately wanted to talk about what was between them. Yet what was the fun in acting like a mature adult when she could race back into her apartment and latch the door behind her?

Maybe Miranda would be surprised, though.

"It was my pleasure." The flirtatious side of Miranda—which made up over two thirds of herself, if she were honest—*really* wanted to bring up what happened right before they decided to ride back to the city. When Danielle wasn't hunched over the bike, burying her face in the depths of Miranda's chest, they were acting like nobody in the world could see them sitting together so boldly out in the open.

But Danielle's response to that had been to slump down into the weed-riddled grass and stare into the flowering abyss before her. Miranda had stayed close, but said and did nothing. It was always better to let Danielle come to her when she was ready. No matter how infuriating it was to be so close to what they used to have.

"By the way," Danielle said, fists clenched at her sides. A car maneuvered through the parking garage, its lights flicking on as soon as it was out of the safety net of the sunshine. A man in a business suit parked near the elevator and paid them no mind as he hopped out with his briefcase and waited for his lift. "I've decided to take some time off while I figure out what to do next. I'm gonna... well, I'm gonna unabashedly ask for money from some people who really owe it to me. To get by, you know."

Miranda sat up in her seat. "Nothing wrong with that." Dare she refer to living off *julah* money for all of her adult life? Far be it from her to tell Danielle she couldn't do the same thing. "Just take care of yourself, okay?" She secured the spare helmet and prepared to put her own back on. If she hurried home, there might be time to do some gardening with the rest of her personal day. "I'll see you around, apparently."

Danielle's face fell when she realized Miranda was about to take off for home. *Are you kidding me?* she thought, simultaneously wondering if she had been too wishy-washy with what she desired most. For every alarm going off in her head, screaming that she should mind herself, there was another one begging her to give in to whatever temptations she still harbored in her heart.

And other body parts.

Seriously, she scolded herself, *you're the woman who can ask out little flops like Alicia, but you're suddenly a ball of nerves around a woman who's a little more butch than you?* Great. Now she had to debate whether Miranda was more "butch" than her. Because that was a fair comparison to make while she mentally begged the woman on a motorcycle to stay behind a while longer.

"Do you want to come up?" Danielle blurted.

Miranda almost dropped her helmet. "Huh?"

"For, uh... coffee. You've been driving a lot today. You might need some coffee to get you home?" How lame did she sound, anyway? While never the suavest woman in town, Danielle had *some* reputation to protect. There went that reputation now. Right down the proverbial toilet.

The only thing keeping Miranda from leaping off her motorcycle and thanking her lucky stars was the confusion still swarming her addled mind. "Depends," she coolly said. "Are we talking instant coffee or...?"

"Oh, well. I've only got instant coffee."

It was almost sweet how despondent Danielle sounded when she admitted that. Miranda graced her with an appreciative smile. "So happens I'm in the mood for instant coffee right now. Sometimes it's good to go back to the modern-day basics."

"Well!" Danielle made an about-face and slowly marched toward the elevator. "What are you waiting for? I've got a whole Tupperware container full of instant coffee!"

Miranda could barely believe it as she swung her legs off her bike and followed Danielle to the elevator. The man in the business suit had already made his short use of it. A few seconds after Danielle pressed the button, the doors dinged open and she stepped inside.

"Remember when we got trapped in an elevator?" Miranda asked, keeping a respectful distance from Danielle as the doors closed again. "Because I certainly do."

"Oh my God." Too late. Danielle couldn't escape now. "Don't do that to me. I still get claustrophobia thinking about it."

"Everyone thought we were fooling around," Miranda continued, knowing damn well the effect it would have on Danielle. "When you hadn't even bothered to kiss me yet."

Danielle was about to fall through the floor, regardless of how quickly it surged upward. "Kiss *you*. I spent five years thinking you were always on the verge of kissing *me*."

"Really? Because that would have been grossly inappropriate and an abuse of my power over you. You should have paid better attention to your officers' training. Because when you're a captain, they spend *weeks* telling you to not fraternize with anyone. *Anyone.* We used to joke that meant you couldn't even give yourself the ol' rub and tug without getting slapped."

"I can't believe we're having this conversation. All I did was ask you up for instant coffee."

"Mmhmm. Is that all you asked me up for?"

"Yes," Danielle was a little too quick to say. She really regretted living so high up now. Made these elevator rides unbearably long when a woman she liked ruthlessly flirted with her. Especially when she could remember what happened the last time they were in a room together... "No." She cleared her throat. "Maybe. Depends on what that coffee does to you, I guess."

"What kind of coffee is this, exactly? Because if it has *that* effect on a woman, I may want to get some for myself."

"Good God, this is getting worse."

"Should we start the kissing now? Or are we too close to the..." The elevator stopped on Danielle's floor. As soon as the doors opened, she bolted out, apartment key in her hand. "Guess that answers that question." Miranda shoved her had in the doorway before the elevator closed. She wanted to take her time following Danielle to her apartment.

Although Danielle had been through Miranda's house a number of times by now, this was Miranda's first foray into her lover's abode. She knew it was probably small—and it wasn't like Miranda's house was a mansion by any means—but she wasn't prepared for the giant floor-to-ceiling windows overlooking the busy street below. Nor was she prepared for Danielle's overwhelming aesthetic of black furniture and white accents. Even the couch was black, which made Miranda want to throw it into every face that ever told her she took her love for Earth tones too far in her own home. *Did this apartment come with the black appliances, and she went with it?* Miranda thought, respectfully removing her boots at the door before stepping onto the off-white carpet. *Or am I looking into the depths of her soul?* That wasn't a joke. Miranda seriously wondered if the Process had this kind of dark effect on Danielle's existence.

"That is quite the view." Miranda helped herself to the windows while Danielle hustled to make instant coffee, because that was *really* the most important thing. "Everybody gives me grief about owning my house in my neighborhood on *my* salary, but I'm starting to wonder if..."

"I got grandfathered into my old rent when I moved in a few years ago. Trust me. It's a long story." Danielle didn't add that she had to be gentle with her money to make it stretch as far as it did. Which was why one of the first things she panicked about when she was informed of her court-martial was how she would pay her rent two months from then. Especially when her water bill had gone up and the electric company thought it cute to raise their rates as well. Cable and internet? It was a monopoly in that neighborhood. She could cancel, but then what would she watch late at night when she would rather stare at TV Land reruns instead of facing her nightmares?

Miranda ran her hand along the back of the couch before stepping into the kitchen. White carpet gave way to black tiles. The countertops were far from the marble in her own home, but the quartz got the job done, didn't it? Although, Danielle really should look into a different product for cleaning out that sink. It could easily smell... better.

But Miranda wasn't up here to impart her opinion about Danielle's apartment. She had come up to admire the view. Particularly, the view of Danielle's ass in those tight jeans.

"Are you checking me out?" Danielle turned away from the coffee maker, disbelief somehow on her face. Didn't she know that this was their plan all along?

Miranda leaned against the refrigerator the moment it began to hum. Oh, what to do? Play ignorant? Pretend that the promises of instant coffee were *so* alluring that she couldn't help but stare at the woman making it, as if that would create caffeine faster?

Or should she be bold?

"Absolutely," she said, Cheshire grin pulling her lips apart.

"Unbelievable." Danielle snatched two coffee mugs out of a cupboard. "You play coy for half the afternoon and now want to eat me alive."

"Is there a problem with that?"

The cupboard door slammed shut with a *bang*. "Yeah," Danielle announced. "It's distracting me from making your coffee."

Miranda *did* love that petulant look on Danielle's face. She had the cheekbones and eye shape to pull off murderously delirious while retaining that tone that played right into Miranda's style of humor. "What if I told you I really don't want coffee right now?" Miranda covered one of the mugs with her hand.

"Yeah?" Although the coffee maker ran, Danielle blocked it with her body, bringing herself closer to Miranda's seductive stance. "So what do you want?"

The haughty way she said it almost made Miranda fall over in laughter. *Some things change in people,* she thought, remembering what Sulim used to be like when she was in a certain mood. *Some things never change. And some things morph in unexpected ways.* Sulim would have never bumbled her way through this like

Danielle did. Sulim was forward, even when inexperienced. Perhaps the Process really *did* do a number on poor souls like Danielle's.

Fine. Miranda could work with that. She had changed in some ways too, hadn't she? She had way more finesse than she used to employ during her days of reckless sexual exploration.

"I want to see your bedroom. That's the real reason I came up here."

Danielle cleared her throat for a whole five seconds before coming up with an even *in*appropriate response. "The view of the city isn't as good in there."

"Who cares, when I'd assume we close the curtains?"

"You're really too much, you know that?"

"Only because you don't have the balls to kiss me first."

Miranda had muttered that, but Danielle perfectly understood her. It was what prompted her to turn around and head toward her bedroom, jacket coming off her torso and coffee unceremoniously forgotten in the kitchen. "Come in here and say that again!" Danielle called.

"Not until you admit how much you like me!" Miranda could play this game. In fact, she rather enjoyed it. "And tell me how much you want me in your bed!"

She had to admit, she much preferred this kind of behavior compared to what happened in her house two days ago. The pressure of the Process and the results of regression no longer hung over their heads now that the initial indulgence was out of the way. Maybe this time would be different. All the fun... without the dissociating. On both of their behalf.

Miranda knew how to take off a jacket. Maybe she'd follow Danielle's suit as she sauntered to the open bedroom doorway.

"Get in here and kiss me!" Danielle demanded.

Miranda closed the door behind her, enjoying the exact view she had come to see: Danielle, dressed down to her T-shirt and underwear, laying across her bed as if this had been the plan all along.

Like it wasn't. They both thought that the moment they both gave in to what they had wanted all day. It only had to start with a kiss unbridled by the terrific weight of the Process.

The more they indulged in each other's bodies, the lighter that weight felt.

Fourteen

Devon had exhausted his small collection of formalwear when he was asked to dine with Commander d'Alacron. She assured him that there was no need for the smallest bit of pomp. They would dine in a private room within the capitol building. The same one the President of the Federation occasionally used to entertain dignitaries and conduct the sort of meetings that decided the fate of the universe.

Yara was quite familiar with it.

"You really must try some of the topal soup if you haven't enjoyed it yet." Yara acted as if this weren't a light interrogation as they sat to eat. Her private guard ensured that the only person to come and go from the kitchen was the same maid who had been working in that wing of the building for the past fifty years. Otherwise, the exits were sealed, and the only way Devon was getting out was whenever Yara decided she was done speaking with him. That could take *hours*. "I may be biased about its flavor, though. It's from my home region here on Terra III. I used to eat it *all* the time when I came home from my schooling."

Devon pulled a napkin into his lap, a habit that sometimes earned him strange looks from the Federation citizens, although Yara couldn't have been assed to care. She was a clean enough eater that she didn't bother with napkins. Nor did she employ the little personal vacuums that many well-to-do Federation citizens loved to cart around in their bags. They were handy for both solid and liquid spills. Assuming a person had that problem. Yara, naturally, did not. Someone keen enough to make it to her position rarely struggled with dexterity.

"I think I've had it," Devon said as the maid deposited a hot bowl of soup in front of him. It faintly smelled of ginger and basil, two things that reminded him of home, while he remained unconvinced that it contained either of those flavors at all. "Thank you," he said to the maid, who dutifully ignored him on her way out of the room.

Yara noted his manners, but did not mention that the maid was mute. Made her perfect for overhearing snippets of confidential meetings. Like this one.

"You know," if Yara knew how to do one thing, it was lay on the flattery when she deemed it time to get what she wanted. Devon was subjected to her decades' worth of experience in the fields of flirtation, ass-kissing, and seduction. It was what made her so formidable in her earliest days of law enforcement, back when she conducted undercover operatives because her superiors saw a remarkable skill in a woman who knew how to make people of all genders quiver in their boots. "You've been hearing this quite a bit these past few days, but I studied you when I was a girl too. Master Marlow's mercenaries are legendary. Quite the little kid's tale to keep the playground burning with games. Whenever children get together to play mercenaries, they're referencing what our stories say about Cerilyn."

"I've been hearing things like that, yes."

Devon drank his water, but he waited for Yara to have a sip of soup before trying it for himself. *If she wants me dead,* he thought, *then I'm a dead man. But I'll be damned if I play right into her traps.*

"Then you know we all burn with torrid curiosity about what it was really like. That's why I enjoyed your interview earlier. We rarely get to hear the realities of for-hire mercenary work. Especially when it comes to Cerilyn. The mercenary troops that you can hire today aren't the same. Poor imitations, really."

Devon wasn't surprised to discover that there were still mercenaries in the Federation. He would've been surprised if they congregated on a planet dedicated to that life, but the mercenaries of the present-day Federation were more concerned with hiding deep in jungles and in frozen tundras. Those who hid out in more cosmopolitan countries took to the underground and crowded slums. If there was one thing that hadn't changed, it was the need for discretion. And to not piss off the law.

"You know a few things about hiring mercenaries, Commander?"

"Sometimes you need a little extra help protecting colonies from separatists. Sometimes, a big, brutish mercenary is the only one who can strike fear into someone's heart. People are used to the Federation uniform. Even if we have the means to put them down, we're at the obligation of a million intergalactic treaties. Everything must be done just so, yes? Mercenaries don't have to play by those rules."

Devon hid his displeasure for the sour soup while contemplating the meaning behind Yara's confessions. Why in the world was she telling him how the Federation forces skirted laws? Was she implicating him? Was he in danger? Or was she lowering her guard—on purpose, of course—so he would be more likely to share the information she sought?

At least one of those things was true.

"We played by our own rules," Devon said. He couldn't be arrested now for what he did back then. Nor could he have been arrested back then! Cerilyn hadn't been Federated. They were a rogue, independent enterprise left untouched due to their warlike numbers and the needed services they provided. "But when you rose to my level, you worked closely with a number of Federation Forces."

"Yes. I have access to countless historical documents, some of them intriguingly ancient and confidential. Seeing what many of my predecessors did to keep and maintain their positions has been fascinating. Some of them certainly couldn't get away with their actions now." Yara chuckled. "Not that I should like to try."

Devon picked at his food, but helped himself to more ice water. This wasn't a polite dinner meeting for Yara to ask him the burning questions she always had about the mercenaries she apparently idolized. For while she never said that directly, Devon picked it up in her mannerisms, intonation, and the glint in her one eye. *Let me guess,* he thought, *in another life, you would've been one of us.* A tenacious woman like Yara d'Alacron truly could have been a great mercenary, assuming she was okay with killing and pillaging for pay. Then again, Sulim di'Graelic had made it her whole ten years without harming a single soul, but she was a great anomaly. Most mercenaries were like Sonall and Cairn: they killed, they looted, and they left the bodies for survivors to deal with. That's what they were paid to do.

Sometimes, murder happened even when pay wasn't on the table. Cairn knew a few things about that.

As if Yara caught the thoughts in his head, she abruptly changed the subject. "There are a few things I'd like to ask you. Off the record, and in confidence."

"Off the record, huh?" Devon didn't realize he had repeated that in English. Even so, Yara did not struggle to know what he meant.

"There are a few holes I'd like you to fill in for me, Mr. Anderson." Yara removed a rudimentary folder from her bag. It no longer mattered that she dressed in her casual eveningwear of a sleeveless blouse and a simple pencil skirt. She was every much the commander in her white uniform. Devon had a feeling that Yara was a woman who showed up in a T-shirt and jeans, and everyone *still* immediately deferred to her as the most powerful person in the room. "I have questions that don't need input from other parties." She meant Marlow, specifically. Although his employees were often a nuisance as well.

"I will do my best, of course," Devon offered. What his best entailed, however, might change depending on what she asked.

"Of course you will. Because you're an amicable guy who wants to help the Federation catch some of the nastiest criminals in the universe, yes?"

He narrowed his eyes. "I've already told you everything I know about Nerilis Dunsman." Before Yara could deny that was who she meant, he continued, "And Syrfila Tograten."

That made the commander let out a pent-up huff that even she hadn't known she harbored. "This is not about Tograten," she hastily uttered. "I would rather not talk about her at all, if it's all right with you."

"No problem. I have no love for her, like you."

"How would you know what I..." Yara recomposed herself. The last thing she needed was Devon learning about some private matters that not even the president herself knew. For Yara and Syrfila went so far back that the only reaction she *could* have to that name was a sneer. And an instinctive press of her fingers to her permanently injured eye.

No, it was *not* something she wished to speak about in present company. Not ever.

Yara opened the folder and presented Devon with a familiar face. He had to double-check that he recognized who he thought he saw.

"Do you know this woman?" Yara asked.

Devon stared at the honey-kissed skin, the shoulder-length hair, and the deep brown eyes that had untold horrors of a thousand years ago contained within them. *Don't express a damn thing.* Curiosity was all right, he supposed. He wouldn't betray anything by simply picking up the photo of Capt. Miranda Hotchner in her dress uniform and pretending he was captivated by her striking beauty.

More like compelled to punch her in the face. Devon often told himself that bygones were bygones after a thousand years of more pressing business—and, well, weren't people allowed to change?—but he couldn't help how he felt whenever he saw his mother's murderer.

"No idea." He returned the photo to Yara's folder and stole a sip of soup. The sour explosion on the tip of his tongue did not deter him from shoving more food into his mouth. Only when Yara glared at him did he realize how guilty he looked. *If Sulim were here right now, she'd tell me the first mark of a man who has much to say is how full he keeps his mouth.* Devon politely swallowed and drank his water.

"Absolutely no idea? That's curious." Naturally, Yara had damning evidence to expose to Devon. Particularly of the last time he had a short rendezvous with Miranda a few weeks before.

They had reluctantly agreed to meet when Danielle's court-martial was going full steam ahead and Devon had been called upon as a witness. Miranda risked much interfering with his testimony, but Devon didn't give a shit if she was next on the chopping block. Their mutual interest was in keeping Danielle safe. Both in her life as Danielle, and in her existence as Sulim.

That meant going over Devon's testimony and deciding how they might intervene should Danielle lose her grip on reality. She was their only true thread still keeping them together, since the last thing either Sonall *or* Cairn wanted to acknowledge was what had transpired on a not-so-forgotten planet a thousand years ago.

Devon wished he could say that Danielle's regression might mean he never had to deal with Miranda again. *More like the exact opposite would happen,* he thought. *Assuming I want to keep Danielle in my life.*

The fact that those two inevitably came as a pair was something he accepted a few months ago.

Still, he had to consider the present. Particularly a present where he gazed upon damning evidence of his meeting with Miranda. Nothing screamed sneaky little buggers like them both wearing hoodies and meeting in the corner of a Thai restaurant on the far reaches of the Bay Area. Everything had been so heavy and clandestine that Devon couldn't even enjoy the disgust on Miranda's face when he told her what had happened over Christmas. *"What if I told you I'm going with the flow, huh?"* he had asked her. *"God only knows what she'll think of me when she gets her memories back."*

"If she ever regresses," Miranda had countered. *"And I should hope to God she wants nothing to do with you after that."*

Their rivalry was as solid as it had been a thousand years ago, only now with a different cause tearing them apart.

"This woman is named Miranda Ann Hotchner." Yara slapped down another paper, written in not only Basic, but bits of English and a few other languages Devon only vaguely recognized. "You have been photographed talking to her in private. Stop lying and tell me who she is." That wasn't a smug grin of triumph on Yara's face. The triumph was in the cross of her muscular legs and the lean of her arm over the back of her chair. She pulled her whole body away from Devon, proving to him that she was not only confident that she could destroy him if necessary, but demonstrating how little she cared about his lies.

"Why do you want to know?" Devon knew damn well *why* someone would want to know more about Miranda. However, he wasn't about to reveal more than Yara already knew. It wasn't a matter of protecting Miranda, a woman who could disappear from the cosmos for all Devon cared. It was about protecting somebody else. Someone he actually did care about. "She's nobody important."

"Then why lie about knowing her? Come on, Mr. Anderson, you've already told me that she's important enough for you to protect. Tell me how you know her. At least."

Devon gritted his teeth. He knew it. He knew that something like this was behind their meeting.

"Why don't you tell me how much you know first?" Devon asked. "Like how *you* even know her."

"My sources remain anonymous, of course." Devon wouldn't know much about Lady Amyran. Not enough for him to be shocked by the revelation that one vindictive *julah* woman sold Miranda's information out to the Federation Forces. Yara couldn't do anything with it until she had corroborating evidence, anyway. "Don't concern yourself with them. I'd rather know about your sources. But, if it will endear you to me a little more... what if I told you that I have reason to believe that you and her go *way, way* back?"

Devon said nothing. His hardened gaze said *everything.*

"Forgive me for not knowing how things like reincarnation and the Process work very well," Yara said with an exaggerated sigh. "Don't get angry with my ignorance for asking this, but... is it possible for me to talk to Sonall? You know, the other person living inside of you."

That was only a tad ignorant, yes. Borderline offensive, when one considered the way Yara said it. "That isn't how it really works, no," Devon said. "Once you regress, let alone break free from the Process, there is no *other person* living inside of you. You just are." There was more to it, of course. Rea d'Eran called the sensation of being at peace with his past while striving for another future as *reconciliation.* It meant he had absorbed memories, skills, and desires that had been latent within him. The things that made a man *Sonall* and made another

Devon could only be represented in a Venn diagram that quickly shared a big, happy middle. Devon would never again be as addicted to drink, dice, and women like Sonall had been, but neither had Sonall been inclined to music and technology. Researchers would spend another few millennia determining when death and rebirth switched parts of the brain around.

"Oh, lovely, so we can have a simple conversation about this woman, then?" Yara punched a button on her communicator. It displayed a small, slightly skewed hologram on the table. The file flickered. Yet it was clear enough for Devon to see the most damning piece of evidence about his connection to Miranda. "Should we call her Miranda? Or should we call her Cairn di'Cerilyn, the chief of Second Tribe when it met its untimely end?"

Devon couldn't stop the blood draining from his face or his eyes widening. It wasn't merely a matter of connecting the dots. When presented with side-by-side evidence of both women's appearances, it was like looking into his own mirror. Cairn and Miranda would never be *identical,* since different parentage affected a few things between lives. For example, Miranda had her mother's jaw, whereas Cairn had *her* mother's jaw. There was still no denying that they were the same person. Not when they shared the same exact father and was bequeathed with their first mother's body.

"Yes. You know her *very* well, don't you?"

Devon regained control of his expressions. Too late, though. Yara had him right where she wanted him. All he could do now was try to survive without sending the hounds after Miranda. Easier said than done, of course, but he didn't make it to Second in Command by being a bumbling idiot who incriminated everyone around him. Sonall may have been drunk half his waking life, but he still had the education being the son of a lord afforded him.

He also knew where his loyalties lay.

"Imagine my shock," Devon said, "when I saw her again."

Yara glommed onto his half-admission. "So she is the same person?"

"It's like seeing a ghost."

Although Devon did not actually say, *"Yes, they are the same woman,"* Yara took it as a win. This was off the record, after all. Devon wasn't being recorded, although she could certainly arrange it. Whatever he said and she committed to memory was as good as gold.

"That is utterly fascinating," she said. "Of course, I already knew the answer, but hearing it from your mouth only makes it more real. Is she in the Process, like you were?"

"As far as I can tell." The answer was yes, and Devon knew it. Miranda had admitted as much to him when he asked her that same question. The only other thing he knew was that...

"So, did Master Marlow have a third mercenary doing his dirty work out there? Because he never once told the Federation a thing about that, and I would be curious to know why."

The only reason Devon answered was to keep Marlow from being investigated even more than he already was. It didn't take a genius for Devon to see how carefully Marlow stepped around human toes. *Julah* may live exponentially longer than regular humans, but the Federation was so big and powerful that it had the ability to handicap his movements for much longer than the average human lifespan. When a man also had a ton of people to protect...

"Marlow is not responsible for her," Devon said. "I'm not even sure he knows about her." "That second part is what I find hardest to believe. You really want me to think that a *julah* like him doesn't know somebody is in the Process?"

"I'm sure they can sense things. I don't really ask about it."

"But you don't think he knows about her?"

"We've never talked about her."

"Why not?" Yara took a long sip of her water. "I would think finding one of your kindred spirits on Earth would give you a few questions."

"I don't pry into her business. Regardless of what any photos of us you may have imply, we are not on the friendliest of terms."

Yara unleashed an unsettling grin. "Such an interesting history between you and your fellow mercenaries. I can only imagine what it was like directly answering to the woman who was responsible for your change in lifestyle."

"You're in the military," Devon said. "You know what it does to you. Any personal feelings I have toward her are simply that. They're personal. I'm not holding it against her anymore, but that doesn't mean I forgive and forget." He wrinkled his nose. "How do you know about that, anyway? It happened over a thousand years ago. I didn't think the tribe kept records *that* well. Not who was responsible for what."

"It's easy enough to piece together when you can access what digital records remain from that era. Arrah was and is a Federation planet. We have plenty of evidence that your family's murder occurred on such and such a day, and that you, your sister, and a few of your family's employees were taken to Cerilyn by Right of Conquest. Hmph. Can you imagine that being a thing today? The universe certainly has changed since then."

"Right of Conquest kept the members up. Few people willingly joined ranks." Devon cut Yara off before she could offer her expert opinion on the matter. "We weren't the military. We had no benefits and so little freedom that it was a miracle if you ever saw your home again. We took exiles and psychopaths, but those don't necessarily make the best stock of mercenaries."

"No. Suppose not. According to that interview you gave, the best ones were the 'normal' people you took by Right of Conquest and broke down until they either survived or died. Like... your sister, yes?"

That was the lowest blow Yara could have thrown. Yet here they were, Yara sitting smug in front of her soup and Devon doing his best to contain his demeanor.

"Yes. My sister didn't make it. She took her own life shortly after we arrived on Cerilyn. I'm sure witnessing the violent death of our parents had something to do with it too." How lovely it was to regress and be once again plagued by those memories for himself. And Yara had to ask why he didn't like looking at Miranda if he could help it?

"Yet you survived and went on to become a legend. Literally. A legend."

"I had nothing to do with that part. I was good for my day, but if it weren't for what happened, nobody would remember me now." He assumed his eventual ascension to chief wouldn't be its own stuff of legends. Probably of how he ran it into the ground because he was inebriated most of the time. "I'd rather not talk about my sister, if it's all right with you. Bit of a sore spot. But you know that, don't you?"

Yara snorted. "Were you this insubordinate back then, too?"

"You adopt a bit of an attitude when you choose to survive instead of die. And what can I say? I take issue with people in power pulling these stunts with me."

"People? Are you sure it's not women in power who shove that stick up your ass?"

"It has nothing to do with gender, I assure you."

"That's what they all say."

Devon didn't doubt that Yara faced her own share of shit, even in the so-called progressive Federation. The president may have been female as well, but that didn't stop the same old shit that cropped up every time a human woman came into power. Not in a world with good old boys and few good old girls. Although, if Yara had her way, she would certainly become the first on the list of *good old girls.*

That didn't mean he was full of shit when he said he genuinely admired women who earned the respect of their peers. However, he didn't think highly of anyone who abused their positions of power, especially to gain some other end.

"Regardless, it's a testament to your innate survival skills," Yara said.

"I was merely good at numbing myself. I was far from the only one there who spent most of his pay on substance abuse. Or women, for that matter."

"No men?"

"Wasn't into that. It was also a homophobic environment, so even if I was... hmph." Part of keeping people in line was imposing archaic rules. While the Federation had recognized same-sex unions long before anyone was born, Cerilyn wasn't exactly known for its progressivism.

Devon had half a mind to change the subject again, but he knew that doing so would bring them back to Miranda. A woman he had a reason to protect, even if he didn't like her.

"Cerilyn sounds like it was a very... physical environment."

Was Devon reading her correctly? Or was this more flirtation for the sake of it? *That would certainly be something,* he thought. *The Commander of the Federation Forces flirting with me.* Nobody would believe it. Well, perhaps they would, because he was a *legend.* Women of all levels loved to flirt with legends, didn't they? Didn't mean Devon was dumb enough to believe it. Yara was as genuine as a card dealer with something up her sleeve.

"You punched people. You then boned other people. It's about as simple as that." Unless one's name was Sulim di'Graelic. She was infamous for doing neither. Something Devon now realized was far from the truth, but Sonall had certainly bought that image up until the end.

Exactly how Sulim wanted it. That was part of her survival plan, like doping up and spending his nights in brothels was part of Sonall's.

"Why are you asking me this?" Devon asked. "Fancy yourself a mercenary in another life?"

Yara considered him for a moment. Devon assumed she would switch topics. Instead, she surprised him by saying what she had always intended. "There are a few things different from technology and spirituality back then. For instance, we now have this thing called *past-life therapy.* Even if you're not in the Process, you can benefit greatly from it. Many people end up living through some of their past lives through it. You know what *hedpah* is, yes?"

"Of course I do." It was an indigenous plant of Yahzen, one heralded for its regressive properties. A good, strong whiff of it would knock a person right back into a previous life. Devon didn't need it, but people who had undergone normal reincarnation used it as their only way to connect to their other lives.

"I've indulged in it a time or two." Yara chuckled. "That's how you know this is a confidential conversation, Mr. Anderson. *Hedpah* is contraband outside of Yahzen, so I could get in a lot of trouble if that information came to light."

"I don't think I'll ever care to share that with anyone."

"I figured. Anyway, every time I've indulged, I've had the same visions. Or flashbacks, you might call them."

Devon said nothing.

"In every flashback," Yara leaned forward, elbows on the table and singular gaze set heavily upon Devon's countenance. "I'm on Cerilyn. It has to be."

The sly smirk gracing Devon's face was not for Yara. It was for the realization that she would most definitely be a remnant from those forbidden days. *"Hey, man,"* the assholes in his subconscious said, *"Remember that time? In the closet? 'Course you do! You were a virgin until then!"*

"How about that?" Devon said, searching every face he knew from back then. Yara being a reincarnation of someone who lived that life didn't necessarily come from Devon's time. Cerilyn had been around as a mercenary haven for several hundred years. The book Devon signed when he was officially inducted into the lifestyle was ancient back then. "What I know of regular reincarnation says that it's a result of a terrible life. I'm sure lots of those poor sods were reincarnated to get a second chance at a decent existence." The Void could be merciful, even if humanity was not.

"I don't want you to get the impression that I romanticize those times." Yara briefly looked away. "I simply want to know everything there is to understand about it. Starting with this woman who played such a pivotal part in your life as Sonall Gardiah. Shall we have dessert? I hope the soup wasn't too sour. I've arranged for something more subtle for dessert. It might actually be a dish common on Arrah. I don't know."

She danced around subjects like she danced around her admiration for him. While Yara d'Alacron would never flat-out admit that she fancied Devon—or, at least, who he used to be—she wouldn't do much to hide it. Devon saw that clearer now. The warnings May had given him were not born from jealousy, but from concern. The more Devon was drawn into this woman's web, the more he was likely to suffer.

Maybe not immediately. There might even be substantial, pleasurable gain in the short term. But in the long run? Devon faced a reflection that was soon to scold him.

He toed that pivotal line. Keep Yara happy and stay in her good graces... and don't fall for her seductive act. If anything in his existence taught him how to survive, it was his instinct around potential lovers. Particularly of the blond variety.

Fifteen

"Do those windows open?" Miranda shoved her foot into one of her boots and bent down to lace them. "This high up, I know some builders skimp out and only give you a piddly five inches."

Danielle propped herself up on her elbow, fingers caressing the wild strands of her hair as they stuck up in every direction. She couldn't remember how much her windows opened in her bedroom. Nor did she care. The temperature was perfect. Or that may have been because she was naked beneath a single sheet. Lots of places felt cooler when one was naked. "Are you trying to say something?" she cheekily asked the woman getting dressed.

"Little stuffy in here, isn't it?"

A boot slammed against the carpet. Why Miranda insisted on going back to the front door to grab her boots to put on in here, Danielle could not infer. That didn't mean she turned down the view, though. Miranda was a sight whether she wore casual jeans or was strewn naked across the bed. Danielle only hoped that her lover wouldn't abscond with the wrong sock. Socks were a hot commodity in her dresser drawer, and now that she was unemployed, it might be a while before she sucked it up and bought more.

Then again... she mused, while Miranda combed her bed hair with her fingers and dashed into the bathroom once more, *she's pretty loaded for reasons I'd rather not know. Maybe I should make her buy me some socks.* Danielle was in a good enough mood to start playing the field. Get some *julah* money out of the old man who ruined her soul's existence. Get some *julah* money out of the woman now coming out of her bathroom with straighter hair and hands that smelled like lavender.

"My God." Miranda stood at Danielle's bedside, phone in hand but eyes locked on the sight before her. "Here's an image I never thought I'd see in real life. Look at you. So smug."

"You'd be smug too if you came as much as I just did."

"I don't need that to be smug." Miranda turned her head away before Danielle could see the blush on her cheeks. "Knowing what you look like naked makes me smug enough."

"And now that you know, you bounce."

Although Danielle said that with a hyperbolic sigh as she flung herself onto her back, Miranda took it to heart. "I'm not a wham-bammer, thank you." Honestly, it depended on the partner. There were certainly a few she couldn't wait to get away from as soon as the deed was done. Sometimes it was guilt that drove her out the door. Mostly, however, she realized two seconds after the final gasp sounded that she had made a grievous mistake. To the ether she usually went. "I told you, I have somewhere I need to be in a couple of hours. I need to go home and freshen up."

"That's right. Wash me off you."

That would be a crime against humanity, Miranda mused, her attempts to contain her cracking smile *not* working. "I was going to take a shower anyway, thanks." She adjusted the cuffs of her jacket. Her arm propped her up on Danielle's bed, a hand snaking its way toward the sheet encasing her body. "Do you *think* I want to wash this loveliness off me?"

"I don't know your motives." Danielle folded her hands behind her head, daring Miranda to pull back the sheet. She wouldn't, of course. That would only invite more fun into their lives, and there was too much to do to allow that to happen. "I barely know mine most days."

"Tell you what. For pulling a screw and flew, I'll make it up to you somehow. Assuming you're down with dinner at my place later this week."

The light flickered in Danielle's eyes. Whether she reveled in a brief regression that showed her a reliable future, or she merely suffered a yawn from the exertions of her day, Miranda could only guess. Her guesses were all wrong, of course.

"You cook?"

Miranda had half a mind to slap a hand against the leg wiggling beneath the sheets. "Of course I can cook! Between the two of us, I'd wager I know more about it than you do."

"I mean, you're probably right. It's hard to beat my regular rotation of stir-fry and meatloaf though. Do you know how long meatloaf lasts? All week, if you stretch it out well enough."

"That should be a crime." Next, Danielle would probably tell her that the leftover meatloaf regularly made it into the after-work stir-fries. That lovely image would be in Miranda's mind for the rest of the day. Right up there with the image before her right now. "At least tell me you make spaghetti sometimes. Literally the easiest dish in the world."

"That would be stovetop ramen."

"I'm leaving." Miranda stood up, the clunking of her boots sending finality through the bedroom. "Before you continue to violate my Eighth Amendment rights."

"You've already violated my Fourth Amendment rights a good amount today."

"Yes, tell me, what did I *seize?*"

"I mean, there was a lot of searching going on. I think I did most of the seizing, though."

If Danielle continued to grin like that, Miranda would be compelled to stay a little while longer and show this US History nerd a few things about other so-called rights and amendments. Did free speech include screaming in pleasure? They should know before the neighbors complained.

"Friday night," Miranda said with a wink. "Come by my place at seven. Or earlier, if you insist on seeing me still in my uniform."

"We'll discuss roleplaying at a later date, Captain Hotchner."

The sarcasm was not lost on Miranda, who was slightly surprised that Danielle would make such a reference so soon after her court-martial. Perhaps it wasn't that raw, however. Miranda knew better than most in Danielle's life that the only reason she enlisted was to find her sense of purpose. Regina may have been told that her granddaughter was sick and tired of college and ready to reap in benefits and sign-on bonuses, but the truth was that Danielle was always destined to be drawn to that kind of life. She was a mercenary, after all. Growing up in a military family meant she had a front-row view into what she could do in this life. If it weren't the military, though, it would have been something. Law enforcement. Security. Underground cage fighting. Anything that let her soul vicariously relive what it understood best.

Miranda understood it, because she had also lived it. Her father may have told her to enlist and be his spy into the American government, but even before he popped into her life, she had known her life would not follow any particular script. Just like it hadn't a thousand years ago.

The fact they ended up in the same branch, in the same office, wasn't coincidence. That was the Void ensuring these two connected souls found each other once again.

A feather-light kiss sealed their thoughts. Before pulling away, Danielle agreed to come to Miranda's house for a proper date on Friday night. What she would do in the meantime, however, continued to elude her. She had a feeling Marlow would be difficult to get a hold of until Devon's celebrity tour was finished.

"Maybe I'll see you around before then." Miranda drew her fingertips down the breadth of the sheet covering Danielle's naked body. "Void be willing."

It was her first time making a casual reference that so many around the Federation did as much as Americans referenced God or Jesus. The code switching that occurred based on present company often kept Miranda from making such references at all. Why risk saying it around the wrong person? She already juggled a multitude of cultures in her life. Bringing Federation language to her everyday life was like asking for invasive questions.

Danielle understood the reference, of course, but she didn't know how to parse it. Another dour reminder that Miranda was part of the world beyond theirs. She knew things that Danielle barely understood, let alone remembered. They had some deeper connection that refused to present itself to Danielle's subconscious. Did it matter how badly she wanted to kiss those lips or feel that skin against hers when it might be her undoing?

Because she knew there was *something* powerful lurking between them. Danielle felt it like she felt the butterflies bouncing in her stomach every time Miranda gave her *that* heady look. She may draw away now with a seductive grin on her face, but Danielle would do well to keep her spring fever in check.

"God willing," she said back to Miranda. "Every time the Void gets involved, shit gets weird. I'll take my chances with the Big Man upstairs."

There were a hundred things Miranda could have said to that, each one more ominous than the last. Yet she left it at, "I have your number if anything comes up. Otherwise, see you Friday."

"For stovetop ramen?"

"Was thinking more Italian, thank you." Miranda hesitated in the bedroom doorway. "If you're getting ramen from me, it's homemade. And I don't really like making homemade ramen when the restaurant down the street will always do a better job."

"But you'd do it for me, right?"

"Let's not make any promises I might not be able to keep."

"Okay, then what is a promise you *can* keep?"

That was a trick question, indeed. For there were few promises Miranda truly could keep without completely revealing who she was to the woman who would hurt most to hear it. She couldn't say *"I'll love you forever,"* or *"There isn't a place in this universe you could go where I wouldn't follow."* Those were the kinds of phrases to send Danielle running. Because the alternative was her remembering something she wasn't yet ready to handle.

Perhaps that gave Miranda an idea.

"If you need anything," she said, attempting to keep her tone light even if what she was about to say was heavier than Danielle anticipated, "you know where to find me."

Although the weight of what she said was immediately apparent, Danielle insisted on keeping things light as Miranda left the bedroom. "Does that include money and free food?"

Miranda said one last thing before reaching the front door.

"Whatever you need, my love."

Danielle stared into the blank space of her apartment before slumping back down into her bed. She didn't have much time to mull over those words. An unprompted nap claimed her only a few minutes later.

A glass of fermented *esti* berries, colloquially known as Estiary Wine in Basic, flowed generously into a glass too big for any human being to consume. "This is how it works," Yara said, presenting a glass to Devon. "You tell me what I want to know, and I'll owe you."

The overwhelming acidity of the wine almost knocked him out. He had forgotten such potency was common in this corner of the universe. Estiary Wine had been a staple in the Gardiah house, thanks to his mother's fine palate, but it was scarce on Cerilyn. If mercenaries were throwing down hard-earned pay for possibly-illegal drinks with high alcohol content, they went with the *julah yaya*, whose tales of use rivaled those of absinthe in late nineteenth century Paris. When consumed by humans, it packed a powerful punch.

"I've already told you what I know," Devon lied. For all he knew, this wine was spiked. Yara wasn't above that, either. They may have been in her private apartment in the capitol compound, but that simply made it easier for her to drug her so-called guests and get what she *really* wanted through truth serums and amnesia tonics. All highly illegal, of course, but the authorities were far from charging their commander with anything as long as it wasn't made public. There was a time in Sonall's life when he could resist such machinations, but the Devon of today wasn't as certain he could survive that level of interrogation without throwing his chief to the wolves. "What you do with that information is up to you. Honestly, her fate is no skin off my back. So if I knew anything else, I'd definitely tell you."

Yara looked at him as if to say, *"That's what they all imply."* Yet the words leaving her mouth were a mere, "Thank you for your candor. It's good to know that there are still strong-willed men out there in the universe."

That was meant to be flattery. Devon had to contain his rolling eyes before they gave away how little she impressed him. Scared him? Certainly, things could quickly go that way. But impressed him? He'd be more impressed if Yara d'Alacron didn't reek with ambition at any cost. This was a woman who wanted to leave her mark in the history books. There had been a hundred female commanders before, so that notoriety had faded. The operations she had conducted and seen through were mere blips in the news. She was good at what she did. Great, perhaps. But good and great didn't make history. Not a history that was already thousands of years long. If she wanted to cement her legacy before she died in a few more decades, she needed to make her mark. Now.

If she couldn't bring in the diabolical Nerilis Dunsman, then she could at least blow a few holes open into his operation.

"I only ask that if you bring her in for questioning, you don't mention my having anything to do with it," Devon said.

"Is that the favor you're asking of me?"

"Hell no. If I'm asking a favor of the Commander of the Federation Forces, I'm making it count."

Yara's smirk followed her across her sitting room, where she set down her glass and withdrew a small container from one of her drawers. *Speaking of illegal contraband,* Devon thought, although he couldn't pinpoint what was in the container. He had a bad feeling, though.

Perhaps it wasn't *bad.* His life was not endangered, nor was his soul about to be torn asunder. But he didn't trust her. He *shouldn't* trust her. The commander was conventionally lovely and flirtatious, but she played up both to get her way. In another life, she was probably a master seductress who stole from her marks when they were asleep. (Or hacked into their devices to steal their identities, more likely.) Yara's privilege had allowed her to follow a more morally acceptable path, however. Yet she knew what she was and how to use it to her advantage. Devon was a red-blooded heterosexual male with a reputation in a past life as a loose philanderer who drowned his trauma in whatever woman he could charm or pay. A woman like Yara would definitely take that into account, even if Devon was savvier now than he used to be.

She knew that. She also knew how to draw the old him out and use *him* to her advantage.

"You're a smart man, Mr. Anderson. Or should I call you Devon? I admit, that's a nice name for where you're from. If I met one more John or Bill among my Earthling contacts, I'd pass out from boredom."

"Imagine how we feel." Devon kept one eye on her as she placed a small handful of green and yellow herbs into an ornate diffuser. A receptacle on the side swallowed a few ounces of a clear liquid. Not water, though. Something meant to dilute the color and scent of what Yara was about to burn. "What is that?"

"Forgive me. I find these apartments to be so stuffy. Security reasons, of course. They don't dare give me too many vents to crawl through or windows to smash. Not even this high up." Yara continued to smile as she turned on the diffuser. The sweet scent of something familiar hit Devon before the dilutant worked its magic. Yara drank half her glass of wine and turned to Devon. "I like to keep it fresh in here, especially when I have guests."

"Yes. I'm a guest. In your apartment." Devon couldn't help but snort. The extra inhale of breath meant he ingested more of whatever diffused into the room. Something tingled in the back of his mind. When he spoke again, he acknowledged how difficult it was to speak in Modern Basic and not the old and familiar form he used a thousand years ago. He swore he knew the differences a few minutes ago. Why was it so hard to use the new verb endings that signified his familiarity with Yara's private quarters? In Old Basic, he would use a simple *do* sound that was cross-class. Modern Basic, however, incorporated a few new endings that differentiated status. Yara was a bit above Devon, after all, and he had done a fair job referencing that in this new tongue he spoke.

"Everything all right?" Yara asked, unperturbed.

"Yes... just..." Devon blinked away the invisible smoke wisping into his eyes. His Earth-minded brain told him it was pot. The side of him familiar with the Federation, however, instantly recognized what was in the diffuser. "Is that *hedpah?*"

He almost couldn't believe it. This whole time, he had worried about truth serums and knock-out drugs. What he should have feared, however, was a drug famed for unlocking past life memories and personalities.

Well. That was one way to interrogate him.

Yara came closer, her breath soon only a few inches away from the man who braced himself against a shelf and fought with the memories flooding back to him in giant, tumultuous waves. Soon, he would be more Sonall than Devon. Whatever control he maintained over his actions was filtered through the men Sonall and Devon shared in the core of their beings. The thoughts and actions that transcended rebirth and made him who he truly was when in the purified clutches of the Void.

Oh, Yara intended to use it to her advantage. Whatever favor he asked of her would certainly include whatever a man like him thought coy. Yara was willing to give him almost anything, though. Anything that was within her reasonable abilities to give. Money? She had plenty at her disposal. Sex? He'd be so out of it that she doubted it would be too bad.

What she did not intend, however, was her own reaction to the *hedpah*.

She had indulged many times before, of course. Yet she had never done so with the likes of Devon around. As soon as the sensation filtered into her body, she likewise took a step back with him and remembered something she had never, ever intended to unlock from the depths of her subconscious.

"You're not doing such a bad job." Whose voice was that? Hers? But Yara had never sounded like an uneducated rube from some backwater planet. *"You're kinda cute, too. Bet you're a virgin, though."*

She was prepared for anything—coming from Devon. Fear. Prowess. Anger. Good humor. She was not, however, prepared for the existential dread overcoming her. To the point she succumbed to her knees, hands bracing against her floor as she held back the urge to scream.

Every waft of *hedpah* entering her brain was like another punch to the back of the head. Her flights of fancy of the mercenary lifestyle of legend were nothing compared to the taste of blood in her throat or the pain she endured more than once a week.

I looked at this boy and hated him. Where had that realization come from? Was it Yara d'Alacron facing the grown man standing before him? Or was it that meek, broken teenager she had completely forgotten about until now? *The chief didn't care about him at all. Meanwhile, she wouldn't stop hurting me and the others.*

Who was the chief? Who were the others? Yara was not in the Process. She would never unlock that side of herself, because her soul had been filtered through the Void the first time she died. But she remained unwashed. She was still a stuck-up brat who wanted things done her way, and would do anything it took to accomplish that. So when the Yara of a thousand years ago beheld the new recruit tending to his family's horses and nursing the wounds of his sister's death? She decided to use him for her own twisted ends.

That's how it was done on Cerilyn. Those were the sides the history books left unrecorded and the legends left unsaid.

"Isn't it funny?" Devon said, struggling to keep his cool as he recognized the woman standing before him. While she didn't strike anger into his heart like Miranda did, Yara was an unexpected surprise. An old, familiar face that made him more depressed than anything else. "Seeing you here after all this time. You think I ever forgot you?"

Yara pushed herself up. She attempted to reach the diffuser and turn it off before this got any worse, but the strength of her fleeting regression brought her back down again. It took Devon helping her up to remember what was happening.

Yet she couldn't talk to him like the girl she once was. That came with the Process, not mere reincarnation. All a reincarnated soul could do when under the influence of *hedpah* was remember.

And act.

Her will told her to jump on him, so she did. And Devon's will told him to go with it and try to forget the bad.

So he did.

Sixteen

Rains did not come often Yahzen, although the lush landscape most of the planet boasted suggested that precipitation was plentiful. Yet when Vikkel and Kalera touched down at Amyran Estate after their sojourn to other parts of the planet, they were greeted with the smell of freshly fallen rain.

"Ugh." Kalera wrinkled her nose as she stepped out of the cruiser. A landscaper looked up and nodded in silent welcome. She did not reciprocate. "I think I'm going to be sick. This humidity is awful."

Vikkel secured their vehicle. Any affection he held toward his wife was reserved for steadying her as she attempted to fly up the cobbled walkway to Amyran House. As usual, she had miscalculated how quickly she could travel with both her belly and her nausea.

The house was in the classical *Ofutah* style popularized when High Priest Tanasoro declared the optimal shaping of the Void and the universe. An ostiary topped the main hall, which was flanked on either side with long wings that once housed the entire Amyran clan during the first great plague to nearly wipe out *julah* kind. An extra wing had been built in the back. A bit stouter than the two great wings, but one of Vikkel's ancestors insisted it was a desirable place for the help to keep their quarters. Indeed, the hybrids and humans the family contracted for their daily tasks enjoyed more modern architecture within their apartments. The same could not be said for the stubborn full-blooded *julah* who came and went over the millennia. They considered their dedication to drafty rooms and creaking beams a testament to their faith in the Void.

Yet Vikkel's paternal instincts kicked in ever since he married his pregnant wife. The newlyweds lived with Lady Amyran to both save face and to give their child a comparable head start over hybrid children born off their families' estates. The more Vikkel walked around his childhood home, however, the more he questioned the logic behind raising his own child in this place. Kalera, of course, preferred living on Terra III with her human father Cornelius. Yet even the ambassador to Yahzen agreed that he'd rather see his grandchild raised the *julah* way. It was the only way he could guarantee a future for his descendants, since human legacy and money only continued for so many generations. *Julah* prestige and wealth was nigh infallible.

As the Amyrans proved after their rise from the proverbial ashes. Everyone—and that meant everyone with a *julah* surname—loved to gossip about little House Amyran and its inability to ever make a decent name for itself. Thousands of years and multiple generations had passed since the Amyrans last boasted any relevance among their kind. Most of their funds came from Lady Lilla Amyran's first two (deceased) human husbands, both men with riches and powerful human families of their own. Her sights were always elsewhere, of course. Since Vikkel's grandparents had failed to secure an arranged marriage for their daughter before their deaths, it was up to her to continue the full-blooded line. She had two hybrid sons, and many human suitors who occupied her bed, but she had yet to find an appealing *julah* willing to marry her, let alone take her name and join House Amyran.

Then again, this was a woman who blamed her family's woes on the plague of six generations before. "It wiped out everyone in the family who was of decent breeding stock," she often told her sons. "Not to disparage your direct ancestor, who was the only surviving full-blooded male of breeding age, but he wasn't the strongest soul in the Void, if you know what I mean. As soon as he obtained his Mastership, he gambled half our coffers away. They called him Master Payday, because everyone else got paid when he entered the halls."

Vikkel and his wife knew their places in this house. The family tree may have been scraggly, but as soon as Lilla found a decent *julah* man to marry and beget at least one child with, they would be demoted in familial status. Their children would be treated fairly enough as long as Lilla was alive to remember her firstborn, but within a thousand years, any hybrid children tracing their lineage back to Lilla Amyran would be scattered to the stars.

It wasn't something either Vikkel or Kalera wished to dwell upon, but they did so every time they returned home to Yahzen. And there was no choice in the matter on this day, for their return marked the annual Gracious Void Feasts, when every *julah* was encouraged to return to their ancestral home to pray, honor their forefathers, and take care of estate matters that had been long-overdue. Since Kalera was pregnant with the Lady's first official grandchild, it was essential she make an appearance so everyone could pray over her womb and beseech the ancestors to please, *please* bring her a competent soul from the Void.

She should not have been surprised to see a certain carriage outside the main entrance.

Kalera stopped short of going into the main hall. Sure enough, the housekeeper popped out of the front door to inform Vikkel that his mother was out back in the *bappah* courts, and she wished to see them as soon as they arrived. "Look who's here, Vikkel. Because I don't have enough old women freaking out over my uterus."

Vikkel had to drag his wife to the playing courts in the back gardens of the house. Wedged between the servants' wing and the south wing, where Vikkel and Kalera kept their marital home, were two courts for playing the traditional pastime of *bappah,* a badminton-like sport that included a whistling ball and two racquets. Lady Lilla had been a fan since she was a small child, and although she would never reach competitive levels, she enjoyed challenging her guests to matches. So it was no wonder to catch her shining golden hair fluttering on the humid air as she raced back and forth on the court, racquet swinging and cajoling cheers echoing across the court.

Her opponent, a woman of similar petite stature but of higher social status, raced to catch the ball before it landed on her side. Dark hair nearly fell from its casement on top of her head. Her fitted *bappah* outfit, consisting of a fluttering skirt and conservative top, suggested that she had brought her own instead of borrowing one from her hostess. She didn't notice her daughter standing at the edge of the court until she shot back the ball out of bounds.

"Kalera, darling!" Nicola Ferran waved to her only child. Kalera was in no mood to wave back to the woman she had only seen once in the past two years. *Right after my wedding,* Kalera thought, shuddering as she recalled those memories. *She got around to visiting us after my father finally tracked her down to tell her I was married and pregnant.* Whatever Lady Ferran really thought about that? She kept to herself. This was a woman who treated her daughter like a curiosity. "How lovely to see you! I did hope that we should meet before I had to leave for home again."

"Mother." Kalera folded her hands on top of her protruding stomach, grateful for the poncho wrapped around her full figure. She had taken to tapping her fingers against her belly when anxious, something she had never done before becoming pregnant for the first time. When facing the woman who used to rap her knuckles for fidgeting? Now was not the time to remind her mother that some things never changed, no matter how quickly a *mah-julah* child matured. "How lovely to see you. I wasn't expecting to see you here."

"It's your home now, isn't it?" Nicola gestured for Lilla to take a break from their game. Lady Amyran traipsed to the edge of the court, where she took a swig of cooled *cageh* from her canteen. Nicola looked after the Lady of the estate as if they were dear old friends. In all honesty, they *had* been in the same social circle growing up as the only daughters of their generation within their families. Although Nicola had married first, she and Lilla became pregnant around the same time and attended the cursory First Time Mother's course in the capital, as expected of all *julah* women, whether they begat full-blooded or hybrid children. It was there they became acquainted, bonding over the styles they wished their children to share and dreaming of what their futures may be like in their fleeting lives. Lilla had been exceptionally curious that Nicola was having her first ever child as a "gift" to her husband. Whereas for Lilla, having a child was her possible ticket to family salvation. All the good it had done her so far...

Arranging a marriage between their children had only been natural when the sexes were determined. Yet they certainly had not counted on one standing up the other at the altar. After the Amyrans' shame reverberated through *julah*-kind, Nicola took personal offense and cut Lilla off from many of a Lady's social spheres. It wasn't until the surprise marriage of their children that the moratorium on Lilla's social graces was lifted and the two began to converse again as if nothing happened.

"Come, come, let me get a look at you." Nicola steadied her daughter, first taking a look at her full cheeks before diving beneath the poncho to take a gander at how Kalera had bloomed in the past several weeks. "Would you look at that! My first grandchild. Do you know the sex yet?"

Blushing, Kalera shimmied out of her mother's grasp and replaced the poncho over her stomach. "N... no," she lied. "You were supposed to arrange my gathering of blessings, but I have yet to hear anything."

"Oh!" Nicola tittered. Both her daughter and son-in-law instantly recognized it for the fakery it was. "Of course! Silly me, I thought we had some time left. Yet you look like you're about to pop open at any time. Well! If it's all the same to you, I shall conspire with Lilla about it. I'm sure she won't mind helping me plan a party."

Those words were divine music to Lilla's ear. She whipped around, *cageh* spilling from her canteen. *A party!* she thought. *Planning one with* the *Nicola Ferran!* Nicola's parties were legendary, from her afternoon garden soirees that saw the who's-who of the *julah* matriarchy and human diplomats, to her clandestine cocktail parties full of carefully sequestered debauchery. When Nicola opened the aged casks of *yaya*, burned the *hedpah*, and surrounded herself with surly hybrid artists and their models...

"Why don't you spend some time with your mother, since she's surprised us with her presence?" Vikkel put a reassuring hand on his wife's shoulder before turning toward his own mother. "If it's all right with you, there's something we must discuss."

Lilla huffed. "Lady Ferran has..."

"I'm sure she'll like to spend some time with my wife, whom she hasn't seen in so long."

Lady Amyran furrowed her brows before tossing aside her canteen and kerchief. "Very well. I shall like to recline in the sunroom, anyway. Let's go."

The sunroom was the first proper abode inside of the manor. With a fishbowl view of the gardens, Lilla could lay on her favorite chaise lounge, drink her fill, and gaze longingly across the acreage her family had called theirs for generations. She often dreamed of razing it to plant *cageh* fields or to build *yaya* breweries. That's where the money was those days, since the humans fancied themselves consumers of *julah* goods. But they required capital to start, and capital was not the Amyrans' strongest suit.

"It's really quite nice of Master Marlow to give you and Kalera a break for the feasts." Lilla collapsed onto her lounge. As if on cue, the family's head housekeeper appeared in the doorway, bearing a platter of finger foods and wine for the mistress of the estate. When asked if he cared for anything, Vikkel slowly shook his head, his mother dismissing the housekeeper. "Sometimes I fear he forgets the proper holidays of our people. But I suppose that only makes him more intriguing."

She shared a knowing look with her son, who had to refrain from rolling his eyes. Lilla had been flirting with Marlow—and poisoning him, ahem—ever since their paths began to cross. When it wasn't to procure her youngest son's referral to the Academy, it was to test the waters of their mutual attraction. Marlow had been a confirmed bachelor his whole life. Lady Amyran thought that a crying shame. Especially with so much money at his disposal.

"Master Marlow is a generous employer. We would've been home sooner, but we had pressing matters to take care of on his behalf."

"Of course! That's how it goes with men like him. His matters of saving the universe are always more important than directly contributing to his home planet. It's a damn good thing Yahzen does not rely on him to function. We would all hurtle into the sun."

Vikkel sat in one of the chairs adjacent to his mother's lounge. "We need to talk about those documents Kalera and I gave you after our wedding."

Although Lilla hesitated, she pretended to not know what he was talking about. "Come again?"

"The documents. You know the ones."

"Ah... yes. When you and Kalera did your little detective work into the fate of Nerilis Dunsman's... uh, genetics." Another word had been on the tip of her tongue, but she failed to say it in front of her own son. "Very scandalous. I daresay I still don't believe a lick of it. What about it?"

Vikkel waited for his mother to stop running her mouth before responding. "You didn't tell anyone or share those documents with someone, did you?"

Lilla whipped her head around, golden hair falling from its casement. "Absolutely not! What would make you think I'd dare share such gossip about someone nobody ever wants to talk about? I couldn't even *sell* something like that. You know, if I wanted."

"Uh-huh." Vikkel didn't doubt for two seconds that his mother wanted to sell it if it meant some quick cash. How else would she buy a new slinky dress to wear to Nicola Ferran's next "art" party? Not that Vikkel desired to think about his mother slobbering over someone he probably went through boot camp with. "There are rumors circulating. Or at least I'm hearing unprecedented talk that Nerilis Dunsman has a child somewhere out there."

"Oh, don't be so quick to accuse your poor mother of things," Lilla said with a huff. "People have been talking about his secret children for thousands of years. Why, I was a little girl tugging at your grandmother's skirt when I first heard of it! If you believe most of the rumors, Master Dunsman has a child in every branch of the government and temple. Most of them full-blooded, if you can believe it."

"I cannot." Vikkel also noted that his mother continued to refer to Nerilis as "Master Dunsman," not that he could extrapolate anything from that. Lilla was old enough to remember a time when Master Dunsman was the High Priest of the Void, and when one did not offer him that highest of honorary titles, they defaulted to his station within his family. Yet since he lost all of his titles, only the most stubborn of the elderly continued to call him *Master*. Or at least without any sarcasm. "Besides, this isn't about rumors of his full-blooded children. This is about a hybrid like me. But you know that already. You've seen the reports."

"That he has some Earthling child? That only makes it all the more intriguing to people who can't stop gossiping. Earth will be a source of mystique until it disintegrates from its sun. The moment people heard he was targeting it, they started churning rumors. What is it to us?"

"Mother." Vikkel wished that, for once in her life, she would look him in the eye when he initiated an important conversation with her. But Lilla often preoccupied herself with whatever grooming was pertinent at the moment. Right now, she picked at her cuticles, wondering if it was too soon to return to her favorite salon in the city. *The hybrid girl there really does the best cuticle work,* she fondly thought. *I need to go as much as I can before she meets her untimely end.* Really was a pity sometimes, wasn't it? Such good labor was hard to find. There should have been a law against humans dying so young when they provided such great service to women like Lilla Amyran!

"Son," she eventually shot back at him.

Vikkel shook off the bristling sensation on his shoulders. "I am serious. My research indicates that the leak definitely came from your corner of the universe. Kalera and I swore you to secrecy when we gave you those files." Not really, but it had been implied. Should something have happened to them, Lilla was to take the information to the *julah* genealogists. Or perhaps the authorities.

Yet nothing happened to us, Vikkel gratefully thought, as his mother winced from a painful cuticle and sighed.

"And I'm serious when I tell you it's not as big of a deal as you're making it out to be." With a mighty harrumph, Lilla eased back into her seat. "You're making things out of nothing. You'll soon realize it's the same silly rumor that's perpetuated every few decades. The planet of origin changes, but the whispers are the same." She finally leveled her gaze upon her son. It was in those moments when their genetic similarities truly shined. While Vikkel would always have his father's chin, hair, and unfathomable posture, Lilla had contributed at least one trademark.

Her eyes, of course. Those stone-cold blue irises were the same exact color as the ones staring Vikkel back in the face every time he looked in a mirror. Not that he ever doubted that this woman had given birth to him. Lilla would have never acknowledged his existence if that were the case.

"You'll also soon realize that there are things greater than what you perceive to be of the utmost importance," Lilla continued. "For a *julah* such as myself, the only things that truly matter are maintaining the legacy of my line and doing service to the Void. Ultimately, it means nothing to me what that man has done with his seed. It has nothing to do with my womb."

That was a strange way to put it, although Vikkel certainly heard the message. *All she really cares about is securing the Amyran name for at least one more generation,* Vikkel thought. *That's all she's ever cared about my whole life.*

"You always give me that dour look when you're reminded of your place in this family." Sighing, Lilla kicked up her feet and folded her hands on her stomach. "You may sulk about your lot in life, son, but you'll have something beyond your own death that any full-blooded sibling of yours could never dream of touching."

Vikkel said nothing, although he kept one ear turned toward his mother.

"You'll always be my firstborn." Lilla looked away. "That means something in our culture. To women, dear. Soon, you'll understand that as well."

Vikkel rose from his seat. The implication that the firstborn always mattered most, regardless of mortality, was something that he had often heard of in his mother's culture. But it wasn't something he usually enjoyed in a family where he was as expendable as the rumors about Nerilis Dunsman and the daughter everyone whispered he had.

Seventeen

Hungover on *hedpah* and still reeling from the memories throbbing in his head, Devon was escorted from Yara's sealed chambers the next morning. The guards who took one look at his disheveled, unwashed self could only exchange an inside joke in some language Devon did not understand.

He definitely understood what he heard when he returned to the guest apartments, however.

"Well, well." Lanelle looked up from her morning caffeine, a diabolical grin growing on her fair face. "Look who's finally back. We were about to file a formal inquisition to the military barracks on your behalf. You know, if you weren't back within another few hours."

Devon tapped his head against the doorframe leading into the Terra III kitchen that boasted the essential amenities. Evan stepped away from the appliance that washed and restocked the dishes so a busy human didn't have to. Or a busy *julah*, for that matter. Marlow was in the next room about to make inquiries on Devon's whereabouts.

"Yooo, there he is! Oh, shit." Evan immediately lowered his voice when he caught the depressed demeanor on Devon's face. Or what was left of it, anyway. Devon was as bedraggled as a cat left in the pouring rain, his reddened, saggy eyes dropping down his face as his jaw likewise slacked toward his chest. Grayish lines colored his cheeks. His hair was so greasy and tousled that Lanelle didn't think twice about getting up and prepping the steam bath in an adjacent room. At the very least, it would make him smell a little better. "What happened to you?" Evan continued. "Did she drug you and make you tell her every crime you committed a thousand years ago?"

The smell of caffeine and breakfast hit Devon. He ran to the sink to dry heave, and it was only then that Lanelle recognized the telltale signs of a man who had breathed in too much *hedpah* in one night.

"She absolutely did drug him, it looks like." She crossed her arms and scoffed. "Here I was, about to bet that she had used her crotch instead."

Devon didn't want to hear that word. In any language. *Makes me think of sponges and fluids. Other bodily functions... ugh.* Here came another dry heave.

"Right. That seals it." Lanelle lowered her arms. Evan went to grab his employer. "That was a horrendous walk of shame, wasn't it? One fueled by illegal drugs the good commander should not be using. But she'll get away with it, of course, because..."

"Please stop talking." Devon clung to the sink. Rather amazing he could speak without losing the bile in his stomach. "The sound of your voice is making me ill."

Lanelle almost took offense to that. Luckily for Devon, she knew what it was like to have a *hedpah* hangover. "Come lie down on the lounge." She took him by the hand and guided him to the plush sofa near the windows overlooking their busy neighborhood of Terra III's go-go-go capital. She snapped her fingers above her head, which prompted the windows nearest Devon to dim and block the morning sunlight from his delicate eyes. "I'll see if I can't throw you together a remedy, but you might need Master Marlow's help getting back on your feet." She didn't tell him that the sorcerer was one of the best at waving away a nasty *yaya* hangover in a young woman's head. Didn't make it any less true.

When Marlow did arrive, it was with a hard clamp of his cane against the floor and the slow, methodical shake of his head.

"The hell did the commander do to him?" Marlow asked. "Besides the glaringly obvious."

Lanelle chuckled. "My diagnosis? A gallon of *hedpah* and one Succubus-inspired..."

"Give us a moment, would you?" That cut Lanelle off so quickly that she frowned. "The man needs some air. Go grab us a bucket in case he vomits."

"Don't say that word..." Devon muttered.

Marlow ignored him. "I need you to tell me what happened. Is this *hedpah?*"

Devon lowered his hand from his forehead. The room spun as he attempted to sit down on the couch. By then, Marlow had pulled a handkerchief from his front pocket and handed it to the young man sweating from every gland in his body. "I don't... ugh..." He hadn't felt this sick since Kalera inflicted him with a *julah* plague a few months before.

"I'm telling you," Lanelle continued from the other side of the room. "I know a *hedpah* hangover when I see one. You remember what I was like that one time I went crazy all over the bad batch? Sick for *days*. You ask me, the Commander doesn't understand usage very well. You have to *ease* the fumes into the room. Not, like... drink it."

"Thank you for your contribution," Marlow said.

"It's not just *hedpah*. Commander d'Alacron sucked him dry, if you know what I mean."

Although Marlow perfectly understood his assistant's meaning, he was not wont to dwell upon the imagery now invading his imagination. "I don't think such details will be necessary."

"To be honest." Devon eased himself into a supine position, his head resting against a pillow that smelled of Lanelle's shampoo. "I don't really recall anything at all. The only things I'm remembering right now are things that happened a thousand years ago. I'm barely hanging on to what's happening right this moment. I think the only reason I know my name is because Lanelle didn't exist back then."

"Either he got the really good stuff," Lanelle said, "or it was *bad*."

"Thank you once *again* for sharing. Now, if you don't mind," Marlow turned around to shoo Lanelle from the room, "you would be a much bigger help if you went into my room and brought me my travel alchemy kit."

Lanelle furrowed her eyes before playing the dutiful assistant. "Alchemy?" she muttered. "Whenever I get like this, he tosses me a pill made of Void knows what and I throw up for the rest of the day." She saw how it was. *Some* people got special treatment.

Marlow waited for her to disappear into the other room before turning his attentions back to Devon. "Be honest with me," he said. "Is this *hedpah?* What happened last night with Commander d'Alacron?"

Devon inhaled the deepest breath he could stand. One he wouldn't choke on, anyway. "We had dinner. Privately."

"Yes, I surmised as much would happen."

"I don't remember what we talked about. I might later."

"Go on."

Devon pressed his face into the back cushion. It didn't do much to suppress the nausea that overwhelmed him when he walked into this room and saw so many familiar faces. "She brought me back to her apartment. I remember that, because I left it this morning. About an hour ago. Some of her guards escorted me back here."

"We were becoming quite worried about you. There was no word about what you and she had done after she insisted you go with her."

"She must have drugged me. I don't think we drank anything. But there was... yeah. That stuff you mentioned. The stuff that makes you remember past lives."

That was an incorrect way to phrase it, since *hedpah* didn't "make" people remember anything. All it did was open the gateway to a flood of memories, but only if the person inhaling the fumes was susceptible. Someone like Danielle, who fought against everything her mind attempted to unlock, only succumbed to crippling anxiety. A soul that had been freed from the Process merely welcomed a few new memories. Or, in Devon's case, made terrifying realizations that he wouldn't recall for another few hours.

Yet Marlow knew what he meant. *Hedpah* was used in religious ceremonies among the *julah,* who were immune to its effects under the assumption that all *julah* were original souls. It was because of those ceremonies that they discovered its side-effects on humans. Humans like Devon, who had a lot of lives to relive if he inhaled too much of the yellowish smoke.

Lanelle brought him his kit, which he set up on the nearest table and used to concoct a remedy for Devon's ailment. It wouldn't cure him, at least not immediately, but it would quell his nausea and help him snooze off the last of the haze. The pills he usually gave Lanelle were a higher dosage that lasted a longer period of time—not that he would tell her that right now. When Lanelle partied, she did it with so much gusto that she was liable to accidentally kill herself. Something Marlow kept in mind for those mornings when he walked into his office and discovered his assistant passed out on the floor after a rough bender. *What Devon is dealing with,* Marlow thought, while the young man quaffed the elixir and immediately fell into a fit of dry heaving, *is too high of a dose for someone not used to it.* There was the other matter, too. The one that Lanelle kept mentioning and Marlow was inclined to believe.

"Do you remember what happened as a result of the *hedpah?*" he asked, once Devon had settled back down onto his back. "Any specific memories? Anything that happened in real life?"

"I only remember being a kid," Devon said. "Way back then. When my sister killed herself and I stopped caring about anything."

That wasn't helping Marlow. Not that he knew what he searched for in the glazed over eyes beneath him. "Did something about where you were trigger it? Was it the commander?"

Devon closed his eyes and sighed. "Ah, shit. I think I slept with her."

Again, this did not help the man trying to piece together an intricate puzzle. If anything, it only made things worse.

"What you two did doesn't concern me right now. I want to know what you remember, exactly, and what triggered it. You wouldn't have specific memories unless you were compelled by some external force."

"I don't knoooow." Of course Devon knew. This was like if Marlow asked him what his birthday was, and Devon played dumb. Yet his brain was so jumbled that Devon was likely to mix up his birth date for his social security number.

"Every time I try to focus on anything, I get thrown back to that time." The same memories replayed in his head over and over. Nothing screamed insecure and juvenile like constantly reliving the very first time he lost his virginity. *It's not like I want to dwell on this right now,* he thought, in between flashes of that girl's half-naked body and the suffocating heat of that supply closet. *I mean, it was so romantic and something I totally didn't regret.* "Oh my God, make it go away."

"That tonic should kick in soon. When it does, try to remember what happened *before* the commander got frisky with the illicit substances."

"What do you think I'm trying to do?" It didn't help that the other memory lurking in his brain had nothing to do with a woman he was romantically involved with. Why the hell was he thinking about Miranda? Sure, she had been related to the person shoved into the forefront of his thoughts, but *why?* "Wait. At dinner, she asked me about..." Ah, here it came. The inklings of what happened twelve hours ago. "She asked me to identify..." That's why he was thinking about Miranda. Her picture had been thrust into his face, after all. Demands for her identity. Insinuations that they were somehow related. That she was *related* to a wanted criminal. "You know what? I don't think I can remember."

Marlow knew enough about Miranda that the information about her wouldn't have been scandalous. But did he need to know that word was getting out? That someone had told the Commander of the Federation Forces? *Think I'll spare him that for right now,* Devon thought. He needed to talk to Miranda about it first. Because he loved nothing more than a reason to talk to her.

"Fine." Marlow furrowed his brows and turned away. "Just get your rest, I suppose. I'll have Lanelle get you something to eat when you're ready."

Devon welcomed the silence overcoming the couch as he closed his eyes and attempted to doze off the remaining effects of *hedpah.* Slowly, more acknowledgments of what happened the night before came. *I can't believe it,* he thought, the bottoms of his palms pressing into his eyes. *There are going to be regrets going beyond a thousand years.*

Eventually, the sobering went straight to his bladder. The compulsion to relieve himself drove Devon off the couch. After stumbling past the tables and chairs surrounding the sitting room, he turned the corner and faced the hallway leading to the bathroom.

May stood there, leaning against the wall, her downturned face saying everything she thought about what she overheard.

"What?" Devon asked.

She shook her head. "I told you that woman was trouble."

"Let me deal with my own shit." Devon pushed past her. "It's bad enough everyone in here is already laughing at me."

Except May wasn't laughing.

Aside from making reincarnated humans see things they were never meant to remember, *hedpah* was often used in ritualistic ceremonies to contact either the Void or the dead. (Contrary to popular belief, they were not always the same.) Whenever a family of *julah* wanted to communicate with their divine ancestors, usually to beseech blessings or advice in times of crisis, they packed in the *hedpah* and burned it until the smell refused to leave their shrines for months. The common person who never studied at the Academy, let alone joined the priesthood or devoted their lives to studying the intricacies of the Void, assumed that it was mere tradition that made it such a precious commodity even among their people.

High Priests, however, knew exactly what *hedpah* was capable of and why it was so important in ceremonies—even the crudest ones.

"If the Vallahars are good for one thing," Nerilis muttered as he stacked small bushels of *hedpah* into the corner of his shack, "it's getting me what I need." The former ambassador to Terra III, the deposed Master Janush Vallahar, now hid in forced exile. Yet his mother and the extensive family they controlled had their way to continue the dirty work while the figurehead took the fall on their behalf. It was Lady Vallahar, one of the most respected soul-seers in the universe, who continued the clandestine transactions to secure Nerilis whatever he might need from his home planet. While he often hid out on Yahzen, it wasn't the safest planet in the galaxy. He could only shield himself from civilization when he was awake, and he was not lazy enough to ask a family like the Vallahars to risk greater punishment by harboring him in the depths of their estate. No, it was enough for him to send the Lady coded messages asking for one and a half tons of *hedpah* to make their way to a shack on the far edge of their property, out by the fields where they cultivated what made up a bulk of their fortunes.

Restless, Nerilis had tirelessly worked to conduct this ceremony since he last saw his daughter. While Miranda giggled beneath her bedcovers and thought herself mighty lucky to finally have something going right in her life, her father forewent sleep and bathing to secure her future as a tolerable sorceress.

He needed answers. He also needed some comfort of his own.

Contacting the Void was risky, even for a man of his experience. Just because he could do it faster and hold the connection longer than anyone else didn't mean he forewent the possibility that this might be the time he was caught by authorities. The amount of *hedpah* could be seen burning from up to five miles away. And the smell! He would be lucky to get it out of his clothing.

He also needed to lower his defenses to conduct the proper meditations and prayers necessary to connect to the Void. For two days straight he chanted beneath his breath, and even when he momentarily disengaged to tend to biological necessities, he still muttered sutras and infused the air around him with his aura. Most people, should they ever try contacting the High Priestess at home, couldn't do in one month what Nerilis did in one weekend. They didn't have his expertise that came with being the former High Priest. Nor did they have his Void-given skills.

They also don't have my determination to see her again, he thought, coming oh-so-mighty closer to establishing the connection that had transcended tens of hundreds of years. Had anyone stopped to wonder if the reason Nerilis Dunsman did such a fine job contacting the Void was because he knew the High Priestess so well?

"What is it, my love?"

He opened his eyes at the sound of her voice. Although Joiya was but a figment of reality, a shadow in the corner of his eyes, Nerilis responded as if she were corporeal enough to embrace. His fluttering heart reminded him, however, that he must continue to concentrate should he desire to see this conversation through.

"There you are," Nerilis said, as if he merely searched for his wife in the endless halls of their home. "I have been meaning to check in with you."

"If you've gone through so much trouble," Joiya's voice reverberated in the air, "then you are doing more than simply checking in with me. You know we do not have much time."

No, of course not. They never had *time.* Not even when they were schoolmates passing such precious time between classes. And definitely not when they were courting! Time flew too quickly. Their whirlwind romance had gone from cordial camaraderie to preparing their wedding at the Temple of the Void as if nothing else had happened in between. Why would they have time now?

"I must ask you about the girl," Nerilis said. "I need to know if this is a fruitless endeavor."

"You mean our daughter."

It was always a strange thing to admit. Nerilis couldn't say he enjoyed admitting his fornications in front of his ascended wife, even if the reason he indulged them was because of a promise he made her a thousand years ago. *When I first confessed what I had done,* he thought, almost losing the connection to the Void, *I never thought I would have her forgiveness. Or her insistence that I keep doing it so our daughter could continue to live.* "Yes. The one I am trying to teach to be more like us."

"You cannot force that which is not natural," she softly chided him.

"No, but I don't know what else to do. Even with Ramaron's power, it's not enough to blend a whole universe into another. I have to recruit and nurture who I can. Who better than the daughter of the High Priest and Priestess?" He allowed Joiya a moment to speak. To reply. To rebut in the manner she always used to when he was hotheaded enough to assert his way. *There are only two people in this universe who can tell me where to stick my hubris,* Nerilis thought, as he longingly gazed at the shadow in the corner of his eye. *And one of them isn't technically in this universe. Not even now.* "Although she is a *ma-julah*. The most unfortunate kind."

Although he extended Miranda the politically correct term for a hybrid, there was no denying the subtext behind his words. "The most unfortunate kind" referred to her *julah* heritage coming from her father's side, instead of her mother's. While it wasn't unheard of for patrilineal hybrids to exhibit grand skills, most accepted that it was passed matrilineally. This made *ma-julah* like Kalera and Vikkel adept to their sorcery, albeit in a more limited way than full-blooded *julah* enjoyed. Vikkel's telepathic capabilities were often considered an Amyran trait, seeing as how his own grandmother passed the juiciest gossip in such a way thousands of years ago. Yet Miranda had not only a human mother against her, but one who came from such entrenched ignorance that the girl never had a chance to come into any of her own powers at the most pivotal time of her youth. The only thing she truly had in her favor was the level of power within her father. If even a trace of Nerilis's abilities resided inside his daughter, then there was hope.

"She may be disadvantaged in her biology," Joiya said, "but she has one grand advantage to her cosmology."

Nerilis dared to turn his head toward the shadow flickering in his peripheral vision. He received the briefest of glances when he beheld his beloved, but it was always too fleeting. In this realm, Joiya could only appear via a mortal conduit or in a flash of light. It was Nerilis's will and skill that made her even this *real*.

"Please, enlighten me," Nerilis said.

A golden butterfly fluttered past the High Priest's face. He did not acknowledge it with more than a glance. He would only have eyes for the woman who had stolen his heart. When she was in the room, anyway.

"There is no other soul like hers in the Void or in the mortal realm." Joiya's voice wavered. Were they already losing their connection? "Were she to be truly ours, she would've been exceptional, but not because of her soul. It was your doing that made her stronger. My body may have been born again from a human mother, but it is a *julah's* soul inside of it. There can be no other type. I daresay that human side of her can barely contain her."

Nerilis considered that for a moment. "You're right. She was not a random soul assigned to your body when you gave it back to the Void. She was always meant to be a *julah*. The Void plucked her from its depths and blessed her with its knowledge. It's a strange change of fate that has brought her into a hybrid form."

"Yes, my dear. I can vouch that she is the one who lived inside of me for such fleeting moments. But the Void had other plans for her. She was meant to be a *ma-julah*, I think. I... was not a suitable mother."

"Don't say that." If there was one thing Nerilis would not stand for in these rare moments he shared with his wife, it was the pain of their past. Why reminisce on the losses they constantly suffered, when so much more was at stake? "The Void had other plans. So must we."

Joiya nodded. "Spiritual power has always trumped genetics. There are humans who have mightier souls than some of our own kind. If you put them into a *julah's* body, they could be as strong as we ever were." That was sacrilege to Nerilis's ears, but he kept his demeanor contained. "And our daughter has the tremendous power of rebirth in her soul. She is doomed to the Process. Even I have seen it."

Her voice trembled. It was not merely the tone of a frightened mother in mourning for her offspring. It was the keening of High Priestess, who beheld the sorriest souls. Yet she had the power to kiss their bruised cheeks and offer them the chance to return Home or to be reborn again for a second chance at happiness. When her daughter, the girl who looked so much like her, came to the Void after her deaths at her own father's hand... Joiya saw it every time. The kiss of the Process. A price her own child paid out of unfathomable love.

The only anger Joiya was still capable of feeling toward her mate was from that moment. When she beheld the soul of the one named Cairn, she saw no hope of escape. Nerilis's power had been too resolute when he set his daughter's soul into the Process. Her own wish, the thing that would break her free in another life, was set to the impossible.

Nerilis already knew that. Like Joiya, he had the ability to see into souls of varying power. He scryed their fates until he discerned their destinies. In his own daughter's case, it was nothing but abysmal circumstances. He often supposed he should blame himself for the sorry part he played a thousand years ago. Yet what was done was done. Even if he could undo it...

"A *julah* soul with the endless potential for rebirth. Yes. I suppose that is the key to her power." Nerilis tapped his finger to his lips. "Unlocking that won't be easy, though. She's already resistant to my teachings."

"With all due respect, Nerilis, you're a very impatient teacher. You often fail to understand that not everyone has even the fraction of power that you do."

"I don't have time for patience. The longer we dally, the emptier the Void becomes. You dare tell me to my face that this isn't so?"

"Why do I have reason to lie to you? With such precious time we get to spend together, you think that's how I'd use it?"

Nerilis chuckled. "I will do it, my love. You won't have to wait much longer. Soon, we will..."

"Just promise me one thing."

Although he was not a man used to having his words cut off, Nerilis honored his beloved's desire to interrupt him with a bow of his head.

"Don't forget that she is still your daughter. You may not know her as well as I do, but I can tell you, my darling, she is as fragile as she is determined. She is *my* daughter. I never gave birth to her, but I remember what it was like to carry her inside of me as often as I did."

Every time she reminded him of those horrible memories, he withheld another wince. There were few things that made him shudder to think about. Personal things, anyway. Nerilis was not a man who took great offense easily, nor did he waste time on humility or embarrassment. Yet there had been pain. Terrible moments in which he swore the universe was out to get him, to punish him for his everyday hubris as he ascended to become the youngest High Priest in the history of his people. Everything was a balance, wasn't it? So many other things had come so easily to him. Sorcery was as simple as breathing. His charms and more lustful ambitions gained him the attention of every young woman who glanced in his direction. The one he was destined to fall in love with? She came to him as readily as the sunlight beams into a flower. The accolades and prestige that followed him into the priesthood meant nothing. His crowning achievement of his young life was either becoming High Priest or convincing his family to allow him to "marry down" and take a Lerenan for a wife. Of course something had to give. The cost of all of this? Watching that woman he insisted on marrying constantly experience the grief of loss. Not even Nerilis had become numb to it after a while. What should have been joyous occasions often turned sour, with Joiya either throwing herself into priestly work or refusing to get out of bed for weeks.

If nothing else, he was inclined to honor her sacrifices by following her advice.

"I know you," Joiya said, her voice growing faint as she drifted back toward the Void. "You are stubborn and push people to be the best they can be. But she has a *julah* soul in a *ma-julah* body. I could not be her mother and nurture her in the Void within my womb. She has endless potential, but you must take care to not push too hard. Mind her mortality. If she dies again..." A cold brush of ice touched Nerilis's cheek. It was the closest he would get to embracing his beloved that night. "I'm not sure I could forgive you."

That was something he had to listen to twice, for it was not often a woman of Joiya's caliber that made comments like that. *So, an ultimatum,* Nerilis thought. He wasn't surprised. Joiya often let her emotions get in the way of logic, and it hadn't changed a bit since becoming High Priestess. She may have given up her corporeal form so her daughter could finally live, but Joiya knew what it meant to stand on the precipice of eternity and stare into its mighty maw. Except she wasn't threatened with eternal rebirth and damnation. She merely oversaw it, assuming the Void continued to exist.

"I must go now," she whispered. "Please, take care. Of everything."

"You know you can count on me. Thank you for the advice."

Nerilis wanted to say more. That he loved her, for one. Yet Joiya was already crossing the intangible boundary between the Void and the mortal realm. Soon, Nerilis would have nothing but the *hedpah* haze to soothe him for a short time.

Besides, after so damn long, she must have known how much he loved her.

Eighteen

Devon had slept off most of his *hedpah* hangover by the time Evan entered the darkened room and delivered porridge for dinner. It wasn't until Devon forced some of it down, his jaw aching and his eyes heavy, that he realized one of the critical spices was native only to his original childhood home.

"Master Marlow suggested something familiar might make it go down easier," Evan said with a shrug. "You haven't eaten all day, so..."

"So he thought I might like something I haven't eaten since the morning my first life was ruined?" Like Devon didn't remember that whole day as clearly as he remembered the other horrors he witnessed. *I ate my breakfast. Got dressed. Prepared for a day of studies and helping my father around the ranch... boom. Here come a shitton of mercenaries with a writ of death for my parents.* The crazy thing? Devon may have been numb to those memories now, but he couldn't downplay how deeply they imprinted into his soul.

"He, uh, had no way to know that," Evan sheepishly said.

"No. Of course not." This porridge was a staple of Arrahite diets. It was so ridiculously simple, much like oatmeal back on Earth, that it was no wonder it hadn't changed much in a thousand years and fifty generations. "Sorry."

"No worries, man. You've had a rough go of what was supposed to be kinda fun." Evan backed away from Devon's bed. "I mean, nobody anticipated the Commander of the Federation Forces taking such an interest in you."

"Yeah, about that..."

"You don't need to share anything you don't want to." The way Evan held up his hands suggested he had no interest in such details. Weird. Wouldn't Evan be the first person to want to hear tales of bedding one of the most powerful women in the Federation? Especially one with such a hardass reputation? *Yeah. Hardass,* Devon thought. That was one way to put it.

"I should probably still talk to Marlow," Devon said.

"I'll send him in if he has a moment. Otherwise, him and Lanelle are out in the living quarters. I've gotta head home before it gets too dark."

"What about May?"

"May? Oh. Shoot. Right." Evan's awkward laughter didn't spur Devon to keep eating his porridge, which went down his throat about as easily as a kick to the mouth. "She took off this morning, saying she had some family nearby she was supposed to visit. Although, if you ask me, she wasn't off to see anyone at all."

"Is that so?" Devon only vaguely recalled the look of disbelief on May's face when he returned that morning.

"Yeah. Uh, that's one jealous lady you've brought with you from Earth, buddy."

"That lady is the daughter of Dr. d'Eran. You know, one of Marlow's friends." Devon still wasn't unconvinced that May wasn't a plant sent by her mother to keep an eye on him. The fact she slammed on a keyboard and wasn't a bad songwriter was a mere bonus, and one he would take as much advantage of if it served the band well.

Evan shrugged. "Doesn't matter whose daughter she is. She's jealous."

"Of *what?*" As if Devon had to ask.

"I mean, it's not super obvious, because some women are *that* good at hiding what they're really thinking, but I dunno. Seems to me she's got the hots for you."

"You're joking."

Talk about a thought Devon wouldn't even entertain. While May was easy on the eyes and knew how to have a good time with the band, she wasn't someone Devon considered a potential girlfriend. Between the baggage of her connections to the Federation, and how little she put herself out there, he didn't see something that screamed, *"Hey, friend, know what's a great idea? Getting involved with that."* He assumed May felt the same way about him. Bandmates first, friends second, potential lovers way, way down in last place. Hell, he'd set her up with Clyde first, not that he thought she deserved *that*.

"Don't shoot the messenger. Just telling you what's glaringly obvious to little ol' me." Evan backed toward the door, a smirk on his face. *Sure,* Devon thought, *go ahead and enjoy this.* Evan must have thought that his marriage made him prime material for doling out relationship advice, but that was the *last* thing Devon needed after a night like the one he suffered. "Anyway, I'll go let the old man know you want to talk to him."

"You're so gracious," Devon muttered, before hauling himself to the restroom. With any luck, he would purge the last of the *hedpah* through his digestive system.

When he had freshened up and stepped back into his private room, a knock on the door sent a bolt of dread down his spine. *It's just... Marlow...* A man who couldn't fathom many of the details Devon wanted to feed him. It wasn't his place to share what he thought about Commander d'Alacron's apparent reincarnation issues. For one thing, Yara probably didn't understand them herself. The way she swung *hedpah* around like it would have no effect on her only worried Devon more. *Her identity is always swimming in the back of my head...* he thought while making his bed and sitting on the end when he was finished. *Every time I've figured it out, she slips away again.* Oh, he remembered those memories quite well, thank you. A young man did not forget losing his virginity in a supply closet even a thousand years later. Nor did he discount every woman who reminded him of his first. *Light hair. Dark eyes. Nothing left to lose.* A girlish giggle that covered the pain and trauma lurking beneath. Reminders that more pain lurked around every corner for those unlucky few who curried the chief's favor.

All Devon knew was that Commander Yara d'Alacron had once been on Cerilyn. What that meant for the eternal state of her soul was something he couldn't decide.

Another knock on the door.

"Hey, sorry about earlier..." Devon wiped his hand over his face, indulging in his own weight against his tired muscles. The door opened and closed a few feet away. He didn't lift his head, but only because he couldn't stomach looking into

Marlow's wrinkled face so soon. "I felt like total shit. Still don't feel great, but I think I'm on the up now."

"No need to apologize for that."

Devon snapped up his head. A move his neck instantly regretted. "I... uh..." He looked at May, who stood by the bed with her hands clasped and demeanor dourer than he had ever beheld before. "Sorry. Thought you were Marlow."

"He stepped out for a moment," May said. "Thought I'd come back and check on you."

That was almost enough to send Devon onto his back, mental and physical exhaustion playing tricks on him. Somehow, he overcame that urge and kept his eyes leveled on May's. Evan's words continued to replay in his head. May? Jealous? Because *she* wanted to be with Devon?

Utterly ridiculous. This was not the face of a woman who had dreams of pillow talk.

"I'm fine," Devon insisted. "Just a bit of a bad headache. I haven't been hungover on that stuff since... well, I don't know when. Not in this life, anyway."

"Like I said... that woman's trouble."

Yeah, she definitely doesn't have the hots for me. Evan would hear that bit of dialogue and assumed May meant the naughty kind of trouble. The kind that sucked a man into a lioness's grip and tore him to shreds. Sexually, of course. The irony? Devon would usually be into that. With almost literally anyone else.

No, May was more like Devon's chastising aunt. The queen of *I told you so!*

"Excuse me for not wanting to piss off one of the most powerful women in the universe," Devon said. "If she says we're having dinner, we're having dinner. I can control what I say to her, but my actions speak louder than words. I had no idea what she might try if I said no."

"What? Like she was going to kill you or something? Do you still not have any idea who you are? There's no way they could off you without raising intergalactic suspicion. It would take *way* more planning than inviting you up to her private quarters and getting information out of you the old fashioned way."

Devon was on his feet before he decided it was a good idea. *Not a good idea…* He nearly toppled back down to the bed, but managed to stay standing as he faced May and said, "I don't know what the hell *you're* smoking, but it wasn't like that. Not once had she planned to sleep with me, and I sure as hell hadn't been thinking about seducing *her,* if that's what you're so worried about."

"Am I worried you might be thinking with your dick on this trip? Maybe!"

"Why do you care?"

May was nearly knocked back by that question. When she regathered her bearings, she squared her shoulders and said, "Heaven forbid I care that you're doing okay and not being torn to pieces by the vultures that inhabit this place."

There was enough hurt in her voice to make Devon rethink what he said next. "Sorry. I know you've been like a second wheel on this whole trip, but I thought it was because you wanted an excuse to come visit."

"Please. I can get a visa to leave Earth whenever I want because of my parents. Which I don't do very often, because quite frankly, I'd rather be on Earth with flip phones and gasoline-powered machines than here most of the time."

"I mean, you grew up there, right?"

"I've had multiple opportunities to get a job in the Federation. My mom has so many connections in the psychological fields that your head would explode to hear them. Shit, if I wanted, I could probably get Evan's job as Earth Liaison. God knows I'd do a better job than Arthur Weasley back there!"

She was so incensed, with her reddened cheeks and puffing chest, that it took Devon a moment to realize he should laugh. "Probably. He's a bit much."

May was not reassured by that. "I'm serious. It's bad enough when you deal with everyday citizens on Terra III. Once you're involved with the government, you've got to watch your back. Commander d'Alacron is not on your side."

"Trust me. I get that. Loud and clear. Last night's dinner was an informal interrogation."

"Uh-huh. And what was…"

"That happened because of the *hedpah*. Which, I should point out, she dragged out to get answers out of me. I don't think she expected to be affected by it too!"

May shut her mouth, but did not look away.

"It's really complicated," Devon said. "And you can't tell *anyone,* not even Marlow or Lanelle. But I'm pretty sure the commander is a reincarnation of someone I knew back then. It's probably no accident that we're both born at the same time and crossing paths. Not sure how much I believe in fate or whatever, but it's really weirding me out right now."

The bottom lip curled into May's mouth. "I see. I suppose it is more complicated than..."

"Than being horny and bumping uglies? No kidding. Nothing about last night was pretty. I kinda want to forget it." That was one way for Devon to face his maturation in the past year. The kid still in college would be replaying every moment in his head until he had burned it into his brain for future use. *I'm not saying it was the worst sex I've ever had,* he thought, *but I am saying it was probably the scariest.* When two people were out of their minds and combatting the overwhelming memories that only existed to re-traumatize them? Yeah. Not fun. The pleasurable aspects only served to make things more complicated. "Guess this is why your mom's job exists. For shitheads like me."

May finally looked away, her hands lowering to her sides. "I know you've got it hard," she said. "And you're going through shit I can only imagine. I won't pretend to know what *hedpah* does or what it's like be triggered into a regression you can't control. Nor will I judge someone for doing something stupid because of it. But forgive me if I see you stumbling in here after a 'private' night with one of the most dangerous women in the universe, looking like you've been tortured."

"I kinda was," Devon said. "But so was she."

"Unbelievable."

"I don't have the hots for her," he reassured her. "Nor do I wanna sleep with her again, even stone-cold sober. But I don't want you getting the wrong idea. She didn't... she didn't *coerce* me. Like I said, I don't think seducing me was anywhere on her radar before she had a reaction to the stuff. We both went off the rails after that. You ask me?" He didn't wait for May to reply. "She needs your mom's business card."

An uncomfortable silence fell over them. May sighed, her shoulders sagging. Devon fought back a new, overwhelming wave of memories that weren't only about the night before—or a thousand years ago. Not on Cerilyn, anyway.

The porridge. Meeting one of his descendants. Realizing that not everything that once made him happy was out of his grasp.

"I might as well tell you before the others," Devon said. "I'm thinking about taking a detour to Arrah before going back to Earth. I don't have to be back at work until Monday, anyway. I think it might help me decompress a little. You know, see a place I haven't been in a thousand years?"

May was not immediately responsive. Something that made Devon clear his throat and shift between his feet.

"As long as you're back by Monday," May said. "We're supposed to go over band stuff on Tuesday, and I don't want to be the one who has to explain to the others why you're not around."

"Right. The band." Jesus. Devon had almost forgotten. Not because he didn't care, but because there was too much going on in his life—and he was looking at a bandmate right in front of him! "So much for the idea of us writing some stuff while we're here. Clyde was looking forward to it."

"Go to Arrah and get some inspiration. I'll cook something up in a minor key to get you all nice and moody."

If her goal was to make him laugh, it worked. If her goal was to leave him banging his head against the bed—well, that worked too.

The hard part wouldn't be convincing Marlow to take him to Arrah once their business was concluded on Terra III. No, what worried Devon the most was the prospect of facing some of his oldest memories. The ones he still repressed, because they were too painful to face.

May might have been right. He would certainly find lots of artistic inspiration on his first home planet. Too bad there was no way to convey what it did to his brain.

In English, anyway.

Nineteen

Whereas Devon was used to the rigors of flashbacks and regressions, his lover of the evening was not so lucky.

Absolutely nothing Yara d'Alacron did relieved the throbbing in her head or the numbing between her legs. At least one made sense. *You fool around like that,* she thought in stewed silence, *and you pay for it the next day.* She was no stranger to the rough, fury-infused kind of "lovemaking" that made a woman take stock of her physiology and wonder how the hell her maternal ancestors had survived millennia of screwing and giving birth.

She was, however, a stranger to feeling like shit in the head the morning after.

Her problem was treating it like a standard hangover. She had *yaya* cures in her bathroom that would perk her right up after a bender, regardless of who she was meeting or what colony she was invading today. *God, that reminds me...* She rubbed her eyes and stared at her holographic schedule that had a giant red blight in the middle of her week. *We're supposed to be quashing an uprising on Weetok II tomorrow.* She had already signed off on the man and gunpower, but the commander was expected to make an appearance before the troops took off for the tiny mining colony that was a year away from declaring full independence from the Federation. Which was rich, considering those backward hicks wouldn't last two seconds without the food stock and medical supplies the Federation gave in exchange for their *subsidized* labor!

Yara didn't have time to get angry about it again, though. She was too busy slumping over at her desk and wondering why the *yaya* cure wasn't working. *Yaya* was supposedly the most powerful vice a normal human could ingest. There was a reason it was regulated more than any other legalized spirit. Humans weren't even supposed to drink it without supervision! This was why they had *yaya* bars with professional babysitters. Not that it stopped Terra III's upper crust from enjoying it at parties behind closed doors.

Yara had so many regrets right now.

"Ma'am?" A woman dressed in the office formal finery of the Forces' headquarters knocked on the door before admitting herself. That knock was enough to make Yara jerk back and grit her teeth in disbelief that she was so rudely interrupted when she felt like such shit. "Your pre-lunch is here. I'm so sorry. I tried messaging you, but you weren't responding. You know the protocol..."

Knew it? Yara damn well wrote it when she ascended to her lofty position and hated the thought of being assassinated in her own office and nobody finding out until she started to smell. *If I don't respond to the official messages from the reception,* she reminded herself, *someone has the right to barge in here and check on me.* That was why her receptionists and personal assistants were armed. One never knew when they might walk in on the Emperor of Isadore choking her for once again refusing manpower to their intergalactic borders, or the Master Chancellor of Yahzen hypnotizing her into giving over whatever the *julah* wanted this week.

"I'm fine," Yara grunted. It took a few seconds for her vision to clear and her brain to register who she looked at on the other side of her office. Mousy brown hair and a clean face announced that it was Earoa Iko, one of the most junior members of the top brass that had immediate access to her commandership. "Finer than a cup of aged *cageh!*"

Earoa grimaced. "Is there anything I can get you, Commander?"

A new head. Yara drummed her fingers on her desk. Too bad that drumming was like punching herself in the head.

Only then did she remember what had happened *before* falling into bed the night before.

Fuck me. It's that goddamn hedpah. Yara had been around *hedpah* before with little reaction. How was she to know that such a large dose in the presence of Sonall Gardiah would make her... whatever the hell that was! Yara had to shield her nausea behind her spread palms as a riot of memories she could hardly parse spread across her inner eye.

"I think I need a *julab*," she said. "Specifically, a healer. Don't ask questions. Just put in an inquiry at the hospital and the embassy. Confidential, of course."

"Yes, ma'am." Earoa backed away. She almost forgot to close the door behind her.

"Fuck," Yara muttered. "Fucking fuck." She turned off her tablet and dug into one of the many drawers behind her. A snap of her fingers both added to her headache and lowered the lights in the room, drew back the shades on her floor-to-ceiling windows overlooking central Terra III, and turned off every screen in her office.

Such a dark silence reminded her of another time. A time when, even in the Federation, having such technological wonders as interplanetary communication was a privilege granted to only those who had proven themselves trustworthy to "the cause."

At first, Yara thought she remembered her earliest days in the Federation Forces. Back when she was a naïve whelp who worked her way up from security grunt to undercover agent. *Partly because I loved the idea of putting my manipulative charms to good use, partly because I knew it was one of the fastest tracks to one promotion after another.* She had been good at it, like she had always been called to a life in the military. Two things she had never questioned. Not even when she was a little girl in her hometown, glued to the advertisements of grown women in Federation uniforms.

"I could be one of them one day," she had always thought. *"I could go home."*

This was her home now. This giant office that had more security than some moons' national banks.

That wasn't what she remembered, though.

She stared at her desk, hands in her lap. Her eyes glazed over. Whatever effects the *hedpah* still had on her came to the forefront now, reminding her of those Void-stricken years as the brainwashed thrall of a force greater than what she commanded now.

Back when she had no use for common sense. Back when she laughed because it masked the pain. Back when she threw herself at anyone who would have her, man or woman. She may be more discerning as Yara d'Alacron, but only because she had her security to consider. Deep down, she was still the same desperate teenage girl who conflated bad sex for a glimpse at love.

Like in a supply closet when I was supposed to be babysitting asshole little kids still crying for their dead mommies!

For an instance, she remembered who she was. Where she came from. What had dragged her to that hellfire of an existence. What had eventually led to her traumatic downfall, dead before the great Tribal Revolution occurred and ushered in a new era of fragrant promises and More of the Same.

Her blood had fueled the engine of that Revolution, completed in a single act, in a single day.

Yara launched away from her desk and dug through her sealed briefcase for the files she had shoved in Devon's face the night before.

She slammed the picture of Capt. Miranda Hotchner onto her desk and stared into those dark eyes. Fiery. Reserved. Determined.

Yara knew those eyes. Those *eyes,* the only part of her body that was truly Miranda's, regardless of who had bequeathed them to her. Humans weren't the only ones who called eyes the window to the soul. That school of thought came straight from the *julah,* and here was a walking example of it.

Devon had confirmed enough of Yara's suspicions. He confirmed that Miranda was the Processed reincarnation of Cairn di'Cerilyn, the chief of Second Tribe at the time of their destruction. What he couldn't have known—nor her, for that matter—was that such a confirmation would now become their downfall.

"You…" Yara snatched the picture into both hands, the edges crinkling as she gritted her teeth and stared into the same eyes she had once known so well a thousand years ago. *I may only have one working eye,* Yara thought, *but I see right into both of yours.*

The anger stewing within her wasn't directed at Miranda, or Cairn, for that matter. The anger came from fear. Fear that any latent memories Lana still harbored from another life would lead her to absolute madness.

Yara d'Alacron was not in the Process. How could she have been, when that rotten little girl she once was had been all alone when she died by her own hands? There were no *julah* on her planet. And the hybrids among them were ignorant to their powers, not that their numbers were great, either. And Yara, for all her suspicions about Miranda's parentage today, had no way of knowing that Cairn had been a hybrid as well.

No. She had been alone. A sad child who had seen too much trauma over her short life. Trauma that eventually took hold in her head and forced her hands with the only knife she was commissioned.

People who committed suicide were almost, by default, guaranteed reincarnation. Anyone who was so miserable that they chose the frozen embrace of the Void over another breath deserved a second shot. Sometimes, that chance was immediate. Other times, the Void bided its time, waiting for the perfect moment to send that wiped soul back to the mortal realm to be born again.

Yara would never regress. Such a feat was impossible for a simple reincarnation. Instead, she was plagued with vague recollections and a terrifying knowledge that she may have once been someone other than who she was now.

Sometimes, though, she remembered such specific things that the second they inhabited felt like an eternity.

"You bitch," she snarled.

A large breath knocked the memory out of her. Yara eased her grip and lowered the photo to her desk, where it lay wrinkled. She placed a hand against her chest and wondered what the hell had come over her.

"Commander?" Earoa's voice beeped across the communicator on the corner of Yara's desk. "There are currently no available *julah* healers in the city. However, I have located a hybrid healer at the local temple who is available for a discreet check-up."

Swallowing, Yara replied, "That's fine. Send them in as soon as they get here. I... I am going to lie down for a bit, so please hold my meetings and calls unless it is an absolute emergency. Do you understand?"

"Yes, Commander."

Yara heaved another breath and placed her head on her desk. Earoa was obedient, wasn't she? Always doing whatever Yara asked. The exact kind of person she liked to have on her staff.

Once upon a time, she would have killed to be in charge. For once, she would have had the power to make her underlings feel the fear and terror she experienced every time the chief summoned her. Back then, it was the only way she could process the jump in adrenaline.

Devon wasn't allowed to go to Arrah without some serious negotiations with Marlow, who liked the idea as much as he liked drinking *yaya* by himself. He had finally agreed to take Devon on the promise that Lanelle would accompany him—which went over *super well* with the woman on the brink of a few days off—and they cleared it with the Gardiah clan still holding down the fort on Arrah. This required a plethora of calls that mostly went unanswered, since the farmers had more pressing things do than communicate with the elite on Terra III.

Just as well they were stuck inside for most of the evening, then. For around dinnertime, they received a most unexpected visitor who commanded enough prestige to bring down every bit of security in a five-mile radius.

It started with a knock on the door.

"Who is..." Lanelle was sent to answer, but within three seconds she was against the wall, a surly middle-aged man wearing a charcoal gray Federation uniform "gently" advising that she keep her hands where he could see them. The second part of the security detail included two *julah* hybrids who walked in with arms spread wide, as if their puny wards were enough to reflect anything Marlow threw at them. Not that the old man had much time to react. By the time he realized they had important company, the President of the Intergalactic Federation of Sentient Bodies and Their Peoples waltzed in as if she made a habit of dropping in on dinner at the Marlow apartments in Terra III.

"Here I thought the great Master Marlow could afford... grander... accommodations." President Madelae d'Errowyn had better posture and greater diction than the commander, who technically took orders from *her*. But one look at her provided the greater context behind her insistence on being the firmest-speaking person in the room. President d'Errowyn did not shirk on the pressed uniform that separated her from her entourage, but still referred to her as a civil servant. The highest ranking one in the entire Federation. "These are quaint."

The snippy way she said it raised greater ire in Marlow than her barging into his home with a small army. Said protectorates formed a perimeter around the living area while a small contingent searched the rooms for threats. That was how May made her grand appearance, since she had yet to emerge from her room for dinner.

She was there now, with both hands held up in the air and her heart racing in ways nobody else could relate to yet. *Well, that's the President of the Federation,* she thought, attempting to keep her cool, *and I'm the only one in this room who both knows who she is* and *has never been this close to her before.* Just another day for Marlow, who had met more Presidents in his long life than anyone else could recite.

"I'm sorry if my accommodations are not grand enough for you and your entourage, Madam President." Marlow lowered his hands, partly because he didn't give a damn, but mostly because he needed to balance himself against the dining table. His cane had clattered to the floor in the kerfuffle. Nobody was in a hurry to pick it up for him. "I was given no notice of your impending arrival. I would have at least changed out of my loungewear."

A small smile tugged at the president's face. It was the closest any of them would get to seeing the latent mirthful side of her. "Last minute decision. I had a sudden opening in my schedule, which meant I had the chance to drop by and say hello to our local celebrity."

She meant Devon, of course, who had been sitting as still as death at the table, *Just once,* he thought, *I'd like to eat my dinner in damn peace.* How fitting was it that his last night on Terra III featured a surprise visit from the president? And he was expected to sit there and keep chewing his food like a dozen goons wouldn't blow his head off if he made the wrong move? Devon could imagine their briefings before they left their cruisers. *"The man is a heavily trained murdering machine. Treat him as such."* Ah, if only they realized he couldn't use their weapons if he tried, and his strength was nothing like it used to be.

Marlow motioned for him to get up. Devon did so slowly, his legs as quick as molasses as he looked the president in the eye.

"I don't believe we've met," he said in English.

"Right. They told me you don't quite speak Modern Basic yet." She switched to her best shot at Old Basic, which she only knew thanks to her secondary degree in linguistics and a helpful interest in old historical documents. There were plenty to read in politics, after all. "I am the President of the Intergalactic Federation. Madelae d'Errowyn, at your service."

Devon would have been impressed, but the only thing he really got out of that was, *"I'm President. I serve you."* Somehow, he doubted that was what she really meant to say.

"Nice to meet you," he said in enunciated Old Basic.

The president extended her hand. Devon was obliged to shake it, although it was like approaching a colonel in the American military, thanks to the way Madelae hid her other hand behind her back and kept her legs locked at five and seven. He half-expected her to tell him at ease when they parted again.

Instead, she looked him up and down and said, "Yes, I suppose you would make a fine soldier again. Bit insubordinate though, aren't you?"

"You should've seen me a thousand years ago."

The tilt of her head was the president's sign of amusement, and her own men and women couldn't discern was it was about. Probably because the only times they saw her smile was when she was about to order the detainment of someone who displeased her. "For all I know, I was someone else a thousand years ago." She snapped her fingers and summoned an assistant to her side. "I don't have a lot of time, Mr. Anderson." A holographic clipboard landed in her hands. Madalae swiped through a selection of files until she found the one she wanted. "But I desired to personally deliver your pardon instead of leaving it to a lower ranking official."

"My... what?"

Marlow intercepted the chip coming out of the clipboard. Nobody stopped him. Especially not the hybrids standing a few feet away, their shaking hands still extended. When they entered the room a few minutes ago, they had been in work mode. Now they stared at one of the most famous men their mothers had ever told them about. Here! In the flesh!

Marlow pressed the button on the side of the chip. A display of its contents soon appeared, written in both Basic and English, supposedly for Devon's benefit.

"Really?" he asked, droll in demeanor and suggestion. "Please tell me this is purely for show, President. You can't really tell me that 'Sonall Gardiah' here was still on the books for a pardon."

"Didn't you arrange it with one of my predecessors about seven hundred years ago?" the president mused. "I found it in my stack of notes I received when I became President. Should your mercenaries complete their missions, they would be granted full ceremonial pardon for their past transgressions as rogue agents from Cerilyn."

"The man in question has been dead a thousand years."

"Am I not looking at him right now?" Madalae knew the answer to that, of course. She had a better understanding of the Process than most humans. One of many things she studied in her preparations to become the woman she was now. "Because I was under the impression that the soul of that man is merely in a new body. Therefore, he may answer for some crimes and transgressions *he* committed, whether in another life or not."

"You have to be kidding... Lanerak's Law clearly states that a person cannot be held responsible for crimes committed in a past life."

"Lanerak's Law wouldn't exist if it weren't for you, Master Marlow."

"Right. Because I lobbied for it on my assistant's behalf."

Madalae lightly snorted. "I meant because you're the one who put her into that position."

Lanelle, who had been standing behind Marlow, chose that moment to speak up. "Thanks, by the way! I like not being in Federation prison."

Devon remained the only one utterly lost. "Let me get this straight... I'm being *pardoned* for my crimes as a mercenary a thousand years ago?"

"Like I said, purely ceremonial." Madalae shrugged. "It's not like we were in the business of hauling you off in chains to make a point. As Master Marlow said... Lanerak's Law prevents us from doing that. You can only be charged for Federation crimes you've committed in your present life. Oh, and you should be pretty grateful. I have it on good authority that you could have been charged for *many* things over the past several hundred years. You mercenaries don't exactly save the world with the law in mind."

"Gets in the way sometimes," Devon muttered.

"It was lovely meeting you. Perhaps we shall meet again soon."

Nobody said a thing as the president was led out of Marlow's residence. She was flanked in the front and behind by a dozen people, and at least two of them always kept their eyes on the people in the room before the last one closed the door. The silence befalling the living area gave May the chills and made Marlow sigh.

Devon was the one to break the silence.

"So... Lanerak's Law?" He looked right at Lanelle, who did not show her sheepishness through a blush or stutter. She was much more likely to fuss with her skirt and sit back down to finish her dinner as if nothing happened. "That have anything to do with you?" Like Devon didn't know the answer before he asked.

She sniffed.

"Like I said to the president," Marlow interjected, "there was no need for such legislation before I meddled with spiritual affairs. It doesn't help that the people I put into the Process are..." He shot Lanelle a look. "Volatile."

"He's saying I cause trouble," Lanelle declared with a mouth full of food.

"Just a little trouble. Rule breaking trouble. *Law breaking trouble!*"

"You know what?" Lanelle wagged a finger in her employer's direction. "You would be drinking a lot by your third life too if you had to work for *you.*"

"It's a miracle you didn't accidentally kill somebody!"

May sat down without a word. Devon soon followed.

"That property was doomed to be torn down anyway." Lanelle asked Devon to pass a seasoning on the far side of the table, as if this were a normal conversation she often had with Marlow. "So what if I helped it along when I crashed my cruiser?"

"It's a miracle you didn't die."

"Okay, but like, that crash screwed up my knees for the rest of that life, so it was like a part of me died."

As the silence fell again, everyone gradually looked in Devon's direction.

"I actually drink a lot less now," he said. "You know, compared to then."

Lanelle guffawed. "No kidding. You were plastered when I boned you."

May dropped her fork and stared at Lanelle, who continued to shovel food into her mouth. Marlow shifted uncomfortably between his feet. Devon was the only one who remained nonplussed.

"You would know, since I can't, you know, remember traveling through time for twenty-four hours."

May poked at her food, although her mouth twitched too much for her to eat. "I really regret coming on this trip."

"How do you think I feel?" Devon asked.

"I don't know how you feel *now...*" Lanelle slammed her fork against her plate. "But you used to be a hot mess. And when I say 'hot' I mean you were..." She made an OK sign, a gesture she picked up from the Earth TV shows Evan binged when there wasn't much to do around Marlow's office. "The fact you could get it up even though you were so inebri —"

Marlow slammed both hands onto the table when he sat down. He didn't have to say anything for the meaning to reverberate across the table.

"So you get into a lot of trouble," Devon surmised.

"I've been an angel this life."

"Absolute doll," Marlow muttered.

Devon needed to change the topic before everyone resented him for existing a thousand years ago. "Do you think they're gonna give Danielle a pardon too?"

"They have to now." Marlow took a hearty bite of his dinner. "Since the president made a big show of finding an excuse to come see you in the flesh."

Wasn't that what Devon predicted? What *Marlow* so astutely observed a few moments ago? The pardon was more than ceremonial. Hell, if it were truly ceremonial, there would have been an actual ceremony to go with it. That? That was Madalae's way of demanding an audience without extending any formal invitations.

Like Commander Yara d'Alacron, President Madalae d'Errowyn did not do anything without mindful precision. That was the only way for determined women such as themselves to reach so high, so quickly, and so devoutly.

It wasn't their individual hungers that should have made everyone in that room uneasy, though.

It was the fact they got along so well... and shared many of the same self-serving ideals.

Twenty

W hat did one bring to a date at another woman's house? What said, *"Thanks for the hospitality and making me some food"* without insulting that woman's house or her cooking?

Because Danielle was not messing with wine. Not when she was on Miranda's doorstep. Friday evening, looking over her shoulder to ensure nobody stared at her a little too much. *She obviously knows waaaay more about wine than I do,* Danielle thought as she impatiently waited for someone to answer the door. The lights were on inside. She swore to God she smelled food cooking. So where the hell was her date? *Probably in her cellar selecting the wine to seduce me with tonight.* That was why Danielle didn't bother bringing a drink. She knew that whatever she plucked from the store on the corner of her block would be laughably cheap and tame compared to whatever Miranda packed. That woman was definitely a wino. Combined with sophisticated tastes and a fat bank account? Danielle braced herself for a glass of wine that was worth more than one month's rent in the Bay Area.

Then again, Danielle had a habit of psyching herself out, especially when it came to Miranda. *Time to buck up and be a damn adult.*

She had sucked in a deep breath the moment the door opened.

"Aww, you shouldn't have." Miranda gestured to the small container of roses in Danielle's hand. She had preferred the four-piece in a tasteful crate garnished with greens to the usual half-dozen bouquets some may have brought to a date like this. *Bouquets are so not me,* Danielle thought. *I wouldn't be caught dead carrying a bouquet of red roses in this part of town.* She might as well put a spotlight on herself and declare it the end of her sanity.

"Hope you're not allergic." Danielle stepped inside as soon as Miranda moved out of the way. The door closed and latched behind her. "Because it was either these or lilies. I went with the safer bet."

Miranda took the flowers. Since they were already in a small vase, Miranda only had to pluck her current table centerpiece and replace it with the roses. She stepped back to admire her interior design skills before turning back to Danielle.

"You look nice." Miranda shoved her hands into the deep pockets of her black cardigan. The dark turtleneck beneath allowed more of Danielle's attentions to travel to the soft brown hair let loose after a long day in an office with strict dress codes. The only thing more distracting than the nape of her neck was the tight pair of jeans clinging to her long legs. Danielle might as well slap herself if she kept up the ogling. "Special occasion?"

"You're kidding, right?"

"Why do you think I dressed up?"

"Yeah, I was meaning to comment on those jeans. They're very distracting."

Miranda stood in front of the stove, stirring noodles in one pot and checking the steaming vegetables in another. "I know my best physical assets. Ass is number one."

Danielle looked down at her own outfit. She hadn't questioned her jeans before, but now she wondered if she looked half as good as her date. What was her best physical asset, anyway? Ex-girlfriend Alicia had been all about the abs that came from military life, but those were hard to show off outside the summer months. *God help me, it's my breasts.* She should have worn a V-neck shirt instead of her graphite gray cowl-neck sweater.

Her subconscious helpfully reminded her that she probably wouldn't be wearing these clothes all night.

"We're about ten minutes away from dinner." Miranda shut off one of the burners and removed the vegetables. "You should start smelling that garlic bread soon. Just threw it in the oven before you knocked."

"Oh, God, the garlic bread."

"Is that a moan of anticipation, or humiliation?"

"Can it be both?" Danielle leaned against the island counter. "I say the dumbest shit on the phone." She referred to a short but pleasant phone conversation they shared when Danielle readied for bed. *I felt seventeen again.*

"If it's any consolation, I could hear the stupid grin on your face when I said all of that the other night."

Danielle stared at her feet. Every time she glanced down, never mind in the kitchen, she almost remembered that a piece of mail had fallen off her counter. Not that she would see it here in Miranda's house. But, perhaps, had she been back home, Danielle would have finally realized she had missed it.

Definitely not tonight.

"How are things at the office?"

Miranda barely glanced over her shoulder. "Really? That's the small talk you're going with? The thing that will make you remember what happened a week ago?"

"It honestly feels like at least a month now."

"Suppose you should get used to it. You're living a different life now."

Miranda bent over to pick a stray uncooked noodle off her floor. Danielle tilted her head, unabashed in the way she checked out the ass in front of her. "Yup. Definitely living a different life. I get to come into your house and ogle you while you cook for me."

Although her shoulders jerked back in surprise, Miranda didn't immediately get up. Her flirtations were more suited for coy gazes and diabolical smiles. "Not a bad consolation prize for losing everything you worked for over the past ten years."

Danielle finally looked away when her lover stood back up. "I haven't lost *everything...*"

"True. You still have your good looks and rugged charm."

"*Rugged?*"

"I really should have made you cut your hair more often. Since you never had any intention of growing it out long. You always kept it too shaggy."

Danielle helped herself to one of the chairs at the dining table, eyes locked on the roses she had so *nicely* brought over, not that someone like Miranda could appreciate them when she was busy running her mouth. "Shaggy? First I'm rugged, now I'm shaggy?" She sniffed the plate of pasta appearing before her. "You didn't put any Scooby Snacks in this, did you?"

"Guess you'll have to find out."

The fact you bring up my hair, Danielle thought while waiting for the rest of dinner to appear, *goes to show that what we have... had... is not appropriate.* Part of Miranda's job was enforcing the dress code in her corner of M-Town, and Danielle was paid no special favors when it came to the haircuts she received or wearing her favorite jewelry. *Great, now I have to figure out where to get my hair cut.* She no longer had access to the M-Town salon that cut and trimmed her hair for free. How much was a haircut these days? Could she still get them for ten dollars?

"You don't get your hair done at the buzzcut barber's, huh?" Danielle might as well ask before she was caught staring at the nape of Miranda's neck when she sat down.

"No." A bottle of wine—ah, yes, definitely out of Danielle's league, since she couldn't pronounce the brand—tipped into a glass. "I don't get it done at the salon either, before you ask. I go to a Japanese salon near Chinatown. I get someone who knows how to cut non-white hair, and they get someone who can tell them stories about celebrity sightings in Japanese gay bars. We both win."

She really is shameless about flaunting her sexuality... Because in the military, talking about going to Japanese gay bars was definitely "flaunting." How in the world had Miranda not been discharged yet? Who had she slept with to get some level of protection? Or, given her obvious affluence... who was she paying, and how much?

"Here I thought I was good knowing exactly who to ask for at the salon and booking two months out to make sure I got her." Not everyone was as lucky as Danielle. Some got the *other* lady, who spent more time chatting and less time paying attention to what her scissors did. For someone with short hair like Danielle's, it was imperative she get a stylist who both knew the dress code rules and had the precision of a sharpshooter. *Just because I was in the military doesn't mean I had to forego some semblance of style...* She had to keep the stereotypes of desk jockeys who never saw action alive. "I don't know what to do about my hair now. How do people find stylists in the civilian world? I mean, I was half-civilian from the beginning of my military career, but I never had to decide where to go to get my hair cut or what to wear to work. Guess there's something to be said for selling my soul to Uncle Sam..."

Miranda drank her wine before offering a toast. *Thank God,* Danielle thought. *This is already weird enough. Last thing I need is a toast to us or something.*

"We've got to figure out something else to talk about," Miranda said with a shake of her head. "New rule: we don't talk about the military while on a date."

"Excuse me? What else do we have in common?"

"We have lots of things in common."

"Name one thing." Danielle held her glass out for wine. She needed it now. "And the word 'Japan' better not be in there."

The words Miranda was about to say stuttered between her teeth. Because she had totally been about to say, *"We both have a Japanese grandmother!"*

"That's not fair. You know a woman wants to state the obvious."

"Maybe a *woman* should put a little more thought into it."

Miranda's brows crawled up her forehead. "You're lucky I know when you're being sarcastic."

"Am I being sarcastic, though?"

"Yes." The wineglass was on the table again. "You're doing your damnedest to not smile."

"Spend a lot of time staring at my lips, huh?"

"They are rather beguiling. Very natural pink. Not like mine." She took the first bite of her salad. "You know what else you've got that's pinker than mine?"

Danielle nearly snorted the wine in the back of her throat.

She was relieved to be reminded that they did have more in common than those superficial things. Once Miranda worked Danielle's grandmother into the conversation, they spent several minutes reminiscing about every time Regina hurried home from M-Town to pick up Danielle from after school strings practice. When asked what the hell she had been playing, Danielle reluctantly admitted she once fancied herself a guitar player, not that it ever went anywhere beyond the customary folk songs taught at school and the pop songs she looked up in songbooks and online. The most embarrassing thing she admitted that night was teaching herself Pearl Jam's "Jeremy" and thinking herself the most badass seventeen-year-old in Marin County.

"You truly are a nineties teen," Miranda muttered. "See, now I feel like some lecherous old woman cradle robbing you from your home, because I remember when that song came out and thinking I was way too old for it."

"To be fair, you struck me as someone who fancied themselves a sophisticated youth."

"You have no idea. I had all the hallmarks of a spoiled rich girl without the affluent home life to go with it. Had the designer bags and shoes, all filled with the kind of contraband that could get a girl kicked out of the country."

Danielle intentionally ignored the reference to Miranda's old habits. "Then you joined the military and had all of that knocked out of you?"

Miranda opened her hands, fingers encompassing the scope of her house. "What do you think? We're drinking vintage Sauvignon."

"Is that what this is?"

"More like that's how special the occasion is."

Danielle could have easily continued to banter with something like, *"You make it sound like it's our anniversary. Don't say the first week anniversary of when we did it."* She refrained, however. They were supposed to focus on their similarities, not what divided them as people first, lovers second.

"This is really good, by the way," she said instead. "I had no idea you cooked."

"I cook anything that gives me an excuse to feel like a sophisticated wretch at my own table. But thank you."

Danielle coiled the last of her pasta around her fork. She was about to bring it up to her mouth when a deathly chill overcame the room.

Her fork clattered to the plate, her hand frozen by her face.

"Are you all right?" Miranda leaned in toward her, but all that did was steal more breath from Danielle's depleting reserves. "You look like you've seen a ghost."

How could she not feel that? How could she not see *that* until she turned her head and immediately froze the moment she saw the creature looming outside her living room window?

A colossal Shadow stood outside, its dislocating mouth drooping toward Miranda's hedges. Its fluttering knuckles kissed the ground, the two beady yellow lights that were its eyes threatening to wink out if it did not soon feed. That's why it was there, yes? To feast upon Danielle's wretched soul, full of endless potential for eternal life?

Those troubled souls, displaced on their way to the Void, had lost the last of their strength. The only thing that could restore them and help them on their journey was a feast of untold proportions. A feast currently residing in Danielle, who had been dealing with these foul creatures for as long as she had lived.

It had been a while since she last saw one, though. How long until this blind monstrosity, with hulking shoulders and a rippling spine, finally gave up and left Danielle the hell alone?

"Do you see that thing?" she dared to speak, albeit in a whisper. Her hand slowly lowered to the table, but she did not raise her head. "Please tell me you see it. I don't want to feel like I'm crazy."

Miranda's shoulders sagged. "Yes. I know it's there. I know why it's here."

Her voice was indifference. Mild frustration. Far from the crippling fear that people like Danielle and her partner Devon felt when faced with a Shadow hunting down their Processed souls. *They feed on those in the Process... or so I'm told.* There were so few in the universe. Only two known people now that Devon had broken free and no longer held endless potential for continuous rebirth. *Me. That woman who works for Marlow.*

Only the hunted could see them.

"Do you *see* it?"

A hand covered Danielle's. "Yes."

"Aren't you afraid of it?"

"No."

Although her mind was nothing but fear and confusion, Danielle rationalized that must be because Miranda was not in the Process. Why did she have to be afraid when her soul was not endangered?

If only Danielle had applied that same logic to Miranda *seeing* the Shadow outside her window. This was a woman who had remembered that Shadows hunted Processed souls. The Void was kind enough to give such prey the "gift" of seeing the hunters. Otherwise, how would they know to protect themselves from the hunt?

Miranda lacking fear should coincide with blindness.

That soft hand squeezed Danielle's. "It won't hurt you."

Easy for her to say, wasn't it? Danielle was the one shaking, her eyes never leaving that *thing* staring right at her. If she made the wrong move, that was it. Her existence was over, and she was left to some of the worst cosmic torture imaginable. *Born again and again,* she reminded herself, *only to die right away.* That was the fate that awaited every poor soul trapped in the Process if they didn't break free before the end of the universe.

"It could attack me."

"It could," Miranda drolly confirmed. "But it won't."

"How do you know."

The truth? That lurked in Miranda's head, which remained pointed to the monster now crawling up her wall, sniffing, searching for its prey.

Because it fears me more than you fear it.

She couldn't say that, though. She couldn't say anything that required more explanation to keep Danielle placid. Did Miranda enjoy letting her lover stew in ignorance? Of course not. But what else could she do? It was imperative that she not shock Danielle into a forced regression that could kill her. *If that's the case,* Miranda thought, *I might as well throw her to the Shadow so those puny souls can at least live.*

Miranda would never forgive herself for that, of course.

"Stay here. Stay still." She stood from the table, dropping Danielle's hand. That was the only movement Danielle allowed herself. Two seconds later, she was as stiff as a board, the only sounds her breath and that little jerk of her chest belonging to her thumping heart.

Miranda slowly approached the living room window, where the Shadow clamored back down to her hedges and slammed its jaw against the glass. Invisible ice encased the room. Danielle wasn't the only one who felt that cold in her bones. So did Miranda, who pressed her hand against the window.

"Get out."

The words were not English. Nor were they Basic of any era. The discerning ear would place it as "slightly Julah-esque," but only because it shared the same root for "out, away, leave." She spoke the Ancient Song, her limited vocabulary supplemented by what she had picked up in the Void nearly ninety-eight times. With the soul of a *julah* and the body of the High Priestess, Miranda couldn't avoid picking things up here and there. Words implanted into her soul between lives. They appeared when she closed her eyes. The Song that reverberated through the Void now throbbed in her veins. The more she wished to protect the ones she loved, the easier it was to sing.

Besides, that was the only language a Shadow understood.

It stared at her, swallowing her aura of endless potential. Every Shadow was drawn to her for the same reasons they hunted Danielle—they sensed that everlasting energy that would more than sustain them on their wayward return to the Void. But unlike Danielle, who was nothing more than a feast to be consumed, Miranda was untouchable. She was as good as their God in their haphazard brains.

When God told you to get the hell out, you got out.

Danielle released her pent-up breath when that Shadow bounded away from the house. A few minutes later, it would collapse into a pile of cosmic dust, the souls that had once made up its form no more. A pang infiltrated Miranda's heart as she turned back toward Danielle. Not even the High Priestess knew what happened to souls that ceased to exist.

"It's gone," Miranda announced. She put on her best smile, not that anyone, including herself, believed in its power. Danielle continued to gape at her. Did she remember what happened after their first kiss a year ago? When Miranda triumphantly turned around and marched down a path lined with Shadows that refused to touch her?

Those were the memories one often questioned the veracity of, after all.

"I... thank you?" Danielle was still as pale as the moon when Miranda sat down and resumed eating. "How do you do that?"

"I don't fear them. They can't hurt me."

Finally, knowledge knocked into Danielle's head. "Wait, you can see them?"

"We've established that."

"But that means..."

Miranda had to think fast. What if finding out she was in the Process was enough to knock Danielle into a regressive spiral she could never escape? They already treaded dangerous waters with every intimate conversation they had. *The closer I get to my dreams coming true,* Miranda thought, *the closer I get to accidentally destroying her.*

"People in the Process aren't the only ones who can see Shadows." Technically, Miranda didn't lie. She just lied by omission. *I can't tell her I'm not in the Process,* she asserted to herself. *I won't outright lie to her, but I won't put myself in that situation to begin with.* "Surely, you know there are others."

Slowly, the scent of half-finished food enticed Danielle to get back to her life, not that she could easily shake the jitters. She had survived many Shadowy appearances, but that kind of familiarity only brought with it a strange trauma that was both nonplussed and life-altering. As the minutes wore by, she would forget that chill. Until next time.

"I know *julah* can see them. Well, the old man I need to ask for money can. But I thought that was because he was a priest or something." She glossed over the fact that Marlow never officially became a priest. His life of wandering and upending academic research across the Federation started the day he realized serving under Nerilis Dunsman was not his destiny. "I don't know of anyone else."

Miranda dithered between shoving food in her mouth and outright answering Danielle. "Yes. That's true." She took a bite of her own garlic bread. If only she could savor it, because it came perfectly out of the oven.

"So..." Danielle didn't realize her fork shook in her hand. These particular jitters were not only born from an encounter with a famished Shadow. "Then it's possible... that you..." Her fork landed in her lap and clattered to the floor. "That you're a *julah*..." The reason her voice tapered off wasn't because she was in awe. More like she sounded so stupid the moment she said it, embarrassment colored her cheeks.

They needed more wine. Miranda tipped the last of the bottle into her glass and topped off Danielle's.

"Oh my God." Danielle almost knocked over her filled glass, a kind thank you to the woman who had saved her nerves, only to rattle them again. *That explains so much!* Danielle didn't know how she never realized it before. What else explained Miranda's old soul? Shit, it explained where all her money came from. The poorest *julah* was still richer than the average Earthling. *That must also be why she had the Third Piece on her person. Seems like the kind of thing julah want to have around for collection's sake!* "How old are you?"

She couldn't believe that was her first question. Like Miranda would floor her with a figure between seven hundred and fifteen-fifty.

It accomplished one thing. It made Miranda double-take at the woman she intended to take to bed that night. "Thirty-five! You know that!" she cried.

"But you're a..."

"I'm half, is what I am. On my father's side." There. That should be enough information without frying Danielle's brain. All Miranda had to do was not mention her father happened to be Nerilis Dunsman, Impregnator of Human Women Across the Universe. "That makes me *ma-julah,* or so I'm told. Nothing terribly special. I don't get special powers. Just... a few other perks."

Danielle continued to stare at her as if she had announced she was President of the Intergalactic Federation. "You're half-*julah,*" she spurted.

"Yes. Hate to break it to you, but my mother really is an everyday woman on the other side of the world. Not my fault she fell in with a horny guy checking out Earth." When Danielle's exasperation didn't ebb, Miranda continued, "I'm not exactly registered in any family book. I'm sure my *julah* relatives have no idea I exist. I intend to keep it that way." Probably a good idea. The Ducah clan would tie her up in their *yaya* cellar and slowly starve her to death. "My mother doesn't even know what kind of man my father was. I only found out because I got sucked into this crazy bullshit of yours."

"I don't recall doing that!"

"I knew about it before you remembered, obviously. Why do you think you worked for me? Because your grandmother coincidentally set us up? Please. I should have been transferred long ago. Shit, the only reason I stayed in the military was because I had to keep an eye on you!"

Danielle gripped the edge of the table. "Under whose orders?"

Miranda looked her right in the eyes before averting her gaze again. "I'm not at liberty to say. I'm sorry. I didn't mean to bring this up at all."

"No, no..." Sighing, Danielle helped herself to a large gulp of wine. So much for savoring it. "People keep things from me all the time. For my own good, or something."

"People don't want you getting hurt. I know it seems like you're being coddled, but..."

"I *am* being coddled. Because for some stupid reason I can't remember who the hell I am. This is the worst kind of amnesia. I'd rather be a coma patient who wakes up unable to piece together what led her to that hospital. At least I'm not at risk for perpetual death if someone walks up to me and tells me everything that happened to traumatize me so badly."

"I can only imagine how frustrating that is." Dare Miranda brave it? Was now the time to reach over and take Danielle's hand on top of the table? *Just do it, dumbass.* Yet Miranda had to contain her anxiety as she entwined her fingers with Danielle's, as if they were on the verge of breaking up before their relationship really began. "If I need to say it again, I will—I'm not your enemy, Danielle. I've been on your side since the beginning. Since before you knew what was going on in your crazy life."

"My life wasn't crazy until a year ago." Danielle squeezed Miranda's hand before withdrawing her own from the table. "Sorry. Those things freak me out. Finding out you're... well, I think I heard rumors about that before, but I never know what to believe anymore. I'd ask what family you're affiliated with, but..."

"I'm not sure myself."

"...But that's probably prying too much. Sorry. It's just I know more about your own family now than I ever knew about mine from long ago."

I know as much as you did, my love. Miranda wished she could tell her, but she didn't risk it. She didn't tell Danielle that her father was a regionally renowned artist and her mother was his greatest muse. There were paintings of her that still existed, and not only because she was the mother of the fabled Sulim di'Graelic. *I know that they died before I met you. Died when their space cruiser malfunctioned upon entering your planet's atmosphere.* At least that kind of death was quick.

At least it meant Sulim was sent to live with her aunt, on a farm that Cairn and her compatriots raided during one of their missions.

We probably would have never met if your parents didn't die...

Cairn sure as hell wouldn't have taken Sulim onto her ship, for the rest to become history.

"I know it's a lot to ask of you after all you've been through," Miranda said, "but you can trust me. I'm not, like, seducing you to kill you."

"You saying that only makes me think you are."

"At least I'm like a black widow, huh? I'll make sure you have a good time before I do you in."

A childish grin tickled Danielle's mouth. "Understatement."

"Come on." Thank God, they were back to smiling again. "Forget that awful thing. We have two rules at this table. We don't talk about the military, and we don't talk about things that could trigger you into hell."

"I don't always know what that might be."

"One more reason to keep me around."

"Why? Because you know everything about me?"

Shoulders slumped, Miranda leaned over and pressed her lips against Danielle's ear. She was not pushed away. "I know enough, but that's neither here nor there." She was not pleased with herself for jumping to seduction in a time like this, but Miranda didn't know what else to do. So she curled her hand around Danielle's thigh, reminding her that this was a date, not an inquisition. "If you could change the subject to anything else, what would it be?"

Although Danielle wrapped her hand around the one on her thigh, she did not let either linger. With the politeness of a royal duchess brushing off an earl she did not care to court, Danielle removed Miranda's hand. "I wanna know how many languages you speak."

"Hm?"

"You heard me. How many?"

"How many am I *fluent* in?"

"Sure, since apparently there are that many for you to make the distinction. How impossibly smart are you?"

"I didn't realize that correlation also led to causation."

"For God's sake, Miranda, you talk like *that*."

Any excuse to laugh, they both supposed. Good. Laughter truly was the strongest medicine, after penicillin and two rounds of *yaya* at the local *julah* watering hole. Some healers swore by it, anyway. The cheekier ones prescribed it to humans when anesthetic was not on hand.

"Four," Miranda finally said.

"*Four?* Jesus Christ. Here I am stumbling with English. What the hell do you speak?"

"English, obviously. Japanese. Those are my two most fluent languages. At least, I can debate philosophy in both. Now, are my arguments any good? That's debatable."

"What are the other two? Polish? Basque? Swahili?"

"Very funny. I don't exactly have a cultural background in either, so I don't know what you're getting at."

Danielle snorted. "So what are the other two?"

"I speak a good amount of Basic." Miranda didn't mention she lumped Old Basic into that. In fact, her Old Basic was as fluent as English, and her Modern Basic was less than her Japanese skills. *The only reason I know that much Modern Basic is because I have to.* "I also understand enough Julah to get by, if I had to. I'm not planning on taking a trip to the home planet anytime soon, though." She wanted to make a joke about burning alive the moment she set foot on the planet, but refrained.

"Like I said," Danielle continued, "I'm lucky I can speak English on a good day."

"You've got Old Basic locked up in your head, at least."

"So I'm told."

"I've heard you speak it."

Danielle kept her eyes on her empty plate, even while drinking the last of her wine. "Do I have an accent?" she whispered.

"Huh?"

"You said you heard me speak it. So do I have an accent? How many accents does Basic got, anyway?"

Miranda couldn't help it. Once her laughter started, it kept coming.

She cleared away the dishes, one eye always on the windows overlooking the street. While there were no signs of more Shadows, Miranda wasn't taking chances. She made a note to herself to ask her illustrious father about ways to protect her house from future visits. If she intended to keep Danielle around...

She turned from the sink, now filled with half-washed dishes, and found Danielle on the living room couch. Her eyes weren't on anything in particular. The whole weight of their intimate world was on her shoulders, and it stopped Miranda's heart in her chest.

When she finished drying off her hands, she approached the couch and hung over Danielle's shoulder.

"Would turning on the TV help distract you?"

"I was admiring it. Big, but not audacious."

"I don't watch enough TV to warrant a bigger one. Besides, these houses are so close together my neighbors would hear it if I lingered on a football game for too long."

"Go Forty-Niners, I guess."

Miranda picked up the remote. She had last left the TV on the news, and it didn't bear good headlines now. The perfect pick-me-up after a dinner like theirs.

"Here. Pick us something good." Miranda handed her date the remote. "I'll be back."

Although Danielle knew Miranda was off to the bathroom, she didn't think anything of it. She was too engrossed in flipping channels, diverting her attentions from what had happened that night, that week, that whole past year. She continued to reel from Miranda's admission that she was half-*julah*. How was such a world possible? For over five years, Danielle had served beneath a *ma-julah,* as if it were nothing. How many people knew? How many people guessed that the reason Miranda was still in her post was because of Danielle? Did this now mean Miranda's job was in danger for other reasons? Did she care if she lost her job? Clearly, she had other things to fall back on.

Did she mean what she said about watching over Danielle? Or was this one big trap?

To what end?

When Miranda returned, she found Danielle on the far end of the couch, the TV left on old sitcom reruns. The kind of thing Danielle normally loved when she needed to escape the terrors of the world. The only thing that had soothed her when she was a child of the '80s, wishing away the voices in her head and the nightmares that haunted her nearly every night.

Did Miranda know anything about *that?*

She did, not that Danielle could know yet. She wasn't yet privy to the nightmares that had clawed out Miranda's eyes on evenings she couldn't close them. Nor could she know about the regressions that had sent her into frenzies her own mother decried demonic. Nobody had been there for her when she regressed, strapped down to a bed in a grungy apartment in one of Tokyo's cheapest neighborhoods. No one but the second most wanted criminal, who was only there because Nerilis Dunsman offered her protection.

"I remember this show." Miranda didn't know what else to talk about when she sat on the couch, careful to not encroach upon Danielle's space. "I had a friend who was obsessed with it."

Danielle's hands mangled one another in her lap. "Could you..." she began, swallowing what pride she had left around Miranda. "I don't want to watch TV. It's background noise."

"I see."

"Could you kiss me already? I want to go straight to that."

Although the words were welcomed, her anxious tone did nothing to ensnare Miranda's cooperation. "When you put it that way..."

"I'm sorry. I know. I sound crazy. You don't get it, though..." Danielle pressed her fingers against her temples. "When you kiss me, I feel good. Not just sexually good. Just... *good.* I don't worry about anything. Nothing bothers me. All I care about is kissing you back and all that other stuff that comes with it."

Miranda bit back a sarcastic reply. Sarcasm had little place in what Danielle so desperately needed now. *One day,* Miranda reassured herself. *When she remembers, I can be as sarcastic as I want and not drive her away.* She used to think that was a pipe dream.

"It must take a lot of trust for you to tell me that."

"Trust?" Danielle shook her head. "I guess. Really, all I'm doing is following my instincts. I don't know what else to do right now. You'd think my number one goal would be to simply stay alive long enough to regress, but that's stressful. I don't want to think about staying alive. I want to think about *living.*"

Miranda averted her gaze to her own feet. Her black flats were perfect for looking semi-fashionable—yet comfortable—in her own home, but now she wished she could see the toes she had taken in for a pedicure two days ago. Danielle talked about focusing on living? It was those little things, like getting her nails done, that kept Miranda from descending into her own head and everything her blemished soul had been through.

No wonder she was so sarcastic.

"So what you're saying is... sex makes you feel like you're living in the moment instead of focusing on staying alive?"

"Sure. Guess you could say that."

The flush in Danielle's cheeks almost made Miranda regret saying it like that. "Out of many things, of course."

A hand slammed against the back of Miranda's couch. She sat up with a start—and did not anticipate the face now hovering so close to her own. Determination was a good color for Danielle. Far better than the tinge of embarrassment she occasionally suffered.

"You're driving me nuts, you know that?" Danielle said.

Oh, was that an invitation? Formally signed and stamped from the woman who had been courting seduction far longer than she had been alive on Earth? What a fine turn of events.

"I can't be any worse than you," Miranda countered. "Do you know how long you've been driving *me* nuts?"

"Not as long as you deserve."

Miranda leaned in close enough to feel Danielle's breath on her lips. "If this is your way of getting back at me, then you're doing a fine job."

"You don't know the..."

Danielle was cut off by the kiss she had demanded only a few minutes before. After a single second of hesitant surprise, she sank against the weight of the woman she had slowly been driving insane for almost a millennium.

You know why I'm so determined to make it work this time? Miranda sent that into the ether as she wrapped her arms around Danielle and pulled her down onto the couch. *Because we were destined to come here one day.*

A thousand years ago, Earth had hardly been on the Federation's radar. The human colonies established thousands of years ago had been left to fend for themselves after the current incarnation of the Intergalactic Federation finally took hold in the wake of devastating wars. By the time technology finally started catching up on Earth again, it was deemed too far away for most gubernatorial interests. It had become a destination planet in a sense. A social experiment, since nobody descended from those initial colonists knew who they were anymore. Earth was an isolated microcosm of greater human activity in the universe. No wonder it was where people retired when they never wanted to be bothered again. No wonder it was a haven for criminals who would rather be free on a backwater planet than do time in a high-tech prison full of amenities.

"It won't be so bad," a woman had said a thousand years before, in a futile attempt to convince her lover to flee with her to Earth. *"We can hide some of our tech. It's what lots of people do. If they say we're witches, we'll find somewhere else to live. But I think you'll like Italia. Everyone I know who's been through there says it's going great places. So much culture. They've worked out the civil kinks recently. We could be at peace there and still find some stimulation..."*

So what if they never made it to Italy? Venice and Rome weren't the point. The mission was to get off their sinkhole of a planet and escape to a new life where they would finally be free.

The thought of being free *now?* While here? On Earth? That was fate, wasn't it?

Sometimes all it took was one kiss to convey that level of belief.

Twenty-One

The atmosphere was exactly as Devon remembered it. The blue skies were occasionally covered in a sheen of red-gold as the sun took a long descent over the horizon. The sweet scent of a gas called *regisphellium* in Earth-based Basic. Hardly harmful to the human inhabitants, but with enough nitrous oxide to make people giddy on a cloudy day. SADD did not really exist on Arrah. This was a planet people with depression came to if they could afford it.

The economy had been up and down since Sonall's life, after all. Currently, it was experiencing a new upturn, thanks to improvements in the Federation's economy. While the towns and small cities on the tiny planet remained, new resorts had popped up in between them, boasting "the greatest lifestyle this side of the Federation." Only a few wild horses remained from Sonall's time. Most of them had either been domesticated or hunted by poachers. The Gardiah horses, which were once some of the most valued in the universe, had been no more for several hundred years. The closest available was a ranch on the other side of the planet from the Gardiah Estate, but those were poor imitations. Perfectly acceptable in the world of riding and rearing, but hardly prize-winning.

The forests were still there, though. Some had grown back now that the horses were mostly gone. The rolling hills of yellow-green were often speckled with dark forest evergreen, with the white and sandy-beach-yellow buildings favored by Arrahites poking through like little beacons of civility. The resorts catered to the middle-class and uppercrusts with plenty of swimming holes, sunbathing spots, and nature therapies, but it was the working ranches and homesteads that illuminated the landscape during sunny days.

Devon stepped out of the space cruiser a few minutes after noon, Lanelle right behind him with her bag strapped to her back. "Ah, darn," she lamented after a hearty sniff. "No *regisphillium* upticks today. Blasted clear skies. I wanted to get a little high."

Devon inhaled a deep breath, the familiar air tickling the lungs not at all used to Arrah's distinctions. After a small fit of coughing, he adjusted, but missed the sweet scent he had anticipated.

"Sorry about the bumpy ride, folks!" Their driver, a middle-aged man with a bald spot and a local accent, stepped out of the cockpit and motioned for his passengers to head down the offramp. The one member of his crew, who also happened to be his oldest son, offered to carry Devon's duffel bag. The only reason Devon let him was because he was too distracted by the memories overcoming him. *This place looks nothing like my old estate,* he thought, brushing something away from his eyes, *but it's definitely the same land, I suppose.* "That first blast off the moon is always the roughest! Now!" He turned to Marlow, who shuffled into the sunlight, the grip on his cane rubbing his skin raw. "Am I taking anybody back up to the moon after your visit? Or is this where we part ways?"

With gritted teeth, Marlow said, "I will be taking care of myself, thank you very much, kind *sir.*" Those same teeth still rattled from the blastoff they suffered twenty-five minutes ago. Arrah's pristine conditions and small geographical size had recently led the government to requesting *all* immigration be conducted through the only moon, which was nothing more than a glorified rock that barely housed enough room for a hotel, a supply shop, and a fleet of independently operated cruisers that ferried the proper visa-holders between the moon and the planet. That meant after Devon put in the overnight paperwork to visit his descendants and his ancient homeland, Marlow was in a pickle. If he simply poofed everyone onto Gardiah Estate, he could have their future visas revoked from the Arrahn government. They were one of the few governing institutions in the universe that couldn't give two shits or a horse's tail about *julah* privileges.

Like Marlow would stick around for another jagged ride to the moon, though. Once he left Devon and Lanelle behind, he was teleporting back to Terra III, and nobody would damn well stop him. Since when did *julah* need visas anyway?

"You sure this is the right place?" Lanelle asked, looking at a map on her tablet. "We're supposed to go to Gardiah Estate. You know the place, right?"

"Of course! This is it! The entrance of the estate."

Devon knew things would be different—after all, his old home had been razed, and the new ones built in different locations every time—but he still expected... more. An archway. A widened road. Hedges. *A sign!* All he saw was an old dirt road winding from the local highway that linked the county seat to the resort town by the shore. An old fashioned mail receptacle sat at the end of the driveway, but a note on the side asked deliverymen to carry all packages and letters with handwriting on their seals to the main house. There was no security. Not even a dilapidated old shed to keep the rain off a weary traveler's head.

During Sonall's time, this land had been tended to by the finest landscapers on Arrah. The Gardiahs had enough to their name—and plenty of horse stock—to warrant around the clock security at every official entry point and around the fenced perimeter. Mail was delivered into an electronic receptacle that transported letters and packages through underground tubes to the main house. The only reason Devon didn't turn around and demand to be taken to "the real estate" was because he recognized the peaks of the neighboring hills, including the rocky outcrop upon which he used to sit as a boy avoiding his chores.

This was it. This was where he had first been born. This was where the real Sonall Gardiah had died before leaving Arrah forever.

Until now.

"Hey!" A voice echoed from around the bend. Soon, the familiar face of Fanar Gardiah appeared. His long tanned legs pedaled an old two-sided tuk-tuk without a proper covering. The seats were empty, aside from a jug of water and a pair of worn riding gloves the driver of said vehicle did not care to use. "Over here! Sorry I'm late! Or is it you who is a little early?" His laughter bounced between the trees.

"Oh, great!" Lanelle cried. "We get the real rustic experience!" She latched onto Devon's arm, her nails clawing into the biceps trapped beneath shirt and hoody. "Please tell me your family has running water. I've heard horror stories about these planets. Some real 1800s Earth shit."

Devon shrugged her off. "I have no idea. It's been over a thousand years since I was last on this planet. They say they had to rebuild a couple of times."

"Great. Great, great, great." Lanelle grounded herself with a deep breath. She pulled back her dark hair into a ponytail, but had nothing to clasp it into place. When she released her hair again, it was with a serene smile that would have unnerved Devon on any other day. "No running water would be hell for my dermatitis. Just saying."

Fanar caught up to them with another wave. Squeaking axles brought the bike and its attachment to a stop. "Welcome to our little slice of paradise! Too bad the pressure is good today huh?" His laugh was louder than the anticipation ringing in Devon's ear. "We had a great nitrous party last week!"

Lanelle rounded on Devon, who slung his duffel bag over his shoulder and walked toward Fanar. "This explains a lot about you. Getting high every other day, that is."

"Explains being up for a good time." Devon tossed his bag into one of the seats. Stepping up made Fanar's mode of transportation creak badly enough that Devon had a moment's hesitation. "But I was an alcoholic. Different kind of high."

When Devon said that in Basic, Fanar looked up from his communicator and slipped his foot off the pedal. His uncomfortable laugh rippled through the clearing. Devon ignored it. He may have been technically related to Fanar by someone's reckoning, but he was so many generations removed from what Sonall went through that making him restless was far from Devon's concerns.

One by one he was joined by Marlow and Lanelle. She sat on the back of the contraption, hat pulled down her face as the Arrahn sun filtered through the tress. Marlow placed his cane across his lap and mused that he should have brought Charlie instead of leaving him in Evan's care again. Devon wished the dog had come along too. Having at least one creature around that gave no shit about the state of his soul was a freedom from burden.

Fanar had to pedal harder now that an extra five hundred pounds weighed down his vehicle. Yet he didn't complain. The sun was warm, the air fresh, and the breeze gently blowing on what was an early summer's day. After announcing that it was about a five-minute ride up to the main house, he whistled a tune considered an old Arrahn classic. A song that had barely been in the public consciousness when Sonall was alive.

Devon leaned against the partition separating him from Marlow. Trees, bushes, and flowers slowly passed them. Most of those trees had been around when he was barely a whelp who had no care for every blade of grass on his family's property. Why would he? The last time Devon was here, he was sixteen and more concerned with staying in his father's good graces and catching the attention of girls whenever he and his sister went into the nearest town to have lessons at the community schoolhouse. Their tutors couldn't cover every subject.

"Is Saranjo still around?" Devon asked his descendent. "It used to be the closest town."

"Saranjo? You mean Saran's Town? There's a town called that about five miles out, but it's far from the biggest thing around. You're thinking of Piyat. That's where everyone around here goes to school. Graduated myself about a year back."

Devon assumed that higher education was not as much a thing. Nor had it been when he lived on Arrah, a whole thousand years ago. For a man who had recently graduated university on Earth, it still felt like a faraway dream.

Kinda like the building that soon came into view.

It was far from the only building, though. Barns, stables, vehicle ports, and sheds dotted the acreage beyond the driveway, but it was the main house that captured his attention. *Can you really call it a house?* he wondered, tracing the seams of where one generation built this and another built that. The hodge-podge of a humble manor didn't have much room for sprawl. Not when there was farming equipment to store and horses to stable. Instead, the house built upward, a fine array of balconies and bright, circular windows harkening to what the locals called "Ferintian style," so named after the famous Arrahite architect who had lived three hundred years before. While he personally had nothing to do with the Gardiah Estate, one of Fanar's ancestors—and, apparently, Sonall's descendants—had been a *huge* fan.

This is stranger than I anticipated. The air was the same. The sky looked exactly like how he remembered. The call of local birds and the sprawl of green trees with pink flowers littered his memories like the scent of fowl roasting and the sounds of his sister's laughter. The big gray house with airy chambers, floor-to-ceiling windows, and columns reflecting the Federation opulence of the time may have been gone, but the ghosts of the Gardiahs certainly haunted the fields. The blood may not have been spilled in this spot, but it fertilized the same earth.

A large woman in a cream-colored cowl waited for them on the stoop separating the house from the dirt. She leaped up as soon as Fanar lifted his hand in greeting. A communicator almost dropped to the ground. The only thing flashing on the screen was Fanar's name written in the local Basic script.

"Welcome!" she greeted with the cheeriest tone she could muster. Too bad for her she had smoked a little too much in her day and the gravely chords were what hit her guest's sensitive ears. "Oh, it's so exciting for you all to be here! Fanar has told me so much about you, Mister... ah..."

Devon had been the first to hop off Fanar's tut-tut, his duffel bag in his hand and his eyes on the grove of green and pink trees in the distance. If he squinted hard enough, he could see the rocky outcrop he once used as his hideout when he wanted to avoid his father's criticisms. "Thanks for having us. I know this was a real last-minute request, but I promise to not bother you too much. It will only be a couple of days. You do much to honor me."

The woman, who fanned the disbelief off her face, gestured for her honored guests to come forward. "I'm Sonjah Gardiah. Fanar's mother, although most people ask if I'm his older sister." That was a lie and a half, but Arrahite culture *did* stipulate that one should always overly-flatter the female head of a household. They were the ones who had the final say in all matters of marriage. "His little sister is around here somewhere. Afraid it's the three of us right now outside of the hired hands. My husband and some of the other family are doing business off-planet. Boy, will they be sore to know they missed your visit!"

Marlow stepped between Devon and Sonjah. Although he was far from breaking height records among his people, and his permanent injuries over the years meant he walked with a cane, he still towered over Sonjah. "I also apologize for such a hasty arrival," he said with much better Basic than Devon's. "Hello. Master Ramaron Marlow of House Marlow."

Sonjah's eyes widened as she stood up straight and accepted Marlow's tip of the hat as a formal greeting. They did not shake hands or bow to one another, although it wouldn't have been strange for them to do either. Yet Marlow was correct to hold off on any physical interaction with Sonjah Gardiah. She would have combusted.

"Wow. A real *julah* on our property! I don't think this has ever happened before. Fanar!" Her voice jolted across Marlow's shoulder and smacked her son right in the head. "Heat up some of the *cageh* I've got down in the cellar! Use the cast iron!"

Cast iron. When Marlow would be the first to tell her that the relatively affordable *julah*-made Flat Metal, as it was colloquially called in Basic, made much better *cageh* than the cast iron still found on rural planets.

Still, hospitality was hospitality.

"I'm afraid I cannot stay much longer, Lady Gardiah. I am needed back on Terra III as soon as I've assured Devon and my assistant Lanelle are situated here. I will return in two days to pick them up, of course."

Lanelle popped an antacid tablet into her mouth. "I'm gonna need more of these," she muttered.

Devon nudged Marlow out of the way. "Thank you again for hosting us, Lady Gardiah."

"Lady! You two keep calling me titles we ain't got for hundreds of years, and I might start believing you! Now, come here! I want to see how much we resemble you! Bet you can't guess that I'm the blood-kin here! My husband married into the family and took my name."

Devon forced a smile as the woman, who was technically his great-great-great-granddaughter—or was it grand-niece, perhaps?—took him by the cheeks and stared into his pale blue eyes.

"Ah, *fiddgits,*" she benevolently cursed. "Ain't nobody in the family got eyes like those anymore. We had a red-eyed boy I called my uncle, but they said he was albino or something. But I see my son in your nose! That's about as proud of a tradition we keep up around here."

Sonjah was kind to say such a thing, since in reality, Devon did not look much like the current crop of Gardiahs homesteading on Arrah. Even when one accounted for the divergence in genetics afforded him in his current life, what was brought over from the Process stopped at dark hair and a penchant for a farmer's tan. The male and female relatives he beheld now were lankier in build and boasted curlier hair. Rounder faces. A receding hairline on young Fanar's part. *I'm supposed to be looking into a mirror,* Devon thought, *yet I barely recognize these people.* Sure, a thousand years and countless generations had passed... Void only knew what brand-new genetics were introduced into the clan over the past millennium, and their supposed female progenitor certainly looked nothing like Sonall... but he expected something. Anything to remind him of Sonall's parents or, God forbid, his sister.

"Your hospitality is greatly appreciated." Devon caught the look on Marlow's face begging to leave. "I think we've got it from here," he said to his mentor. Did Marlow want out of there because of his involvement in this family's fall? While he had nothing to do with the assassination, it was because of Ramaron Marlow that Sonall was never able to return to Arrah and reclaim his birthright in any way. Because, deep down in the most Pollyanna depths of his subconscious, Devon wanted to believe he would have cleaned himself up and taken some of the stolen horses back to Arrah to start over again. It would've been much easier when the rightful heir showed up to contest the man who had illegally hired assassins so he could grab his neighbor's prize.

"You know how to contact me, should the need arise." Marlow turned around and headed back toward Fanar's vehicle, not that he intended to use it. "And if you don't, Lanelle knows how."

"Well!" Devon wasn't given a moment to watch Marlow take off into the ether. Sonjah was too busy hustling him into the cramped entryway of her family's estate. "Who is this lovely young lady, huh? The future new Lady Gardiah?" Although she meant the title as a joke, nobody would be surprised if *someone,* be they government or *julah,* paid Devon reparations by throwing his old lands back at him and hoping he would be complacent for the rest of his final life. "I'm sorry, I didn't catch your name, dear."

Lanelle choked up her antacid tablet and grabbed her bag. "Yeah, right! Although..." she switched to English which, thankfully, nobody but Devon understood. "I did bang your great-great-granddaddy."

Devon had never been so grateful that Lanelle knew when to code switch. "Try to behave, huh?" he said, making way for her to follow him into the house. "These are probably nice people who are very generously letting us stay here."

"Only because you busted a nut a thousand years ago."

"You know about my busted nuts, huh?"

"I know of at least two." Lanelle left her bag in the entryway. After checking for a signal on her communicator, she said, "Personally, that is."

"I *know.*" The greatest irony was that Devon had absolutely no recollection of it. Not because Sonall had been taken advantage of during his impromptu trip to "the present," but because the spell that brought him forward through time wiped his memory when he returned. Great for him. Not so great for Devon, who now lived with the fact that he had bent the laws of time and physics to have sex with Lanelle in another life. *Do I call it a thousand years ago?* He mused, navigating the stacks of old books lining the front hallway, *or a few months ago?*

If there was one thing he *did* know, it was that he and Lanelle would never be a thing. Not only was she wholly disinterested in Devon, he couldn't say the attraction toward her would be mutual.

He didn't know what he wanted, really.

He certainly didn't know what he hoped to find here in this house he did not recognize.

The smell was much different from his old house, too. The tighter corridors and smaller windows in every room meant a lack of proper ventilation. Musty scents and sensations followed him around every corner he turned. Floorboards creaked. Dust swirled in the air, and not for a lack of attention on anyone's behalf. The first thing any Arrahite farmer would tell someone was that it was nearly impossible to keep the dirt off the windowsill and deep in the floorboards.

As Sonjah insisted on Devon and Lanelle sitting down to *cageh* in the modest dining room, he glanced out one of the framed windows and beheld the rolling green hills and slight yellow hue to the air that occurred around this time of day. Although they offered familiarity, it only served to remind Devon of one crucial thing.

The phrase *"You can never go home again"* was more real than the memories he couldn't touch.

The rattling of plates and cups was the same in every café throughout the universe. A romp at Starbucks, therefore, was similar to a visit to Moonlight's, the Federation's answer to cheap, ubiquitous caffeine chains.

May sat in one of millions around the Federation. Specifically, she was in store #345, which had been operating since it opened as the first wave of expansions three hundred years ago. What set Moonlight's apart from its predecessors and saw it turn into the third biggest corporation in the known universe was simple: coffee. While some claimed Earth's greatest export to be either its "maddeningly hilarious entertainment" or the fresh water harvested from the Arctic, it was actually coffee. While Earth hadn't seen any money from humanity's collective love for the bean in at least a hundred years, thanks to the crop now taking up entire moons and planets to keep Moonlight's in business, everyone still attributed it to

Latin flavors that took up the Federation by storm faster than Ricky Martin in 1999.

There was something to be said about the Federation's approach to coffee, of course. For one, technology and plenty of people with time to burn meant the Art of Coffee had reached unprecedented heights. May had to admit that Moonlight's beat out her local favorite coffee shop back home any day of the week. What she *hated* to admit, however, was that her favorite thing to get when visiting Terra III was a Bosconian Roast with two shots of Vallaharian *cageh*. Humans couldn't give two shits about the Vallahars' recent falling from grace, so Moonlight's continued to advertise it as "the premier blend from Yahzen, home of *cageh*." Not like Moonlight's was big on the *julah* planet, anyway.

"You're not eating your biscuits," Rea, the illustrious mother of May, said. "Aren't they your favorites? Oh, I know. It's because I got you a year's supply for Christmas last year. Did I ever tell you that they looked at me the *strangest* way when I handed them the bag I wanted them to wrap it up in? It was the bag with the dancing Santas. You know, lots of people here know the image of Santa and sometimes he pops up during the winter for kitschy parties, but they still know diddly squat about Earth. I think they thought I was taking your coffee and biscuits to some party!"

The only delightful thing about this conversation was that it was completely in English, since Rea spoke it fluently and May was a native speaker. They occasionally garnered strange looks from the tourists and office workers who only heard English on broadcasts and thought it a novelty language before something to seriously study.

"I'm not really hungry," May said. "I had a pretty big breakfast at Master Marlow's."

"Really? With whom? Don't tell me it was with Mr. Evan. He thinks a real Earth-based breakfast is five links of sausages and a stack of twenty pancakes. He probably puts mustard on them both for good measure."

"No, it was mostly a Terra III breakfast."

That should have pleased Rea, who was always on her daughter about eating healthier than was normal on Earth. Rea was barely old enough to remember the switch between fresh foods and highly processed shit that now littered the American shelves. *"It was supposed to be the one good thing about living on Earth,"* she once told a colleague. *"Now it's almost no better than the processed shit we get on Terra III. Only with even fewer regulations!"*

"Then what in the world is getting you down? Don't tell me you miss Earth already. You've barely been here a week. Oh, I know. You're having sugar withdrawals..." Rea shoved the small plate of biscuits across the table. "You *really* should have a bite or two. Perk you right up."

"It's been a stressful trip," May explained. "I knew it wouldn't be a walk in the park, but since I'm not, you know, famous, I thought I'd at least be spared *some* of the stress."

"What did you expect? Nobody gets off the hook when they play sidekick to a celebrity in any part of the universe. I still can't believe you agreed to participate."

"Like I said, I didn't expect it to be so stressful."

"Stress is one thing, hon. Are you sure another part of your problem isn't how you're handling things with Devon?"

"How *I'm* handling things? Not sure I want to know what you mean by that."

"Before you twist your hair around your neck," Rea said, "I'm *not* implying you have a romantic fascination with the man. I know you too well to think that. Besides, you have much better tastes."

"Mom..."

"I'm guessing, though, you're seeing the 'real' him behind the mask he presents to the world. I've seen the interviews. I've had his ass on my couch. The more the weeks go by, the more he blends into who he used to be. The young man you met a few months ago isn't the same one you know now. Trust your mother when she says this. She's got a degree in reincarnation psychology."

"That's not a thing," May spat.

"The hell it isn't. Who do you think pioneered it? The *julah?* Please. They'd rather pretend that their actions never have any lasting consequences on us mere mortals."

May nibbled her sugary biscuit. It went with her Moonlight's take on coffee better than anything she ever had in America, but that wasn't why she had a few tears in her eyes. That was born from frustration, and lest her mother assumed it was because of *Devon Anderson,* of all people, May said, "I can't tell you some of what's going on here. I'm not sure I could tell you even in private. It has to do with..." she lowered her voice. "The government."

Her mother sat up straight, arms crossed on the table and ears listening for eavesdroppers. "Strange bedfellows, huh?"

"Oh, you could *say* that." May sighed. "I can't wait to go home. Two more days. If it didn't put people out so much, I might ask to go back early. I miss my apartment and Earthling technology. It's so much quieter. Can't feel it go through you like I can right now." That was one thing May always claimed to hate about visiting the Federation. *"I can feel the waves, Mom!"* She had said that when she was ten, and she said it now at twenty-three. Her sensitivity to all things that led to overstimulation practically smacked her as soon as she was off Earth. She could handle her large American city. Any outpost in the Federation? She might as well court a panic attack for fun.

"I know you don't care much for your mother's home planet," Rea said, "but she always appreciates it when you come for a visit."

"Like she always appreciates talking in third person like she's crazy?"

Before Rea had the chance to defend herself, two men in plain clothes entered the café, although the looks in their eyes were easy enough for any discerning person who wasn't on the brink of falling asleep to interpret. They may not wear a uniform, and they may not brandish their holographic badges, but two of Yara d'Alacron's most loyal officers couldn't hide their affiliation.

The fact that they bypassed the line for coffee and directly approached May and Rea's table only solidified that message.

"Rea d'Eran?" the shorter man, with a bald spot and half a grown-in mustache, asked.

She did a double-take, fingers prancing around her throat. "Excuse me? That will be *Dr.* d'Eran to you, young man."

"We need you to come with us, *doctor.*"

"What is the meaning of this?" Rea asked.

"Official business, ma'am."

"Am I in trouble?"

The stoic face both men gave them implied she might be if she continued this uncooperative attitude. May nudged her mother's foot beneath the table, as if to say, *"You know to never ask Federation Forces those kinds of questions, right? Exercise common sense, Mother!"*

"What is this about?" Rea asked again.

"Come with us, ma'am. Your assistance is requested."

"In an official capacity?"

Both men jerked their heads toward the door. It gave Rea the perfect opportunity to see the firearms strapped to their hips. It wouldn't be the first time a government goon threatened a civilian in recent days...

"My daughter stays here." Rea stood, bag strapped to her shoulders. "May," she continued, in English, "Stay put here. I'll be back. Just... stay in public, honey."

"Mom..."

"Do as I say." Rea never snapped at her daughter like that. By all accounts, May was a spoiled child who had both never wanted for anything and never understood the reach of her parents' money and influence. She didn't ask questions when her mother used that tone with her, though. If Rea went from zero to sixty on that scale, there was a reason. One that someone raised on Earth probably could not understand when the Federation Forces were involved. For every "bad cop" story in America, there was "gang of rogue Forces" in the Federation. "I'll be back as soon as I can."

Rea did not fear for her life, but she also took no chances as she kept her elbows at nine and three, keeping either man far from her person. One stood in front and the other behind her as they escorted the renowned psychologist to the back street cutting behind Moonlight's and past the trash receptacles of the commercial towers they stood against.

A car with government plates idled a few feet beyond the last receptacle. While boxes and greasy papers shot down a chute into the underground incinerators, the man in front of Rea opened the back door to the car and motioned for her to get in.

"I'm not..." she began, assuming the backseat was empty.

A hand extended to help her inside. "Dr. d'Eran. I've been hoping to meet you for some time now."

The only reason Rea instantly recognized that voice was from hearing it on broadcasts often enough over the past two years. Around the time Commander d'Alacron was promoted to her position and began appearing in weekly statements, aired both on monitors and across radio waves. She wasn't merely a commander of the greatest force in the universe. She was a public liaison, meant to build good will between the government and the people they lorded over like it was nothing. The only voice more famous than hers at the moment was the president's.

Rea caught her breath. Luckily for her, nobody thought it prudent to shove her into the car against her will. "Commander?"

"Please. Have a seat. I wish to speak with you while we drive around the block a few times. I am much in need of your... opinion. And perhaps your professional services."

Rea looked at the men hovering near her. The ones who knew exactly where her daughter was. *May wouldn't actually stay there, would she?* Rea fretted. No. Surely, May would wait a few minutes before high-tailing it back to Marlow's residence. She was much safer there than anywhere else right now. May knew that, yes? It was all Rea could think as she slowly lowered her rear to the backseat of Yara's government car.

"Thank you so much for humoring me, Doctor," Yara said with a saccharine smile. "So sorry to interrupt your day. I know how busy a doctor's life can be."

"Surely not as busy as the Commander of the Federation Forces?"

Yara's smile did not let up. "Let me set the scene for you, Dr. d'Eran. Guilez?" She referred to the driver in the front seat. "Let's drive."

The doors were locked and the windows sealed. The car pulled forward. Rea was Earthling enough by now to know that the Commander opting for antiquated transportation meant this was as clandestine as possible.

It was also possibly the end of her life, if those espionage movies had anything to say about it.

Twenty-Two

Danielle didn't want to think about how long it had been since she last woke up next to another woman, let alone one she was romantically involved with. At least, waking up without a sense of dread or shame hanging over her head. *It must have been Alicia,* she thought, slowly blinking away the sleep from her eyes. The sun was bright, although a cloud cover would soon take care of that. Yet it wasn't the sun that had awoken her. Nor was it someone snoring or kicking her in their sleep. The honor went to the rumble in her stomach and the cramp in her back.

That day, she couldn't say she had woken up next to another woman. Miranda's side of the bed was empty, the covers thrown back and the imprint in her pillow gone. The only evidence it was her bed was the lingering scent of her perfume that had yet to wear off so soon after applying it.

Danielle didn't bother to cover herself as she sat up and stretched her arms across her body. Fine thing for there to be nobody else in a certain woman's bed, but Miranda was certainly around there somewhere, yes? Maybe she was making breakfast, if Danielle were such a lucky woman. What time was it? Eight? How had she slept so late when she fell asleep around ten the night before? *You can't call what we did a workout,* she thought, a flush to her cheeks. *Not a big enough one to knock me out for ten hours.*

It explained why Miranda was already up, though, wherever she was. Which wasn't in the bathroom, the first place Danielle inspected when she dragged herself out of bed.

Did she have anything decent to wear? Not like she packed an overnight bag. The best she could do, if she didn't want to put on her dirty clothes from the night before, was pick through the second drawer in Miranda's dresser and throw on an old and worn T-shirt that its owner probably didn't care too much about. Not that Miranda owned a nice collection of size L shirts for Danielle to feel comfortable in, because that would be too convenient. The best she could ask for was a black shirt, size M, that said *7th Annual Run for the Cure.* Whatever they had been trying to cure had since faded.

It barely covered Danielle's ass. At least it wasn't tight in the shoulders. That was the worst.

Probably looks like a tent on her... Danielle shuffled down the upstairs hallway, wondering how this shirt would look on a woman Miranda's size. She may have been technically one inch taller than Danielle, but her frame was much smaller. Instead of bulking up, her exercise regime merely made her toned. Did she even have stretch marks? Because Danielle had plenty, and it was the physical aspect of her body she most derided. *Note to self,* she thought, peering into the second bedroom's ajar door, *double-check this phenomenon the next time you get between her legs.* To think, Danielle had three chances the night before, and she never took a single one!

"Good morning." Miranda saw her before Danielle had the chance to adjust to the sunlight streaming through the second bedroom's window. "See you became acquainted with my clothing drawer."

"Do you have a problem with it?" Someone else had been through her own drawer. Gone were any of Danielle's worries that she may have stepped out of bounds, since Miranda stood in a pair of cotton sleep shorts and a T-shirt that may or may not have implied she attended Coachella once upon a time. In fact, she had, but she was so blazed she barely remembered it.

"Problem? With you wearing my clothes in my house? I'm not sure if you recall last night very well, but that's practically a dream come true."

Miranda returned to her painting. Danielle side-stepped behind her. She didn't know what she expected to see Miranda working on, but a still life of a daisy in a clear plastic vase was not one of those things. Only then did Danielle realize that there was a half-dead daisy in the corner of the room.

"So this is what you do on your Saturday mornings, huh?"

"When I'm inspired enough," Miranda said. "Or in a good enough mood, I suppose."

"I thought you were some big artist who had gallery showings on the other side of the world?"

Danielle may have said that with her tongue implanted in her cheek, but Miranda took her with enough sincerity that she put down her palette and cracked her knuckles one by one. "Big? Of course not. I lucked out with a couple showings because of who I am." She meant her ethnicity and nationality, but Danielle could figure that out for herself. "I still have a lot to learn. I don't do still life because I find it particularly stimulating, but it helps me practice things like shading and figuring out my style. Makes it easier to apply to my original works. Although... I'm a bit blocked, creatively speaking."

"I'm not posing nude for you anytime soon."

"Wasn't about to ask."

Danielle turned to the wall behind her, where Miranda had neatly arranged a stack of finished paintings. Or finished enough, if one asked her for an honest opinion. Among the still life practices were the works Danielle was more familiar with. Cast-offs from Miranda's recent collection of reincarnation-inspired paintings reminded Danielle that they had almost too much in common. Was it a coincidence that Miranda favored butterflies in her motifs? Even the darker paintings, full of grim reminders of what it meant to have once been alive, contained delicate little insects shining brightly despite adversity.

"You really like butterflies."

Miranda wiped her hands on a handkerchief. "I like beautiful things, you could say. Besides, it goes to show what a novice I still am. Butterflies are ridiculously easy to paint." She hopped off her stool. "Are you hungry? I haven't had anything to eat yet. I could go downstairs and —"

"Is this about reincarnation?"

Miranda stopped halfway to the door. "Excuse me?" Danielle currently had her hand on a still-life practice of Miranda's front window on a day shortly after it rained. Of course, that wasn't the one Danielle meant. That would be the one behind it, the first draft of a painting that had made it into the final collection. Two butterflies flying free in the night sky, their stardust trails entwined. "What makes you think that?" Perhaps, if Miranda laughed it off enough, she could convince Danielle that it was about something else.

"Sometimes you get a vibe about things," Danielle said. "I also know that *you* know a thing or two about it."

"About what?"

Danielle put the paintings back into place. "Reincarnation."

"That's a bold assertion. Here I thought you were at the forefront of such things."

"Cut the crap. You know more than you ever let on to me."

Miranda bristled. "I know a few things. About the Process, for instance, and how unpleasant it seems."

"Seems?"

"Most of the information is conjecture. I wouldn't claim to speak on your behalf."

"Yeah." Danielle put her hands on her hips, as if the change in stance would encourage her to also change the subject. "Guess I have a pretty unique perspective. Kind of why I see a painting covered in butterflies and assume it must be about reincarnation."

"It may not be common knowledge here, but it's a popular motif in Federation culture, thanks to the *julah*. Butterflies are one of the only creatures that can be found naturally across the universe. In fact, it's believed they were imported here thousands of years ago. So were a few other creatures, come to think of it."

"Right. I had already forgotten your big reveal last night. Guess I can say I've slept with a *julah* now. My mentor will be absolutely thrilled."

Miranda held back a gasp. "Perhaps it's best that you don't mention me to him. I have to keep it on the downlow, so to speak. I've been unregistered for so long that it would be more drama than it's worth if it got out I'm a *ma-julah*." She didn't mention why that was. Sure, the genealogy department would be most put out having a brand-new adult to suddenly shove into their records, but they would have to know *who* her father was. Wasn't like anyone could lie in her father's stead, either. After they got one real look at her, they would know she was somehow related to Nerilis Dunsman. Probably because she was the spitting image of his wife.

"I don't think he'll care enough to report you." Not that Danielle had confidence when she said that. For all she knew, that was the one aspect of his culture Ramaron Marlow was a hardliner about. "But don't worry. I won't mention it to anyone. I'm still trying to process stuff... like..." She leaned against one of the only empty spots on the bedroom wall. Miranda's shirt was tight enough on Danielle that it inched up her torso when she stretched her arm above her head. "How ridiculously hot you are at 8:30 on a Saturday morning."

Miranda's mouth twitched. Holding back laughter to save Danielle's face was not her strongest suit.

"That was cheesy, huh?" Danielle asked.

"Some cheese can be appreciated." Miranda carted her dirty brushes to the bathroom. "That reminds me, though. I wanted to talk to you about something before you left."

Was I going somewhere in a hurry? Danielle thought. "Hopefully it's not a talking to about my suave debonair. I've worked hard on it, you know."

"There's the woman I let into my house. Cynical with a touch of black humor. I do love me some familiarity."

Danielle didn't know how to take that. She had some time to think about it, though, as Miranda washed her brushes in the sink and left them to soak in their plastic container. "Guess I'm not good at being flirty," was what she said when the water shut off again. "Probably wasn't in any life."

A small smile cracked over Miranda's shoulder as she thought of something she couldn't say to Danielle.

You never were good at flirting, but that's what made it fun when you tried.

She grabbed a small hair-tie off her nightstand and pulled back the extra inch of hair that hung on the back of her neck—something Miranda should have done before settling down to paint that morning. Instead, she'd take the opportunity of getting hair out of her face to start breakfast downstairs. Assuming she could get Danielle to follow her, of course. Someone was a bit taken aback at the look passing her on the way to the staircase at the end of the hall.

"I know, right?" Miranda said, reading Danielle's mind. She held onto the handrail at the top of her stairs before giving a swish of the hips at the start of her descent. "Take a picture and share it with your friends. This is the most casual Saturday morning me you've ever seen. Shall we watch cartoons?"

This was the perfect opportunity for Danielle to try flirting again. Something like, *"Can we watch them on your bedroom TV?"* If only she thought of that before another three minutes passed and she was expected down in the kitchen.

"You really don't have to make me breakfast." Too late. Miranda had already cracked the eggs. "I mean, I could help."

"I've heard the legends about your cooking." Miranda reached up to grab the pepper from her cupboard. She wasn't the only one who struggled to keep her shirt covering her abdomen. "I prefer my food not blackened, thank you."

"That happened *one* time." Danielle drummed her fingers against the counter, a nervous habit she would soon berate herself for in present company. "I only burnt that dinner because somebody who shall remain nameless got a call from his boyfriend who was breaking up with him and I had to abandon the stove to make sure he didn't punch a hole through my wall."

"Ben always had a way of handling his breakups with grace." Miranda turned away from the stove, not that she would let the food burn. "Look where such skills landed him a few years later." The coffee pot announced it was finished. Only then did they both acknowledge the aroma, and Danielle could hardly wait for Miranda to place a cup down with a nice choice of creamers for every occasion. "Which brings me back to what I wanted to talk about."

Danielle didn't need that hanging over her as she had her first sip of coffee. "Does it have to do with last night?"

"There's a loaded question. Do you mean the scary thing outside the window, or the sex?"

"As my grandmother would say... why not both?"

Miranda caught the bread coming out of the toaster. "No, nothing to do with last night. I was thinking more about the future."

Although Danielle had a feeling she knew what this was about, she could not help herself from saying, "If this is you asking if I want to go on a tropical getaway weekend with you, then by all means, pack my bags and buy me a new bikini." She drank more coffee. Her mouth needed to stop talking.

"You? In a bikini?" Miranda plated the toast and the first round of eggs. "Are you trying to kill me?"

Danielle poked through the basket of jams and jellies kept on the far side of the counter. Apparently, Miranda was a fan of driving up the coast and hitting roadside stands, from the Bay Area of California to the Bay Area of Oregon. *Marionberry?* Danielle mused. *I'll try any berry once, I guess.* "So what was it that you wanted to talk about? Don't tell me I snore."

"No, but you do sweat more than I anticipated when you sleep."

"Gee. There's a revelation." Also explained a few things...

Miranda refrained from cooking her own eggs. "I wanted to talk about... well, I mean... wow. Think this is my first time having this conversation in years. Always thought it would happen more organically."

"Honey, you're cute and have fingers like honing missiles, but it's a bit early to be talking about marriage."

Danielle had been joking, but Miranda nevertheless took a step back in surprise. "Nothing like that, I assure you."

"What, like it could never happen?" Perhaps this was too much fun. Maybe Danielle had a hand on this flirting thing, after all! All she needed was a better handle on determining the best time to flirt in the first place. "You know how this whole lesbian thing works. We go out for a week, this time next month you're renting me a U-Haul, and within six months we've adopted either a pair of dogs or cats and argue over who gets to park in the driveway." She caught the look on Miranda's face and relented. "That's what I've heard, anyway."

"Suppose you're not too far off from the truth."

Danielle shot a hot breath across her lips. "Called you out ahead of time, huh?"

"I was *going* to suggest... or ask you, I suppose..." Miranda sipped her coffee, in dire need of that extra boost of caffeine to get her through this. "If you might want to... uh..."

Danielle did her best to be patient, but it was almost nine in the morning and the coffee jitters began their happy dance in her limbs. "I've always wanted to go to Montreal. Hint, hint."

"Damn it, would you let me finish?"

"Not if it's this much fun watching *you* squirm for a change."

"Would you go steady with me? For Void's sake, I can't believe I said it like that..."

Danielle was trapped between laughing her ass off and reveling in how sweet that moment could have been—if she wasn't too busy trying not to crack up like Humpty Dumpty at the local comedy club. "Go. Steady." Those were real words. Put together. Like this was 1958.

"If your goal is to make me feel embarrassed, congrats, it's working. I feel like I'm fifteen and asking another girl out for the first time. Trust me. I wasn't half as suave back then as I am now. You girls make me nervous!"

Both of Danielle's elbows touched the counter. "You're adorable. Especially with that poufy little ponytail. I can see your roots." They were not the same color as the rest of her hair, as if Danielle needed proof that Miranda had been dying it for decades. "Gee, I haven't been asked *to go* steady in like... well, not by a woman, in ever." Her only other serious relationship with another woman had been with Alicia, and that was all Danielle's doing in the beginning. Or so she liked to tell herself when looking back on those years.

"Just say yes or no, would you?"

This was fun. This was a side of Miranda that Danielle had been dying to see since they met. The verklempt side. The blushing, eye-avoiding side. This woman had no problem getting others into bed, but when it came to making things officially monogamous for the foreseeable future, she could hardly hold herself together. *Everyone has a weakness,* Danielle thought. She was the complete opposite. Terrible at initiating relationships, even one-night ones. Not too shabby at reading the room a few weeks later and going for the next stage if it felt right.

Well? Does it feel right now?

Danielle knew what she wanted to say. Every instinct she dared listen to screamed at her to say yes. Why shouldn't she? She and Miranda had the kind of chemistry that had been boiling for years. Finally giving into it hadn't changed its power. A whole week had gone by, and Danielle was still throwing herself at someone who could've easily been a one-night-stand of orgasmic magnitude, but nothing more once the fog cleared and they both got it out of their system. *Honestly,* Danielle rationalized, *if I get to see more of her dressed like this, making me food and letting me into her painting studio like I'm Level 1 Clearance? Worth it.*

Too bad there were some good reasons for her saying no. At least for now.

"I... don't take this the wrong way." No wonder Miranda was so nervous. She must have known Danielle was about to shoot her down. This was a woman who had a great poker face, but around people like Danielle, she struggled to keep the fear out of her eyes and the twitch out of her fingertips. "I'd like to keep seeing you. Maybe have some real dates? The kind that start *outside* of your house for once." Her forced laughter did not alleviate the tension over her cooling toast and eggs. "But I don't think I should be committing more than that to anyone right now. I don't know what's going to happen. Nor do I know how I'll be feeling a few days or even weeks from now. I'm kinda barely holding it together right now. I don't want to say I'll be your girlfriend if it turns out it's more trouble than it's worth for you."

"Sooo..." Miranda said with a thoughtful roll of the eyes, "it's not me, it's you?"

"I'm not breaking it off. Come on. You make me breakfast."

"That's fair." Miranda finally returned to cooking her own breakfast, but not before gesturing that Danielle should get started eating her own. "I'll have to keep working at convincing you to make me your full-time girlfriend. I've got a lot of tricks up my sleeve, you know. Starting with how good my cooking is. Start with dinner, level up to breakfast and dessert. Wine and dine you the only way I know how." She winked over her shoulder. "That's pretty fancy, by the way. I have expensive tastes and don't mind throwing the wealth around. Play your cards right, you'll be the most spoiled woman in the Bay Area, and I'll be happy to keep that a reality."

"See? This is the kind of confidence I like in you." Danielle brushed off any discomfort she felt from Miranda's words. It was too easy to succumb to the weight of expectations. "By the way, I've always wondered about the money thing. I mean, there was no way you could afford a house like this, let alone in a neighborhood like this, on a captain's salary. I don't care how many grants you got."

"I didn't get any grants," was all Miranda said. "I paid for this house and my car in cash."

"Your car isn't as nice as this house. Just saying."

"You make it sound like I live in a mansion up on the hills. Like I've got a view of the bridge of the ocean. You know what view I've got? Bob's ass when he bends over to inspect the base of my side of the fence. Bob's ass and Tina's ugly PT Cruiser full of screaming kids going off to soccer practice."

Danielle rolled her eyes. "You know what I mean. I could never afford this house with the way prices are jumping here. There's all those murmurs about a crash too."

"Bet you're glad you don't work for the government anymore, then."

There she went, skirting the overarching question once again. "Do you have so much money because you're half-*julah?*"

Miranda bristled. While it was definitely brazen of Danielle to ask such a direct question about finances—let alone so early in the relationship—what made her uncomfortable was the sudden reminder of where her funds came from. *Hush money. Blood money. Pick one.* That's what she thought as she watched her breakfast sizzle and heard the toaster ding again. Her "father" thought that by throwing around money he pulled out of his ass, he could somehow make her existence more palpable.

Nerilis didn't do it because he loved Miranda. He did it because he felt guilty. Besides, money meant absolutely nothing to him. Even if he hadn't been one of the richest men in the universe at one point in time, his con-artistry and sorcery was so advanced he didn't have to think twice about tweaking anybody's bank accounts. Never mind when it came to Earthling technology. The most effort he put into it was ensuring Miranda stayed under the radar. Multiple offshore accounts below reporting minimums barely kept her head above the proverbial waters. This was a man who occasionally called her up and ask how much was too much for Earthlings to process. A trillion dollars had no meaning.

The only dollars in Miranda's American bank accounts came directly from her paycheck and a few investments her father made on her behalf. She paid taxes on all of those. To offset her guilt about having a billion dollars across multiple accounts in the Caribbean and Switzerland, she made numerous donations to charities under anonymous names. Nerilis Dunsman had the power to use her as a tool to completely wreck Earth's global economy, but instead she occasionally donated a few hundred thousand here and there under the name Gregory Hotchner.

She also drank really expensive wine. It was one of her few real indulgences. *Excursions to Napa, where half the people behind the wineries know me by name now.* Having someone to take with her was always a plus. Like she told Danielle, she genuinely enjoyed spoiling women. She always figured her father's imaginary money should go to *something* good besides keeping her comfortable while she waited for her soul's obliteration.

"My father is very well-off, yes. You know how those *julah* are. They have no concept of money and economics compared to humans. But I guess when you've been living so long and amassing wealth in a humanoid microcosm for so long, you lose all ability to reason about it. These are the same people who can't comprehend living only two hundred years. Or two thousand, for that matter."

"I should ask the old man what the number one cause of death for all *julah* under a thousand years old is."

"Dumbassery, like anyone else."

"So your father actually pays his child support, huh?"

"Guess you could say that. It's definitely agreed that I won't talk about him, let alone to somebody who likes to flap her gums."

"Don't know who you could be talking about. I'm the one who probably lucked out that her dad died before she was born, because he was such a deadbeat there's no way he would have paid *his* child support."

"Guess, in a way, you lucked out ending up on your grandmother's doorstep."

"Quite literally. I remember the day my mom dropped me off for dinner and then drove away to do something. I don't know what. All I know is that she died on the way to wherever she was going."

Miranda plated her breakfast and turned to Danielle. "You remember your mom, huh? Weren't you really young?"

"Like... five? What? Are people not supposed to have memories from before that age? I mean, I don't remember much. Just a few things. And I don't remember her mother at all. I don't remember when she died, exactly, but you'd think I'd remember something about a Japanese grandmother who everyone called Setty because they couldn't be bothered to remember her real name."

The barstool scraped across the floor as Miranda sat down. She wasn't in a hurry to eat. "I'm sorry you've had so much loss in your life. Could be worse, I suppose. You could have my shitty family who did the bare minimum to acknowledge my existence."

"Yeah, you've mentioned some things before. I'm sorry."

Had Miranda? Or was Danielle extrapolating her information from rumors? Because it wasn't a secret that Miranda came from a broken home. *Started in San Jose with a bunch of conservative Japanese immigrants, made my way back to Japan and went to Catholic school.* There was a memory Miranda could live without. The only boon in her life was her grandmother. It definitely wasn't her father. She knew nothing about her extended *julah* family, although the internet was at her fingertips. Like the existence of the deep web, there was another part of the internet that allowed people to access Federation-based information. There was a wiki-like website for *julah* genealogy and living people. Because of course there was.

Miranda never investigated it, though. What was the point? She had no cultural ties to those people. Her life was rough enough trying to pass as either American or Japanese while on Earth. Her human half held all the cards. She would always be human before she was *ma-julah.*

"Just so we're on the same page," she began, desperately wishing to change the subject. "We're dating, and we're sleeping together, but we're not going steady. Yet."

Danielle put down her forkful of eggs. "Yet."

"Right, right. I don't have plans to see anyone else for now. Don't let that discourage you from living your best life, though. You wanna keep your options open? Find yourself? Extort old powerful men for money? Honey, I'm fluent enough in Julah I could write the request for you. Just not in the polite dialect, I suppose."

"Trust me, he doesn't deserve 'polite dialect.' The man ruined my whole spiritual existence. Translate 'hey you fucking fuck muncher, pay me some goddamn reparations for what you did to my fucking soul,' for me, would you?"

"I might have to get out my dictionary for that."

"They got dictionaries here for that shit?"

"Oh, honey." Miranda put her hand on Danielle's arm. "The things I could show you."

For the first time since discovering the existence of life beyond her microscopic corner of the universe, Danielle was somewhat curious about learning up on it. But only if she learned the curse words first. She often indulged in her juvenile side like that.

Twenty-Three

F or many *julah,* Sah Zenlit was the first place they learned to teleport to, since it was usually a part of the Academy's admissions interview. When Nerilis Dunsman casually popped into where he damn well pleased, let alone a place he once considered his personal stomping grounds, it was only a matter of time before some idealistic young student stuck his nose in the air and asked, *"What's that smell? Smells like somebody who could annihilate me at Theoretical Astrophysics."*

It helped that Nerilis was one of a handful of *julah* who had mastered teleportation. As in, distance didn't matter. Nor did he lack for energy, even after zipping around the universe every half hour to collect this, barter that, and finally settle down to have a drink in a mining outpost that didn't know his aged face from the town drunk's.

However, even a man of such outstanding magical caliber was prone to the minor mistake now and again. Especially when he was distracted at his point of departure. For most people, this would be a forgettable incident—arriving in the wrong room, but in the right building, was not much cause for concern when one traveled home or to the official entry points around the Federation. For Nerilis Dunsman, though, appearing in the wrong room meant certain people found out he was *there.*

"Oh!" Calseeth Ducah, the first cousin he saw about once a year, dropped the empty cup in her hand. It landed with a pitiful *plop* on the other side of her couch. "Good afternoon."

Nerilis took a step back, cursing himself for not concentrating enough only a few moments ago. He had gone from one of his hideouts in a dark pocket dimension to the bright, illustrious rooms of his old mentor's apartments at the Academy. Calseeth, who was Master Obello's full-time steward, was one of the only people aside from Master Obello who knew Nerilis often came around.

Nevertheless, he could have lived without seeing her.

"I, uh..." He straightened himself out. Calseeth picked up her cup, checked for a stain on the couch, and looked back up at him through dull brown eyes. *I can hardly believe she's my cousin, let alone a first cousin,* Nerilis thought. Calseeth was the old maid of his generation, and he had no one but himself to blame, since he became the universe's pariah right when she entered prime marriable age. The only reason Calseeth saved some face instead of holing herself away in the family estate for the rest of her life was because Nerilis convinced Master Obello to shirk public opinion and hire the woman. Something only possible because Calseeth had little to no career as a sorceress—otherwise, she would have been the biggest security threat since somebody turned their back on a younger Nerilis detonating experiments in the great fields out back. "I came to see Master Obello. He is in, I hope?"

"He is resting." Calseeth nodded to the door leading to Master Obello's personal chambers, the place where Nerilis had *intended* to appear. "Exams were this week."

That's all she said, but her meaning was clear. *"You did well picking the right time to show up. One week earlier and you might have been spotted by one of his mentees."* Once upon a time, that would have been a young and foolhardy Nerilis Dunsman—or a younger and foolhardier Ramaron Marlow, who managed to upset the old Master more than Nerilis ever accomplished.

More damned bygones.

"Would you like some *cageh,* Master Dunsman?"

She was probably the last woman on earth who called him that so casually. It was stranger to think that she had grown up thinking of him as the future head of her family. *By the time she was of age, I was High Priest.* What was it like, being this woman of blood-kin and looking at the man who had fallen so far?

"*Cageh* might be lovely," he said. "Thank you. I'll check on the Master."

With a curt nod, Calseeth stood and carried her cup into the kitchen.

Master Obello was in his favorite chair, head back and mouth open as his chest slowly rose and fell. Nerilis kept to the far wall by the door, lest he stood too close to the wide, unshuttered windows lining two walls. No matter how quiet he attempted to be, Nerilis could not avoid awaking the Master, who snorted so hard that his chair rocked backward.

"I hear exams have finished," was how Nerilis greeted him.

It took Master Obello a few seconds to realize he wasn't dreaming. "I suppose you don't miss those."

"On the contrary," Nerilis helped himself to another chair by the door, "I sort of miss the rush of taking something that does not really matter seriously."

"Ah, yes, I recall your aloof attitude to something as inconsequential as final exams."

"When you've lived the life I've lived, Master, you realize how truly inconsequential it really was."

Master Obello would not refute him on that. He would, however, wait for Calseeth to bring in the *cageh* before continuing. "I take it that recent events are what bring you here again? You rarely drop by for a pleasure call."

"Only because my wanted status makes it a pain in the horse's ass. You know I can't stay long, either."

"You have a little time. The maids have already been through for the week, and most of the students have returned to Yahzen for the holiday. Or to run off to Sah Zenlit to do whatever it is the youths do these days to blow off steam."

"I doubt much changes with drinking, drugs, and sex, Master."

"No, but I don't much remember it myself. You have an edge over me on that one."

"You've been an old man for a long as I've known you. I can only imagine what you do and do not remember."

"You're not younger than I was when we met."

Although Nerilis knew that, such a fact hit him right in the chest. *Yes, I'm an old man now too.* He was the age most High Priests rose to their stations. *Truly puts into perspective my record-breaking age of 1,080.* He had been the youngest ever. To this day, no one had come close to touching it, not even the current High Priest, who held the title of second youngest ever at 1,823.

Doesn't matter, they would've found a reason to oust me by now. Nerilis had been a novelty back then. Even if Joiya had never Ascended to the Void and they lived a normal, priestly life without panic from beyond, fatigue would have been strong among his people. There was something to be said for those in power eventually dying off, be they human or *julah.*

"So..." Master Obello folded his hands over his stomach. "Since you can't stay long, I suppose we should cut right to the chase. What brings you here, Young Master Dunsman, and how can I help you?"

Nerilis was not the kind of man who liked to be taken aback. Yet if there was one man who knew how to throw him off balance, it was the only man to have ever called him a "simpering blemish against your family's name" long, long before he had ruined his reputation.

"How did you know I needed help?"

"You're not going to risk being spotted here unless you really needed me. Maybe you don't care about your own safety, but you care about mine. Your whole reason for being here is to seek my aid. So, seek it."

The door opened with a soft knock. Calseeth helped herself into the room, a tray of *cageh* in her hands. Two cups steamed and cooled. She added a generous touch of powdered nutrients to Master Obello's cup. As soon as Nerilis looked away, she added some to his as well.

Nerilis didn't hold back from talking in front of his cousin. She knew most of what he was up to, thanks to him popping into Master Obello's office over the years. Nevertheless, Nerilis sucked in his breath and reformulated his words before saying, "The experiments with my... *ma-julah*... have not been a success." It wasn't merely Calseeth's presence that made him refrain from properly acknowledging Miranda or her relation to him, but the fact that he was still embarrassed by her existence a thousand years later. Master Obello had been shocked to hear about her at first, but he claimed it was due to the mysterious nature of the Void, not that Nerilis had slept with any other woman after his wife's Ascension. Yet only one of those things brought shame to Nerilis's cheeks. "Even with me as her sire, she has no natural skill. She might as well be a record-keeper for the genealogy department. If she were properly brought up as my daughter, I'd be ashamed of her faulty talents." He glanced at Calseeth. "No offense."

She shrugged, cleaning up some of the dirty dishes from Master Obello's chamber.

"Not everyone can be the next in line for your fantastic throne," the master drolly said.

"But she's my daughter. You'd think that me being the *julah* side of her would at least provoke *something*."

"Ah, it never works out that way. Just ask the families I've had to explain this to over the millennia. I say a prayer to the Void every time two of our best students marry and have children. That's a lot of pressure when most of it comes down to luck."

"I like to think that my own skills aren't all luck."

"No, but you can't eliminate the possibility that you had a nice leg-up from your genetic draw when you were born. I see it all the time. Proteges who walk out of their unremarkable families becoming the next High Priests, and magical dynasties putting out a dud of a generation. If all the training and education can't help some full-blooded children, what luck does a *ma-julah* with no natural talent have?"

Nerilis hadn't come here to debate genetics with his old mentor. He came for answers. Advice. Anything that would put him on the right track toward his intended purpose of saving the Void from its own annihilation. "You had to put in that bit about unremarkable families creating magical monsters."

"If you don't want to talk about Young Master Marlow, say so."

"I didn't come here to talk about him, so I will say so."

"Yet for some reason, the only man of your generation who could possibly come close to your skill level, is not the one you're relying on to help you," Master Obello said.

"It's not enough. We need at least one more person strong enough to take on such a task. Unfortunately, even with that blasted League working on my behalf, I was unable to find a single *julah* among their ranks with the kind of power I need. Not even Ramaron could suggest somebody."

"So you turn to your own fruit of your loins."

Nerilis chugged his *cageh*. "Naturally."

Master Obello considered this information while Calseeth carried the tray full of dirty dishes out of the room. She made sure to close the door behind her. "I see that you've already considered what your own child may be capable of. And, to be sure, had you and Young Lady Lerenan ever seen a child to term, there would have been great expectations of their abilities."

"Says the man who blasted the other children of known talents."

"I said it can be unfortunate when they're incapable. To be sure, most of the time powerful sorcerers pump out powerful children. While it's not surprising your child with a human woman is not talented, another might be."

Nerilis was on the immediate defensive. "I do not have any other children. There isn't even the possibility. She has been the only one for a millennium."

"I didn't say there might be one out there right now."

They were silent. Calseeth returned, her quiet steps echoing in the room.

"I don't care for what you're implying, Master," Nerilis said.

"No, I suppose not." Master Obello settled back into his chair, as if he were preparing for a new nap. "You are loyal to a fault. Only one woman has ever had your heart, and I daresay the two of you would have completely ruled our kind under a benevolent theocratic dictatorship should things not have happened as they did. I've seen the way you talk about this daughter of yours. And I remember the first time you confessed to her existence. You considered her a necessary fault of your character."

Nerilis grimaced. "I am mortal after all, and therefore have moments of weakness."

"Hundreds of years had passed since the death of Young Lady Lerenan. Who would blame you?"

"Me."

Master Obello sighed. "Your candor is commendable, but it does you no favors. You know what must be done if you want a child with the potential to be as powerful as yourself."

Nerilis could hardly believe he was hearing this from his oldest, most trusted mentor. Master Obello was not a man who inserted himself into the personal affairs of others. When he first heard that Nerilis and Joiya had befriended one another in their classes, he warned them both to not lose sight of their studies. When they were officially dating, he did not go easy on them during their exams. The only time he intervened was when they wished to become engaged, but the Dunsmans of the era were not thrilled with Joiya's pedigree. Only then did Master Obello personally speak with Lady Dunsman about how Joiya had single-handedly brought unprecedented honor to her family, and any other should be delighted to have their son marry her.

Now here he was, swearing that this wasn't about gossip or moving on. This was about saving the universe, as it always had been since Nerilis Dunsman first confessed to Master Obello about the torture within the Void.

"Even if that were possible," Nerilis began, "where would I find an agreeable woman? I may not be as in the know with current sociopolitical affairs, but I have a feeling that available full-blooded women willing to propagate with me are few and far between."

"To be sure." Master Obello set aside his *cageh* cup. "It's a precarious world out there. Our kind is seeing dwindling numbers. Academy enrollment is at an all-time low, even after lowering admission standards. Everyone is nervous about the state of the Void now that it's becoming common knowledge in the *cageh* houses and *hedpah* clubs. I was shocked to hear the other Masters openly talking about it at a recent staff meeting. I'm sure some of them were former members of

that League. If nothing else, that lot spread the word unlike anything else. But..."
He tapped his finger to his chin. "There will always be someone who does not
mind as much as others. Do you think you would have enough time for there to
be a child that is born and grows enough to come into its own?"

"Are you asking me if the Void will collapse tomorrow or a hundred years from
now? If I knew the answer to that, I would either have given up already or still
have more hope."

"Then you must try."

"Ah, yes, I shall go straight to the nearest matchmaker and ask for a woman
with some magical ability who is willing to spread her legs for a mass murderer
who brought so much shame to his house that they had to change their names."
He shot his cousin a look. "Sorry about that, by the way."

She said nothing.

"I will tell you what I tell every student here who worries about his or her future
romantic prospects," Master Obello said. "There is always someone. Perhaps they
will not be a perfect match, but they will suit your needs. Do not go into it
looking for anything but a means to your ultimate end. Calseeth?" He turned
to his steward, who had remained in the middle of this awkward conversation
for one sole purpose. "You have connections in some ladies' circles. Perhaps you
could ask around in case there is a young lady out there of... an open mind." That
was the nicest way to put it. "She must be a full-blooded *julah,* with no history of
unremarkable magical use in her recent bloodline. Do you understand?"

She curtly nodded. "I will be attending a function soon. The perfect place to
ask."

"Then please, do so. And bring us some more *cageh,* would you?"

With another nod, Calseeth departed Master Obello's private chambers.

"I can't believe this," Nerilis continued. "To bring a life into this world at a time
like this would be the most irresponsible thing I can do."

"Think of it this way," Master Obello said, appealing to what ego was truly
left inside of the man before him. "With optimism, you will see your quest
through. With or without the child you need, you will overcome the obstacles

before you and save us from ourselves. Then, what shall you do? You may be younger than me, but you're older than you think. Right now, you are the last of your full-blooded line. Will you depart this mortal world and return to the Void without ensuring your line? You are the last Dunsman. The Ducah have forsaken you, but you could rebuild your own house, your own way."

Nerilis did not want to admit that the thought of leaving behind some real genetic legacy appealed to him. Such things, after all, still lingered from his youth. When he was the future head of his family, who was responsible for the lineage and continuing the bloodlines for the next few thousand years. Since the death of his wife, however, he had left those thoughts behind. Not until he fell into bed with the madam of a brothel on a since-abandoned pleasure moon had he remembered what it's like to court shame—and to see a child of his be born.

A child he did not know existed until he happened to see her face on a broadcast one day. The chief of some barbaric tribe was coming to Terra III to talk treaties, and everyone on Yahzen shouted that she looked like the High Priestess.

Because, in a way, that's exactly who she was.

I'll never forget the day I first saw her. It was like the first day I saw Joiya. Except in the place of adulation stood apprehension. The queasy feeling that shot up his throat and told him he had messed up so badly that he had bent the very essence of the Void and brought into the mortal world a person who was never meant to exist.

Of course, now he knew that had been its plan all along. As a former High Priest, he knew not to question it. Figure out what the hell was going on, by all means, but questioning it? He might as well ask the Void why it ever came into existence in the first place.

"How are we to know that any child born by next year would be powerful enough to help in another twenty years' time?" Nerilis asked, poking more holes in the plan. Anything to get him off the hook that was looking more and more attractive as the minutes wore on. "You're the first to tell me that I was a fluke, and it still took me decades to qualify for admissions."

"You let me take care of that, assuming you go through with this. Depending on the mother, I might be able to access the child myself for personal tutelage."

Nerilis scoffed. "Why in the world are you going through all this trouble?"

"Because it must be done," was all Master Obello said at first. Then, "The most important thing for us to fret about is the Void. You are the only one I know who has come up with a viable solution, but you cannot do it alone."

"Viable solution, huh? Where were you a thousand years ago?"

Master Obello narrowed his eyes. "That was *not* a viable solution."

"Yet you had no problems harboring a fugitive for those first few decades."

"I may not have agreed with your methods, but I agreed with your reasoning. You were always a brash young man. It's been good to see you stray away from the unilluminated paths you forged for yourself in those dire days after Young Lady Lerenan's passing."

That was one way to refer to Nerilis Dunsman's rise to power in the Temple.

"I will, of course, continue to work with my daughter. In case there is truly untapped potential there. But I do not hold much hope for a *ma-julah*."

Master Obello nodded. "Bring her to me. I can assess her for myself."

"I don't know if that's a good idea. If somebody sees her... there is no guarantee she will obey my wishes, anyway. She is willful."

"Ah, she must get that from her *julah* side."

Sometimes, Nerilis couldn't tell when his old mentor was joking—and when he was merely stating the obvious.

Twenty-Four

The weather remained pleasant during Devon's stay on Arrah, although the days were longer than he remembered. At the end of the second day, Lanelle made the offhand comment that the planet's axis had slightly tilted since Devon's spirit was last there. *"Not enough to, like, destroy everything, but it's hotter and days are a little longer."* The parts of him that hated how much she knew about his home planet were only mitigated by the parts of him inspired by how casually she flitted through the house like she belonged there.

Devon couldn't say the same for himself. From his first night there, he was aware of how out of place he was among his own kin. Oh, the Gardiahs were plenty hospitable and over the moon to have him around—even better when they gave him a tour of the property, showing what they had done to change their fortunes over the centuries. Yet as much as Fenar and Sonjah insisted that he was the biggest thing to happen to them in the past five years, Devon knew that he really didn't belong there. He wasn't going to find what he had been looking for. Whatever that was.

On his last evening there, he ascended one of the staircases leading up to a deck overlooking the nearby forest. Although Sonjah had offered him *cageh*, he declined it in favor of the clean well water he took with him alongside a small plate of *fofarin* biscuits and goma berry spread. It was one of the simplest snacks anyone in the universe could have asked for, but it was native to Arrah, and something that still survived from times long ago.

The first bite wasn't as nostalgic as he anticipated. Perhaps that was part of the problem. He expected too much.

"Oh, come on." Lanelle crept up behind him, two clay mugs in her hands. "Are you seriously up here moping like you aren't a *god* to these people? You've got a great-great-great-great-whatever down there who wants to tell everyone in the universe that he's related to you, and you're..." she sighed. "Let me guess. Trying to remember what it's like to be from here."

Devon didn't look twice at the mug sitting next to him. Nor at the woman making herself at home in the other chair. Lanelle wasn't dressed in anything more than comfy, casual pants and a giant sweater, and her lazy look was complemented by the mighty sigh she let out when Devon shifted in his seat.

"Guess you would know about that, huh?" he asked.

"Been around that block a few times. I've given up on it, though. It was around my third life I realized I was never going to get that feeling of being at home again. You're talking to someone who was able to meet some of her first family during her third life. Remembered them perfectly. Didn't look a day older to them. Awkward as hell. So awkward I went and got absolutely toasted that night and vowed to never meet my old family again. Most of them are dead now, anyway."

Devon wished he had something to get toasted with right now. He may not recognize any of the people on his old property, but he still hated the feeling that he didn't really belong there. *I have nothing else to compare it to.* He had heard the phrase "you can never go home again," but it didn't mean anything to a man who never had a real home to begin with. None with any meaning. He had the apartments he lived in with his Aunt Laura, who raised him after his drug addict of a mother chose vice over family. But one did not have an "Aunt Laura" without the accompanying cold personality and the teaching of self-sufficiency from an early age. The woman had taken on an extra job to raise him. It was the least he could do at ten years old to warm up some cans of soup and bagels for when she came home from the evening shift at the neighborhood supermarket.

Arrah was the closest thing his soul had to a true home. That and perhaps Cerilyn, the one place in the universe he could stroll through like he still owned the place.

Too bad it was gone now. The one time in his existence he thought that.

"I don't know why I came here," he said to Lanelle. "Guess I wanted to see what it was like after so much time. See how they changed the place. See what my descendants are like."

"Yeah, can't say I have any of that." She sipped her drink and took in the sunset beaming across the treetops. "No ancestral lands. No surprise descendants. You know what's crazy though?" she drank like a fish, which surprised Devon if only because the *cageh* was still hot. "Your genetics are completely different from your so-called family. You could bang your great-infinity granddaughter and those chromosomes won't give a shit."

Devon raised his eyebrows. "This is what you sit around and think about, huh?"

"Honey, I've gotten into bed with old cousins to prove I could without it meaning a thing. Any weirdness is all in your head."

"I don't think I would be in a hurry to sleep with my mom if I went back in time right now."

Lanelle chuckled. "How's the drink, huh? Hitting you yet?"

"What are you talking about?" Devon sniffed the *cageh,* which was still almost too hot for him to drink. He took a whiff and didn't find anything out of the ordinary. Then again, he barely remembered what *cageh* smelled like.

"Go on," Lanelle said with a mischievous smile. "Have a sip or five." Her cup was back at her lips. "Took what they had in the kitchen and spiced it up a bit. Figured we could use it for our last night in rural paradise."

Against his better judgment, Devon took a sip. At first, it tasted like the bitter tea the *julah* favored for their daily constitutions. Then the punch to the head hit him.

"What... did you put in this?"

Waggling eyebrows greeted him over the rim of Lanelle's cup. "Found some other stuff while I was snooping around in there too. Come on! It's enough to loosen up and stop feeling so down on yourself. You've been like a sad duck ever since we started your rock star tour. Enjoy the last day of your vacation before you go back to being an Earthling who doesn't enjoy the pleasures of instantaneous teleportation."

"I do have access to that now, you know," Devon said. "It's how I get to LA every other weekend for my therapy."

"Mmhmm." With a roll of the eyes, Lanelle sat back in her seat. "We go to the same therapist. I know enough about that."

Devon pinched his nose and had a larger sip of his spiked tea. "This is awful," he said. "But I've had worse."

"The more you drink it, the better it gets."

Hearing her say that made him glance in her direction again. "Has living a whole five lives really turned you into a depressed ingrate that has to get her jollies via drinking and whatever the hell else you do?"

She shrugged. "I was pretty much an ingrate even before I started working for the *magnanimous* Master Marlow. And let me tell you, he is one worldly bastard. I can tell you the names of most of the people he's slept with. I mean, a few are under my radar, but if you spend as many lives with a man like I have, studying him and his cronies, you learn stuff about where they stick their dicks."

"He sleeps with people, huh?"

"In the past thousand years? Eh, sure. Hey! Ask him about the bar he owns on Bah Zenlit! Make him *really* flustered! It's worth it!"

"Think I'll pass. Remember, I'm too stuck up my own ass to give a shit about other people." That's probably what he looked like to other people right now. *To May.* Ugh. Every time he thought about their minor spat, the more embarrassed he became. She had been right that certain people were trouble. But Devon was also correct that there were some people you could not turn down, no matter how many "bad" feelings they gave you.

He drank mouthfuls of spiked *cageh*. As many mouthfuls as he could stand without gagging. He didn't know how hard the alcohol would hit him when it finally did, but it couldn't come soon enough. Not when he was trying to push aside the memories of his ancient family. A part of him would never forgive his older sister for leaving him behind on some shithole planet. Staying here in Arrah kept reminding him of those sour feelings.

"I've been staring at this outcrop over here." Devon pointed to the gray stone cliff jutting out of the woods, the setting sun casting it with a warm glow. "I'm half-convinced it's the one my sister and I used to play on before we were deemed too old to have imaginations. Well, I was too old, being a teenage boy."

Lanelle grunted. "Uh-huh. Let it out, kid. All that pent-up rage at your daddy you've been harboring for a thousand years."

"What rage is there? It ain't at my parents. Any issues I had with them were killed the day they died. It's amazing how much you don't care once they're gone."

"You've got rage." Lanelle took another judicious drink of *cageh*. "Looots of rage at somebody here."

Devon didn't have to think too hard about that. "I'm angry at what tore me away from this place in the first place. Finding out what happened to the man who hired mercenaries to assassinate my father isn't enough. I'm mad that... well, guess I'm mad I wasn't also killed that day."

Lanelle was silent for a few moments, and for good reason. She may have had her own demons lurking within, but they didn't compare to seeing one's life go up in flames and blood while total strangers made off with any young bodies they could convert into killing machines.

Devon needed another drink.

"You know part of my job was to read a lot about you, yeah?" Lanelle said. "Looots of research. To go with looooots of rage." She chuckled. "But no matter how much I read about it, I still can't fully comprehend everything any of you went through. I've never had to kill anybody. I'm not in the Process because I need to take down a bad guy."

"I was in the Process because your boss decided I was special enough to keep around for a thousand years," Devon said. "I was the guy you could point in any direction and say, '*Go kill 'em, boy*' and I'd go kill 'em in five seconds. I could make it clean or leave as many entrails behind as you wanted. Best part? I saved a modicum of sanity that let my bitch of a chief think it a grand idea to make me her second-in-command. So, you know, when I finally had my own clean chambers for the first time in years and could access what passed for the internet whenever I wanted, I was nice and fucked. Couldn't leave even if I wanted to. As long as you were a mercenary, you were granted an ongoing pardon as long as your supposed crimes were a result of a paying customer. Even if you don't commit another murder or steal some shit again in your life, you could be snagged by the Feds the moment you got away without them shooting you in the back. So imagine what that was like. Watched these people you might lead one day kill everything you knew and loved. The only thing keeping you loyal to them was the fact they had broken you down and you had no choice. You either went along with it, or you died. And if you died, it was like they won."

"You could have changed things when you became leader."

"Yeah, right. That's what every chief thinks. They're going to change things. Work on recruiting instead of kidnapping. Better living conditions. More freedoms. It never works. The whole system was corrupt from the ground up. That's what happens when you deal in death and secrets, and the only way people can cope is if they keep themselves numb in between gigs."

Lanelle didn't say what was on her mind. *Wasn't your Chief supposedly one of the greatest ever?* That's what history said about Cairn di'Cerilyn, who implemented many of those practices mentioned. Of course Devon would think that way, though. That was the woman who killed everything he loved, long before a man named Nerilis Dunsman came to Cerilyn.

Lanelle was one of the few people who knew that Cairn had been reincarnated, let alone as whom.

"Yup. That's definitely where we used to hang out," Devon continued. "You know, if there's anyone I would bring back if I could, it's Graella." He decided he had enough of the spiked *cageh* and put the cup down with finality. "I think, since I've regressed, I've been holding the most rage about her. You know, she killed herself on Cerilyn. The parts of me that are angry she left me behind are also angry that she was driven to it. She was a really sensitive soul. I dunno. You ever have siblings?"

"A couple times. Not this life. Not the first life. I get loving somebody like that, but it's not ingrained into my soul."

"Yeah. Ingrained. That's one way to put it."

Devon leaned his head back against his seat and sighed. Soon, he would be back on Earth, trying to move forward with his existence. The ghosts of his past would remain scattered across the universe, but some of their souls were always a part of his. Moving on, especially after lasting so long without knowing about who remembered him, meant forgiving the people who had screwed him over in the first place.

Then again, maybe he wasn't ready for that yet.

The upside to meeting in a public place like a diner was that it was too loud for anyone else to hear what Danielle and Miranda said the moment they sat down in a booth. Especially on a Sunday morning, when the place was packed with both the pre-church and post-church crowds.

"Look at you, Miss Fancy With Her Schmancy Wine." Danielle grabbed a menu from the side of the table. "In a greasy spoon with the plebs."

Miranda leaned forward, her whole look the kind of thing Danielle had not been prepared for that sunny Sunday morning. T-shirt, jeans, and a fitted black jacket that would make most women double-take, if not outright fall in love with her. Yet at the same time, that was probably Danielle's bias for women like Miranda showing through her beleaguered soul. *She's also wearing that ring...* Danielle noted the Third Piece, a garish blue, plastic-looking stone slammed onto a faker piece of metal. The kind that looked like it left behind green stains on the skin. That thing had been the bane of Danielle's life a year ago. Since then, it had occasionally appeared on Miranda's finger. Was she taunting Danielle, or did it have other significance?

"What if I told you," Miranda began, "that I'm actually a big fan of greasy spoons?" A waitress in a white and red plaid uniform approached. "They've got the best coffee. Melts the skin right off your bones."

"God, I want coffee." Danielle turned to the waitress. "One coffee, please."

"Make that two," Miranda said.

The waitress left to get them coffee while the two women on totally-not-a-date flipped the menus over and stared at specials with slightly gentrified twists. Danielle took one look at the price and thanked the Lord Miranda had offered to pay for breakfast when she texted her probably-not-girlfriend that morning and asked her out. *"I'll buy you breakfast,"* was what greeted Danielle when she rolled over in bed that morning and picked up her phone. *"To complement cooking it for you yesterday."* Danielle belonged to any woman who knew the difference between "compliment" and "complement." Good thing she was already sleeping with Miranda, otherwise she might have had to start.

"So is there a reason you asked me out this beautiful morning?" Danielle had already decided what she wanted. A big, fat Belgian waffle with blueberries and whipped cream. "I mean, something in particular, not just an undying love to see me."

"You got me." Miranda had also decided. Brunch-sized burrito, complete with chorizo and cilantro, the two things her mother decried the most when she first moved to America in the '70s and had authentic Mexican food. "Went twenty-four hours without your presence and couldn't take it any longer. I had to see you. Had to breathe the same air as you." The deadpan way she said that made Danielle look up from the packets of artificial sweeteners and snort.

"I knew it. You're obsessed with me." With a dramatic sigh, Danielle accepted her delivered coffee and told the waitress what she wanted to eat. After commending Danielle for the excellent choice in waffle toppings, she took Miranda's order. "Kinda like how you used to stalk me in cafés."

"I did not," Miranda said.

"Did too. Remember? A year ago? When you sat down with me in the café when I was trying to not have a massive freakout over saving the world?"

"Ah. I do now, yes. You were reading a book. What was it? *One Flew Over the Cuckoo's Nest?*"

"Not even close. Pretty sure it was *To Kill a Mockingbird.* Only because I reread that one a lot."

"Right. You were that kid who actually liked the reading assignments in high school."

"What did they make you read in Japanese Catholic school, huh? The Bible? In what language?"

"For your information, it was bilingual. It was also used as a guide for English class, which I excelled at for the first time in my life."

"Too bad it wasn't Basic, huh? There's something they should teach in schools here."

Miranda tipped some cream into her coffee and blew the steam off the top. *If only she knew that it was Old Basic I was more fluent in,* she thought. "If you must know, I had zero plans today and couldn't bear the thought of going back to work without you being there."

"Just as well," Danielle said, red touching her cheeks. She would power through her embarrassment, though. "It would be super inappropriate now."

"Luckily, it's not."

Danielle finally unleashed the giggle she had been withholding. "I can't believe I'm having breakfast with you out in public like this."

"I know! And we didn't even sleep together last night! Crazy, isn't it?"

"You know what I mean!"

Unfortunately, Miranda did. Danielle continued to be utterly flabbergasted that there could be anything real between them. *Can't blame her,* Miranda rationalized. *She had her whole life turned upside-down a year ago, and now she's lost the only job she's ever had. Now here I am buying her breakfast.*

"In all honesty, I had a feeling that you may be unavailable for a while, so I thought we should get good and sick of each other. So you could properly miss me."

That drew another playful smile out of Danielle. Was that a record since her breakup with ex-girlfriend Alicia? "My grandmother called me last night and invited me to dinner tonight, so I'll probably be spending the night there. You know she's worried about me."

"Have you told her about us?"

"I haven't told anybody about us."

"Nobody?" Miranda was genuinely surprised. Somewhat. "Thought you would have told your closest friends." Including someone who currently wasn't on the planet.

"It's been a crazy week for a lot of people. I mean, in case you forgot, we've only been seeing each other for a week, and yesterday you asked me to be your girlfriend."

"I did, didn't I?"

Groaning, Danielle said, "It's a good thing you're rich, because I have a lot of stuff to shove into a moving van."

"You think I'm making room for all your stuff? I've seen it. All that black isn't good for my aesthetic."

"Just let my little gothic heart keep the bed sheets."

Miranda's phone buzzed beside her hand. "Absolutely not." She checked her iPhone, a Christmas present to herself when she realized the whole smartphone thing was probably the future. Although it had cost her a few points of respect in her other homeland, where five keychains attached to a flip phone remained the reigning champion. *Keychains on smartphones are so impractical.* She squinted at the text notification on her screen. *So is this asshole.*

She slid her father's notification off her screen. The message, *"We need to talk. Reply when you're available and I'll call you,"* was filed under H for Hot Garbage.

Miranda barely had a few seconds to decompress from her father shoving himself into her date when a familiar shadow loomed over the table.

"You have *got* to be kidding me." Ben Kallman, dressed in a white fitted T-shirt and a pair of denim cutoff shorts, held an iced tea to his chest as he looked between Danielle and Miranda. Danielle immediately covered her face with her hand and looked out the window. Miranda sighed, having forgotten that this diner was a popular weekend morning haunt for some of the people she worked with—and used to work with. "Like, you have to be messing with me." His finger jerked between the two women caught fraternization in their private time. "The moment I'm no longer in the betting pool for how long you two have been going out, you guys flaunt it right in my face."

"We're not flaunting anything," Danielle spat, her elbow sliding across the table. "Get your mind out of the gutter."

"Morning, Kallman," Miranda said with pursed lips.

"Hmm. No. You don't get to call me that anymore." That saucy tone was reserved entirely for Miranda, whom Ben turned his whole body toward, iced tea sloshing in its glass. "Not since you gave the worst testimony supposedly in favor of my character a few months ago. It's Ben now." He glanced upward, a wistful look on his fuzzy countenance. "Or DJ Baby Ben. I haven't decided yet, but you girls can come see me turning tables over at Rodrigo's any Friday night. Except you." He pointed to Miranda again. "I can't believe you. Just dragging your lesbian BS all over town and daring to not get court-martialed." His head whipped toward Danielle. "No offense. You're still cool. How's the civvy life treating you? Real drag, ain't it?"

Danielle shrugged, the disbelief that this was happening still clouding her eyes. "It's only been a week. I'm still adjusting to a lack of an income, insurance, or a proper retirement on the horizon."

"Sucks getting shoved out so close to the twenty, huh? Meanwhile, this one over here is made of Teflon and could start tonguing a girl right now and still somehow not get in trouble. Clinton's paradise, everyone!"

"Are you quite done?" Miranda asked. "We're preparing to enjoy our Sunday brunch."

"Oh, wouldn't want to interrupt Sunday brunch." Ben gestured his iced tea toward the group of guys in backward caps and pucca shell necklaces conversing over mimosas and new gym fliers. "No, heaven forbid. We can't go interrupting brunch around here. That would be *sooo* inconvenient."

Danielle braved lowering her hand from her face and giving Ben her undivided attention. "It's not what it looks like, all right? I may already be out on my ass, but I'd love it if you didn't tell people about this and start spreading stories."

"I'm not going to tell anybody anything. Not *willingly*." Both sides of his mouth dragged down when he said that. "I love you too much. And I don't wanna put *Troy* in the crosshairs. That would be a dick move. And I may be a dick, but I try not to throw my friends under proverbial buses."

"Appreciated," Miranda said.

"Mmm, you're not one of my friends, Hottie."

"Making a girl feel real good about getting up on a stand under oath and saying what a gentleman you've always been."

"Didn't work, so..." Ben cleared his throat. "Sorry, Danielle. Didn't mean to interrupt your lovely brunch, even though I question the company you keep."

"You make it sound like she single-handedly got you court-martialed two years before your twenty was up," Danielle said.

"Her? Single-handedly? Nah. I'm just a jealous guy who can't believe she cavorts with half the women in the neighborhood and is stilllll enjoying that promotion that should've been mine."

"If it makes you feel better," Miranda interjected, "I will probably never get another promotion before I retire."

Ben inhaled deeply. "Nope. Doesn't make me feel better. Ah, well, your secret is safe with me. I only wanted to make sure I knew what the hell I was looking at." He nudged Danielle, who braced herself against the table. "By the way, if you need a job, I know someone over at Lucy's who's hiring. Waiting tables, but she'll train you after hours on the bar where the *real* tips are."

Danielle managed a stunted smile. "Thanks, Ben. I'll let you know. Right now I'm taking a forced vacation."

He scoffed at Miranda once more before waving at them both and returning to his friends on the other side of the diner. Danielle shoved her face into her coffee while Miranda slowly shook her head. "It really is only a matter of time," she said.

Danielle's coffee cup touched the table. "Until..."

"Until I'm in trouble, of course."

They were silent until their food arrived a few minutes later. Danielle didn't know what to make of what Miranda said. In truth, Miranda didn't know what to make of what she said, either. Did she mean getting caught with a woman and being the next to go? Or did she mean something else?

Such as something to do with the person sitting across from her?

Twenty-Five

Nobody looked twice at the nondescript woman from a fallen family tip-toeing her way through Nicola Ferran's party. In truth, half of the attendees would have no idea who she was, even by name, since they had been born centuries after the restructuring and renaming of House Ducah. They saw someone like Calseeth and wrote her off as an introverted entity, either there at the insistence of someone else or because they were the sober +1 of a rowdier guest. Everyone who was enough in the "know" to get an invite also knew that Nicola's parties were built on the backs of naked servants and uncorked *yaya* that flowed as freely as the clothing of every guest ripping off their garments and either dancing on the tables or touching each other in adjacent rooms.

Calseeth had her own opinions about these depraved parties, of course, but she always kept them to herself. She did not attend the odd Ferran party because she wished to indulge in drunken revelry, talk poetry with the leading *julah* and hybrid artists, or find a one-night stand that would let her to relive her wild days of unfettered *inkep*. (Not that Calseeth's family allowed her to indulge the services of backroom agencies on Sah Zenlit. Her youthful hormones had to chew their way through human servants and the male hybrid escorts she saved up to pay when she joined her parents on a trip to Terra III.) Calseeth came because it was the best place to connect with liaisons, broker deals that helped a member of her family, and because Nicola Ferran remained a powerful ally whether she was married to the current human ambassador to Yahzen or not.

Besides, it gave her an excuse to get off Bah Zenlit for a few hours. A woman of her social standing could only go to so many places on Yahzen without attracting dirty looks and sympathy, and she avoided Ducah Estate outside of the obligatory festivities. It was better for her sanity.

Although one could argue that these parties were not much better for her mental energy. Conservative and reclusive Calseeth had to wade through a *hedpah* den in the room where Nicola's great-grandmother had penned one of the classic *julah* novels and search beneath drunken bodies in the ballroom until she finally found the dice game commanded by Lady Nicola Ferran.

"Calseeth!" The woman was spotted before she had the chance to observe some of the game. "What a wonderful addition to this party! Come, come, let us make room at the table." Nicola moved her smoking holder out of the way, inviting her other guests to scoot their chairs and allow Calseeth to have a seat at the end of the table. There was no declining it, since Calseeth's goal was to get to Nicola in the first place. "Everyone, please meet Calseeth. She's a very old friend. Her mother went to the Academy with mine. We're practically cousins." That was the politest way Nicola could introduce Calseeth in front of so many strangers, since Calseeth was a good several centuries older than the Lady commanding the party. Unlike the Ferrans, the Ducah women had married younger back when they were named The Dunsman Women. Back when someone like Calseeth would have been seen more for her connections instead of the untouchable spinster she was now. If a Ducah did not practically sell herself to a youngest son, she could kiss her marriage prospects to full-blooded *julah* goodbye.

"Very gracious of you to invite me to your get-together once again, Lady Ferran," Calseeth said with a bow of her head. "I always enjoy an excuse to exit the Academy for a night."

"That's right. Calseeth is the steward for Master Obello." Nicola fluttered her eyelashes and hunched her shoulders as she picked up the dice and tossed them between her hands. "She's also woefully sober." That was met with hearty chuckles and a snap of Nicola's fingers. "Come, come! Telulah, dear, bring us some more *yaya!*"

A fresh round of intoxicating spirits appeared at the table. Calseeth would have been remiss to reject a drink straight from the hostess, so she picked it up, joined the toast, and took a long sip. Most everyone else downed theirs in one gulp.

"Calseeth…" A man with heavy-lidded eyes and a slight slur to his speech turned to the interloper at the table. "That name sounds familiar. What is your family name? Or are you *ma-julah?*"

"How could she be a hybrid when I told you that our mothers went to Academy together? My mother died of old age." Nicola took a puff of her herbs. "Her being a hybrid would mean her own mother was one foot in the grave when Calseeth was born. Stop smoking so much, Gilbrent."

Calseeth's eyes widened. "Gilbrent Wellems?" she asked the man next to her. "The painter?"

"The very same, lovely Calseeth." He offered her his hand, sparking whispers around them. "Forgive me if I'm not at my most sophisticated tonight. None of us come to Nicola's party to sound insightful through the glasses of *yaya.*"

"One might say that the *yaya* makes us *more* insightful," Nicola said. "Will you join us for a round of dice, Calseeth?"

She consented, but only because Gilbrent looked at her like *that.* He knew who she was. Whatever his judgment, he did not visibly pass, but Calseeth was almost awestruck to be sitting next to one of Yahzen's most celebrated modern painters of the past five hundred years. There had always been artists, young and old, who pushed the cultural boundaries with their daring takes on *julah* sexuality, but none raised such ire as Gilbrent Wellems, who was most infamous for his series of nude portraits depicting young ladies mere hours after their *inkep* liaisons. For every daughter of a "good" family who publicly protested because of her recognizable flushed cheeks, there was one who went to the publications to tell all about his "unbelievable strength," which even Calseeth knew was a euphemism for his genitals. Even she was not sheltered enough to forget that the matchmakers favored prowess above all else, and Gilbrent had candidly written in his memoirs that he had been a part of "over a hundred professionally arranged liaisons with as many ladies." A Daughter for Every House, as some liked to say. *Including his own*, Calseeth thought with mild scandal.

"Calseeth," Nicola curtly said, rousing her guest's attention. "Shall we make room for you on the scoreboard?"

Calseeth nodded, but only because she had to stay in Nicola's good graces. She wanted an audience with the hostess, after all, and she would be damned if she came all this way to botch it.

This meant playing a delicate game. While everyone around her made merry, from downing a fresh glass of *yaya* to rolling their dice at every turn, Calseeth took careful sips of the alcoholic beverage and pretended she knew a damn thing about the game. She was required to put up a little something. Nicola assured her this was far from high-stakes, but what was the fun if they didn't risk losing *something* that night? To prove her point, she shimmied out of her underwear and plopped it on the small cart of empty glasses. Whoever won got her knickers.

One by one, players put up coins, membership cards to private *cageh* houses, and an unlit candle some *ma-julah* carried in her bag for no damn reason. Calseeth had nothing of small value to part with, aside from a handful of coins that soon joined the pile. She hoped the allowance Master Obello gave her would be more than enough.

Rowdy dice shaking and exclamations of winning and losing commenced. Nicola always managed to be in either first or second, which led to someone accusing her of using sorcery in a "game where we decided to not use sorcery!" Nicola, who was a decent sorceress in her own right, handwaved this away by insisting she was simply a lucky woman. Besides, how could someone accuse a soon-to-be-grandmother of such a thing? She was pure of Voided soul!

Calseeth was always toward the bottom, but that wasn't what she focused on while Nicola played hostess and dice bounced on the table. Every so often, Gilbrent leaned in toward her, *yaya* on his breath and hair grazing her cheek. "It's all in the wrist, see?" He pointed to Nicola, who flicked her wrist and watched the dice tumble to a decent number. "No sorcery required. She's been gambling for as long as she's been alive."

"You and she go back, Mr. Wellems?"

"We certainly do, Ms. Ducah."

She bristled. "You know who I am, huh?"

"The lot of your generation has a distinctive look. No name change is going to change the dark blond hair and sloping noses. I knew your father before he passed. Looked like his brother... who looked like his son."

At least he did not say Nerilis Dunsman's name in present company. This was exactly the type of party for recruiting to the League of Spiritual Awareness, but people were also likely to swap stories of interactions with the mass murderer or discuss how his priesthood would have gone in another timeline. The Dunsmans were a favorite topic of the philosophical crowd, but they kept it to themselves when someone like Calseeth was around. Sometimes, someone slipped and called her by her birthname, Calseeth Dunsman, and instantly regretted the hurt appearing on her face.

She had always liked that name.

"Here." Gilbrent washed away those thoughts as he took Calseeth's forearm the moment she picked up the dice for her turn. "Keep this part of your wrist locked. Flick only your hand. Your fingers should fan out with your pinky closest to your chest and your index finger near your neighbor. Go on. Try it."

With the tables' eyes on them, Calseeth released the dice with a flick of her wrist. They bounced together until upturning the highest number of points for her yet.

"See?" Gilbrent said as competitors clapped and spoke to one another. "It works."

Calseeth did not celebrate her small victory. She was too busy staring at the place where Gilbrent's hand had been, her skin still warm and her mind wondering when the last time she felt anything like this was.

Nicola had noticed this little interaction and didn't hesitate to bring it up as soon as the game was over and the other guests broke off to flirt on couches and talk of politics by the snacks. "Gilbrent has taken a small liking to you, I see." She took a decent drag from her *hedpah* holder and leaned back into her seat on a couch. "I want to warn you that his attentions tend to be fleeting, but hell, you should live it up a little, Calseeth. A fling with a man like that could be good for you."

Calseeth pretended she hadn't heard that. *I am much too old for "flings,"* she thought, reminding herself why she was there. "I hardly believe he even remembers me now." She sat directly beside Nicola. "If you have a moment, Lady Ferran, I should like to speak with you privately."

Those immaculate black eyebrows perked up. "Privately? Oh, this must be juicy. Why don't you follow me into the other room? I can ensure nobody follows us."

Nobody may have followed, but that didn't mean there weren't people already in that room. Nicola broke up a make-out party that was about to head to Conjugal City. The two young people already drunk on *yaya* feeling themselves on the *hedpah* stumbled out of the small study with their clothes half-off and their glasses askew on their faces. Nicola latched the door behind them and motioned for the very couch where those two were hard at work creating the next generation of hybrid *julah*.

"This is as private as it gets at one of my parties." Nicola lifted her smoking stick to her lips and leaned against the back of the couch. "Especially now, when everyone is starting to split off and pass out. Ugh. And I'm getting a headache. I'll do my best to hear you out, but I might need to get more of this stuff to keep the headache at bay." She lifted her stick. Calseeth politely avoided the smoke filtering in her direction.

"Thank you for your attention, Lady Ferran."

"*Please,* call me Nicola. Lady Ferran is what people call me when they want to suck up. Even my own husband calls me that in front of his dignitary friends. Which reminds me, I should surprise him on Terra III next week. These parties always make me sentimental for my pet human."

Calseeth would not comment on Nicola's attitude toward her human husband. Unconventional? Hardly. Nicola Ferran was far from the first *julah* aristocrat to marry a human while young. The more disconnected from both *julah* society and human culture one was, the easier it was to see a human spouse as nothing more than a phase—a passing fancy that a lady or master might consider a practice round for "real" marriage with a fellow *julah* later in life. Nicola had her pick of *julah* suitors. She was even sleeping with some of them, since she figured her husband Cornelius only had three or four decades left in him. Time to start sampling the goods before the proposals hit her mailbox three weeks after her husband's funeral. Nicola was mindful of her image, however. A years' worth of mourning, then she might openly court. But she probably wouldn't marry until her daughter Kalera had passed away as well. Then it would be appropriate to completely start over with a new family, while her hybrid grandchildren decorated parts of her house.

Calseeth, however, found such frivolity unnecessary. No jealousy involved, either.

"It's about one of my Master's acquaintances..."

Nicola leveled a sober gaze on Calseeth, who minded her demeanor. "We've been over this before. I have no desire to join the LSA, especially right now with its petty squabbles and bad PR. I already have enough drama with the capitol investigators infiltrating my parties. I had to have one escorted out before you arrived." She sighed. "Truly ridiculous times we are living in."

"It's not about the LSA," Calseeth said. "But it may be... slightly related."

Nicola may have been half-stoned and swimming in drink, but she had been partying for so many centuries that it was easy enough to snap out of it when necessary. It helped that her last round of *yaya* had been half an hour ago. "Dare I ask?"

"My Master's acquaintance needs a match. She must be full-blooded. Perhaps a lady who is wont of marriage and children, but can hold her own with her husband out of the picture. She must come from a family with strong genetic ties to sorcery. I suppose she must have close family members who have attended the Academy, if she herself has not. It does not matter which family she is from, as long as she is not from mine."

Nicola never looked away from Calseeth, who now shifted in her seat. The Lady Ferran was as quick and discerning as the wittiest matriarch, and there wasn't a shred of gossip that didn't go through her ears at one of these parties. Someone always let something slip. Sometimes, people like Calseeth came into her life and asked for a monumental favor.

"This acquaintance you speak of..." Nicola lowered her voice. "Wouldn't happen to be a cousin of yours, would it?"

Calseeth hesitated. Neither of them would speak Nerilis's name out of fear of someone accidentally overhearing and glomming on to the conversation. Yet it was difficult to be clear when all she could do was speak in simple riddles. "A rather infamous one, yes."

"Interesting." That was all Nicola said for a minute, as she contemplated the ceiling of her sitting room and smoked. Calseeth did not say anything as well. Not until she was sure that Nicola was about to cast her from the party. *Yet she said "interesting,"* Calseeth thought. *If I have piqued her interest, then I'm still her good acquaintance. Maybe even a friend.* "What does an old Forces dodger like him need with a wife? I thought part of his whole sorry story was that he was *so* distraught over the death of the first one. Did he finally move on a few thousand years later?"

"It's not a wife he's truly searching for," Calseeth said, ignoring the rest of Nicola's musings. "He's more in want of a... vessel."

"I daresay that's the way most men of our kind would put it if you truly asked. I tell you, Calseeth, I am *dreading* marrying a *vah-ke* one day." Her use of the old fashioned word for "*julah* male" would have amused Calseeth, but this was not an amusing conversation. "If they're not marrying you to advance themselves, they're doing it because their mothers are hounding them to continue the precious line. I see that such panic has finally come to the classic take on House Ducah."

"It goes deeper than that, hence the need for a talented woman. Magically talented, that is."

"And I suppose you're asking if I know of anyone desperate enough for children that she would risk her very freedom to bed the bastard and carry more bastards?" Nicola snorted. "So this is what happens when you spend most of your life in a haze of fancy. You become a flesh peddler for criminals." Her sigh brought with it a rearrangement of her body on the couch. "All right. I'll see what I can do. Should I go straight to you or your Master, should I think of anybody?"

"I suggest you ask me."

"Of course." Nicola absentmindedly scratched behind her ear. She might as well have been telling Calseeth to take her bidding elsewhere. "Dear Void. That is quite the favor to ask of me. No matter what I think of the man, I could get in a *lot* of trouble for talking about this." She glanced at Calseeth. "Meanwhile, I have no reason to believe you won't double-cross me the moment I bring you a name."

"To be fair, Lady Ferran," Calseeth said, already having anticipated this discontent, "I have no way of knowing you won't go straight to the authorities after tonight. Both my Master and I have much to lose if this gets out."

"Your Master, yes, I'm sure. But what do you really have to lose, Calseeth? You're the daughter of a fallen family. You were practically sold off to your Master because nobody would marry you, poor thing. You have no title. No real inheritance. No family of your own. No career you've carved for yourself outside of being the mousy little steward of a well-to-do Master of the Academy. Don't get me wrong, honey, you've done well with what life has handed you, but you're not exactly risking your life here."

"No." Calseeth's gaze moved to the hands folded in her lap. "But I am risking my freedom." She could end up in Federation prison for this, assuming her own government didn't prefer to put her in a cushy *julah* penitentiary where she would wear the same brown outfit every day for three hundred years while reminiscing with other low-offense women. Perhaps five at most were currently in the women's penitentiary house in the capital. Calseeth knew who most of them were, and she did not care to spend the next part of her life in their endless company.

Nicola studied her for a moment before speaking again. "Why? Why risk it for a cousin who never did you any favors?"

Calseeth squeezed her hands together. "He ruined our family. But he's also the only one with the ability to rebuild it."

"Yes. He is legendary enough that there is surely a woman out there desperate enough to beget him at least one child. I'll see what I can do. After that, it's all luck to your family."

That was all Calseeth had asked for.

Master Marlow fetched Lanelle and Devon on the arranged day, although he had asked them to meet him on the moon, where immigration demanded to process them anyway. Since Marlow did not set foot beyond intergalactic soil, he did not have to do anything more than sit at the only bar behind the checkpoint and sample Arrah's wine while waiting for his charges to arrive from planetside. When they stumbled past immigration, who once again pointed at Devon and grinned at the idea that he was one of their own, Marlow was already talking to the television set above the bar.

"What an idiot," he muttered, referring to the current Grand Chancellor of Yahzen, a man who had been his senior at the Academy. "I remember when you used to go to the pleasure club and get so wasted on *yaya* and *hedpah* that you passed out in a pool of your own vomit."

He had said that in Julah, a language the bartender conveniently did not understand. But Lanelle did, and that was enough for her to come up and say, "Would that be the pleasure club you own now?" She hopped onto the seat next to his while Devon stood behind them, a conspicuous baseball cap pulled down his face. Everyone—and that meant *everyone* who passed—pointed at him. Baseball caps were for Earthlings.

"No," was all Marlow said at first. Then, finishing his drink and leaving a tip for the bartender, "This was a place that's long since closed now. Mostly because my club ran it out of business when it refused to get with the times and start offering decent accommodations for students looking to blow off their most carnal steam."

"You're a smut peddler, sir." Lanelle patted him on the shoulder. "Just think, you might be semi-responsible for the children of your peers making little grand-babies!"

"I assure you there are rarely babies made at one of my clubs."

"Right, right. Except for when I'm there. Those boys like to try it, even though I'm as sterile as Devon here. Hey, maybe that's why they like me! No little hybrid babies to explain to Mom and Dad back on Yahzen."

Marlow sighed, preferring to assume that Lanelle was once more gassing herself up as a loose woman who blew off her spiritual trauma by fooling around with people most humans would never interact with, never mind mate. Because even if a human woman went to Bah Zenlit with the sole purpose of hooking up with Academy students, she would not usually do it at the kind of establishments Ramaron Marlow owned through a shell company. Most women weren't ad-mitted to begin with. They ruined the *vibe.* The drunken, smoking, pants-losing *'whatever, I'll try anything once'* vibe Marlow had spent his youth embracing while his best friend called him a pervert through clenched, jealous teeth.

Good memories, Marlow thought, staring at the Grand Chancellor. *He came to a party there once. Too bad I blacked out. I could probably blackmail him now.* If he needed the money, which Marlow did not.

Devon had blocked out the conversation he couldn't understand even if he wanted. Instead, he checked the time back home on his phone, since they were due to depart for Earth any second. *One in the afternoon,* he thought. *And I have to be back at work tomorrow.* He didn't want to consider the jetlag. Neither Arrah nor Terra III had a twenty-four-hour clock, so it was impossible for him to know how many days it would take to jump from early morning on Arrah to mid-afternoon in California.

Either way, he was sleeping a few dozen hours, God help him.

"Hey! Didn't think you guys would be back so soon."

It was strange hearing English—let alone *American* English—after two days of the heavily accented Modern Basic and whatever concoction of languages Lanelle spoke around Devon. Yet there was May, emerging from a ladies' restroom with her sweater buttoned up and her laces rethreaded right on time for traveling across the universe.

"Trip was quicker than going down," Devon said, his West Coast drawl attracting the attention of those around them.

"Great." Lanelle dragged herself away from the bar and stood between Devon and the looky-loos. "Move along, folks. No need to get security involved, right?"

May glanced at the small crowd forming. "Perhaps we should get a move on."

"Yes, of course." Marlow sighed, finished his drink, placed his hat on his head, and tapped his cane against the floor. He did not need help getting up, but he appreciated Devon's aid as they rounded the corner in the hall and kept to the far side of the wall. Families returning from intergalactic trips soothed crying babies and fixed the hair of daughters who were discombobulated in Arrah's instantaneous teleporters. A few day laborers on return from a business conference had manually flown in on a space cruiser that left them a little worse for wear than the teleporters, but they both agreed that particle rearrangement was *really* not their thing. Everyone, from Lanelle to May, was relieved they didn't have to travel by either method as long as a master *julah* was around.

Assuming Marlow didn't stumble from his two drinks, anyway.

A representative of the docking station and teleportation gate showed the party to a private waiting room they would use for their own teleportation. After filling out the same questionnaire he suffered through when he arrived an hour ago, Marlow motioned for everyone to huddle together and, "For the Void's sake, hold onto your belongings. I'm not coming back for something you may have dropped." For some reason, that was pointed to Lanelle, who was already dropping a handkerchief out of her bag and almost kicking it toward the wall.

"Coming to my place, huh?" Devon asked her. "Hope you like an old sink that backs up when it's cold."

Lanelle scrunched her nose. "Eww. You really do live like a bachelor, huh?"

"That's what most places around where we live are like," May said. "My heater clangs."

"What the hell is wrong with Earth? Hey." Marlow didn't get a chance to concentrate on what he was doing before Lanelle snapped fingers in his direction. "Get this boy some money so he can get a real place to live. Just because he lives on Earth doesn't mean he has to suffer in squalor."

"Thanks, Lanelle." This was the last thing Devon had the chance to say before they disappeared from Arrah's moon. "It's good to know you only have the best intentions in mind."

Before any of them knew it, they were in Devon's cold and abandoned apartment. The light came straight through his windows. Before taking the time to reorient himself, Devon stepped forward and lowered the blinds on his living room windows.

May inhaled deeply. "Ah, yes, backed up sink that hasn't been touched in over a week. Just like home."

"Eww," Lanelle said again, shielding her eyes from the fright of a half-empty studio apartment in the city. "I thank the Lady every day that I was not reborn on this planet. Especially a few hundred years ago, when I started doing that shit. Bet you guys didn't even have delivery in... ugh, what year was three hundred years ago here? This is supposed to be what Evan studies."

"Do you have everything?" Marlow asked, helping himself to one of the only two chairs in Devon's apartment. "If things seem to be in order, Lanelle and I will be departing for Terra III. Or, as she might like to call it, civilization."

"California is one of the biggest economies on Earth," May pointed out.

"Compared to what? Even Arrah's moon makes more money in their scam of a travel system."

"Ladies," Marlow said with a sigh. "There are things to be done."

Lanelle was all too happy to return to Terra III after first roughing it on Arrah and now standing in the midst of bachelor funk. She waved goodbye and stood next to her employer, already waiting to get the hell out of there. Devon wasn't upset about it, since he was prepared to collapse onto his bed and bury his face in a familiar pillow. Besides, he could contact Marlow whenever he wanted now. May, on the other hand, checked her cell phone for any updates from her mother.

They were due to meet in LA the next day, before May turned around and came back for band practice.

She still hadn't received an update about what happened to her mother after the Forces requested her presence.

"Finally." Devon opened one of his cupboards and grabbed a plastic cup. He bypassed the kitchen sink and filled the cup with juice from the fridge which, thankfully, had not spoiled while he was away. "Some peace and quiet."

May sat in the chair Marlow had been in. "Hope you don't mind if I chill for a few minutes before heading out."

"Sure. Want something to drink?"

Devon's phone lit up now that it had local service again. Old voicemails and texts from family, bandmates, and other friends listed themselves in no particular priority. May had long switched to an intergalactic communication provider that had bought the rights to certain American towers. Eventually, someone would convince Devon to do the same. "No, thank you," she said. "I'll probably stop at the corner coffee shop and get some caffeine after I leave."

The coffee pot hummed to life in the small kitchen. "Sorry about the smell."

"Please. If old apartment smell bothered me, I wouldn't be living in the city." May yawned. "Are you going to be ready for practice in a couple of days? Because I might sleep through it."

They barely hung on to their small talk while Devon made coffee and May pretended to be in fit condition to take the bus back to her own place. Maybe she should have accepted some caffeine, after all. *That would only keep me here longer,* she thought, watching the back of Devon's head as it moved from one end of the kitchen to the other. *Things are already awkward enough as it is.*

"By the way," she said, when Devon leaned against his sink with a coffee cup in his hand, "I haven't heard from my mom since I saw her however many days ago. I don't think I told you this, but she was escorted to the Forces' HQ by some no-thank-you grunts. I really hope she's okay."

Devon stared at her through the steam of his coffee. "You mean Rea?"

"That's my mom, yeah."

"What did she *do?*"

"I dunno! That's the freaky thing. I'm assuming they needed her expertise for something. They wouldn't... she didn't do anything wrong, so they wouldn't make her disappear, right? You were with..." May stopped. "Sorry."

"It's fine." It had to be. "I'd rather not talk about the commander, if it's all the same to you. Bit too complicated when I have intergalactic jetlag."

"I won't pretend to know what it's like to be in your position," May said. "My mom definitely makes it sound complicated. All the more reason to hope she's all right."

"I'm sure she is. She's a smart woman."

May gathered her skirt in her hands, pressing the fabric against her knees. "Everything's crazy lately. I don't know why I agreed to go on the trip. I don't even like Terra III. I hate the teleportation." Although, she had to admit that traveling with a *julah* sorcerer was so much nicer than the bastardized technology humans used to mimic the way talented *julah* altered the state of reality. "Everything's so crowded. The housing is so sterile. Nobody's shoving Jesus down your throat, but when the whole universe basically follows the same religion, you get tired of the Void shoved down your throat."

"How do you think I feel?" Devon muttered. "I've been there more times than most."

"Right. Sorry."

Devon put down his coffee and sighed. "I go back to work tomorrow. I've specialized in tech that is laughably obsolete in most of the universe. I'll probably walk into the office, where hardly anybody knows me, and get yelled at by my boss because I didn't fix a networking problem while I was on a sanctioned vacation. I can't decide if I'm excited about nobody giving a shit about me, or resenting it."

"If our band ever becomes popular, you'll already know what fame tastes like."

"I get the feeling you're not into it."

"Fame? No. I get enough attention working at the record shop. Serge talks a lot about his plans for the band with us. It takes all of me to not look him dead in the eyes and say, *'Devon and I are descended from aliens from another galaxy.'*"

For the first time in much too long, Devon laughed.

They both needed the laughter. Between May worrying about her mother and Devon remembering a mysterious man with an interest in the band, there was too much weight resting on their shoulders. Besides, they still hadn't fully healed after their fight a few mornings ago, when Devon returned from a night of bitter memories and a fouler taste in his mouth. May still believed he had been legitimately seduced by the commander. Devon still believed she was truly jealous.

They may have been bandmates first, friends second, but neither denied the curiosity simmering between them. Yet neither could say exactly what kind. Was it even a curiosity that was sated by being around each other more? Matters weren't helped when May felt guilty for getting close to Devon because her mother asked for her help getting through to him. And when Devon stewed in his failed relationships, he had no time for the other women in his peripheral. Yet even he had to admit that May would make a convenient girlfriend. She knew who he really was. She was familiar with the Federation—shit, she was a citizen—and could not only show him how things were done a thousand years after Cerilyn, but she wouldn't freak out about it, either. They both shared a love of music, and her preference for Earth's level of technology and communication meant they would never argue about what planet to live on should it come down to it.

She wasn't bad to look at, either. Her thin brown hair and long body may have been trademarks of modern Federation genetics, but compared to other Earthlings, she was striking in her own way. Devon didn't care that she was taller than him, but he was aware that some women were weird about it.

May wasn't weird about it, though. She had been thinking a lot of the same things about him. The only major downside *was* his real identity, since May could live her whole life without dealing in more Federation drama and whatever shit Devon was dragged into on a weekly basis. He may not have believed it, but she knew he wouldn't be doing networking for hardly another year. He was too high-profile. By the end of that year, Devon—and Danielle—wouldn't be able to cross the street without some nitwit freaking out. May didn't want that level of attention in her life. Not even if their band became the biggest in the country.

Still... that past week had proven something to the both of them. They cared enough to fight over Commander d'Alacron. May had shown her jealousy beneath the façade of concern. Devon had already insinuated that he needed someone who could understand him so well in his life.

May picked at a bump on her finger. "I should apologize for anything I might have said this past week that put unneeded stress on you. I knew this trip wouldn't be easy for you. But I had no idea how it might really affect you."

"To be fair, I didn't either." Devon shook his head. "A year ago, I would've thought it the coolest shit ever. But that's before I started remembering everything. Those people wanted to push an idealized image of what my life was like. I know it's been a thousand years since a planet full of trained mercenaries existed, but I can't believe people thought it was anything but a prison. Even those who made the best of it like me were miserable."

"Are you miserable *now?*"

"No... but I can remember. It's ingrained into my soul. It's trauma."

May didn't say anything. She merely stood up, thinking of her mother's studies on the effects of the Process and regression therapy. Lanelle Lanerak had been her star subject for the past several decades. That woman was a lot like Devon, and it showed every time they were in a room together. Their old and tired souls had seen more life, more experiences, more trauma than the average human. For all May knew, she was a reincarnation of someone who had known trauma and died, but she would never remember. She would never carry around that weight like Devon and Lanelle did.

"I'm sorry," May apologized again. "If there's anything I can do, let me know. As a friend."

"Yeah. A guy could always use some friends."

He hadn't meant to sound sour about it. What Devon said was true. He needed friends more than ever, perhaps. Friends who could deal with who he might become as his soul finally settled into his body.

He and May stood awkwardly in the middle of his small living area. Every time they made eye contact, their gazes shifted again.

What was there to say? Did they even know what they *wanted* to say? Were they so caught up in who should make the first move that they became paralyzed with fear? After all, if the experiment went belly-up, there could be hurt feelings. And those hurt feelings might spill over into the band they were both attempting to launch into something better. Something more permanent.

First thing a manager told any band was *don't shit where you eat.* Which made perfect sense for a man who currently had a lot on his plate and a woman trying to get by day by day.

"You know what? I'm going to go." May brushed the dust from her skirt and headed toward the door. "I'm tired. I'm sure you are, too. This whole past week has been a roller coaster, then you went back to your planet..."

"You went back to your planet," was not a normal thing for a woman to tell Devon, let alone so nonchalantly. Not even Danielle would say that. Not in her current state, anyway.

"Yeah, probably take a nap. Restock on groceries. You gonna be okay going home?"

"It's a simple bus ride away."

"I mean, I could give you a lift in my car."

May gave him such a pathetic look that Devon almost felt silly for making such a suggestion. Of course May didn't need—or want—a ride from him. But what could he say? That he didn't want her to go because he didn't want to be alone?

"Hey..." He approached her as she reached the front door. "Thanks again. For everything this week."

She stared at him as if she still wasn't sure what he really wanted. Then again, *she* didn't know what she wanted either.

They might as well get this over with.

If Devon ranked the first kisses he experienced in his life, the one with May would place third for notability... but first for pure, willful passion. May flung her arms around his shoulders, and he grabbed her by the waist with the intent of not letting her go, but it was for show. Devon was more wrapped up in the presentation of that kiss than the actual emotions welling up inside of him.

Perhaps because there *were* no emotions.

He may have been broken. Maybe she wasn't into it, either. Maybe this was a terrible idea and they would immediately regret it the moment they pulled away. Void knew they would make a convenient pair, though. Their close proximity, their understanding of each other's lives—and May's ability to look past Devon's fame and simply see who he was now, while respecting who he used to be—and their shared interests made for a generous relationship. Yet so many conveniences could not orchestrate chemistry. Devon felt that the moment he put his lips on May's. The regret was instantaneous. The physical passion may have burned, but he could think of at least two other women he'd rather have a mediocre kiss with right now.

They broke it off at the same time, Devon lowering his arms and May holding her hands to her chest. They shared one glance before May said, "That was..."

Devon sighed.

"Oh, thank God, you think so too?"

The relief on May's face was what made Devon laugh. "At least we got that out of our system." He walked her to the front of his building before waving her off. He had already forgotten about the kiss by the time he returned to his coffee.

Twenty-Six

The main office of data entry division was eerily quiet Monday morning. Miranda didn't make eye contact with anyone as she came into the building, and she sure as hell didn't acknowledge any of her subordinates as they hustled to their desks and logged into their assigned computers. There was never much for her to do, outside of taking a head count and reporting absentees. Usually, there was a small stack of weekend notices on her desk. Most of them inconsequential. Occasionally, a missive from a higher-up that someone was in trouble.

Big trouble, as of late.

Today, she walked into her office and turned on the light to discover a familiar manila envelope in the center of her desk. Shelley, who had been her secretary for the past three years, started her day an hour earlier than Miranda and was the only other person in the division who had a key to the private office. The way she neatly lined up the captain's mail was more recognizable than the view from the simple rectangular window allowing Miranda a glimpse of freedom.

"*Notice of re-assigned officer.*" Lieutenant Anne Wilson was pictured side by side with herself, once in her dress uniform and once in everydays. The same stern expression looked back at Miranda in each. *I can't look like that in my photos even when I try,* she thought, remembering how the photographer had admonished her for "smiling" too much in her photos. She hadn't been smiling, though. The military did not offer many reasons to smile.

Turnover could be high in data entry. The office was a healthy mix of those who had been there for years and those who wouldn't be remembered in a few weeks. "Purgatory" was a common nickname throughout M-Town. Lieutenants with nowhere else to go after their promotions often sat at a desk and received software training before their inevitable reassignment papers arrived. Those who stayed for more than a few months often found it their new home, where they languished until retirement or discharge, whichever came first. The overflow of lieutenants who never made it to captain used to depress Miranda when she first arrived as a fresh Second Lieutenant. Having been captain of the division for the past few years, however, taught her that she was one of the lucky ones.

Lieutenant Wilson's file came with a handwritten note from her former CO. Miranda was used to those too. It usually meant that the *real* reason a transfer to Purgatory was granted had nothing to do with the official reason on file. In Wilson's case, that was *Insufficient Performance at Former Post.*

The note bent over backward to say that DADT was sniffing around Wilson's personal life. Which meant she was not only sent to Purgatory—for her own safety, presumably—but to the other, lesser voiced nickname for data entry: Gays and Gimps, home of the closeted homosexuals and those too disabled to see action, but hale enough to sit in front of a computer screen. Out of every lieutenant who was transferred out of Miranda's department, only a few were sent overseas.

There was only one cubicle available for Lt. Wilson. Danielle's old desk, which she had personally cleaned out during her official walk of shame and military IT later decommissioned and rebuilt from the computer up. The same dog and pony show every time someone was dishonorably discharged or court-martialed.

Too many lately.

Still, this was the only one to hurt more than Ben Kallman's escort from the premises. Miranda may have had her dream girl warming her bed as of late, but it didn't stop her mouth from drying as she prepped to receive a grim-faced lieutenant five minutes after nine.

"First Lieutenant Anne Wilson reporting for duty, ma'am." Her hat was tucked beneath her arm while she saluted her new CO. Miranda barely acknowledged that someone had entered before she was forced out of her chair. "Captain Jackson sends his regards."

Jackson had once worked alongside Miranda when they were both desk jockeys in that office. He was promoted first and sent to another division while Miranda became the queen of Gays and Gimps. No wonder he thought to have Wilson transferred to her domain. That buzzcut was for more than ease of care.

"At ease, Lieutenant." Miranda hated how rigid so many of these transfers were when they first arrived in her office. They reminded her too much of who she used to be. "You're five minutes late. The shift started at nine."

"My apologies, ma'am. I did not receive my orders until fifteen minutes ago."

"You came from Jackson's department... that's on the other side of M-Town."

"I marched right over, ma'am. Haven't even cleaned out my locker there yet."

Miranda sat back down in her chair and rubbed her temples. "Since this job is about as simple as throwing rocks into the water, we can go over your training in another hour. That will give me time to get through this paperwork and afford you my undivided attention." She dragged over a piece of paper that was stamped with URGENT. "Return to your former post, gather your things, and report back. If Captain Jackson gives you grief, tell him Hotchner says hello." Her voice couldn't get any droller. "He'll know what it means."

"Yes, ma'am!" Wilson marched out of the office. Nobody paid her any mind as she hauled ass out of the department.

The military court-martials one big ol' queer only to send me another one, Miranda thought that the moment her phone buzzed on the edge of her desk. She wasn't supposed to entertain personal use during work, but unless brass kicked down her door and asked what she was doing, she could spare an extra five minutes to check her texts. Preferably out of sight from where she was *pretty* sure someone had installed a hidden camera to keep track of how often she bit her nails and poked a tissue up her nose to get that *one thing* bothering her breathing.

There were two texts awaiting her. The first that caught her attention was from Danielle, who had sent her a grainy photo of the view from bed. Miranda vaguely recognized the bedroom window with curtains closed and the sun bringing on a new day.

"Still not used to staying in bed on Monday mornings. Aren't I supposed to report to work by 0900 hours?"

Miranda was sentimental enough to see the veneer of serious contemplation in Danielle's simple text. The rest of it was flirtation. Always appreciated.

"I like you where you are right now." Miranda texted. *"If only I could leave this office and come straight to you. You're not even here anymore. What's the point?"*

"Keeping the secret that we're actually banging now that I'm out of military jail. Everyone would explode to see us make out. Bet you five bucks."

"I explode when we make out."

"Is that what that stain is on my shirt?" Danielle asked.

Miranda kept a giggle to herself as she scrolled to their older texts. They were careful to not send anything too risqué, although the references to making out and banging wouldn't help Miranda's case should she be court-martialed. *So I won't submit my texts as proof I'm really straight. If I get court-martialed... I don't care. It would almost be a relief, now that she's not here anymore.*

"I keep remembering what you looked like on my office floor, doing pushups because you were a few minutes late again."

"Quick question," Danielle replied. *"I always wondered if you made me do fifty pushups instead of the standard twenty because you thought it was hot."*

"Oh, absolutely. I also liked the way you held in your grief over the situation. Although over the years you did get a little whiny about it. I should have made you do seventy."

"I'm still doing my pushups and sit-ups. Before the end of next month, I plan on showing you what I can do with one hand."

"My God, Cromwell! It'll practically be my birthday by then!"

"Are you going to tell me to do my pushups then?"

"Do you want me to? I didn't realize we were heading toward roleplay so soon."

A figure caught Miranda's eye through the small two-way mirror to the main room. Shelley had stood a little too close to the mirror and caught the fluorescent lights above her. When Miranda looked back down at her phone, thinking about getting to work and saving the flirtations for lunch, she noticed the other text alert.

It was written in Julah.

"You must practice," was all it said.

The message came from an unknown number, which didn't shock Miranda. Her father could make up a number and have it show up on her phone, like he pulled money out of the air and sent it to whatever overseas accounts she currently kept. The sorcery behind it wasn't the point. It was the message. *"You must practice."* A daily reminder that she wasn't any normal woman falling in love all over again.

She was destined for something else. No, not greatness. Whatever machinations her father practiced on any given day.

Practice. How was she supposed to do that at work? Set aside the folders and stare at her paper weight until it moved?

Miranda pocketed her phone and got up. She might as well make the morning rounds while she thought.

She bumped into Lt. Wilson a few minutes later, fresh from her run across M-Town and none the sweatier for it. Miranda would have been impressed, but she had looked forward to a mindless surveillance of her shoebox kingdom—much like she once spent her late evenings staring out across the jungle canopy of a planet that hosted her tribe of violent misfits.

If the Pentagon knew she could run such a ruckus...

"This is your new station, Lieutenant." Miranda escorted Wilson to Danielle's old cubicle. There were no signs of the other woman left behind. Not even a hint that she had been court-martialed instead of reassigned. "Your login information has been provided in your file. IT should have set up the computer to automatically begin your tutorial programming as soon as you log in. I expect you should have it completed by lunch."

"Yes, Captain."

"James?" Miranda interrupted Troy in the middle of his morning work. As soon as he removed his headset, Miranda continued, "Lt. James can finish showing you around and answer any questions you may have." They had an understanding that she would look the other way if he didn't meet his quota that day as a result. "Welcome to our little family of misfits, Lieutenant."

"Thank you, ma'am." Yet Anne Wilson looked between Troy and Miranda as if she were missing key information. "Misfits, ma'am?"

Sighing, Miranda returned to her office. She hadn't meant to actually say that word.

Is it wrong for me to miss the woman who used to sit there, even though I'm now closer to her than ever? Miranda shut herself up in her office and sat in front of her window. She didn't know how much more of this job she could take, what with her primary reason for enlisting now free from its constraints.

Danielle... no, Sulim...

Miranda's hands curled around her armrests. Her breath had a habit of leaving her as of late. When she was alone, balancing the reality of the present with the gift of the past, it was like her subconscious abandoned her. What gave her strength? Balance? The inner eye required to see the truth lurking deep within her Processed soul?

I shouldn't be here, Miranda thought. *I should be with her. What if she regresses?* Yet as much as Miranda worried that Danielle might need her, she also worried what would happen the moment Sulim awakened as well.

Will she love me? Kill me?

Miranda consoled herself with one fact. If Devon hadn't killed her moments after regressing, Danielle probably wouldn't. But she could do something worse. *She could leave me,* Miranda thought. *What if the pain is too hard to bear and she leaves me?*

If those thoughts weren't proof that Miranda was always looking for reasons to abandon ship on her existence, she didn't know *what* would be. Here she was, watching one of the biggest dreams she had harbored in the past one thousand years come true, and all she could think about was how it would inevitably crash in flames.

Her paperweight caught her eye. Lest she brushed off her father's instructions, Miranda snatched the weight off a stack of slender folders and placed it before her. She folded her hands beneath her chin and focused all of her attention on the glistening, marble-like qualities of the glass paperweight.

It didn't move.

Of course it didn't. She hadn't put enough thought into it. Nor had she embraced the purpose of such an exercise. *"As important as it is to learn basic sorcery,"* Nerilis Dunsman could be heard saying much too long ago, when he addressed a young class of Academy students, *"none of it will matter unless you have conviction behind what you are doing. The Void, of all things, knows this."*

Unlike Miranda Hotchner, who didn't know enough.

Commander Yara d'Alacron still nursed her emotional wounds when she called the captain of the Federation's intergalactic secret police into her office.

The Covert Investigators of the Federation always came and went from the Forces' headquarters, but Yara didn't make a habit of talking to them directly if she could help it. More than a few of her predecessors had tanked their careers thanks to plucky journalists who uncovered unbelievable conspiracies that had seen coups on moons and meddling with non-Federation planets. Not that Yara was *above* contracting their services. Sure, Captain d'Kerni reported directly to President d'Errowyn on all matters official and secret, but Yara had an understanding with the esteemed president. That's how things worked in the Federation.

That's how they work everywhere, Yara thought, as she greeted Captain Joel d'Kerni in her office. The man, who was old enough to be her father, carried himself with such pride and conviction that Yara often thought her own private guard could learn a thing or two from this man, who had fought in two wars, including a little uprising called Sunset on the former capital planet Terra II. Although Terra II, the unfortunate predecessor to the current capital planet of the Federation, had been lost to human carelessness thousands of years before, Captain d'Kerni often joked that he remembered the wars that ended it.

Now here he was, having been summoned under the air of top secret black matters.

He offered the Federation salute before accepting Yara's invitation to sit beside her desk. Since the matter was not only top secret, but the commander had a blistering headache to still nurse, she did not offer him any refreshments.

"Thank you for coming on such short notice, Joel." Yara didn't hide the pain pill she swallowed. She did, however, keep the alcohol accompanying it within a common water bottle. She was far from recovered from her night with Devon, and the illustrious Dr. Rea d'Eran had informed her that it might take "several weeks" for not only the *hedpah* to completely wear off, but for the commander to accept the weight upon her soul. The good doctor was also the one to prescribe the pain pills now soothing the past-life memory receptors of Yara's brain, so there was that. "I know you are a busy man, but what I must ask of you cannot wait. It's a matter of intergalactic security."

The captain looked around the office. Drawn blinds. All technology shut down, covered, or decommissioned. Hell, most of it was out of the room, since Yara would not risk a single device recording this meeting for her future infamy. "Considering what I see here," he said, "it is either an assassination attempt against the president, or..." He snorted. "Nerilis Dunsman, I presume?"

"Astute." Yara licked her finger and pressed the pad against the fingerprint lock on one of her desk drawers. Inside the drawer was a box that could only be opened with one of her tears. Not hard to muster when all she had to do was think about what had haunted her memories so shortly after her plans backfired. "Yes, new information has come to light. I called you in because I have an important *covert* job for you, Joel."

His shoulders slightly sagged from the gravitas her words commanded. "I see. Dare I ask if he's up to his old tricks again? Or is it finally time to run in and bring justice to the old bastard?"

"I wish, but we are one step closer." Yara unearthed the condensed folder she created shortly after Lilla Amyran left her office several months ago. "The time has come for me to tell you about this. I have been sitting on it for a long time, deciding the best course of action, but I feel that my hand has been forced."

Yara flipped open the folder and slid it toward Captain d'Kerni. He snatched it off the desk and held it before his face, consuming information that held the highest level of confidentiality. Not even Yara's second-hand man knew the contents of these folders.

"Bring that woman in for questioning," Yara said. "Whatever it takes, short of killing her. Although I hope she comes willingly. Make her feel like an esteemed guest before I lay it into her." *I honestly can't wait,* Yara thought. It had been a long time coming, and she hadn't even known it yet.

Joel lowered the folder to his lap. "This is beyond Federation control."

"It's a matter of intergalactic security, and we have a duty to follow through. The trillions of people we supposedly protect and serve would expect nothing less from us."

"The president..."

"You let me worry about d'Errowyn," Yara snapped. "Do you, or do you not also take orders from me, Joel? We won't harm a hair on her pretty head. Not if we get the information we need. I'm prepared to offer her immunity, depending on what she gives up." And depending on how Yara felt by the end of the confrontation. It could go either way, honestly. She might let the woman go. She might slit that pretty throat.

The captain looked down at his supposed orders once more. "I will need access to the teleporter for any and all men I take with me. Inform the local chief of police that we will be doing covert work and to politely look the other way. And..."

"Joel," Yara interrupted, "I know how to run an operation like this. I only need you and your closest men to do the dirty work. Preferably as soon as possible. Can you do it tomorrow?"

"Tomorrow?"

"Time is of the essence. I need to extract information from her before Dunsman makes his next move, whatever it might be. Hell, I need her to tell us his next move. Where he's staying. What he might be willing to negotiate should..."

"All right. I get it. Time is of the essence." Joel sighed. "I will see what I can do. It will require pulling some of my top men away from their assignments on short notice. One of them is undercover on Yahzen. Some of the very same work you're looking to do right now."

"Do whatever you must. I expect to be informed of how it's going within six hours."

"Six..."

"Did you not hear me? I expect a prompt response ASAP. Starting now, Joel."

He took that as his cue to leave, not that he was in the business of staying behind for an idle chat with one of the biggest headaches in the upper echelons of Federation control. When Joel showed himself out of the office, he didn't bring with him a copy of his orders. Nor did he ask any further questions. His mind was sharp enough to remember the important details.

Besides, the pictures included within the file were not easy to forget. Captain Joel d'Kerni was a pious man who never missed a scheduled service with his local Priest of the Void. Half of his generous paycheck went right to the Temple, and he was no stranger to the charity events that required volunteers and high-profile men such as himself. It was what made him a solid choice for his promotions over the years, when the Federation Forces were eager to capture a heretic traitor like Nerilis Dunsman. In fact, no one had more elegantly slanderous things to say about that man than Joel, who took something that happened a thousand years ago as a personal affront to his faith.

He had seen the official photographs and paintings of every High Priest and their spouse going back countless years. He knew what Nerilis Dunsman's beloved looked like.

What did he think of the picture he saw? He didn't let it overcome him until he was in the elevator, checking that he was alone before heaving a sigh of heresy. As far as he was concerned, he was off to pick up the High Priestess herself for a round of Federation-style interrogation.

Hopefully, the Void would have mercy on his unclean soul.

Twenty-Seven

The days of twirling a phone cord around her finger may have been in the past, but Miranda found ways to express her giddy girlishness as she flopped on her couch late Monday evening and partook in what was now her favorite part of the day. She didn't even mind the bulky, flat phone in her hand that had taken some getting used to after many years of flipping and folding her old phone.

"Okay, but how gay *is* she?" Danielle asked, taking the news that she had already been replaced quite well. "Is she gayer than me? Because I guess it's okay if someone new is moving in on my best friend if she's gayer than me."

"Normally I wouldn't play the 'who's gayer' game," Miranda paused to sip her herbal tea, "but this woman is pretty damn gay. And a damn better soldier than you. Did you know she *ran* back across M-Town to get her things after I gave her the order?"

"I would have walked."

"You would have taken your sweet time, no matter how fast your legs were moving."

"Yeah, well, you know me..." A wistful sigh like that was liable to send Miranda crawling over the back of her couch. How else was she to filter the excitement always bubbling in her veins? "My legs don't have to be moving to get the job done."

"Your mouth is always running, though."

"Damn it, that was your chance to make the obvious joke."

"Sometimes it's more fun to toy with you than give you what you want."
Miranda chuckled. "Speaking of things I already know..."

Danielle muttered that she didn't see why she couldn't come over right now
to put that theory to the test. Miranda was inclined to invite her, but something
had felt off since the moment she stepped through her door at five-thirty. She
had intended to spend the evening purging her feelings another way. But before
she made the segue from dinner dishes to upstairs art studio, she decided to call
Danielle and tease her from a neighborhood away.

"You know what I should paint?" Miranda took her time ascending the stairs.
Whenever her bare foot landed on the carpeted runner, she remembered a little
over a week ago, when Danielle graced this house with her ephemeral presence.
"You. Naked. There. Is that blunt enough for you?"

"Thought you weren't into painting pictures of people," Danielle said with a
chilling sigh.

Miranda pushed the studio door open with her shoulder. The light flicked on.
In the corner was a brand-new canvas, her recently completed project propped up
against the wall. She had to kick away paint-splattered newspapers and search for
her smock to get to her stool and easel, but that was any other night spent in her
studio. *I've got one hour before I should head to bed,* she thought. With any luck,
Danielle would keep her company that whole time.

"I didn't say it had to be a literal painting of you naked." Miranda considered
her color options before committing to picking up a brush. "Abstract art, my dear,
does an excellent job of getting the sensual point across."

"Dunno. Are you sure you've seen me naked enough times to get an accurate
depiction?"

A brand-new brush popped out of its plastic wrap. "You're killing me." The
midnight blue paints drew Miranda's attention. She dipped the virginal brush
into the paint, the smell hitting Miranda right in the pleasure center of her already
fantasizing brain. "Next thing I know, you're moaning and groaning over the
phone, and I wouldn't even be convinced you're touching yourself. You're just
doing it to drive me nuts."

"You're already on to my tactics?"

"It's almost like I know you well enough by now to know what a needy pillow princess you are." Streaks of blue appeared on the canvas. Was tonight a chance to test a new technique? How much did she want to depict the night sky as it embraced the lovers dancing in their private oasis? "As it so happens, I love women who incorporate pillows into their diets."

No matter how many times Danielle attempted to say something, she betrayed the giggles throwing her across her own bed. "That's because you don't give me a chance!"

"Why would I do that?" Miranda leaned back from her canvas, considering the mess she had already made. "It's so much fun tossing you around my bed!"

"And my bed, apparently."

"Is that where you are right now?"

"Aha!" Triumph blew across the line. "I knew this is where everything was headed. You want to phone sex me while you paint!"

"Do I? Sounds incredibly distracting. I'm trying to be a serious artist over here." While Miranda let that stew on the other end of the line, she glanced outside the small window overlooking her street. Shadows moved beneath the streetlamps. A large van came to a slow stop in front of the neighbor's house. Miranda thought nothing of it. Although it was well after eight, it wasn't unusual for utility maintenance to park on her street for most of the night. "I don't know if you recall, but my paintings hang in galleries on the other side of the world."

Danielle was silent while Miranda swapped her brush between hands.

"You there?"

"Yeah." Danielle cleared her throat. "Sorry." The flirtations were over. Danielle's distracted voice and Miranda's busy hands would bring this conversation to a close before they ran out of things to say. "I had this really weird feeling. Been getting them a lot. But I might just be traumatized." She laughed that off, but Miranda remained fixated on the nervous charge in Danielle's tone. "There's this huge change in the air, you know? I don't just mean all the crazy stuff in *my* life. Don't really mean whatever's going on between... us..."

This was Miranda's chance to put the idea of going seriously steady out there again, but somehow, it wasn't the proper time. "What do you mean?"

Her curt demeanor brought Danielle to another sudden silence. "I dunno. Maybe I'm picking up a sixth sense for shit hitting the fan. Or maybe I'm anxious about the future. I guess I should call some people and make sure they're doing okay. I haven't talked to my ex in a while. Is that a weird thing to say to someone you started dating a week ago?"

Who was the ex, again? Miranda *should* have known it was Alicia, the woman she had met more than once during Danielle's younger years. *A woman I was jealous of,* Miranda thought. Yet her brain tricked her into thinking it was Devon—and if she was jealous of Alicia? She seethed with disdain for the man who was now her rival. Not just in love, but *everything.* Devon's inability to let go of what happened a thousand years ago was understandable, but his concurrent inability to realize that Miranda was no longer that person shoved a pinecone up her ass.

"Not weird. Wouldn't I rather date someone who was on friendly terms with her exes? I mean, if you have nothing but awful exes, I would assume the problem was with *you,* huh?"

"I guess. I haven't talked to her since the... you know what."

"Her?"

Danielle scoffed. "Yeah. You remember Alicia, right? I dated her for a couple years. We broke up because I asked her to move in with me and she freaked out about her homophobic parents finding out."

"Oh. Right. I remember her now."

"Who do you think I meant? Some guy?"

"I mean... there was that guy..." Miranda couldn't remember Seth's name to save her life. Nor could she recall how long he and Danielle had gone out. Was it a date? Five years? She was in the hot seat now, and her memory might as well go out with her trash.

Danielle wasn't thinking of Seth, though. She was thinking of the only man who might qualify. Because that *wasn't* Seth.

"*Anyway,*" Danielle continued, "tell me I'm not losing my mind and everything will be okay."

Before Miranda could offer such reassurances, someone rang her doorbell.

"Uh, hold on a sec." Miranda set aside her materials and slipped off her stool. She didn't bother checking her hair or smock as she hurried down the hall and stepped down the stairs. The doorbell rang again before she made it across the living room.

When she poked her head through the front window curtains, she was met with the dour face of a man wearing black and sunglasses. At night.

He wasn't alone. Not according to the small entourage on Miranda's driveway and the driver keeping the van idling across the street.

"I had a caller come to the door," Miranda said. "I'll have to call you tomorrow, babe." She waited a few seconds for Danielle to say something, but there was no time to anticipate a farewell. Miranda had to hang up now, before the man in all black and sunglasses knocked down her door with his bare fist.

The curtains closed. Miranda inhaled a deep breath. Nobody outside her house possessed a particularly aggressive stance. While they didn't scream *cops,* she still had a despondently bad feeling regarding her safety.

After another large breath, she smoothed down her hair and cracked open her front door.

"Yes?" she asked.

The man leading the procession lowered his sunglasses. It wasn't enough to see his eyes. "Miranda Hotchner?" he asked, accent thick. "Please open the door."

That wasn't English. That wasn't anything but Basic, a language Miranda knew well enough thanks to her previous life—and knowing too many assholes on Earth who spoke the lingua franca of the Federation.

Not cops, she thought. *Federation Forces.* If only she knew how bad it could get yet.

After unlatching her door, she opened it wide enough to block the entrance with her body. The lack of cool air was daunting. The lack of any emotion on Captain d'Kerni's face brought newfound levity to Miranda's consciousness.

"What is this about?" Miranda asked in Basic. She hoped her accent wasn't tragic enough to offend these men. "Are you with the Federation?"

"We can tell you more as soon as we've sequestered you to an interview room. It's not safe in the street like this. Please, come with us. You are not under arrest."

The "yet" hung unsaid in the air. Miranda clenched her teeth. The last time she was asked to go with someone like this, she died.

"Who are you? Tell me that before I come with you."

"I am Captain Joel d'Kerni of the Federation Forces. We request your presence for an interview. This is a matter of intergalactic security, so you're coming with us either way. I *highly* suggest you take the peaceful route, Ms. Hotchner. You will be returned to your home as soon as your interview is complete. I repeat, you are not under arrest."

"Yet I'm coming with you either way." Miranda glanced over her shoulder. She swore she heard someone lurking outside her back door. "All right. Allow me five minutes to take this smock off and grab my bag. At least give me that."

She hid her fear to the best of her ability. Fear wouldn't get her anywhere. The more these men knew she feared them, the more likely they were to take it to their advantage.

While they gave her five minutes to remove her smock and grab a light sweater from the coat closet, Joel motioned for his men to get back in their vehicles. He and two others awaited Miranda at the front door, where she emerged with the keen awareness that *someone*—perhaps a *ma-julah* among the ranks—cast a temporary illusion spell over the neighborhood. All the better for Miranda's sanity as she was marched past her neighbors' houses and watched cars pass right by them without regard for what happened.

She was escorted into the back of the van parked across the street. While dark inside, she was greeted with the scent of *hedpah* and her escorts wearing masks to filter the shit out of their own heads. Miranda was not offered such a mask.

She looked at Joel, who sat across from her, mask snapped against his face and arms crossed against his chest. These were two people who were well-trained and used to showcasing the best poker faces in the business. For Miranda, that meant hiding the anxiety reaching her fingertips and draining her mouth of saliva. For Joel, that included silencing the part of his brain that demanded he cease his heresy right away.

It already took every ounce of restraint to refrain from asking Miranda the questions that burned within him. Looking upon her face was nothing like beholding it in photographs. She was more like those paintings he saw at every service in the Temple of the Void than anything had led him to believe.

He was not the only one who swore she looked like someone they had seen before. But only Joel d'Kerni knew who she was, and the urge to stop the van and release Miranda was strong enough to save his soul.

Instead, he said, "Does the *hedpah* not affect you?"

Miranda chose her words carefully. "Of course it does." The van hit a bump in the road. The inexperienced Federation driver had taken it much too fast, and everyone in the back braced themselves. "But I don't think of anything I haven't spent my whole life thinking about already."

That only unsettled Joel more.

"From one captain to another," Miranda continued, "let's pray we get this over with quickly."

He couldn't agree more.

Twenty-Eight

C ommander Yara d'Alacron possessed two separate offices in the headquarters of the Intergalactic Federation. The first was her primary office, where she did her paperwork, spoke in confidence with those right beneath her command and those like Joel d'Kerni, who knew her well enough and what the headquarters were about. Then there was the second, almost identical office, where Yara kept nothing of importance besides a few tasteful paintings she favored and the occasional knick-knack those with power gifted her to curry favor.

This secondary office was one floor beneath her primary office. Here, she entertained those who weren't on the clearance lists that allowed possible enemies of the state to see her true chambers. Whenever she wanted someone to feel welcomed—and, dare she admit it, *privileged*—she came downstairs in her dress uniform that boasted fewer accolades and showed a little more skin. Her underlings didn't know who she was off to speak with, of course, but they saw where she was going, what she was wearing, and that little skip of excitement in her step. They might as well assume she had caught the third most wanted man in the universe, a grifter who was famed for his otherworldly beauty and ability to steal billions of dollars out of some of the Federation's wealthiest coffers.

She was off to meet a decent candidate for that man's next victim, however. Yet nobody looked at Miranda, currently escorted through the back hallways so late on a Terra III night, and thought her one of the richest women they had ever met. Not in those paint-stained clothes and hardly any makeup on her face.

In fact, they didn't see her at all. Joel ordered the entourage to shield Miranda's face from anyone they came across in the building. From the moment they arrived at the meeting point where one of the few full-blooded *julah* to work for the Federation Forces offered to teleport them back to Terra III, Miranda had either worn a shawl over her head or was shielded with the light blue flags hanging from the walls of the Federation headquarters. Joel's men looked askance at him when he made that strange order, but none of them were about to argue. There was nothing sacred about the Federation's light blue flag. It was merely a nuisance pulling some off the walls and holding them up so Miranda's face wasn't seen by anyone. Not even them.

Joel's paranoia that someone might recognize her was so high that when they reached Yara's secondary office, he offered to personally escort Miranda to her interview. This included pulling off his own scarf, a piece of his uniform that only the highest-ranking members of the Federation wore to be easily identified from far away. The scarf had been blessed by the High Priest of Terra III's Temple of the Void and the only thing on his person that didn't feel like blasphemy to throw on her head.

Miranda entered the office with this scarf enshrouding her face and a strange man who spoke Basic reverently escorting her with one hand hovering near her elbow and another about to rest on her shoulder. Yet he personally never touched her, too afraid to upset some echo across the universe. Miranda was unable to determine what the hell this was about, but she knew she was on Terra III—and she quickly deduced she was in one of the capitol buildings. Gold fringe on the blue flags meant government officials, such as the president, her cabinet, or any number of her staff. Deep red fringe, like what ensconced her as she walked the halls? She knew that was military. In case she couldn't tell from the uniforms surrounding her.

She didn't expect to walk into Yara's office, however. Nor did she expect to see *that* face, the infamous one that occasionally graced the stations broadcasting from the Federation. Whenever Yara made a statement concerning public security, she interrupted some of Miranda's favorite intergalactic shows to announce that someone was on the loose, had been caught, or threatened one of the Federation's foremost institutes.

So Miranda knew that face. Specifically, she knew that blond hair always worn loose around Yara's visage, since the commander was not one to pull a patch over her blinded eye unless circumstances called for her hair to be pulled back. She most favored her long, silky bangs over her right eye, shielding the world from the scar that brandished her as a former undercover agent for one of the Forces' foremost anti-terrorist divisions. That's all Miranda knew about it, though. She had never read one of Yara's official biographies, released when she was first promoted to Supreme Commander of the Intergalactic Federation Forces.

"Thank you, Captain." Yara's expectant voice was lighter than it usually was on TV. When the scarf lowered from Miranda's head, fraying her staticky hair around her face, she beheld that seismic grin coming from the other side of the room. "That will be all. You may stand guard outside the door, if you wish, but I doubt I will need your services until I personally call for you to escort Ms. Hotchner back to her planet."

Joel hesitated, eyes glued to the back of Miranda's head. Occasionally, he glanced in Yara's direction. He knew he must obey his commander, but the urge to take Miranda by the hand and haul her to the Temple only a few blocks away was... staggering. That's when he knew he must take the next few days off and pray for his sins.

"Pleasure." Unlike Joel, Yara had no inhibitions extending her hand to Miranda. "I am Commander Yara d'Alacron of the Intergalactic Federation Forces. Do you speak Basic?"

Miranda slowly raised her hand. Her grip was so strong that Yara winced when they shook. *Good,* Miranda thought. Some psychology transferred among all humans in the universe, and that included the intimidation tactic that was a death-grip of a handshake.

"I speak Basic fine," Miranda replied.

"Thank goodness. My English is... well, non-existent. I watch some of the shows, but quite frankly, it's not a language worth learning for most of us." With a sigh that put a little emphasis on her words, Yara motioned to her desk and the chairs around it. "Have a seat, Ms. Hotchner. Miranda, yes?"

"Either is fine."

That hadn't been the question, but Yara went along with it as she sat in her large, comfortable chair and forced Miranda to take one of the starker, harder chairs. She would hardly be uncomfortable in that thing. Wasn't it the point? This was an interrogation, after all. *Make her want to go home as soon as possible,* Yara thought, pressing a button on her holographic intercom and requesting refreshments from her personal assistant. She didn't ask what Miranda wanted. She would get whatever form of *cageh* was in the kitchen. And, maybe, some water. If she were a good girl.

"I am so sorry to disturb you. It is evening where you're from, yes?"

"Yes," Miranda replied, hands in her lap and elbows on the arm of her chair. She had fixed her hair as soon as she sat, but she couldn't do anything about the wrinkled paint clothes. *Then again,* she thought, staring at Yara, *she can't do anything about that nasty gash in her face.* Yara had access to the best surgeons in the Federation, so really, her eye wasn't too garish to look at. But even Miranda found it disturbing enough to silently request the commander to keep it covered. It didn't help that what little Miranda knew about this woman said it was basically a war wound. "But it's not too late." If she weren't careful, she would slip into Old Basic, a language she wanted to keep from the astute commander.

"Still, I apologize it had to be done this way. You see, it has recently come to my attention that you are a... person of interest." Yara perked up when the door opened. Joel admitted Yara's assistant, a young, obedient man who kept his head down and his uniform pressed to perfection. The insignia on his lapel marked him as a member of the Service class, which either meant a hefty promotion with little action for those who performed well, or a demerit for those who were soon cast to military bases in the far corners of the universe where nobody could hire local help to clean privies and feed soldiers. This man was already high ranking for his division when Yara picked him out of a lineup. He was easy on the eyes—and so, so obedient. The only reason she refrained from speaking until he was gone was because she didn't want to show her fondness for him in front of the deadliest woman to once command an even deadlier force beyond the Federation's reach.

Miranda likewise waited for the man to retreat. Joel closed the doors. Yara kept her eyes on Miranda, that smug smile hardly comforting in a room filled with empty imagery and a ticking clock that bored right into Miranda's skull.

"You can be candid with me, Commander," Miranda said, careful to enunciate every syllable of a language she did not often speak. "I am in the military. Perhaps not one as great as this one, but it's considered one of the greatest on my planet." She loathed utilizing that rhetoric, but when necessary, she could bullshit as well as any other American.

"Of course, Ms. Hotchner." A ruthless smile slapped Miranda on the cheek, but she did not turn it. Nor did she heed the blotching red swarming her skin. "Or should I say Ca..." Yara swallowed her words, hands fumbling on the desk and something swelling her good eye shut. "Excuse me." She rubbed her eye with one careful finger. "Captain. I should say Captain."

"It is not necessary. Not a part of my identity like your position might be, Commander."

"No need for flattery from either of us. So..." Yara revealed a condensed version of the folder she had presented to Joel earlier that evening. "Let me get down to it so you can go home faster, hmm? Tell me. Do you know this man?"

She presented the last known photo of Nerilis Dunsman, a man spotted on the streets of a Yahzen city only a few months before. His graying blond hair was pulled back into a ponytail, and his wrinkled brow presented the same confident decorum he once harbored as the High Priest of the Void. Anyone on Yahzen would recognize him. Yet Miranda couldn't be surprised that her brilliant father would put himself out so openly like that. He must have had a reason. Like implicating someone had associated with him—probably to get back at that person. A power move, and as socially stupid as he could be sometimes.

As it so happened, someone in Miranda's position would have to recognize him too. And she knew that Yara knew *that* about her.

"Of course I know who that is." Miranda tapped her finger to her chin, as if perplexed that this was in front of her. "That is the most wanted man in the universe. Dunsman, is it not? Who doesn't know him?"

Yara pretended that didn't faze her. Too bad Miranda had seen right through her bullshit and decided to pull *Who doesn't know him?* as her primary dueling card.

"Have you ever met this man?" Yara continued. "In real life?"

Miranda hadn't initially known why she was summoned to meet with the head commander of the Federation Forces. *I knew it wasn't good,* she thought, *but this goes beyond not good.* Her poker face was on full display now as she considered her responses. Did Yara know who Miranda was? *Even that question alone is so loaded.* She might know who Miranda was in a past life. She might know she was Nerilis Dunsman's daughter in each of her pathetic lives. But the two facts didn't necessarily cross in the commander's mind. Miranda had to guard her words.

"I've known many men who look like him. But none who have gone by that name." It was a half-truth. She was never asked to call Nerilis anything. Not even *Father,* which suited them both well. He didn't like being reminded that she was his daughter as much as she didn't like the reminder that he was her father.

Yara was not impressed with the lack of information. *She's good,* she thought, unable to penetrate the look on Miranda's face. In a perfect world, Miranda would falter like every good interviewee who was two seconds away from being offered immunity in exchange for the name of a cold-hearted killer. Yet Yara didn't know if Miranda was qualified for immunity. Surely, a crime had been committed along the way—but what if Miranda was as bad as her supposed father?

"You know that your planet was targeted by this man only a year ago, don't you?"

Miranda pursed her lips. "I follow the news."

"Did you consider evacuating?"

"An acquaintance asked me to evacuate with them, but the thing you have to understand about us Earthlings is that we're *very* connected to our planet. One does not simply pack her bags and leave Earth, no matter how often we lament that we wish we could."

Another fantastic non-answer. Yara would need to bring out the big guns a little sooner than she anticipated.

"Much like Cerilyn, I presume."

"Excuse me?" Miranda asked.

"Oh, it's only what I've heard about life on Cerilyn. Do you know Mr. Devon Anderson?" Yara continued to speak through gritted teeth. "He's told me so much about it. His interviews in his recent press tour were something else. So much information to glean." She pulled away the picture of Nerilis and replaced it with one of Devon, particularly his government photo that went onto the passes and ID cards he was assigned during his trip. Again, no reaction from Miranda beyond a cursory glance. "As someone from there yourself, I'd thought that..."

"Someone from there?" Miranda echoed. "So, you know?"

"Why do you think you're here, Ms. Hotchner? Because you were randomly selected among subscribers to The Federation Times?"

"Suppose not. What do you know?"

Maybe her military has trained her well enough after all, Yara lamented. "You are the reincarnation of this woman, are you not?" Beneath Devon's picture came a copy of an old photograph that had survived preservation in the Federation's records. She didn't have to tell Miranda who it was, even if Yara had completely misunderstood who her guest was. After all, the name *Cairn di'Cerilyn* was typed at the bottom of the photograph, followed by the year and the exact location of the state dinner the illustrious chief of Cerilyn's Second Tribe had visited toward the end of the civil war that had torn at the Federation for over a hundred years. Back when business had been better than ever for a planet of mercenaries.

"You already know the answer to that," Miranda eventually said.

"I will need your verbal confirmation."

"I cannot help who I am," Miranda said. "But I am, in fact, the reincarnation of the woman in the photo." She couldn't very well deny it. Playing dumb would get her nowhere, especially with her literal face from a thousand years ago staring back at her. Few things had changed in her genetics since then. Her eyes were a bit narrower, and her jaw a little longer, but those were still her father's prim lips and his pride simmering in her sinew.

Yara could hardly hold back the glee manifesting inside of her. "Fascinating. You know, I always wondered about the name. That wasn't the name you were born with, is it? I mean, the di'Cerilyn name is farcical, obviously, but where in the world did *Cairn* come from?"

Miranda snorted. A question she had not anticipated—never in a million years. "No, it wasn't the name I was born with. I was..." She shuddered, the first sign of weakness since she was taken into custody by Joel d'Kerni and his men. "I was originally named after the High Priestess of the Void. My mother at the time was a big fan. Real religious nut."

"Of course you were. I saw it in your records that survived." *Joy* had a different meaning in Old Basic than it did in Modern English, but it was a common human derivative of the *julah* name Joiya. The Miranda of the twenty-first century, however, thought it an awfully ironic name. What joy was there in being born on a pleasure moon? Where one's mother was the drug-addicted madam of one of the sorriest brothels on the whole moon?

She sold her own ten-year-old daughter to the predatory chief of Second Tribe, after all. Sold her for what amounted to fifteen-hundred dollars. *And the only reason she got such a low price for my life is because she had already sold my first bed-rights to the woman who decided she liked what she sampled,* Miranda recalled. *Enough to make me her favorite punching bag for the next ten years.* Until Cairn killed her. That had been a satisfying day.

"That's my only connection to this man," Miranda lied, pointing to the picture of Nerilis. "My mother loved his wife. Which is weird when you think about it. She would have been dead long before my mother was even born."

"I know it's been a while since you were incarnated into the Federation, Ms. Hotchner," Yara said. "But we say that the great and venerable High Priestess *Ascended,* not died."

"Whatever. They say the same thing about Jesus on Earth."

That only took Yara back a little bit. While she was far from pious, she was still raised with respect for the Temple and everything they did for the mortals in the universe. *Just because I have to occasionally arrest them for genocide and high treason,* she thought with disdain, *doesn't mean the Void doesn't exist.* Which was more than anyone in the Federation could say for the whole Christianity thing, which was designated a "cult with no basis in reality" alongside the millions of other religions that had been disproven over the millennia. Still, it permeated Earth-based media that was popular within the Federation, and there were die-hard followers that hung out on this planet or colonized that moon… so Yara was unfortunately familiar with the metaphor about Jesus.

"You didn't answer my question," Yara said. "Where did your chosen name come from?"

"When I was sold to Cerilyn," Miranda said, "I changed it. There was no point going by my old name anymore. I had no association with the woman who gave birth to me from the time I left my birthplace to when I died on Cerilyn." *Like I'm telling her the real way I got my name,* Miranda thought, unappreciative of the memories this conversation triggered. *It's none of her business what that woman did to me.*

"I see. Sorry for the questions. You see, for being such an important figure in that part of history, there's so little known about you. Everyone knows about the stories and backgrounds of the two infamous mercenaries quested with entering the Process and leading a crusade against the most powerful man both in and outside of the Federation. But all we know about the woman who contracted them out to Master Marlow is what the Federation gleaned during her tenure as chief. There were many spies keeping tabs on Cerilyn, as I'm sure you know."

"Unlike you, Commander," Miranda grunted, "I can actually remember that time." Like she remembered uncovering Federation spies among her ranks. Right up there with uncovering spies from the other tribes that stood to lose coins as Second Tribe commandeered the contracts coming from all corners of the universe. Unfortunately for *those,* they were quickly dispatched into the same pit that every dead body to ever be uncovered in the fortress soon called their final resting place.

"Because you are in the Process, are you not?"

There was no point denying it now. Yara already knew the answer to that, and if Miranda wanted to stay on her good side, she would comply as much as she safely could. "Yes."

"Interesting." Yara pretended to look through another file, although it didn't say anything that wasn't already pulsing at the forefront of her mind. "It's *so* interesting because anyone a master *julah* commits to the Process must be registered with their own government, let alone *ours*. As far as we know, only three people are in the Process. Granted, Master Marlow only went through the proper channels for his assistant, but the other two are properly accounted for. I don't pretend to know what logistics my predecessors had to encounter hundreds of years ago. I can only *imagine* the red tape, you know?" Her diabolical smile should have unnerved Miranda, but this was a woman used to dealing with unbelievable sociopaths and their nicey-nice acts they adopted in their search for power. "Which begs the question. Who put you into the Process, Ms. Hotchner?"

This was the make it or break it point. Not only did Miranda finally have to *lie,* but she also had to be so convincing that Yara wouldn't dare question the veracity of her statement. *And I have to count on some man who barely knows I exist going along with it.* Because Yara would undoubtedly follow through on her investigation. Why else would she have Miranda dragged out of her home in the middle of the night to have this *personal* interview?

"Why, Master Marlow did, of course."

"Is that so? Strange. He's never mentioned you before."

"Why would he? It was quite the embarrassing scene when I died." Wincing as she drew her teeth across her lip and hugged her arms across her body was a nice touch. One she did not willingly commit. "I had to beg him. I was there when the others died. For all I know, I was the last survivor of Cerilyn before it winked out of existence." And took her life with it. "I'd rather not talk more about it, if it's all the same to you. Besides, I don't think your government wants to know what my final moments were like. You're concerned with who did the deed, and now I've told you."

"Be sure I will follow up with Master Marlow about this, of course. And if it's true, he could be in very big trouble."

"From what I understand, he gets into trouble a lot."

"Yes, well..." Yara couldn't contain her sigh of frustration. Dealing with *julah,* let alone one who did as he pleased like Ramaron Marlow, was a continuous point of consternation for the human government. Catching the only man stronger than him made Marlow the means to the end. "Understand that this is all part of our investigation into Nerilis Dunsman. A man whose wife you're named after..."

"Was. A really long time ago."

"...and whose name is connected to yours."

Miranda had been waiting for it. No way they would drag her all the way here unless they had real dirt on her. If this were a matter of bureaucracy regarding the status of her soul, then to hell with it, who cared? But this always came back to Miranda's father. Almost like, from the very beginning, he controlled her entire existence.

Not bad for an absentee father, Miranda thought.

"You say you've never encountered him, to your knowledge." Yara leaned back in her seat, elbows resting on the arms of her chair and fingers steepling before her face. Some of her hair gently fell to the side, revealing the garish scar left across her right eye. "Yet your first mother named you after the High Priestess, his bride. And isn't it *quite* fascinating that you look so..."

Miranda had never before wished to be wearing her usual face of makeup. At least her hair was dyed and cut in a way Lady Lerenan would have never worn. *But I can't change my face,* Miranda lamented. The eyes were wholly her mother's—both of them. The spiritual one who had Ascended long ago, and the mortal one who was unfortunate enough to meet a man in a bar. Her hair would always naturally part the same way it did in those paintings. Her complexion may have altered from life to life, but nobody looked at her and thought, *"Isn't her skin unfortunate?"* The High Priestess was renowned for her natural beauty. Miranda may be muddied with her father's genetics and whatever mortal birthed her in this life, but men like Joel d'Kerni looked upon her in awe for a reason.

"You're a dead ringer for the High Priestess of the Void," Yara concluded. She backed up her statement with a photograph of Joiya Lerenan when she was still alive. *Her wedding day...* Miranda had seen this photo before. It was the last known picture of Lady Lerenan, shortly before she was called to the Void. The cream-colored gown layered in the "tears of the ancestors," iridescent gems mined from some far corner of Yahzen and heralded to contain spiritual properties nobody bothered to explain, weighed down her small frame. The veil was pulled back from her face but covered her long, black hair. Minimal makeup highlighted her youthful visage. Sometimes, even Miranda forgot how young her real mother was, considering all she had accomplished in her short life.

To think, Miranda mused, *she was probably pregnant with me when this picture was taken.* Or had miscarried yet again. Nerilis was never good at keeping the details straight when he was yelling at Miranda for daring to exist.

"I have been told there is a resemblance," she finally said, looking away from the picture. *Looking away from my own face, really.* "Your own captain was looking at me quite strangely our whole trip here. Is that why they made such a big to-do about concealing my identity?"

"Captain d'Kerni is a religious man. Pious, really." Yara snorted. "Whatever he thinks is not relevant here. What *I* think is relevant. And what you think, I suppose. So. What do you think?"

"About what?"

Yara merely smiled at her. "Let's not play these games. It's late wherever we live. I'm sure you have a life to get back to." This was the moment Yara had been waiting for. While she had plenty of other evidence to tie her to Nerilis Dunsman now that she knew of Miranda's existence, that wasn't going to shake the suspicion. What Yara needed was the *one thing* to knock Miranda out of her seat when the photo slid across the table.

Sure enough, Miranda's face paled when she saw a stealthy photograph of her and Danielle having brunch that weekend. While they weren't touching, their body language heavily implied that they were friendly, if not intimate, with one another. It was the perfect fodder to show Miranda that she was not only being watched, but the Federation knew of her relationship with Danielle.

"I have more," Yara said. "Photos of her leaving your house. Recordings of what you said to each other on the street. Nothing in your house, I assure you, but I'm sure I've pinged your paranoia already." She sniffed, as if this were a nuisance of an investigation to her. "Isn't it something? You and the reincarnation of Sulim di'Graelic, one of the most famous mercenaries to ever live on Cerilyn. Oh, I'm sorry. I forgot that was supposed to be you."

Miranda quickly regained control of her twitching muscles. "I don't understand why you care about this. Obviously, we know each other."

"Know each other? Yes, that is obvious. From what I understand about the Process, that's what happens when people go into it together. None of that is shocking now that we know who you are. What I find so curious is the other side to your relationship. You are lovers."

Miranda remained silent.

"I'd venture a guess that you were lovers on Cerilyn too." When Miranda didn't take the bait, Yara continued, "Wasn't the mercenary life extremely bigoted? Every man and woman for themselves. Everyone found reasons to hate you. Like if you weren't from the popular planets of the time, or if you had a lot of money when you were taken... ah, and it was extremely hard for women, I'm sure. But what was it I remember reading about that time? It could be quite homophobic, right? I believe it was the chief before you that really turned opinion against it. Oh, the stories I've read... they're practically adventure novels these days. Historical pieces for young boys and girls who want to play mercenaries and soldiers. I will say that some of the dramas that attempted to recreate Cerilyn haven't done *you* justice. You're far prettier than any of those actresses. Which is a shame, because we have photo and video of you from that time. When you came to Terra III for the treaty renegotiation, as a special guest of the parliament. What did they offer you? Complete amnesty, relocation services, and stipends for all your people if you vowed to disband your tribe and depart Cerilyn? That must have been a tempting offer. Even the queen of a mighty rich kingdom must know the dangers that lurk in her shadows. Being a chief was always looking over your shoulder, wasn't it? You should know. You were the one who murdered the chief before you. The one who made homophobia all the rage among your people."

She was good. *Too good,* Miranda thought. Yara was an excellent example of the kind of sociopath who made her mark on the world. Even if Miranda's life wasn't on the line at the moment, it very well could be if Yara thought it would serve her career.

"She deserved to die," was all Miranda said. Then, "Nobody missed her."

"Yet her legacy lived on. Because of her, you couldn't be open in your relationship. It must be a blessing in disguise to see it play out today."

Miranda kept her mouth shut and arms crossed. Her body language may scream that she was uncomfortable, but as long as she didn't say anything, Yara couldn't corner her.

"I understand that Ms. Cromwell is in a delicate situation. She hasn't regressed, yes?"

"I suppose not," Miranda muttered.

"So it would be a huge detriment to her health if I were to bring her in for an interview next. I would have to show her these pictures and ask her disturbing questions about your relationship to the man she was sworn to stop. Does she even know, Ms. Hotchner? Does she know who you are?"

Yara wouldn't ask that if she didn't already know the answer.

"How did you find out about me?" The façade fell. Miranda was no longer the collected daughter of a well-to-do lady and the most powerful man to ever be born from the Void. She was a desperate orphan who didn't want to be sent back to the planet of prisoners, exiles, and forgotten children left behind by the Federation's broken systems. *Death, madness, and pain.* That's how Miranda always remembered it, since it was the bulk of her youth as an up-and-coming teen mercenary who numbed the pain with women, drugs, and dice. *Pain. So much pain.* When she wasn't having her ass kicked in the training yards, she was being shot at on the field. And when she was allowed some peace at night?

All it took was that cunt of a chief to ruin her night. Many, many nights.

Perhaps it was the *hedpah* while in transport. Maybe it was the plethora of memories Yara foisted upon her. All Miranda knew was that when she opened her eyes again, she didn't see photographs of her distant past and recent life. Nor did she see the Commander of the Federation Forces before her. The woman was recognizable, but it wasn't Yara d'Alacron, the decorated undercover agent who transformed her career into what it was today.

She saw someone else. Someone Miranda had once known so well that it was no mistake that she was the first to find the bloody body one night a thousand years ago.

"You..."

Her eyes were wide, absorbing the woman before her. Much like Devon had not so long ago, when his brain clicked and his soul screamed at him to run far away, Miranda now faced one of the more unpleasant memories to ever beset her trauma-logged brain.

Yara tilted her head. "Me."

"It's you." Miranda's hands landed on the desk. Yara did not flinch. "Do you know it's you?" Her bearings slowly returning to her, Miranda leaned back in her chair, catching her breath. "What the hell is happening?"

Yara twirled her long hair around her finger, noticing a small blemish on her right index finger. She opened one of the unlocked drawers and located a nail file with a fine laser that both buffed and trimmed. Did either of them even smell the *hedpah* now? Miranda hadn't been aware of the yellowish fog before. Yara was used to it by now.

"I'm sorry. Do you have a headache?" Yara folded her hands over her stomach, chair slightly turning with her budding excitement. "You know what's funny? You were always in my visions whenever I partook in the *julahs'* favorite escape. I didn't understand it, though. You look so much like the High Priestess that I always assumed I was having a religious experience as a child." The more they inhaled, the faster they devolved into using Old Basic. "Now I get it. Because I used to know you quite well, didn't I, Cairn?"

Miranda pressed her palms against her eyes, but that didn't keep the *hedpah* smoke from entering her lungs and wrapping her brain in a warm, invasive blanket.

"Reincarnation is such a funny thing," Yara continued. "I'm not in the Process. I don't have access to regression and memories like you do. But I've always known that I was carrying an old weight on my shoulders. I understand now. I was one of you. I suppose that gives me grounds for reincarnation. Anybody who died there was probably reincarnated at some point. May the Void have mercy on us all."

Her lips curled into a vampiric grin while Miranda slowly lowered her hands and gazed upon the woman she once thought of as a "scrawny, no-brained girl." That ditzy blond had come a long way in the short time Cairn had relatively known her. From training together to becoming partners in their teen years. *From suffering at the hands of the same madwoman... to what she did to her.* Yara may have been free from the lucid memories the Process provided, but Miranda wasn't. She would never forget it. The screams of torment. Some stupid girl begging for forgiveness, to be loved, to be acknowledged by the woman with the power to end her life without repercussion.

They had been the chief's chosen, and that came with it no boon.

Yara was far and away a physical step up, but that girl had never stood a chance in her youth. Yet when Miranda looked beyond the healthy head of hair, the glowing skin, and the admirable fat-to-muscle ratio that represented a fit soldier, she saw that scared whelp who used to cry herself to sleep. *Sometimes in my arms.*

Miranda had never forgotten her. She also never anticipated seeing her again.

"Kila..."

Yara perked up, a renewed fondness for Miranda touching her lips. "My name was always on the tip of my tongue. It's nice to hear someone finally say it."

"What are you doing here?"

"If I had to hazard a guess..." Yara glanced up toward the ceiling. "Living the life I was always meant to claim as my own."

Miranda was about to vomit. The *hedpah* fumes made her feel nauseated, but that wasn't the only thing sending her bile up her throat. *Her... the blood. So much blood.* Miranda's memory was too foggy to remember what made her crawl back to their small dormitory early one morning. *I almost remember...* That hadn't been important. Not when all Miranda recalled was standing outside their door, fearing a ghost on the other side.

Indeed, she had opened it to reveal the only thing to have made her cry in a long, long time.

"I know you're not in the Process," Miranda spat. "Because I was there when you died!" She may have been half-*julah,* but if Miranda didn't have hope of becoming a great sorceress? Cairn was a bigger lost cause. She couldn't have put a soul into the Process if she studied a thousand years at the Academy.

"I don't recall many details about my death, but it's heartening to know I wasn't alone. Maybe that's why I remember *you* so well."

This was impossible. Even if only slightly improbable, Miranda refused to believe it. She could handle an interrogation about her father. A slap in the face like this? This must have been planned. Yara knew exactly what she was doing riling up Miranda and sending her into a tizzy.

This had been personal from the beginning.

"I'm hoping that this renewed relationship between us will mean more open communication." Yara pulled a mask across her face. One that filtered out the *hedpah* as more of it swarmed the room. She enjoyed the sight of Miranda slowly slumping into her seat, eyes fluttering shut and mouth open. "The interview may be over with not enough information, but I've made my point. And, for once, I got something over *you* for a change."

She stood, hand dragging along the desk as she slowly approached Miranda's languid body. That freshly trimmed nail started a trail from Miranda's cheek and traced the length of her throat, shoulder, and left arm. Yara had no other interest in Miranda's body, but it thrilled her to touch the woman who had betrayed her love and trust a thousand years ago.

Yara didn't remember the details. They didn't matter. The raw emotions of a traumatized teenager fighting wars for nations and planets said everything she needed to know. The only reason Yara didn't wrap her hand around Miranda's throat was because she *was* no longer that brash youth who ended it all while lying in her bed.

It wasn't comforting to know that Miranda had been the one to find her. All that meant was what Kila knew all along back then...

She was out getting into trouble with that appalling bitch. Little Miss Perfect. The trainee whom Yara and Miranda had been tasked to help blossom into her full potential. Watching the love gradually bloom between two battered girls hadn't bothered the Yara of back then. What did was knowing their chief also fancied someone new. Younger. *Better.*

Yara called for Joel to come fetch Miranda. In the few seconds it would take him to come, she indulged in her bubbling aggression and snatched her hand around Miranda's throat. The single squeeze she gave it was enough to sate her. For now.

Joel entered, mask on and head down. Yara held her hand up as if she were checking Miranda's pulse. "I'm afraid that the interrogation was too much for our Earthling friend," she said, turning back to her desk. "Have her checked out and sent home. She knows what must be done now."

"Yes, Commander." Yet Joel hesitated as he gazed upon Miranda's unconscious body. Two small white spots, the exact size of Yara's fingers, slowly faded from her flesh.

Miranda stumbled down the sidewalk, her head throbbing and breathing shallow. She would be all right, but waking up from a *hedpah* hangover after her whole night was interrupted meant she looked drunker than someone coming out of a bar at midnight.

She could hardly believe what happened. Had it really happened? That face. That voice. Not until the *hedpah* truly kicked in did she recognize Kila, one of her only confidants in those dark days on Cerilyn, long before she tasted the chiefdom. *Back when being chief was akin to being a megalomaniacal dictator.*

The only one to get it worse than Cairn was Kila, who was foolish enough to love her abuser.

"Ugh." Miranda pressed herself against the wall outside a brightly lit convenience store. A homeless man stared at her. At first, he considered asking her for money, but she looked like she was having it worse than him that night. "What a mess."

Joel had intended to drop her back off at her house, complete with apologies, medicine, and a prayer for her. Miranda could do without all three, but she took the medicine anyway. Like anything else, it took a good twenty minutes to a half-hour to kick in, and by that time she had insisted on being dropped off in another neighborhood. If only she knew where the hell she was going.

No. She knew.

Miranda approached her destination with a clearer head. At the same time, she couldn't say who she was in that moment. Did it matter? She slipped into the lobby when a resident came out, pretending to live there. Like she belonged there. *I absolutely belong here.* She helped herself to the elevator, hand covering her mouth as she fought back the memories the *hedpah* forced her to relive. Her phone was in her hand. She should call ahead. Leave a text. Anything other than show up on Danielle's doorstep with a dire need to see her.

I don't know what's going to happen, she thought as she knocked on the door. Her stomach tumbled in anticipation. Or vomit. She couldn't tell. Not until the door opened and Danielle, dressed in her pajamas, expressed a modicum of surprise at Miranda's disheveled appearance. *She might come for you next. We need to get out of here.*

Instead of following through on her half-assed plan, though, Miranda made the most boneheaded move that would have made any iteration of her cry.

She greeted Danielle with a kiss and slammed the door behind them. Luckily for her, Danielle didn't ask any questions. Miranda wanted to believe that was the old soul in her lover understanding the dire consequences they faced if they mucked it all up—again.

Twenty-Nine

D evon wouldn't say he was excited to go back to work as a networking grunt in a high-rise commercial office, but it was the normalcy he craved after the past two weeks of insanity. In his office, where he was required to wear slacks and a polo shirt regardless of what dusty maw he had to crawl into, his boss didn't care who Devon had been in a previous life or what he had done to save Earth a year ago. If Devon wasn't single-handedly bringing internet back to the security office on the third floor, then what good was he?

Sure enough, he walked into work Tuesday morning to the immediate call to see to complaints about "email troubles." His coworker, a man named Neil who had the social skills of a kid who never heard the word "no" in his life, made it clear that nobody wanted to hear about Devon's vacation or what was going on in his life.

Suited Devon fine. After clocking in and throwing his stuff into his locker, he inhaled a deep breath and hopped to the fifth floor, where a corner office manager was at her wit's end trying to send "very important" emails to someone in Los Angeles.

"I've *tried* turning it off and on again," she snapped, long before Devon even opened his mouth. "So don't give me that crap." She rolled her eyes when she saw the indifference on Devon's face. "Never mind. What do you need to do to fix it?"

"First I need to get a handle on how the internet is working here. Is it only email you can't send, or can you not access any webpages, either? What does the networking icon say in the corner of your Windows tray?"

The woman stared at him as if he spoke gibberish. The sad thing? Devon didn't know how to speak plainer English when it came to networking.

"Can you access, say, the CNN website?" Devon tried.

The manager snorted. "Why would I want to read CNN?"

"That's not the point. I'm asking if you can access any other website but your email hosting."

"My email isn't online."

"But... it is. I mean, it's supposed to be. How are you accessing it?"

"Through the Firefox icon, of course."

Devon wanted to smack his head against the manager's desk. It was more productive than this conversation. "If you wouldn't mind, I'd like to check it out for myself."

Of course she minded. What if it started working and he saw her important emails? They did *incredible* things in this office! For all she knew, he was a Chinese intelligence spy or a Russian hacker. Devon wished. He would be living a much more exciting life.

You already do live an exciting life outside of this office, idiot, he admonished himself, while crawling beneath the manager's desk to check her fiber connection. *Isn't this what you wanted? To be back in a place where people treated you like dirt instead of some war hero who needed to publish his memoir yesterday?*

Devon had comforted himself with those thoughts the exact moment the head of the IT department burst into the office and called his name.

"Anderson!" He hustled up to the desk, practically shoving the office manager out of the way as he searched for Devon, still beneath the desk. "That you, Anderson?"

Devon almost hit his head coming out of the desk. "Huh? It's me."

Pete, the IT department head, heaved a sigh of relief and slammed his hands upon his hips as if this were proper protocol for all networking investigations in the building. "Good to see you back from your vacation! Not sure what you're doing *here,* though." Pete turned to the woman currently on the phone with her own boss. "We'll send someone here in a jiffy to look into your problem," he said with a customer service voice. "I actually need him in my office. Five minutes ago."

"What?" Devon brushed some dust off his charcoal gray slacks. "I didn't hear anything about it from Neil."

"Neil is actually on his way right now to take care of this." Pete looped his arm around Devon's shoulder and escorted him toward the door. "I need *you* downstairs to talk to me about a little something."

Devon hated this already. Usually, he assumed this meant he was in some sort of trouble—he was a *grunt,* after all, and they were the first to be blamed for anything that went wrong. But the smile that continued to beam on Pete's face long after they got into the elevator did not sit well with a man who was too tired to deal with a smiley boss.

"So..." Pete nudged Devon with a sharp elbow. "I had no idea that we had a celebrity in our midst." The man hiccupped. *Hiccupped.* Was he possessed, or drunk? "Then again, until a week ago, I had no idea there was life beyond our planet, but here we are!"

Devon nearly gagged on his own spit.

One of his fears had followed him back to Earth. Not only was Pete one of the most recent inductees into the Federation Hall of Those in the Know, but he now knew who Devon *really* was. *So much for going incognito at work to have a sense of normalcy,* Devon thought as he sat at Pete's desk and was served coffee in "the best mug in the break room." That simply meant it was the mug without any coffee stains baked into the ceramic or chips along the rim. *High honor right here.* Devon grimaced when Pete sat down in his chair and looked at his subordinate as if this were the best damn of their lives.

Devon had every right to dread this. Pete looked at him as if he were one man's ticket to fame and fortune. For a guy who had only learned of the Federation a week ago—thanks to someone from intergalactic security checking up on Devon's workplace—he was quite accepting of it. Pete had always been a man of big, global aspirations. He believed in countries coming together to achieve world peace. He thought the Euro was the coolest shit. The concept of highly advanced humans living light years away from his humble planet? Thrilling! The only thing better was finding out that one of the recent hires in his company was on vacation to do a media tour that Pete could now watch on this handy-dandy cable station that he hooked into his TV for only a hundred bucks more a month.

He hadn't slept in about four days. The man was going to teach himself Basic before the end of the year.

Devon hated what this meant for his future in the company. Anything he did now wouldn't be because he earned the promotion or raise. It would be because Pete and anyone above him didn't want to look like they were being "unnecessarily" harsh on a young man trying to make a living. People were watching them. The whole galaxy was watching them, if security details standing outside on the sidewalk could be counted on. The only reason the whole building wasn't hopping on Devon's back was because most Earthlings still had no clue the Federation existed.

One thing was for sure, though. Devon would no longer be going into a lowly manager's office to tell her to try resetting her computer. He would have a role much closer to home in Pete's office. Oh, and a raise. Actually, did Devon *really* want to spend his days working IT, *juuust* because that was his training in college? There were much better things for him to do. Pete wanted to learn more about the technology they had in the Federation. Ethernet cables were a thing of the archaic past. How much technology was wrapped up in *julah* magic, anyway? Did Devon know? Wouldn't he much rather further his training by learning the Federation systems... and reporting back to Pete? Forget it. Pete had some friends in higher places that already knew about the Federation and would love to take Devon under their wings! And maybe have him marry their daughters. He was straight, right? Ah, it didn't matter! They had sons too!

"I just want to do my job," Devon said at the end of one of Pete's spiels.

"And you will! You'll earn your paycheck like anyone else." What Pete didn't say was that further research—which mostly amounted to Federation articles translated into English for the masses like May who preferred that language—indicated that Devon qualified for possible reparations from the *julah* government thanks to the "undue spiritual duress" one of their own subjected him to for a thousand years. What was a pittance in hush money to them could buy Devon a nice life in an expensive American city. He didn't have to fret about work at all if he was content with a one-bedroom apartment complete with security. Pete needed to sell this new position to Devon if he wanted the young man around for years to come. They needed Devon more than Devon needed them.

Which is what Devon realized halfway through their conversation, and he didn't know anything about reparations yet. Nothing beyond what Danielle wanted now that her own career had gone down the drain, and he had no idea she was about to get exactly that.

His mood was so sour by the time he left work that he was grateful to leave the building unmolested. A part of him worried he might see a Federation news crew or some adoring fan on the sidewalk. Instead, he saw someone he had almost completely forgotten over the past two weeks.

There, pulled up along the curb, was a black limousine. Standing outside of it with his electric cigar and cane was Pauloso d'Whain, a man who had been patiently waiting for Devon's return to Earth.

It took Devon much too long to recognize him. Probably because his brain was fried and every inch of his body begged him to go home and take a well-deserved nap. *I'll sleep forever at this point,* he thought, following Pauloso into the back of his limo. The driver was told to do a few laps through the blocks surrounding Devon's work. Meanwhile, Devon was offered an assortment of refreshments, both locally curated and imported from the greater parts of the Federation. According to Pauloso, this was a friendly cause for celebration. After all, he had gotten to Devon long before any other music distributor in the galaxy, and that was a win for them *all.*

"I don't know what to tell you," Devon said as they passed the same building for the third time. "I can't make these decisions on behalf of my band." He pulled out his phone, pretending to look for one of his bandmate's numbers. Instead, he was hoping to God that someone he considered a friend had texted him. About anything. He'd even take a text from Alicia that started with, "...*and furthermore, when my father told me that you were a wimpy sack of shit, I should have listened!*"

There were no messages, though. No follow-ups on how he was doing. No calls to hang out after he was done working. Even Clyde had gone radio silent, and he was usually the first to text Devon about some random shit going on downtown. *I would love for that right now.* Random shit that had nothing to do with Devon Anderson or his previous incarnation, thank the Void very much.

"I don't want to be pushy," Pauloso said while drinking cider straight from the bottle—Devon continued to decline, preferring a beer when he finally got home, whenever *that* would be, "but you're in a very enviable position, Mr. Anderson. It would be natural for any discerning music man such as myself to recognize your talents and attempt to sign your band right away. But it's me we're talking about. I don't have to tell you again that my company has the biggest market reach in the Federation. I sign the biggest pop stars and rock bands. Hell, I sign some of the biggest acts on their home planets that nobody else in the Federation has heard of, because I want those distribution rights. I can get you in any store and book any venue if the sales warrant. And yours will, because everyone wants to see Sonall Gardiah in person. Hearing his own music? His artistic expressions of what he has been through?" Pauloso chuckled. "You will become a very wealthy man, even if you unfortunately only tour here on Earth. But, on the other hand, my company does facilitate tourism packages for citizens of the Federation who wish to come to Earth and see their favorite artists in person. Nobody tells you about the additional shows that come to the major tours. Federation-locked, I assure you."

"That sounds... like the deal of a lifetime," Devon muttered.

"I'm sure you're concerned about your artistry. I assure you that I'm not interested in telling you what to write or how to write it. I can provide producers if you have a specific sound, but bring your own for all I care. Produce your own tracks. It makes no difference. Your name alone will sell your albums and make your friends' dreams come true."

"Our drummer and lead guitarist know nothing about the Federation," Devon was quick to interject. "I'm not even sure I want to drag them into it."

"Understandable. But I think they'll come around when they figure out how rich and famous their music will make them."

Devon was talking to a brick wall with only one motive. From the moment he met the man, Devon knew that Pauloso was only interested in growing his wealth by making dollar after dollar off Devon's name. *Would I even be allowed to perform under my real name?* Devon wondered. *Or will I have to use my dead name to make him happy?* This wasn't what Devon imagined when he spent his high school and college years fantasizing about becoming a star like his favorite musicians. Hard work, good personality, and great music. That was supposed to be the secret sauce Karma concocted over the years. Devon knew they were capable of all three, but if they were to get signed to a decent label and become instant classics at the launch of their first album, it was because the masses liked what they did. Not because their lead singer happened to be the reincarnation of a man murdered a thousand years ago.

"Let's pretend I entertain your offer," Devon said. "I would still have to talk it over with those who *do* know about the Federation. I don't care how much money and fame you promise us. Honestly, I'm not interested in fame. I've had enough for the rest of my natural existence."

That was supposed to remind Pauloso that he was messing with a man who had seen a millennium's worth of life. For a human, that was staggering. Unnatural. Pauloso couldn't fathom the natural lifespan of a *julah,* never mind what Devon had been through. *My soul is older than his,* Devon thought with slight disdain. *Yet he has the audacity to tell me he knows what's best for me?*

"I think you'll find that with my help in the industry," Pauloso began, "you can control the exact level of exposure you desire. Of course, once your band's name is out there, you will have to take security precautions. Continue to live on this charming planet if that's what you want, but you'll have to move into a home that supplies better security than your current accommodations."

"That gets incredibly expensive in this city really quickly." Did Pauloso think that Devon was *into* his trashy studio apartment? Even student housing had provided a better residence, and the only reason he and Alicia swung that was because he lucked out in the lottery that assigned apartments to seniors.

"Rest assured I will provide a generous signing bonus to *all* members of your band, but especially you, Mr. Gardiah."

Devon had heard enough already. Luckily for him, the car was stopped at a red light, giving him adequate opportunity to open the door and step onto the sidewalk. "My name is Devon," he said. "Devon Anderson. That's the first thing you need to understand if we are to *ever* work together." He shut the door. While he wished he could say this gave him the impetus to continue his trek to get *someone* to understand who he really was, all it did was anger him more.

Not to mention the sheer anxiety he experienced when he wondered how the hell he'd bring this up to May and Clyde, two people who would probably have opposing ideas and bring them right back to square one.

He began the trek back to his car a few blocks away. As Devon always did now, he pulled out his phone, his small anxiety crutch that may or may not be making things worse for his mental condition.

He didn't expect to see a familiar initial leaving him curt text messages to *"Call me as soon as you can. It's important. VERY IMPORTANT."*

The crazy thing? Life was so upside-down right now that for the first time since regressing, Devon didn't care that the woman pulling him back into more drama was Miranda.

Thirty

Although Danielle had been in Miranda's house before, she never thought she'd have it practically *memorized,* never mind find some misplaced comfort in it.

Yet here she was, sitting in Miranda's house for the second day in a row. It would have been five days, perhaps, if she hadn't spent all of Monday in her own apartment. *My apartment doesn't feel this homey, though,* she thought, staring at the soft, cream-colored walls and the wooden furniture that brought an earthen look to Miranda's simple tastes. Every time Danielle walked through the door, she was bombarded with the mild scent of potpourri and whatever air freshener Miranda used to attempt to mask the smell of cigarette smoke. That was the only thing that jarred Danielle back to reality, not that she smelled it for long. Olfactory fatigue compounded with the honeymoon period blooming in her mind, and she often forgot that Miranda smoked at all—which was a feat, considering Danielle's disdain.

Comfort often messed with her mind, though. By Tuesday that week, she was helping herself to the TV remote and flipping through channels. One of the first things Danielle noted was that more than *one* Federation channel existed, although, based on the icons in the corner, they were owned by the same company. The one Danielle received was all news and documentaries, whereas this one broadcasted variety shows and fictional serials that she couldn't understand even with the English subtitles. Granted, her eyesight was far from the best, and the TV was at least ten feet away, but the technical and cultural terms appearing in this Terra III family drama made her head spin.

"You understand what they're saying?" Danielle asked, as a bowl of salad hit the dining table. Miranda was halfway back to the kitchen when Danielle turned up the volume on the TV. She recognized Basic, but she couldn't understand it—not even with Old Basic locked away in the depths of her mind.

"I understand it well enough when it's the news." Miranda held back a yawn as she plated the fried rice she whipped up after work. She hadn't known Danielle was coming over for dinner until the text exchange invited her. Much like Danielle was finding comfort in Miranda's house, Miranda was in turn appreciating the presence of a loving soul that wasn't out to harm her. For once. Such a novel concept. "Dramas and such are much harder, since they speak casually and have a lot of accents. This is a Terra III show... so... it's not as hard as some other shows. I honestly don't watch these much. Just the news."

"Is the news any better than what we have here on Earth?"

Miranda sat down with both of their dinner plates. "It's always good to see another perspective. Even the most progressive countries on this planet pale next to the system the Federation has set up."

Danielle turned off the TV and turned toward her plate. It wasn't rude to grab the salt and pepper in this house. Nor was she against making a face at the hot sauce Miranda generously added to her rice. "You make it sound like some utopia. I've met a lot of those people in charge, and they're all fascists waiting to happen, if you ask me."

Miranda didn't mention that was Sulim's latent paranoia about authoritarian governments talking. Not that she blamed Sulim for it one bit. "No place is a utopia, but the thing about a giant government that crosses galaxies is that there is a lot of autocratic institutions throughout it. Hell, even Cerilyn was..." She stopped. The last thing she should talk about at the dinner table was *Cerilyn*. It didn't matter if Danielle had regressed yet or not. There was always something better to talk about. "Healthcare is completely free and accessible for citizens of the Federation. They also have a UBI based on where they live, as set by more localized governments. Retirement funds, generous maternity and paternity leave, free childcare whether you go public or private... I mean, it's not surprising. They've had thousands of years to figure it out."

"Mmm, yes, and from what I understand, thousands of wars to make sure those planets, autonomous or not, fall in line."

"Maybe you're getting your memories back after all," Miranda muttered, as she shook some salt onto her dinner. If she had more time to think about what to cook for them, she would have steamed some edamame. Oh, well.

"Huh?"

"Nothing."

Miranda leaned back in her seat before taking a single bite of her food. As much as she wished to gaze upon the lovely woman sharing her table, her mind continued to wander toward her TV and the black screen that reflected her chagrin. *I remember when we used to do this all the time...* she thought, recalling those final months leading up to the end of their lives. Although Miranda grew up speaking only Old Basic back then, eventually, she taught herself Julah. She picked up languages easily regardless of what life she lived, but monolingual Sulim had once asked her a similar question while they watched the news from the chief's personal chambers—one of the only places in Second Tribe's fortress where someone could access the media.

"Can you really understand what they're saying?" Sulim had asked.

"Of course I can. Do you want me to teach you some? It's a very simple language. It's the only reason I picked it up as a kid."

"Oh... no... I don't see why I should need it."

Sulim's intellectual insecurity had annoyed Cairn back then, and it further frustrated Miranda now.

"What is it?" Danielle asked.

Miranda suddenly remembered the cooked food before her. She supposed she should eat before it got cold. "Nothing. Just thinking."

Danielle almost asked what she was thinking about, but decided against it. They both tacitly agreed to not speak of those things while having dinner. Besides, if Miranda was to continue offering Danielle some semblance of a safe space... such matters had to be set aside unless Danielle brought them up herself.

"You know what's not fair?" Danielle said, breaking right into Miranda's thoughts. "You're such a good cook. Meanwhile, I would've burnt this."

"Which is why we're not having dinner at your place."

"I mean, we could, but you would have had to cook."

"I've seen your kitchen. Nothing goes where it's supposed to."

"I didn't realize kitchen gadgets had specific places they were supposed to go."

Anyone else, and Miranda would have been annoyed. Looking at the smile attempting to crack on Danielle's face, though, made Miranda laugh as well. "I'm not that good at cooking, but I am great at presentation." Her phone, which she had left on the other end of the dining table, rang. "You can make anything look good. Even the zucchini I burnt on the bottom of the rice." She didn't bother looking at who was calling her before she answered. "Sorry. It might be my-"

"Put me on speakerphone."

Miranda's throat swelled shut at the sound of her father's cracking voice. "Ex... excuse me?" Maintaining her composure in front of Danielle, who looked at her over a fork full of rice, was harder than lying about everything they used to have. "Why would I do that?"

"Because I told you to."

"I don't have to..."

Danielle perked up at the sound of Miranda's rising voice. "Everything okay?"

No. It wasn't. How could it be okay when Miranda's father interrupted everything she had attempted to build for herself in those past few weeks?

"I will speak English for her benefit," Nerilis continued to say in Julah. "She needs to hear what I have to say, since you're so hellbent on courting her in this life, too."

Was this his sassy-dad way of saying he didn't approve of his daughter's choice in partner? *Bet my mother would have been fine with it.* That was Miranda's defiant thought as she laid her phone on the table and switched it to speakerphone. Her final glance in Danielle's direction was one of pure apology.

And a little regret too. There was no going back from this.

"What's going on?" Danielle's chest was already constricted before she heard the god-awful sound of *that man's* voice.

"I remain disappointed." Nerilis's voice wasn't any less caustic in English. Which didn't help Danielle, who lurched back in her seat, eyes wide and air trapped in her throat. She couldn't get away from him. No matter where she went, or whether she regressed, this man was right behind her, threatening her again.

"I don't know what you want me to do about your disappointment." Miranda was careful with what she said. She didn't need Danielle to know—not now, perhaps not ever—her relationship to Nerilis Dunsman. *The only child he's ever had,* she thought with nothing but bitterness in her mouth. "I'm not responsible for any of it."

"Our universe will soon implode." Nerilis was always so nonchalant when he spoke of the end of the world. What excuse did Miranda have for wanting no part of it? "If we do not fuse with another, we can say goodbye to our sorry lives. No. Not just death. An end of all existence. There will be no Void, either. Do you want all those poor people who were sacrificed to have it be for nothing?"

"You..."

Danielle interrupted Miranda with her own thoughts. "What the hell do you want with us? Why are you calling her?" She kicked back her chair when she stood up and almost knocked over her plate. "I don't know what is going on here, but I want nothing to do with you. Do you understand?"

When Nerilis finally spoke again, it was to a small child arguing for the right to run into traffic. "It doesn't matter if you want nothing to do with me, girl. Your soul may be old, but your mind is terribly young. How can you not see past your own nose? When I say the universe will implode, I mean *everything will cease to exist.* Including the blasted Void and all souls within it. An unprecedented event no universe has ever seen. There's no telling what affect it might have on others around us. And you want to sit on your ass and count your duty done because your planet is not in immediate danger any longer? This isn't about Earth. It's not about you, either."

"So you agree it's also not about you?" Miranda drolly asked.

Danielle, who had little time to wonder how Miranda knew him so well, continued, "Get the hell away from us. You've broken me enough. *You've* ruined my existence, not the goddamn implosion of the universe."

"Ask yourself this, *girl.*" Nerilis's voice was terrible enough to send Danielle back into her seat. "Would you rather exist beyond the end of time? Because that's your current alternative. I should think you want neither to happen. Since I cannot force you to regress without compromising your soul, I have dedicated my life to ensuring nobody ceases to exist. At all. As a former High Priest of the Void, I can't think of anything more diabolical than allowing such a thing to happen. Or are we here to argue about ethics? Because I can't be assed to rehash this with you yet again."

"What do you mean *again?*" Danielle said with a huff.

"I'm sorry. I can't keep all your lives apart. You've had so many."

Danielle's first thought? *When did you get so catty?* Her second? *Forget this bullshit.*

"Sorry being a hybrid hasn't turned me into a master wizard," Miranda said. "Your disappointment in me is duly noted, however."

"If this is your way of saying you're angry about how things have turned out, I pity you."

Miranda rolled her eyes. Danielle was still confused—and still concerned that she might soon have a panic attack.

Before her father said anything else, Miranda took Danielle's hand and whispered, "He's not going to do anything to hurt us." She scoffed. "Just annoy us."

"I heard that," Nerilis said. "I know you think there are more important things right now, but I would *love* to inform you that the clock is ticking. Not just for Earth. For the whole blasphemous universe. I'd rather not spend eternity in a state of forgotten nothingness. I doubt you do either, even if you've convinced yourselves it's not a big deal."

"Would it be possible for us to have this chat tomorrow?" Miranda switched to Julah. Not only for her father's benefit, but for Danielle's. She didn't need to hear this. "I'm in the middle of something right now. We're working on getting this young lady regressed."

Danielle sat back in her seat. She may not have understood what Miranda said, but she knew what that *was*. The fact that Miranda was half-*julah* didn't bother Danielle any. What did was knowing that she was perfectly fluent in the ancient language.

She was about to put two and two together when Miranda cut the call with a grunt of frustration. Her phone was subsequently shut off so Nerilis couldn't call her back—because he would. He didn't understand things like *"Stop calling me, Dad."*

"I'm so sorry," she apologized. "He really is uncouth like that."

Danielle placed her elbows on the table and folded her fingers over her mouth. "That man is calling your personal phone," she hissed through her hand.

"Yes. He is." Miranda cleared her throat. "Like I said, though, I promise he won't do anything to harm us. I get that he can still be intimidating, but…"

"The man who is responsible for my grievous shit is calling your personal phone."

The color drained from Miranda's face. "Yes."

"Let me guess. You can't explain this to me because it might kill me."

"Danielle…"

"No, no." Danielle's hands flicked away the words coming toward her. "I knew when I started fooling around with you that something like this might happen." She let out a deafening sigh, head soon meeting the table. "You think I forget what you were doing a year ago?"

Miranda's hands curled around the edge of the table. "No." A year ago, she was doing some of her father's dirty work. Dismantling Earth. Attempting to double-cross him.

She had succeeded, but Danielle had seen her face. She had been in this house, stealing from Miranda.

"I'm on your side," Miranda reiterated. "If you think I can fake what we have? Then give me a goddamn award."

Danielle shook her head. "What the hell do we have, huh?"

Miranda didn't want to say it. She was too afraid of embarrassing herself. Too afraid of Danielle rejecting her answer.

"It's fine." Danielle sniffed and grabbed her fork. "Let's not think about it right now. Don't let that asshole ruin our dinner." She stabbed her noodles, but did not eat them.

"Are you... sure?"

"Yeah. I mean, if this is a ruse to kill me, at least I'll have fun before you do it."

Out of everything she could have said, that perhaps shocked Miranda the most.

Thirty-One

"I'm surprised you get a whole hour off for lunch." Danielle dropped into the chair nearest the window. The view of the city center was a sight to behold, but she barely had enough time to admire it before the restaurant host asked if she and Devon might like to move somewhere "a little more private." At first, she assumed he thought they were a couple. When Devon brushed him off, Danielle was allowed to speak again. "Not bad for an entry-level job, huh?"

Devon's elbow slid across the table as he peeked through the window. Although Danielle had arguably the better seat, relief on his face implied he was grateful to not be the one in full view of the window. "It's a recent development. My boss informed me this week I'm getting quite a few perks I never anticipated."

Although Danielle noted the depressing lilt to his voice, she didn't immediately address it. "Oh... well, that's good, right? You must be doing something right."

Devon bit his tongue while a waiter fussed with their place settings and poured them ice water from a carafe.

"By the way..." Danielle looked over her shoulder once the waiter was gone. Her fingers fidgeted with the menu, but she didn't open it. "This place is really nice." She didn't mean to imply that neither of them could afford it, but it was what she thought. Waiters in tails in a high-rise restaurant that played recorded piano music over the speakers? It reminded her too much of the place where Marlow first asked to meet them. *Talk about a whole lifetime ago...* she thought. "How did you find out about it?"

"My boss actually suggested it. Don't worry about the tab. It's covered."

"Huh?"

Devon pointed to a building across the street and to the right. "See that? I work there. This place is really convenient."

"Have you eaten here before?"

"Nope."

Danielle held up her menu. *Thank God it's in English.* She had fretted the menu would be in either French or Italian, cementing her fears that they *definitely* couldn't afford it. This was the kind of place Miranda would bring her, not Devon, who was working a starting wage. Even though he said the tab was covered... Jesus, how was she going to rationalize a French dip for twenty-five bucks?

"Okay..." She lowered the menu alongside her face, which hovered above the table. "What's going on here? When you asked me out to lunch today, I thought we would be hitting a café or diner." She peeked at the menu again. Although written in English, she couldn't make out half of the entrees, such as *"Plum-pickled Ertu'ah with Roasted Wopa Sprouts."* She might have been having a stroke for all she knew. "You know. A bit more lowkey than this place."

"Sorry. Like I said, my boss recommended it. It's his new favorite place."

A man in a three-piece suit and a gray handlebar mustache emerged from another room. After searching the room, he conferred with the nearest waiter, who pointed in Devon and Danielle's direction. The mustache was the first thing to perk up as soon as he recognized two of the Federation's most famous people. He asked the waiter if he looked "presentable" before hustling up to the table, where Danielle was about to grill Devon about things he could not readily answer.

"M... Mr. Anderson." The owner of the restaurant, who had never met Devon in the flesh before, gave a curt bow while tugging at his own suit jacket. "Ms. Cromwell. It's an honor to have you two dining in my humble establishment."

Perhaps his slight accent didn't give him away to Danielle, whose mouth was too agape to properly respond, but it did to Devon. "Hi," he said. "We're here to have a peaceful lunch, if it's all right."

"Oh, of course. I'll make sure that you are not bothered and that you receive prompt service." He motioned for the waiter to return to his side. "A bottle of the '95 Willamette we have," he said in Basic. "There should be three of them left. Go!"

"That's not necessary," Devon said. Danielle was only more confused, although the realization of what kind of restaurant this was slowly dawned on her. "Although, I wanted to know if you serve any dishes from Arrah."

"Ar..." The owner smacked his hands together in an eager fist. "I don't believe we have any Arrahite cuisine on the menu, sir, but our head chef hails from Qahrain and should be familiar with some dishes. Modern, of course. We might have to research..."

"Don't worry about it." Devon continued to speak in English, but it wasn't for Danielle's benefit. Although he understood Modern Basic better than ever now, he wasn't yet confident speaking it. A part of him was afraid to slip into Old Basic, and he would never fully explain why that brought him a modicum of shame. "We'll have whatever sounds good today."

"Of course." The owner's smile unnerved Devon, but all Danielle saw was an older gentleman who was probably not of this world. When he turned his eye to her, however, she knew things were about to get awkward. "You are originally from Qahrain, are you not, Ms. Cromwell?" he asked in English.

"Uh..." She turned her dropping bottom lip to Devon. For help.

"Yes. You are." He stiffened where he sat. "Qahrainian cuisine should be fine. Something easy."

"Absolutely, sir." The owner picked up the menus and retreated to the kitchen with the waiter. As soon as they were gone, Danielle folded her hands before her face and cocked one eyebrow toward Devon.

Embarrassment crashed over him, but he somehow kept his shit together while answering the look on her face. "This is a Federation-friendly restaurant, obviously."

"This isn't just a *friendly* restaurant," she said with sarcastic fervor. "Pretty sure this is where Federation people come to hobnob and eat their grandmother's home cooking from whatever planet they hail from."

"Like I said, it's my boss's new favorite place." Never mind the fact Devon had yet to tell Danielle all about that. "I thought this would be a decent restaurant to meet since it's close to my work and nobody will bother us."

"That plan is clearly working so far."

"The past two weeks have been a shitshow," Devon explained. "Right now, that guy fawning over us for simply being who we are is the least of what I've had to deal with."

"Being a celebrity is hard, huh?"

"That goes for you too."

While Danielle didn't appreciate his tone, she admitted—at least to herself, anyway—that he was right. The only reason Devon's face was all over the Federation media was because of his recent tour of interviews. It could have easily been Danielle as well. Right now, the only people who readily recognized her were those who paid closer attention to her photos.

"So... that guy knew what planet I used to be from, huh?"

Devon's face softened alongside his shoulders. "It's public information."

"I mean, *I* don't know that."

"I didn't either until I regressed." Devon steeled himself for possible backlash. "I mean... this isn't what I expected to talk about today."

Danielle let out a relieved breath. "Right. Uh, why did you ask me out for lunch?"

"Just thought we could catch up face to face for a bit. Oh, and... well, I guess this crazy thing happened. On top of the other crazy things. This something is more personal though. Guess I wanted an outside perspective from someone who doesn't have a stake in it."

Danielle waited for him to continue. Whatever she expected, it had nothing to do with his music career. Never mind a producer she had never heard of, and probably never would again.

Yet Devon couldn't think of anything else more important to talk about. Not their futures as two reincarnated mercenaries who had fulfilled their mission and were, theoretically, allowed to live out the rest of their natural lives. Not what their new celebrity meant for those lives, which would never know true peace, even with a powerful *julah* on their side. And definitely not their personal love lives, which remained rife with potential jealousy that couldn't be explained away as anything more than "one of those things that happens when you're injected into the Process with somebody."

So Danielle listened to his strange meetings with a man in a limousine, as if they were suddenly living in a teen movie from the '80s. As much as Danielle loved a good John Hughes flick, something about this was *weird*. Yet she couldn't quite put her finger on it until Devon finished speaking and his entire demeanor was imbued with the perfect broody look for a bad boy wanting to play rock 'n roll for his adoring fans.

"If you go with this guy, you'll probably be set for life," Danielle thought out loud. "You'll get to make all the music you want. I mean, that could be your career, right? I'm guessing it's what you've wanted. You got into the computer stuff because it was practical."

Devon didn't respond, but his eyes implored her to keep going.

"But you won't be famous because of your music. Your band will be famous because of who you are. Even if people end up genuinely liking your songs, it's not why they checked you out. You're gonna have to live with that for the rest of your creative life."

"Yeah." He hated her for putting so succinctly into words what had been keeping him up those past two nights. "It feels like selling out in the worst way possible. At least 'selling out' the way we used to know it meant a big label shoving a producer who knows how to make top forty hits into our direction. This is like..." Devon scoffed. "I've talked to one of my band members about it. You remember May? She's the doctor's daughter."

"Yeah. What does she think?"

"I don't think she likes the idea of being recognizably famous, but she also says that this is really the opportunity of a millennium for everyone else in the band. She's right. This isn't only about me. This is about my bandmates too. If I can use my name and face to take us to that level..."

"But I thought only your best friend knew about all of this?"

Devon nodded. "That's the hard part, really. I figure it's best for certain people to remain totally ignorant about what's going on out there."

"Wow. Wish we had that option, huh?"

His downcast glance was not as cynical as the bite to Danielle's voice. "Some people take it well. Some don't. It's not surprising." When he caught himself sounding like those first days he survived in a city of blood of vice, he jerked himself out of his haze and changed the subject. "Anyway, enough about me. I keep going on about what's going on in my life."

"Not like you don't have a lot going on."

"What about you, though? You've been through a lot lately. Have you talked to Marlow about..." He dropped his voice. "Reparations."

Danielle took her time answering. "No. I've been, uh, distracted." She couldn't look at him when she said it. Instead, she looked out the window, as if she had never seen her own city's skyline before.

"Distracted? Good? Bad?"

She met Devon's gaze halfway across the table before looking away again. "You know how sometimes one door closes and another one opens...?"

"Oh, job opportunity?"

"Umm... not really." As badly as Danielle wanted to make a sugar mama joke about her new girlfriend, now really wasn't the time. *Although it does explain why I'm not hurting for a job right now.* She didn't have to worry about rent with... well, her new sugar mama. For however long this was going to last. "Something nice, though. I'm not really sure how it's going to go, so I haven't talked to anybody about it yet. Ahem."

Devon still wasn't following. Then again, he had an idea. Perhaps his brain simply didn't want to process it.

"I'm sort of seeing somebody," Danielle blurted.

Obviously. Devon even surprised himself when he thought that. After all, just because his subconscious knew exactly what was going on with Danielle, didn't mean *he* wanted to admit it. He held no fantasies that they would magically end up together, no matter how much the old him wanted it to happen—the modern Devon was keenly aware of all the reasons it would fall apart around them. *Probably five weeks in,* he continued to muse, as his fingers drummed on the table and he attempted to maintain a nonplussed countenance. That was the most genuine look he had seen on Danielle's face for a long time.

He would dare say she was excited about the news.

"Oh." That was all he could manage. No matter how much he attempted to smile on her behalf, he couldn't do it. Because he knew damn well who she might be talking about. "That's good, right?"

"Right." Danielle's shoulders slumped with relief, casting aside all the weight she had carried in the moments leading up to telling Devon the truth. "I mean, I wasn't mentioning it before because I thought it would be a casual thing that didn't go anywhere, but if I'm being honest, we're already exclusive. I don't know what that means yet." She said that with a growing smile on her face, as if she didn't know *what* she wanted it to mean. The more naturally relieved she looked, the more Devon saw the writing scrawled across the wall. His heart hardened into a lump. His stomach prepared to catch it when it fell. "Trying to not be a total stereotype right now. I mean, I took things slow with Alicia when we started dating. Then again, that was my only real relationship when I think about it. So how can I really know what I'm like in an average relationship?"

"Stereotype?"

"You know..." Danielle blushed. "U-Hauls and stuff."

"Ah. You're seeing a woman?"

"I mean, I might as well, right?" Her laughter grew awkward. The waiter who was about to overcome the butterflies in his stomach and ask if a substitution from the chef was acceptable suddenly turned around and retreated to the kitchen. Danielle didn't notice him. Devon did. "Everyone knows I'm queer now. Even the military." She cradled her chin in her hand. "There's no reason to hide it anymore. I should celebrate being totally out of the closet by dating the first woman to ask, right? Wait." She sighed, hand sliding up her face and pressing against her nose. Devon had a great view of the unflattering angle. "It's not like that. I'm... I'm actually feeling pretty positive for the first time in a long while." She straightened herself up, hands pressing against the end of the table. "Yeah." She blew air through her pursed lips. "Guess I'm not used to feeling optimistic about things. Is that weird?"

Devon slowly shook his head. "No. You should feel optimistic. Shouldn't everyone?" He cleared his throat. "Is it anyone I know?"

Danielle had to think about that for a second. Her natural inclination was to make a crack about Alicia—specifically, how her girlfriend was *not* their mutual ex—but it wasn't appropriate. "I think you know her. Maybe not personally. Actually..." The smile disappeared. "That's why I haven't mentioned it to much of anyone. It's kinda scandalous when you think about it."

Devon grunted. How could he possibly like where this was going?

"Just don't do anything stupid, huh? That's my job right now."

"What do you mean?"

He grimaced. "Sorry. No. I'll tell you later. Not here." He glanced at the waiter, still waiting for his chance to approach. "You should talk about your good news. It's good, right?"

"Uh, right." Finally, Danielle noticed the waiter dancing from the corner of her eye. "Does that guy want something?"

"Our autographs, probably," Devon muttered. "Don't be surprised if they want you to sign it using your dead name, though."

Danielle took a moment before giving Devon her attention again. "You know who it is," she whispered, not wanting this total stranger to hear about her love life. "It's kinda embarrassing because of how you know her."

"Nothing could be more embarrassing than dating Dr. d'Eran." Devon didn't mention it had nothing to do with her being his therapist, and everything to do with kissing her daughter.

"You might be surprised." Danielle ran her fingers through her hair. Although she had rehearsed this since the day would inevitably come when she had to tell Devon about her relationship, she was still too nervous to say. "It's..." She met his eyes from across the table. "It's my former commander."

That was the best way to address that elephant about to come crashing through the fine Federation-cuisine restaurant. Although Devon expected that, he still wasn't prepared for the cataclysmic avalanche of emotions crushing him to hear that the one woman he held so much personal disdain for was finally with the one he had gone to the ends of the earth for—and would do it again.

At least my heart hasn't...

He thought too soon. His heart plummeted into his stomach, disrupting the acid that was already bubbling to attack his esophagus. As long as he kept the color in his face, Danielle should never notice. Regardless of how Devon felt about the news, he wasn't about to ruin it for her.

Because it's personal. In the past. A thousand years old. Different people. Different times. That's what the rational Devon of now said. Angry, bitter Sonall from a millennium ago?

Best to not dwell upon it.

"You know," Danielle continued, "the woman who..."

"Yeah. I know who she is." Devon winced. "Sorry. I know her better than you might realize."

Although Danielle offered him a curt nod, she couldn't say she knew what he was talking about today. "It's not like we're getting married anytime soon," she said for some confounding reason. "But it might end up getting more serious down the road. I dunno." Danielle attempted to shake the conflicting feelings from her limbs, but they continued to cling to her like her most intimate layer of clothing. "It's not only the fact that we've always had this... chemistry... between us." She would leave it at that. "But she knows about me already, if you know what I mean. I don't have to dump any big reveals on her. Screw it, she knows more about the Federation than I do. Actually, I'm probably not supposed to share this, but she's also half-*julah*. Which explains a *lot*."

Devon perked up at that. "She's what?"

"Yeah. On her father's side. She hasn't told me who it is. She also said something about being unregistered, so I guess I better not go around telling people, huh?"

"Guess not." Already Devon's mind was reeling from the information. *I had no idea she was half-*julah. Even if he had heard it before, it hadn't stuck to his brain. Certainly, like Danielle said, it explained much about Miranda, both in this life and the first one. "Remember what happened when you-know-who came to Earth?"

"Yeah?"

"Uh-huh. Remember what happened to *her?*"

Something clicked inside Danielle's head. *"This used to be my body."* That's what the High Priestess had said in those few moments when she possessed Miranda and addressed the two mercenaries sent to save yet another doomed planet. If there was one thing both Danielle and Devon knew from Federation history, it was that the High Priestess was once the tragic wife of the High Priest who would go on to ravage the universe...

Her father... that call from last night... Danielle's throat was about to close.

It couldn't be. Best to shove it aside for now.

"Anyway," Devon said, "I'm happy for you."

Danielle looked up from her empty place setting. "Really?"

"Yeah. Of course. If you're happy, then it's a good thing, right? You deserve to live a little after all you've been through."

Danielle didn't know what surprised her more—that Devon would be supportive of her moving on from whatever thing they once had, or that he would feel that way after hearing who it was.

A part of her was still paranoid, after all.

"So you think it's not a problem that it's her?" she asked.

"What do you mean?"

"The person I'm dating." Danielle was careful to not mention her by name in the restaurant. "You think she's good for me?"

Devon was grateful that she hadn't asked, *"You think she's a good person?"* Because that was a much harder question for him to answer.

"I think you'll be very happy with her."

There was something in the way he said that... something that both surprised and reassured Danielle's paranoia. *He wouldn't say that for no reason, right?* she wondered, as the waiter finally gained the courage to ask if they might accept a change from the chef. To Danielle, it was nothing. After all, she barely remembered her old, dead name. To Devon, however, it was a chance to request one food that Danielle didn't recognize. The waiter sputtered for an answer before rushing back to the kitchen to ask the chef.

"What did you order?" Danielle asked.

"I asked if they had this one dish that used to be really popular on..." He halted. "You-know-where."

"You can say it, you know."

"Cerilyn."

Danielle sighed. "What was it?"

"Something that would have been considered peasant food everywhere else. Bread and a type of gruel you can dress up any way you wanted it. Super protein-fortified, although I think these days they would skip the powders and go straight for real food substitutes."

"Ooh, like crickets?"

Devon had to do a double-take at that one. "Why are you mentioning cricket protein?"

"Why wouldn't I be mentioning it? Sounds like the kind of thing we have done."

"Don't think crickets survived in that environment. Beetles, on the other hand..."

By the time the waiter returned with an answer, Devon and Danielle were laughing over gruel filled with beetle guts and bread loaves teeming with spiders. The waiter politely waited for them to stop clutching their stomachs before informing them that the chef was delighted to attempt something so out of his usual realm of cuisine expertise.

There wasn't anywhere near enough time for him to make their meal *and* for Devon to get back to work on time. He didn't care. Even if his boss wouldn't look the other way, Devon was about two days away from quitting, anyway. If Danielle was out there finding her happily-ever-after, then maybe he should get on with his too.

For the first time in way too long, Evan brought back a sandwich big enough to share with Lanelle during their lunch break.

"I made sure they left off the relish." He slapped the foot-long monstrosity onto the main panel separating their bodies from the holographic computer screens. Lanelle held back her disgust as her coworker unwrapped a pile of meat, condiments, and bread with a flick of his wrist. *God,* she thought, *you can see him drooling.* Evan loved his sandwiches. He loved Earth sandwiches the best, since he claimed Earth produced the best sauces. Lanelle, on the other hand, only ate when necessary. Which was probably why Evan had noticed her skipping lunch lately.

It would have been sweet, except Lanelle was in no position to give a shit.

"I'm telling you, convincing the CEO of Subway to expand to Terra III was the best work I've done yet." Evan kissed his fingertips before pulling apart the sandwich. A pile of napkins joined half the sandwich as it landed beside Lanelle. "Soon it's not gonna only be the biggest restaurant chain on Earth. It's gonna be the biggest one in the universe."

"Oh, no," Lanelle drolly said, eyes locked on the screen before her. "And beat out the Rusty Red?" She referred to the intergalactic soup superstar chain that was featured on almost every street corner that boasted a population more than 500. Lanelle had seen the rise of Rusty Red through her four lives, and every life they got a little worse. Or a lot worse, since she had passed some time between lives while the then-CEO of Rusty Red sold out to a corporate conglomerate that immediately swapped ingredients for cheaper varieties and convinced customers that a few more hundred calories per meal was nothing. *"Just run more,"* had been a popular slogan when Lanelle was growing up in her current life.

"We could get some Rusty Red soups to go with these sandwiches."

Lanelle finally gave him the attention he craved. Albeit in the form of a glare of pure disbelief, but Evan could smile for the first time since returning to work.

"How are you not five hundred pounds?" Lanelle snapped. "Don't tell me it's vitamins. I've seen your wife's cooking." That was a jab at the fact neither Evan nor his wife cooked. Most of their meals were ordered in, which was only possible because Master Marlow was so disconnected from human budgets that he let Lanelle set their salaries. Which she was always *more* than happy to do, because a girl wanted a swanky condo overlooking the ports. Even better if she had enough cash leftover to spend her downtime in the pleasure plazas, where she was on a first-name basis with half of the android wranglers. She may or may not have been dating one.

The communicator on the panel lit up. Lanelle turned toward it with a sigh.

"Seriously. You should be dead by now," she muttered. "Meanwhile, I gain five inches around my waist when I look at this thing." She pushed aside her half of the sandwich and picked up the communicator, her customer service voice making Evan shudder. "Greetings. This is Lanelle Lanerak, First Assistant to Master Ramaron Marlow. How can I help you?"

"Lanelle?" Devon's voice was faint from Earth. Lanelle not only switched her brain over to English, she fiddled with two dials on the communicator until reception was better on Devon's end. "Sorry if I'm interrupting. I really need to talk to Marlow. Like, serious talk."

Lanelle glanced at the screen in front of her. She swiped away the boxes of emails and scheduling graphs that ran Marlow's professional life and brought up the *Where the Shit is He?* app that only worked in certain locations. Like Terra III, where Marlow happened to be, thank the Void. This was a man who liked to up and disappear to the interdimensional rifts or, worse, his family's estate. *Can't track him there,* Lanelle lamented. *It's like he doesn't want me to find him sometimes.*

If anyone could find him, though, it was her. More than once she had tracked him down in those pleasure plazas. It was how she met the guy she was dating!

"You're in luck," she told Devon. The sounds of English caught Evan's attention, who dropped a bite of sandwich from his mouth. "Master Marlow is currently in his Terra III office. I'll patch you through in a bit." It was easier than giving Devon and Danielle the *real* number that went directly to Marlow's pocket. Sometimes, they ended up there anyway, but Marlow was so strict about who could call him without preamble that both Lanelle and Evan often had to hack their ways back onto his communicator. "Should I tell him what you're calling about, or do you want the honors of dropping the bombs yourself?"

"What makes you say that?"

The fact you asked, for one. Lanelle rolled her eyes. She didn't have time for this. There were sandwiches to ignore and schedules to make. *And coworkers to chastise for filling this room with mayonnaise.* Oh, look. Some squirted onto the console as she spoke.

"You wouldn't be calling unless you knew something about the commander's office blowing up this line when you're not." Yara d'Alacron's cronies sniffed all around Marlow's office, which was easy enough to do when they were only ten minutes away by hovercraft.

"I'd rather tell him myself. This is really, uh..."

"Say no more." Lanelle put him on hold and looked at Evan. "Wanna spend the rest of your break listening in on this call?"

He swallowed. "Absolutely."

Lanelle pushed the button that patched Devon through to Marlow's personal line. As soon as she heard the ringing, she motioned for Evan to get closer so he could also hear. She didn't even mind his peppery breath for once.

Thirty-Two

"You honor me by responding to my request, Master Marlow." Yara was at the door to personally greet the man who ambled down the hallway with a military escort. He was keenly aware, of course, that any of these humans could do something funny at any moment. While a *ma-julah* could do even more damage, they might have more loyalty to him. No wonder Yara made sure everyone in her employ today was nothing but pure human.

"When the Commander of the Federation Forces personally rings me," Marlow began, removing his hat and shoving it into a grunt's hands. He slammed his cane into the entryway to Yara's office, urging her to step aside, "I am inclined to answer when time permits. You made it sound quite serious."

"Rest assured that I would only bother you if it were a matter of intergalactic security." Yara followed him, shutting the door behind her. Her men had their orders. *"Stand guard unless I call for you."* They would. These were her most loyal men. More loyal than Joel d'Kerni, who was currently kept far away from this meeting. Imagining his reaction to yet another interview with Master Marlow, a former acolyte turned spearer of the cause to save planets from the old High Priest, made Yara sick. She didn't have time for that.

She did, however, have plenty of time for one of her keenest pet projects.

"May I offer you some *cageh,* Master Marlow?" Yara remained standing while Marlow helped himself to the couch on the far side of the room. No matter how many times she asked him to sit at her desk, he knew better than to condone any optics that implied she had *any* notable power over him. While it may have been true according to the hierarchy of the Federation, he had a good few thousand years on her, and he was too old and too tired to play along with those theatrics. Hell, even when he was a student at the Academy, he would have laughed at the request and left the room. This was a step *up!*

"I am not in need of refreshments." Marlow eased himself into the couch. As much as he didn't want to admit it, his old hip injury had not only put more pounds on him, but had entrusted his ass to flop wherever it pleased, with or without his express permission. *God help me if Nerilis saw me now,* he lamented to himself. *He would never let me hear the end of it. He'd have me running laps.* Probably in some other dimension. One with higher gravity, just to spite Marlow.

Yara kept her thoughts to herself as she brought over her tablet and folders to the coffee table in between two identical sofas. She sat across from Marlow, spreading her materials across the table while taking care that her hair did not fall away from her face. She preferred to go without an eyepatch in present company, but she didn't want Marlow seeing her injury until she decided it pertinent. For a little psychological warfare, of course.

"You honor me with your time." She didn't hide her disdain for this meeting any longer. Marlow propped his hands atop his cane, the rubber tip digging into the hard floor and his pinky tapping against the motion sensor that was currently in hibernation. Like Yara presented herself in a certain way, Marlow knew the advantage of sitting like an injured old man who could barely move without medical aid. "And without your entourage. An unprecedented feat."

"Don't doubt that my two chaperones are waiting for me. Your guards were quite adamant that they not make it past the lobby."

"It's really for the best. We don't allow pregnant women past the final checkpoint, anyway. One of my predecessors used to scent these rooms with *weepil,* long before we knew about the birth defects it could cause."

"Kalera can take care of herself."

"When is she due?"

Marlow leaned forward, the couch creaking beneath his weight. "I don't believe you truly care about my bodyguards' wellbeing. Why am I here, Commander? I've already answered all of the questions you could possibly throw at me."

"New information has been brought to light." Yara saw no reason to hold back her trump cards now. Marlow wanted to play this way? He wanted to be rid of her and on his way? Fine. She could slap him upside the head with everything she now knew about certain humans beneath his thumb. "Remind me. How many souls have you registered into the Process?"

He kept his demeanor neutral, but Marlow wouldn't deny the fuzzy feeling in his head. "Three, of course. They're all accounted for."

"Ah, yes. Your assistant, Ms. Lanerak." Yara turned her tablet around. There was Lanelle's Federation ID, her scowl as lovely as ever. "And the two so-called mercenaries, Mr. Anderson and Ms. Cromwell." She purposely dropped Danielle's old military title. It wasn't necessary any longer, was it? "It's strange. I've recently interviewed another soul who claims to be in the Process. She was kind enough to tell me who put her into it." Yara finished swiping through her photos and presented Marlow with the photo of Miranda that now haunted her subconsciousness. "She says it was you, Master Marlow. You put her into the Process."

Marlow sucked in his breath, which Yara noted before he had the chance to master every facet of his physical reactions. *This never gets easier, does it?* he thought, gazing upon Miranda's dour visage. Unlike his old friend, Marlow didn't immediately see Joiya's features. The hair wasn't even the same. Yet he saw it, of course.

She looked so much like Joiya that it was natural for Nerilis to lose his mind every goddamn time. But Marlow saw another person in that face. Specifically, behind those glowering eyes that dared him to ruin her life again.

"She claims to be the reincarnation of Cairn di'Cerilyn." Yara left the tablet on the table for Marlow to behold. He was not easily wont to look away, either. "To be fair, that's why I interviewed her. I had my suspicions. Every bit of my harvested intelligence told me to interrogate this Earthling until I got the truth. It's rather amazing how readily she gave it up too." Yara's sigh of self-indulgence accompanied the gentle tug of her hair. There was what was left of her eye, catching a modicum of Marlow's unsettled attention. "So interesting. There has never been a recording of Cairn di'Cerilyn's reincarnation. You'd think there would be, considering she was once the most recognizable face of Cerilyn. Until you got your hands on her number one and two, of course."

"You think I do not recall?" Marlow sat back again. "A thousand years ago is like two months ago, sometimes. I recognize the young woman, of course. Why shouldn't I? She is correct. I was the one who put her into the Process."

Yara's elbow slipped off her knee. She quickly corrected her posture, but she had to turn away before Marlow caught the scowl on her face. This was *not* how it was supposed to go. Marlow was supposed to be shocked. Deny his relationship to Miranda, let alone that he was responsible for her soul's turmoil. Yara would believe him, too, since she wanted to catch Miranda in the egregious lie she told a few days ago. *I know it was Nerilis Dunsman who put her into the Process. I know she's connected to him.* More than that, Yara already knew that Miranda was Nerilis's biological daughter. She merely needed to prove it to a court of Federation law!

"You did." Yara absentmindedly scratched at her forehead. When she caught Marlow watching her, she straightened her back and shoved her hands into her back. "Why is she not registered, then?"

Her accusatory tone did not make him flinch. "Simple. I didn't realize it had worked until recently. She was a very last-minute addition. I hadn't quite finished the spell when I had to get off Cerilyn. I don't know if you've ever been on a dismantling planet, Commander, but it's not a very safe place to be. The woman we both knew as Ms. di'Cerilyn was as good as dead by the time I left. How was I to know it worked? She never came forward to me until recently."

"You mean Miranda Hotchner did not come forward?"

"It is possible she is the first I am aware of. Who is to say? They all run together after a while."

As much as Yara was used to the verbal runaround *julah* loved to give her, Marlow's non-answers made her clench her fists in her lap. "Walk me through the events as you remember them, Master Marlow."

He had already rehearsed this story. Lanelle had helped, since she was the only one in his employ who knew who the hell he was talking about after Devon's fateful call. *"They're going to ask you about Miranda Hotchner being in the Process. You're going to take the fall and claim you're the one who put her in the Process,"* Devon had said. *"Don't even argue with me about it, Old Man. We're doing this for Danielle."*

Marlow had no issue with taking the fall for Nerilis, who had gone out of his damned way to put them all in this mess. Marlow's issue lay in Devon's tone. *When did he get so bossy?* Marlow thought about that now, while Yara glared at him from across the table.

"My only relationship with Chief di'Cerilyn before the destruction was purely professional," Marlow insisted. "I approached her when I discovered Nerilis Dunsman was going to target Cerilyn as his first planet with life on it. I paid her for the best of her best, and she supplied the best. I paid good money for them too." Cairn had been reticent to provide *the* best at Marlow's insistence, and it wasn't until later that he realized why. Sonall had been her Second in Command and retired from missions. Sulim? She was the chief's personal bodyguard. And, as Marlow finally realized, her lover. "Once she realized what was at stake, she was quick to provide the best team she had. Brought them out of retirement, so to speak. But, ah..." This was where Marlow always fumbled his brand-new story a little. "They didn't quite make it. The last I saw them alive was in the inner sanctum of their fortress. I was desperate and had little time to make decisions. They were dying. Literally dying." The reports over the centuries were clear that both Sonall and Sulim received mortal wounds from Nerilis Dunsman before the planet collapsed. Marlow had always assured himself that they were dead before the true end came for them. "When you're dying and desperate, you agree to stupid deals. To be fair, I was also desperate. I knew what a threat Dunsman posed to the universe." Marlow sighed. "I regret ever putting them into the Process, but after it was done, it was too late."

"That's fantastic. What about the chief?"

Marlow scratched his ear. "She begged me to do it to her too. Since she had been a valuable asset, I decided to help. Like I said, though, before I could finish the spell, I had to depart to save my own hide. I always assumed it hadn't taken. Why would I, when she never contacted me afterward? My own mercenaries never brought her to my attention. I had no reason to believe that Cairn di'Cerilyn was anything but returned to the Void after the destruction of her namesake planet."

Yara wrote something in her personal notes while keeping one eye on the man who brought her so much ire. "You do realize I must forward this to the proper authorities, yes? You will be at the very least *fined* by both the Federation and the Priesthood of the Void."

"Let me worry about that, Commander. Now that I know the truth, I can make legal amends among my own people."

"Oh, I'm sure you will. I'm not telling them what to do about it. I'm telling them you've confessed to such a spiritual transgression."

Marlow tilted his head to the side. "You have a great interest in this person, don't you, Commander?"

She stopped writing. "Excuse me?"

"Cairn di'Cerilyn. Something about her name raises your hackles. It almost makes me think you have a personal relationship to her. Of course, that is impossible. You are not in the Process." Marlow chuckled. "I'd be able to tell if that was the case. No..." He rubbed his chin, his other hand dancing around the top of his cane. "If I take a good, hard look at you, I can tell something else, Commander. You're reincarnated."

Yara lowered her tablet. "What does that have to do with anything? Billions of people have been reincarnated."

"Yes, but your interest in this case is not natural. If you were *merely* reincarnated, you would only care as far as your job commands you. Your energy reads completely different when you talk about this person. I don't suppose you're..."

"This is none of your concern. All I wish to share with you, Master Marlow, is that I am currently seeing Dr. d'Eran about any spiritual concerns of mine."

"Ah, yes, of course. Quite a good idea. I'm sure she'll help you more than I could."

"She is the professional on these matters, yes."

Marlow shrugged, preparing himself to stand. "If that's all you need to ask me, Commander, I should like to take my leave. I have other appointments to attend before the end of the day. Apparently, I must make a few things right with the proper channels regarding a certain soul shoved into the Process."

"If it's all the same to you, Master Marlow," Yara snapped, "there is one more thing I should like to ask."

Marlow was still on the edge of his seat. "What is that, Commander?"

She showed him the picture of Miranda, this time side-by-side with the official portrait of the High Priestess, which hung in every Temple and was printed in the back of every holy book regarding the Void. Marlow was so exhaustingly familiar with it that he didn't even look.

"Care to tell me what I'm looking at here?"

Marlow barely glanced in her direction. "Now you play with fire, Commander."

Yara was taken aback. "Excuse me?"

When Marlow stood, it was with a mighty grunt that put to rest their conversation. "There are some things that go beyond the reaches of the Federation's grasp. You asked your questions about the identity of these women and how they came to be. I answered. That is all there is for you to know."

"Excuse..."

Marlow helped himself to the door. "Oh, before I go," he interrupted, "may I be so bold as to give you a little bit of advice, Commander?"

She did not respond.

"When it comes to matters of intergalactic security, there is little information to be had in the identity of one inconsequential woman from a thousand years ago. Now, I shall make matters right with the governing bodies that bother themselves with what I do with my life and time!"

It was the most *julah* thing he could have said, and Yara was convinced he did it on purpose. *One day,* she thought, as Marlow was escorted back to the lobby where his bodyguards awaited him, *we won't have to deal with these smug degenerates any longer.* That was beyond the scope of her lifetime, however. For now, Commander Yara d'Alacron would have to secure her legacy through other means.

Personal means.

Thirty-Three

Although Danielle was no stranger to the dreams that haunted a woman not yet regressed, she had enjoyed a recent reprieve from them. How long had it been since she last awakened in a cold sweat, wondering where she was? *Who* she was?

Since discovering her job was about to come to a traumatic end, Danielle had been nightmare free. Well, free from the terrors that used to haunt her a thousand years ago. Her brain had too much else to focus on now. Like how she would move on from the only career she ever had, and how badly she wished to live in another world. Maybe even another time.

Now? As she lay in someone else's bed and recounted the previous day? She was taken to a time long ago. Her brain insisted on it.

The sweat brewing on her skin translated to the sweat Sulim always felt when she stood on the balcony overlooking the jungle below the fortress's rocky outcrop. Sometimes, she caught the rainclouds rumbling across the trees, driving the people conducting business in the neighboring town into their huts. The first time Sulim beheld the strange geography of Cerilyn, a planet that boasted a jungle on one side and desert on the other, she feared those rainclouds rising up and dumping upon her unprotected body. Indeed, when she used to live in the lower dormitories, she occasionally heard the rain beyond her wall and pretended she was back on her native planet, where the rains fell upon farm fields and the sun baked the life into the earth.

A threat loomed over that place, though. One that was now known to Sulim and the others closest to her.

Sulim knew anxiety. She knew fear. She didn't know *this*, though.

She slipped into the secret passage connecting her room with Cairn's apartment. While she didn't see her companion right away, she heard rummaging in the bedroom, followed by muffled sounds coming from the closet vault.

"What are you doing?" Sulim leaned in the doorway, beholding Cairn shoving the valuables and money the two of them had saved and embezzled into luggage.

Cairn stopped long enough to acknowledge Sulim. "We must leave in the morning. We will tell Sonall and the others that–"

"Are you nuts?" Sulim had a headache. She had hoped to find some solace in her lover's arms. Instead, she had more bullshit on her hands. "We can't leave now! We're needed here!"

Cairn kicked aside a half-empty bag and approached Sulim. "What we need is to save our skins. Everything we ever worked for is for naught if we don't leave as soon as we can. Now, I need you take these bags and sneak them on board before we head out in the morning. It's too suspicious if we take it all down at once tomorrow."

"Do you hear yourself? Are you even the same woman who just gave a huge speech about how to not put your own life above everyone else's? There's no coming back from defecting now. We would be toast the moment survivors get a hold of us. I don't even want to think about what some of those brutes on our roster would do should they lose the last shred of respect they hold for us."

"It won't come to that."

"Why do you think that is?"

"Because our resident madman will undoubtedly get the other Relic, do his thing, and we're all gone. The moment we leave, I'm sounding the evacuation alarm, anyway. Then, it's every man for himself."

"Which you should oversee! We should be the *last* to evacuate!" What kind of leader did Sulim talk to right now, anyway?

"There will be no ships left, and you know it. Everyone will be too scared to come back to pick up more evacuees. Sulim, please..." Cairn reached for her lover's hand. "We have to go. Grab whatever is most valuable to you, see anyone you need to... we have to *go.*"

That desperation shook Sulim's floundering resolve. "I can't believe I'm hearing this right now."

"Tomorrow morning is the latest we can wait. You heard him earlier. He will give you and me just enough time to get out before carrying out his plan. It's only a matter of time before

he finds the other Relic!"

"Yeah, can we talk about that?" Sulim backed away from the closet, the bed's gravity pulling her down until her legs finally had the chance to regain their strength. "When were you going to tell me about that man hanging around here? How long have you known? He's your father, isn't he?"

Cairn dropped her bag and stood in the closet doorway. "Which question do you want me to answer first?"

The fact she wasn't shocked by any of them told Sulim everything she needed to know. Nevertheless, she desired to hear the words from Cairn's own lips. "Is Nerilis Dunsman your father?"

Cairn pushed her bangs out of her face. "Apparently. Was a bit of a shock to me, you know."

"Why didn't you tell me?"

"There are many things I've never told you. About my heritage. About my childhood. About the chief before me." Cairn cocked her head. "Usually because it's not worth talking about."

"I think knowing that Nerilis Dunsman is your *father* is noteworthy."

"I had no way to know he would target Cerilyn. We were planning on leaving, anyway. Sulim..." Cairn stepped forward before Sulim got up from the bed and left.

She rubbed her forehead. Her fingertips were not enough to relieve the pressure assaulting her body. "What happened earlier? When he was here?" She sat up. "You scared him off somehow. What was that? Do you... have powers like him?"

She didn't know what she expected from Cairn, a woman who had more secrets than anyone else Sulim knew. *Over ten years of sharing her bed, and I still barely know who she really is.* There were times when Sulim questioned if the chief even *loved* her. *She might not be capable, for all I know.* Her fears that Cairn had moments of disloyalty were long gone, but that didn't mean Cairn was the most honest woman on Cerilyn. Chiefs were rarely honest at their cores.

"I don't know. Something like that has never happened before." Cairn bridged the gap between her and Sulim. "I think he was shocked into leaving because he's always thought I'm incapable of that kind of... ability. You have to understand, hybrids like me tend to not have sorceric abilities if we're *julah* only on our father's side. It's mostly matrilineal."

"But..."

"But I saw him hurting you." Cairn sat on the bed next to Sulim, their hands entwined. "I didn't know what he would do to you. For all I knew, he would kill you before my own eyes. I was... I don't want to say *scared.* I was angry. The man has been nothing but a hindrance since the moment he made himself known to me. His goal of getting in the way of my own happiness was finally at its final straw. I just... exploded."

Sulim allowed Cairn to lean her head against her partner's shoulder. "This is a lot to take in," Sulim said. "And now you want to leave in the morning. You want to abandon your people to whatever fate your father has planned for us."

"It's not like that. Of course I don't want 'my' people to suffer. That's why I'm giving the evacuation order as soon as we leave."

"Once we're gone. Once we've taken a ship that could carry five more people. We should be transporting civilians, if nothing else. At least take some of the girls from Honeydew..."

"There's not enough time. Besides, they'll talk. Nobody spreads gossip faster than courtesans."

"I can't be here right now." Sulim stood up, shaking Cairn off her. "Do what you want. I need... I need a moment to think. There's gotta be another way."

Cairn did not chase after her. "You're smarter than anyone else I know. If anyone can come up with the perfect solution, it's you."

It was those reassurances that always drew Sulim back into her partner's web. *Because I love her. Because we're in this together.* Cairn had her moments that made Sulim question everything about what they had, but in the end, she always came back around: to their feelings, their dreams, and the legacy they'd give up at a moment's notice if it meant peace.

Sulim would do whatever it took. She and Cairn only had one life together. It was either this or throw themselves into the pits of despair that had claimed more than one of their kin.

Better to be a traitor and free than beholden to the tastes of honor that came with being one of Cerilyn's top mercenaries. Anything was truly better than that.

Danielle awoke with a familiar pang to her chest—and an all-too-familiar disorientation that mutilated her sense of where she was... or who she now was.

She pried the covers away from her throat, the sheets and pillowcase beneath her head doused in sweat. Her eyes refused to open as she gasped for air. The pain radiating from her brain to her fingertips was enough to make her finally cry out in terror.

Where? Who? Why? She grabbed her throat, choking on the memories still too vivid for her to set aside. Deep inside her head screamed a dormant voice. Danielle couldn't make out the words. All she knew was that the sleeping identity within her was coming closer and closer to forcing herself upon Danielle's consciousness.

Soon, a weight was upon her.

"Danielle." Miranda's firm voice didn't penetrate Danielle's trauma. When she recognized that frightened whiteness in Danielle's eyes, she changed tactics. "Sulim."

The thrashing only stopped when Miranda grabbed Danielle by the wrists and held their hands close between their chests. Miranda, now wide awake in the middle of the night, entrenched her weight around Danielle's waist and thought of everything she could to make this moment pass peacefully.

Of course, she considered that Danielle might finally be regressing, but it didn't make sense. There had been no triggering catalyst. Nothing that Miranda could pinpoint as she stared into Danielle's vacant eyes, cursing the darkness for obscuring the parts of their features that they once treasured most.

"*Maita-ya...*" Danielle whispered, her body continuing to tremble beneath Miranda's gasp. "It's our fault..."

Miranda didn't know what spurred this in Danielle's psyche. It was bad enough she knew what Danielle was talking about.

"It's not our fault." Miranda didn't mean to speak with so much conviction. Perhaps it wasn't really *her* saying it at all. Nearly twenty years after regressing on her own, she still sometimes battled with another voice within her. "Do you hear me? We couldn't have prevented it. It's not our fault. We did everything we could to stop it."

Danielle whimpered where she lay, hands shaking in Miranda's grasp and voice as broken as the spirit that struggled within her. "We're going to die," Danielle said in Old Basic. "We're all going to die—and it's our fault."

Miranda hung her head, her grasp on Danielle's wrists slackening. "No," she said. "We're not going to die. Not this time. That's over. That's in the past. Danielle? Danielle, baby, wake up." Why was Miranda the one trembling now? Was it the smack of the past hitting her upside the head when she heard Sulim's far away voice full of fear? "We're on Earth. We made it. Nothing's going to touch us. We're safe. *You're safe.*" She sniffed something disturbing her nose. Tears? No. There was nothing to cry about now. "I'm safe."

Those reassurances worked well enough that Danielle's breathing finally stilled, her eyes fluttering open and pupils returning to their proper place. When she spoke, it was with the familiar warmth of the woman Miranda had taken to bed that night. "You mean it?"

"I don't know what you saw in your dreams," Miranda whispered, "but that happened a thousand years ago. That's over. We're here now." Her hands clenched Danielle's. *I can't let her go,* Miranda thought, ankles and kneecaps digging into her bed. "I love you."

She had been holding back those words for more than two weeks. *My whole life...* From the moment Miranda met her father and the woman he hired to babysit her when she was a teenager. From the moment she regressed, alone and forlorn in a dirty apartment. *From the moment she walked into my office to report for duty.* These weren't words to say while Danielle continued to wrestle with her memories. Nor were they for so early in a normal relationship. Miranda didn't want to make such a mistake that scared Danielle away. Everything was always so... tenuous.

Danielle remained frozen for one whole, maddening second. As the sweat disappeared from her skin and the breath steadied in her chest, she achieved a clarity that had been elusive for much too long.

"I love you too."

Although they were words they both longed to say and hear for an age, the impact was far from earthshaking. If anything, the mutual feelings settling into their bodies and placating their erratic heartbeats were merely...

Relief.

The weary sensations cast out from the universe could have consumed Miranda. They could have sent Danielle into another stupor—one she would not remember in the ensuing morning. Instead, they clung to the darkness.

And to each other, their hearts full of ancient relief and joy for the first time since they last shared their dangerous dreams on a sun-soaked balcony.

Thirty-Four

Word from the head office summoned Captain Joel d'Kerni early the next morning, when he was fresh from his bath, breakfast, and a kiss to his older children's cheeks on their way to school.

When he heard who called him, he stopped in front of his in-home shrine and made an offering to the High Priestess. His wife stood silently beside the front door, offering him a pat on the shoulder and a silent look that said, "*Good luck.*"

Although he knew strange things were afoot in the Federation, nothing prepared him for the look on the Commander's face when he stepped into her office.

"Ah, Captain." Yara looked up from her desk, which she loomed over with a dictator's confidence. The men following one another out the door, brushing against Joel and deferring to him with nods and "sirs," beneath their breaths, were filled with pent-up energy that made Joel look twice. The more steps he took into Lara's office, shutting the door behind him, the more he already resented what this job asked of him some days. "Lovely morning to you. I'm glad you could come in on such short notice."

He stood a respectful distance away from her desk. "I was told you have direct orders for me, Commander."

She motioned for him to come closer, that smirk of self-indulgence dancing upon her pinkened lips. "Yes. I want you to personally helm the arrests that are on the docket today. Off the record arrests, I might add. This is a classified mission." She cocked her head. "I take it there will be no issues with that?"

What a trick question from a tricky woman. Her simply saying *that* much meant Joel was already beholden to the mission. To turn it down was to compromise not only his position, but the sanctity of this mission's classified nature. If Joel valued his life and career, he would do whatever Yara wanted.

"I aim to serve the Federation, Commander." His back was rigid and his deep voice even. "Who is it that I am to arrest today?" For him to be personally called in must mean that this was a high-profile arrest. No wonder he had a sick feeling in his stomach.

Yara swiped the screen built into her desk. From the depths of personnel files and documents apprehended from one of Earth's more cooperative agencies, she pulled up the three bookmarked IDs that both the Federation and the American government earmarked as *crucial*.

Joel hoped to the Void that Yara did not notice his growing reticence.

"This is a matter of Intergalactic Security," Yara calmly said, studying his reaction. "These three are not only required for individual interrogation. They are to be secretly arrested and put into our protection. Do you understand? I don't care what you have to do to bring them in. By the end of the day, I want you and your men to be back from Earth, and these three secured in the cell of highest clearance." Luckily for the Federation, it was currently empty.

"Ma'am…" Joel stared at the pictures of Devon, Miranda, and Danielle, each one scowling at him through a DMV lens. "I don't understand. What are the…"

Yara cut him off with impunity. "The charges, since you are an honorable man and must announce them when you make your arrest, are conspiring with an enemy of the Federation and interfering with an intergalactic investigation. You leave the rest to me."

Joel still did not approach the desk any more than he had to, since between that placid look on Lara's face and the strange pressure in the air, he was convinced that to come closer to his boss was to invite the power of the Void into the room. He was a pious man, but he didn't think bringing about the end of the world for the sake of it was a good idea.

"Is there something you don't understand, Captain?"

Oh, Joel hardly understood anything right now. He didn't understand where this sudden vendetta came from, nor did he understand why *his* loyalty was being tested. He was far from the only man serving beneath the commander who had the authority to make such a high-profile arrest—and do it quietly. Yet Yara bringing up his background and making a show of his qualifications didn't sit easy with him. Surely, she knew how hard this would be for him? It wasn't just Devon and Danielle's relation to the Void and how highly they were put on some pedestals, even if they didn't know it.

It was that face looking back at him. The one in the center.

When he made his offering to the High Priestess earlier, he had seen such a face. The standard portrait that hung in every Temple was easy enough to get, but a man of Joel's standing and the money he kept in his coffers afforded him a hand-painted recreation straight from Temple artisans on Yahzen, who embellished the High Priestess's hair with glittering paint and coated her wedding gown in crystal. Joel's youngest daughter used to sit before the altar and stare at the painting of Joiya Lerenan, asking her father questions he could not answer.

Today, that daughter attended the capital's School of Spirituality to hopefully one day become a professional human liaison to the Temple. The day she enrolled was one of the proudest of Joel's life. Although he had no explanation for what he saw before him, he couldn't stop imagining his daughter's reaction should she discover whom her father was off to arrest.

"Permission to ask for clarification, Commander."

Yara slightly furrowed her brows. A move innocuous enough—to someone not looking for signs of discomfort. "What is it?"

"Who is the woman in the middle?"

Lara's huff of indignation was Joel's first sign that he screwed up by asking. Yet he wouldn't back down. Not when he was already on trial. "She is the woman you picked up for me the other night. I've decided based on our prior interview that she is more than a person of interest and someone we must have in our custody. That is *all* you need to know, Captain." Lara's face softened. Already changing tactics? "I think I know what's spurring this question. Let me assure you—she is not who she looks like. She is a sick woman who impersonates a holy figure to grift adherents such as yourself."

Joel didn't believe her, yet what could he say? Besides, "Isn't she the woman associated with the criminal Syrfila Tograten?"

"Yes." Yara slammed her ass into her chair. "And both of them are associated with Nerilis Dunsman. What of it? I want them *all* in custody. I'd send you after Tograten too, if I knew where she was."

Joel had been in charge of more than one investigation into Syrfila's whereabouts, but he never heard of Miranda, nor had she come up in his intelligence gathering or from interviews with people who had known Syrfila under her Earth-based pseudonym. *How did the commander find out?* he wondered, while maintaining a straight face. *And why the urgency? A grifter? We don't go after petty grifters.* Miranda would not be the first person to pass herself off as the second coming of the High Priestess. Why did the commander care enough to put her best men on the job?

But he wouldn't find out, would he? This was all need-to-know, and he wasn't in the know.

"Of course, you can pamper them all you want, if that's what you desire, Captain." Yara waved him off as if he were no longer a great concern to her. "But once they're in this building, they are under *my* possession. Do you understand?"

"Yes, ma'am."

"Get along and make it happen. I want them in the cells before the end of the day. I have interrogation questions to prepare."

Joel girded himself before leaving her office and gathering his closest men and women for the mission briefing. If the three arrestees were to end up in the basement cells... *That's not an interrogation,* he thought, while putting together the materials for the plan of attack, *this is state-sanctioned torture.*

Truly, his loyalty was on the line. Yara had specifically chosen him from the handful of trusted captains to helm this mission because she trusted him the *least*. If he proved himself worthy of her trust after this, the world was probably his.

If he failed, however... God only knew what a vengeful Commander of the Federation Forces could do to him and his family. He supposed he might find out soon.

After all, everything about this mission screamed personal revenge. Joel d'Kerni simply didn't know how Yara was connected to Miranda Hotchner, the woman who set him on edge in all the most perplexing of ways.

He did, however, know how Yara was related to Syrfila Tograten. Those two went so far back that anyone with the clearance to look into old personnel files could find out how the young undercover operative Yara d'Alacron infiltrated a terrorist organization that contained Tograten in its high ranks.

Everything was personal with the commander. It always had been, and now, someone was about to suffer the consequences.

Thirty-Five

"Of all the stunts I've seen you pull," Danielle said, descending the staircase with her phone in her hand, "calling out sick to visit my grandmother is up there. How the hell do you still have a job? Seriously."

She hopped off the last step, almost losing her balance and slamming right into Miranda, who packed one of her larger purses for a jaunt out to the countryside. The late morning air wafted through the open living room window—for once, Miranda hadn't opened it so she could smoke a cigarette. *I haven't smoked in two days,* she realized, holding a half-empty pack of cigarettes in her hand. She decided to forego shoving them into her bigger purse.

"I have sick days to still use this year," Miranda said. "Not sure what else you want."

Danielle grabbed her cup off the island counter and filled it with water from the sink. "See, if *I* had called in sick, I better have a note from a doctor. And the M-Town clinic won't write you a note for your superior unless you're bleeding from three orifices or hacking up an actual lung."

"Yeah, you were basically a grunt." What Miranda didn't mention was that the people who looked over these things were easy enough to bribe. And with her father's money, it was simply a matter of having the right connections. Although now that Syrfila was no longer around, greasing wheels and seducing the woman who headed one of the personnel departments, Miranda should start assuming that her days of easy time off were over. Something for her to think about while she cleaned old tissues and lint out of her everyday purse.

"I'm offended by that," Danielle said in the kitchen.

"Does this mean we're canceling the trip to your grandmother's? We can't do that to her." Miranda entered the kitchen, where she crept up behind Danielle and wrapped her arms around a T-shirt fresh from an overnight bag. Soon enough, Danielle would have her own drawer in one of Miranda's dressers. It was too soon to talk about moving in together. Not until someone regained her memories. *If that happens soon,* Miranda thought, while enjoying the giggles and sweet admonishments her surprise had garnered her, *it won't be a matter of if, but when.* "She's been waiting for *years* to hear that we're hooking up."

That almost knocked the water right from Danielle's hand. "I swear to God, if you say 'hooking up' in front of my grandmother, I will die. Right there on the Formica table."

Miranda rolled her eyes. "I'm a complete lady in front of other people. You're the only one who hears the words 'hooking up' from my lips."

"Liar." Danielle leaned against the counter, phone in front of her face. "Anyway, what time do you think we'll be there? I want to let her know I'm coming so she isn't covered in horse dung when we tell her."

"Tell her what? That we said the L word last night?"

Red consumed Danielle's cheeks. With a cracked voice, she said, "You're awful. Bringing that up before I've even found her number in my phone..."

"Regrets? Already?"

Danielle attempted to say something, but all that came out was a sputter.

"While you're doing that," Miranda snatched her purse off the back of her couch, "I'll be rehearsing my answers to her inevitable barrage of questions."

No matter what, neither Miranda nor Danielle could say this was a terrible turn of events. Miranda already planned to call out that day and treat Danielle to whatever she wanted, as a mini-celebration of the day they first said *I love you.* She didn't anticipate Danielle wanting to visit her grandmother—with Miranda, no less—and tell her the good news. Regina would find out soon enough, anyway, because her two favorite girls both had the terrible habit of spilling beans when around their only real maternal figure. Danielle joked that it must have been destiny that Regina would undoubtedly approve of a relationship she had been trying to make happen for almost ten years. Miranda, on the other hand, knew the truth.

Nothing was destiny, like nothing was coincidence.

"I'm about to do it!" Danielle called from the kitchen. "I'm gonna tell her I'm visiting!"

"Are you saying you're with me? Or are we letting her be surprised by that?"

"Oh, I think she deserves a little heart attack right-"

They were both startled by a heavy knock at the door.

Miranda's purse landed on the end of the couch as her head whipped around, hair tickling the tip of her tongue. Something about that knock—both familiar and strange—sent a chill down her spine.

"Miranda Hotchner!" came a heavily accented voice. "This is Captain Joel d'Kerni! We kindly ask that you open your door!"

The air was gone from her throat.

"What the..." Danielle was soon behind her. "Who the hell is that? Is he speaking Basic?"

Another pound. This one made Miranda jump and Danielle take a giant step back.

"Fuck," Miranda whispered. "Fuck, *fuck.*"

"Three fucks." Danielle stayed behind while Miranda approached her door. "That can't be good."

What Danielle didn't share was that her heart was already racing and her throat dry. She may not have known that one of the top captains to serve beneath Yara d'Alacron had come to ruin their day, but she understood instinct and bad feelings—this interruption brought *both.*

"Miran—!"

Miranda cracked open the door, revealing the imposing captain and his small entourage of armed and highly trained soldiers. To anyone else, they looked like common military personnel at a house of a known American military captain. Neighbors like Bill and commuters like the woman who took a shortcut down Miranda's street to head to her finance job would take one look and assume it was something that had nothing to do with them. The plain Federation uniforms helped. They were drabber than a sailor with nothing else to do besides read his letters from home and make his bed.

"I heard you the first time, Captain," Miranda said. "What do you need now?"

Joel, who lost his voice the moment he saw Miranda's face, had to fight for his words. "May we come in?"

"Not until you tell me what this is about."

Danielle hovered close to Miranda, but attempted to stay out of sight. Her phone was sweaty in her hands. Before she accidentally called her grandmother's number, she went back to her address book and scrolled until she found someone more likely to understand what was going on. Her thumb hovered over the call button. She didn't yet press it.

"I'm afraid you don't have much choice." Joel handed Miranda a piece of paper, completely written in Basic. She could barely make out the first few bold letters before Joel pushed her into her own house and entered with his entourage. "We have a warrant."

"For what?" Miranda attempted to grab her phone from the coffee table, but one of the soldiers blocked her from retreating farther into her own living room. "What is the... who..." She saw Lara's signature at the bottom of the paper and immediately turned to Danielle. "You need to get out of here," she said in Japanese, knowing damn well that Danielle was far from fluent. Which was why Danielle relied more on force of her words than anything grammatical—never mind *formal.*

Yet Danielle was cornered by the kitchen, phone clutched to her chest as she was surrounded by Joel's men and women. The moment Miranda's hands were pulled behind her back was the exact moment she realized she wasn't the only target that day.

"Hey!" Danielle attempted to shrug everyone off her, but she was one woman versus three. Joel approached her, holding another warrant of arrest. "What the hell! What did we do?"

"Don't say a thing!" Miranda shouted in English. "You hear me? Don't..."

One thing both Miranda and Danielle quickly discovered was that when the Federation wanted to take prisoners deemed enemies of their order, all the rules went out the window. That included refraining from any use of force. When Miranda was knocked to the ground, her words turning into harried grunts, Danielle slammed her thumb against her phone. Two seconds later, it was knocked to the carpet, where it was almost stepped on by three pairs of feet as Danielle was shoved toward the front of the house.

"What is going on?" Danielle shouted as loudly as she could muster. "What do you want with us? What have we done?"

Miranda was half-dragged toward her front door, where Joel d'Kerni read the pertinent parts of the warrant out loud. "You are under arrest for aiding and abetting a known fugitive and enemy of the Federation..." He cleared his throat. "Two people, actually."

"Who!"

"Syrfila Tograten, for one." He handed off the packets of syringes they often brought to such public arrests on Earth. Better to drug the accused and have them go peacefully than to have ignorant Earthlings ring up 911 and blab to the media. "Nerilis Dunsman, for another."

Miranda scoffed. Although she saw the syringe, she wouldn't go down without her piece heard across the neighborhood. "If this is coming straight from Lara, then you need to know who she is!" The needle jabbed into her arm. She had about ten seconds. "She's no better than us! She just died before she joined us!" Her head whipped toward Danielle, who was already fading out from the effects of the drug. "Don't believe anything they say about me! Sulim!"

Danielle didn't hear her. She was propped up between three soldiers and quickly carried toward the van that would drive them straight to the Forces' Earth-based intergalactic transporter. Miranda held out longer. Long enough to trip on her front step and say one last thing to Joel.

"My mother would be disappointed in you."

She didn't mean the one who raised her, and Joel knew that.

Devon returned from his morning break to find his boss standing in his office door.

"Hey! Dev!" An awkward chuckle choked the air. "You won't believe what I heard from the first desk. Apparently some more of your Federation buddies are on their way up to speak with you. Don't worry about being on the clock." Pete turned back to his office with a wink. "Take all the time you need."

"Huh?" Devon may not have had enough caffeine yet that morning, but he knew when things sounded *off*. His Federation buddies? Why would they announce their arrival downstairs unless it was some official business? Marlow and his employees wouldn't announce a damn thing. They showed up and took him off to do whatever they needed from him.

Devon pulled out his phone to check for messages. Indeed, he had one from Danielle.

A voice message.

At first, he didn't understand what he heard. Instead of her saying what was on her mind, there was nothing but knocks, yelps, and grunts in Basic.

"....You are under arrest for aiding and abetting a known fugitive and enemy of the Federation..."

Devon held himself against the hallway wall. The message kept playing, complete with Danielle demanding to know what was going on and Miranda's voice carrying above them all.

"If this is coming straight from Lara, then you need to know who she is! She's no better than us! She just died before she joined us!" Devon sucked in his breath at the mention of Lara's name. "Don't believe anything they say about me! Sulim!"

The elevator doors opened to Devon's right. Before he saw whether they were friend or foe, he jetted down the hallway, swinging around the corner and hauling ass to the nearest fire escape. He wasn't taking any chances. Even if the Federation merely wanted a "friendly chat" they could do it from a safe distance. Far enough that it was physically impossible to arrest Devon for crimes against the universe.

Devon didn't have time to call ahead and tell Marlow's office that he was on the way over. Not that it had ever stopped him from showing up unannounced before, but rarely did it accompany the thundering of feet and his voice yelling over the swinging pendulums of Marlow's interdimensional hideaway that someone needed to show up. *Now.*

Nobody was there. Not until Devon slammed his ass in a chair and pushed the button that connected him to Marlow's office on Terra III. Something he didn't dare do until he was secured in a realm he didn't *think* the Federation Forces could access without Marlow's express permission.

"Hey, buddy." Evan's face appeared on a screen that had been blank a few seconds ago. Devon jerked back in Marlow's chair, hand clasped over his heart. *Just a little jumpy, great,* he thought, while collecting his breath and thanking his stars that it was Evan and not someone else. "What's up? If you're looking for the old guy, he's currently at home taking a day off. Or something." Evan shrugged. "I dunno."

Lanelle's hair hovered on the edge of the screen. "Who is it?" she asked, before the rest of her face appeared. "Oh, no. What happened?"

Leave it to Lanelle to know that something must be wrong for Devon to be out of breath in an interdimensional lair that few people could access. "Yara had Danielle and someone else arrested." He slammed his hand on top of his head, leaning far back in the chair and stressing the bolts that held it together. "They were coming after me next, but I managed to slip away."

Evan perked up. "Whoa, what?"

Already, Lanelle's fingers flew across her holographic keyboard. "You're *sure* that's what happened?"

Devon held up his phone. He replayed the phone call as loudly as it allowed into the microphone, the dread that had been hanging over him finally crashing down onto his head. "Literally two seconds later I find out somebody from the Federation was at work and wanted to see me. What exactly am I supposed to make of that?"

"Looks like there's no record of an arrest warrant like that in the system." Evan looked between his screen and Lanelle's. "We have access to those here. Not to mention, both you and Danielle's names are in our pings. Anytime an official missive goes out with either of your names, we get an alert."

"Yeah, like this is *totally* public, since they know we can see it." Lanelle's fingers flew, her eyes never leaving her screen. "I'll have to access the commander's internal, classified documents to find out for sure. It's going to take a little while." The only time Lanelle stopped typing and looked in Evan's direction was to gently shove him. "Call Marlow and get over to Devon. Double-check the connection from the hideout is encrypted. They'll still crack it eventually, but hopefully we'll have Devon out of there by then."

"Isn't that harboring a fugitive?"

"I've been in Federation prison before. It's not that bad. Hell, it got better the second time."

Evan shook his head. "Be right over, Dev. I'm gonna tell Marlow what's going on and hopefully he'll meet us there before any goons show up. 'Cause I make an awful meat shield. I don't even have magical abilities."

"You think I do?" Devon asked. "I don't know any non-*julah* who does."

"Excellent idea." Lanelle snapped her fingers in Evan's direction. "Call Marlow, and get Vikkel and Kalera there."

Evan held up his personal communicator, but wasn't calling anyone yet. "Are we having some kind of standoff with the Federation Forces? Maybe *you* guys wanna..."

"Call 'em now!"

When Lanelle barked orders, it wasn't much different from having Marlow himself roll through the room and demand to speak to the person in charge of the entire Federation. In this case, the president, who may have been the one to sign-off on Lara's secretive arrest warrants.

Devon collapsed back in Marlow's chair. He hoped to God that Danielle and Miranda hadn't been tossed on their asses into the great abyss of the Void.

Thirty-Six

No ideal situation existed when someone was apprehended by the top brass of the Federation Forces. The best anyone could ask for was the red carpet treatment as they were led into a quiet room, offered fresh *cageh*, and kindly asked, *"Are you sure you weren't with so-and-so on such-and-such night? It's really important that we know."* Before that poor person was unceremoniously dumped on some outcrop of a moon, of course.

Danielle and Miranda were not given the redcarpet treatment. They weren't even given the dirty rug treatment.

The first sign that awful things were afoot? Danielle's head thundered in discomfort when she finally woke up and realized that she wasn't in Kansas any longer.

"Holy shit." Her head weighed a hundred pounds. Yet the only thing worse than her chin permanently fusing with her chest was the threat of her neck muscles rioting against her. So Danielle slowly forced her head up, eyes blinking open and voice croaking in her throat.

She couldn't move her arms.

"Where the..." Danielle had to stop and collect her breath. Although more of the room came into focus, it didn't answer her most pivotal questions. *What the hell happened? Where am I? Why can't I move half my body?* Did her head awaken before the rest of her?

Was it a miracle her lungs were still functioning? Was that smell from her own blood trickling down her nose, or the sewage spewing through this room? "What...?"

Her hand flexed, but her arms still couldn't move. As the dark pipes in the large storage room came into view, she realized that she was tied to a chair, like the victim of a bad '80s mob movie. That same hand she now so expertly commanded soon found itself wrapped in another.

"Welcome back." Miranda had been awake about twenty minutes longer, her whole body a giant lead weight against her chair. Filling her lungs with stale air took more effort than it was worth. The sedative hadn't even been that high of a dose, but the Federation took no chances when they secretly arrested prisoners. They had been given the *good* stuff. Shit so good that it went for a hefty price on the black market.

The same shit we used to use back in the day, Miranda lamented, realizing that this was far from the first time she had been subjected to the chemical concoction slowly wearing off in her body. That also meant she had a good idea about how long they had been out. Two hours. Three hours? Possibly four, based on how heavy they *really felt.* "You holding up okay? They didn't bang your head up, did they?"

"What the *hell* happened?" Danielle yanked against the heavy binds securing them back-to-back on uncomfortable chairs. "Where the hell are we? Last thing I remember is..." It all came back to her. Danielle groaned. What else could she do?

"This is how you're treated by the Federation when you're a special interest in a millennium-long case of mass murder and treason." Miranda chuckled. "Some things haven't changed." She didn't elaborate. Now was not the time to bring up some of the more "creative" tactics she and her fellow clever mercenaries enacted over a thousand years ago. *By that time,* she remembered, *they were already old, tested, and true.* "Are you okay, though?"

"Do I sound okay?" Danielle once again croaked. She was in desperate need of fluids, both in her throat and her body, but such sustenance would not be forthcoming anytime soon. She didn't need Miranda telling her that this was part of the upcoming interrogation. "For God's sake. I feel like someone slammed this chair against my face and knocked me out cold."

"Yeah, you sound like hell."

"Thanks. You sound like Maria Callas as well."

Miranda reached her fingers toward Danielle's, head leaning back until it found the back of her girlfriend's. "They didn't separate us for a reason." She told herself that more than anything. "I don't know why, but they want us together when they come in here to either collect or interrogate."

"Sounds like that could be a bad thing. Why are they even arresting us? Something about being in bed with the same guy I've banged up more than once?"

"You ask me, this is a personal thing." Miranda sighed. "The commander. Yara d'Alacron. She has a personal vendetta against me, I think."

"Oh, great. Great. Want to fill me in on that, so I can make sure this story is properly corroborated?"

"It's a long story. She and I... we go back." What Miranda conveniently left out was how they *went back* over a thousand years. *I didn't do anything to her back then,* Miranda thought. *If anyone in this life would have a good reason to torture me a little before slitting my throat, it's Devon.* Poor bastard would have to deal with her again in the next life. Yara, though...

Yara was not in the Process. Miranda would stake a piece of her damned soul on that fact, but it didn't stop the commander from seeing things in her memory that weren't really there.

"That stuff they were saying about you and Nerilis Dunsman." Danielle would never get comfortable in her chair, but as the sedative wore off a little more, she relaxed against Miranda and allowed her fingers to uncurl and her palms to touch the back of Miranda's hands. "Was it true? Because God knows there has been crazy shit I've wanted answers to."

Instead of directly answering that question, Miranda said, "What kept you from asking these past few weeks?"

"Seriously?" Danielle drolly asked. "Been a little busy."

That was the first thing to crack a smile on Miranda's face since waking up and realizing they were in dire straits. Water dripped from the ceiling, barely missing Miranda's head by two inches before splattering to the floor. The dank air and the lack of light pinpointed the location in some forgotten basement of the Federation Forces' main building on Terra III. This was where the lowest of the low criminals—who didn't pose a magical threat—were holed up for off-the-record questioning. This wasn't like having an escort to Yara's office, or sitting down in one of the official interview rooms several floors above them. Nope. This was where the commander shoved those she didn't want the public and media discovering through official channels.

I've been in worse situations. Miranda thought that, yet her fears weren't for herself. She was more worried about Danielle, whose volatile soul could be triggered into a regression over the smallest admittance at this point. Miranda had been preparing herself for the inevitable—at some point, being around Danielle in a romantic manner would lead to her regressing. Finally. After a thousand years, Danielle would not only regress, but be freed from the Process.

Miranda had to be there for that. Not only to protect Danielle during her most violently self-harming moments, but to reap the reward of a thousand-year wait.

Like this, though? The danger was too much to risk. Miranda couldn't say or do a thing that might accidentally set off the chain reaction in Danielle's brain. And Void help the Federation Forces if they thought they were going to hurt her.

Either of them, for that matter.

"Personal reasons," Danielle muttered. "The commander of every Federation military personnel in the universe doesn't like *you* for *personal reasons.* Come on. You can't leave it at that. And if you're joking, you better tell me. I'm tired of being caught up in this crap. Do you know how many times I've been kidnapped or apprehended by people who want to mess me up this past year? I'm trying to live my goddamn life."

"Yes, you're the reluctant protagonist every English teacher harps about," Miranda said with a sigh. "I might have been joking a little bit. I honestly don't know what her issue with me is. She's under the impression that I've worked for Nerilis Dunsman in the past, but that's not true. I've never supported his endeavors. I should certainly hope you believe that, considering."

"Yeah, not really looking to move in with someone who's down with the death and mass destruction of half the galaxy. Don't care how good in bed you are. That's a toxic relationship right there."

"Good to know you still have your sense of humor. By the way, I'm being a little cagey because I'm under the assumption that we're being watched. These bastards will stoop to every low to catch us in a gotcha. So, be careful what you say to me. Maybe be careful about what you're thinking. I don't know what kind of crazy technology they might be trying on us."

"Why? You think they can read our minds?"

"No. But they have masters in body language and people who can pick up what you're really thinking based on your tone. Don't think not speaking Basic will help either. That's how good they are."

"Sounds like you have some experience with this."

"Just be prepared for anything they ask. Everything is an attempt to catch you in a lie they can use as an excuse to lop off your head."

"So this is how it feels to go from hero to zero in two days." Referring to herself as a "hero," no matter how sarcastically, only made her think of something else. "Oh my God, what about Devon? I wonder if they got him too."

The thought had crossed Miranda's mind, but she wasn't about to bring him up on her own. "Worry about him later. We need to figure out how to get ourselves out of this mess. Especially since you of all people are perfectly innocent. You're only guilty of being associated with me."

"Thanks, by the way. Was finally starting to feel pretty good about my crazy-ass life. Should have known that anyone I actually fall in love with is bad news."

Miranda craned her head around. "So you *are* in love with me?"

Danielle closed her eyes after realizing what she had said. "Goddamn it."

If Miranda could move, she would nudge her shoulder against Danielle's. "Good to know that last night wasn't a fluke."

"It's gonna be a fluke if we don't get the hell outta here. And if you turn out to be a more embarrassing choice of a lover than that guy who got on the stand and called me a gay slut."

"Honestly, the more I think about it, the more you really shouldn't be making your own dating decisions. I've seen them all over the years. When you're not dating college kids, you're dating people way too old for you. Pick a generation and stick with it."

"Hate to break it to you, but we're both Gen X shills."

"At least we got the best music." Miranda snorted. "Ugh, I have to pee."

"Me too."

"On the count of three, we both go at the same time. That should make them want to get us out of here faster."

"Flawless plan. Really upsell the value of the average Earthling. We all reek of piss."

Miranda finally managed to encircle her whole hand around Danielle's. "We're going to get out of here. I promise you."

Danielle's body softened against the chair. "I'm trying really hard to not freak out."

"I know." Miranda sagged alongside her. "They don't train you for this in the American military." Before Danielle responded, she further murmured, "But they did in your old life." She was so careful to not say *"In our old lives"* that she almost forgot to include herself.

"Too bad I don't remember shit."

"You remember plenty in your sleep."

Now was not the time to be embarrassing Danielle, and that was as far as Miranda would take that. Yet she couldn't deny how good it felt. A little. Just a bit.

Reminding her that there were times, long ago, when things were much worse. How had they moved on from that, again? *Dying. Being reborn. Whatever it took to build up an impossible resistance to these kinds of situations.* Miranda—and later Danielle, when she had the wherewithal to regress—often thought about that. As corny as the movies made it sound? Death and rebirth were truly *only* the beginning.

"I never remember anything later," Danielle said. "If only people would let me move on." She shook in her binds, the frustration building up within her only tangible to anyone within five feet of her. "But nope. Gotta keep getting my ass handed to me every time I stop to take a breather. No wonder I'm so attracted to you. Might as well walk right into the fire, right?"

"I was always told I had the whole bad girl thing going on," Miranda said. "Can't say I ever invited that badge of honor. Just kinda keep stumbling into it." Or, as was more truthful, she was pulled into it by nefarious characters who didn't have her best interests at heart.

But she always made do. They both did, and this would be no different.

"But *why* are they after me?" Devon corrected that once he realized he left out a pivotal piece of information. "I mean *us*. Why do they want us?"

The only people he trusted beyond Earth surrounded him. While Devon took up the entirety of a couch not too far from Marlow's desk, the Master was fixated with the screens before him. Evan leaned over his shoulder, occasionally pointing to something that Marlow was quick to return to with a flick of his finger. Lanelle stood between Devon and the desk, head craning this way and that as everyone talked at once.

Meanwhile, on the very edge of the room, Kalera sat in a lone chair while her husband Vikkel stood guard by the only real-world entrance to the hideout.

"You are a person of great interest!" Was Marlow's forceful tone supposed to make Devon feel better? "Thanks to Lanelle's skills…"

"It's okay to say *hacking*, sir," she interrupted.

"…We were able to find the original, classified arrest warrants for the three of you. The charges are inconsequential, of course, because I have a feeling the real reason the commander wants you in custody is because of personal issues."

"You're telling me." Devon rubbed his hands down his face. Forgetting that unfortunate night with Yara was not the easiest thing. Would have been lovely if he could have written it off as a mistake on both of their parts, but the more he thought about it, the more he realized how terrible the universe could truly be in matters of the soul.

She's someone who should have solidly stayed in the past, he thought, recalling the look in Yara's eyes when the *hedpah* took control of her memories. Devon only had a rudimentary understanding of how reincarnation worked for souls not in the Process. He was used to remembering everything from the moment he regressed. For those who were merely reincarnated, their memories should have been stripped from their soul before being returned to the mortal world. Yara, though...

Devon remembered plenty about who Yara used to be. A sorry wretch of a woman who had sent herself to a grim end. *Not like it was an unusual one back then,* he thought. Life wasn't merely hard on Cerilyn. It was brutal. Those who didn't voluntarily enlist for the life of a sword for hire were ripped from their homes as the spoils of war. The only way to exist on Cerilyn was to accept that a person was now a slave to a violent oppression they couldn't understand even if they had *wanted* to be there.

My sister ended her life shortly after we were taken. Graella hadn't been a weak girl, but after witnessing the bloody deaths of their parents and the ransacking of their ancestral home, it was no wonder that a girl who had been raised to enjoy the softer side of life had decided to poison herself before she was transformed into the very thing that had destroyed her.

Yara's former incarnation had met a similar end. Only instead of poison, she had been found in her room, arms cut open and the soul gone from her eyes. Devon hadn't been the one to carry her bloodless body from her dormitory, but he had seen who had.

It was the day the leadership changed...

No wonder so much swarmed those wretched souls. In one day, Yara's death had led to a quick, violent coup and the changing of the proverbial guard. That was the day Cairn became chief through regicide.

Blood, death, and murder... Every time Devon sank into those memories, he covered his head with his arms and had to force himself to breathe.

"Hey." Lanelle put a hand on his head while Marlow and Evan continued to argue by the computers. The couch was soon joined by Charlie, who bypassed Lanelle with his stubby body and struggled to hop up next to Devon. The dog whines were the only thing to snap Devon out of his stupor and encourage him to pick up the Basset Hound now settling into his lap. "Now's not the time to get bogged down in whatever shit is going through your head. We're going to figure it out, though. I promise."

"They've got them." Devon sighed, Danielle's phone call continuously playing through his head. "I mean, the Federation has Danielle. And..." He could hardly bring himself to say Miranda's name, if only because the memories were still too raw. *My sister. My mother. My father.* People who had died over a thousand years ago and were barely remembered by their descendants.

"They can't be dead, because we would know about it." Lanelle put her hands on her hips and lowered her head toward Devon's. "Good thing they're military, huh? Have more than a few tricks up their sleeves when it comes to surviving interrogations. Because I won't sugar coat it. Commander d'Alacron and her predecessors have never been known for anything short of torture when they think they're going to enjoy the bounties of a big spill."

"Would really rather nobody be tortured today. Including myself."

"You won't be taken into custody, so help me," Marlow said from his desk. "Of course, everyone in this room is now guilty of harboring a criminal, but I have more than a few strings I can pull to keep us out of trouble."

Lanelle huffed. "What he's conveniently leaving out is that he's about to burn up every bridge he still has on Yahzen. I swear, you've called in more favors this past year than the whole time I've known you. Have you earned yourself more favors at all since then?"

"Rather difficult to earn the kind of favors I have in my life when you get to be my age and have mobility issues." Marlow stabbed one of the keys on his tablet. "Believe it or not, I'm not as popular in the Bah Zenlit bordellos as I used to be."

Evan popped up with blush on his cheeks. Lanelle could only roll her eyes.

"Surprised you don't have more offspring out there, sir." Evan patted Marlow on the shoulder before pacing between him and Lanelle. "Real lady killer."

"You and I both know he was never killing no *ladies,*" Lanelle muttered.

Devon shot up from the couch, dog falling from his lap with a small yelp. Eyes turned to him, but at least the mouths shut up. *Can't take it anymore,* he thought. *Everyone is focusing on the wrong thing!*

"Let me talk to Yara." Yeah, that was the kind of thing that made heads turn in his direction. Even Marlow, who had Void knew what up on his monitors. "I'm the one she wants. I won't turn myself in, per se, but I'll at least have one last interview with her."

Marlow hooted as his hand hit his knee. "That's how it works, of course! Just let me call her up and arrange a meeting for you! Have some tea and shoot the breeze, like old times!"

Although Devon was well aware that Marlow was mocking him, he still said, "Yes, that's what I was thinking. I'll answer whatever questions she has. I'm innocent of any wrongdoing, according to the treaties, so they have no grounds for holding me. I'm sure as hell not aiding and abetting anybody! The only reason they want to arrest me is so they have an excuse to work me over until I talk. Well, the only person who can talk to her better is someone already in her custody." He didn't mention who that was. "She knows who I am, and I know who she is. At the very least, I'll get Danielle released before anything shitty happens to her." As usual, that was his top priority. Although even he would admit that his own safety was listed in there as well, he would have been a terrible companion if he didn't at least *try* to get Danielle out of trouble. Again.

What was this? The third time in a year?

"Don't cut off your nose to spite your face," Evan said in impeccable English. "You'd be walking into a lion's den. Only instead of being cute little kitty cats, you're looking at one of the most powerful people in the entire universe. I'd argue even the president herself doesn't come close to the kind of shit the commander can stir."

Devon deigned Evan with one meaningful glance before pushing past him toward Marlow. "The commander is stirring shit because of a past life regression. I don't think she's in the Process…"

"She's not," Marlow confirmed. "I sized it up myself the last time I saw her, which was as recently as yesterday." Had it only been a day? Felt like several. "She is most definitely reincarnated, though. I'd say an overdose of *hedpah* has her acting off her rocker, but I'm no medical doctor when it comes to these things. But a lingering overdose would only affect her this long if she had a volatile previous life to begin with, and that's a big if."

"Trust me. She did."

Marlow narrowed his eyes. Devon may have loomed over him, but the gravitas of Master Marlow's life experience and station in the universe almost brought Devon down to the old man's level. It was in those moments when everyone in the room was grimly reminded that Marlow was capable of more than he let most people see.

"You're *sure* you know who she used to be?"

"Right now?" Devon sagged his shoulders and sighed. "She's still that person. A scared, neglected, jealous girl who never stood a chance. That's why she's taking all the power she has right now and shoving it in our faces. She's jealous because we've been able to move on and she hasn't." And other reasons Devon didn't quite understand, but he would damn well fake it. "I don't care what you people think you know about that life." He turned to Evan and Lanelle, both of whom were their own brand of silent as they watched Devon take command of the room. "Unless you lived it, you have no idea what kind of lasting stain it leaves on your soul. You don't have to be in the Process to see it when you look in the mirror."

He entered a short-lived staring contest with Marlow, who only turned away to hit something on his holographic keyboard. "Fine. I will see what I can do. Understand that we are *all* putting our necks out for this. I will not allow my employees to suffer at the hand of the Forces if I can help it. That includes squirreling you away where I deem safest, even if it means sealing your lips shut myself. All that said…" He glanced at Vikkel and Kalera in the corner of the room. "Wherever you go, they're going with you."

"That's not…"

"Devon." Lanelle grabbed his hand with both of hers and attempted to pull him away. He only relented because she had caught him so off guard. "You better do as he says. For your own sake."

He rounded on her. "What do you-"

"You're not as tough as you think you are." Lanelle jammed a finger in his chest to reiterate her point. "You think you're still that dickhead who crushed skulls and took out at all his pent-up rage on the people he was paid to fuck up, but you're *not.* Trust me. I've met that guy, and you're not him anymore."

"Yeah. I remember that. Thanks for the lovely reminder."

Lanelle would not blush at the memory of her easily seducing the previous incarnation of Devon who came through during a botched ritual meant to send him back to the past. "It's not a bad thing, you know? That guy was a helluva mess. You? You've still got plenty of strengths to play up. Strengths you couldn't dream of having in *that* life. If you go into the commander's grasp, don't think for two seconds you'll mow her over or she'll get out of your way. You'll have to do better than that."

It took Devon a few seconds to get what she was saying. "Sorry. Those goons are doing Void knows what to Danielle and…"

Lanelle's brows lifted up her forehead. "And Cairn. We know." When Devon said nothing, she continued, "I get that this is complicated shit for you, but *please* leave it up to Marlow to figure out. We dunk on him all the time, but there's a reason he's still head of his family even after all the stunts he's pulled since long before either you or I ever met him in our first lives. The man is a goddamn prodigal sorcerer even *today.* Never forget he's one of the only men in the history of time to successfully not only put one person into the Process, but *three.* You know who the only other person who has done it in recent *julah* memory? Meaning thousands of Void-damned years?"

Devon didn't need her to say who. He had a pretty good idea.

"Do as he says," Lanelle reiterated. "We all want you out of here safely as much as you do."

Although he couldn't argue with that, Devon could think of one person he cared a little less about.

Thirty-Seven

Danielle and Miranda's predicament wasn't looking any better. Miranda knew they were in bigger trouble than she originally anticipated when she felt the first water drop land on her scalp. Then another. When she looked up at the ceiling, she encountered two subsequent drops that landed right between her eyes. As much as she hoped that would be the last of them, another soon hit her ear.

She couldn't tell if the Forces were doing this on purpose, or if they *happened* to leave them beneath a leaky pipe that would soon drive Miranda absolutely insane. *Definitely on purpose,* she thought. They were going for the most innocuous form of torture they could swing on a budget.

Honestly, she had to hand it to them—she would have done the same thing.

"You know," Miranda mused, in a consistent effort to keep Danielle talking, if only to know she was still conscious, "they really don't train you for this in the military. Or at least I don't remember this in any war games."

Danielle groaned. "The last time I did a war game, I was barely out of BT. Once they decided my eyesight was a bust for actual action but not for data input, that was the end of the fun and games for me."

"Hey, I saw your marksmanship scores. Pretty good for someone told to get contacts or ship out."

"I'll never be a sniper, but I'm okay with that. Fat lot of good it would do me right now."

Miranda considered the barrier between encouraging Danielle and attempting to change the subject. Unfortunately for her, the chance to say something else never came. Not when a large metal door creaked open, and they were unceremoniously joined by two armed guards who made way for Yara d'Alacron.

Back straight. Shoulders up. Arms behind her back. She wasn't wearing her uniform. Instead, the Commander of the Federation Forces entered the room in nothing but a dark brown pair of slacks and a black turtleneck that did not denote her rank nor her experience in making someone's life a living hell.

The only significant marker of who she was—besides her ineffable demeanor—was the coif of blond hair that covered her right eye. When she stood before Miranda, highlighted by a remnant of meager light, someone with better eyesight than Danielle's could make out the gash that marred her useless eye.

"So sorry to interrupt your story corroboration," she said in English with a mild pout. "And my further apologies for taking so long to greet you two, my most esteemed guests of the moment."

Miranda scoffed. "You've learned English, huh? That was fast."

"It's much more garish than Basic," Yara said, "but learnable with a little bit of spare time. Why, the only reason I bothered is because of you, Ms. Cromwell. I'd call you Lieutenant, but I've heard the unfortunate news."

Danielle turned away again with a huff.

"Captain Hotchner, though," Yara continued, walking a lazy lap around her two captives, "has still managed to retain every rank and honor bestowed upon her over the years. While not the most illustrious of military careers, it's perfectly acceptable." She stopped beside Miranda, who refused to grant her eye contact. "It's *so* interesting to me that you haven't been demoted, demerited, or outright discharged for any of your own flaunting of your country's rules. Just the strangest thing."

Miranda opened her mouth but immediately closed it again. Yara wasn't worth the breath.

"I'm sure you two are wondering why you have been arrested and kept in such intense conditions." Yara's laps resumed. The two guards she entered with stood side by side near the closed door. She did not acknowledge them, but they awaited her orders with perked ears. "You two are the best link I have to Nerilis

Dunsman, the most wanted man in the universe. Oh, and you?" She kicked the back leg to Miranda's chair, shaking her entire foundation and almost making her bite her own tongue. She let out a hiss of dissatisfaction. "You're also a known accomplice and confidant of Syrfila Tograten, the *second* most wanted person in the universe. Trust me, I was not satisfied with our interview the other night." She paused for effect. Had Danielle heard her? Did she know what that meant? "Although Master Marlow corroborated your story about him putting you into the Process..."

Danielle jerked in her seat. "What?"

Miranda slowly closed her eyes and bit her lip. Although Danielle was barely within reach, her discomfort was so palpable that Miranda wished she could erase everything Yara had said.

"Oh?" That was the real reason Miranda wished she could get them the hell out of there *right now*. Now Yara knew. "Does she not know? Honestly, I'm a little surprised. And disappointed in the both of you. Isn't that the kind of thing you share with your lover?"

Miranda lifted her head, a threat lingering in her eyes. "Do your men enjoy their jobs peeping into my window? I hope they've been enjoying the shows."

Yara flashed her the smallest of smirks. "I assure you there has been no 'peeping.' But you do a terrible job hiding your relationship. Which continues to beg the question how you've been spared your military's current rash of discharges. *Terribly* run military, if you ask me. But that's not what we're here to talk about." She bent down low before Miranda, daring their noses to touch. "I'd rather talk about the fact your love muffin over here didn't know you were in the Process. What else doesn't she know? That you're the potential reincarnation of the most important religious figure in the history of mankind?"

"Yes," Miranda spat, sarcasm dripping from her lips. "I'm the Dalai Lama. You got me." While Danielle continued to stiffen behind her, Miranda said, "I am *not* the reincarnation of the High Priestess. That is preposterous."

"No, you're only the spitting image of her." Yara looped around to Danielle, whose lips had dried in shock. "What do you make of that? Have you ever noticed? Or do you not remember what the Holy Mother of our people looks like? I've heard that you haven't regressed. How incredibly unfun for me." Yara straightened her back. "Or is it? You didn't know she was in the Process. What else is she hiding from you? That *I* know?"

Danielle sucked in her breath. "I have no idea what you want from me, but..."

"Your arrest is unfortunate. By all accounts, of your entire brethren, you're probably the most innocent one today. Hell, even if reincarnation law didn't forbid it, I'd hardly have a thing to charge you for based on your previous life. 'The Mercenary Who Doesn't Kill.' What use is that? A soldier who won't kill for hire isn't worth a dime to me. Yet people paid you untold amounts. So what is the truth? Was it all marketing? Did you *really* kill people? No. Suppose you don't remember. But *you* might." She kicked Miranda's chair again. "After all, you're-"

"What the *fuck* do you want from us?" Miranda interrupted. "Come on. Let her go. Like you said, she's done nothing. She knows nothing. You're right I haven't told her a thing."

"Is that because you don't think she can handle it? Or because telling her would..." Yara chuckled. "Oh. I see. Telling her would shock her into a forced regression... and possibly kill her. Is that how it works?"

Miranda furrowed her brows. "Let her go."

"You have to be kidding. You think you give the orders around here? Let me tell you, *Captain,* you know nothing about giving orders." There was that smirk again. "Or do you?"

If she says, "Or do you" one more time... Miranda couldn't let Yara know her plan was working. Everything about the commander was prime pettiness. Miranda would *know* that, absolutely. After all, this was an incredibly petty arrest that served a dual purpose. On one hand, Yara came *this* much closer to figuring out the truth behind Nerilis Dunsman's actions, but the reason she took pleasure in tying up Miranda and threatened her with Danielle's torture was to get back at her for something that had happened a thousand years ago. Something Yara couldn't even *begin* to understand. Whatever her soul clung to from a past life was a mishmash of traumatic energy and vague recollections in the deepest pits of her dreams. Not only could Miranda not understand that for herself, but she could also barely figure out how to circumvent Yara's anger over something she couldn't remember in detail.

Everything was emotional. The emotional had become nothing but political.

"I had an interesting conversation with Master Marlow yesterday." Yara's fingers wrapped around her chin. "After you told me he was the one responsible for putting you into the Process, well, I had to go to the source for myself. He corroborated your story. But you know what?" Yara stood right before Miranda, elbow coming dangerously close to the prisoner's cheek. "I don't believe him. I think it was the fallen angel himself who put you into the Process. I don't put it past Master Marlow to still have his best friend's back."

Miranda said nothing.

"What do you think, Ms. Cromwell?" Yara stretched her arms around her head, feet carrying her to the ends of her own interrogation. "What do you make of that accusation?"

"I have no clue."

That dark, foreboding tone did not sit well with Miranda, who already worried that Yara might have revealed too much. *I swear to God,* Miranda thought, *if she forces Danielle into a regression, I'll kill her with my own hands.* Yara already played fast and loose with the rules of reincarnation and *julah* sorcery. Miranda may have only known a small fraction of what her father carried in his head, but she knew one thing: to play God with the Void was an undertaking barely understood by the men who had claimed such lofty heights before.

How useless and weak did she feel now? She couldn't punch her way out of this situation. Only a real *julah* of her father's—let alone her mother's—caliber could get them out of this situation unscathed.

"Surely my accusation must make you feel something," Yara mused. "She's not even denying that she's in the Process. Then again, she's already confirmed it with me. I thought you already knew."

"Some things hadn't come up, I guess," Danielle muttered.

That got a laugh out of Yara. "I was once in a relationship like this. My partner was a master of keeping important information from me. They claimed it was to *protect* me. I suppose they were afraid that I wouldn't be able to handle the truth about them. Some really awful things in a person's history. For all you know, they might be the daughter of the most wanted man in the universe."

Miranda had done an admirable job keeping her reactions to herself. Yet that moment, when Yara revealed she knew the truth about her captive's ancestry? Ears didn't simply perk. Miranda's whole head jerked up, eyes wide enough for one of the guards to catch the pallor on her face. When he nodded to Yara, Miranda knew she had screwed up.

"This is getting ridiculous," Danielle said. "What do you want us for? I know nothing about the man you're looking for. I haven't seen him since I kicked his ass a year ago. What's it to me what he's up to? I've paid my dues. I want to go home and-"

Yara interrupted her with a heavy sigh. "I *know* you haven't had anything to do with him. Trust me, that's not why you're here. You think you have any real information for me? Absolutely not! The mere thought makes me laugh. And maybe I would have been inclined to leave you alllll alone to your miserable life before I found out about you and the real person I want to interrogate here today."

Danielle hung her head. Had she already accepted that Miranda was the real reason they were both tied together like this, in a room where nobody could possibly save them without losing their own life or freedom? Of course she had. For the past two weeks, Danielle had known everything was too good to be true. To her, being trapped in the Process was as good as being a spiritual punching bag. Perhaps there was no real "God" up there, creating and curating like a true master of the universe, but there was still *something*. Some entity that wanted her to suffer for the mistake of being in the wrong place at the right time.

Something had always drawn her to Miranda. For as long as she wanted to believe it was chemistry, personality, and a passion for the same things in the bedroom, in the end, it was the universe playing tricks on a woman who simply wanted to be left alone.

If she had really fallen in love with Miranda? Clearly, this was what happened.

"You're collateral damage. Who you *are* is of no importance to me. If I can use you to find out how to reach the former Master Dunsman and take him down? I'll have more than earned my place in history. Why, I'll have done what *you* and your partner could never achieve. Not that you stood much of a chance with Dunsman's own flesh and blood working against you at every turn. But you already had a feeling this woman was more than she seemed, didn't you? Go on. You can tell me *everything*."

"Why the hell would I do that?"

"Don't piss her off," Miranda muttered over her shoulder. "This is the Federation. You think the American military would make you disappear? Try being obliterated from history."

"You give us too much credit," Yara said. "I can't *obliterate* you from history. By a number of treaties and conventions, I can't even legally torture you! Not physically." Nobody believed that a little treaty would keep the Federation Forces from torturing anyone, and they would be correct. Yet if Yara could get away with it even easier? Better! Nobody had ever said anything about not torturing people *spiritually!* "But don't think I'm above getting what I want, no matter what. When I'm *this* close to achieving my destiny..." She grabbed either side of Danielle's chair, her breath hitting nose, lips, and a chin that ducked out of the way of the commander's spittle. "I grab it by the goddamn balls and crush it."

"Let her go," Miranda pleaded once again, this time her voice releasing a squeak that betrayed her rising fears. "Please. I'll tell you whatever you want. Just let her go."

Yara sharply inhaled. "You're lying. I'm not going to release the one bartering chip I have. What, do you think I got to my position by being *stupid?*" Her hand caressed the top of Miranda's head. No matter how hard she attempted to shake Yara off her, however, Miranda consistently came up against a woman whose grip was too strong—and her will? Impervious. "You and I go way back." She grabbed

Miranda's shoulder-length hair and yanked back her head, soliciting a gasp of adrenaline-fueled shock that rippled between both chairs. "Don't we, Cairn?"

"Fuck you!" That fear reverberating through Miranda's voice wasn't for her own safety. The sound cracking through the leaky basement was dedicated to the word soon escaping from Danielle's lips.

"What?"

Miranda's hair was released. Her head flung forward, chin sinking against her chest as her arms thrashed against the ropes binding her to her chair. "Fuck you," she repeated. "Fuck. You."

Yara only had eyes for Danielle, who attempted to crane her head over her shoulder. "What the hell?"

"Remember what I said when we were arrested?" Miranda didn't sound so convincing when every other word was accompanied with a harried breath. "Don't trust a thing they say. They don't actually know *anything!*"

"What did she call you?"

"Are you going to deny it?" Yara asked Miranda. "You told me yourself that you are the woman once called Cairn. It wasn't even your real name, was it? I have each of your records dating back to around year 4600. Few know what your real name was, but *I* know. Because you told me that too." Yara paused for an agonizing second. "Joy. Hardly the name one would expect of the infamous Chief of Second Tribe, the most expensive, most sought-after batch of mercenaries in over a hundred years. No wonder you changed it. Cairn sounds like someone who wants to bash my skull in. How about that?"

Danielle's arms were shaking. "Is she lying about this too?"

"Yes, Cairn. Am I lying?"

"You're doing this on purpose," Miranda accused the commander. "You know she doesn't remember any of this yet. You're trying to-"

"What? Get answers out of *you* by dangling regression in front of *her* face? What is it to me if she dies? Like we've already established, I have no use for her. Besides this."

"Don't listen to her, Danielle." Miranda would get through to her, somehow. "She will tell you things you're not yet ready to hear. If you're forced into a regre—"

"Why don't we let *her* decide what she wants to hear?" Yara kneeled before Danielle, who refused to look her in the eye. "Must be tiring, having everyone around you decide what's best for your brain. I've seen your files too. All of them. We have a file for every life we know about. Because, sometimes, you unfortunately perished before anyone even knew who you were. That's how you cram a hundred lives into a thousand years. I wonder how many times you died as a little bitty baby. See, I only have files for over fifty of your lives. Sometimes, you were so young, you barely knew who you were before you died. Other times, you magically made it to thirty before your whole world crashed around you. Honestly, as someone who has lived and died so much, I think you've more than earned the right to hear the straight truth from people. After all, according to your very first file, you were one of the smartest mercenaries anyone could have hired. If what I read and hear is true, you would have been recruited by the Federation if you ever defected and asked for clemency. In fact, I have a letter from one of my predecessors who once suggested that his tech unit poach you for themselves. But I guess you were making so much money as a mercenary that by the time you were given privileges like the ability to even access the internet, you had no reason to leave. Or... was it something else that kept you on Cerilyn? Or someone?"

Danielle's head was heavier than a boulder resisting gravity. *The more Sisyphus pushes that piece of shit up the back of my neck...* she thought, wishing everyone would get the hell away from her, *the more I want to scream.* "You tell me. I don't remember a thing."

That was a white lie. She remembered bits and pieces that barely cobbled together a story. She had dreamed the night before, after all. While she couldn't recall details now, she remembered the warmth she felt in someone's embrace. The promises they made. The hope she felt in her heart, until she awoke in someone else's bed and clung to them until she could breathe again.

That person was behind her now, begging her to close her ears for her own good.

Who the hell could she trust? Something had always warned her to stay away from Miranda. No matter how enticing she was, trouble swam in her veins and clung to the bottom of her shoes. She was the kind of woman to never scrape it off, either. Not when it brought her life some hollow meaning...

If she really were Nerilis Dunsman's daughter... what did Danielle even *do* with that? Miranda had admitted to being half-*julah* on her father's side, but to be *his* daughter? Let alone in the Process? The reincarnation of a woman Danielle couldn't remember, but whose name she now recognized?

What did she do with that information?

"*I* think," Yara said, "that you two also go really far back. Now, maybe you don't remember me at all, yet, but our friend Cairn remembers me. That's one reason she's trying so hard to keep me from talking to you. Because I know some of your dirty little secrets, I'm a danger to you and your soul."

"She only knows what's in your files," Miranda said. "She died before she could have known a goddamn thing about what happened on Cerilyn."

She really wasn't denying it! *I don't know what to do...* Danielle closed her eyes, shutting out the women who barraged her with words and promises. Warnings. *Threats.* Because Danielle wasn't stupid! She knew a threat when she heard it, and Yara was threatening to ruin her to get to Miranda!

"Be that as it may," Yara said, "I'm *very* good at reading files I've obsessively studied since gaining access to them. If there's one thing I've deduced from our own archives, Ms. di'Graelic, it's that you were very dedicated to your chief. *Very, very dedicated.*"

The way she enunciated each syllable drove the stake of disbelief farther into Danielle's heart. Little by little, the truth that Danielle had been suppressing for a thousand years came forward.

She continued to push it back. Now was not the time.

"I could only be so lucky to have one of my own men so devoted to my personal safety. But I have a feeling I would have to be sleeping with him for that to be a reality. That's the only way it works. Pay with pussy and get the best protection available."

"You have *no* idea what you're talking about," Miranda snapped. "What is this crazy fanfiction you've written?"

"Are you denying it? Everyone back then knew that Cerilyn was nothing but drinking, sex, and gambling. The three honored vices of a people who have little to live for and enough trauma to fell most normal armies. Why would you two be any different? I'm sure there's a salacious story in there, but ask me, it's as simple as trying to keep your enemies off your backs. After all, the tales that were passed down about the impressive Sulim di'Graelic was that she was a virginal wunderkind who couldn't be swayed by even the most beautiful clients. We have more than one record of you shooting someone in the foot because they came on to you after you did the job they hired you for. Impressive marksmanship skills are also in your file, I might add."

"Fascinating," Danielle muttered.

Yara chortled. "You know what I *really* think, though? *I* think that story was purposely pushed out by your chief to cover up the fact that you two had a very special relationship."

"For the love of God," Miranda interrupted. "Stop the nonsense."

Yara stood up straight, the countenance of playing games wiped from existence. "I want answers about the whereabouts of Nerilis Dunsman and what he plans on doing next. You will give me *everything* you know, Cairn di'Cerilyn." Her hand landed where the two chairs met. "Or I will make sure your bed warmer knows *all* about you. The High Priestess can only save her soul after that."

Miranda's head jerked around. "You *bitch*."

"Stop. You're flattering me."

"Both of you shut the hell up!" Danielle shrieked, her head already pounding and her stomach churning. "Fuck this! Fuck you!" That was addressed to Yara, whose eyes widened with delightful surprise that she was already getting to Danielle. "You have no right to detain me like this. Do whatever you want to her, but let me the hell out of here before-"

"Before what?" Yara asked with a chuckle. "Before you shoot me in the foot? Before you call Master Marlow to come pick you up from your big-girl interview? Because he's not going to come save you. *Either* of you. You'd be better off praying to whatever God you happen to believe in. The *julah* have no reach here. They don't even know you're here."

Something rancid shot up Danielle's throat. "Before I throw up on your shoes."

"Oh, for the Void's sake." Yara had barely hopped out of the way when Danielle coughed up the bile that had been burning her esophagus. "This is ridiculous." Once Danielle had found her breath again, Lana grabbed her by the chin and forced her whole head back. As fingers dug into Danielle's cheeks, Yara basked in her infernal satisfaction. "The cunt you've been having a great time with is none other than the bitch who sold your soul to the highest bidder a thousand years ago. She is the reincarnation of Cairn di'Cerilyn, the chief of Second Tribe who directly dealt with Master Marlow and offered your body for sacrifice. She, like you, is in the Process, but unlike what she says, was thrust into it by her *father,* Nerilis Dunsman, the former High Priest of the Void and the man responsible for destroying your soul over such a long, *long* time." Yara released Danielle. Chin and cheeks fell. More bile shot up Danielle's throat. "And you were fucking her, you barbarian whore."

Yara immediately met the derisive glare of the only woman who knew more about her than Commander d'Alacron herself. While that intrigued her, the commander was more enamored with how she had so effectively cut through Miranda's tough demeanor and reached the scared, broken bitch inside of her.

"Enjoy getting to know one another again." Yara motioned for her two guards to step outside. She slowly followed. "When you're ready to talk, we'll only be a scream away."

At that point, the fact that Miranda had already told her she would know whatever she wanted as long as Danielle was safely released no longer mattered. Yara had achieved what she set out to accomplish. After all, that was Danielle growing listless in her seat, limbs lax and head hanging so low that she might as well have been unconscious.

Miranda jerked against the binds holding them together. She searched for Danielle's hand while the door closed, enshrouding them in the darkness they had awakened to find. When Miranda's skin finally touched Danielle's, all she felt was the clammy palm of someone who was quickly losing grip on reality.

"Hang in there," Miranda said in English, before slipping into Old Basic. "Hang in there for me, Sulim."

Miranda bolstered herself with fake confidence. It was too late to turn back. The words had crashed upon Danielle's head.

The only thing Miranda was grateful for was that there was at least *one* thing Yara had not guessed about a love from a thousand years ago. Otherwise, there was no hope for Danielle's recovery as she began to regress against her will. Some things doomed them from the start.

Thirty-Eight

Yara helped herself to a bottle of *yaya* she saved for days like this. Days when she basked in the culmination of all her hard work and whatever personal trauma she subjected herself to if it meant getting the job done.

Not her fault if she sometimes enjoyed the spoils.

She reclined against one of the couches in her office, warm glass in her hand. Like wine, aged *yaya* was best savored in a snifter glass that evoked the aroma of a plant that could only grow on Yahzen. *Bless the families that keep up the more sacred traditions,* Yara thought, as she sipped the fiery liquid that soon burned an ashen trail down her esophagus. Few humans could drink *yaya* like the *julah* did, but Yara had spent most of her youth partying outside of her schoolwork. When she joined the Forces, one of her trainers singled her out as a candidate for undercover work. That often meant learning to hold her liquor against the drug lords, terrorists, and hardened mercenaries of the world. While she wasn't likely to knock back a few glasses now, she would take a potent bottle and save it for the high-intensity days that asked for a *moment's* respite.

She had Danielle and Miranda right where she wanted. One drawing the truth out of the other.

At about this time in an hour... She sipped her drink again. *I'll know everything there is to know about Nerilis Dunsman.*

Someone knocked on her door. Without giving anyone permission to enter, the door flew open, and there was Joel, marching toward her with news on his face.

"Report, Commander," he grunted.

Yara savored the last drop going down her throat. "Either Cairn wants to talk, or you've finally found and arrested Sonall Gardiah for me."

Joel completely glossed over her use of their old names. "As it so happens, we have Mr. Devon Anderson down the hall right now."

That certainly piqued Yara's interest. "Down the hall? If you've arrested him, I want him in the interview room four."

"He has not yet been arrested, ma'am."

"Are you daft? Did I not personally give you the warrant?"

"That's the thing." Joel's visage remained firm against Lara's disbelief. "He hasn't been apprehended, nor is he here to turn himself in. He's come with a contingent of Master Marlow's employees and wishes to talk to you as a free man."

Yara sighed so hard that her body sank into the couch. "You must be kidding. Of course he's being harbored by those who think they're above the law. At this point, I wouldn't be shocked to find out Master Marlow has been harboring his old friend for all these centuries. Whatever. What is this about, again?"

"Mr. Anderson is here with an escort and wishes to speak with you." Joel cleared his throat. "Now."

"Quite presumptuous of him to waltz in here with an *escort* and demand to talk to *me*. Doesn't he know that I'm a busy woman?" Yara pulled her legs up onto the couch and drank the rest of her *yaya* like the *julah,* each little drop scorching her stomach as she dumped it all in there. "I have information to extract before I go to bed tonight."

Joel shifted on his feet. "I'll send him in, then."

"For the love of..." Yara pressed the glass against her forehead. "Make it *clear* that us not arresting him on the spot is a sign of good faith that he will fully cooperate." Her voice grew louder the farther away Joel walked. "I don't care how many bodyguards he brings!"

Was Yara surprised to see who accompanied Devon when he entered, eyes burning like fire and posture stiff enough to inspire a healthy dose of skepticism on her behalf? No. Nor was she surprised that a pregnant woman like Kalera Amyran was the one to walk in first, her entire countenance shooting daggers at the commander. Of course Marlow hadn't believed Lara's warnings about substances that might still linger in the air. Nor did Kalera care, clearly.

Nor did her husband, who brought up the rear and kicked the door shut behind them.

"Have a seat, Mr. Anderson," Yara said with a lazy shrug. "I'd offer you a drink, but you caught me on my break."

Devon planted himself on the couch across from Lara. Not once did he remove his eyes from the woman who held his fate and those he loved in her hands.

"Where are they?" No greetings. No due deference to the woman who commanded the entirety of the Federation's Forces. *Really bold of him to waltz in here like this,* Yara thought with a dire sigh. "Don't pay me lip service either. I want honesty, or I walk out of here and you will never see me again."

Yara peered into the bottom of her glass. If this man hadn't suddenly made demands of someone who was used to men making *such* pithy "requests" of her time and power, she would help herself to a second glass. Maybe half a glass. Yara held her liquor well, but there was only so much her body could do when she started drinking. Never mind at her job... "Such a bold promise, Mr. Anderson. Especially when you've been cutting quite a new life for yourself thanks to the fame and fortune about to come your way." She kicked her feet off the couch and sat up with a creak in her bones and a groan in her throat. "If only I could take some credit for it."

"Where are they?"

"Who are you to ask such demanding questions? Tell me, why should I entertain your inquiries? You're a wanted man! What is stopping me from having you arrested on the spot? Your bodyguards? Please. There are five thousand soldiers in this building that I can call upon at any moment. You saw a hundred of them on the way in here, and they're not even the cream of the crop. You have no idea where those are."

"I'm guessing they're guarding Danielle and..."

"Cairn di'Cerilyn. Yes. She's in my possession."

That didn't startle Devon, but it did shut him up. "So, you know?"

"There's very little that I don't know now. Just trying to fill in a few blanks. Don't suppose you could help me with that, could you?"

"Depends. Will giving you information result in the release of Danielle at least?"

Yara chuckled. "What? You don't want the other one released, too? I wonder what she would think about that."

"I doubt it would surprise her much."

"Right. She killed your mother and stole your woman. That would sour me, too."

"I think you have some things backward," Devon retorted. "She only did one thing."

Yara leaned forward, empty glass touching upon the table separating her and Devon. "Here's the thing, *Mr. Anderson.*" When she sniffed, it was with the air of a woman who couldn't believe that she was entertaining him in this matter. "Ultimately, I only care about our mutual person of great, intense dislike. You and Ms. Cromwell are... ah, you're collateral damage, I suppose. So while I fully intend to arrest you when I have the chance, I'm actually making great headway with my downstairs interrogations. What information do you have that Ms. Hotchner will not be forthcoming with?"

The word "interrogations" did not inspire confidence within Devon, who already worried that he may have been too late to save Danielle and Miranda from whatever fate Yara d'Alacron intended for them. *What trouble have you gotten us all into?* That thought was telepathically sent to Miranda, who would more than likely never, ever hear Devon's thoughts. "I'll tell you anything you want to know. *Anything.* Assuming I know the answers. You want to know who assassinated Senator di'Rael when he was on his way to the Federation Council to testify against the Boardrun Company drilling in his territory?" Devon snorted. "I could tell you who ordered the hit."

"I'm not interested in cold case files from a thousand years ago," Yara said. "I want information about the current whereabouts of Nerilis Dunsman and what he plans to do next. Nothing is more important than bringing him to proper justice."

Devon gritted his teeth. Did he know a damn thing about Nerilis, let alone where he was or what he planned next? Of course not. It was enough for him that the man wouldn't be bothering him any longer. "Are you sure that's all you care about, Commander?"

Yara shrugged. "There are always little bits and pieces I crave to taste, but don't think for two seconds I care about anything more than what is happening *today*. Now, unless you know of Ms. Hotchner's paternity..." She glanced up at Kalera and Vikkel, who stood right behind Devon's couch, arms crossed and eyes disturbingly pasted to Lara's forehead. A quick look told her that she might be able to take all three of them out, but Yara would be injured before she had the chance. Perhaps fatally, if she didn't keep a straight head on her shoulders. *The woman is a decent sorceress,* she remembered from the files. That was the main reason Yara didn't want Kalera in her office. That and the idea of potentially wounding the pregnant daughter of the human ambassador to Yahzen sounded like a PR nightmare. "I'm not sure what we have to talk about. I'm willing to act in good faith, though. Give me one decent piece of information and I'll cancel your warrant. No promises about the fate of your female comrades."

This wasn't what Devon sought, but it was better than nothing. If there were no warrant for his head, he could better help Danielle—and Miranda, he supposed. *Why do I have a feeling they're a two-for-one deal now?* No matter how much he bemoaned it, however, he knew what he had to do.

"You asked about her paternity..." Devon sucked in his breath. Problem was, he wasn't 100% sure, either. Most of it was conjecture on his part. While he hadn't been as *bright* back then as he was now, there were things that Sonall saw—and heard—that had stuck in his mind for all those years. Devon was simply better at analyzing them now. "I think I know."

"You better have something better than a *julah* male. Because I already know that."

"Yes. I know who he is."

Yara attempted to hide her mild excitement, but gave it away with a tap of her finger against the table. "Tell me who it is. I want a name, and an explanation."

"An explanation? I'm not sure I can give you that, considering I know jack shit about how *julah* function. But I can give you a name." Devon steeled himself for what he was about to admit. "I'm absolutely certain that her father is Dunsman."

Although Devon had no idea what to expect, he was not anticipating Yara to smugly sit back in her couch, a small chuckle echoing in her throat. "Thank you for confirming what I already knew."

Devon furrowed his brows. "If you already knew it, then..."

"I've known for a while. There are people in this world who have not turned their backs on the Federation and how we try to protect our people. *All* of our people." Lara's glare traveled toward Vikkel, who had maintained a silent, expressionless vigil since coming into her office. Now? He faltered a little. It was the first reminder to Devon that he was not alone. "That goes for the *julah* as well. You might be surprised to know that there are those who will turn in their own."

Vikkel lowered his arms. He exchanged a look with his wife before directly addressing Lara. "What are you talking about?"

"You're not surprised to hear that the former High Priest, the most reviled person to ever exist among the *julah,* has sired a woman trapped in the Process. I wonder why that is?" Lara's haughty laugh echoed in her office. "I never reveal a trusted, anonymous source, but..." A whistle tickled her words. "You really shouldn't be surprised, Young Master Amyran."

"You *mother!*" Kalera spat. "That thrice-damned bi—"

"Oh, please," Yara interrupted. "No need for that. She is your child's grandmother, after all."

Devon's voice was the one that soon raised above the rabble. "I do not know what other information to supply you, then. But I do have a question to ask you, Commander."

Yara fought to still herself. "Yes? What is it?"

Devon was not laughing. He hadn't uttered a single chuckle since coming into the room. "Are you really willing to destroy everything you've worked for in this life to satisfy some old grudge from a life you are incapable of ever truly remembering?"

Yara wasn't laughing any longer. That wasn't *laughter* huffing out of her throat when she looked Devon in the eye.

"You want information nobody else is willing to give you? Fine. I'll tell you everything I know." Devon's hands lifted into the air. Finally, he smiled—but it wasn't the smile of a man who had something funny to share. "About your old life, that is."

He finally had her right where he wanted her. That was a powerful thing to command when so much was at stake.

Thirty-Nine

The silence was only broken by the constant drip from the pipes above. Miranda shifted her body far enough away that it stopped tapping her on the forehead, but she still heard that constant *drip, drip, drip* as it pattered against the far side of her chair.

She had long stopped asking Danielle if she was all right. How long had passed since Yara marched out of the room with her small entourage? Nobody knew. Could have been an hour. Could have been five minutes. Time meant little to someone whose soul had been around nine-hundred years too long.

Miranda leaned back and inhaled a deep breath that constricted her chest against her jacket. Somewhere, down by her zipper, something was caught on the bindings and pulled against her shoulder every time she tried to move. She had to pee. God knew she was dehydrated on top of it. Yet nothing frightened her more than the fate of someone else's wellbeing.

When Danielle finally spoke, it was both a cause of relief and a punch to Miranda's gut.

"Is it true?"

She had been conscious that whole time, yet the concept of *conscious* was one neither she nor Miranda comprehended at that moment. For while Danielle was awake, her soul was in flux. The shock of what she had heard however long ago didn't simply throw her current self into a tailspin—it yanked the old her, the one lying dormant, to the surface. Right now, as the Federation played chicken with her life and the destiny of her soul, she was both Danielle and Sulim at once. The parts of her who couldn't believe what they had heard waged war against the ones that calculated what to do to get out of this hellish situation.

Danielle wanted answers; Sulim wanted out of there.

"True..." Miranda slowly shook her head. "She has some of her facts scrambled, but I'm not surprised. It's not like she *actually* remembers us. It's fragments in her head and remnants left on her soul. She wasn't supposed to ever remember us."

"So it's true. The part about you."

Miranda could no longer hide it. To deny it now might borrow them more time, but inevitably, Danielle *would* discover the truth and might hate Miranda more for it.

"Yes. I am in the Process. I was put into it at the same time as you and Devon—because I was there. I outlived you both by one precious minute." Miranda shuddered. "You died in my arms, and I died next to you."

That confounding silence continued to haunt Miranda. Was Danielle still with her? Yes. Was that necessarily a *good* thing?

Not even Danielle could answer that. Her head throbbed, and her chest ached. Every time she lifted her chin, she was met with the insurmountable weight pressing upon the back of her skull. If only she saw the shadow looming over her, daring her to regress.

There was one upside, both she and Miranda supposed. If Danielle died of spiritual shock, she would be trapped in the Process forever, and the force of her soul expending a timeline's worth of energy at once would possibly replenish the Void and save them all.

It wasn't a worthy sacrifice, however. Especially since that meant Miranda would go down with her.

"So you are who she says you are."

"Unfortunately. Why do you think I've always kept my eye on you?" Miranda held back a tearful smile. "You were my number one."

That heartfelt expression was lost on Danielle, who focused on one key point. "You never told me. When were you going to tell me? Were you laughing at me the whole time?"

"What?" Did it sound like Miranda was laughing *now*? *All those years ago, when you first walked into my office and reported for duty.* Miranda would never forget that moment. She knew it would happen, eventually, but she had not been prepared that day. Not for the missing half of her soul to look her in the eye and dare to say she didn't remember. "I would never laugh at you. I couldn't tell you, that's all."

"Why? Thought I was too weak to understand the truth? That we were lovers?"

"I wish it were that simple. We were *more* than mere lovers. We were soulmates. Don't you get it?"

No, Danielle didn't get it. Wasn't that the problem haunting their ill-fated relationship?

"For a thousand years I've followed you," Miranda said. "And for a thousand years you've forgotten me."

Danielle snorted. "Maybe there was a reason I never remembered you."

"Of course there was. It's the reason everyone is so delicate with you." Miranda did not intend to unleash her anger, yet her voice grew in agony the longer she spoke. "At any point we could have sat your ass down and told you the whole truth. You could have regressed on your own by now if it weren't for your own blind stubbornness that keeps you from remembering what *I know.* You and me... we fucked up. We fucked up so badly that it..." Miranda clamped her mouth closed. No. She still couldn't risk it. Danielle hadn't regressed. She might be on the cusp, but until that time...

It was still too dangerous.

"Fuck this." Danielle's arms rattled in the binds holding them to her side and to the chair behind her. "*Fuck. This.*"

Her outburst shook Miranda in her core, but all it did to their chairs was make them creak beneath their asses.

"I'm sorry," Miranda muttered.

Danielle hadn't heard her. She was trapped in her own chaotic thoughts, screaming in her head until all she beheld was the constant echo of conflicting opinions and memories she barely upheld as her own. Every time Danielle squeezed her eyelids shut, she reopened them a little less herself.

The shock of everything she had heard in the past hour was flaring up—soon, she might not even be herself. She might be someone else entirely.

"I'm so pissed at you."

That piqued Miranda's interest, not because of what Danielle said, but *how* she said it. Old Basic wasn't exactly in her repertoire of spoken languages, after all. Not when spoken with such a flawless accent that sounded *slightly*... oh, what was the name of that planet again?

Qahrainian.

Sulim threw back her head and grunted with a roll of her eyes. "I told you to stay put. Did you? Nooo. You never listen to me. Sometimes I think that *you* still think you know so much more than me. Wish I could say I've gotten used to it. Know what this reminds me of?"

Miranda had no idea how to respond, never mind what language to speak. "I... uh..." She switched to Old Basic at the last moment. "No. I have no idea what this reminds you of. Why don't you enlighten me?"

Sulim was either losing grip on reality, or pausing for effect. "That time you picked me out of a crowd like, '*Oh, yeah. That one. I'll take her back to my cave and have my way with her.*'" Right. Pausing for effect. Miranda was delighted to know that Sulim was as droll with her wit now as she had been a thousand years ago.

"Yes. You're right. This is exactly like that time." Miranda didn't think she could get as equally pissed as the woman tied to her back, yet here they were, bickering in a dead language. "I totally picked someone to take based on how much I wanted to sleep with them."

"Oh, well, it was either me or my cousin who *shit himself.*"

"Now he shat himself? You always told me he pissed himself when I crashed your party. Which is it, hmm? How bad did he smell when I rescued you from that *literal* hellhole?"

Sulim clenched her fists and flared her nostrils in pure, unfiltered derision. "Rescued me," she muttered. "Just for that, you can play here by yourself."

Three seconds later, Sulim had freed herself from everything holding her to the chair. She stood up, brushed the water droplets off her clothes, and stood in front of Miranda, hands on hips.

"Impressive," Miranda said. "Was wondering how long it would take you to figure it out." She cocked her head. "You *always* do."

"They're Tier A Federation knots. Bit of a bother, but nothing I can't handle."

"The fabric isn't the same as what we're used to. Times and technology have changed. We're not playing with dragline anymore."

Sulim shook out her arms and twiddled her fingers at her sides. "Like I said. Nothing I can't handle when I'm determined."

"Are you going to untie me now?"

That hoot in Sulim's throat caught Miranda off guard. "Yeah, right. Think I'll let you stay here and think about what you've done."

"Do you even remember what I've done, Sulim?" Miranda made sure to say that name, as if a part of her couldn't quite believe she was really talking to the woman who had changed her whole existence.

"I know Madam Vaus has been telling stories about you again. Rumor is you've been frequenting her brothel while I'm gone."

Wow. Miranda had absolutely no idea what to say to that. *Bit late for this argument, aren't we?* "I really can't discuss anything with you when you're like this."

Sulim stretched her arms high above her head. After adjusting her shirt so it covered her abdomen once again, she marched past Miranda, kicking another empty chair toward the far side of the room.

"What are you doing?" Miranda craned her head over her shoulder, but could barely make out Sulim's form as she climbed onto the chair and punched something in the ceiling. "Are you kidding me?" Panic swelled in Miranda's chest. Not only was she being left here by herself, but Void only knew what the hell kind of trouble Sulim was getting herself into! "This isn't the 4600s anymore! They've developed new ways to smoke your ass in the vents! Get back here!"

In true insubordinate fashion, Sulim was doing her own thing—and Cairn could kiss her ass.

Forty

Every time Devon told Yara something she hadn't yet discovered for herself, she hid her shock with a cough into the back of her hand. Or she pretended she had hair in her eye—both the good and the bad one. By the third round of her fussing with the bangs she used to cover her defunct eye, Devon had caught on to her ruse. Did he get a little something out of it?

Absolutely.

He was careful to not share any falsehoods, however. And if there was something he simply didn't know, he was honest about it. This wasn't a time for satisfying himself with sordid tales he pulled from his ass. If Yara caught on to it at all...

People he cared about were in her grasp. She had the power to ruin them all. Better to stick with the facts he knew, no matter how pretty they might not have been.

"You remember the day I died?" Yara leaned in closer, finger pressed against her pursed lips. Devon kept a respectful distance. Arms crossed. Legs remained firmly clenched together. Although Yara had not truly intruded upon his personal space, Devon wasn't giving her even a *sliver* of a chance. "Obviously, I have no recollection, and I haven't found a decent record of it."

"Digging into the records of your old life isn't the wisest thing to do. Especially if there are things you don't want to see."

"But I *want* to see them, don't you get it?" Yara licked her lips in the anticipation of having everything she ever felt in this life finally validated. "Such pain. A terrible existence that eventually led to my own demise. Yet here I am, a thousand years later, more successful than I could have ever anticipated back then. It's a story for the ages. The kind of shit they'll put in my biographies for centuries to come."

"I have a feeling you weren't thinking about that back then. Death on Cerilyn was never a pleasant thing."

"How did I die?"

"Don't you know by now?"

Yara laughed. "I have an inclination. I don't do things neatly, so it wouldn't have been poison. A gunshot, perhaps?"

"One is closer than the other."

"Hmm. What else can you tell me?"

Devon shook his head. "I was there for your funeral, but not when they found you, so I don't know a whole lot about the details." Before she could ask more uncomfortable questions about what her funeral was like, Devon continued, "That day was a bit overshadowed. Everyone thought it would be just another funeral we were subjected to so we remembered what happened to us if we didn't fall in line. Then the chief was murdered in the middle of it. Quite the spectacle. *That* I was there for."

Was that smile on Lara's face one of fascination or dejection? "You truly are a font of stories, aren't you?"

"Honestly, most of my stories of that life happened way after you died. All I personally remember about you is dealing with your constant tough-girl shtick and eventually sleeping together." Nothing glamorous. A supply closet and two traumatized teenagers with nothing else to occupy their time. Besides work.

Kalera put a hand on Devon's shoulder. "Master Marlow has called and wants to know how much longer this is going to take."

"Suppose it depends how long it takes for your husband to get back," Yara said. Vikkel had stepped out many minutes ago to call his mother and find out what the hell had happened with the confidential information she was given. He had yet to return. "Don't know about you, but I'm enjoying our time together, although

I do have *work* to return to at some point." Yara had hoped to be back downstairs by this point. She had more *interviewing* to do.

Too bad all of that was soon circumvented.

"Commander!" An officer appeared in the opened doorway without invitation. Yara shot up from her couch, while Devon lowered himself, completely out of the young man's sight. "Situation!"

Yara shot Devon a deadly look. "You're coming with me. I have no doubt that whatever it is, you and your cohorts are somehow involved."

Kalera inserted herself between Devon and Yara as they marched down the hall. Devon didn't ask questions, although he burned to know what the hell had happened. Lara? She expected anything, from Master Marlow making a sudden appearance or both of her interviewees falling over dead in their bondage.

She certainly did not expect what she saw on the closed-circuit security cameras on display in a room down at the far end of the hall.

Joel was already there, sitting next to the guard on duty at the time of Danielle's miraculous escape from her chair. The man shook in his seat every time the captain asked him a question or to replay a specific period of footage. Yara walked in the moment Danielle's form chastised the other woman, still tied up to her chair, and waltzed across the room like someone had left her ropes a little too loose.

"Ma'am!" The guard on duty leaped out of his seat and acknowledged the commander when she shoved herself into the room. "I alerted the captain as soon as I noticed Ms. Cromwell was missing. She got up like it was nothing and jumped up into the vents! I've never seen anything like..."

"Show me the current footage," Yara barked. "How did this happen?"

The cameras switched to live. Three armed guards surrounded Miranda, hounding her for information about Danielle's whereabouts. Two more guards poked the vent entrance and used body-heat detectors on every part of the ceiling. They were already under orders to keep both Miranda and Danielle alive, but that didn't soothe Devon as he watched with wary guards point their weapons toward the vents.

Nevertheless, he choked down a chuckle.

It was loud enough for Yara to hear. "What's so funny?" She was *this* close to grabbing him by the collar of his shirt. "Do you know what's happening here?"

"Gee. Suppose you're dealing with one of the best of the best in there. If anyone knew how to get herself out of a fix, it was Sulim di'Graelic. Why, her second home was the vents. How do you think she directed every mission we went on? I couldn't fit in them."

"It's so..." Joel stood up straight, his eyes locked on Miranda as she was lifted from her chair, "rudimentary."

"Yeah, they don't make them like that anymore," Devon muttered.

Yara shoved him out of the way. "I want someone at *every* vent in the whole building. Do you understand me, Captain?"

"Yes, ma'am," Joel said.

"Bring the other one into interview room one and have an armed guard on her at all times. I'll have this whole building turned upside down before the end of the night if it means finding a *missing suspect*. As for you," her finger jammed into Devon's chest, "you're not going anywhere. For all I know, you had something to do with this."

"I wish. Feels like the old days, not that you would remember."

"Lock him and his bodyguards in my office with *armed guards*." Yara continued barking orders as she marched into the hallway. "I want Master Marlow here before I count to ten! And do *not* tell the president about any of this!"

Devon didn't even mind the way Joel's men manhandled him on his and Kalera's way back down to Lara's office. Knowing that the woman he once knew so well was currently up to her old tricks like it was a thousand years ago made him happier than the thought of her finally regressing and being free from the Process.

He only wished he knew what she was really up to, because things could either get interesting... or very, very ugly.

Ugly. Everything around Danielle was *ugly*.

She clambered through the tight vents, peering into the slats that occasionally appeared beneath her nose. Dust, grime and the webs of Terra's III native arachnid slid against her clothing and marred her hair, still wet from sitting in a leaky, cold room that no man was meant to inhabit for more than ten minutes at a time. Did she care? Did Danielle prowl through the vents of a building she didn't know because it titillated her?

No. Then again, she barely knew who she was right now.

She wasn't quite regressing yet. Figments of who she had once been inhabited the forefront of her mind, but it wasn't triggering her into the embrace of the Void's not-so-soothing answers. To regress meant going to a point of no return. Regressing meant completely obtaining the memories she had at the time of Sulim's death a thousand years ago. All that had happened was Yara triggering an episode that could have grown out of hand like a piece of dry grass catching fire in the woods.

Every so often, she stopped crawling, wondering what the hell she was doing or where the hell she was. Those moments were characterized with the creeping sense of claustrophobia and the vague memory of Miranda tied up behind her. Where was she now? What had happened? How in the *world* did Danielle end up in the very place her old self deemed safest?

Danielle couldn't remember, but Sulim could. That was her endless problem.

Once, when Sulim was the most sought-after rogue of espionage and kidnappings that left loved ones quaking to pay a hefty ransom, she had figured out one of the best ways to infiltrate a building or oversee a mission she headed was by sneaking into the vents. Back then, it didn't matter what kind or who had built them. From the old-school fans pushing air through rattling ducts, to the precise lasers that heated up their insulated surroundings, Sulim wasn't afraid of what she might find. She knew how to turn things off with a remote hack via her own communication device. Cameras? Most of her targets were either too stupid or too unassuming to ever think they needed cameras in the *vents*. The funniest thing? The intergalactic headquarters for the Federation Forces was old enough that such things hadn't been upgraded in centuries. Repairs kept things running as they should, but *cameras?* Heat-seeking scans? Those were things included in the new parliamentary building a few blocks away, but not in the military headquarters.

That money was better spent elsewhere, after all.

Danielle hovered above a spinning fan that cooled off a young woman in uniform on her meal break. She spent the whole hour in a private room, eating food out of a small packet and flipping through the news on her tablet. Occasionally, she slurped through a straw and let loose the gas trapped in her body. This was when Danielle should have noted the name on her lapel or memorized the codes she punched into the security door separating her from the hallway that led to the ladies' restroom. Unfortunately, Danielle's body was as blind as the proverbial bats crying in her belfry. Sulim could have seen it in two seconds, but that body—and those eyes—had been dead for a thousand years. It was moments like those that reminded her she was no longer in the body that once steamrolled entire governments and made grown men piss themselves once they realized she was in the room.

Sulim sighed within her. Danielle batted those thoughts away and continued on through the vents, driven purely by instinct she barely understood.

She looped back to the room she and Miranda had been tied up in, but there was no one there now. Nobody she *cared* about. Just two goons decked out in riot gear with their guns pointed at the vents. The chairs were empty. Danielle waited around long enough for someone to mention the "prisoner in Interview Room One" before backing up without a sound. Just in time, too. One of the soldiers pointed a heat-scanner at the vents where she had been a second before.

That was the moment she completely gave in to instinct. The only way Danielle was getting out of this alive was if she surrendered to the silent voice within her.

That voice wasn't always so silent, however. Occasionally, she whispered something that Danielle should have known. *Remember, this building existed long ago too.* Sulim had seen the blueprints more than once. Some of the plans were part of a payment, since the tribe was interested in currency beyond gold and credits. Information was sometimes as valuable, especially to a woman who spent most of her hard-earned money on the latest devices and intergalactic signals that bypassed most of Cerilyn's censorship protocols. If she was expected to infiltrate, she had to know what it looked like, inside and out. No one knew when she might be given the deal of a lifetime to infiltrate the Federation's own headquarters. Any of them.

Assuming this building hadn't changed much outside of necessary upkeep over the past few centuries...

The main interview rooms for persons of great interest were on the upper floors. Unfortunately for Danielle, there were no directories. Nor was there any way for her to go up a floor through the vents.

If she wanted to get upstairs... she had to take the stairs. Or the elevator. Both of which were plenty dangerous, even if she knew what she was doing.

Danielle caught the woman on break as she recycled her trash and picked something out of her teeth. After a mighty sigh and stretching her arms above her head, she untucked her credentials from beneath her blouse and turned on the sensor that allowed her to pass through the security checkpoints throughout the building.

Danielle quickly scanned the small break room. *No visible cameras. Does that mean they're right beneath me?* The woman tucked her coiled hair beneath a hat that would fit nicely over Danielle's head. It was either now or never.

She pushed through the grate separating her from the small room. The moment the woman looked up, Danielle was no longer herself.

She had effectively become the woman who knew best how to handle these situations.

"Ah—!" The woman, whose nametag said *d'Rena,* passed out the moment Danielle dragged her beneath the cameras and put her to sleep with a constricting hold. Not the kind she practiced in the military. The kind that was declared illegal when on *official* Federation business, not that it ever mattered to a mercenary who did things her own damn way. If someone died in the process? Oh, well.

Then again, she *did* have a reputation for not killing anyone...

"Sorry," Danielle whispered as she lay Ms. d'Rena against the wall and stripped her of her hat and jacket. The hat was easy enough to pop on Danielle's head. The jacket barely fit over the clothes she already wore. Should she try on the skirt? No. As long as she was convincing enough in the hat and jacket, the security pass would do most of the work for her. It was a hop, skip, and leap away to the nearest elevator, and Danielle already knew where the cameras were in those.

Still, she hesitated before stepping out before the camera and entering the hallway.

If there was one thing both current and past Danielle could accomplish, it was imitating a soldier who was used to being watched by superior officers. So the trickiest part wasn't convincing those who didn't really pay attention to her that she belonged there—it was eschewing the lingering looks and possible questions someone might ask her. Current Danielle didn't speak Basic, after all, and Sulim could barely piece it together with her Old Basic. As long as she kept her eyes down and marched as if she had somewhere important to go, she would make it to the elevator.

Thank God there was a directory in the nearest one—and it was *empty!*

Danielle couldn't completely hide herself from the camera, but all that showed up was the top of d'Rena's white hat. How much time did she have before the next person looking to take a break walked in on the woman without her credentials? Or her jacket, for that matter? Hell, d'Rena might wake up and sound the alarm before Danielle made it to the top three floors, which apparently required a separate security clearance that might not have been included in d'Rena's sensors.

Danielle would worry about that when she finished riding the elevator to the highest level it could go. According to the directory, the commander's office was on the top floor, but there were no details about what room or how to get there, of course. *Need-to-know basis, I take it,* Danielle thought. She scanned the other labeled rooms and offices until she realized there was one more interview room drawn out than was labeled.

She had a feeling that's where she would find the woman she was paid to protect.

The elevator door dinged open. Instead of finding an empty hallway, however, Danielle saw a group of soldiers being briefed on "the suspect who had eluded custody."

She decided to shut the door and ride down to the next floor.

That floor was a bit less crowded. *Not only that, but is that another elevator I see?* Down the hall. Across from an important-looking conference room. One man with accolades decorating his lapel stood in front of the double doors, scanning his tablet with such fixation that Danielle snuck up right behind him and muttered something in Old Basic.

"Huh? What was that?" The man turned, barely catching a glimpse of Danielle as she ducked around him, ID and keychain with his personal sensor now in her hand. Although the man certainly felt *something,* it didn't register in his mind until Danielle was nothing but a blur in the corner of his eye. He shrugged off the interaction as someone jogging past him and went back to his emails. He wouldn't notice that his belongings were missing until he attempted to use the restroom in fifteen minutes.

Plenty of time for Danielle to sneak into the next elevator. Once the sensor on this one worked, she chucked d'Rena's behind a plastic plant and read the name *Ernhard* on the new one.

The elevator didn't travel one floor before it stopped and opened again. The briefed soldiers were on their way to board, their CO right in front with his sensor out and head turned over his shoulder. Just as one of his men called out for Danielle to hold the door, she slammed the button. The soldiers were running to catch the door the last she saw them.

Only then did she let out a sigh of relief. It was short lived, of course. She always had to be "on." That meant giving into the thoughts that constantly pounded against her skull.

Don't let them see you. Be discreet, but courteous. Be quick, be swift, be soon forgotten. Go where is necessary and leave out the rest. Focus on the task. Focus on getting back home.

"Home" was the concept short-circuiting her brain. To be fair, it had broken her brain more than once when she was a single-souled organism on a barbarian planet. *Home* meant nothing.

Home was a person.

The elevator stalled before reaching the top floor. Voices were heard through the wall. Something about a woman found in the basement, missing her hat, jacket, and credentials. Where had her sensor last been scanned?

They stopped this thing because they know I'm in here. Whether it was true or not, Danielle had to get the hell out of there.

She braved having her face caught on camera if it meant kicking through the top emergency compartment of the elevator, pulling herself up with pure upper-body strength she had conditioned for the past ten years, and looking for the nearest escape before the elevator moved again.

Vents. Excellent.

This particular panel did not want to budge, however. It had been decades since it was last touched, and the clasps holding it to the wall had rusted into place. It took such a mighty lurch of Danielle's body that not only was she knocked backward—and toward the hole dumping her eight feet to the elevator floor—but it made such a sound that echoed through the shaft she had fewer than five seconds to sneak in. The grate landed in the elevator with another loud thud, but by then, Danielle had pulled herself into the vents of the top floor. She was long gone through the ducts by the time the elevator resumed movement and the soldiers flooded the carriage, each one pulling at the abandoned grate as if it would give up the clues they desperately sought.

If only Danielle had a weapon. *Then* she would feel a little better. As it was, she only had her body, and the old her felt the same restrictions Sonall had felt when he reawakened in Devon's body.

When was the last time you got a decent workout? Danielle didn't know if she thought that or spoke it aloud. Didn't matter. Either way, it was a wild thing to ask, considering she had to be in prime condition even if she hadn't been sent to the front lines across Earth. Yet her current life wasn't anywhere near as physically demanding as the old one. Before the end, Sulim had thought herself going *soft*. To even think that now...

Her hat was soon caught on a screw sticking out of its socket. One hand slammed down on the metal before her, the sound bouncing through the ducts and probably alerting half of the personnel beneath her. Danielle remained still until she was sure nobody was coming after her. Only then did she ditch the hat in the vent and continue on, hoping to God she correctly remembered that directory.

She knew she was close when she found the first (empty) interview room. Then the next. Then the next.

There should have been one more. The unmarked one on the loose outline of a map in the elevator.

When she finally came upon the head of brown hair chained to a barren desk, her heart skipped a beat.

"*Psst.*" Danielle cupped a hand around her lips. Miranda's head slightly turned. "Sit tight! I'll find a way to get you out of there."

Miranda snorted, careful to not turn her full attention to the vents. Had she been surprised? Yes. No. *An eclectic mix of this and that.* She hadn't expected to hear Danielle's voice in that exact moment, but she knew she was loose. And if the Federation hadn't caught her yet? She was much closer than anyone anticipated. Including the woman who knew her best.

Nevertheless, Miranda had no idea how the hell Danielle was going to get them *out* of there. The only way Miranda was leaving was if she was released—or if the whole building went into meltdown and she slipped out the back. But then she would be a fugitive on the run. Where would she go? To her father's embrace?

Danielle had better know what she was doing.

Except Danielle had no damn idea. She was fueled by nothing but instinct as she took one last, longing look at Miranda and continued through the vents. Even above the hum of the computers locking tightly onto Miranda's visage, she heard the faint clanging of someone moving somewhere they shouldn't be.

Yet a glimmer hope was still a glimmer, wasn't it? *If only I knew what I was hoping for at this point,* Miranda thought. Because she sure as hell wasn't hoping for a personal interview with a man who walked into the room the moment Danielle was out of earshot.

"Captain Hotchner." Joel slapped his tablet onto the table before sitting down. A guard stood at the door, one eye on them, one eye on the hallway. "The commander doesn't know I'm here yet, so we have a few moments to ourselves." He cleared his throat, aware that Miranda's gaze was completely focused on his refusal to make eye contact with her. "I have some questions I desperately need clearing up."

She pursed her lips and stared at a spot on the floor. "I don't know where she is."

"That's what the commander is going to grill you about as soon as she remembers you're here. That's not what I want to ask you."

Miranda rolled her head back. "Then I'm all yours, Captain."

He hesitated before asking his first question.

"Are you the reincarnation of the High Priestess Joiya Lerenan, her name forever in our souls?"

Miranda laughed. How could she help it? The man sounded like a zealot. A zealot who *almost* knew the right questions to ask.

"No," she said. "You've got it all wrong. I don't look like her because I *am* her." She waited for Joel to finally look up from his tablet, interest piqued. "I look like her because I'm her daughter."

Although Joel had prayed for direct answers, he still wasn't expecting that.

Forty-One

"Excuse me?" Joel folded his hands over his tablet. "Could you repeat that for me?"

"I think you heard me." Thunder clashed behind Miranda's eyes when she finally locked on to his once more. "Joiya Lerenan. Your hallowed High Priestess. Wife to the former High Priest Nerilis Dunsman. Yes. Her. She's my mother. I inherited her body." Miranda shrugged. "Isn't that what you want to hear?"

"That doesn't mean I believe such a preposterous claim. There are no records of the two ever having children. I would know."

"You're discounting all of her miscarriages. I kept trying to come, but the Void had bigger plans for my mother. It couldn't have her bloodline living on and compromising her role in the universe. Or so I've been led to understand. My father is a terrible teacher. Very impatient man. He hates the fact I'm nowhere near as powerful as him."

Joel had to pick his jaw off the desk. "Your father. Are you saying he is Nerilis Dunsman?"

"What, don't believe I'm half-*julah?* Use one of your fancy DNA scanners. You'll find out very quickly that my father is a *julah* male."

"You already have a mother on record in your Earth-based files. A miss Kyo—"

"There's always some woman around for my father to knock-up and make sure I arrive safe and sound on the next planet he targets. Like I said, awful father. Kept killing me and bringing me back to life like a nutjob. He could have paid child support like everyone else after the first time he goofed and lost a nut in some woman."

"I..."

"You already know who I'm the reincarnation of," Miranda interrupted. "Look up who my mother was. A madam from the pleasure moon. Eros. You might have heard of it. You may be a religious shit, but you're still a man who probably wishes it was still around."

"That doesn't mean..."

"From my understanding, my first life was a total accident. My father had no idea I would be the result of his one-night stand with some forgettable courtesan. He didn't even know I existed until he came to my planet to wink it out of existence. Let me tell you, that was a rough reunion. He looked at me like you are now." Miranda grinned. "Like you saw me in a painting yesterday. Except his obsession was based in reality. Yours is a lifetime's worth of religious conditioning."

"I want to get this straight." Joel either had to keep talking or succumb to the shock rattling his brain. "You are claiming that not only is your father Nerilis Dunsman... but that your mother is *the* Joiya Lerenan. Although she's never once given birth to you."

"Mmm, not successfully, no. I mean, I don't remember being miscarried. Hard to remember something that never formed memories. Trust me, I have enough, otherwise."

"That makes no sense."

"The Void works in mysterious ways, Captain." Miranda attempted to open her hands in admission, but the chains attaching them to the table rattled until she gave up. "Then again, I don't think most people know that my mother's body was still 'alive' when she Ascended."

While it was true that the common man did not know of Joiya's "death" as how it happened, Joel thought himself a slightly more educated individual when it came to the history and legends of his own religion. The story disseminated to the masses told of a young bride who Ascended to the Void on the morning of her wedding. In truth, Joiya's Ascension occurred the night before, her body left behind as a lifeless, soulless shell.

Someone had to end its suffering. It might as well have been her betrothed.

"I don't know how it works," Miranda continued. "All I know is that one day, several years after my father left the priesthood, little ol' me was born. When he found me on Cerilyn, he didn't merely know it was me because I *looked* like my real mother. But because I *was* her." She shrugged. "Until he started talking to me, of course. He wasn't prepared to bring his wife's body back into the world with a different soul, yet here I am. Honestly, if you ask me, I think I was always meant to be the spitting image of my mother. The Void took it to an extreme."

Joel did not betray the tension in his heart. Looking at Miranda as she spoke certainly did give credence to her being who she claimed to be, but looking away? If he hadn't seen videos or heard audio recordings of the High Priestess when she was mortal, he would never make the connection. Joiya Lerenan was, by all accounts, a sophisticated woman of vast intelligence and talent. Nobody questioned why the Void chose *her,* the youngest student at the Academy in thousands of years and a woman deigned good enough to marry the future High Priest. Joiya's position, both in the Academy and as Nerilis's lover, elevated her small family in ways the Lerenans still could not fathom. Their daughter was a martyr and a holy figure. The Temple of the Void had no central iconography since its ancient origins, yet here came a woman specifically chosen to help rein in the horrors happening from within the Void itself.

Martyr. Joel squeezed the stylus in his hand. *Holy Mother. Prophet.* He flattened both hands against the table. *Hero.*

This woman before him was none of those things. She may be the reincarnation of a woman who once held insurmountable power on her planet and almost heralded a new age of relations between the Federation and the mercenary cult, but that's where the similarities ended.

"Sir," the guard standing in the doorway poked his head in toward Joel, "the Commander is coming soon. She'll want..."

"Yes. Of course." Joel gathered his things and stood. "Thank you, Captain Hotchner. This has been... very enlightening." He turned to the guard. "I want a warrant for a DNA test," he muttered. "Get it ASAP. The twenty-minute kind.

This woman's DNA will be tested before the Commander lays a finger on her, understand? If d'Alacron does anything... stall her, and inform me. I have some calls to make."

"Yes, sir. Ah..."

"What is it?"

The guard hesitated. "Do you really believe her?" He glanced at Miranda, sitting primly in her prisoner's seat. "That was a wild tale."

Joel took a step into the hallway. "We'll find out, won't we?"

The guard bounced between both of his feet, eyes dancing from Miranda to Joel as he sauntered down the hall. As soon as the guard was relieved from duty, he hightailed it to the warrant office five floors down.

Although Devon had not been taken into formal custody, Yara *helpfully* reminded him that agreement came before Danielle disappeared into the bowels of the building—and hadn't been found since. Occasionally, they overheard the tale of the woman found on the floor of a basement break room, or the officer who lost his sensor—oh, and who could forget the vent grate found on the elevator floor?—but Danielle's whereabouts remained unknown, no matter who was looking and how many took up the cause. Until she was located, Devon was considered an accomplice, and there was no talking himself out of it.

"Sit." Yara had the honors of slamming Devon down into the seat in front of Miranda. Unlike Miranda's hands, which were attached to the table between them, Devon's had been tied behind his back from the moment they left Yara's office. She stood at the head of the table, a handheld firearm on her waist and a knife strapped to her arm. Both Devon and Miranda had to admit she looked more formidable now than she had earlier that day, and neither of them cared much for it. "Let's see if you two can jog each other's memories. First, I want to know where Danielle Cromwell is and what she's doing. Second, I want to know where Nerilis Dunsman is and what *he's* planning."

Miranda rolled her eyes and head simultaneously; Devon choked down a laugh. Yara's broken record was more obnoxious than the water droplets falling from a basement pipe.

"No. Idea." Miranda scoffed. "About either. Doesn't matter how many times you ask."

Yara turned her attention to Devon. "I told you everything I know," he said before she could harass him. "Sulim feels at home in the vents. That's all I know." Although he was not wont to throw Miranda under *every* bus to cross their path, he couldn't help it this time. "She knows more about the crazy asshole than anyone else."

"Thanks," Miranda said, "but I still don't know where either of them are."

"If you knew, would you tell me?"

Did Yara think that was some kind of *gotcha?* "If I did know where she was," Miranda said, assuming she was speaking both for herself and Devon, "it would depend. Are you going to hurt her when you find her? Because I don't think I want to help with that."

"Ultimately, all I care about is finding Nerilis Dunsman. Can you *not* understand why I care about that?"

"Oh, I understand."

Both of her prisoners had said that at the same time, yet with incredibly different inflections. Miranda heaved her words with the wariness of a woman who was tired of being asked the same question over and over. Devon was about to hit the table with both of his knees as he lurched toward Yara, who jerked back, hand on her firearm. The guards at the door likewise moved into position. Once Devon realized that acting out was likely to get everyone killed, he forced himself back into his chair and avoided Miranda's gaze.

Yara lowered her guard only a little. "I see I've hit a nerve."

This time, it was Miranda who couldn't bite back her words. "All you care about is yourself. Finding your wanted criminal is simply to solidify yourself as some great champion of the Federation. Your name and your legacy. That's all that matters to you. Ever since you became the commander, it's all about cementing yourself as the bitch who caught the most powerful *julah* to ever live."

Devon didn't disagree with her, but that wasn't what he meant when he almost got them killed. "You're also so obsessed with who you used to be. How many times do I have to tell you that you don't *want* to remember that crap? Count yourself lucky that you're not in the Process and living that nightmare at various points throughout your goddamn day."

"You two are... spicy." Yara sniffed up her pride. "My personal business has nothing to do with-"

"Would you just hit me already?" Miranda interrupted. "It's been clear all day that you want to punch me in the face. Go ahead. Get it out of your system and live the rest of your damn mulligan. I don't know what's clung to your soul and made you so pissy about me, 'cause it's not like I killed your mom in front of you or anything."

"Why do you have to do that?" Devon asked.

"In fact, the only thing I remember you having a serious problem with was how popular I was compared to you. Is this some mean girl shit? Does my mere presence trigger you so much that all you can think about is how much the chief liked me more than you?"

Miranda knew she threw more wood onto a raging fire, but couldn't help herself. Much like Yara barely contained herself when she snatched Miranda by the throat and pressed her head against the back of her chair.

Both guards looked as if they didn't know what to do. Devon tugged at the cord holding his hands behind his back, but couldn't free himself in time. Yara's hand squeezed Miranda's throat, and the only thing keeping her from murder in the interview room was that so many eyes were on her.

But that didn't mean she was in a hurry to release her hold.

"You got everything you wanted," Yara muttered in Old Basic. "You were the chief's favorite. Everything you wanted, she gave you. You didn't even appreciate it. What did I get? I got her crumbs. She barely knew I was there except for when you dragged me into your shit. And then what did you do? You killed her. Couldn't take it anymore, huh? You couldn't wait. She was grooming you, was going to make you her Second the moment you turned twenty. She told me herself. The night before I died, she told me all her plans for you. Made sure I knew how much I had *failed,* and how disappointed she was in me. She was going to make you all hers, and I was going to be left in the *dust.*"

Her hand tightened around Miranda's throat. She wasn't stopping until Miranda finally gave in and winced for her life.

Yara snatched her hand away. An imprint reddened against Miranda's throat, which gasped for air as the rest of her fell into a spasm of laughter.

"Me? Had everything? Oh, I was definitely her favorite! I really loved the part where that meant she beat the crap out of me whenever she felt like it! Not to mention what she did when we were alone." Miranda was still laughing. "You were there, sometimes! Telling me how bad you felt for me. Then you offered yourself up like the willing victim you always were. You know why I killed her? You know what sent me over the edge, *Kila?*"

Yara jerked back. When Miranda looked her right in the eye and said that name again, it was like staring into a mirror that reflected the lives they should have been desperate to leave behind.

"Your funeral." Miranda wasn't stopping, even with a constricted throat and a desperate desire to cough. "That cunt pretended that she was your best friend whom you confessed all your deepest dreams and desires to. Completely absolved herself of her involvement in your death." She turned her attention to Devon. "Didn't she? That's what the chief said."

Devon sighed. "Something like that. That wasn't the highlight of the day."

"No. Suppose not. Was probably me ramming my knife into her stomach and spitting on her writhing body. Sooooo much blood. It got in my hair, and you both know I didn't have much hair back then."

"I thought the bodyguard or literally anyone else would take you out the moment it happened," Devon said.

"You know why nobody did? Not that I would have cared..." Miranda bit her lip. "Because everyone hated that bitch. I simply did what everyone else wanted to do. There wasn't a soul there that day that didn't hear what she said about you and think something should be done to stop it. So... I shut her up." Miranda wasn't finished, though. "You know what really pisses me off about this situation right now? It's not you acting like an entitled brat because your soul got wired wrong when it was reincarnated. It's you accusing me of all this twisted shit when you know damn well that she was my worst nightmare. Out of all the trauma I've spent the past thousand years unpacking, *her* shit is what haunts me when I go to sleep. This is the woman who hit me so hard I got a concussion from her bare fist. Hmph. Let's not forget she *bought me* from my mother when I was a kid, and didn't let her purchase go to spoil that first night."

Devon winced. Some things had been assumed, but never confirmed.

"And to top it all off," Miranda said, "I was the one who found you. While I was off dissociating through another night of her bullshit, you were in our room dying because you wished it was you. You knew damn well I would be the one who found you in the morning. That's what you wanted. To punish me for being her favorite punching bag. Well... if your goal was to make sure I never forgot you, it worked. I don't know how you lost that eye, *Commander,* but it in no way compares to what we both lost back then."

Yara squeezed her fingers against her hips. "I lost this eye," she said, pulling aside her bangs so Miranda could get a good look at the healed gash that had once been Yara's right eye, "when someone I cared for betrayed me. You know why I've never had it replaced? Because I don't need to forget what happens when someone I trust throws me to the wolves."

"So you became the wolf instead." Miranda chuckled. "Poetic. By the way, I still don't know where Nerilis Dunsman is."

Yara's frown was caustic enough to make Miranda squirm a little, but neither of them backed down from their unholy causes. The Commander scoffed as she stepped away from the table. Her attentions were soon turned to Devon, who had been wishing he could forget everything Miranda revealed.

"Commander." One of her many guards pushed through those before the door and stood to attention once he caught Lana's eye. "Sorry to interrupt, but Master Marlow is here and demanding an audience."

Yara smacked the back of Devon's chair. "Of course he is."

"He's in your office right now. I'm sorry, we... we tried to hold him and his assistant back, but because most of our men are currently searching the–"

"Of *course* he is." Yara couldn't decide whether to glare at Devon or Miranda for this interruption. Surely, one of them was behind it. Never mind the fact she had taken into custody a man she had brokered a deal with, and had in her possession a woman Marlow knew more about than he cared to admit. "Keep them in there. I shall handle this." She poked her finger into the guard's chest on her way out of the room. "These two do *not* leave this room, do you understand. And I want the rest of you quiet. If they talk to each other, we need it easily recorded on the cameras for later."

Yara flew down the hallway. The guards were about to close the door—two of them inside guarding the suspects, and two outside guarding against invaders—when one of Joel d'Kerni's top men chose that moment to appear.

"I have a warrant from downstairs." He presented it to the men outside, who soon summoned those inside. "To acquire the DNA of the female suspect."

After perusing the document, the man was ushered inside. He already had on him a sterilized DNA scanner and a kit to take a physical sample downstairs.

If Miranda thought she was getting out of a needle, however, she was sorely mistaken. Much like her arm after the man jabbed her. As she looked away and sucked in her breath, Devon rolled his back against his chair and continued to wonder how the *hell* he kept getting in these situations.

"Much obliged," the man said, slapping a bandage on Miranda's arm. "Now, please open your mouth."

"You already have my blood," she snapped back. "Does that not tell you everything you need to know?"

"Please open your mouth."

While her arm throbbed in displeasure, Miranda reluctantly dropped her jaw.

"What the hell was that about?" Devon asked as soon as the man was gone with his samples. "Could have lived my whole life without seeing that."

"Aww, do needles make you woozy?" Fine thing for Miranda to ask that when she was feeling a bit woozy herself.

"By the way," Devon said through gritted teeth, "you look like shit."

"Yet here you are, staring at me. You haven't thrown up yet, so the sight must not be too bad."

Devon hated it when she was right.

Forty-Two

There was no pretense of civility or hospitality. No offers of *cageh* or suggestions that they take the interview to a more "comfortable" place. As far as Commander d'Alacron was concerned, Marlow could eat shit and choke on it.

Her glare said as much when she appeared in her office, boorish gaze hitting the old man right in the face.

"Very presumptuous of you to assume I have all the time in the world to entertain you, *Master* Marlow." The only reason she extended the use of his title was to say it with disdain. Sure enough, Marlow got the message—he didn't wait for her to sit down across from him, after all. He actually turned around on the couch, hands slipping off the top of his cane. "Give me one good reason I don't arrest you for treason right now."

He snorted. Although he played her words off as nothing more than the inane ramblings of a short-lived human, he chose his own carefully. "Treaty of Dah comes to mind. I know neither of us was alive when it was signed between our races, and my politicking isn't as good as my spiritualing, but I definitely remember what it implies."

Yara loomed over him. "Take your treaty of privilege and shove it up your useless ass." Yara shot a look at Lanelle, sitting right next to her boss. "Why the hell are you here? Fancy getting arrested as well?"

"Commander," Marlow said, redirecting her attention. "There seems to have been a mistake somewhere along the way today. Are my employees correct when they tell me you have taken Devon into custody? After the agreement we had that he would come freely to speak to you in exchange for his own freedom?"

Yara's smirk did not reassure the man whose breath tightened in his chest. "Things have changed, Master Marlow. Mr. Anderson is a man of great interest right now. See, things are not going to plan today. I'm afraid that your other mercenary, whom you so *helpfully* unleashed upon this world, is out of her mind and currently, as we *speak,* crawling around the building's ventilation doing Void only knows what."

"Huh?" Lanelle looked toward the ceiling. "Run that by us one more time."

"I do not take orders from you. In fact, it may shock you, I do not take orders from *anyone.*" That included the President of the Federation, a person who was more figurehead than someone like Yara to take *seriously.* When it came to listing the most powerful people—politically speaking, of course—in the Federation, the commander swam among the names of the President and the High Priest of the Void.

The president? A pebble in the commander's shoe. What the hell could she do, hmm?

"I am a very busy woman, Master Marlow," Yara continued. "So unless you have information that I care about, I am afraid I must ask you to either leave, or be taken into protective custody."

Marlow heaved himself off the couch. Lana readied to tell her men behind her to take one of the most powerful *julah* to cross their lifetimes into custody. Marlow may not go quietly, but he would be reserved in using any sorcery that might either compromise his position in the Federation or the lives of the soldiers following orders.

"Am I correct in understanding that you are currently holding *three* delicate souls without any true representation? Dare I assume you have not offered it to them? If that is the case, then I insist that I represent the needs and interests of the three you have taken into custody today!"

Yara laughed right in his face. "Considering you're not a certified man of the law, I find that hilarious. I hate to break it to you, Mr. Marlow, but not everyone we interrogate is afforded the same paltry rights. We're not talking about embezzlers or thieves. This all traces back to the biggest terrorist in our history. I am well within my right as Commander to arrest and interrogate anyone I believe may be harboring or abetting such a fugitive. Why would I agree to let *you,* of all people, represent them? The only reason none of my predecessors ever raked you over the coals is because of your treaties."

Marlow curled his lips back into a feral frown. "You do not read back far enough into your own appointment's history, Commander," he snarled. "For I have very blatant memories of what it means to be taken into *your* kind of custody. One thousand years ago, I was taken down to this very building's basement and left there to rot for *days* until I was 'ready' to talk about what the ex-High Priest had done to two uninhabited planets. So don't think for two seconds I don't know what you're doing with my charges. The only reason they're probably not dead right now is because of the spite they've been carrying with them over a hundred lives."

"A hundred lives. How many planets does that make, Master Marlow? How many trillions dead? Fuck their collective three-hundred lives. There are an innumerable number of people dead because of one man's crusade, and I *will* see justice brought to him before the end of my tenure."

"You do not know what you play with, Commander," Marlow said. "Out of the three people in your possession, only one has completely broken free from the Process. If the other two die while in your custody, not only will you be guilty of a spiritual manslaughter nobody has ever witnessed before..." He rounded the couch, cane smacking against the floor. "But the whole universe will hear their screams when everyone goes to sleep tonight. Do not try it, Commander. Even you are not that cruel."

"Cruel," Yara spat back at him. "You think what I do is *cruel.* I ask you, Master Marlow, who was the fool who put those three in that position in the first place? Will you shirk your place in their 'spiritual manslaughter' and put the blame upon your companion's shoulders?"

"He has been no companion of mine since the Ascension."

Lanelle raised herself up from the couch and put a hand on Marlow's shoulder. "We should go. We are not going to do them any good here. We'll rendezvous with Evan and–"

"You think I do not know my place, Commander?" Marlow spat, every speck of his aura enveloping the women around him. While Lanelle sank back down to the cushions, Yara pretended that she was not the slightest bit intimidated by the sight of a fully-grown *julah* who knew how to break her neck with the snap of his fingers. "I was there. I left the priesthood that day. We saw the greatest spiritual sight of the past hundred-thousand years and couldn't bear to look again. So do not ask me if I shirk my place in this universal farce. I may have been desperate, but I knew what I was doing when I enslaved those two to the whim of the Void."

Yara lowered his arms. "Those two."

Finally, the anger cracked on Marlow's face. "I mean..."

"Those two," Yara repeated. "Sonall Gardiah and Sulim di'Graelic. Those are the only two you put into the Process. Don't lie to me any longer. I knew you were lying the moment you claimed to have put Cairn di'Cerilyn into the Process." She spun her foot around and huffed her way to the door. "Either get out of my office *now*," she cried, "or fuck the Treaty of Dah!"

Lanelle grabbed Marlow by the arm and pushed him toward another door. "We need to go. Now. We're no use to them if we're taken into custody, too. Evan barely knows what the hell he's doing out there."

"All right," Marlow relented, shame coloring his cheeks. "Let us gather the Amyrans and–"

He was soon interrupted by none other than a familiar voice popping out of every speaker in the building. Even Lara, who had been angry enough to strangle one of her own soldiers, stopped dead in her tracks and turned her ear toward the nearest speaker.

"No way," Lanelle muttered, hand sliding off Marlow's shoulder. She and her employer were the only ones around who understood every word of Old Basic dripping from the crackling speakers.

"Still looking for me?" Although it was Danielle's voice, one could only characterize the person speaking as *Sulim*. "You will never catch me. Send your best men in this age and they still won't find or catch me. I am among you right now. Every step you take tickles my throat." She paused, laughter peppering her words. "If you feel me on your fingertips, I slip away. See me in the corner of your eye, and I disappear. Do you not know my worth? Because I know yours. Once upon a time, I would have been paid millions to help eliminate every single one of you, and I would have done it."

"Find her!" Yara yelled over the ensuing rabble. Her soldiers did not understand what Sulim said, but Yara did. She understood well enough that she was at Sulim's mercy. "That communication must be coming from the seventeenth-floor broadcast center! *Find her!*"

"Commander d'Alacron," Sulim called her by name, bringing the whites of Lara's eyes out as prominently as the white of her throat. "If you do not want this building to be compromised, then you will bring both of your captors to the basement garage. After you release them to me, I will shut down the security's self-destruct mechanism. No, no, not the new one you must have installed in recent centuries. The *old* one I've found deep in the ass of the records room. Looks like one of many I tampered with once upon a time. It will be faster and easier for you to give in to my demands than to find someone who knows ancient tech like I do. Do you want to play with all the lives of the people in this building? In this neighborhood? How close are we to the capitol building, Commander? I hear your President is currently entertaining the *julah* ambassador. Would be a shame if all of them got hurt because *your* crusade endangered them."

"This isn't good," Lanelle said.

"No," Marlow agreed. "It sounds like she's skirting the edge of regression. If nobody's careful..."

"I know." Yet Lanelle was helpless as Lana disappeared from the room, a contingent of soldiers following her. "I will take the Amyrans and find Evan. We'll go with Plan B immediately."

"Do be careful." Marlow's hand lingered on her arm before she slipped out while every soldier was distracted with the Commander's orders. "Remember, you can exit the Process anytime you wish."

Lanelle hesitated at the end of the couch. "It won't come to that," she assured him. "Just like it won't come to you missing a well-timed teleportation at the very last minute. I hear you're grand at those."

Marlow's face retained its pallor. "I'm getting old."

"Until you start paying me to change your diapers, you're not too old to get yourself out of trouble."

She always joked when facing the unpleasant realities around them. Yet Marlow couldn't smile as Lanelle disappeared. Nor could he ignore the voice continuing the pound over the speakers.

"Bring them to me, Commander," Sulim demanded. "Or I'll give you a real reason to remember us with nothing but spite."

Marlow's freedom lasted for approximately twenty more seconds. Once Yara remembered he was in there, seven soldiers arrived to apprehend him with barely an apology in their eyes.

He could have felled them all if he truly wanted. Yet Marlow went peacefully, because there was no point finishing what Sulim threatened to start.

Forty-Three

There were times when Danielle snapped out of it—when she gazed upon the people below her and no longer knew what the hell she was doing, let alone how the *hell* she was going to get them all out of this deplorable situation.

Then she saw the depraved look in Yara's eyes as she stormed down the hall, and Sulim didn't have to think twice about what she was about to do.

The people she cared about were in trouble. Most of all, the woman she had sworn to die for was about to lose her ass. If Sulim of a thousand years ago wouldn't have let that happen, how would the Danielle of today fare?

Perhaps that was the scariest thing. Danielle was well-aware that she was losing herself to a person who technically shouldn't exist, but it wasn't like the micro-regressions which had plagued her all her life. This felt *real*. Like she both commanded those memories and channeled the angel born a millennium before. She peered through a crack in the grate above Miranda and Devon's heads and only thought of them as the people she trusted most in the world. For they weren't merely Miranda and Devon, two people who should have been completely oblivious of one another in this life. They were her lovers. Her partners. People who had saved her life more than once and not only valued her soul, but had heard her express how she really felt about being a mercenary on a "barbaric" planet.

They were her family. And not in the *"we're all in this together in this life"* kind of family that Cerilyn pushed to make people compliant and reliant on one another. She had chosen them. When her real family abandoned her to her fate, a handful of people from all sorts of backgrounds stood up to take her in and make her one of them.

She loved them. She would die—and even kill—for them.

When thoughts were put that way, there was no denying it. Danielle relied on Sulim's knowledge and instincts as she made her way through the top floor of the building and set into motion the only thing a former top mercenary of her time could achieve.

Thank the Void this structure was *old*. The tech was mostly updated to the past two decades, which made Sulim's head spin when she stole an officer's tablet and attempted to hack the system. Deregistering the device's alarm was difficult enough. So was getting into the OS itself. Danielle's technophobic brain was of absolutely no use—not only did she barely know how to hook up a DVD player, but the Federation technology of a thousand years ago was well-beyond advanced compared to present-day Earth. Sulim once knew how to fly a space cruiser across the Federation without breaking a sweat. Now? She almost lost her lunch hacking into a personal tablet.

But she did it. And the permissions she found within it must have been divined by the Void. Within two minutes of punching buttons in the vents, she accessed the security camera network. From there, she made her way into the PA system.

She only had a flimsy plan, but a flimsy plan was better than no plan when time breathed down her neck.

There was still one big problem, though. This erratic, tenuous link between Danielle's current and past lives meant she wasn't making the soundest decisions. Her instincts said, *"Bring them down to the basement parking structure."* Yet there was no idea beyond that. What did Sulim think she was going to do? Knock out the small army the Commander brought with her? Run away with her family and never look back? Where were they going? Nowhere was safe. This wasn't the Federation of then. There were no longer lawless planets that harbored criminals. After what Nerilis Dunsman did, the Federation made sure of that.

Who would protect them? The *julah?* Even if Marlow wanted to, he could only construct a half-hearted pocket dimension for them to inhabit. And for how long? Wouldn't they miss the sunlight? The fresh air? How long would they live there like house-arrested prisoners, and what would happen when the Federation finally realized what he had done?

Yet Sulim couldn't think of those things. She was beholden to one idea. That one-track mind may be dangerous, but she hadn't been in her right mind for a long, long time.

To the basement.

She estimated it would take her half an hour to slide down the vents, assuming she didn't hurt herself or her passage wasn't blocked along the way. Climbing back up wouldn't be possible, though, so she had to make sure this was the plan she wanted all along.

She stole one last look at Miranda and Devon as they were rounded up by Lara's soldiers and pushed out of the room. Once Danielle realized Marlow wasn't too far away—and his hands were bound as well—she knew she had to go through with her plan.

Down she went.

Yara flanked herself with two of her best men before leading the procession down to the basement garage. Two elevators connected the top floor with the bottom, so she personally escorted Miranda into one and had Devon ride down in the other. Marlow and his guards had to wait for one of the elevators to come back up before Joel d'Kerni had the honors of taking the old man with no one else around.

"Please forgive us, Master Marlow," he apologized after the doors closed. "It's been a hectic day."

"Yes, I suppose scaring the shit out of some innocent people is quite taxing." Marlow declined Joel's offer to be steadied without the proper aid of his walking stick, currently left strung across the couch in Lara's office. Marlow didn't need it with his hands behind his back, but he needed something to steady his bad hip while the elevator lurched downward. He propped himself against the handrail with a sigh. "Your Commander truly does not know what she plays with."

Joel did not appreciate hearing that, if only because he had received the results of Miranda's DNA test a mere minute before he was asked to escort Master Marlow down to the basement. *It confirmed that she is indeed Nerilis Dunsman's daughter.* Joel still didn't quite believe it, if only because the theory was so preposterous. How could that man have a daughter who was the spitting image of a woman who had not given birth to her? Multiple times? If this wasn't such a damn busy day of committing heresy, Joel might go down to the archives and order everything they had on the three suspects. The more photos and written reports, the better.

"The commander has her agenda," Joel agreed. "She believes they can tell her where to find Nerilis Dunsman."

"If anyone knows where he is, it's me," Marlow said. "And I have no idea. The man has pocket dimensions between here and the Void. I've never seen someone who has such an effortless approach to sorcery. There's never been a man like him before, and there never will be again."

Joel turned toward Marlow as the numbers ticked down above them. "Is that how he's able to do alchemy with flesh and blood?"

Marlow snorted. "You're a man of the Temple, are you not, Captain?"

He was hesitant to respond. "Aren't we all, sir?"

"Some more than others. Just because you know the Void is real and that what happens there affects us all, doesn't mean you bother yourself with it. When I was a priest, I was assigned to the Temple you probably attend now. Granted, I was nothing more than an acolyte before I eventually left, but I saw things that we boys of the Academy didn't get in our youth. I personally saw how little humans cared for the place they came from and returned to after death. It was a thing most of you lived with. And here I was, a man who had known almost nothing but the Void from the time I was old enough to look up into the dark sky hovering above my family's estate. So when a man whose life ends in a little over a hundred years takes interest in spiritual matters, I notice."

"I may attend weekly service. My wife may be a core volunteer at our neighborhood shrine. We may have met at a social function put on by the city Temple where you once served a thousand years ago."

"Way more than a thousand. Oof. I was much younger then. I could move around without aid. I had a walking stick even when I chased Nerilis across the universe."

Joel urged the numbers to go down faster. "I don't pretend to know what's going on, sir. I–"

"Merely follow orders? Tale as old as time."

"I wasn't going to say that." Joel finally looked Marlow directly in the eye. What did he expect to see, let alone what did he expect Marlow to look like? This was a man who was older than Joel's direct family line—and he could count back almost a hundred generations. Marlow barely looked older than Joel's own father. He moved like someone who would rather be playing board games in the park than babysitting everyone in the capitol building. As for Joel, who had seen numerous pictures of the man next to him, but had never had a private moment to chat? He might as well ask what had been plaguing him for many nights.

Yet Marlow beat him to it.

"It's heresy, you know." Marlow kept his eyes on the metallic doors before them. "Oh, it doesn't mean much at the end of the day, but if the commander has her way, she will be committing a heresy the likes of which the Temple hasn't seen since my old friend started killing in the name of the Void. If either woman under her watch dies? That's a kind of pain that is not comprehensible to men like you and me. I'll have my own guilt in the situation, but at least I'll know I wasn't the one who killed them. I have a feeling your commander doesn't see things the same way. She's suffering as well, spiritually. But it's no excuse for what she might do to the woman who has inherited dear Joiya's body. In a way, that woman might be the High Priestess's daughter. I wonder how she would feel about that, considering she gave up her own life to stave off the end days for us." What Marlow left out was that the Ascension had only bought the universe a couple thousand more years, and the clock was quickly ticking down. "It's bad enough she's had to see her own daughter come and go from the mortal world because of me. Perhaps I should apologize one day to her."

"It is a shame, sir."

The elevator doors popped open. Marlow patiently awaited Joel to escort him out to the garage. "Not as big of a shame as watching the universe crumble around us."

Marlow was already a master of guilt trips and passive-aggressive jabs, thanks to his short-lived career in the Temple and the ensuing politics that came with his true life's work. Besides, as he had told Joel? He knew a man of pious devotion when he saw one.

"We better get going." Joel urged Marlow to step out ahead. "The commander doesn't want to see us missing, and we don't want to live in a world where she knows we're missing."

Marlow walked, hoping for the best.

"All right!" Yara called to the echoing concrete park around her. "We're here! Let's make this quick!" When she didn't receive a response, she glanced at Miranda, standing not so far behind her. "Please kindly tell her we don't need this building going down in such a busy commercial district. Let alone with us inside. That is assuming," her voice raised again, "you actually have that ability! Last I checked, the self-destruct feature takes quite a few overrides to put into place!"

"She knows how," Miranda muttered. "Unfortunately for us."

"So then let's get this party started. Or do I have to put you in mortal danger for this to get underway?"

What Yara sorely did not understand—and Miranda didn't either, unfortunately—was that Danielle was the least of their problems. Mortal danger only came into play when someone had the sorcery to parry a threat, and that someone was not Lara.

Yet there was no time to consider that when a clatter erupted in the corner of the garage and every gun in the vicinity turned toward the empty vent that *should* have contained a person. For every soldier confused about what they didn't see, there was another looking up at the ceiling and back at the door they used to enter the garage. Yara kept her one wary eye on her men before turning her back toward Miranda and Devon, both of whom were too close for her liking.

"What the hell happened down here?" Devon asked in Old Basic, as if no one around them parsed his words. "What's got Danielle going loco?"

Miranda slowly shook her head. "The fearless leader here wanted to get to me through her, and oh-so-helpfully revealed that I am the reincarnation of her lover."

Devon withheld a gasp as he too looked toward the ceiling, as if he could spot Danielle any better than the trained personnel around them. "You mean the one thing we've all been keeping from her this past year."

"The very same."

"Did she use your name?" That *she* was heavily implied to mean Lara, whom Devon was not wont to mention by name.

"Yup."

"Fuck."

"Yup."

Yara heard them chattering and shot them a glare of warning. As soon as she confirmed both of their mouths were sealed, she turned back to the empty garage before her. Step by careful step, she approached the darkness only protected by the heavy artillery vehicles used for riot control and terrorist threats around Terra III's capital. She kept one hand on her holster, and she was prepared to shoot if spooked.

That was the thing about Yara d'Alacron. She was far from the perfect soldier. She was "perfect enough" to pass every test with flying colors, and the Void knew she had proven herself more than capable in both a soldier's shoes as well as an officer's, but she was still human. She had at least one glaring flaw that superseded her talents in the war room—and on the battlefield.

She was vain. Every time glory touched the tips of her fingers, she forgot most of her training.

Yara turned toward her men and captors. "Where the hell is she?" she demanded of anyone who could answer. "I don't believe for two seconds this place is actually going to blow. Joel!" she snapped at her captain. "Have any of your men found her yet? Make sure the security system hasn't been compromised. Check it ag—"

Guns raised and laser sights focused on the shadow leaping behind Yara and grabbing her by the throat.

Forty-Four

The only gasp louder than the commander's was Miranda's. While her life did not flash before her eyes, she clearly saw Danielle's go through every stage of existence, if only because the end was about to drop down upon her neck like a guillotine released from its starting position.

Was that fear in Danielle's eyes? No. The woman inhabiting her consciousness had dozens of weapons pointed at her before. This might as well be a trip to the market for a woman who could look danger right in the eye and no longer feel her knees tremble.

Then again, that was a time when she had better control of her environments. Today, Danielle held a weapon to the commander's head, and she wasn't sure she knew how to use it.

"Let them go!" Danielle demanded, one arm firmly wrapped around Yara's shoulders while the commander futilely pulled at it. The other arm held the gun to Yara's temple. Yet no matter how much the commander wiggled in Danielle's embrace, nobody budged from that spot. All Yara's wiggling did was make Danielle tighten her hold, slowly choking the commander until she lost most of her strength. Danielle looked as crazed as she sounded, eyes glaringly wide and hair dusty and mussed from her time in the vents. The jacket she had stolen was brown in spots and wrinkled against her muscular body. If nobody had recognized her, they would have mistaken Danielle for a terrorist who had managed to stumble in at the right time.

Except this was no terrorist in the traditional sense. This was a spiritually compromised human machine made for killing.

"I'll do it." Danielle continued to speak in Old Basic, but the gist of her words and the tone of her voice made it clear to the modern humans what she meant. "I'll kill her right here if you don't let them go. *Both* of them. Let them go and let us get the outta here."

"Where we gonna go?" Miranda yelled back at her. "What are you doing, Sulim?"

"She won't kill me!" Yara called out above them both. "That's her whole shtick, right? The useless mercenary who won't kill a fly."

"She might not have killed them," Devon muttered, "but she definitely hurt them a time or two. I *really* don't think you want to push her!"

Danielle tightened her hand around the back of Yara's neck. "Have you not heard me? Let them go!"

"For the love of God..." Yara couldn't believe she had to translate this—not while her airway was constricted and her feet slid against the concrete beneath her. "Release them!"

Miranda and Devon could hardly believe it, but were they truly surprised that Yara caved so easily? *That means she has a Plan B,* Miranda surmised as her wrists were finally freed and she was pushed forward. *What could she be planning?* Devon had as much hope as the woman next to him when he joined Miranda only a few feet away from Danielle, who recognized them with a flick of her eyelashes.

"Sulim." Miranda held up her hands by her chest. "Put the weapon down and release Commander d'Alacron. Let's not get any of us killed here today." The reality choked Miranda like Danielle choked Yara. "We need to make sure neither of us dies today."

The most concerning thing to Miranda wasn't her own fate—it was that haggard look in Danielle's eyes that was neither "her" nor Sulim. One second it was the same visage Miranda remembered from years so long ago that only the *julah* were around to remember. The next? She saw the unassuming woman who had kept her head down for ten years and was still fed a court-martial for breakfast. Miranda might as well have been watching the numbers tick down on a bomb.

"You two get out of here." The words wavered between Old Basic and English—barely intelligible enough for most to get the gist of what she said.

"Where are we supposed to go?" Devon held out one hand, his futile attempt to get Danielle to hand over her weapon not making him friends. "We're not going without you."

Danielle plucked the knife off Yara's arm and kicked it toward Devon. He didn't dare bend down to grab it. Nor did Miranda act more than a little bit interested in the firearm coming out of Yara's holster and sliding toward her.

"Come on. Grab them and get the hell out of here."

Miranda thought of the most tactful way to tell Danielle—or was it Sulim?—that her brain was officially fried by the Void. "If we grab these weapons, they're going to take us out. That's all there is to it."

"You should listen to them," Yara said. "It's you versus everyone here. And we don't negotiate with terrorists. They'll let me die before giving you what you want."

"So then go ahead and shoot me."

"No!" Miranda drew more attention to herself than to Danielle, at least. Did it feel great having all of those firearms pointed toward her? About as swell as the sword of Damocles grazing her neck hairs. "Danielle. Sulim... you don't want to die right now. Not only are you not yet free..." She couldn't believe she was doing it, yet once the first tear fell down her cheek, she was capitulating like one of Yara's toadies. "I didn't wait a thousand years to lose you like this. Okay? Please, we will sort this out. You're not in your right mind right now. You've been triggered into a regression, but it's not really *you*. This isn't how it's supposed to be. *Please.*" She both begged Danielle to come back to her wits, and for the soldiers around her to give mercy when apprehending them all over again. Because it was going to happen. No way were they letting Danielle walk away after what she had pulled.

Sulim looked her right in the eye, barrel of her firearm still pointing into Yara's temple. *She's not going to have the strength to hold that woman much longer.* Miranda hated to admit it, but regardless of how fit Danielle was now, it was nothing like she had been during the glory days as Cerilyn's upper echelon of talented mercenaries. Her stamina, in particular, was lacking. Meanwhile, Yara was still in her physical prime. As soon as she gathered her bearings, she'd ruin Danielle's day.

"Do something!" Miranda yelled at the old man still in his cuffs. "She's going to get herself killed!"

How helpless was she that she couldn't do a damn thing, even with her hands free and her fully-actualized brain in her head? Miranda had been in plenty of deplorable situations in this life alone, but nothing had compared to this. She saw her lover's demise flashing before her eyes, and it would happen right here, right now, if someone didn't do something.

But there were too many weapons pointed at them. The law wasn't on their side. Danielle blew her chance at a pardon when she held the Commander of the Federation Forces hostage. Yara hadn't exactly proven herself incapable of holding a grudge after so long. Did Sulim even know who she held in her arms? This didn't add fuel to the fire—it destroyed the very foundation the fire blazed upon.

Yara knew that. As soon as Danielle proved herself more confused by Miranda's spectacle than anything else, the Commander took her chance to fling her legs into the air with a grunt mighty enough to knock Danielle back on her feet. The firearm clattered to the ground. The only thing that kept the soldiers from opening fire was the fact that Danielle's gun did not go off when it made impact.

Instead, she was the one shrieking when she made impact.

"I have had *enough* of this shit!" Yara didn't simply slam her body weight upon Danielle to keep her in place. She returned the suffocating honors by wrapping her hand around the back of Danielle's neck and nearly snapping her shoulder out of its socket. The cry of alarm was enough to make most of the soldiers take a step back while Devon and Miranda resisted the urge to rush forward and tackle the commander. Joel d'Kerni held up his hand to ensure nobody fired *anything*. "The three of you are all going away for a *very* long time, so help me the goddamn Void and the bitch that made this all happen!"

She looked at Miranda when she said that. While Miranda knew Yara referred to the High Priestess, she also knew when to take things personally. That was directed at her as much as it was anyone else.

Which meant Joel saw the ultimate heresy when it slapped him in the face.

"What are you waiting for?" Yara shrieked. "Take them all back into custody! Marlow too! I want them in separate cells within the hour!"

The captain hesitated before he grabbed Miranda by the arm. "I'm sorry," he said. "I'll make sure none of you are harmed."

It wasn't good enough for Miranda, who saw the fear in Danielle's eyes as she pushed away the intrusive thoughts that claimed her conscience. Sulim wasn't going to save any of them now. It was impossible. This wasn't the world of a thousand years ago, and her body wasn't the same. Even if Danielle could overthrow Yara once more, the standoff was over. Everything they did only led to a higher chance of death.

"No..." Miranda saw the future now. Their lives were ruined. This had gone beyond a misunderstanding that her father may or may not get her out of—and he would get no one else out. How long would they waste in prison? What would happen to their lives on Earth? Would she and Danielle ever have that life they worked so hard for not so long ago?

This was it. Her final chance to halt the madness.

She just had to want it.

"Stop!"

That was the word she thought, yet it wasn't the sound she made when she broke free from Joel's hand and flung her hands before her. The single syllable that coated her tongue was neither English nor any age of Basic, and it didn't cease its echoing as Miranda's thoughts compounded upon one another.

The thing about Julah was that it was the closest language to the Harmony of the universe. No matter how hard Miranda thought in another tongue, when her desperation manifested before her, only the Harmony spoke through her actions. There wasn't a soul in the room who didn't understand the metaphysical voice of the cosmos. It rang in their ears and sang in their veins, touching an old, hardened *julah* who had seen everything in his longer life—and slapped a pious human across his cheek when Miranda reached for the commander.

Yara understood that word, too. For a moment, she no longer felt the burden of trauma pricking her skin when she looked upon the three former players of an old life. Instead, she was assuaged by the Harmony that had soothed trillions of wayward souls since the dawn of life.

When the echo finally faded, weapons clattered to the ground and Yara was frozen where she stood. As long as Miranda locked her eyes on the woman intending to do harm, Yara wasn't going anywhere. Her muscles had long lost their ability to flex and move. Her skin bristled beneath the burden of ancient magic that was never meant to leave its sieve. Her tongue dried and flopped out of her mouth.

With a flick of Miranda's wrist, Yara was flung across the ground. The moment she landed, gravity pulled her back down toward the core of Terra III, and her knuckles struggled to twitch as her heart slowed in her chest.

Joel likewise fell to the ground, but it wasn't because Miranda had directed her ire at him. The man was in such shock that he collapsed between Miranda and the man dancing around him.

"Careful." Marlow was the only one brave enough to touch Miranda, who kept her glare fixated on Yara and Danielle. The only reason Danielle had yet to get up was because of the shock claiming her as well. "You don't want to kill her. All the sorcery in the world won't save you if you're caught killing the Commander of the Federation Forces." Marlow placed a gentle hand on Miranda's wrist. Only then did she tremble, her righteous anger overflowing. "You're not as strong as your parents."

Stubbornness attempted to rule over Miranda's conscience, but she eventually resigned to the fatigue now consuming her. As she wobbled against Marlow's frame, the soldiers attempted to pick up their broken weapons.

"Don't! That's an order!" Joel pushed himself back up to his feet. Before Devon had the chance to go to Danielle, the captain slapped a hand on his shoulder, a friendly—but firm—insinuation that anyone who didn't want to get into any further trouble should stand stark still. "Are you all right, Commander?"

Yara groaned.

"Suppose a metaphysical punch to the face doesn't feel that good," Marlow quipped. "Can't recall. It's been so long since it was my turn."

"Master Marlow," Joel turned toward him, "I am going to clean up this mess and see to it that the commander is sequestered to the medical center next door. Is there anything I should tell the personnel there about how to treat her?"

Marlow kept one wary eye on the commander's ailing body, but it wasn't her physical health he considered. "See if you can't find Dr. Rea d'Eran and send her down. For all of them."

"The reincarnation specialist?"

"Are you daft and don't see what's happening to these people?"

Joel relented, but only because he was in over his head. Especially when he considered the woman whose chest heaved so hard that Marlow had to put both hands on her shoulders.

"Get a hold of yourself." He made sure he had Miranda's attention before continuing. "You don't get the luxury of witnessing the first time you've done something like this in the comfort of your own home. Or the Academy for that matter. You did a very *legally* controlled thing in front of the top brass of the Federation Forces. I need you to snap yourself out of this if you want to get out of here a free woman."

"Not gonna lie," Devon said, not hiding the fact he had been eavesdropping. "Not sure how any of us are getting out of here a free *anything*."

Marlow cleared his throat and lowered his hands from Miranda's shoulders. "Yes, well... depending on how things go for Lanelle and Evan at the capitol, we might be able to pull some pardons out of our asses. But that will be it. After tonight? I don't think there's a damn thing I could ever do again to keep you three out of legal trouble. I've burned every bridge and used up every favor I had to my name." He sighed. "After this, I'm looking at a forced vacation to my family's estate."

Devon wasn't one to announce how humbled he was. The best he could do was mutter a thanks before asking the captain if he was free to check on Danielle now.

"Or maybe…" He gestured to Miranda, whose anger had depleted into a deep, aching doom. "Maybe it's best if you do it. Who knows? Maybe she's still triggered and needs to see you're safe before we do anything else."

Miranda spared him a single, sorrowful glance. "No." She conceded with a turn of her heels. She didn't know where she was going, but she knew she shouldn't be around when Danielle regathered more of her bearings. "It's too volatile for me to do it. You weren't there when we were…" She sighed. "The real Danielle is pretty pissed at me right now. I wouldn't want to trigger her further into a forced regression by hanging around. You do it." This time, when someone put their hand on someone's shoulder, it was with the reassurance of wanting to see a job well done. "She'll know where to find me."

"But…"

"Someone she trusts should be by her side," Miranda said. "That's not me."

"Where the hell are you going?"

Miranda stood before Joel, ignoring Devon. "Do you believe me now, Captain?"

Joel snapped his fingers for two of his underlings to fetch the commander. "In the face of so much evidence?" he asked. "I'd be a fool to deny what I've seen here today. Forgive me, though, if it takes me a while to fully accept it. I also doubt hardly anyone would believe me if I said a damn thing."

"Probably for the best," Marlow said behind Joel. "The Temple does not know of her existence. Probably. Honestly…" His sigh was so loud that more than one person looked in his direction. "I have no idea anymore."

Miranda waited for Marlow to be distracted by a soldier looking to put him in bondage once more. "You must get me out of here, Captain," Miranda said. "Your commander has a grudge against me, personally, but I've done nothing wrong. Like he said, though," she referred to Marlow, who finally talked himself out of more handcuffs, "the authorities do not know about me. If you want to help my mother in any way, you'll forget about what happened here today and make sure the commander doesn't continue this farce of an 'investigation.' I do not know where my father is. Trust me, if I did, I might be inclined to tell you to get him off my ass."

Joel held up his hands. "I can't make any promises, but I may be able to get you out of here under cover of darkness. As for them..."

Miranda didn't have to turn around to know whom he meant. "They can take care of themselves. Devon is more than equipped to handle her should she truly regress." Just saying the words made spit choke her throat. "It's for the best if I'm not personally around for it if it's to happen under these circumstances."

"I'm not sure who you *really* are..." Joel said with mild wonder, "but..."

"Captain!" A soldier leaned out of the door leading back into the main building. "The bus is here for the commander. Should I send in the medics?"

"Are they military?"

"Of course, sir."

Joel motioned for the team of medics to enter with their small hovercraft that would keep Yara's body still and stable as they maneuvered her into their ambulance and relegated her to the private military suite next door. When Joel asked his own top soldier what else he had heard, he received a small dance between feet and a mouth that wouldn't quite say what was on his mind.

"Out with it," Joel said.

"We've made contact with Dr. d'Eran." That wasn't all, apparently. "And the pres... the president is on the secure line when you're ready."

"The president?"

"Yes, sir. President d'Errowyn apparently knows of the situation here and wants to talk to you." The soldier's eyes darted toward Devon, who leaned over Danielle's half-unconscious body. "And him. But you first."

Joel caught Marlow's attention. "This is your doing, I suppose?"

Marlow shrugged. "The Void works in mysterious ways."

With a grunt, Joel announced that he would take that call in another moment. Right now, he had a more pressing matter.

"I will do my best to erase what happened here tonight," he said to Miranda. "I make no promises, though. Once the commander comes to, it could be my head. But I took an oath when I joined the Forces. One you probably remember well."

"Let me guess," Miranda drolly said. "Service to the Federation, which includes matters both physical and spiritual." She chuckled. "I've never taken an oath like that, but I can respect it. Especially if it gets me out of trouble."

Joel nodded. "As you may imagine, unless I think you've done something reprehensible enough to keep you apprehended, there is no reason to keep you here."

"What about them?"

"Since they are known entities, we will do this the diplomatic way. As for you... it's best that you go now. You and Master Marlow can slip out the back. My men will look the other way." His next few words were reserved for Marlow, whose attentions he had to seek one last time. "After you take her where she needs to go, please do come back and answer a few questions regarding the future of your charges. I will be personally taking them to the medical center as well, since that is where Dr. d'Eran shall be."

"I do hope we haven't created *too* much of a mess this time, Captain. Seems like only a few months ago we were having another standoff with the commander. Remember a few of my own kind there as well."

"I missed that fracas," Joel said, "but if you ask me, most of this mess is because of the commander, who is clearly not in the right mind. I will be working closely with Dr. d'Eran and the medical staff to find out if a leave of absence might be in order."

Miranda stuck close to Marlow while Yara was loaded onto the hovercraft. A lone medic knelt next to Danielle, who slowly stirred between him and Devon. Soon, both men leaned back to give her air. "Some time off would do her good. She has a lot to think about." *And hopefully not think much about,* Miranda personally added. "I only wish her peace."

"Sir!" Joel's soldier was back. "The president can't wait for you much longer."

"Allow me to take this, Master Marlow. Miss... ah..."

"I'm a captain as well, Captain." Miranda's fingers spread across her hips. "Just don't call me Chief. Those days are long behind me. I think the three of us would be quite happy to keep moving forward with our present lives, regardless of how much the commander should like to drag us back in time with her."

"Right." Joel stepped backward. "Captain. You should probably get going."

Although Miranda was relieved to steal away from the scene with the only man whose power compared to her own father's, she was not wont to look away from Danielle, who was finally sitting up with the help of the medic. Her confused countenance wouldn't linger for long. The moment she saw Miranda, she might launch into a spell nobody could save her from—least of all the woman who wanted nothing more than to hold her right now.

"Quite the feat back there," Marlow muttered, distracting Miranda from looking over her shoulder as they walked into the darkness. "I had heard... ah..." He initially switched from Basic, which they had all been speaking with Joel, to English, but that didn't sound right either. "Do you speak Julah?"

"*Sa.*"

Her accent was a bit off, but Marlow knew a "yes" in his native language when he heard it. "Of course you do. Let me guess. Your father taught you, because he never much cared for becoming multilingual."

"His English was fine." Miranda scoffed. "It was his Japanese that made my ears bleed."

Once they were out of everyone else's line of sight, Marlow finally allowed his shoulders to sag. "Did he teach you how to do that?"

"I... I don't know what that was." Miranda could hardly remember it now. "I only knew I had to do something to stop her from hurting–"

"Your father is an incredibly impatient teacher. He is the type to throw you into the abyss and hope you can swim your way out of it. Trust me, as much as I hate to admit it, there were many times when I needed his tutoring when we were in the Academy. And he *liked* me."

Miranda wasn't sure where this was going, but she let him keep talking.

"I've long expected he'd get desperate enough to try to tap something out of you. You are, after all, your father's child. And, well, you have your mother's... eyes."

"Literally, so I hear." Miranda scoffed. "Hate to break it to the both of you, though, but just because I look like her doesn't mean I have her actual genetics. I'm still a hybrid through my father's side. Doesn't matter if he's strong enough to wink a planet out of existence. Some things skip a generation."

"Be that as it may... that was real."

Miranda's blushing didn't herald any real humility. "Don't tell him, all right? If he pounces on you in the middle of the night and asks what happened..."

"Don't go assuming he hasn't been watching us the whole time."

Miranda wished he hadn't voiced what she was already thinking. "Please," she whispered. "Can we leave? I'm exhausted. And I need you to get back here so you can–"

"Yes. Of course," Marlow interrupted. "If I'm tired, then you must be exhausted."

"I was going to insinuate the other way around."

"I may be old, but I'm not *that* infirm. Yet. Your father continues to drive me toward an earlier grave."

Miranda only found it odd in passing that she should hold Marlow's hand while he took her back to Earth. She wished she could say that she no longer heard the cries, shouts, and confusion of the world on Terra III when she stepped into her own house only a few minutes later, but they continued to haunt her while she fumbled through her dark kitchen for a glass of water and enough melatonin to knock her out for the next day.

She wasn't escaping her fate, she swore. Just putting aside the urge to get into more trouble.

Forty-Five

D ue to the highly classified nature of their visit, the staff at the medical center across the street sequestered Danielle to a windowless room after her vitals were checked and wasn't deemed an "immediate physical threat." The room didn't even look like they were in a hospital: the bed was a plush, elevated couch that kept the head upright while the wires within the cushions monitored heart rate without the need for anything else touching the patient's body. A single hologram appeared with a push of a nurse's finger, displaying the charts pertinent to Danielle's well-being. Otherwise, it looked like a comfortable waiting room, with a TV on the wall and beverages available on the coffee table between two normal couches for visitors.

Devon didn't sit on a couch. While Danielle curled up on her side and stared at the wall before her, he pulled up the chair the nurses and doctors used for up-close examinations and sat in silence. Occasionally, he glanced at the TV, although he finally turned it off when he continued to see his face advertising a "highly demanded" rebroadcast of his interview with the TV journalist. Had it really not been so long ago?

"Has anyone been by since I last left?" Marlow, one of the few allowed to come and go from Danielle's room, looked older and more tired than ever before. Devon didn't ask where he had disappeared between the end of the stand-off and the rest of them making it to the medical center, but he didn't care. A part of his subconscious made note of Miranda's disappearance and knew the two were connected. That was enough. "Sorry I keep stepping out. There's a nurse here who will not rest until she's poked every one of my limbs and made me breathe into her insufferable bag." What Marlow left out was that the particles in the bag were used for testing susceptibility to ailments that affected *both* humans and their older, more experienced cousins. Marlow wasn't likely to keel over from a stroke, though, no matter how pale he looked or how slowly he walked even with his cane in hand.

He would, however, help himself down to one of the couches.

"We haven't seen the nurse in a while," Devon said. "She said we were waiting for Dr. d'Eran to have some time to drop in and see us."

"Good luck with that. They have the doctor locked in with the Commander upstairs. It's going to be a long night. She, uh..." Marlow flicked his fingers in Danielle's direction. "She showing any signs of being in trauma?"

Devon hated that he knew what Marlow meant by that. "She hasn't been regressing, if that's what you mean. She's conscious, but not saying much."

"I can hear you assholes," Danielle muttered. "I'm not dead."

"That's good!" Marlow couldn't exert any more energy on Danielle's behalf than that.

"I want to go home," Danielle continued.

Devon placed his fingertips on the edge of her couch. "We should wait for Dr. d'Eran to sign off on you before we go."

"Ah... well, I'm not sure you're going anywhere yet, Devon." Marlow sighed. "Part of the reason I was out so long is because the president is here."

Devon looked over his shoulder. "She's here? Now?"

"Yes. She won't be coming down here, but she wanted to see the commander for herself. I have a feeling that d'Alacron will be going on mental health leave very soon. I put in a good word for that captain to temporarily take her place, at least for local administration. He's got a decent head on his shoulders." Marlow paused for a well-deserved breath. "The president wants to talk to you, though, Devon."

Although the words were rather shocking, Devon couldn't muster up the energy to show it. "Of course she does. Everyone wants to talk to me."

"You're an accessible man."

"You're a pushover," Danielle muttered.

Devon patted her side. She did not shrug him off. "Thanks." To Marlow, he said, "I don't think that's a good idea right now. Tell her I'll see her tomorrow."

"Oh, yes, right, I'll tell the President of the Federation that you will see her at your convenience, not hers."

"It's more important that someone stay close to Danielle. It might as well be me."

"I want to go home," Danielle reiterated.

Marlow sighed. "I've got one last trip to Earth in me. As soon as I get back, though, I'm sleeping for twelve hours. If you two want to go, I'll take you."

Devon swiveled his chair around. "Really? They made it sound like–"

"There's no way Dr. d'Eran is going to see Danielle anytime tonight, barring a horrible emergency. They'll have her monitoring the Commander for as long as they can. Honestly, it's for the best. The Commander has things going on that even I barely understand. As long as it seems that Danielle has not been sent into a forced regression, it probably is for the best that she go somewhere she feels safe."

Danielle buried her face between her hands and the thin pillow beneath her head. "Just get me out of this place."

"What about the staff?"

Marlow was back on his feet. "I've already done as I pleased so much today that it might very well be my last chance to still be a bit of a flippant boy. Quick, while nobody is looking. That's how I've always preferred it."

Danielle snorted in mild amusement. Devon didn't get the joke.

"...And *then* he brought me this really expensive bottle of wine from France. I'm not sure how he afforded it." Lanelle finished pouring the cheap wine she and Devon found in Danielle's cupboard. It was dark in the quiet kitchen. Quiet enough for the clicking and clinking of glasses and elbows on the counter to make Danielle gnash her teeth while she curled up on her living room couch. Only a few feet away, Lanelle regaled Devon with tales of Evan's adventures around Earth. The man himself wasn't there. He was too busy playing Marlow's mediator back on Terra III, a job that usually fell on Lanelle's shoulders. "This is the man who once got in trouble for 'smuggling' hydrangeas from Hawaii. He really thinks he's above the local laws sometimes."

Devon sipped the wine. After blanching in mild disgust, he forced himself to drink more. "Never been to France. Never been to Hawaii."

"But you've been to how many other planets now?" Lanelle drolly asked.

"It's different. When I'm here on Earth, perspective changes. The Federation might as well not exist here."

"It is quite the experience compared to back home." Lanelle sniffed her wine before shrugging and sloshing it down her throat. "No offense, but I don't get what Evan sees in this place. The man didn't only build his whole career on a bankable niche. He genuinely gets excited about Kardashians. Whatever those are."

"I mean, I kinda get it. Earth was a hot topic back when I was a kid." Devon didn't realize how that sounded until he heard it come out of his mouth. "I mean, way back then. My sister and I would watch every documentary and think piece about it. Kinda crazy to think there really is all that video and sound evidence of Earth's history out there, yet we don't have it here. I can still remember listening to the Leif Erikson tapes." Devon didn't remember the contents. Something about a land that would one day be known as Canada. Young and adventurous Sonall found the Vikings the most interesting thing about "current events" on Earth. His sister found them barbaric.

"Whew, yeah, that was long before my time. By my first life, everything was about the Age of Enlightenment."

Devon thoughtfully studied the plastic glass in his hand. "You remember us from past lives, don't you?"

"If it makes you feel better, this is my first time truly meeting you in this life. I was technically alive in my last life the last time you died, fat load of good it did me. I was trying to retire so I could die peacefully between lives, but you know how that old man is." Lanelle poured herself more wine. "He literally works you to *death*."

"You still haven't really answered my question."

"If you're asking me how much you've changed over your lives... I'd say about as much as I have. Which is to say, we're still the same people we were when a man named Ramaron Marlow hobbled into our lives."

Are we really the same people, though? Devon glanced in Danielle's direction. She had covered her face with her hand, but looked far from asleep. The woman who had attacked the Commander only a few hours ago was a stark contrast to the one asking to go home. Devon also couldn't see himself going back to being the dissociative loser who used to think the answer to all problems was to knock heads and boots, not always in that order. "At the end of every mission we had to give our body counts to pay the fines, you know?" He referred to the ten thousand dollar fine every tribe paid per person killed in private contracts. "I always had the highest, no matter how many people were with me. If the next asshole killed five, I killed ten. If he killed thirty in a total shootout, I killed fifty. You know. Real upstanding citizen stuff. Everyone told me after I killed my first person it would get 'easier.' I don't think they realized how 'easy' it would become."

Lanelle was silent for a moment. "Not everyone killed somebody."

Devon knew exactly who she meant. "That was the one thing I always resented about her. She always found a way to incapacitate, but not kill. She'd injure the fuck out of someone in her way, but they wouldn't lose their lives. But it was all I knew. And when we started getting paired up for missions and commanding a higher and higher price for our skills, I knew it meant I had to kill even more to make up for her. I don't know how many people I killed back then. I think I've tried to forget over a hundred or whatever lives."

Lanelle continued to sit in silence.

"Some aspects of me may be the same, but not that. I'm never killing again. I don't want to be that person. That man deserved what he got."

A hand appeared on his.

"When I say we're the same people, I'm not talking about our actions. I did plenty of things I'm not proud of in my previous lives." Lanelle retracted her hand. "You're not so different from who you were before, because you care about the people you love and you want to see justice for the wrongs you've witnessed. When you were a kid back then... what did you dream of for your future?"

Devon had to think about that. "I guess... taking over the family business, of course. It was the practical thing to do, and I was proud of it. But my real passion was in art. Something my father tried to knock out of me, and something I abandoned for other vices when I became a mercenary."

Lanelle snorted. "And who are you now? With a practical, respectable job you're proud of, but you also really love making music. So? What's the damn difference?"

"Guess you're right."

Danielle's head appeared over the back of her couch. "You guys are obnoxious. Get outta my house."

"Good evening, Sleeping Beauty." Devon held a glass of wine up in her direction. "Nobody's going anywhere tonight. Maybe you should go to bed."

"Dibs on the couch," Lanelle said. "You can sleep on the floor." That was for Devon.

"I dunno..." Danielle stood up out of her own volition for the first time in hours. Although she wobbled where she stood, a part of her was alert enough to smooth down her hair and straighten out her dirty clothes. "Might need help getting ready. Devon, would you be a dear and pick out something for me to sleep in?"

Devon raised one confused eyebrow. "*Dear?*"

"Guess you can turn on my shower for me." Danielle said that to Lanelle, who was as startled as Devon to be given orders. "I smell like hell."

Both of them slowly slid off their stools, leaving the glasses of wine behind. "Whatever you need," Devon said. "Just glad you're feeling better."

Danielle remained stoically still while Devon wandered into her bedroom and Lanelle muttered something about "asinine Earth plumbing" that was a not-so-covert way of saying Danielle better not complain about temperature or water pressure.

She waited until both were out of sight, Devon opening dresser drawers and Lanelle fumbling for the light switch in the bathroom. Once she knew she had a few seconds, Danielle grabbed a jacket from the back of a chair and made sure her keys were still in her pocket.

She didn't bother putting on her jacket until she was in the parking garage heading for her car.

Forty-Six

D anielle ignored the speed limit as she zipped down the highway. Most of the route heading north out of town was autopilot. As long as her muscles remembered the exact moments to turn, and her reflexes allowed a little give for sudden cars and deer in the road, she'd be fine. Probably.

Never mind her car was almost out of gas. Nor did it matter that she had forgotten to turn on the radio, the one thing that always serenaded her when she drove by herself. Her eyes occasionally glazed over and something threatened to stop her heart, but she would get to her destination on time. She wore it.

She lied to me.

That was the constant thought that made Danielle wipe her watering eyes and renew the fury in her veins. Miranda, the woman Danielle had begun giving her heart and body to since they first met each other in this life, had lied to her.

Lies by omission, but still lies.

When was she going to tell Danielle the truth? When she had Danielle completely ensnared in the honey-coated trap that lured her in with promises of forgetting her woes? Or when Danielle finally got a clue?

The clue was here. It was in her mind. She couldn't stop thinking about it as she drove down the road.

When was anyone going to tell her anything? Why did she have to be so coddled? Why did everyone treat her like she was two seconds away from succumbing to the worst spiritual torture imaginable? All it did was make Danielle feel like a fragile doll that anyone could throw down and destroy at any moment. Was she really so useless? Was this a cosmic joke? Who was laughing?

Was Devon laughing? Was Lanelle? Or, God forbid... Miranda?

Was she laughing when she kissed me? Did she think it hilarious when I finally got into bed with her? Did she only have herself to blame?

Danielle had a few near misses on the highway. An opossum almost lost its life beneath her tires because she didn't see it in the road. A car pulling out of a driveway nearly met her front bumper because she refused to slow down. More than one driver saw the way she swerved and cursed the police for not being out that night. The more Danielle succumbed to her memories that were still in that fog of reincarnation, the bigger danger she became both to herself and everyone around her.

Good thing her grandmother didn't live *that* far away.

It was the only place she wanted to be right now. The only safe place. *I was supposed to come here today,* she thought, putting her car in park behind her grandmother's truck. A light flicked on in the living room. *I was supposed to come here with* her. How happy Regina would be to know the two women she always wanted to get together had finally done it. Danielle had only mentioned herself coming over that morning, and Miranda was to be the surprise. They had joked about it so much that Danielle still clearly remembered it before the posse came to arrest them.

Felt like days ago, not hours.

The Danielle standing on her grandmother's porch knocking on the door wasn't the same one who had planned to visit that day. Something had permanently changed within her physiology. Her mind swung between two such unforgivable extremes that Regina hardly recognized her when the door swung open.

"Sweetheart! Where have you been?" Regina tightened her white bathrobe around her body. "You said you were going to be here for lunch, then nothing! Not a call or anything. I was worried sick and must have called you a hundred times!"

Danielle had noted the missed calls from her grandmother, but could hardly respond to them when she returned to Earth. "I'm sorry, Gran. Something came up on my way out the door. You see... I guess... can I come in?"

"Oh, yes." Regina moved out of the way. Danielle shuffled inside, the familiar smells of her childhood home plucking her nostrils and caressing her cheek. This was the first and only place she remembered living as a child. Her old school photos still adorned the mantle and the hallway walls. A few of the horse riding ribbons she had earned during her days of junior rodeo decorated the shelves, right between Regina's old military commendations and photos of her mother and father, both of them gone back to the Void.

Back to the Void... She had never thought of it that way before.

"Do you want some tea? How about a water?"

Danielle turned to her grandmother. "I need some Tylenol if you have any."

"What in the world happened to you?" Regina beat her granddaughter to the kitchen, where she opened one of the cupboards and filled a glass with water from the sink. "You were so chipper this morning."

"I was." Danielle didn't want to slump into a kitchen chair. Instead, she stood by the entryway, wondering how awful she must have looked. "I had planned on telling you that I was seeing someone. I was... really excited."

Regina stood before her, pill in one hand and glass of water in the other. "Oh?"

"Yeah. Didn't work out. I don't want to go into details but... I'm not talking to her."

"I see." Regina patiently waited for Danielle to take her medicine. "Anybody I know?"

"Honestly..." Danielle handed back the glass. "I barely knew her, come to think of it."

Danielle wasn't about to tell her grandmother the mystery woman was Miranda, of all people. Maybe one day, but definitely not tonight, when all Danielle wanted was a hug and the comforts of her childhood room.

"Are you hungry?" Regina smoothed the bangs hanging on Danielle's forehead. "I've got some leftover burrito stuffing in the fridge... my goodness, honey, you're sweating like you've got a fever." She pressed the back of her wrist against her granddaughter's skin. "Are you sick?"

"I have a really bad headache. And maybe a broken heart. They often go together."

"I hope this isn't like Alicia all over again..." Regina went to the fridge, staring at food she barely remembered buying or cooking. Her thoughts were only on Danielle, who leaned against the kitchen entryway with a grimace.

"Think I'll go on up to bed. Maybe we can talk in the morning, when I've gotten some rest. I might stay here a couple of days, if that's all right."

Regina closed the refrigerator. "Of course. Stay as long as you need. You've been through so much."

"You don't know the half of it."

"What was that?"

Danielle rubbed her pulsating eye. "I said..."

"Are you even speaking English?"

No. Danielle wasn't, and she now knew it. Whatever came out of her mouth had probably last been spoken several hundred years ago—whenever Old Basic eventually morphed into Middle Basic.

"I'm going to go up to bed." Those words took concerted effort to deliver in English. "I don't want to worry you. I really need some rest, Gran."

"All right." Regina sucked in her lips.

Danielle pushed herself up the stairs and used the last of her energy to open her old bedroom door and trudge toward the twin bed pressed up against the window overlooking the fields behind the old farmhouse. The covers had only been mildly updated since her high school years. The purple and black quilt was the same. The pillow was fresh, though. So were the sheets Danielle couldn't be assed to pull back, much like the clothes she didn't bother to remove before flopping down on the bed with a sigh.

Her eyes were so heavy, yet she gazed up at the clear sky and the full moon illuminating the night. Perhaps one of her greatest mistakes was ever leaving this place. At least in high school, fraught with boredom, puberty, and grunge music, she had been safe. Her mental health issues, as she saw them back then, were under control. She had embraced her newfound sexuality and dreamed of a day when she would have a girlfriend who looked at her like the moon gazed upon the earth.

All of that hurt now.

Danielle curled up in the fetal position. As her eyes grew heavier, she remembered the last time she saw a moon like that.

Terra III had a single moon much like Earth's.

"I hear Earth has a moon like that," a voice echoed in her head. *"One day, we'll put all of this behind us and go there. Just you and me. Nobody has to know. They'll never find us there."*

Danielle couldn't see the sight that she had once treasured a thousand years ago, but she felt the arm around her and the lips hovering near her cheek. The warmth of another body was always with her. No matter how much she attempted to forget.

She wanted so desperately to forget.

You can't forget. Who was that? Was it her own voice? Taunting her? Remnants of a past life reminding her? *How do you forget someone like that for so long? She was the best thing to ever happen to you.*

Danielle pulled her pillow over her head. "No..."

No matter how much it hurts. We must remember.

"No..."

They're all waiting for us. Some have been waiting longer.

"Please..."

I want to breathe again. Even if the truth hurts so much... surely, happiness is worth it.

Tears ran down Danielle's face. The pillowcase couldn't wipe them quickly enough.

Every time her mind wandered, she saw more and more of that face, both romantic and tired. Heard that voice among the rabble of fear and boredom. Tasted sweet kisses and dusty air. Every time someone attempted to harm Danielle, there was another person willing to catch her or put their body on the line for her.

Someone. *Someones* who loved her enough to die for her.

The words now floating through her head belonged to no one while echoing the Harmony that flowed through the river of souls that kept the universe alive. Danielle was never imbued with unnatural power. She didn't speak the original language of the Void. Nobody, in any of her lives, claimed *julah* heritage. Yet she knew the Harmony when it came for her, whispering in her ear. Reassurances that it would all be over soon. Apologies for the trauma she had endured in her long existence.

Really, a thousand years of one soul going through so damn much was the unnatural part of her human life.

Danielle lay in her childhood bed while the flashes of Sulim's life exposed themselves to her eyes. *Remember the farm? Remember Aunt Caramine? She sold me out for our cousin. When the mercenaries came to Qahrain, the girl who found us in the cellar could only carry one of us away as her prize. She was going to take the boy. My cousin. Instead, my aunt sold me for free. I thought I was going to die. In reality, my life was saved.*

The way Sulim stoically accepted her fate as a new recruit to Cerilyn's Second Tribe wasn't recorded in the history books. Those only cared about her feats and how much money she had made. They speculated about her love life and dissected her unremarkable lineage. The day-to-day life she slowly absorbed? The acquaintances she made who would one day become her family? Some of them were more charming than others, but even Kila, the girl who would one day take her own life while Sulim was off on her very first mission, had spared her a kindness here and there.

Sulim had been popular because she didn't cause drama and took her training seriously. She had wanted to survive, and people saw that in her. Even the chief. The first one. She had liked Sulim a little too much...

Who had spared her that fate? Who put herself in the chief's way whenever her eyes lingered in Sulim's direction?

The one who brought me there. The one who felt the most responsible.

In the end, Sulim became the responsible one. She remembered railing against Cairn's decision to make her lover a personal bodyguard, under the premise of "we'll never be apart now." Sulim had assumed she'd be made Second. Instead, that had gone to her partner, a man who had lost most of his childhood memories to drink.

He had been in love with her. So had the new chief, the one who had taken the life of the woman who wanted to hurt Sulim when she was a new recruit.

Sulim remembered that first kiss, beseeched the night before she went on her first mission. There had been promises of more, but Cairn didn't take her attraction seriously back then.

She remembered finally coming back two years later, to a new chief she hardly recognized—but still wanted in her arms.

She remembered those years of adoration and promises. Betrayal and disbelief. Childish arguments and a selfish plan that could have easily destroyed their tribe. A plan that was well underway when an old *julah* with a cane waltzed in one day and put those plans on hold.

We tried to go through with it anyway...

Deep down, Danielle had always known she had been in love with that woman. Enough to destroy their tribe if it meant their unmolested freedom. But the name, the face had always eluded her. Something that should have brought her joy in her new life was verboten. To remember the curve of those lips and the texture of that hair, never mind the whisper of Harmony on that voice, would have brought the greatest pain at all.

It was our fault... Sulim and Cairn's selfish desires to escape to Earth, where they would live in hiding in a medieval world, had accelerated Cerilyn's downfall and spurred the reign of terror that Nerilis undertook for the next one thousand years. It was because of them that so many people had suffered. *And why we died...*

She remembered dying.

Regret. Pain. And a tearful face begging her to stay.

Their selfishness had been their downfall.

Selfishness.

Verboten.

Here. Now.

Time froze for a single moment in Danielle's room. When her silent scream became reality, the piercing wail of her remorse shook the foundation of the house. The moon shuddered in the sky. Blades of dewy grass shriveled up and died. Somewhere, from the corners of the Earth, wayward souls turned toward her cracking voice and shared her grief.

Danielle's unwavering cries of fear brought with them the pain that contorted her limbs and made her spine leave the bed. No matter what she did, she couldn't shake the cracking of her skull as her soul screamed for freedom.

Sulim was coming for her. There was no going back now.

I won't be forgotten. Danielle's hand smacked against the wall while her foot twisted in such a strange way that her shoe slid right off her. *You won't keep me hidden anymore.* The bed creaked every time Danielle's back arched and her head threatened to slam against the wireframe headboard. *Fuck you. It's time.*

Her mouth wouldn't close. Her throat wouldn't stop screaming.

"Danielle!" Regina flung into the room, her granddaughter's ungodly sounds summoning her from downstairs. "What is it! What's wrong!" She hadn't moved like that in years. Yet when Danielle uttered the first wail of regression, Regina didn't question what her body did. "Baby! *Baby!*"

Danielle's uncontrollable thrashing hit her grandmother right in the diaphragm. Regina fell backward, catching herself on the headboard while Danielle continued to lose control of herself.

"Danielle..." Somehow, after thirty years of watching her granddaughter slowly succumb to an illness Regina had no name for, she had known it would come to this. It had been inevitable. "I'm going to call–"

"Help!" That was one word Danielle managed to gasp when her tongue was hers to momentarily control again. "Call... Dev..."

"911? I'm calling an ambulance." Regina found Danielle's phone on the floor, where it had fallen out of her pocket in her thrashing. There was no password on the flip phone. Only a million missed calls and texts from a panicked man named Devon—a name that was now familiar to Regina.

"Devon!" Danielle's knuckles smacked against the window. "Call him!"

Regina's wrinkled fingers fumbled with the address book. When she couldn't access it, she gave that up and instead went into the most recent text message from Devon and smashed the gray shape of a phone on the keys.

Devon immediately picked up.

"Danielle! Where the hell are…"

Her screams were loud enough to wake the dead, let alone be heard from the other side of the room.

"Hello?" Regina hovered near her granddaughter while pressing the phone to her own ear. "Is this… this must be Devon. Danielle told me to call you. This is her grandmother."

"What the hell is going on over there?"

"Help!" Danielle gasped once again.

"I don't know what's going on." Regina couldn't take her eyes off Danielle, but she didn't dare get closer. "She came here, said she had a headache and something bad happened today… now she's losing her damned mind!"

It only took a moment for Devon to figure out what must be happening.

"Holy shit. Where are you? We'll be right over."

"My house! I think you've been here before!"

It also took a moment for Devon to remember that Regina lived a whole hour outside of the city. He was already grabbing his coat and motioning for Lanelle to high-tail it out of Danielle's apartment with him. "I have to go find my car. *Don't* let her hurt herself!"

"How?"

"Strap her down if you have to. Extra padding. Wherever she is, she might land on the floor at any moment."

Regina looked at the hardwood floors and immediately pulled the extra blankets out of a chest and rushed into the guest room to steal pillows from the queen bed. It wouldn't be enough for the night, but it might buy Devon and Lanelle time to get there.

And then? It was all up to Danielle. Regression wasn't easy even on the most willing soul.

Forty-Seven

If there was one small favor to be thankful for, it was that Devon's workplace was much closer to Danielle's apartment than his. Since that's where he last left his car, it made his life a *little* easier when he realized he needed to hightail it out of the city. Now.

Still required hopping one of the last trolleys of the night, which meant Lanelle got a crash course in handling fare while Devon pushed away the panic attack quickly overcoming him. To most of the third-shift workers trying to get home in the middle of the city, he looked like a haggard lunatic hauling around his grumpy girlfriend, and neither of them spoke particularly *good* English. For every person thinking about calling the cops on them, there was another cranking up the volume on their iPod and plastering their eyes to the rainy windows.

"What the hell is this thing?" There were only a few cars parked in the employee parking lot at Devon's office building, and the one he rushed toward was *not* one of the BMWs or the manager's Fiat in the far corner. Instead, Devon yanked open the sticky door of his 1996 Ford Taurus and motioned for Lanelle to get into the passenger seat. "I am *not* getting in that!"

After Devon started the engine and threw his hands toward her, Lanelle relented, but only because she knew time was of the essence.

"She just had to run off on her own," she muttered, while Devon focused on the traffic leading them out of the city. "Typical. Guess that's what happens when you regress for the first time in a hundred years. We got off easy with you!"

"Please don't remind me." Devon rushed through a yellow light the moment it started turning red. A car honked somewhere to his right. If he got a ticket, so be it.

"Do you know where this lady lives?"

"I have a vague idea. I know what highway to get on and about how far we have until we get down to the details. Wish this was happening during the day. Lot easier to recognize landmarks. I've only been there a few times."

With a sigh, Lanelle booted up her communicator, hoping to the Void she could make a connection as long as they were still in the city. There was a reason most who worked for and still had connections to the Federation stayed in major cities. The only ones who moved to small towns around the world wanted to get *away* from pesky Federation people like her, because the only way to contact them was by directly patching into an Earth-based line.

"For the High Priestess's sake I hope you're conscious," she said the moment Evan connected to her. "I need you to do Devon and me a huge favor. Fast. Like two minutes fast, because we're about to leave the city here and I dunno how long the connection is going to hold."

Evan was barely conscious, since he had spent the latter half of his day riding the anxiety train to Panicville. Being tasked with contacting the capitol once it was apparent Commander d'Alacron had gone off the rails had only added to his fatigue. The *only* reason he was still awake and in Marlow's office was because it was either that or try to sleep in his own home, where his wife was likely to pester him with questions about why he wasn't "so much himself."

"What's up?" He sounded like he was about to drop his head onto his desk at any moment. "If you're looking for Marlow, he's already as–"

"Look up the address of Danielle's grandmother. *Now.*"

"Okay, okay. Sheesh." While Devon almost missed his exit and suddenly swerved, Lanelle squeezed her eyes shut and said a prayer to the High Priestess. *At least be there to greet me when this dumbass kills us both!* This would be how she went out in this life—in the rusty can of metal that only Earthlings still used.

She should switch places with Evan. He'd *love* to go like this!

Lanelle relayed the address as soon as Evan told it to her. He promised to forward the instructions as soon as they downloaded to his communicator. Earth satellites were *just* advanced enough to tap into Lanelle's GPS and lay out a map for them to follow, but she wasn't sure how much more juice her communicator had. It was supposed to last eight days with "mild to moderate use," but fuck her if she could remember the last time she charged it. The indicator light changing from yellow to red did not inspire confidence.

"I will get us there," Devon assured her while Evan kept asking why they needed to know this info. "*Don't* tell them what's going on unless there's a real emergency. If I know Danielle well enough by now, it's that she doesn't want a huge to-do over this."

Lanelle cut off her connection to Evan and tapped her palm-sized communicator against her lips. "From the sounds of that screaming over your phone, there's plenty of a to-do already."

"Yeah, well..." Devon's knuckles turned white against his steering wheel. "Don't remind me. I can't get that sound out of my head."

He flew ten miles over the speed limit in the hopes the fifteen minutes it saved would make a difference to Danielle, never mind her horrified grandmother who had been yelled at by two different people to *not* call 911. Devon relied on Lanelle to tell him when to get off the highway and high-tail it down the rural road that bypassed a number of farm acreage that was barely lit enough to see what was right in front of him. The closer they got to Regina's house, the easier it was for Devon to recognize the bright blue mailbox and the dilapidated white fence.

Good thing that pop of color was there, because Danielle's black car was less than noticeable from the dark road.

Devon laid his hand on his horn to alert Regina that they were there. She popped out onto the porch, tears in her eyes as she grabbed Devon by the arm and didn't even register that she hadn't seen Lanelle in many, many years.

As far as Lanelle was concerned, this was her first time coming to Regina's house. Evan was usually the one posing as so-and-so to check in on Danielle after Marlow caught wind that she was one of his mercenaries reborn in this corner of the galaxy. That didn't mean, however, that she didn't stop to reorient herself when she stepped into the cozy living room and had déjà vu.

That episode was dashed when a painful scream ripped through the walls.

Devon rushed up the stairs before Regina could get an answer out of him. She turned to Lanelle, who was prepared to redirect Danielle's grandmother to the kitchen—and maybe slip her a sedative. Only a few seconds later, Devon's voice boomed down the staircase.

"Lanelle! I need your help!"

"Please wait here." Her customer service sweetness was completely lost on Regina, who barely understood Lanelle's accent right now. "We're going to make sure she's safe." With hardly any reassurance in her own heart, Lanelle hauled herself up the stairs with one hand on the creaking banister.

When Devon had entered Danielle's room, he had been prepared for any number of scenes. Yet any mental preparation was now dashed as he beheld the dangerous situation before him: Danielle, with her feet twitching and her chest shoving upward into the air, was always a hair's breadth away from toppling out of the twin bed and onto the pile of quilts and pillows Regina had placed on the floor. Danielle had lost one of her shoes and torn her own T-shirt thanks to the thrashing that commenced every ten seconds. The pain in her cheeks and the fear in her eyes when Devon landed on the edge of the bed and grabbed her wrists was unlike anything he had ever seen in a person before. Yet he knew exactly what it was, because he had been there himself only a year ago.

Danielle had helped him through that traumatic moment, and he would be damned if he wasn't there for her in the same way.

"Grab her feet!" There was no time for Devon to take in what he saw. Not when Danielle's safety was on the line. "We have to keep her from hurting herself."

Although Lanelle knew that perfectly—having regressed a time or two herself—she didn't give Devon flack once she saw how badly Danielle still suffered a whole hour after she screamed over the phone. Only now she was incapable of saying a single word. The only sounds coming out of Danielle's mouth were long, painful moans that still didn't convey the fire in her veins and misfiring neurons that told her she was being drawn and quartered. Every time she thought she had found respite, another meteor crashed into her chest and sucked the air out of her lungs. Every terrible, unforgettable memory she had locked away in the depths of her brain screamed into her ear. It wasn't just death. It was guilt. Regret. The everlasting fears that she would never break free from this tortuous cycle of needless death and rebirth.

"We need to tie her down," Lanelle shouted in Basic. That only startled Regina more, who had been standing in the doorway with both hands on her chest. "Hey!" It took Lanelle a moment to realize she needed to scream in English. "This is like a farm, right? You got anything to tie her down until it's over?"

"Tie her... what is *happening?*"

"No time, lady! Get the leather belts!"

Regina was shaken enough to thrust herself out of Danielle's bedroom. Lanelle returned to carefully removing Danielle's other shoe while Devon pinned her hands to her bed. Neither of them could stop her arching back or the erratic movements of her hips without further harming her, but the least they could do was keep her from falling.

"How long does it take?" Devon barked over his shoulder. "It's already been an hour!"

Lanelle didn't take his terse tone personally. "A couple hours. Hopefully she'll be through the worst of it soon. Then again..." She almost got kicked in the face. "It's not like we know what she's like when *she* does it. There's a reason she never has before, right?"

Devon didn't answer. He was too concerned with the sweat dripping off Danielle's skin and how unflattering the tear in her shirt was. It had been enough she ruined half her clothes by crawling in disgusting building vents and being toppled to a grungy concrete floor earlier. She hadn't changed since then. Hadn't even showered. Now here Danielle was, in a rickety old bed with her stomach hanging out and the last thousand years clouding her eyes.

"It's gonna be okay." Devon said that as much for him as he did Danielle, who occasionally recognized his face and cried in terror once more. "Lanelle and I are here. We won't let you get hurt."

The sooner those restraints came, though, the better.

Regina dumped what she rounded up from the kitchen tack, where she kept the belts and harnesses that didn't necessarily fit in the barn. Even in her frenzy, she had been careful to only pick up the full-grain leather that would withstand Danielle's feverish trashing.

"If you hurt her…" Her growl hit Devon right in the back of the head. He kept his focus on Danielle, his fingers reddening as he struggled to keep her arms and torso pinned to her bed. Lanelle picked up what she could from the floor and didn't hesitate to start tying Danielle's ankles to the foot of her bed. "I swear to God, your head is dead."

Devon caught one of the belts flying in his direction. "Trust me, this is all to keep her from hurting herself."

"One of you better tell me what's going on later." Regina's hand braced her heart, breath catching in her throat as she watched these two relative strangers tie her belligerent granddaughter to the bed. "Her mother was a very sick woman, you know. What if…?"

"She's going to be fine soon!" Devon tightened the knot that kept Danielle's wrists shackled to the sides of her bed. He was not wont to tie them above her head—the last thing he wanted was her shoulders popping out of their sockets. "I promise. Please…" He spared Regina a tired look. "We'll explain everything later."

That still wasn't good enough. "Tell me what to do."

"Go… boil some water."

Regina hurried out of the room. Lanelle looked up at Devon.

"It's something we say," he explained. "Keeps people busy and out of the way."

"Boil water, though? What are we going to do? Steam the demons out of her?"

"For God's sake, let's focus on this for now!"

Now that Danielle was no longer an immediate threat to either of them, Lanelle sank down to the floor and Devon steeled himself against the very edge of the bed.

He loomed over Danielle's midsection, careful to not impede her air but close enough to keep an eye on her breathing and hear whatever nonsense she uttered.

"I know it hurts." During a rare lull in her movements, he used the back of his sleeve to wipe the excess sweat off her forehead. "It'll be over soon. You'll get all the rest you need after that. We're here, okay? We won't let anything bad happen to you."

"Help..." she whispered.

"Help is here. We'll untie you when the worst is..."

"Call her. Please."

Devon hesitated before removing his phone from his pocket. He didn't have to ask what Danielle meant. There was only one woman she'd want to call while regressing.

He dialed Miranda's number and held his phone to his ear. While he waited to be sent to voicemail, he saw the clarity in Danielle's eyes. Her hands continued to uncontrollably flex, but her vision was hers once more.

"She's not picking up." Once Miranda's prerecorded spiel began, Devon closed his phone. "And I don't know where she is. I'm sorry."

"Please..."

"I wish I could."

"Do you?"

Devon braced his hand against the windowsill. "Yeah."

Danielle closed her eyes and let out the deepest breath trapped in her lungs. Slowly, her body stilled.

It didn't last, though.

Both Devon and Lanelle had to hang around for another hour, coaching Danielle through the hardest moment of her life. They tried every language they cumulatively knew to get through to her, but the only words she spoke were a mishmash of Old Basic and English. Lanelle took a moment to check in with Evan, but still did not tell him what had happened, only that, *"It might be a while before I get back. I'll call you when I need Master Marlow to pick me up."* Devon didn't move from his vigil as long as Danielle was suffering. The last thing he wanted was for her to feel like someone else had abandoned her.

"It's all our fault..." Danielle moaned more than once. "You died because of us."

After that next hour passed, Danielle collapsed without a word. Her eyes fell as heavy as her body. Her hands and feet were limp. Once Lanelle checked that she was still breathing, she patted Devon on the shoulder and told him to remove the restraints.

"I'm going to have a long talk with her grandmother, I guess." Lanelle's sigh implied she couldn't think of anything else more painful right now. "Don't think she's got any alcohol here, do you? I'll even take the really rancid stuff from this planet."

Devon began untying the belts holding Danielle's wrists to the bed. "Good luck. I don't envy you. I'm going to stay here, if that's all right."

"Of course. Somebody should keep an eye on her anyway." Lanelle hesitated. "She'll be fine in the morning. I promise."

"But are you sure?"

"Man, I'm not sure about *anything*. Just go with it, okay? Otherwise, you'll drive yourself crazy." She shook her head. "I'm going downstairs before that lady calls the authorities on us. Holler if you need anything, but I don't think you will."

Lanelle's footsteps faded from the room. Devon sat up, fatigue claiming him as he finally allowed himself to relax for the first time since that harrowing phone call.

He could hardly believe it. If Lanelle were right...

Devon gazed down at Danielle, who fell into such a fitful sleep that not even a mighty earthquake could rouse her until her brain was done rewiring itself. The ache of regression didn't stop when she finally accepted her old self back into her body. It required a complete reset from the inside-out.

She'll be Sulim again, he thought while kicking off his shoes. *The three of us will have no more secrets.* He hoped, for Danielle's sake, that her regression also brought with it freedom from the Process. The desperation to know she was finally safe to die a final time was as strong as his need to wipe the last of her sweat away and to make her as comfortable as possible.

Even if they would both be comfortable with him changing her, though, it didn't matter. There were no fresh clothes between the two of them. Nothing in the closet still fit her. Danielle would have to be stripped to her underwear, and what was the point of that?

Devon could hardly keep his eyes open. He waited five more minutes to make *sure* that Danielle wasn't either waking up or falling back into a fit.

She was as still as death, aside from the very slight rise and fall of her chest.

Devon considered making himself a bed out of the quilts and pillows on the floor. When that proved fruitless, he slapped a pillow onto Danielle's bed and gently nudged her over toward the wall. It was a tight fit, but as long as he lay on his side with his arms around her, they both fit on the small bed that was never meant to hold two grown adults.

For as long as they had known each other in this life, Danielle and Devon had been linked together. They had entered the Process at the same time, under the same circumstances—and with the help of the same man. Their souls were entwined in ways that would have never been possible without the spiritual magic that carted them through the Void, bypassing every gate and failsafe that was supposed to ensure they didn't stay the same exact person between each and every life. Regardless of what repercussions that havocked upon their souls.

Knowing that for the first time in a thousand years, the woman he held would *know* him in ways she had yet to understand both shattered and elated Devon. Of course he was elated that his best friend, his partner, the woman he admired more than any other and had literally killed for would be back. The only way it could have been better was if that newfound freedom brought with it the kind of mutual attraction he had ached for a thousand years ago.

That's why he was shattered. Once Danielle woke up with Sulim's memories glowing in her eyes, there would go the last shred, the last *shadow* of a chance for something to be "there." Something more than an intimacy that only came with being in the Process together. It still couldn't make her fall in love with him. Her heart would always belong to someone else.

I don't care, as long as she's safe. I don't care, as long as I have my best friend back.

Even now, as Devon hugged her close to him, he didn't think they could ever possibly be physically close enough for him to be sure that she was still alive.

Forty-Eight

D anielle didn't have a single thought when she woke up the next morning, the sun shining high in the sky and her body aches slowly spreading from one muscle to another.

No thoughts. Until she recognized her childhood bedroom and the sweat-logged quilt beneath her.

Wasn't it strange that she wore such dirty, ill-fitting clothing? Wasn't it even stranger than she felt... not quite like herself? For one thing, her body shouldn't be this sluggish. Even accounting for the long night—and longer day before—she should have been stronger. More agile. Ready to take down anyone who tried to get in her way.

Ludicrous, wasn't it?

Danielle forced herself up, hand on her head and fingers untangling her hair. She shrugged out of her sleeves and stared outside, eyes adjusting to the morning sunlight while memories slowly returned to the forefront of her mind. Eventually, she turned around and saw the pile of quilts and pillows bunched up by her bed. They happened to form the outline of a grown person, as if someone had been sleeping beside her for most of the night. Danielle only had a foggy memory of who that could be.

Voices murmured downstairs. Her room was over the kitchen, but she couldn't make out what they were saying. She only knew there were at least two people. Her grandmother, perhaps, and a man. Occasionally, one of them laughed like it was another Friday morning. Dare Danielle believe that it really *was* "just" another Friday morning in her grandmother's house?

Her legs turned to mush when she attempted to get out of bed. After righting herself and rediscovering her balance, Danielle trudged toward the floor-length mirror that hadn't been dusted in years. *I'm a mess,* she thought, pushing back her bangs and beholding the wrinkles and stains on her clothes. A giant tear ruined a perfectly good V-neck. The only reason her bra got by unscathed was because it was so old, it finally reached the point where nothing could destroy it now.

"God..." Once she realized she couldn't go downstairs looking like this, she pulled the ruined shirt over her head and tossed it onto the floor. Only then did she realize that her stomach and upper arms had scratches and bruises dotting the skin. Every time she opened a drawer or rummaged through the closet of old clothes to wear, another vague memory of the day before returned.

None of it mattered now. Now that *all* of her memories had returned, she realized that the Federation couldn't touch her. Not with the wild look that had been in Yara's eyes when Danielle pulled her to the ground. The commander would be lucky if Danielle didn't come after *her* for the undo duress and cruel and unusual punishment that was using Danielle's status as someone still in the Process as a torture device against...

Danielle found a baggy T-shirt from her high school days. She had never been into team sports, but she had a shirt from the Powder Puff game that one of her friends had *insisted* she join senior year. While the T-shirt was a little snug now, it was comfortable enough for driving home and taking a decent shower. God knew Danielle needed to change her underwear and maybe light her jeans on fire.

This is absolutely not what I'm going to wear for long, she thought, already imagining the outfit she'd pick out from her apartment closet. After she showered, of course. There was so much to do to get ready.

Like go downstairs and face the music.

She had guessed it was Devon in the kitchen with Regina, but Danielle didn't expect to come off the final step and find Lanelle half-asleep at the Formica table, her plate of eggs and sausage completely untouched. One might assume that Lanelle's refined Federation palate said *no* to such basic Earth foods, but in reality, she was too tired—and too nauseas—to touch anything to her tongue, no matter how much her stomach growled.

Any conversation peppering the breakfast table was interrupted when Danielle appeared in the entryway.

"Honey!" Regina leaped up from her seat, nearly knocking over her chair as she rushed toward Danielle and pulled her into a strong embrace. "Are you all right?" She cupped her hands around Danielle's face and checked her eyes and teeth, as if she were a horse up for inspection. "My God, after the night we've had..."

"I'm fine." Danielle spared her grandmother a reassuring smile before shrugging out of the hold and addressing the pair sitting at the table. "Thank you," she said. "Last night was rough, but I remember you both being there."

Devon slowly stood, his dirty clothes no match for the hair he barely had time to smooth down with tap water earlier that morning. "Is everything...?"

She didn't let him finish his thought. "Everything is as it should be."

Regina tucked some of her granddaughter's errant hair behind her ear. Devon came closer, disbelief clouding his face. "Does that mean the worst of your regression is over?"

Although she didn't smile, the relaxing of her cheeks and the unclenching of her jaw said everything Devon needed to know. When he opened his arms to her, she was inclined to meet him halfway, her heart skipping two, three beats when she realized that this was the man who had been with her when she died.

"Told myself I wasn't going to cry, so best believe I won't." Devon released her, only for Danielle to be pulled back into her grandmother's arms.

"Good. Let's not embarrass us both."

"Oh, sweetheart, why didn't you ever tell me what was going on?" Regina grabbed a washcloth off her counter and smacked Danielle on the arm. "Do you know what that was like last night, huh? Do you know what it's been like these past few months with you coming and going like you're doing an undercover op for the CIA? In all of my goddamned years I never thought something like this..." When her words failed her, she shook the towel toward Lanelle, who had both arms on the table and fingers pressing into her half-asleep face. "I had to find out about all of this... about why you came into my house screaming for your life... from an *alien!*"

Lanelle snapped out of her stupor. "Hey. Rude. I am a lady."

"You were never going to tell me. You were doing all of this crazy shit... you were *famous*... and..."

Danielle calmed her grandmother down with two soft hands to the shoulders. "Gran." Her voice remained even, although the air around them was far from it. "I did what I had to do. Telling you anything could have endangered you more than you already were. But don't worry about me, okay?" She lowered her hands. Regina, who wasn't used to such a candid yet confident aura from her granddaughter, remained awestruck. "The worst of it is now in my past. Already this life, the one you helped give me, is better than anything I had before. I know it must feel like you've been nothing but a pawn of the Void's, but... I'm not my mother. I'm not my father. I'm sorry you and your family got caught up in my reincarnation, but it's over now. There's only moving forward." She realized how all of that sounded when fear crawled into Regina's eyes. "I'm still your granddaughter. There's simply more... layers to it now." She gestured toward Devon. "If this guy can still get on my nerves as much as he did before he regressed, then I'm guessing I'm not changing too much."

"Happy day," Lanelle muttered from the table. "Can't wait to tell Master Marlow about this."

"How much did you tell my grandmother exactly?" Danielle asked both Devon and Lanelle. "How much am I going to have to fill in after today?"

Lanelle stabbed the eggs on her plate. "Let's say I didn't get any sleep because I was *chatting* all night. I am now officially fluent in English. I'm putting it on my résumé now that I'm about to be out of a job."

"You can tell me the rest right now," Regina insisted. "I left some food hot on the stove for you. Do you want cof—"

"I have to get going," Danielle said, cutting off her own desperate grandmother. "There's something I really, really need to do, and I need to go home and clean myself up for it."

Devon caught the look on Regina's face and said, "I'll go with you. I can–"

"No, nope." Lanelle's mouth was full of eggs. "You're due back on Terra III. You've got a date with the president."

"The president?" Regina echoed. "George Bush?"

Lanelle washed her breakfast down with orange juice. "Who is that?"

"Different president," Danielle surmised. "A bigger deal than Bush."

"Is that like the Obama guy?" Lanelle picked a piece of cilantro out of her teeth. "Or am I mixing him up with Clinton? Forget it. You guys go through leadership so fast. My name's not Evan. This ain't my thesis defense."

Devon sighed. "Yeah. Guess I'm seeing the President of the Federation in a couple of hours. I should go home and freshen up too."

Lanelle shook her fork at him. "Please! You smell like my socks!"

Even with that decided, Devon walked Danielle out to the front porch, if only because he wanted to make sure she was truly fit to drive by herself. Although he had been more or less "normal" the day after his own regression, he had always been more susceptible to embracing his past self. What if Danielle continued to fight it long after the fact?

Regina wasn't pleased that Danielle was leaving so soon, but there was a promise to come back the next day and fill in any missing information. Danielle simply "had to do something" now that her mind and body were her own again. It helped that Lanelle distracted Regina with an album she accessed through her communicator. Lanelle was, after all, one of the few people authorized to drag up photos of both Devon and Danielle's past lives. Wouldn't Regina *love* to see them?

"So..." The screen door closed. Devon was alone on the porch with Danielle, who only offered to entertain him for a few more minutes. "It's really you, huh?"

Danielle snorted, her posture finally relaxing. "Me who? Because I'm the same person I was yesterday."

Devon couldn't fault her for that logic. "You know what I mean. You spent the whole night regressing. It was... well, honestly, it was pretty terrifying. Wasn't sure what to expect with you."

"Yeah, well..." Danielle gazed out at the front yard, where three cars were haphazardly parked next to the empty road. She wasn't sure how she was going to successfully back her car out and around Devon's, but it would work. Probably. "Rough night. Remembered some things I had repressed for a really long time."

"There was a reason, you know."

"That people were keeping things from me? Yeah. No shit. Well, now I remember."

"Would be nice to hear you say it, though." Devon crossed his arms. "That you really are her after all this time."

"Make you feel better, wouldn't it?"

Devon should have expected that. "It's not about me."

"Great. Now you're my therapist."

Devon opened his mouth again, but decided against saying anything that might set off his friend. Besides, he didn't need her to verbally confirm it. He could see it in the way she walked, how she addressed those around her, and how her aura oozed the frustration of not having the kind of fit body a woman in her physically demanding position anticipated. *Even her eyes are different,* he noted, since Danielle's had never been quite so... green. Usually, her hazel eyes veered a little more brown than green, but Sulim had noticeably green eyes.

Danielle's shoulders sagged. "Yes. It's me." She switched to Old Basic, which flew off her tongue in ways it hadn't in over a thousand years. "My name is Sulim di'Graelic, and I have shit to do."

So terse. So flippant. So unabashedly her.

Yet there was something else that made Sulim not only herself, but had crossed over to the woman she was today. Danielle wasn't the type to push away her friends when they needed her, and nor was Sulim—they simply had developed different strategies for the high-stress situations they usually found themselves in, but this moment didn't count.

When Devon took another step closer, Danielle flung her arms around him and held back the tears of relief that had threatened her eyes since the moment she awakened as her old self. This wasn't a time for crying. Once she completely settled into her new life, she would have plenty of time to shed both happy and regretful tears alike.

Devon held onto her with all the strength in his body. Unlike the night before, however, he wasn't searching for reassurance. He had it now.

"I've missed you so much." Perhaps he was the one shedding a tear. "I've seriously missed my best friend."

"Who said I was your best friend, you loser?" Danielle laughed through her brutal use of Old Basic. "Me too. I'm sorry it took me so damn long to come clean with myself. The things I didn't want to remember..." She stepped back, taking in the sight of a man she now saw through greener eyes. "Maybe I'll tell you about them soon. When I've had time to process them."

"I'd like that. I'll buy you a drink back in town."

"We'll laugh about the old times. Like when I bum-rushed you in the brothel when your pants were down because it was the third time you stood me up for a debriefing."

Devon certainly was not expecting *that* anecdote, yet here it came, flooding his own memory like it had only happened yesterday. "I was a mess."

"Me too," Danielle said. "You look good. I mean, now. I mean..." She gave up trying to sound diplomatic with a few tears in her eyes and a frog in her throat. "Better. Happier."

"I'm trying. New life, new chances. Just taking it one day at a time while worrying myself sick over you of all people."

"Never asked you to."

"Like I wouldn't? Didn't I call you my best friend?"

"Yeah. Guess we are. Go figure."

"Anyone looking at us would wonder how such a pair had met."

"Unless they're from the Federation, I guess."

"That reminds me," Danielle said, "don't you have a date with the president about something? Try to get me out of trouble, would you?"

"Forget that. Don't *you* have somewhere you need to be? I mean, don't you have someone you should go see?"

Danielle bit her lip. "You know about that, huh?"

"Come on. It's like the biggest elephant in the room 24/7. From the moment *I* regressed, I've been struggling to keep my mouth shut about who you should really be seeing."

"And you're okay with it?"

"Why wouldn't I be? We all deserve happiness after the amount of shit we've been through. I don't want to forget what's happened, but I want to move on. Can't exactly do that if I'm not willing to forgive people for doing what they thought they had no choice but to do. Now go." He gestured toward Danielle's car. "Let me know if you need me to let you out. I kinda parked anywhere last night."

Danielle stepped into the driveway. "Thanks, Dev." She wiped the drying tears from her eyes. "You're a good guy."

"Better guy than I was?"

She hesitated before unlocking her driver's side door. "In a different way."

Danielle slid into the seat and allowed herself two seconds to decompress. The moment her hands touched the wheel and her foot hovered over the gas pedal, she glanced up and saw Devon standing in the middle of her grandma's porch, his stance as confident as a man who knew how to bash heads—but his demeanor softer than anything she had seen in the military.

M-Town. That's where I need to go.

With a wave of her hand, Danielle started her car and began the arduous process of backing out into the road without smacking into Devon's vehicle. By the time she had pulled out, everyone was on the porch, Lanelle with her plate of food in her hands.

Nobody said anything. They merely watched her go where she needed to be the most.

Everything Danielle did between getting home and leaving again was dedicated to one tough decision after another. Should she shave in the shower? What about exfoliating? Did she have time for that? What should she wear? Her feet were heavy when she stepped out of the shower and blow-dried her hair for the first time since she last cut it. The cuts and bruises on her arms and stomach wouldn't be covered up with simple makeup. Should she wear makeup at all?

On one hand, everything had to be perfect. On the other? She knew she could show up in dirty pajamas and smelling like shit and she'd be welcomed. That almost made it worse.

A clean pair of jeans was obvious. But what about up top? The weather was warm, but not hot. A little humid, but not about to rain. Danielle picked through every item in her closet, dithering between a sleeveless turtleneck or a fitted T-shirt. It wasn't until she tried on the sleeveless white top that she realized it was what she wore when she appeared on Miranda's doorstep several months ago.

She grabbed the same scarf she had also worn and secured it around her neck. After combing her hair a third time, she looked to her hand and realized that it felt so empty.

Once, a thousand years ago, she had worn a ring on the only finger it fit. That ring was out there now, somewhere. The memories, feelings, and passion associated with its owners had crossed time and space to eventually become the third Relic of Earth.

Danielle understood now. So much made sense, even if it hurt her heart to think about.

She grabbed her phone the moment a text came through from Devon. *"About to meet the president. Good luck with your day."*

Danielle stood in her living room. The silence was a golden opportunity to remember what it was like to breathe.

You are Sulim. Those thoughts were in her own voice—Sulim's voice. Yet that woman was no longer a piece of her brain attempting to unlock. She now freely flowed through Sulim's veins, basking in the warm glow of a new life and the freedom to live it as she saw fit. There was still the matter of the Process looming over her soul, but no longer would she awake in the middle of the night, plagued with the trials of regression that had yet to touch her. *You are Danielle. You are the same.*

Anything Sulim had desired... anyone she had loved... they had been born in Danielle's heart, prepared to direct the very course of her life. Destiny had a name.

She snapped out of her stupor. It was almost noon. The plan was to go to Miranda's house and either find her there or wait for her to come back from work. Yet the sights of M-Town continued to flash before her. The place where they had once again met.

She knew me. She must have recognized me the moment I walked into her office to report for duty. Yet she held it in.

Danielle had a lifetime's worth of apologizing to do. The least she could do was start by going where she knew her destiny awaited.

If Danielle truly knew her heart well enough, then she had gone to work as long as she was physically able. She had already taken the day before off. No matter how much Cairn opined that there weren't enough days off in their line of work, she always took her position of power seriously. Lives were in her hands. Every day required her utmost attention.

There was a place in their large, imposing fortress that offered few comforts. Something Cairn had installed when the money started pouring in and her people needed a few things to make their days a little brighter. Something that was as costly to install as it was to maintain, since it required digging deep into the earth of a hostile planet.

Sulim had loved that thing. Every chance she had, when there were no other duties, she was often found near it. Cairn had once said she looked like a guardian angel sitting among the spray and foam.

Danielle knew where to go. She didn't even bother to take her car. As soon as she remembered, that aching longing that had haunted her for a thousand years took control of her body and thrust her onto the street. The wind was in her face, blowing back her scarf and kissing her cheeks. The thumps of her footsteps matched the beat of her heart.

Although she was anxious to get there, she knew she had all the time in the world. For the first time in her existence... there was time.

Forty-Nine

Devon barely had enough time to shower and change into nicer clothes before Marlow appeared in his apartment, collapsing into a chair and bemoaning, "After I bring you back later, you better kiss my damned feet. I am so tired!"

Lanelle wasn't with him. Just as well, because she was more likely to criticize whatever Steve Jobs-esque outfit Devon pulled out of his closet. *It's up there with what I wore to my job interview.* Such a strange thing to think about now. A job. An everyday 9-5 where he was a nameless cog in the machine.

Yeah. That wasn't happening anymore. As of Monday morning, Devon was handing in his resignation. Marlow might not know it yet, but he was about to fund Devon's endeavors at doing whatever he wanted for the rest of his final life. Even better if he could swing some money Danielle's way.

That reminded Devon of something, but as soon as he was ready, Marlow swept him back to Terra III, where the frenzy of the capital kept them from saying anything more than questions and instructions. More than one person looked up and paid a little extra attention to Devon, who thanked his stars when his phone connected to a signal in the building. The capital was, after all, the hub of all communication to and from the far reaches of the known universe.

"You won't believe what's happened these past few days..." He texted that to the first person on his alphabetically ordered address book. *"And you won't believe where I am right now. About to meet the President of the whole freakin' Federation."*

He didn't expect an answer before Marlow commanded his attention.

"They have a president, huh?"

"Yup."

"Good luck. I'm sitting outside an appointment with my doctor."

Devon didn't mind being brushed off like that. There were things to take care of, anyway.

"When you go in there," Marlow began, "be sure to address her as *Madam President.*" He said the Basic equivalent, not that Devon really caught it. He was too busy thinking of something else.

"Danielle regressed last night." Devon wrapped his hands around his knee. A man in a pristine black uniform piped with gold and flashing chestnut-brown buttons approached them, posture impeccable and gait more sublime than anyone stumbling around the Forces' headquarters down the street. "Thought you might want to know."

"Wha–"

"Master Marlow," the uniformed man interrupted them with confidence. "And you must be Mr. Anderson. The president is ready to see you."

Devon stood, pocketing his phone and pressing one last wrinkle out of his sweater. "Time for me to find out what's going on." He turned to Marlow momentarily, but only because he wanted to behold the shocked look on his face. "Wish me luck."

Marlow was still slack jawed when Devon walked away. As soon as he pulled out his communicator to call Lanelle, Devon was escorted into the series of hallways leading back to the president's heavily guarded office.

Unlike the Commander's office, President d'Errowyn's was gigantic enough to be comedic. The walls were flanked with soldiers in dress uniform, the man escorting Devon nodding to them as they passed through a heavy door that required both a handprint and an eye scan to access. The only furniture in the room was the president's angular black desk that centered the room that must have been big enough to house the whole building's mess hall. The woman herself sat behind the desk, her bald head illuminated by the one lamp—after all, the walls were pitch black, and the rest of the room so dark that no assassin would think they could get to the president before the dozen or so soldiers hidden in the shadows took them out first.

Yet the cavernous room was silent, aside from the echoing of Devon's footsteps and the breath of the man escorting him.

"Mr. Devon Anderson, Madam." The escort caught the president's eye. She looked up as if she had not been expecting them. "Will you be needing anything?"

"No, thank you," the president responded in Basic. She stood and extended her hand over the desk. The escort stepped back to allow Devon room to press forward. "Mr. Anderson. Thank you so much for agreeing to see me on such short notice." Her clipped, professional tone made Devon feel like he was about to be interviewed for a job he was *way* underqualified to have. Nevertheless, he shook her hand and sat in a chair when prompted. The escort bowed out of the room. "It is highly appreciated."

Devon waited for President d'Errowyn to sit down before responding. "You're the one with such a busy schedule, I'm sure... Madam President." Her head slightly tilted when he struggled with the title, which was perfectly fine to say in English. In Basic, however, it required a flick of his tongue in the back of his throat. Not like Old Basic, which had kept the tongue toward the front of the palate. "It's an honor to meet you again."

"The honor should be mine. I'm the one who happens to be President during a moment of such occasion."

"Much like the commander happened to be in her position when this all happened?"

The president's shoulders tensed. No matter how much she set her jaw or clamped her elbows upon her desk, she still could not betray the thoughts really going through her head. "Yes. Thank you for bringing up the reason you are here. First, I would like to apologize on behalf of the Federation for anything that may have transpired yesterday. You will be assuaged to hear that Commander d'Alacron has been placed on immediate extended leave to address her... health."

"Keep the *hedpah* away from her, please."

"Yes, her penchant for Class C controlled substances will be thoroughly investigated." Somehow, that did not assuage Devon's fears that Yara would not really get the help she needed. Again. "You have my word, Mr. Anderson."

He waited for the other shoe to drop.

"The Federation is aware that many of yesterday's injuries and damages could have been avoided if our Forces had taken better care to treat you and your cohort's special conditions as something beyond their understanding. I want to make it clear that it is the Federation's official position that you, Ms. Cromwell, and Master Marlow are all welcomed members of the Intergalactic Federation and its Sentient Bodies."

"All right."

President d'Errowyn waited for him to say more, but Devon was content to lean back in his seat, waiting for the scene to play out as if he had total control over the situation. *What can I say?* he thought. *She's admitted that what happened was wrong. I have my best friend back. Nobody I care for got hurt. This can finally be put behind us while moving forward.*

"Well…" The president cleared her throat. "That said, Mr. Anderson, we would like to know if there is any way we can personally make up for what happened yesterday. As a way to soothe the soul, so to speak. We want to make it *clear* that you are a valued member of our history and culture. You and Ms. Cromwell both."

"A favor." Devon scratched his chin. "You're asking if you can pay us back with favors."

"Let it be known that I never said such a word, Mr. Anderson."

"Of course. Can't let that little nugget get out. Ah…" He propped his elbow up on the arm of the chair. "What *can* you do to make our lives a little easier? I don't want to speak on behalf of Ms. Cromwell, but… I can think of a few things that might make her happy." He considered his options, although he realized he didn't have much time. Devon had to consider what would make *him* happiest… as well as Danielle, who certainly deserved as much happiness as anyone else.

Two things popped into his head, neither of which never had much to do with him.

"How much pull do you have with the American government?" Devon asked. "How much influence do you have over its military and its congress?"

"American..." The president glanced down to her right. "I'm assuming that is the Earth country you currently inhabit. Yes. I am quite familiar with it, unfortunately."

Devon didn't question that last bit. "Could you influence policies? And even... laws?"

President d'Errowyn already didn't like where this was going. "You'll have to be more specific than that, Mr. Anderson. It highly depends on the matter of the fav... I mean, request."

"Two things." Devon held up the appropriate number of fingers. "Legalize same-sex marriage." He dropped a finger. "And any court-martials that happened in the past year should be reviewed due to the legalization of same-sex marriage."

The tension dropped from the president's shoulders. "That's it?"

"No. I also want immunity from any future legal issues regarding whatever happened yesterday or *any time* before, crossing a thousand years. For all of us."

"All of... you."

Devon grinned. "Don't tell me you don't yet know, Madam President. I'm not an idiot."

She certainly wished he were.

Danielle was on autopilot, but not because she was dissociating. Nor was she afraid of what she might find at the end of her trek across town, beyond department stores, office buildings, and the hole-in-the-wall restaurants that defined her nights out. Danielle was on autopilot because her brain was filled with everything she wanted to say and do the moment she reached her destination.

People bumped into her, snapping that she should watch where she was going. More than one cab honked as she helped herself across intersections. The higher the sun shone and the more she felt the chill of the wind on her arms, the more she realized that she truly had been alive after all this time.

Her heart pounded in her chest while she grew closer to the center of downtown, where businesses gave way to government enterprises. Once, she had driven to and from work every day along these streets, a commute that often lasted twenty minutes depending on traffic. Today, while her mouth dried and her eyes grew large at the chance to see everything she desired, she remembered what it was like to go home and see the person she had most looked forward to being with.

Home wasn't always a cozy place filled with baked goods, warm beds, and hot showers. Sometimes, it was purely defined by the people who made a family she had never asked for, but was given by a merciful Void.

"There's no such things as soulmates," she had once been told, long, long ago. Was it her aunt? The woman to whom Sulim had been entrusted when her parents died so young? That woman enjoyed life as much as she enjoyed having her eyes gouged out with red-hot pokers. *"Whoever told you that at the Temple was loose a screw. The Void only knows who they pump out of their academies these days."*

The young and impressionable woman who had been ripped from her aunt's home and taken to a backward planet in the throes of the universe came to soon believe in soulmates, however. It was the only way to describe fate's hand in bringing her to the one thing that had ever actually made her happy.

She was closer. Always a little bit closer.

Once she spotted the administrative buildings that made up the bulk of M-Town, Danielle took off into a run completely powered by that feeling she had once embraced every time she flew a space cruiser closer to a planet out in the middle of nowhere. A truly inhospitable place only occupied by the few thousand who had no choice but to call it home.

Her feet flew across the pavement. She instinctively avoided the car checkpoint that regulated every vehicle, both personal and corporate, coming through the gates. Danielle was no longer authorized to bring a vehicle into M-Town. The only way she was getting in was through the one pedestrian walkway that cut across the unassuming plazas and civilian cafés that set up shop thanks to government subsidies.

More than one person in uniform watched her fly by as if Hermes himself had gifted her his winged feet. The only ones who recognized her were those forced to do a double-take to make sure she wasn't a crazed lunatic come to cause trouble in a heavily guarded area. It wouldn't be the first time someone attempted something funny in M-Town out of protest...

But anyone whose suspicions were slightly raised were soon blinded. Not by the sun, not by her clothes, but by the bright glow of the warmth radiating from her cheeks—and from the protective embrace of the one entity in the Void who cares.

Of course soulmates existed. When Sulim went to the Temple shortly before her capture, to bring an offering to the newly installed statue of the High Priestess, she overheard the Temple Priestess say, *"I wasn't supposed to get this post originally. I can't remember who was supposed to have it. Sometimes, the wind tells me she went to another timeline to find her soulmate."*

Only the High Priestess could peer into that Timeline That Never Was and see the truth. In another life, where the Void was not under constant threat of collapsing, Joiya never Ascended and lived her life as the proud wife of the High Priest and the mother of their only child. Since her father was the last to play favorites with any daughter of his, it only made sense that her first assignment as a priestess would be on the same backwater rock that any other acolyte would have discovered in her résumé.

It was always meant to be. Perhaps the High Priestess had nothing to do with Cairn showing up on Qahrain one fateful day, but she had seen it coming, several years before destiny set it in stone.

When the pigeons pecking at the cobblestone plaza centering the leisurely side of M-Town took flight to make room for Danielle's flying feet, her eyes locked on each person going about their day. Her pace did not slow until she spotted it.

The fountain.

Not a grand one. Barely big enough to get a decent spray on a hot day. Honestly, the only reason it was there was to "raise the spirits" of the uniformed employees and to make the civilians working custodial and food service think their taxes went to anything decent.

The sun was high in the sky. The lunch hour foot traffic wasn't as heavy as it usually was on a sunny day. Almost as if anyone who thought about going that way was suddenly inspired by the cosmos to take another direction.

There were more important things. Like a reunion that had been a thousand years in the making.

Miranda was the only one who didn't hear the Void's whispers to give the fountain plaza some space. Even if she had heard it, she would have probably ignored it, since the fountain was one of the few places she liked to eat lunch on a sunny day. Didn't matter if someone joined her or she had a bench to herself. The fountain reminded her of those days back on Cerilyn, when she took her first official earnings as chief and installed a little piece of paradise in a place that wasn't used to seeing such "fancy things" for the sake of them being there.

The fountain didn't mean much on its own. Not until Sulim had taken to spending a lot of her downtime on its edge, her blond hair sparkling with drops of spray and the bottom of her boots wetter than a fool dumped into the other side as a prank. Whenever Cairn wanted to find her out and about, odds were good she'd find her there, either reading over reports or indulging in a *book,* of all materials actually allowed out among the masses.

Like most days, Miranda sat there now, poking at her salad and wishing she had heard anything substantial from either Danielle or Devon.

She did not expect to look up from her phone and see someone come flying around the bend.

Danielle suddenly slowed to a walking pace the moment she saw Miranda sitting alone on the bench. The fountain was between them, but every time the spray lowered and revealed Miranda's hopeful face, Danielle's smile grew.

The plastic container and fork clattered to the ground the moment Miranda launched to her own feet, although she didn't dare move. Danielle could have been an illusion. The Void knew she had imagined this moment a hundred times over the past few years.

The moment when Danielle finally recognized her.

"Oh my God..." Miranda couldn't breathe. Lettuce was on her uniform, and a cherry tomato plunked unceremoniously to her flats. "Is that... are you..."

Danielle stopped a few antagonizing feet away from her. No matter how seriously she attempted to approach the situation, she couldn't stop smiling—not with so much unanticipated joy in her veins. "I was about to say the same thing to you."

A tear of disbelief flooded Miranda's face. She stumbled one foot forward. "It's you." Like Devon, she recognized that cognizant look in Danielle's eyes. The one that had been a part of Miranda's dreams since she first drew breath on this planet.

Sulim. *Her* Sulim.

But it wasn't the cloudy haze of a woman trapped in a momentary regression. This was her, in every sense of the beautiful word, and she was taking another step toward their long-awaited reunion.

Danielle's fists curled against her thighs. It was either that or make a fool of herself. "It's me."

What did it mean if Miranda's first reaction wasn't to cry in joy or to throw her arms around the partner of her heart? What if all she was capable of was wrapping her arms around herself, barricading her soul against the chance that this was a deceitful trap? That she was still asleep, fantasizing about a moment that could not possibly come for another thousand years?

She had spent all of her lives since the first one trying to get through to Sulim, the woman who had been too scared to remember her.

"I waited so long..." Miranda said, choking back a sob.

"I know. I'm sorry."

"You look..." No matter where she put her hands, Miranda could hardly contain herself. "You're more beautiful today than you were yesterday."

Danielle closed the gap between them. "So are you."

Their embrace cracked the earth beneath their feet, sending word to every soul walking among them that the first step toward righting the wrongs of the universe had been corrected. The pigeons that had fled at Danielle's arrival now returned, cooing on the fountain and tilting their heads at the two women who held each other so tightly while the forgotten song of the Harmony reverberated between their souls. Even Danielle, who had managed to keep it together, shed renewed tears now that her beloved was back in her arms.

Sulim, the woman sleeping deep within the subconscious of ninety-eight bodies, had never forgotten what this felt like.

"It was all our fault." Those were the first words that fell from her lips, and they were a hodgepodge of English and Old Basic, as if her soul didn't know how to talk anymore. "This whole mess. Forgetting you for so long... I'm so sorry." Her arms clung to Miranda, afraid to ever let her go again. "All those people died because of our selfishness."

Miranda pulled away, only to clasp her hands around Danielle's cheeks and to press their foreheads together. "Listen, we had no control over that, do you understand? Everyone was doomed from the moment that man set his sights on us. We couldn't... there was no way... even if we were a day faster getting our shit together..."

Danielle interrupted her, thoughts bouncing from one concept to the next. "We made it to Earth, huh?"

Miranda lowered her hands, thumb tracing the unforgettable outline of Danielle's lips. "Yes. We did."

There were no more words. Not now, when the only way they could be assured that the other was there was through a kiss that opened the crack beneath them. From their small corner of the world, to the far reaches of their isolated galaxy, every soul—both ensconced in a body and making its way back to the Void—stopped and heard their mutual cry of happiness. For a thousand years, the universe had held its breath. Now, it exhaled.

So did Danielle, when their kiss ended and a giant weight was lifted from her shoulders.

"What is it?" Miranda braced her hands against Danielle's shoulders so she wouldn't fall over. "Are you...?"

Laughter echoed across the plaza, louder than the splash of water or the cooing of pigeons. "I just..." Danielle bit her lip, savoring the taste of a kiss she had been yearning to indulge for so long. "This feeling in me..." Stress evaporated from her soul. The weight she had been carrying within her heart since she first died? It crashed through that planet, bottoming out and dissipating into the silence of the cosmos.

Everything was peaceful. Everything was as it should be.

"I'm free."

Miranda melted around her, cradling both head and shoulders as if Danielle would collapse at any moment. But all Danielle did was hug her back and laugh, her heart so light, her soul so airy, that a spell was broken.

"I remember now," Danielle said. "When I died..."

"I was there. I was there when you died in my goddamn arms..." Another sob cracked Miranda's face as she was the one who collapsed, Danielle's body the only thing propping her up.

"When I died, I only thought of seeing you again." *I wanted to feel that love again.* "You're here. I'm free."

Those were the magical words that made Miranda cry harder. It hadn't been enough that she find Sulim again—that Sulim even remember her and what they once had. *Something so strong yet perverse that we watched an entire world fall at our feet,* she recalled, as if she still tortured herself with that memory.

Cairn had to know that her beloved would never be in danger of succumbing to the worst fate imaginable. Sulim could never, ever be at risk of being trapped in the Process for the rest of time—and beyond.

"I'm..." Danielle held her hand to her face, holding back the realization as it manifested on her twisting tongue. "I'm free!"

The only language she spoke now was the Harmony that whispered all around them. As Miranda clung to her and Danielle deliriously laughed from the happiness chiming in the bones of her final physical form, the water of the fountain slowly stopped splashing and the pigeons fluttered away.

Miranda opened her eyes, and through the sheen of tears she now harbored, she saw the vague outline of her real mother standing where the water had been only a moment before.

"I'm so happy for you."

Miranda's hands slowly slid down Danielle's back. Knees hit the cobblestone. Danielle kneeled before her, a reassuring hand on Miranda's arm.

"It was always fate."

That's what Sulim used to say whenever Cairn bemoaned that she had brought such a "decent" person to the hell that was Cerilyn. Only now, when Miranda looked up into those crystal green eyes, she remembered what she used to say in return.

With a wan smile, Miranda pulled her beloved's face closer.

"We were always soulmates."

This time when they kissed, it was to the normal flow of Earth's life force. People wandered into the plaza, sparing open glances to the couple who flouted the rules. Cars rudely honked on the street only a block away. Someone complained outside one of the cafés that their sandwich had been incorrectly made by the civilian in the red T-shirt and black baseball cap.

None of those people mattered now. Anything could happen to their Earth-based fates, and it wouldn't matter. Miranda's impending court-martial might as well be a kiss-off from the prison she had endured as long as it meant being close to her fragile soulmate.

Someone who wasn't so fragile anymore.

"I love you," she said through her tear-stained face. "I never stopped."

"I know. I never stopped, either."

Their hands clasped together. How exhausting it was, finally experiencing the moment they had been waiting for since death first kissed their cheeks.

Fifty

The crystal blue skies of Sah Zenlit hardly ever saw a storm. The regular light rains ensured that Yahzen's biggest moon was always lush with beautiful greens and the bright, popping colors of both the native flora and those brought from the planet hanging high in the sky. It wasn't like Bah Zenlit, which enjoyed the bountiful technological progressions of terraforming (which was now on its thirteenth millennium of being "fully habitable") and the early *julah* who looked to their moons and said, *"We really should do something with those."*

While Bah Zenlit was molded into the home base of the Academy and provided intergalactic respite for the hybrids who came and went from Yahzen, Sah Zenlit had long been the pleasurable holiday moon that the heads of families retired to multiple times a year while their young children and middle-aged cousins saved up for a yearly sojourn that usually included a ridiculous amount of illicit substances and so much sex that a whole industry cropped up around it. Although Yahzen's laws extended to both of its moons, politicians enjoyed the revelry too much to enforce it on Sah Zenlit.

So when Nicola Ferran invited Lilla Amyran to an "escape to my favorite little hideaway," it wasn't just an invitation to elevate Lilla's standing among Nicola's peers. It meant something big was about to happen. With only Lilla invited along, did Nicola want to make her the new trusted confidant of the century, or was this a celebration of becoming first-time grandmothers, as little as it meant to the both of them?

Well, they were the heads of their families. And women, to boot. Any excuse to go live it up on Sah Zenlit was a good one.

Only Lilla, who had been to the moon more times than she could dare to count, wasn't expecting to arrive at The Celestial Palace, the most exclusive timeshare that only the most influential of men and women could hope to purchase a suite in at any given time.

Did Nicola really exert so much influence over *julah* politics? Because this was the home away from home for the world leaders, Temple heads, and cultural artisans that were so important that they were bequeathed with the Medal of Artistic Integrity as befitting a person who had contributed much to *julah* art and culture. One of the last few figureheads to receive such an honor was Ramaron Marlow's father, the acclaimed novelist, whose books were still in every tutor's bag.

Lilla wondered if the Marlows had a seasonal suite at The Celestial Palace. Not that it mattered now, because he had turned down her advances how many times?

"This place is simply..." Lilla didn't often like to let her plebian guard down, but Nicola had such an affable air about her that day that Lilla didn't care if this was later used against her. "I don't know how to put it. I've never been to this part of the moon before. By the High Priestess's flawless hair, look at that *view!*" She referred to the image of Yahzen in the sky. Sah Zenlit was closer to the planet than its smaller cousin, meaning that on an ordinary clear day the blue atmosphere of one of the oldest inhabited planets of the universe loomed lovingly in the sky. No wonder a place like this was often reserved for the artists and spiritually inclined. Lilla already considered a new career as a poet. "Oh, it's simply to die for. I don't know how I can ever contain myself." Her giggles touched Nicola on the cheek as they helped themselves to the front steps leading up to the main atrium of the timeshare, where staff clad in royal blue uniforms awaited to take their luggage and check them in. "You truly own a little piece of this paradise?"

Nicola's smug look was exactly what Lilla fished for when she asked that. "Been in the family for about a thousand years now. We don't often get to come, so I usually loan it out to friends looking for a getaway and wanting to bypass the *inkep* matchmakers trying to make a side-dollar. My father got it for quite the steal back then. You see, the family that used to own it rather... fell out of favor and had to sell their parcel to make ends meet when the government came calling."

It took Lilla a few seconds to glean who Nicola meant. "No," she whispered. "You mean the Dunsmans?"

"Careful, darling." Nicola greeted the woman at the top of the steps with her most amiable smile. "It's the Ducahs now. How are you, Calseeth?"

Nicola exchanged kisses to the cheek with Calseeth Ducah, who had hopped over from Bah Zenlit for this auspicious occasion. Lilla didn't recognize the dowdy woman in a gray shift dress at first—the timeshare staff in their glistening blue uniforms were *so* much more eye-catching. Especially the young man with abs chiseled out of marble. Lilla's eyes lingered on him far longer than was kosher for a professional establishment such as this one.

"Absolutely content, Lady Ferran," Calseeth said. "You must introduce me."

"Of course. Calseeth, please allow me to introduce you to my newest, dearest friend and the most recent addition to my extended family. This is Lady Lilla Amyran, my daughter's mother-in-law. Lilla, sweetheart." Nicola motioned for the two to come closer. "This is Calseeth Ducah, Master Obello's steward at the Academy. She's one of my most closely guarded confidants as of late."

Although Lilla recognized the name Ducah, she still couldn't quite place Calseeth. Probably because Calseeth was the ultimate "never seen, rarely heard" member of her employer's household. Only when Lilla happened to glance at the dim blond hair and the slope of the nose did she realize Calseeth was one of *those* Ducahs—the ones most genetically linked to the last Master of House Dunsman.

"Calseeth is behind that wonderful opportunity I told you about." Nicola acted as if she had not dropped some bomb on Lilla's head. "Come along. Let us go inside and get settled. I am dying for an early dinner out on the balcony."

While Lilla went ahead with the manager—who had been slipped a heavy stack of bills to keep Lilla occupied—Nicola fell back with Calseeth. "Is everything ready, dear?" Lady Ferran muttered to the steward.

Calseeth offered a curt nod. "He is waiting."

A chill went down Nicola's spine. It was the first and only time she would show any distaste for what she had agreed to do with poor Lilla. "Don't worry. I'll play my dunderheaded part. This is for the good of the universe, after all." She sighed, striking ahead of Calseeth. "I do love the universe. It has me in it."

She caught up to Lilla, who had been thoroughly distracted by the vintage *julah* artwork on display in the Palace lobby. The hostess who had come to greet the Ferran party pretended to be delighted with Lilla's rube-like wit which, of course, was merely her sad act of playing the socialite she thought herself. Lilla always outstayed her welcome, but she had her uses—beyond sacrificing her to a world Nicola wanted nothing to do with.

That wasn't to say Lilla had no agency. Ultimately, everything would be her own decision. But since Nicola knew her well enough by now, she had a feeling that Lilla would sell her soul to the devil himself if it meant advancing her social standing and securing the genetic legacy she so loudly sought.

"Lilla, my dear sister of the Void." Nicola placed her fingertips upon Lilla's forearm and offered her the most genial of smiles. "I've been informed that there is a resident who would greatly like to meet you. Alone."

That perked Lady Amyran's ears right up. "Is that so? Who is it? A painter? A travel writer? Oh, perhaps a politician on holiday away from his family?"

Nicola was compelled to play along with Lilla's ambitions, if only to keep them both placated enough to head down the front hallway. With a wave of Nicola's hand, the hostess forgot what she was doing and returned to her post at the front of the Palace. Not like Nicola didn't know where her family's suite was located.

"You might say it's a man of grand standing taking an extended leave from his family." Nicola looped her arm around Lilla's. As they strolled down the hallway, their full skirts swished together and the strings of beads in their hair tickled their scalps. Lilla looked around to ensure that the staff and other guests saw her walking arm-in-arm with *the* Lady Ferran. *It's one thing for these people to know we are loosely related by law now,* she thought, as Young Master Hylem looked up from his tablet by the big bay windows. *What a handsome young man! I wonder if he's available...* So what if he was a good 1500 years younger than her?

Everyone knew the Hylems—of the political sect, that was—were some of the most strapping specimens of *julah* masculinity in the past thousand years.

"What was with Calseeth Ducah saying hello to us just now?" Lilla asked when they reached the end of the long, well-lit hallway. "I didn't know you were acquaintances with the Ducahs." That was said with a slight hiss of the breath and a flick of the wrist. "Couldn't that be scandalous? I know you parley in scandal, but..."

"The Ducahs are perhaps the dowdiest, most nothing family around right now, darling." Nicola urged Lilla down another hallway. One shorter, narrower, and darker. Had it been there only a minute ago? Lilla swore that when they first came down this hallway, only a staircase and a large set of doors leading out to the monumental labyrinth and one-room café were seen. Now the wall was solid. A painting of Vallahar Estate, where *cageh* was grown and families faced a recent scandal, took up most of the wood panels. "Even when you deduct the crimes committed by some of their own, they have long been like that, so it's not only them staying low and rebuilding face." She shrugged. "Calseeth is a sweet dear. She attends some of my parties I must invite you to soon. She has quite the wrist at dice. Sometimes, we don't always need outlandish, flirtatious, and hilarious friends."

Lilla chewed on that for a bit, afraid to admit that she still didn't quite get it. Nobody associated with the Ducahs aside from lower families that didn't have much to lose from it. That a man like Master Obello had hired Nerilis Dunsman's first cousin to be his steward had long been a point of contention behind closed doors. The Obellos were the kind of untouchable family who had enjoyed grand privileges and adoration since before Lilla's own mother could remember. Then again... perhaps that was why he didn't think twice about it when he saw the opportunity for a skilled steward who would keep to herself and live longer than another hundred years.

Still... *Calseeth?* She looked like the dowdy tutor who had educated Lilla when she was a child. All intellectual substance, no *fun!*

"You know what?" Nicola turned to Lilla, interrupting her thoughts. "I forgot something in the coach I would be mighty sore to leave in there. It's... ah... it's my daughter's ultrasound! Yes, yes, I was going to share it with you tonight over dinner so we can enjoy the first true signs of our mutual grandchild. Do be a dear and go ahead without me, Lilla. The Ferran suite is right here on the grand floor, down that narrow hall."

Nicola grabbed her skirts and flew back down the hallway as if the painting of Vallahar Estate had scared the panties off her. Lilla cocked her head for a moment before turning toward the dim hallway that showed no signs of being recently traversed. Quite the shocking sight for a place so exclusive that Lilla considered it the highlight of her year to be here—more exciting than the birth of her first grandchild!

"Hm." Nobody else was around. No staff, no stewards to ask for directions. Even when she glanced toward where they had come from, she swore the hallway had extended, toying with her. The only way to go was forward, so Lilla hiked up her skirt and carefully stepped down the darkened hallway.

Surely, this was a magical trick of the senses. Perhaps a parlor game that The Celestial Palace employed to entertain their snobby guests. *Julah* were like that, always bored and looking for new ways to bend the universe to their daily pleasure. Why shouldn't this secluded corner of Sah Zenlit be any different?

The moment Lilla glanced down to ensure she didn't step on her honey-colored skirt, her head banged into a door that had not been there a second before.

"My...!" Her back straightened, her hand on her head and her fabric falling from her grasp. "What is the meaning of this? Is this some kind of prank?" She spun around, hoping to the Void that Nicola was right behind her.

No. Lilla was alone. Abandoned to whatever fate awaited her.

The door didn't budge. Not when she attempted to turn the handle. Surely, this was the entrance to the Ferrans' suite. What in the world was keeping Lilla from getting to it?

"This is preposterous." After jiggling the handle a little longer, she splayed her fingers across the panel and concentrated her energy on opening the door with a little *force*. "Absolutely... oof!" Her frustration mounted when she imagined one of the staff or, worse, Nicola coming upon her having a fight with a simple door! Even if this was the wrong way—and why would Nicola do that to her?—Lilla would rather be caught accidentally trespassing than looking like a Void-cursed fool!

With a swipe of her frustrated hand, she unlocked one of the mechanisms stuck inside of the door. A low, green glow appeared around the handle. When Lilla realized this was a more advanced spell thwarting her progress, she gave the door a small kick and muttered a curse that she would have the head of whatever ancestor had produced such awful offspring to do this to her.

It took her five minutes to focus her concentration on the puzzling door. Once she had her wits about her, however, it was only a matter of convincing apparatuses she could neither see nor touch that they should sway beneath the movements of her hand. Confounded her, didn't it? Yet she prevailed, since if the Amyrans were good for one thing, it was producing offspring with enough magical fortitude to get into the Academy.

The door eventually swung open. Lilla, who had debased herself in front of that blasted door, smoothed out her clothing and cleared her throat before stepping inside.

"Hello?" she greeted the shadowy nothingness inside the Ferrans' suite. The only reason she knew she had the right one was because of the family portrait hanging in the small foyer. Was it Nicola and her husband and daughter, though? Of course not. More like a much younger Nicola and her own parents, both of whom were now deceased. "Is anyone here? Nicola, sweetheart? Oh, don't tell me I'm being–"

A feminine silhouette appeared from a back room. Before Lilla had a mild panic attack, however, Calseeth bowed to her.

"Right this way, Lady Amyran. He is waiting to see you."

"Who...?" Yet Lilla took the necessary steps forward, for if there was anything that intrigued her, it was the mysterious promise that something might be waiting for her on the other side of a door. "Is this an early birthday present, or am I being singled out for a prank? Tell me the truth!"

Calseeth said nothing. She merely opened a single door and urged Lilla inside. Naturally, the door was closed behind them.

"What is this…" Yet Lilla's attentions were soon stolen by the man sitting in the lounge chair by the window, a glass of warmed *yaya* in his hand.

Nerilis looked right at home in a suite that was not his own. Yet hadn't it been, only a thousand years ago? This was a place he could enjoy the fruits of his family's labor without dealing with the family itself. A place he had often brought his fiancée, back when they had any sliver of hope or joy for the future.

Those were the things he contemplated as he gazed out the window. Once Lilla was before him, however, her jaw dropping and her hand on her breast, he finally gave her half of his attention.

"This is the Lady Lilla Amyran, sir," Calseeth said. "The one I procured for you with the quiet help of the Ferrans."

"Yes, the Ferrans will be remembered, even if they did take my family's blasted timeshare." Nerilis barely sat up in greeting. Lilla attempted to take a step back, but that wouldn't do. With barely a nod of his head, she was stuck where she stood, her feet glued to the floor and her balance only held upright with the might of a man who could turn her body inside-out if he wanted. Except that took more effort than he was willing to give right now. "That will be all for now, Calseeth. I'll call upon you when Lady Amyran is ready to leave."

Calseeth left as quickly as her feet allowed. The door was locked behind her.

"You… you are…!"

Lilla grabbed her throat as her airway was unceremoniously closed. Nerilis never once laid a hand on her, but he didn't have to— he merely needed her to not *scream*. Not only was it more work for Nerilis, who would have to silence everyone in the palace, but it took so much effort to overcome the agency of another full-blooded *julah*. The only reason he found Lilla so malleable was due to her lowered defenses and the fact that, while the Amyrans were adept sorcerers in their own right, they didn't come close to the legacy in his line.

"Silence is the greatest favor you can grant me right now, Lady Amyran." Nerilis leaned forward in his chair, aware that he would have to let Lilla breathe again shortly. "I'm assuming you were led here under false pretenses. The odds you knew you were going to see *me* are insurmountable." He finally let her breathe, her airways unlocking and the gasps rattling her ribcage. Lilla fell to her knees, hands bracing against the carpet as her travel dress was marred by old dust and the wrinkles creasing the folds. "But I am grateful you are here. You might be... adequate."

"What..." Lilla struggled to look at him, the man she instantly recognized but could hardly believe was in her presence. "What is the meaning of this?"

"You got in here on your own, so you have passed my simple test of sorcery. I also hear that both of your sons are students of the Academy, although they are only half of our blood." Nerilis stood before the window, hands behind his back. "That's impressive. Although I'm sure my old friend Ramaron Marlow helped you with getting the youngest boy in. I've seen him in his classes. He is... well, he tries."

Lilla propped herself up on her own feet, her heart racing and her interest piqued. The man hadn't killed her, so there was that. She was worth more to him alive than dead. "What do you want with my sons, Master Dunsman?"

"Please," he drolly said. "Call me Nerilis. We should be on a first-name basis, Lilla." He pursed his lips. "Your family. The Amyrans. I knew some of your kin well. One of your cousins was an acolyte alongside me in the Temple. Too bad what happened to your family. I don't keep up with our social politics, but it's always a travesty when one must fall out of favor so another can rise. It is the ebb and flow of our people's culture. However, it is a bane when it happens during *our* generations."

"I don't understand," Lilla said. "Why are you here? What do you want with me?"

"My cousin tells me that you are a woman known for your feminine wiles and your interest in furthering your family's prospects in the present age. Yet because of the standing of the name 'Amyran,' you may not have your pick of suitors.

Travesty, that. My cousin knows it all too well. She remains a spinster because the only proposals she can garner are insults to the Dunsman name."

"Master... I mean... Nerilis." The name fumbled on Lilla's tongue. "I'm still not following."

"Of course not. You have no idea what is happening beneath our very feet or above our heads. Out there, right now, the universe quakes for help. Yet what choices do I have to fix it right now? Something beyond even my own reach. I need help."

Lilla was stunned into silence.

"Don't worry," he continued. "I'm not asking you to end life alongside me. Why in the world would I ask a random woman to partake in that? Instead, I am asking you to create it."

She took a step back.

"I don't have much time before my hold on this place falters," Nerilis said. "Let me make this short for you. I need a new wife. You need a husband befitting your perceived standing. Most of all, I'm sure you would love a child that will cement your legacy."

"Are you... are you asking me to *marry* you?"

"I'd actually prefer to not *really* get married. You see, I don't consider myself a proper widower of the soul. It's bad enough I'm even considering this. But if it makes you more likely to join me, then sure."

"I... I...!"

"You may take some time to think about it, of course. I'm sure this is a great shock to you. But I can't grant you much time before I must find another woman who might be willing. Time is very much of the essence. Considering how many tries it may require, how long it takes to gestate a child of our kind... the wait for it to mature well enough to aid us in crossing dimensions is almost too long. I would need an answer within a week, and we would start immediately."

"How many..." Lilla was too hung up on *that* to consider everything else her potential suitor said. "How many *tries?*"

"I think you'll find I am more than adequate. Helps that I hear you're quite the wildling yourself. You and your son have both proven to be quite fertile, it seems. That will be a help."

Lilla half-fainted against the chair Nerilis had been in when she entered the room.

"Like I said. I will give you one week. When you have made your decision, reach out to my cousin and she will act as our go-between. Should you decide to turn me down, however... or if you tell a single soul about what happened here today, including Lady Ferran..." He narrowed his brows. "I'd threaten your other children, but I don't think you care too much for them. No. I'd have to threaten something else. Such as your family estate. Have you been thinking about remodeling?"

"If I turn you down, you will destroy my *home*?"

"No, that's if you tell anyone. If you turn me down, I will merely wipe your memory of this day. I can't have you out there blabbing."

This was more than a little "much" for Lilla, who was more starstruck than fearful. Within two minutes of entering this room, she had not only come to face to face with the most hated man in history—but had received a ludicrous "proposal" from him.

But there was a reason Lady Amyran's name was one of the first on Nicola's lips when Calseeth approached her. Not only was her family known for its slightly advanced sorcery skills, but the woman was desperate. Enough so that she would entertain a proposal from *any* man who checked all of her boxes.

It also helped that her heart and body were depraved enough to do it.

She said she would think about it, but everyone who knew about the proposal already knew her answer from the look of endless possibilities in her eyes.

FIVE MONTHS LATER

Forgetting the whirlwind of the past year and a half was easy when a woman had much to occupy her mind in the present time. Women like Danielle had so much on her plate that it was easy to watch time fly by, one day after another, as if nothing mattered except what people wanted from her on one specific day.

Where to even begin?

The Federation's interest in her had piqued after the events with Commander d'Alacron, who had recently returned to her post after an *extended* leave of absence that almost cost her a career years in the making. No longer was Devon the go-to guy for interviews, research studies, and flights of fancy from faraway "fans" who sent strange letters and made the *weirdest* gifts, like effigies that could only be described by Danielle as, "This is some hexing shit, and I want it de-demonized before it's destroyed."

Or, perhaps it should be said, no longer were people placated with only Devon's presence when either both or *just* Danielle was requested. Gone were the days when she could feign ignorance and laziness as an excuse. As soon as the parliamentary government called upon her to testify about that day's events, she was in the crosshairs of every news network and would-be biographer. The way music producers stalked Devon had now become true about book publishers and Danielle, who asked her—no, *harassed* her—to write a memoir or ten. Neither she nor Devon were wont to become full-blown celebrities, however. While Devon's band signed an intergalactic contract with Pauloso d'Whain, the head of one of the biggest labels in the Federation, Danielle told the would-be publishers of her biography to take a hike. The only thing she could stand to write was a letter to her grandmother.

Devon had stayed true to his convictions to change the direction of his final life. After resigning from his job, he dedicated himself to his band, whether that meant writing songs or negotiating contracts. The biggest hurdle was telling the rest of his bandmates about what they were signing up for, since Serge was as oblivious to the Federation as Devon had been only two years ago. The hardest thing wasn't accepting Devon's role in the machinations of the universe—it was acknowledging that, yes, May really was an "alien" and her family had only been on Earth for about a generation. By the way, did they know that humans in the Federation lived much longer than those born and raised on Earth? May was destined to outlive them all by about fifty years, so they better get along with her since she would one day own the rights to their whole catalog.

Devon also stayed true to holding Marlow financially accountable for the people he had hired a thousand years ago. After all, Devon had to fund his new lifestyle, and Danielle deserved her own money in *her* bank accounts. Even lush with funds, there was so little time for personal lives as the weather warmed up and people became more demanding. Devon and May attempted dating one last time before, two dates in, they officially called it "hopeless." Devon took it as his cue to throw himself into his work and the company he already kept. After all, he had some catching up to do with someone who had been dormant for over a thousand years.

But for as much as Danielle would have liked to have more quiet evenings at home, life on Earth and beyond continued to hound her. The greatest shock had nothing to do with the Federation, or at least as far as she knew. No, that came in the form of the federal government announcing that they were repealing "Don't Ask, Don't Tell" and overturning any related court-martials in the past two years. When General Noyes personally showed up at Danielle's door—when she had *company*, no less!—he told her as much, and that, due to her contributions to the

Federation over the past thousand years, she would be granted a promotion to Captain and assigned a "lowkey" spot as a liaison to the local Federation outpost near M-Town. She almost turned it down, but the extra money and benefits made it too hard to pass up. Especially since she was a petty woman who would have loved nothing more than to stick it to the very institution that had fucked over her and her friends.

Becoming Captain and returning to military life wasn't the craziest thing. Two months later, the Californian Supreme Court announced that denying gay marriage was unconstitutional. The feds soon followed suit, with the Supreme Court of the United States declaring the same. During an election year, no less. The two top Democratic Party candidates had to revise their platforms since "gay marriage good" and "Don't Ask, Don't Tell bad" had been one of the few things they had in their arsenal. The only people who knew this was a direct influence from the Federation were those in the top political echelon... and Devon, who made a point of not telling Danielle he had asked for those favors.

Not everyone reclaimed their posts, however. When Danielle met with Ben and a few others who had been court-martialed, most had decided to cash out the retirements they had been denied and go on with civilian life. With her new rank and assignment, Danielle said goodbye to M-Town for most of the week and instead spent easy workdays hanging around the Federation outpost near the mayor's office.

All while covertly planning something she dearly hoped the media would miss.

Danielle sat in her car on a hot August day. The heat didn't get to her, though. She may have worn a black jacket and trousers that sucked against her legs, but the only thing making her sweat was nerves. She had checked her hair half a dozen times before realizing her problem wasn't that she thought she was too ugly to exit her car: it was the crippling knowledge that life was about to be very different after that day.

Cold feet often cooled a girl down from the heat hanging over her head.

She opened her glove compartment and unearthed one of the packs of cigarettes she had confiscated from Miranda a few weeks ago. Danielle didn't care about being a hypocrite. She cared about calming down her nerves, and if that meant she smelled a little when she walked across the street, so be it.

She had barely stuck a cigarette in her mouth and lit it before someone knocked on the passenger side window.

"Are you smoking?" Devon called through the glass. "I'm gonna tell on you."

Danielle leaned her elbow against her door. She might as well open it and extinguish the cigarette beneath her shoe. *Caught red-handed,* she thought, while unlocking her car and allowing Devon into the passenger seat. *Can't have anything without the Void spying on you.*

"Narc," Danielle muttered.

Devon ignored that. "Is there a reason you're sitting in your car right now instead of going inside?"

"What, were you sent to come find me because I'm not ten minutes early?" She flung herself against her seat, wrinkling her clothes. "Nice outfit, by the way. You clean up decently."

"Decently?" Devon didn't even have his suit jacket on since, unlike Danielle, he deemed it too hot. Instead, he adorned Danielle's car in a powder blue button-up and expensive aftershave that he had imported from Arrah. Much like most of the things now in his home. The few trips back to his old home planet had resulted in *way* too many gifts from his descendants and the local folk who became more curious about his appearances. "Do you know how much I paid to look like this today? Did it for you, by the way. So get your ass in there so this wasn't a huge waste."

"I'll *go.*" Yet Danielle wasn't in a hurry to move. "I just want some peace to myself before I commit."

"Commit to what's happening today?"

"Commit to getting *up.* God." Danielle's elbow rested against the door handle. "You're worse than our ex-girlfriend. Did you learn these mind games from her?"

"Probably." That prompted Devon to get out his phone. He had recently up-graded to the second iPhone, which purported to have *3G* capabilities. Made the communicator he purchased for use in the Federation look like an intergalactic satellite, though. "I got the best camera on the market for today."

"All right, just don't sell any of the pictures to the press. I'd have to kill you."

"Nervous, huh?"

"No," Danielle was too quick to say. "Just, you know... sitting here, thinking about my entire existence." She sighed. "Feels like so much has been leading up to this moment. Doesn't quite feel real."

"Yeah..." Devon fired off a text and pocketed his phone before Danielle noticed. "Sure has been a looong time coming."

Danielle stared at the horn in the middle of her steering wheel. A part of her was compelled to slam it. Another part—the ancient part filled with useless, even older tech—saw this whole vehicle as incredibly beneath her and charmingly obsolete compared to, say, the space cruisers she once flew.

I learned how to fly during my first assignment, she recalled. Quite suddenly, since that was how most of those memories flooded back in her direction. *Two years on an empty moon, quarantined by the Federation Forces when we were only supposed to be gone seven days.* There had never been much more to do except watch TV, read the scant few books available, and go for spins around the moon. Hell, that was how *everyone* in Sulim's squad learned to fly space cruisers. *When they weren't doing the fourth thing, which was fucking anything slightly warm and alive.* She had not partaken.

Damn it, why did she suddenly feel like a party killer?

"I need a drink," she announced.

"There's alcohol inside. I've already scouted the bar."

"I told her to not spring for the open bar."

"You've been denying a smoker her cigarettes for how many months now?" Devon received confirmation that his text was read. "You're expecting her to *not* have an open bar?"

Danielle closed her eyes. "Shut up. Just five seconds of peace and contemplation. *Then* I'll go inside."

Someone came out of the building and hustled across the street. Devon pretended he didn't notice. "Uh-huh," he said, eyes forward.

Knuckles rapped on the driver's side window, jerking Danielle awake. The knocks kept coming until she rolled down the window and saw Miranda's face flushed red with frustration and her perfectly kempt hair tangling in the breeze blowing by outside. What had been hair freshly styled and dyed at her favorite Asian salon the day before was now a veil before her face, and the white three-piece suit that hugged her body caught on the wind as well. The only thing static about her was the wide-eyed glare that now slapped Danielle across the cheek.

"Is this my cigarette?" Miranda hissed, hand reaching into Danielle's car to grab the pack off the dashboard. "You were out here *smoking?*" She gestured to Devon before Danielle had the chance to rebut. "With him?"

"I don't smoke," Devon said. "I didn't think she did either. Today's full of surprises."

"Would both of you shut up?" Danielle braced herself against the steering wheel. She was *this* close to starting the engine and jetting down the street. "This isn't what it looks like!"

Devon leaned over the armrests. "She has cold feet," he proclaimed.

"Thanks, Dev." Danielle switched to Old Basic to really rub it in his face. "You're truly my best pal."

Miranda wasn't amused. "There are two dozen people in there waiting for us," she reminded Danielle, who rolled her eyes. "My own grandmother flew three-thousand miles all by herself to get here. She's currently in there having a very one-sided conversation with *your* grandmother." Miranda jabbed Danielle right in the arm. "If we don't get back in there in the next minute, God only knows what the *julah* are going to do. My father's friend is probably going to start telling dad jokes and do party tricks. My grandmother is *not* ready for aliens to be real."

A car whizzed by behind her. Miranda was completely unflustered.

Sighing, Danielle gave in. "Just wanted five minutes of peace before I sell my soul to the rest of this day. I see now how foolhardy of an endeavor that was."

Miranda opened the door. "Five minutes of peace? I've spent the past four months planning this shit. Did I ever get peace? No! Because you took all of my cigarettes for yourself, apparently!"

"Uh-oh." Devon slowly opened his door. "Mom's mad. You better do what she says before she puts you in timeout and takes away all your birthday presents."

"Speaking of your birthday," Miranda continued. "The whole reason I put a rush job on this was because you were so adamant it happen before your birthday."

Danielle's own fault, really. She was turning thirty-one in two weeks, and some part of her *refused* to officially enter her third decade on Earth without proving she was capable of achieving certain rites of passage that came so easily to other people.

"You guys suck." She grabbed her few things and stuck her keys in her pockets. Devon joined her in getting out of the car, if only so she could lock it before crossing the street with Miranda right behind her. "Suck, suck, suckity *suck.*"

"When did she become such a whiner?" Devon shouted to Miranda in Old Basic. "Do you remember her being a huge whiner?"

"I remember *you* being a whiner." Miranda shoved aside an usher as the three of them entered the church at an unassuming cross-street. She stopped in front of a mirror in the reception room and vainly fixed her hair. "Make sure she gets in there, would you? Last thing I need is her hopping the next cruiser to Qahrain because she has to go find herself or something."

"I wasn't going *anywhere,*" Danielle protested. She barely acknowledged Troy as he approached from the main room, which remained heavily guarded against outsiders. Or was the Federation personnel with stun guns there for decoration?

"Somebody who speaks a language I do not know," Troy began, fixing the corsage on Danielle's jacket, "is in there complaining about something to do with his butt. I think he might have hemorrhoids, and I'm sorry, but I did not bring my special bottom pillow from home."

Devon pushed Danielle toward her real best friend. "Take this, would you? Make sure she's actually present when the fun starts. I've gotta go find my seat." He clapped Danielle on the right shoulder. "See you on the other side, tiger."

Troy gasped at Danielle. "Were you going to stiff a lady?" he hissed.

"Stiff? Is that what we're calling it now?" Danielle followed Troy into the main room. What looked like a plain community church was actually the Bay Area's own Temple of the Void, complete with altar bedecked with offerings to both the Void and the High Priestess. A life-sized ivory statue stood behind the altar, the High Priestess's gaze locked on the open skylight above her. Mahogany benches did not come with Bibles, but instead sported literature in both Basic and English about the Temple's history. They also suggested popular prayers to offer the Void. But what the Temple best dealt in were the rites of passage of Federation members while also consoling the souls that came and went from the Void. The *ma-julah* priest assigned to this little outpost had happily told Danielle that the local Temple was so shoestring that they didn't even have a statue of the High Priestess until a few months ago. *"A generous donation from a patron who doesn't stop by much."*

That priest was now deeply engaged in discussion with Marlow, who stood off to the side with a dog leash in his hand. Charlie, who had been scarce enough to make Devon and Danielle wonder if he was dead, kept quiet because Evan was only three feet away entertaining him with treats that occasionally flew up into the air and landed in the dog's mouth. Lanelle shared a bench with him, eyes half-closed and mouth slacking open as she sorely attempted to catch up on lost sleep. The work of Ramaron Marlow's personal assistant rarely ended, especially when that woman also liked to party.

"There you are!" Regina jumped up from the front-row bench and met Danielle halfway down the aisle. "I've been looking for you, honey. This place gives me the creeps." She sensed the priest right behind her, his body bedecked in the robes and linens befitting his ceremonial station. Did he look right at her when she said that? Naturally! "I mean, I've never been someplace that's so... evangelically Catholic."

"It's neither, Gran. Okay? We've been over this like twelve times."

"Don't mind her." Troy patted Danielle on the chest. "She's got a case of the cold feet."

"I do not have cold feet!"

"Thank God for that." Miranda breezed past Danielle, pausing only to kiss Regina on the cheek. "I'd be mighty pissed."

"Oh, isn't she lovely?" Regina looked after Miranda with a sigh. "Oh, you're lovely too, sweetheart." She fixed the corsage losing petals on Danielle's suit jacket. "I can't... believe..." Regina lifted her glasses and wiped both eyes. "That this..."

"God," Danielle muttered. "I can't deal with this right now."

"Danielle!" A hand shot up from the second row. "Holy shit! Look at you!"

Alicia leaped out of the bench, her silk skirt and bushy blouse sashaying with her ladylike steps that clicked in kitten heels. As she flung her arms around Danielle and smushed the corsage, Danielle was compelled to return the hug. She hated to admit it, but her nerves calmed a bit with her ex-girlfriend in her arms.

"Me? I should look half as cute as you right now." That's what Danielle said when Alicia finally hopped down and gave everyone some space. "Uh, thanks for coming. Hope you didn't have to travel far."

"I've actually moved back to the area." Alicia grinned. "Finally going back to law school in a couple of weeks. Term starts right around your birthday."

"Make sure you get some fun in, all right? I mean, you didn't get to come to my shindig the other night, so for all I know you haven't partied since we last dated."

Danielle wished she could stop and actually talk to the people who made it out there for her that day, but the priest soon motioned for her to approach him. She drew in a deep breath and went ahead, leaving Alicia to awkwardly stand between Regina—who had no eyes for anyone but her granddaughter—and a representative from the Federation who didn't speak English.

"Hey."

Her head whipped around to find Devon standing only a couple feet away. "Oh, hey." She absentmindedly tucked her hair behind her ear. "Long time no see. You, uh…" As much as either of them hated to admit it, her eyes were prone to a quick perusal of how he was dressed that day. "You look good."

"Just good, huh?"

"Yeah, you've been working out?"

All Devon could do was laugh at that question. The man hadn't stopped working out since he first regressed, and to say he looked "different" from his graduation photos a year ago was like saying Danielle had a rough year. Didn't help that Danielle's regression had sent her running to the gym as well, and Devon having a buddy to ring the lunk alarm with him was going to bring down their corner of the neighborhood.

"Sorry." Alicia tucked hair behind her other ear. "I never know what to say anymore. Everything's so… yeah."

As other people sat down on the few rows of benches, Devon gestured to where Alicia had been only a moment before. "Need someone to sit with? I don't really have any friends here." He had invited both Clyde and May as his plus ones, but neither felt comfortable being there that day. A part of him was glad of it now—and glad that Alicia hadn't brought a date either.

"Sure." Alicia backed up into the bench and slid over to give Devon room. "Reminds me of that time we went to my cousin's wedding in the Hamptons."

"Yeah, it's *just* like that time." Devon was stuck on the aisle while one of the armed guards made his rounds. *Absolutely a normal day. Yup.* He thought that while Alicia pinched her skirt beneath her thighs so none of her clothing touched him. He tried not to think about how they had been living together only a year and some change ago. Honestly, having Alicia as a girlfriend felt like another lifetime, as if Devon had died and been reborn at least once since then. *I broke into her damn room to say I was sorry.* Not one of his better moments. At least he had nothing on Danielle who, a mere three days after regressing, broke into *his* apartment in the middle of the night and woke him up "to talk." The effects of regressing could last weeks, and often included brash decisions that sounded perfectly normal at the time.

"So, uh…" Alicia's fingers twiddled in her lap. "How are things? I haven't heard from you in a while."

"Things have been crazy. And I sent you a text like two days ago you never responded to. Too busy moving?"

Alicia blushed. "You could say that."

"You staying with Jenna?"

"No, she has a boyfriend now she lives with. I got a studio near campus. Nowhere near as spacious as the apartment we used to have, though. You still around?"

"Yeah, I reupped my lease. Month to month, though. Dunno. Might move soon. Keeping my options open." For one thing, he might want a place with a proper bedroom. And security. Security was becoming a bigger concern. Just because he could knock a stalker on their ass didn't mean he wanted to. *Not to mention,* he thought, *stalkers from the Federation know how to use some crazy weapons.* "This town is starting to get expensive, though."

"Thought you didn't have to worry about that anymore?"

Devon couldn't fault her for bringing that up. He had been the dumbass who told her during one of their phone conversations that he was probably set for life. This final life was his to live, after all. And at only twenty-three, there was plenty to do and accomplish.

He didn't have everything figured out like Danielle did.

"You ever been to one of these before?" Alicia whispered in his direction. "I feel like we're in a church, but instead it's all idolatry."

"Never been to one on Earth, no." Devon had been to quite a few ceremonies in local Temples of the Void, but not in this life. Or the last one either, probably. "I figure every place has to come up with their own ways of doing things. Plus, you know they're not that, uh, spiritual. It's going to be quick."

"Hopefully not too quick." Alicia pulled out her phone and saw that Devon had sent her a text, asking if she was already there. As she struggled to react, she continued, "It would be nice to catch up afterward, though."

Was that an insinuation? "I don't know how long the reception will last. I think they said it'll be at some tiny Federation bar. Something about 'where it all began,' whatever that means."

"Knowing Danielle, she'll want to bounce from that after an hour. Guess we'll have the whole place to ourselves soon enough."

That was *definitely* an insinuation. One Devon wasn't sure how to navigate. For months, he had struggled with what he felt every time he remembered his relationship with Alicia. The urge to text her was always there, so it wasn't a surprise that they had communicated off and on since breaking up. Yet Alicia's insistence on moving on from him and Danielle had left him searching for closure in other women, as well as himself. So to hear her say *"We should catch up"* and *"we'll have the whole place to ourselves"* only brought back those confusing, nauseating feelings.

He shouldn't read too much into it. Right?

"I'll finally show you my pictures and videos from my original home planet," he said with half a smile.

"I'd like that. Maybe I'll see it for myself one day."

Someone sitting in the front row turned around and gave them a critical glance. "What is going on back here?" Troy muttered, arm looped over the back of his bench. "Uh-huh. You two up to no good, I see. Do I have to come back there and sit between you?"

Although Alicia was embarrassed, Devon shrugged. "It's a day for merriment," he said. "And cold feet in the parking lot."

The priest clapped his hands to get everyone's attention. Marlow sat down next to Troy, who immediately inched away to give an old man his room. (That, and Marlow's walking stick came obnoxiously close to Troy's foot.) Someone quipped that the old *julah* was missing his bodyguards, but what few knew was that Vikkel and Kalera were at home on Amyran Estate, welcoming their first child. They were a little busy for the likes of *this*.

"I've been informed that we are to get this over with," the priest jested, garnering a few nervous chuckles. None as nervous as Danielle's, who was so red in the face that she almost excused herself to use the bathroom. *It's not that I don't want to do this.* That's what she wanted to tell everyone, including Miranda, who wasn't exactly *thrilled* to be the center of attention, either. *I just want it to be over with.* Like a filling at the dentist, Danielle preferred to be numbed up and in-and-out. Unfortunately, when she made that joke to Miranda a few days ago, she had been met with a look of sheer belief and a warning to *not* show up drunk. After a thousand years of death and destruction, Miranda would be damned if today wasn't at the very least *nice.* Just "nice" would cut it. Which meant Danielle had to grin and bear all the uncomfortable feelings swelling within her. At least she didn't smell like cigarettes.

The priest launched into the usual speech in Basic, before switching to English for other attendees' benefits.

"It's not every day we see something like this..." He gestured to Danielle and Miranda, who kneeled before the altar, heads pointed low and ears perked up as the priest fumbled for words. "Something so... out of this..."

Miranda's head sagged. Danielle turned hers toward Marlow, as if to say *"Do something."* The more the priest failed to put into words how monumental the occasion was, the more Danielle refocused her attentions from her own discomfort to ensuring her beloved's dreams came true. *Just nice would suffice!*

"As it so happens..." Marlow launched himself off the bench. His walking stick grazed Troy's foot, which he pulled out of the way as if it had been a personal affront. "As an ex-priest myself, I am fully qualified to do this." As the priest of the Temple began to protest, Marlow merely pushed him away from the altar. "There, there. Thank you. Need this, please." He yanked the golden shawl off the priest and wrapped it around his own shoulders, if only to make him look a little more official for the inevitable photographs "Now, where was he? Oh, yes. He was going to lighten the mood."

Marlow extinguished the incense and replaced the censer with *hedpah.* Good thing Evan had already paid off the guards to look the other way.

"You need to calm down." Marlow leaned against the altar and addressed Danielle, who was still white in the cheeks and shaking in the knees. "This will help. Remember why the hell you're here today."

"Because of you," she snapped.

"Babe." Miranda put a hand on Danielle's arm. "We've already signed the license. It's not like this actually changes anything. Besides..." She fixed the lapel on Danielle's jacket and brushed away another corsage petal. "This is for my mother."

Only then did Danielle take a closer look at the statue. There, on the small plaque before the altar, was Miranda's Japanese name in the donor slot.

"You've gotta be kidding me."

"I want it done right," Miranda hissed. "Please. Breathe in the fumes and remember how much you love me and have been waiting for this day."

When she put it that way, Danielle didn't have much choice. Neither did anyone else in the room, who quickly had their brains addled by the fumes. Anyone who had ever been reincarnated soon fell into a stupendous haze that reminded them of confusing times. In a way, it was exactly what Danielle needed, not because it calmed her own reincarnated nerves but because it took more attention off her. When people like Lanelle were nodding off to sleep on Evan's shoulder, Danielle no longer had anything to prove.

Danielle took Miranda's hand. There, on her left ring finger, was the priceless blue jewel they shared, both in this life and one long before.

It was filled with not only their memories, but the strenuous time when all they had were dreams and passion. A reminder that they had once been bound and determined to get the hell out of their sorry situation and to a place where they could live peacefully, together.

The long road leading to this moment brought a sob to Danielle's overwhelmed and *hedpah* influenced body. Only now she wasn't embarrassed, nor was she afraid of what commitment she might bring upon her shoulders. The only thing that *slightly* bothered her was the man standing before them. The one who had brought this ruin upon them so long ago.

No, not Marlow, although he shouldered much of the blame as well. Danielle—and soon, Miranda—thought of the reflection shining in the statue's plaque.

Marlow didn't do such a bad job conducting the Temple wedding ceremony, really. He didn't even lose his place when he looked up and saw a most uninvited guest standing in the doorway, two sleepy guards on either side of him.

Nerilis didn't stay long. He never cared much for weddings after what had happened at his own.

CHARACTER REFERENCE

HUMAN

EARTH

Aiko Takeuchi – Tokyo housewife who is a friend of Miranda's and the life partner of Reina.

Alicia Greene – The "mutual ex-girlfriend" of both Devon and Danielle. Currently in law school with her eyes on non-profit law. Her long struggles with her identity can make her volatile on a good day.

Andy Dupont – Serge's girlfriend. Andy's eclectic style and punk-rock leanings make her the focal point of every room she enters. Like her boyfriend, she speaks fluent French.

Ben Kallman – A First Lieutenant in Unit #207. Ben has been there longer than almost anyone else and is a peer of Miranda's, rank aside. His flamboyant personal life and cynical outlook toward his military career makes him the kind of person others either love or hate immediately.

Clyde Harris – Devon's best friend and the bassist for KARMA. Clyde was one of the first civilians to find out about the oncoming storm and is a staunch supporter of Devon and Danielle's missions – even if he cautions Devon about his attraction toward Danielle.

Danielle Cromwell – First Lieutenant in Unit #207 on Earth, and one of Master Ramaron Marlow's reincarnated mercenaries. Danielle's acerbic personality is both a reflection of her struggles in the Process and how she simply views the world. Danielle has a great reluctance to regressing due to a perceived trauma that occurred right before her original death. She is the reincarnation of Sulim di'Graelic, a famed Cerilynian mercenary of Second Tribe who became the personal bodyguard of Chief Cairn di'Cerilyn.

Devon Anderson – An IT entry level worker, and one of Master Ramaron Marlow's reincarnated mercenaries. Devon is also the lead singer and second guitarist of his band KARMA. Since regressing, he has embraced a more confident and healthier lifestyle while also dealing with the traumatic memories of his time on Cerilyn. Devon makes friends easily but has the softest spot for strong-willed women who aren't afraid to put him in his place. His thousand-year-long infatuation with Sulim/Danielle makes him particularly protective of her, although he is also close to his bandmates and his fellow reincarnated souls. He is the reincarnation of Sonall Gardiah, a famed Cerilynian mercenary of Second Tribe who was the Second in Command at his time of death.

Emily Smith – Danielle's birth mother on Earth. Emily was the biracial daughter of a WWII veteran and his Japanese war bride. After becoming pregnant with Danielle, she often experienced disturbing hallucinations that greatly impacted her mental health. She died in an intentional car crash when Danielle was five.

Hana Furusawa – The young daughter of Yuri and Hiroyuki.

Hiroko Kawazama – Miranda's grandmother on Earth. Although she is ignorant to her granddaughter's plight, Hiroko is the only family member Miranda has a positive relationship with. Hiroko lives in Tokyo and raised both of her children as a single mother.

Hiroyuki Furusawa – Yuri's husband. He is a salaryman who works in Tokyo and often has to stay overnight. He is not involved in Yuri's personal life, and the feeling is mutual.

Jennifer Anderson – Devon's birth mother on Earth. She is a drug addict who has been mostly absent from Devon's life.

Kyoko Kawazama – Miranda's birth mother on Earth. She blames Miranda's birth for ruining their lives and has often taken this sentiment out on her family. The volatile – and oftentimes abusive – relationship between mother and daughter has led to them mostly going no contact.

Laura Anderson – Devon's aunt on Earth and his legal guardian. She is the sister of Jennifer and took on parental responsibilities for Devon from the time he was a baby. Laura's no-nonsense attitude has maintained a cordial but not loving relationship between herself and her nephew.

May d'Eran – The keyboardist for KARMA and one of Devon's friends. May is the daughter of famed Federation reincarnation therapist Rea d'Eran, but was born and raised on Earth. She prefers the slower paced lifestyle offered on her home planet than in the Federation, but is fluent in Basic and understands most of the common cultural norms around the Federation.

Miranda Hotchner – The Captain of Unit #207. Although she was technically an agent of Nerilis Dunsman's over the past one thousand years, her true allegiance has always been to the mercenaries. She is particularly loyal to Danielle and has often kept an eye on her over the years, with romantic interest her main motivation. She is the perpetual daughter of Nerilis Dunsman and, as a half-*julah*, possesses minor powers in spiritual sorcery. Her reincarnated body – and appearance – are the result of Joiya Lerenan's Ascension. It is heavily implied that Miranda's soul was the one originally destined to be born to Nerilis and Joiya, although constant miscarriages prevented that from occurring before the Ascension. She is the reincarnation of Cairn di'Cerilyn, the famed final Chief of Second Tribe.

Regina Biggs – The former Captain of Unit #207 and Danielle's grandmother on Earth. Regina took on formal guardianship of Danielle after Emily's death and raised her from child to adult. Currently, Regina is retired from the military and spends her days tending to her horses in the countryside. She maintains a good relationship with Danielle and is also close with Miranda, who was one of her charges in Unit #207.

Reina Yamada – Miranda's best friend from high school in Tokyo. Reina is the life partner of Aiko and works as a salaryman in Tokyo. Her masculine appearance and demeanor lead many to believe she is a man, and she likes it that way.

Serge Lavigne – One of Devon's friends and the lead guitarist of their band KARMA. Serge manages a record store in the Bay Area but dreams of being a full-time musician. He is ignorant of the Federation until the band's signing with Pauloso Whain. Serge is the son of French immigrants and speaks the language fluently.

Seth Elliot – A former date of Danielle's with a chip on his shoulder. He testifies against her character at her court-martial hearing to get back at her for what she did to his younger brother, Phillip.

Setsuko Smith – Danielle's grandmother on Earth and the mother of Emily. Setsuko was born and raised in Japan before marrying an American serviceman shortly after the end of WWII.

Syrfila Tograten – An intergalactic terrorist who is currently hiding from the Federation Forces on Earth after escaping arrest for previous crimes. As the "second most wanted person in the Federation" she had no issue agreeing to work for Nerilis Dunsman when he approached her to help with his destruction of Earth. Syrfila has little regard for herself or others, both in physical and mental health. Even so, associates like Miranda are convinced that there is some humanity in her soul. Syrfila is a *huling*.

Troy James – A First Lieutenant in Unit #207. Troy is Danielle's best friend and confidant at the beginning of the series. His reluctance to get involved with the mercenaries' mission and the subsequent diversion of Danielle's attentions has meant a gradual drift in their relationship.

Yuri Furusawa – Danielle's ex-girlfriend who currently lives in Tokyo with her husband and daughter. She is a neighbor and friend to Aiko and Reina.

THE FEDERATION

Cairn di'Cerilyn – The final chief of Cerilyn's Second Tribe. Cairn came to power at the age of 19 through right of regicide. Through her direction over the next ten years, Second Tribe saw unprecedented wealth and improvements to quality of life. Most of her biographies have been heavily romanticized, leaning into the improvements she implemented and her "ethereal, *julah*-like" beauty. Unbeknownst to the public, she was the daughter of Nerilis Dunsman and a madam on the pleasure moon Eros. Cairn entered the Process at the end of the planet's existence. She was later reincarnated as Miranda Hotchner on Earth.

Cornelius d'Ferran – The human ambassador bridging the Federation government with Yahzen. Cornelius is the husband of Nicola Ferran and the father of Kalera Ferran. He shares a stronger bond with his headstrong and magically inclined daughter than with his *julah* wife, who considers him a passing fascination with added political benefits.

Evan d'Aranara – Master Ramaron Marlow's assistant who specializes in Earth's cultures and history. Evan is one of the foremost experts on Earth in the Federation and speaks English fluently. This has led to a side career in translation. Evan's fanatical approach to all things pop culture leads to some people not taking his expertise seriously. He has a close – but abrasive – relationship with his coworker Lanelle. Evan has a wife that is also good friends with Lanelle.

Fanar Gardiah – A direct descendent of Sonall Gardiah and one of Devon's current "spiritual" family members. Fanar's family still resides on Arrah as farmers, although at a much lower class and socioeconomic status than their forebears. Fanar is sent to Terra III to meet Devon and reintroduce him to the family.

Joel d'Kerni – A captain of high status in the Federation's Covert Investigations division. Joel reports directly to both the President of the Federation and the Commander of the Forces. He is a pious man who puts the spiritual matters of the universe above his own orders – most of the time.

Lanelle Lanerak – Master Ramaron Marlow's personal assistant going on a few hundred years. Lanelle was put into the Process so she could return and continue to assist Marlow even "beyond death." After five lives she has become not only fluent in Julah, but a human expert on *julah* customs. She is the one human who knows Marlow better than himself, and the burden of the Process has led her down various roads of addiction and other vices. Lanelle has a close relationship with her coworker Evan and even gets along with his wife, who is one of the only people to make her blush.

Madelae d'Errowyn – The current President of the Federation. Like Yara, she is interested in solidifying her place in human history instead of becoming a mere footnote in archival records.

Pauloso Whain – One of the Federation's most notable rich elite who has made his fortunes in entertainment and media. Pauloso's pet projects include scouting talent on Earth and bringing them to the intergalactic audience. He takes special interest in KARMA because of Devon's marketable identity.

Rea d'Eran – An intergalactically renowned therapist who specializes in reincarnation trauma. Her ongoing research into the Process's affects on the soul keep her perpetually involved in Devon and Danielle's lives. She coincidentally already lived in Los Angeles at the start of the series but has since relocated to the Bay Area to be closer to her research subjects (and clients.) She is the mother of May d'Eran.

Sonall Gardiah – The son of a prominent horse breeder on Arrah and later a "spoil" for Second Tribe on Cerilyn. Sonall became one of the most sought-after mercenaries under Cairn di'Cerilyn's rule before becoming her Second in Command. He was hired by Ramaron Marlow to thwart Nerilis's plans to destroy the planet, but failed. Sonall was put into the Process and was later reincarnated as Devon Anderson.

Sulim di'Graelic – One of the most prominent mercenaries of Second Tribe before the fall of Cerilyn. Sulim was known for her tactical approaches and technological manipulations. Perhaps the things she is most known for, however, is the fact she never personally killed anyone. She was the chief Cairn's personal bodyguard before taking on the final contract to stop Nerilis Dunsman from dismantling the planet. When she failed, she was put into the Process. She was later reincarnated as Danielle Cromwell.

Yara d'Alacron – The Commander of the Federation Forces who raised to prominence as an undercover operative responsible for bringing down large intergalactic terrorist organization. Her career was fast tracked after the arrest of Syrfila Tograten. Yara is concerned with her legacy in human history and becomes obsessed with being the one to bring Nerilis Dunsman to justice. Her ruthless machinations often skirt on the spiritually blasphemous. She is the reincarnation of Kila di'Cerilyn, a junior mercenary who died several years before the end of the planet.

JULAH

Calseeth Ducah – The first cousin of Nerilis Dunsman, who has since adopted the family's new last name. She is the steward for Master Obello at the Academy, a position that has her overseeing both his apartment and his day to day activities as he approaches advanced old age. Calseeth's homely appearance and banal personality has her labelled as an "eternal spinster."

Eneral Adelah – The current High Priest of the Void. He is the first younger priest to be elected since Nerilis Dunsman's abdication, and straddles the line between political suicide and maintaining the julah status quo. He occasionally has contact with Nerilis, but does not necessarily agree with his homicidal actions.

Joiya Lerenan – The High Priestess of the Void and the former fiancée of Nerilis Dunsman. In life, Joiya showed such spiritual and magical promise that she was fast-tracked to the Academy at a younger age than was usual. Alongside becoming closer friends with Ramaron, she entered a romantic relationship with

Nerilis that would last until their time in the Temple and see multiple miscarriages that suggested the Void was unstable. On the eve of her wedding, Joiya fulfilled the Prophecy of the Void and completed the Ascension that left her mortal behind body. She is the spiritual mother of Miranda Hotchner and bequeathed her body to Miranda as well. It's implied that Miranda's soul was the miscarried child who could not form her own body.

Kalera Ferran – The daughter of Cornelius d'Ferran and Nicola Ferran. Kalera is a human-*julah* hybrid with strong sorcerous powers. Her specialties include telekinesis and biological disruptions. She uses a special ball developed for her skills to perform many of her "spells." She was a high-ranking member of the League of Spiritual Awareness, charged with murdering Danielle and Devon on behalf of Nerilis Dunsman. Kalera is currently employed as part of Marlow's security team and is married to Vikkel Amyran and expecting a child with him.

Lancin Amyran – The second (hybrid) son of Lilla Amyran and Vikkel's younger brother. Lancin shows adequate sorcerous capabilities but is developmentally hindered by his mother's narcissism.

Lilla Amyran – The current matriarch of House Amyran and the mother of Vikkel and Lancin through two different human husbands. Lilla has inherited a "fallen" house and is determined to rebuild its status and monetary worth in Yahzen society. She is still searching for a full-blooded *julah* husband who will help her build a legacy worthy of House Amyran. She considers her sons to be temporary failings until she can give birth to "real" children that will carry on her legacy for thousands of years to come.

Master Obello – The current Master of Spiritual Sorcery at the Academy. He is also the patriarch of House Obello, although his named heir is the practical administrator of the estate. When he was younger, Master Obello not only scouted Nerilis and Ramaron for tutelage in the Academy, but became their primary advisor and is one of the few to understand their true motives and relationship to one another. His steward is Calseeth Ducah, whom he hired in the wake of House Dunsman's fall to ensure her future. They both skirt the line between following the law and aiding and abetting intergalactic criminals for the sake of the Void.

Nerilis Dunsman – A former High Priest of the Void and the current most wanted man in the universe. In his youth Nerilis was a star pupil at the Academy and a close, inseparable confidant of Ramaron Marlow. He is also the former fiancé of Joiya Lerenan before her sudden Ascension to fulfill the Prophecy of the Void. After becoming the youngest High Priest in recorded history, he discovered that the Void was about to collapse and retired to take matters into his own hands – this has led to him being branded a genocidal terrorist that resulted in Sulim and Sonall entering the Process to stop him. Currently, Nerilis remains the most powerful sorcery in the universe, which has allowed him to elude capture while he researches Crossing. He is the perpetual father of Cairn / Miranda and is still close with Ramaron.

Nicola Ferran – The current matriarch of House Ferran, a position she shares with her older brother, is the technical head of the family. She is the aloof wife of human ambassador Cornelius d'Ferran and the mother of Kalera Ferran. Nicola is known for her hedonistic lifestyle, often throwing lavish parties for artists, politicians, and academics. She has little interest in her family's matters and is mostly preoccupied with her own fancies and pleasure.

Ramaron Marlow – A former priest and currently one of the most powerful sorcerers among *julah* kind. He is the patriarch of House Marlow, although one of his cousins runs the practical matters of the estate. For the past one thousand years, Ramaron has dedicated his life to stopping Nerilis's "reign of terror" across the universe. While viewed as a celebrity figure among the human populace, *julah* see Ramaron as an unfortunate figure and high-ranking Federation officials view him as a nuisance. However, Ramaron's natural sorcerous abilities maintain his grace. He is the only *julah* in recent recorded history to successfully place souls into the Process, and is the one responsible for Sonall and Sulim's eternal spiritual turmoil. He is a confirmed bachelor with a long trail of engagement and betrothal requests behind him.

Vanush Vallahar – The head of House Vallahar and the former *julah* ambassador to the Federation. Before entering politics, he was an intergalactically renowned healer who specialized in finding a cure for the *julah* plague before trailblazing the sorcery behind competent sex reassignment. He is a former classmate of Ramaron and Nerilis's at the Academy and still maintains a friendly relationship with House Marlow. Currently, he is deposed from Federation life after it was discovered he was the leader of the League of Spiritual Awareness.

Vikkel Amyran – The hybrid son of Lilla Amyran and the husband of Kalera Ferran. After graduating from the Academy, he defaulted on his original betrothal to Kalera and joined the Yahzen Defense Forces. He joined the League of Spiritual Awareness at the behest of Cornelius d'Ferran to keep a covert eye on Kalera. Currently, he is an employee of Ramaron Marlow's and serves as the head of his security.

TERMS & PLACES

PLACES

The Academy – The premier university for *julah* kind, located on Yahzen's moon Bah Zenlit. Admission to the Academy is free and based on merit, as its mission is to "nurture and grow" the sorcerous properties of *julah* kind. The three primary schools within the Academy include The School of the Clergy (spiritual sorcery studies), The School of Diplomacy (politics,) and The School of Hybrid Advancement. Only full-blooded *julah* and hybrids are allowed admittance. Humans are rarely allowed on Bah Zenlit without just cause.

Arrah – A small agrarian planet within the Federation and the original birthplace of Sonall Gardiah. Arrah is characterized by rich ecological resources and pastoral living. The Federation has earmarked it as a planet with limited industrial advancement to preserve the environment that results in many of the crops that are sent across the universe. Arrah's atmosphere occasionally experiences "nitrous oxide days" where the inhabitants report feeling more upbeat and silly, making it a popular tourist destination. Because of these factors, travel to and from Arrah is highly restricted and all interplanetary travel is funneled through its only moon.

Bay Area – The name given to the larger metro area that encompasses coastal Central California. In other dimensions, it is known as San Francisco and Oakland. The Bay Area is the birthplace of Devon and Danielle on Earth and the location of both Relics.

Cerilyn – The home of the three mercenary tribes that once sold their business to the Federation and beyond. The planet had a breathable atmosphere but experienced hot, humid weather that made it less than ideal for agricultural or even touristic pursuits. The three tribes colonized the only three places on the planet where humans could live, and were situated between the dense, tropical jungles and the arid deserts. Cerilyn was the first planet containing life that was targeted by Nerilis Dunsman and is now destroyed.

Earth – A "colony" planet on the far reaches of the galaxy and out of the Federation's control, although the government has an invested interest and Federation citizens are allowed to migrate on a case by case basis. Most everyday Earthlings are ignorant to the existence of the Federation. World leaders and high-ranking military officials are made aware upon induction, however. Earth is well-loved in Federation media and is often a source of creativity and inspiration. Although there are many arguments today about how much the Federation shaped the course of Earth's history, most agree that the earliest civilizations on Earth happened organically.

Eros – A "pleasure moon" named after the Roman (Earth) God. Eros was one of several pleasure moons that had few laws outside of murder and theft. Eros specialized in sexual services and claimed to boast the highest density of brothels in the universe. It was the original birthplace of Cairn di'Cerilyn.

The Federation – Shorthand for The Intergalactic Federation of Sentient Bodies and Their Peoples. The largest political force in the known universe, the Federation is the central governing body of humanity. Although the Federation is primarily tied to humans and their planets / outcrops, it also includes the *julah* home planet Yahzen, the *huling*, and other humanoid races that saw a benefit to joining. The Federation is led by a President who is elected via The Federation Council, which is made up of locally elected members from different planets.

Garlahza – The second largest city on Yahzen and home to the Temple of the Void. It is known as the "spiritual city" of the *julah* and is the most outsider-friendly city on the planet – although pilgrims and tourists must be approved before entering.

M-Town – Short for "Military Town." The military district in the downtown neighborhoods of the Bay Area. In previous decades, the American government bought up land and redeveloped it into a large military complex containing multiple blocks and buildings. Most of the departments are focused on administration for the west coast. Civilian-owned services are allowed, but entry and exit to the M-Town blocks are often guarded.

Qahrain – An industrial planet within the Federation. Due to its population and location within the universe, Qahrain was unfortunately the sight of many of the battles that occurred in recent uprisings against the Federation. Since the wars, however, Qahrain has been allowed to advance technologically and is now a popular "bedroom" planet for those retiring from full-time Terra III life. It is the original birthplace of Sulim di'Graelic.

Temple of the Void – The headquarters of the Yahzen clergy in Garlahzah. Outside of training acolytes into the priesthood, it is where the High Priest of the Void resides and gives his sermons. Administration is conducted by a council who oversee not only the training of priests, but delegate their posts throughout the universe. It is commonly believed in *julah* lore that the inner sanctuary of the temple is where the connection to the Void is the strongest, with the altar marking the place where life began in the universe.

Terra III – The capital planet of the Federation and host to one of the largest populations of humans in the universe. Terra III is also the cultural and academic capital of humanity. A "planned planet," Terra III was chosen for development as the future capital after its predecessor, Terra II, became uninhabitable due to unchecked climate change. Advances in technology have allowed the newer capital to thrive while having few natural green spaces left. The central city of Terra III shares the name of the planet and is home to The Federation Council and the headquarters of The Federation Forces. While also being the home to many of the universe's biggest corporations, Terra III boasts the most racial and sentient species diversity. Every single consulate and embassy is located somewhere on Terra III.

Yahzen – The home planet of the *julah* and supposedly the first inhabited planet in history. Yahzen is characterized by its picturesque landscapes, atmosphere, and culture that reaches back millions of years. Populated by only a handful of cities for a mid-sized planet, each city serves a specific purpose and is more about function than population. Instead, the 100 families of *julah* kind maintain their own vast estates across the planet. These estates often function as small towns or villages, based on the size and prominence of the family at the time. In Julah, Yahzen means "original celestial body."

Yahzen also has two moons that serve their own purposes. Bah Zenlit (First Moon) is the home of the Academy and the small towns servicing it. Sah Zenlit (Second Moon) is a resort moon that caters to the wealthy and is known for its vibrant "inkep" industry. Most matchmakers meet with families on Sah Zenlit.

TERMS & HUMANOID RACES

The Ascension – The prophesized moment when a mortal *julah* woman's soul was called to the Void to become its High Priestess. The term "Ascension" is used to describe that the soul willingly went without its body dying. This historically recorded and witnessed moment occurred in the sanctuary of the

Temple of the Void, where Priestess Joiya Lerenan heeded the call and reluctantly Ascended the day before her wedding to Nerilis Dunsman.

Crossing – A theoretical ritual mentioned in The Old Ways. Crossing is the act of either slipping into different dimensions or fusing one into the other. It has never been accomplished in written history.

The Harmony – The first and original language in the universe, and believed to be the linguistic precursor to Julah. According to *julah* legend, the Void sang the Harmony and brought life and law to the universe. In modern times, the Harmony is only reportedly heard by those of high spiritual awareness and those who have a physical connection to the Void. It cannot be transcribed in its purest form.

High Priest of the Void – The spiritual leader of the Temple of the Void. Like the Pope of Earth's Catholic Church, the High Priest is the highest religious authority and is often considered in even higher esteem than the Grand Chancellor. Usually, the High Priest (who is always a man) is a *julah* of great sorcerous power who has proven himself both as an acolyte and as a priest. Outside of conducting ceremonies and giving sermons that are broadcasted to the universe, the High Priest is responsible for enacting religious policy. The position only ends with death or retirement due to advanced old age or illness. To become High Priest, a man must be voted in upon the vacancy. The High Priest has direct access to the Void, although this has been limited in recent years.

High Priestess of the Void – A prophesized position that is fulfilled when the Void is on the verge of collapse. The High Priestess is a mortal woman chosen by the Void to Ascend and maintain balance. Since the High Priestess's soul is separated from her body, this is an eternal position. Joiya Lerenan is the mortal name of the current High Priestess.

The Huling – An endangered race of humans who live on the fringes of the universe. Their forced annexation to the Federation in recent centuries has led to much civil unrest and rebel activity, leading many throughout the universe to view them as a terroristic culture. The origin of the *huling* as a race is hotly debated, with many believing they are an ancient offshoot of the *julah* with much shorter lifespans and no known sorcerous abilities. However, the *huling* are known for their longer than average lives and self-healing properties. They are able to withstand many mortal injuries and high concentrations of poisons or intoxicants. Naturally, the *julah* deny any involvement with their creation.

Hybrids – The term given to those born from a *julah*¬-human pair. While hybrids are often members of *julah* society (if recognized by a House,) they tentatively live a second-class status that limits their career outlooks as well as their marriage potential. Hybrids can have sorcerous abilities and even attend the Academy at their own special school for Hybrids. Many become priests, enter politics, and even enjoy high-ranking stewardship positions for their families, but can never become leaders. They only live about twice as long as the average human instead of the thousands of years of *julah*. Hybrids can only genetically breed with other hybrids, and alliances between Houses are often formed with them.

The Julah – According to legend, the *julah* were the first mortals born into the universe and have been the keepers of the Void ever since. Unlike other humanoid races (including humans,) julah have an average lifespan of three thousand years and can live much longer. They are also the only race capable of sorcery and have built an entire society around it. Culturally speaking, the julah have formed an advanced hierarchy among their own kind that revolves around the 100 families, often referred to as Houses. Politics, education, and economics are all driven by this (mostly patriarchal) family structure. The home planet and cultural core of the *julah* is Yahzen.

League of Spiritual Awareness – An underground political group of *julah* who believe in the actions of Nerilis Dunsman and their subsequent destruction. Many are high-ranking members of society who keep their opinions out of the public sphere.

Mercenaries – For-hire, apolitical armies that are often used in interplanetary conflicts or even for personal assassinations. Those who were officially a part of a "tribe" on the planet of Cerilyn were legally absolved from completing contracts that would otherwise result in arrest and imprisonment. All contracts and payments were negotiated through a tribe's respective chief. Since their destruction a thousand years before, the mercenaries of Cerilyn have been heavily romanticized by Federation media.

The Old Ways – In *julah* lore, The Old Ways are the fabled sorcerous practices that helped bend and shape the known universe in its early stages. Most of these practices have been lost to time, but some are still taught as hypotheticals in the Academy and have even been achieved by powerful sorcerers.

The Process – A once-theoretical practice of The Old Ways that has recently been proven possible. A powerful sorcerer can instruct a mortal soul to enter the Process at death, sending it into an endless cycle of rebirth until the soul is "freed." The only way to free a soul from the Process is by achieving the goal set at the original death and to completely regress. (See: Regression.) Depending on the goals set at death and any trauma carried from life to life, breaking free can be as simple as willing it or a constant struggle. A person trapped in the Process will continue to be born and killed past the end of time and the universe.

Regression – In spiritual sorcery, regression is a part of the Process and necessary for breaking free. It is the act of remembering one's first life and reconciling one's soul with the current subconscious. While most people in the Process aren't that different from life to life, regressing will potentially trigger shifts in personality and desires to more closely match how a person once was.

Relics – The (often) two physical manifestations of a planet's soul. Relics are divided into two categories: the cultural and the personal. The cultural Relic represents the spiritual power of a large body of people on the planet, and the personal represents strong power from an individual. Relics can change shape and take on new form as spiritual power is transferred over the centuries. When both of a planet's Relics are brought together, instability and natural disasters occur. Ritualistically destroying the Relics forces a planet to cease to exist.

Third Piece – Sometimes called the Wild Card or Detonator. The Third Piece is a highly spiritually charged object that appears when a planet is on the brink of spiritual collapse. It was not known from The Old Ways until recently, and has always manifested as a ring originally crafted a thousand years ago. Alongside the Relics, the Third Piece can be "destroyed" to quickly end a planet's existence. Not much else is known about its properties.

The Void – Often referred to as the afterlife or the underworld, the Void is the spiritual origin of the universe and where all souls are born. According to ancient *julah* lore, the Void sang the universe into existence and brought life and law to the cosmos. (See: The Harmony.) Besides its existence and a few properties (such as how reincarnation works,) not much is known about it, even among the *julah*.

JULAH VOCABULARY

Bappah – A badminton or tennis-like game that is a popular sport on Yahzen and in other parts of the Federation. The game comes in singles or doubles, but singles is the most common form among the *julah*. Equipment includes rackets and a lightweight birdie that is easy to hit over a net or other barrier. It is customary to wear special athletic outfits, even when playing at home.

Chazah – A chess-like game in which two players "battle" with their respective pieces. *Chazah* is "as old as the *julah* themselves" and is culturally revered as the national sport. Since *chazah* challenges both the brain and reflexes, it's often taught to young children in the hopes of honing their foresight and fine-motor skills. Humans throughout the universe have picked it up as well over the years, and two separate leagues exist in championship circles to cater to both *julah* and humans.

Cageh – A tea-like drink that is grown and brewed all over Yahzen. The leaves of *cageh* plant are full of antioxidants that make it the perfect lifelong companion to any living body. The caffeine to keep students focused on studies makes for a fine marketing ploy as well. *Cageh* houses exist across Yahzen and in Federation cities with a sizable enough julah population. It is customary to serve guests *cageh* when they visit.

Dodda fed – Lit. Blessed ending. A more formal way to say "farewell."

Fahpar – Male genitalia.

Fed h'dadda – Lit. Also a blessed ending for you. A formal response to "*dodda fed.*"

Gerupah – Poisonous amphibians that have made their home throughout Yahzen for thousands of years. Although an invasive species from other parts of the universe, the term gerupah is used among speakers of Basic.

Hedpah – The *hedpah* plant grows across Yahzen and nowhere else. The entire plant can be burned through a diffuser and has no effect on unreincarnated souls. However, any human who has been reincarnated will experience "flashback euphoria" which allows them to tap into locked memories and may even trigger regressions. Among the *julah*, it is mostly an incense-like substance used in common religious ceremonies pertaining the Void. *Hedpah* is illegal outside of Yahzen, including at Temples. It and *yaya* are the two most controlled substances from Yahzen.

Inkep – A period of time that occurs in most *julah* women after puberty. Inkep literally means "unstable unpredictability" and refers to the extreme hormonal fluctuations that occur during this time, which can last from a single year or two decades, depending on the woman. During this time young *julah* women experience sexual hyperactivity, but may also have other volatile side effects such as violent tendencies, pyromania, and a higher addictive state. In *julah* lore, *inkep* is described as a woman's body connecting with the Void to prepare to conceive and grow future julah within their bodies. In contemporary culture, however, it's a nuisance that has created its own lucrative industry. Astute *julah* mothers will often ship their daughters off to women-only retreats in nature or, most likely, contract with a matchmaker to hire one or more young men to "court" their daughters in an effort to curb their hypersexuality. A nice side effect of this is that it sometimes leads to fortuitous marriages, but it can also lead to unwanted pregnancies if birth control is not properly observed. After *inkep*, it's customary for families to start seriously finding suitors for their daughters as she is considered of age for public betrothal. *Julah* women are not expected to be virgins at marriage because of *inkep*.

Ju bi-lah – Lit. "Your Holiness." A term of respect for the High Priest of the Void and, less commonly, higher ranking priests across the universe.

Kidwip – Small, docile mammals that originate in the wilds of Yahzen and are occasionally domesticated for casual purposes. Due to their "blank stares" and erratic movements, *kidwip* is also a derogatory term for anyone deemed an "idiot."

Masalah – A ceremonial hat mostly used in academic and political situations. It is cone-shaped and usually comes in black or dark blue.

Oolahvi – A savory porridge commonly consumed for breakfast or lunch.

Orvah – A ritual.

Oyyu – Iridescent stones mined for jewelry and clothing.

Poppu – Lit. "Daddy / Papa." A term of endearment for one's father.

Ralez – A (living) sacrifice.

Terah kopah – A fermented cake.

Tesatah – A flavorful berry that is indigenous to Yahzen and has been developed, crossbred, and imported to other planets. It is the most common berry used in *julah* wine. While most crops go toward wine, *tesatah* are also used in desserts and as dried snacks. It is most akin to cranberries or tart grapes on Earth.

Tumti – A buttery, savory sandwich. Like most sandwiches, it can have any number of additions depending on region or family.

Ulilah – Female genitalia.

Umyah – One of the breakfast staples of the *julah* going back millions of years, *umyah* is a nutrient-dense but easily digestible curry paste. Unfortunately, it tastes very plain and comes in an unappetizing green color.

Urfahtit – Large mammals that make their home in the rare swamps of Yahzen. Due to their slow, labored movements and "lazy" lifestyle, urfahtit is also a derogatory term for someone deemed a "fat slob."

Yaya – A high-proof alcohol that originates from Yahzen. Because of the *julah's* higher-tolerance for substances, yaya has to be extremely potent to get the desired drunken result. Therefore it is restricted in the universe beyond Yahzen, and even on the Academy moon Bah Zenlit. This has not stopped the underground yaya trade, however, and some houses may be making quite the cut from black market sales.

Zatbah – Often translated to "memory stone," the *zatbah* is a blue mineral that is mined only in certain parts of Yahzen. In ceremonial lore, *zatbah* stones are believed to house the powerful spiritual energy of their owners. Due to its rarity and suspected powers, *zatbah* jewelry is only available to those who are at least half-*julah*. Some houses make their living from the mining and mastercraftsmanship of *zatbah*. The mines are primarily staffed by hybrids descended from the families and, occasionally, humans.

Zazipah – Lit: Recycled. A derogatory term for reincarnated individuals.

Zenlit – Moon.

About the Author

Hildred M. Billings is the epic fantasy pen-name for literary and lesfic romance author Hildred Billings. Although all of her stories have WLW relationships at their heart, it was paramount to separate fantasy from contemporary literature and romance - thus, she crammed her middle initial in there, and is forever grateful that her mother didn't name her Margaret Diane instead. Margaret D. Billings just doesn't have the same ring.

A long time lover of all things fantasy, Hildred got into the genre when, at the tender age of 11, she discovered her mother's cache of first edition Anne McCaffrey novels. Since then, she's spent untold hours reading works like *A Song of Ice and Fire, His Dark Materials,* and *The Kushiel Trilogy.* She is also an avid gamer who enjoys fantasy RPGs and action-adventure works. She grew up with *The Legend of Zelda* and graduated to *The Elder Scrolls* as an adult. She likes character heavy fiction that tells a bigger tale than the action itself.

Even when writing fantastical fiction that tests the boundaries of the universe, Hildred wants all of her stories to have, at their heart, a relatable emotion that can speak to most of humanity.

Currently, she lives in Portland, OR, and spends most of her time daydreaming about what her characters will do next.

CPSIA information can be obtained
at www.ICGtesting.com
Printed in the USA
BVHW041946231122
652684BV00001B/2

9 798986 724126

CROSS//Regress

Hildred M. Billings

BARACHOU
PRESS

CROSS//Regress

Copyright: Hildred M. Billings

Published: November 28th, 2022

Publisher: Barachou Press

This is a work of fiction. Any and all similarities to any characters, settings, or situations are purely coincidental.

All rights reserved. No part of this publication may be reproduced, stored in retrieval system, copied in any form or by any means, electronic, mechanical, photocopying, recording or otherwise transmitted without written permission from the publisher. You must not circulate this book in any format.

This story is set in a universe parallel to our own, with its own quirks, conventions, and views of their world. What is true in our universe may not be true in theirs.

Of course, this may not always be true, ever.

Series Order